Acclaim for *Elizabeth I* by Margaret George

**Named "Required Reading" by the *New York Post***

"This is one of the best historical novels I have read in ages, a stunning tour de force. It conveys a vivid and authentic sense of Elizabeth Tudor and her world. Extensively researched with the highest integrity, and deeply engaging, it sets a new benchmark for the genre. I cannot recommend it highly enough."
—Alison Weir

"With her usual flair, historical savvy, and storytelling abilities, Margaret George does it again. Her latest book, *Elizabeth I* . . . is dramatically told and once started, this is a book that is hard to put down."
—Barbara Taylor Bradford

"Like all of George's novels, this one has great depth and detail and provides fresh insight even on familiar historical incidents. Her vision of Elizabeth is a convincing one . . . and conflicts are beautifully portrayed as the clash of heroically flawed people."
—Diana Gabaldon, *The Washington Post*

"Like her heroine, George possesses an eye for beauty and a knack for detail, creating a vibrant story that, for nearly seven hundred pages, enables readers to experience firsthand Elizabeth's decisions, triumphs, and losses. Rather than turn Elizabeth I into a romantic heroine, George painstakingly reveals a monarch who defined an era."
—*Publishers Weekly* (starred review)

"Finally, a rare unfusty take on the Virgin Queen."
—*Vogue* (included in the Books: Anglomania! roundup)

"Phenomenal."
—*Passages to the Past*

"This is a magnificent, stay-up-all-night page-turner. . . . Margaret George dazzles."
—*GoodReads* (Movers & Shakers)

"The epitome of a well-researched book . . . This novel is by far the most human look at Elizabeth [and] an absolute must read for Elizabeth I fans."
—*Dallas Examiner*

"Beautifully researched, evocatively written . . . So many books about Elizabeth revolve around the love story between her and Robert Dudley. This is not that kind of novel—it is a thoughtful book, not a love story—unless you consider it a love story between Elizabeth and England."
—*The History Lady*

"Impeccably written . . . perfect and enthralling . . . Margaret George is just in a class by herself." —*Book Drunkard*

"Gripping and transcendent . . . Not simply content to give us the historical backdrop of Elizabeth's age through her relationships, her victories, and her failures, George gives us far more. . . . By far, the best book I have read in a long time." —*Historical Novels Review* (Editors' Choice)

"[A] lavishly imagined historical bonbon." —*The Star-Ledger* (Newark)

"Dazzl[ing] . . . George showcases her extraordinary talent for making history riveting and revelatory, and for making historical figures spring to life." —*The Daily Page*

"By carefully blending rich historical detail with her own equally rich imagination, George presents a fascinating portrait of a smart, brave, and politically savvy leader who was nevertheless also human and emotional."
—*Fort Worth Star-Telegram*

"George's mastery of period detail and her sure navigation through the rocky shoals of Elizabethan politics mean this lengthy novel never flags."
—*Booklist* (starred review)

"Wonderful. You get the true sense of Elizabeth as a person. That is perhaps what is so great about this book." —*Working Writers*

PENGUIN BOOKS

# ELIZABETH I

Margaret George is the author of several bestselling novels, including *The Autobiography of Henry VIII; Mary Queen of Scotland & The Isles;* and *Mary, Called Magdalene.* She travels widely to research her novels and lives with her husband in Madison, Wisconsin.

# ELIZABETH I

MARGARET GEORGE

PENGUIN BOOKS

PENGUIN BOOKS

Published by the Penguin Group

Penguin Group (USA) Inc., 375 Hudson Street, New York, New York 10014, U.S.A. • Penguin Group (Canada), 90 Eglinton Avenue East, Suite 700, Toronto, Ontario, Canada M4P 2Y3 (a division of Pearson Penguin Canada Inc.) • Penguin Books Ltd, 80 Strand, London WC2R 0RL, England • Penguin Ireland, 25 St. Stephen's Green, Dublin 2, Ireland (a division of Penguin Books Ltd) • Penguin Books Australia Ltd, 250 Camberwell Road, Camberwell, Victoria 3124, Australia (a division of Pearson Australia Group Pty Ltd) • Penguin Books India Pvt Ltd, 11 Community Centre, Panchsheel Park, New Delhi—110 017, India • Penguin Group (NZ), 67 Apollo Drive, Rosedale, North Shore 0632, New Zealand (a division of Pearson New Zealand Ltd) • Penguin Books (South Africa) (Pty) Ltd, 24 Sturdee Avenue, Rosebank, Johannesburg 2196, South Africa

Penguin Books Ltd, Registered Offices: 80 Strand, London WC2R 0RL, England

First published in the United States of America by Viking Penguin, a member of Penguin Group (USA) Inc. 2011
Published in Penguin Books 2012

10 9 8 7 6 5 4 3 2 1



*Publisher's Note*

This is a work of fiction. Names, characters, places, and incidents either are the product of the author's imagination or are used fictitiously, and any resemblance to actual persons, living or dead, business establishments, events, or locales is entirely coincidental.

THE LIBRARY OF CONGRESS HAS CATALOGED THE HARDCOVER EDITION AS FOLLOWS:
George, Margaret.
Elizabeth I : a novel / Margaret George.
p. cm.
Includes bibliographical references.
ISBN 978-0-670-02253-3 (hc.)
ISBN 978-0-14-312044-5 (pbk.)
1. Elizabeth I, Queen of England, 1533–1603—Fiction. 2. Great Britain—History—Elizabeth, 1558–1603—Fiction. 3. Queens—Great Britain—Fiction. I. Title.
PS3557.E49E65 2011
813'.54—dc22 2010035382

Printed in the United States of America
Designed by Carla Bolte

*For Robert,*

*My son-in-law,*

*A loyal subject of*

*Her Majesty Queen Elizabeth*

*Past and Present*

## THANKS AND ACKNOWLEDGMENTS

As always, family—my husband Paul, daughter Alison, son-in-law Robert, sister Rosemary—were supportive and helpful, and my agent Jacques de Spoelberch and editors Carolyn Carlson and Beena Kamlani made the book shine brighter after it came into their hands. I want to thank Professor William Aylward, Classics Department, University of Wisconsin–Madison, for his help in Latin translations, Dr. Mary Magray, Irish historian and lecturer, Department of Liberal Studies and the Arts, University of Wisconsin–Madison, for her knowledge and help with the intricacies of Irish history in Elizabeth's period, and my friend Miki Knezevic for thoughtful ideas about the characters. Dr. Lynn Courtenay and Dr. Nathaniel Alcock ferreted out the exact wording on the Dudley family tomb in Warwick, invaluable help for the story. My father, Scott George, first told me about Old Parr when he looked for his grave in Westminster Abbey. The friendship and support of my SCC sisters—Lola Barrientos, Patsy Evans, Chris Thomas, Beverly Resch, Mary Sams, Diane Hager, and Margaret Harrigan—over the years has meant a great deal to me. And finally, my thanks to fellow Elizabethans Jerry and Nancy Mitchell, who appeared one night at Hatfield House and made the banquet magical.

And the spirit of Elizabeth herself, I believe, hovered over the book as it was taking shape and whispered her guidance.

ARCHBISHOP CRANMER:
In her days every man shall eat in safety,
Under his own vine, what he plants; and sing
The merry songs of peace to all his neighbours:
God shall be truly known; and those about her
From her shall read the perfect ways of honour,
And by those claim their greatness, not by blood.

. . .

She shall be, to the happiness of England,
An aged princess; many days shall see her,
And yet no day without a deed to crown it.
Would I had known no more! But she must die,
She must, the saints must have her; yet a virgin,
A most unspotted lily shall she pass
To th' ground, and all the world shall mourn her.

KING HENRY VIII:
O Lord Archbishop,
Thou hast made me now a man. Never before
This happy child did I get anything.
This oracle of comfort has so pleas'd me
That when I am in heaven I shall desire
To see what this child does, and praise my Maker.

—William Shakespeare, *Henry VIII*, V, iv: 33–38; 56–68

# ELIZABETH I

# 1

*The Vatican, March 1588*

Felice Peretti, otherwise known as Pope Sixtus V, stood swaying before the stack of rolled Bulls.

They were neatly arranged like a cord of wood, alternating short and long sides, their lead seals hanging down like a row of puppy tails.

"Ah," he said, eyeing them with great satisfaction. They seemed to radiate power. But one thing was lacking: his blessing.

Raising his right hand, he spoke in sonorous Latin: "O sovereign God, hear the prayer of your servant Sixtus. Acting in accordance with my office as the vicar of Christ, his representative on earth, who has the power to bind and loose, to forgive sins or withhold forgiveness, I have pronounced judgment on that wicked woman of England, the pretender queen. She is hereby excommunicated from the body of Christendom until such time as she repents. In order that those living under her rule do not go down into damnation with her, we bless the Enterprise of England. Aboard the ships of the great Armada will go these Bulls of excommunication and sentence upon Elizabeth, the pretender queen of England, calling for her deposition, in order that her subjects may be rescued from her impiety and perverse government. They will see the happy light of day when Christ's avengers set boots upon English soil. There they will be distributed to the faithful. Merciful God, we ask this in the savior's name, and for his Holy Church."

The sixty-eight-year-old pope then slowly circled the pile, making the sign of the cross and sprinkling it with holy water. Then he nodded to the Spanish envoy standing quietly to one side.

"You may transport them now," he said. "The Armada leaves from Lisbon, does it not?"

"Yes, Your Holiness. Next month."

Sixtus nodded. "They should arrive in plenty of time, then. You have waterproof canisters for them?"

"I am sure they will be provided. King Philip thinks of everything."

# 2

*The South Coast, England, April 1588*

he old hermit shuffled out of his shelter, as he did every morning. He made his bed in the ruins of St. Michael's Chapel, perched near the peak of a jutting piece of headland stretching out into Plymouth Sound. He stood on the rim of the cliff, the ocean far below him, his eyes darting left and right, searching. The morning sun, glinting off the water, made it hard to see. He shaded his eyes and squinted, trying to detect the telltale shape of sails on the horizon. Nothing. Not today.

Muttering, he turned to attend to his other business—preparing the beacon. He had found an abandoned dolmen, an ancient monument, at the pinnacle of the peak and had been carrying twigs, straw, and kindling there for days. The fire that would flare out from the cone-shaped mounted brackets must be visible for miles, until the next beacon. And this was likely the first. This would be the place, if any place, that the Armada would first come into view. And he, the hermit of St. Michael's, would keep vigilant watch as long as there was a whisper of light to see by.

He patted the dolmen. Pagan stuff. Made long ago by vanished people. But who cared, if it helped in the fight against the Spanish enemy?

# 3

## *The Tower of London, May 1588*

"Quiet!" Philip Howard motioned to the priest.

Someone was coming. The guard was making his rounds. His footstep on the stones outside was a sound that Philip heard even in his dreams. He bent his head down, resting it between his knees, his hands hanging limply. He must look asleep. The priest did likewise, drawing his cloak up around himself. The others in the room fell silent, turned to stone.

The footsteps paused; the shutter over the iron grille in the prisoners' door lifted. Then it clanged down again, and the footsteps continued.

Philip stayed still for another few minutes to be safe. Finally he whispered, "He's gone. He won't make rounds again for two or three hours. Let's begin. Let's begin God's work."

The others in the chamber stirred. The priest threw back the covering on his head. "In the name of the Holy Mother Church," he said, "I will perform this Mass."

Philip shook his head. "It must be dedicated to another intention," he said. "I was not a traitor until they sought to make me one. Now, held for five years here in the Tower, I have seen the evil of the queen and her so-called church firsthand. It must perish. She must perish. And my godfather King Philip will ensure that."

In the dim light the priest's eyes glittered. "And who will the Mass be dedicated to?" he asked.

"To the success of the Armada!" said Philip. "May it wreak revenge on this godless nation!"

"To the success of the Armada," the others intoned.

The priest began laying out his holy implements, an earthenware cup for a chalice, a wooden saucer for a paten, a rough scarf for a stole. "Let us pray," he began.

"O most high, you have looked down in sorrow upon the blasphemy and sacrilege here in England, once your obedient servant, now a renegade. As of old, when a nation went a-whoring after false gods, you used a rod to chastise them, you now send your son, King Philip of Spain, a devotee of the True Faith, to smite them. Just as there was no mercy for the Amorites or the Philistines or the Canaanites, there can be no mercy for these straying people. If we perish alongside them, we are willing. Look what your servant Philip, Earl of Arundel, has carved here on the wall of his miserable prison. See his fine words: *Quanto plus afflictionis pro Christo in hoc saeculo, tanto plus gloriae cum Christo in futuro*—The more affliction we endure for Christ in this world, the more glory we shall obtain with Christ in the next. We know, O Lord, that that is true."

"True . . . true . . . true . . . ," murmured Philip and his companion prisoners. "O Armada, come quickly to deliver England! Bless all her exiled sons who are aboard, taking up arms to deliver their homeland!"

Their heated cries echoed within the dank stone chamber.

# 4

# ELIZABETH

*May 1588*

The whip cracked and snapped as it sought its victim.

I could see the groom cowering in the bushes, then crawling away in the underbrush as the whip ripped leaves off a branch just over his head. A stream of Spanish followed him, words to the effect that he was a worthless wretch. Then the face of the persecutor turned toward me, shining with his effort. "Your Majesty," he said, "why do you keep my whip?"

It was a face I had thought never to see again—that of Don Bernardino de Mendoza, the Spanish ambassador I had evicted from England four years earlier for spying. Now he rounded on me and began fingering his whip as he walked toward me.

I sat up in bed. I could still smell the leather of the whip, lingering in the air where it had cracked. And that smirk on the face of Mendoza, his teeth bared like yellowed carved ivory—I shuddered at its cold rictus.

It was only a dream. I shook my head to clear it. The Spanish were much on my mind, that was all. But . . . didn't Mendoza actually leave me a whip? Or did we just find one in his rooms after he hurriedly left? I had it somewhere. It was smaller than the one in the dream, useful only for urging horses, not punishing horse grooms. It had been black, and braided, and supple as a cat's tail. Spain's leather was renowned for its softness and strength. Perhaps that was why I had kept it.

It was not light out yet. Too early to arise. I would keep my own counsel here in bed. Doubtless devout Catholics—secretly here in England, openly in Europe—were already at early Mass. Some Protestants were most likely up and studying Scripture. But I, their reluctant figurehead, would commune with the Lord by myself.

I, Elizabeth Tudor, Queen of England for thirty years, had been cast by my birth into the role of defender of the Protestant faith. Spiteful people said, "Henry VIII broke with the pope and founded his own church only so he could get his way with Anne Boleyn." My father had given them grounds with his flip quote "If the pope excommunicates me, I'll declare him a heretic and do as I please." Thus the King's Conscience had become a joke. But out of it had come the necessity of embracing Protestantism, and from that had grown a national church that now had its own character, its own martyrs and theology. To the old Catholic Church, I was a bastard and usurper queen; thus I say that my birth imposed Protestantism upon me.

Why must England, a poor country, be stuck with subsidizing three others—the French, the Dutch, the Scots—and facing Spain, the Goliath champion of Catholicism? God's teeth, wasn't it enough for me to defend and manage my own realm? The role was a sponge that soaked up our resources and was driving us slowly but inexorably toward bankruptcy. To be the soldier of God was an expense I could have done without.

Soldier. God must be laughing, to have handed me his banner to carry, when all the world knew—or thought it did—that a woman could never lead troops into battle.

Mendoza . . . His face still haunted me, as if the dream clung inside my head. His black, searching eyes and snake-thin face, his shiny skin and receding hairline—if he was not a villain, he looked like one. He had plotted and spied here in England, until he was exposed and expelled. His last words upon boarding were "Tell your mistress that Bernardino de Mendoza was born not to disturb kingdoms but to conquer them." Since then he had settled in Paris as King Philip's ambassador, creating a web of espionage and intrigue that spread across all Europe.

He was evenly matched, though, by our homegrown spymaster, Sir Francis Walsingham. Did Mendoza have hundreds of informants? Walsingham had at least five hundred, even as far away as Constantinople. Was he a devoted, even fanatical, Catholic? Walsingham was equally passionate about Protestantism. Did he have no scruples? Walsingham's motto was "Knowledge is never too dear"—and he was willing to pay anything. Both men felt they were waging spiritual battle rather than just political war.

And the great clash, the long-postponed Armageddon between England and Spain, was imminent. I had done all within my power to deflect it. Nothing was too base or lowly to be employed: marriage negotiations, subterfuge, obfuscation, outright lies, as when I assured Philip I was only a Protestant by political necessity but not by conviction. Anything to buy us time, to let us get strong enough to withstand the blow when it finally came. But I had run out of ruses, and Philip had run out of patience—yes, even he, the man about whom it was said, "If death came from Spain, we would all live a very long time."

The dawn had finally come. I could arise now.

---

My astrologer John Dee puts much stock in dreams and omens. In this case he was correct. I had barely dressed when I was informed that William Cecil, Lord Burghley, my chief minister, wished to see me on urgent business.

It must be urgent. He knew I did not conduct business before noon.

---

I welcomed him, while dreading his news. He was dear to me; if anyone must bring bad tidings, I wished it to be Burghley.

"Forgive me, Your Majesty," he said, bowing as low as his rheumatic spine would permit. "But it was imperative that you see this." He thrust a rolled-up scroll into my hand. "It's from Philip."

"Addressed to me? How thoughtful!" I clutched the parchment in my hand, feeling its importance in its very weight.

"Hardly, Your Majesty."

"He used the best vellum," I said, trying to joke.

Burghley did not smile.

"I meant to be witty," I said. "Have I lost my touch?"

He forced the corners of his mouth up. "No, Your Majesty. I marvel that you can find humor even in such as this." He took the scroll from me. "Hundreds of them, loaded in the holds of the Armada. Like seeds of evil, to be sown here in England."

"Unlike dandelion down that floats by itself in the wind, these cannot be planted unless Spanish boots walk the land. And they will not."

"Secretary Walsingham's agents managed to steal this one, and also a copy of a letter drawn up by one of King Philip's advisers. It *almost* seems there is nothing he can't procure, or uncover."

I took the letter. It was in Spanish, of course, but that was no problem for me. As I read it, however, I almost wished I could not have understood. It was a carefully thought-out memorandum and recommendation to the Spanish king about what should be done once they had conquered England. I was to be taken alive and conveyed to the pope.

"I do not need to guess what His Holiness would decree," I said. "The Bull states that"—I twitched my fingers, signaling Burghley to hand it back to me, and my eyes found the quote—"that my deeds and shortcomings are such that 'some of them make her unable to reign, others declare her unworthy to live.' He pronounces that he deprives me of all authority and princely dignity, declaring me to be illegitimate and absolving my subjects from obedience to me. So, His Holiness—the former Grand Inquisitor of Venice—would prepare a fine bonfire for me." I shuddered. It was no joking matter. It went on to order everyone to ally with the "Catholic army" of the Duke of Parma and of the "King Catholic"—that is, Philip II of Spain. He concluded by promising a plenary indulgence for all those who helped to overthrow me.

At the last, I did laugh. "Indulgences! Now there's something the world still wants!" It was the abuse of indulgences that had led Martin Luther to start his rebellion against the Catholic Church. "They are not very creative in finding new rewards, are they?" I flung the Bull down.

"He has also offered a million ducats to the Spanish as an incentive for invading England."

I stared at Burghley. "He is putting a bounty on us?"

Burghley gave a dismissive cock of the head. "The Peasant Pope, as he likes to be known, is a clever haggler. The money will not be awarded until the Spanish actually set foot here. There is no payment in advance."

"So either way, he wins." Shrewd old bird. Did he hope to make England into carrion he could scavenge? Never! "Call Secretary Walsingham and the Earl of Leicester to a meeting. We should discuss the situation before the full Privy Council meets. You three are the mainsprings of the government."

Burghley shook his head.

"No false modesty. You know it is true. You are my Spirit, Leicester my Eyes, and Walsingham my vigilant Moor. Call the meeting for this afternoon."

I rose, signaling that our talk was ended. I carefully put the damning papers in my correspondence box and turned the key.

---

It was time for the midday dinner. Ordinarily I ate in the withdrawing chamber with a few attendants, although a ceremonial table was always set in the Great Hall. The lower-ranking courtiers and household servants ate there, but my place remained empty. I wondered, fleetingly, if I should put in a public appearance today. It had been a fortnight since I had done so. But I decided against it. I did not want to be on display now. The Papal Bull and call to arms against me had rattled me more than I wanted to admit.

"We shall eat together in here," I told my ladies of the bedchamber.

Three were closest to me: Catherine Carey, my cousin; Marjorie Norris, a friend since the days of my youth; and Blanche Parry, my nurse from even longer ago.

"Open the windows," I asked Catherine. It was a light, fine day, the sort to make butterflies dance. Some Mays were just green winters, but this one was fresh and perfumed. As the windows cranked open, the outside world came in in a puff.

The small table was set in the middle of the chamber, and here we dispensed with the ceremonial trappings, except that we always had a taster. The servers presented the dishes in quick order, and we made our selections with no ado.

I had no appetite. The Papal Bull had quite taken it away. But I usually did not eat much, and so today's almost untouched plate did not attract any attention.

Marjorie, a strapping country woman from Oxfordshire, always ate heartily. Today she was attacking a mound of pork stew and washing it down with a beaker of ale. Catherine, who was small and plump, never went beyond nibbling, so it was a mystery why she had such a round face. Marjorie was some fifteen years my senior, Catherine fifteen years my junior. Old Blanche Parry had seen eighty years. However, she saw them no more, as she had lost her eyesight recently and had to turn her duty as keeper of the royal jewels over to the younger Catherine. She sat now at the table, eating only by habit and feel, her filmed eyes staring at nothing.

Suddenly I had the urge to lean over and pat her hand. It startled her.

"I did not mean to frighten you," I said. But the touch of her calming hand was soothing to me.

"You should be ashamed, to scare an old lady so!" she scolded me.

"Blanche, you are not an old lady," I said.

"If eighty isn't old, when does it start?" she retorted.

"A few years beyond whatever one's age is," I said. "Obviously, ninety." Was there anyone still at court at ninety? I could not think of any. It was a safe age to target, then.

"Well, my lady, there are some who say *you* are old," she shot back.

"Nonsense!" I said. "Since when is fifty-five old?"

"It ceased being old when you reached it," said Catherine.

"I shall have to appoint you to an ambassadorship," I said. "Such a diplomat! But, dear cousin, I couldn't bear to lose you. And would you really want to live with the French or the Danes?"

"The French for fashion, the Danes for pastries," said Marjorie. "Not a bad choice."

I barely heard her. "The Armada is going to sail," I blurted out. "It will bear down on us soon."

Marjorie and Catherine laid down their spoons and their faces grew rigid.

"I knew it!" said Blanche. "I saw this coming. Long ago. I told you. Like King Arthur."

"What are you talking about?" Marjorie demanded. "Is it more of your Welsh mumbles? And don't give me the nonsense about the second sight."

Blanche drew herself up. "I just knew King Arthur's legacy would come round. The queen is descended from him. We all know that. My cousin Dr. Dee has proved it. Arthur left unfinished business. A final battle. A great test of England's survival."

"It has nothing to do with King Arthur," said Catherine. "The astrologers long ago predicted 1588 would be a year of great moment. All Dee has done is confirm it."

"The prediction, made two hundred years ago by Regiomontanas, said that 1588 would be a year of complete catastrophe for the entire world," said Blanche calmly. The exact wording was 'Empires will crumble, and on all sides there will be great lamentation.'"

"Yes, but which empires?" I replied. "Didn't the oracle at Delphi tell King Croesus that if he invaded Persia, a great empire would be destroyed? It turned out to be Croesus's, not the Persians'."

"There are supposed to be three eclipses this year," said Blanche, undeterred. "One of the sun and two of the moon. We have already had the one of the sun, in February."

"Let them come," I said. As if I could do anything to stop them.

---

I needed to be alone. Even my faithful trio did not soothe me. After dinner was over, I went out into the Queen's garden. Whitehall was an enormous, sprawling palace that had grown from a riverside mansion into a near-city of its own that even boasted a street running through it and two gatehouses. With its tiltyards, cockpits, tennis courts, and pheasant yards, it was difficult to find a secluded spot. But the garden, folded between the brick walls of other buildings, shielded me from curious eyes.

Grass walkways, bordered by low white and green striped railings, made geometric patterns, crisscrossing the plot. Everything neat and within its own boundaries. God's death, if only the world were like that! If only Spain would stay within its boundaries. *I* had never had any territorial ambitions. Unlike my father and his vainglorious attempts at warfare abroad, I have been content within my own realm. They murmur that it's because I am a woman. They ought better to say it is because I am sensible. War is a sinkhole that sucks money and men into it and is never filled.

I took a sharp turn as one path dead-ended into another. A painted pole marked the corner, with a carved heraldic beast, flying a standard, atop it. This was the red Welsh dragon, its beak open wide, its wings spread, its talons gripping the pole. The Tudors were a Welsh family, supposedly descended from King Cadwalader. Blanche had filled my childish ears with tales of Wales, and even taught me the language. But I had never been there. Staring at the carved wooden dragon was as close as I had ever come. Someday . . .

But that day was not now. Now I must make sure that England herself survived, and that included Wales.

I knew one thing: We could not withstand the Spanish army. It was the most finely honed fighting force in the world. We did not even have an army, just armed citizen militias, and whatever private retainers could be mustered by the wealthy on an ad hoc basis.

So the Spanish must not be allowed to land. Our ships would have to protect us and prevent it. The ships, not the soldiers, must be our salvation.

---

The three most powerful men in the realm stood before me—William Cecil, Lord Burghley, lord treasurer; Sir Francis Walsingham, principal secretary and head of the intelligence service; Robert Dudley, Earl of Leicester, most recently supreme commander of the English forces sent to help the Protestant rebels in the Netherlands as they fought to free themselves from Spain—using English money, of course.

It would be a long session. "I pray you, sit," I told them. I myself remained standing. Behind me was the massive Holbein mural that covered one entire wall, depicting my father and grandfather. In it, my father crowded the forefront of the painting, making his own father look as if he were cowering in his shadow. Now I stood in front of *him*. Did I draw strength from him, or was I telling him I now dominated the monarchy?

Instead of obeying, Robert Dudley stepped forward and handed me a lily, unfurling on its long stalk. "An unspotted lily for an unspotted lily," he said, bowing.

Both Burghley and Walsingham looked long-suffering, shaking their heads.

"Thank you, Robert," I said. Instead of calling for a vase, I pointedly laid it on a table behind me, where it would quickly wilt. "Now you may sit."

Burghley said, "I trust everyone has seen the 'Declaration of the Sentence and Deposition of Elizabeth' document? If not, I have copies here."

I clenched my teeth. The very thought of it! "God's feet! Must the Spaniard plague me from hell?"

"Your Majesty, it's old news," sniffed Walsingham. "The wording is little changed from the first two—the one in 1570 by Pius V, and then the follow-up in 1580 by Gregory XIII. Another pope, another Bull."

"A shipload of them is a new twist," said Burghley. "It's disgusting."

"For them it's a religious crusade," said Walsingham. "All their ships are named after a saint or an angel. The standard of the flagship, featuring the Virgin and the Crucifixion, has been blessed by the Archbishop of Lisbon. Why not Bulls in the holds? Oh, and you'll appreciate this. I have the list of their passwords. On Sunday it's 'Jesus,' on Monday 'Holy Ghost,' on Tuesday, 'Most Holy Trinity,' on Wednesday 'St. James,' on Thursday 'the Angels,' on Friday 'All Saints,' and on Saturday 'Our Lady.'"

Leicester gave a snort of laughter. "With the likes of Drake and Hawkins, I'd not like to guess what our passwords are," he said.

"Oh, and all the men on board have been confessed and carry a little certificate to prove it," finished Walsingham.

He continued to amaze me. Where did he get this information? "You must have corrupted a priest, to supply you with such details," I said.

His silence proved that I was right. Finally he said, "And there are those here in England, yes, in London itself, who pray for the success of the mission."

"If you claim this, you must know their names," I said. "Tell them." To anyone else it would have been a challenge, but I knew he had the facts. I merely wanted to have them, too.

"Philip Howard, Earl of Arundel," he said. "Even in the Tower, he managed to gather adherents and get a priest to say a Mass for the Armada and for the Englishmen who are aboard. And yes, I can supply the names of all who were present."

"Englishmen aboard!" said Leicester. "The shame of it!"

Walsingham shrugged. "Lucifer and all his legions recruit far and wide. And Arundel *is* Philip's godson. What can you expect?"

"When did the Armada sail?" asked Burghley. "Has it sailed?"

"It is still in Lisbon. My reports say there are some hundred and fifty ships in it. Not all, of course, are fighting ships. Many are merchantmen and supply ships."

"It will be the largest such fleet ever to sail," said Leicester. "*If* it manages to sail. Losing their commander two months ago"—he mockingly crossed himself—"set them back. Santa Cruz knew what he was doing. This replacement, this Medina-Sidonia, does not know much. He even gets seasick. Some admiral!"

"Getting their hands on Portugal eight years ago, with her ships and her harbor at Lisbon, was the best stroke of fortune they could have had, and the worst for us," said Burghley. "The wonder is it has taken them so long to organize. Of course, they kept hoping that someone would put Mary Queen of Scots, on the throne here for them, and make England Catholic without their lifting a finger."

"We have *you* to thank for ending that," I said to Walsingham.

He allowed his saturnine features to soften a bit. He always looked so dour, my spymaster. Even in victory he could not celebrate. He merely nodded. "She ended it. I only exposed her plots and lies."

"Today England remains the greatest threat to the triumph of the Counter-Reformation. Rome has turned the tide elsewhere and begun rolling back the Protestant victories, retaking territories. But we have emerged as the one country where someone opposing Rome can be safe and pursue a career and a life. For that reason, they need to eliminate us. It's religious, but it's also political," said Burghley.

"Is there any difference?" asked Leicester.

"How long do you think we have before they strike?" I asked Walsingham. "How long do we have to prepare?"

"They may sail any day," he said.

"We've been readying the beacons and repairing the coastal fortifications all winter," said Burghley.

"But we all know—and we can speak freely here with one another—that we have virtually no castles that can withstand Spanish siege artillery. They would most likely land in Kent, just across from Flanders. Kent is open country and easy to traverse. We don't have enough weapons, and those we have are outdated. And then there is the great unknown—what about the English Catholics? Will they rally to the Spanish? Where does their primary loyalty lie? For that reason, my good councillors, our only hope of victory lies in preventing the Spanish from landing to begin with," I said.

"Summon Drake," said Burghley.

"Where is he?" asked Leicester.

"In Plymouth," said Walsingham. "But he'll come quickly."

# 5

s they rose to take their leave, I motioned to Robert Dudley, Lord Leicester, putting on his hat. He halted and waited expectantly.

"Come, stroll with me in the garden," I invited—ordered—him. "I have seen little of you since your return from the Low Countries last winter."

He smiled. "I would like that," he said, turning on his heel to follow me.

Back in the Queen's garden, three gardeners were busy setting out herbs in the raised beds, their backs bent over their task. Should I send them away? Whatever we said would be overheard and, doubtless, repeated. No, they should stay. I did not plan to say anything that could not be repeated.

"You are looking well," I began.

"I would take that as a compliment, but I was ill and looked dreadful when I first returned. So anything is an improvement."

"True." I studied him. His face had regained some of the flesh and animation that the Low Countries had drained from him. Still, he did not look healthy. And he would never look young, or handsome, again. Time had not been kind to him, my "Eyes," the man who had been the most glorious creature in my court thirty years ago. The thick chestnut hair had thinned and turned gray; the luxuriant mustache and beard, sleek and shiny as a sable pelt, were wispy and pale. The soul-searching deep hazel eyes now looked watery and pleading. Perhaps it was not just the Netherlands that had wasted him but the ten years he had spent with the notorious, demanding Lettice Knollys as his wife. "The Netherlands were cruel to you," I told him. "And to me." I thought of all it had cost, and no resolution in sight. "So many deaths, so much drain on our resources."

He paused in our slow walk down the grassed path. "Without us, the Spanish would have crushed the Protestant rebels already. So never think it was in vain."

"Sometimes I think all we have done is to give the Spanish some battle practice, the better to attack us here."

We resumed our walk, winding our way toward the sundial in the middle of the garden, its centerpiece. "I have seen the Duke of Parma's army first-hand, and it is all it is reputed to be," he said.

"You mean, the best fighting force in Europe? Yes, I know."

"But it is weakened by illness and desertion like any other. He started out with thirty thousand men, and hearsay is that he is down to seventeen thousand. That counts the one thousand English exiles, the ones fighting against their own country. They are also"—his eyes lit up like the Robert of his youth—"short of money, and there will be no more until the next treasure fleet arrives from America."

I joined him in a mischievous smile. "Which our loyal privateers will try to intercept. You were out of the country, but did you know that Drake's raiding meant that in the last half of 1586, no silver at all reached Spain?"

We both burst into gleeful laughter, as we had done so many times, and so many places, together. His laugh was still young. "None?" he cried.

"Not a sliver," I said. "Not an ingot. And besides that, the raid he led on Cádiz last spring injured their ships and supplies so greatly that he single-handedly has delayed the sailing of the Armada for a year. That has given Parma's men more opportunities to die or desert."

"Even we knew all about that. Sailing right into their own waters, striking over a thousand miles from his English home base—it was brazen and unthinkable. At least, the Spanish did not think it possible. Now they are all frightened of him. A captured Spanish captain I myself questioned believed that Drake had supernatural powers to see into faraway ports. I did not disabuse him of the notion. Certainly Drake seems to have an uncanny ability to guess where treasure is, what's guarded, and what's not. And he moves with the speed of a striking cobra."

"Amusing, isn't it? He looks so innocent, with his round face and red cheeks."

"His ships are his fangs. He uses them like an ordinary man uses his own hand or foot—as if they were part of his own body." Robert shook his head in wonderment.

We had reached the sundial, a faceted cube that told time in thirty different ways as the sun played on each surface. It had been a gift from Queen Catherine de' Medici as her princely sons, one at a time, came courting me. Perhaps she thought one big gift from the mother of them all would make more of an impression than many little gifts. It was an ingenious device.

One of the faces even told the night hours by moonlight, if the moon was bright enough.

It said four o'clock on all of its faces. Today it would stay light until almost nine, one of those sweet lingering twilights of spring. There was even a face that could read the time as the last light ebbed, a twilight dial.

Robert leaned on one of the sundial faces. "Did you mind the lily?" he asked.

"No," I answered, feeling bad that I had been so dismissive of it. But it was out of place for him to offer it there, then. "It was so like you to do it."

He looked around the garden. "Why do you have no roses here? How can a Tudor garden have no roses?"

"They are too tall for the rails. It would upset the order of the garden. But near the orchard, there is a whole plot of them."

"Show me," he said. "I have never seen them."

We left the little enclosed garden and made our way out along the path leading past the tiltyard with its viewing galleries. Iron brackets lined the fence for torchlight tournaments. Robert had taken part in many but would ride in them no longer. I noticed he was out of breath from the short walk. Then I remembered something else.

"You resigned your post as master of the horse," I said. "Robert, why?"

"All things must pass," he said, lightly.

"But Burghley is still serving me! You two were my first appointments, at my very first council meeting!"

"I still serve you, my Be—Your Majesty," he said. "Just not as master of the horse. Although I will still breed horses."

"So . . . who now serves?"

"An energetic young man I discovered. Christopher Blount. He did well in the Netherlands. Got wounded. I knighted him. You'll be pleased with him, I am sure."

"That title belongs to you."

"No longer."

"In my mind, it always will."

"Our minds see things that our eyes cannot," he said. "I suppose something continues to exist until the mind that sees it no longer exists."

Yes, the young handsome Robert Dudley existed now only in the mind of Elizabeth and in portraits. "You are right."

We had reached the rose garden, where beds were laid out according to color and variety. There were climbing eglantines, their pink petals spread open like frames; small ivory musk roses studding their prickly bushes; sturdy shrubs with many-petaled reds and whites, damask roses and province roses; beds of yellow roses and pale red canell roses that smelled like cinnamon. The mingled scents were particularly sweet this afternoon.

"I was wrong to call you a lily," he said. "I see now that roses reflect your true nature better. There are so many different kinds, just as there are so many sides to you."

"But my personal motto is '*Semper eadem*'—'Always the same, never changing.'" I had chosen it because I thought unpredictability in a ruler was a great burden for the subjects.

"That is not how your councillors would describe you," he said. "Nor your suitors." He looked away as he added, "I should know, having been both."

It was good that I could not see his face, read his expression. "I only play at being fickle," I finally said. "Underneath it I am steady as a rock. I am always loyal and always there. But a little playacting adds spice to life and keeps my enemies on their toes."

"Your friends, too, Your Majesty," he said. "Even your old Eyes sometimes does not know when to believe what he sees."

"You may always ask me, Robert. And I will always tell you. That I promise."

---

Robert Dudley: the one person I could almost bare my soul to, could be more honest with than anyone else. Long ago I had loved him madly, as a young woman can do only once in her life. Time had changed that love, hammered it out into a sturdier, thicker, stronger, quieter thing—just as they say happens in any long-term marriage. The Russians say, "The hammer shatters glass but forges iron."

I once told an ambassador that if I ever married it would be as a queen and not as Elizabeth. If I had ever been convinced marriage was a political necessity, then I would have proceeded despite my personal reluctance. But at my coronation I promised to take England itself as my spouse. Remaining a virgin, not giving myself to anyone but my people, was the visible sacrifice they would prize and honor, binding us together. And so it has proved.

And yet, and yet . . . at the same time I spared them the horrors of foreign entanglement and the specter of domination, I left them with the very thing my father turned his kingdom upside down to avoid: no heir to succeed me.

I cannot say it doesn't worry me. But I have other immediate decisions to make, of equal and urgent concern to the survival of my country.

---

It took Francis Drake the better part of a week to travel the two hundred miles separating Plymouth and London. But now he stood before the full

Privy Council, and me, in the meeting room at Whitehall. He had wanted not to rest but to come straight to us.

The sight of him always made me feel safer. He had such buoyant optimism that he convinced anyone listening that his plans were not only attainable but reasonable.

The group had expanded beyond the inner three—Burghley, Leicester, and Walsingham—to include Sir Francis Knollys; Henry Carey, the Lord Hunsdon; and John Whitgift, the Archbishop of Canterbury, as well as Charles Howard, the new lord admiral.

"We welcome you," I told Drake. "Your feeling about our situation?"

He looked around. He was a stocky man, barrel-chested. It was fitting for the man who had destroyed the barrel staves for the Armada last year. His sandy hair was still thick, and although his face was weathered, it looked young. He was sizing up the possible opposition in the council before he spoke. Finally he said, "We knew it would come, sooner or later. Now is the hour."

No argument there. "And your recommendation?" I asked.

"You know my recommendation, gracious Queen. It is always better to attack the enemy and disarm him before he gets to our shores. An offensive is easier to manage than a defensive action. So I propose that our fleet leave English waters and sail out to intercept the Armada before it gets here."

"All of it?" asked Charles Howard. "That would leave us unprotected. If the Armada eluded you, they could slip in with no resistance." He lifted his brows in consternation. Charles was an even-tempered, diplomatic man who could handle difficult personalities, making him an ideal high commander. But Drake was hard to control, or to appease.

"We'll find them," he said. "And when we do, we do not want to be short of ships."

Robert Dudley—Leicester in this formal setting—chafed at this. "It makes me nervous," he said, "to send out all the ships at once."

"You sound like an old woman!" scoffed Drake.

"Then there are two of us," said Knollys. He was notoriously cautious and scrupulous. Had he been a monk, he would have worn a hair shirt. As it was, his militant brand of Protestantism was a good substitute.

"Make that three," weighed in Burghley. William Cecil always favored a defensive strategy, wanting to keep everything within English bounds.

"It would depend on getting the accurate information about when the Armada leaves Lisbon," said Secretary Walsingham. "Otherwise it is a fruitless, and dangerous, venture."

"I thought that was your job," said Drake.

Walsingham stiffened. "I do the best I can with the means at my disposal," he said. "But there is no method for instant transmission of facts. The ships can go faster than my messengers."

"Oh, I can see faraway ports," said Drake with a laugh. "Didn't you know that?"

"I know that the Spanish credit *El Draque*—the Dragon—with that feat," said Walsingham. "But they are credulous simpletons in general."

"Granted," I said. "Enough of that. What of the other defenses?"

"I would propose that we divide the fleet into two—a western squadron to guard the mouth of the Channel, an eastern one to guard the straits of Dover," said Charles Howard.

"I see what the enemy's plan is," announced Drake, interrupting. "The Armada isn't coming here to fight. Parma's army of Flanders will do that, and the Armada will escort them across the Channel. They will guard the flat barges loaded with soldiers as they make the short trip. It's only twenty or so miles. The entire army could cross in eight to twelve hours. *That's* their scheme!" He looked around, his clear eyes taking in the councillors' doubts. "We must disable the fleet. We must prevent them docking on the shore of Flanders. Our Dutch allies will help. Already they have kept Parma from securing a deep anchorage port, and they can harass him as he tries to use the smaller waterways. The great size of the Armada, meant to ensure a safe crossing, can be its very undoing." He paused. "Of course, an alternative plan for them would be to capture the Isle of Wight on our side of the Channel and make a base there. But if they pass it by, there are no more ports for them until they reach Calais. It is up to us to hurry them along. That is, of course, assuming they even get up here. Now, if we follow my original plan to intercept them—"

I held up my hand to quiet him. "Later. For now we must decide on the deployment of our overall resources. So, Admiral Howard, you recommend two separate squadrons of ships? Would it not be better to station all of them at the entrance of the Channel?"

"No. If they got past us there, they would have clear sailing the rest of the way. They would own the Channel, unless we are already waiting for them farther east."

"I don't think—" said Drake, out of turn.

"Quiet!" I silenced him. "What of our land forces? What say you, cousin?" I spoke to Henry Carey, Lord Hunsdon.

He was a big man who always made me think of a bear. Like a bear, he seemed to belong outdoors. He was warden of the East Marches and stationed near the Scottish border. "I will be responsible for your safety," he said. "I will have forces based at Windsor. Should things become more . . . uncertain . . . I can secure a safe place for you in the country."

"I shall never hide in the country!" I said.

"But, Your Majesty, you must think of your people," said Walsingham. "You must appoint deputies to oversee the administration of supplies and control the defensive preparations, while taking care of your most precious person."

"God's death!" I cried. "I will oversee it all myself!"

"But that is not advisable," said Burghley.

"And who advises against it?" I said. "I rule this realm and I shall never delegate its high command to anyone else. No one cares more for the safety of my people than I myself."

"But, Ma'am, you are not—" began Leicester.

"Competent? Is that what you think? Keep your opinion to yourself!" Oh, he maddened me sometimes. And only he would have felt safe in voicing his low opinion of me as a war leader. "Now, what of the rest of the forces?" I turned to Hunsdon. "How many men can we raise?"

"In the southern and eastern counties, perhaps thirty thousand. But many of those are boys or old men. And hardly trained."

"Defensive measures?" I asked.

"I will see to it that some of the old bridges are demolished, and we can put up barriers across the Thames to stop the Armada from sailing down it to London."

"Pitiful!" broke in Drake. "If the Armada gets that far, it will only be because I, John Hawkins, Martin Frobisher, and the good admiral here are dead."

This was a turning point. I motioned with my hands downward for them to be quiet. I closed my eyes and brought my thoughts to bear, trying to sort everything I had been told. "Very well, Sir Francis Drake," I said. "You shall have your experiment. Sail south to take on the Armada. But return the instant you feel we are in danger. I want all the ships here to face the enemy if she comes." I looked at the other faces, ringed around me. "You, Admiral Howard, shall command the western squadron, to be based at Plymouth. In addition, you will be overall commander of both the land and the naval forces. Your ship will be the *Ark.* Drake will be your second in command. Do you hear that, Francis? Admiral Howard is your commanding officer."

Drake nodded.

"Lord Henry Seymour, whose usual post is admiral of the narrow seas, will command the eastern squadron at Dover." I looked at Hunsdon. "Lord Hunsdon, you will command the forces responsible for my safety, based near London. I will appoint the Norrises, Sir Henry the father and his son Sir John, alias "Black Jack," as general and under-general of the southeastern counties. Young Robert Cecil shall serve as master of ordnance for the main army. And you"—I looked straight at Robert Dudley—"Lord Leicester, shall be lieutenant general of land forces for the defense of the realm." He appeared stunned, as did the others. "See that you do it better than you did in the Netherlands." There, that was my reply to his earlier insult.

As they left my presence, I noted they looked surprised—and relieved—to have had all the appointments settled. Good warriors all, their thoughts were already with the battlefield and the work ahead.

---

Now, evening having finally fallen, the quietness of night descending like a gentle rain, I could rest at last. My bedchamber, facing the river, bathed in reflected light for a few moments before the gold faded. It caressed a painting of my late sister, Queen Mary, hanging on the opposite wall. I had kept it to remind me of her sorrows and, while taking heed of her mistakes, not to judge her soul. I had always thought it sad, the hopeful little glint in her eyes, her mouth curling as if she had a secret. Dangling from a brooch on her bosom was the creamy, tear-shaped pearl that her bridegroom, Philip, had presented to her. But now—was it a trick of the light?—her eyes seemed not wistful but sly. The curve of her mouth seemed a sneer. The whole picture pulsated with a reddish glow, as if fiends were backlighting it. She had brought the evil of Spain to our shores, entwined us with that country. Philip's wedding entourage, in its Armada, had arrived in July thirty-four years ago, as it would again, coming to finish what it had started with the 1554 marriage to Mary: returning England to the papal fold.

I would store the painting away. And as for the pearl—costly though it was, it had brought a curse with it. Back to its owner it must go. Even selling it would not rid me of it. When this was over . . . When this was over, let Philip have his cursed pearl back. It had killed my sister and now it was tainting the room.

The sunset glow ebbed away, and the painting returned to normal, its demonic tint gone. My sister's face reverted to that of the proud, hopeful girl who had welcomed Philip as her bridegroom.

Marjorie and Catherine were standing behind me, tactfully quiet but most likely wondering what I was doing. I turned. "We may make ready for sleep now," I said. "I wish to keep you two close by, but I shall send the younger ones away until the danger is past." I had made Marjorie's husband and her son, the Norris soldiers, head of the land forces in the southeast, and I had appointed Catherine's husband to be overall commander of both land and sea forces. In addition, her father, Lord Hunsdon, was to see to our personal safety. "I fear we are all bound together in this. My Crow. My Cat." Under duress, I reverted back to my old nicknames for them: Marjorie, with her dark eyes and hair and her raucous voice, I called Crow. My gentle, quiet, purring Catherine, my Cat.

---

I lay in the darkness that in early summer is never true darkness. The usual sounds of merrymaking had vanished from the river flowing past the palace. The realm was holding its breath. Nothing was moving on the water or on the land.

It had come down to this moment. Was there any way I could have avoided it, taken a different path that would have led elsewhere, to a safer destination? Not if I had remained true to what I was. My birth itself sanctioned the bringing of Protestantism to my country. To abjure it once I reached adulthood would have been to deny my parents and to reject my assigned destiny.

I had seen firsthand what that meant—I had seen my sister do it. In submitting to our father and agreeing that her mother's marriage was invalid and herself a bastard, she trampled on her deepest-held beliefs. Hating her weakness in surrender, she later sought to quiet her conscience and undo the damage. The result was her unhappy attempt to reimpose Catholicism on England. It led to much cruelty, yet she was not by nature a cruel woman. A ruler's wounded conscience exacts too high a price on his subjects.

Fate had cast me as a figurehead of Protestantism. Therefore it was only a matter of time until the champion of the old faith would take me on.

# 6

he night seemed interminable but the dawn came too early. This day I must call my attendants in and send them back to their homes, without distressing them. Little by little I was stripping myself for battle.

There were normally some twenty women of all different ages and stations who attended me. Some were much closer to my person than others. The ladies in waiting were the most ceremonial; they came from noble families and were more ornamental than functional. They were not in regular attendance but were called upon to be present for formal occasions when foreign dignitaries were visiting. But I did not plan to welcome the Spaniards with a state reception, and none were on duty today.

Some ten women were serving now as gentlewomen of the privy chamber, and out of those, only four senior ones personally served me in my bedchamber. Being a lady of the bedchamber was the highest honor my attendants could have. Three of those four, my Crow and my Cat and my Blanche, I would keep with me now. The fourth, Helena van Snakenborg from Sweden, I would send home to be with her husband.

I had six maids of honor, unmarried girls from good families who served in the outer chamber and slept together in one room, the maidens' chamber. All of them must depart.

If the ladies in waiting were the ornamental regalia of my entourage and the ladies of the privy chamber a mix of companions and assistants, the maids of honor were the youthful jewels that shone and sparkled for a season or two. They were apt to be the most winsome and tempting of the small number of women at court. A king's eye was often drawn to them. My mother had been a maid of honor, and so had two other of my father's wives. Here, however, there was no king's eye to catch, only those of predatory courtiers.

They lined up obediently, tremblingly. Excitement vied with apprehension. "Ladies," I said, "it saddens me that, for your own safety, I must send you away. It may be that I will have to move quickly to a secret location, should the Spanish land, and I will not need your services. I pray that this is an unnecessary precaution. But I could not expose any of you to the dangers of enemy soldiers."

One of the maids of honor, Elizabeth Southwell, tall and graceful, shook her head. "Surely our lives are not more precious than yours. We should be with you when—when—" Her large blue eyes brimmed with tears.

"As Charmian and Iras were, when Cleopatra took her last stand against the Romans!" said Elizabeth Vernon, shaking her abundant reddish curls.

"I don't plan to kill myself with an asp," I said. "Nor would I require you to follow suit. I wish you to go home, for now. Do you understand?"

"Is the danger very great?" asked Bess Throckmorton. She was the daughter of a late favorite councillor. But Bess always had a hint of insolence about her, and the other maids of honor seemed to admire it.

"That depends on how close they manage to get," I said.

The older ladies of the privy chamber said little, merely nodding.

"You may pack this afternoon, to be gone by morning," I said.

Bowing, they took their leave. All except young Frances Walsingham and Helena.

Frances waited until we were alone, then she said, "Your Majesty, I wish to stay. I feel it is my duty to remain by your side."

I looked at her. She was a plain little thing, not at all befitting the widow of the glorious Sir Philip Sidney. Ever since his death, she had effaced herself so that she was hardly visible. Even her name made her invisible, being the same as her father's—Francis Walsingham. I thought it very odd for father and daughter to share a name. "Frances, it is your duty to obey me."

"But my father is embroiled in running the war! I am not just a little girl to be sent home. I know too much ever to be free of fear and worry. I will do better to remain at the center of things. Please, please, let me stay!"

I shook my head. "No, Frances, you must go. For my own peace of mind." I turned to Helena. "And you, too, my dear friend. You must return to your husband and children. Families should be together now." That made Frances's request all the more unusual. "Frances, your little daughter—my goddaughter, let me remind you—she needs you. You must be with her when there is threat of war and turmoil."

So they departed—Frances glumly, Helena lovingly, kissing my cheek and saying, "It will not be long. I shall soon be back."

---

Drake, Hawkins, and Frobisher were out to sea, along with a goodly part of the navy. I suddenly had questions about the ships and the agreed-upon deployment, details only a seaman would know. Of all my able-bodied seafarers, only Walter Raleigh was still on shore to be consulted. Oh, how he had protested against his assignment—to be responsible for the land defenses of Devon and Cornwall. To stay at home when the others would set sail. To yield his custom-built fighting ship, the *Ark Raleigh*, to Admiral Howard as his flagship, now renamed the *Ark*. But he had bowed to necessity and done an excellent job not only fortifying Devon and Cornwall but inspecting the defenses all along the coast and up into Norfolk. He argued for heavy cannon to protect the deepwater ports of Portland and Weymouth as well as Plymouth, the port closest to Spain. It was essential, he said, to prevent the Armada from securing a protected, deep harbor to anchor in.

Raleigh had managed to levy an impressive number of citizens to serve as land defense. But they were armed with home weapons—billhooks, halberds, longbows, pikes, and lances—which were no match for a professional soldier's musket and armor. Our land defense was puny. Only our sailors could save us.

Walter arrived in his best attire, his face glowing with hope. I quickly dashed it. I was not going to alter his assignment and send him to sea.

"Your Majesty," he said, trying to hide his disappointment, "I am here to serve you in any way you in your wisdom deem best."

"Thank you, my dear Walter," I said. "I rely on that." I always enjoyed his company. His compliments were not so extravagant that I could not believe them. He was attentive without being fawning. He was pleasant without straining to be ingratiating, and he was not above gossiping. He also was good-looking and every inch a man. That was why I had made him captain of the Queen's Guard, an entire company of two hundred tall, handsome men in gold and red livery. Their duties were to protect me and attend on my person. I certainly encouraged them to attend to that duty.

"The reports I have received about your work on the coasts have been excellent. I am only grieved that they were such a shambles to begin with," I told him.

"We are so seldom invaded that it is natural we neglected to see to them. Not since your father's day has an invasion been a serious possibility," he assured me.

"There have been some successful ones. The Romans, for one. The Vikings. The Normans. It is certainly not impossible."

"We had no navy to counter any of those," he said.

"The navy, yes. That is why I have called you. Do we have the exact figures for the makeup of the Armada now? "

"Not an exact figure, but we believe that it has around a hundred and thirty ships. Not all those are fighting ships; many are just supply boats and scouts. They have very few purpose-built fighting ships, and those twelve they commandeered from the Portuguese, who are much better seamen. They also got four galleasses from Naples. But whether an oared gunboat can really be effective outside the Mediterranean remains to be seen."

"On paper we are stronger," I said, to reassure myself. "Ever since Hawkins took over the finances of the navy and redesigned our ships, we have become the most modern navy in the world. We now have thirty-four redesigned galleons out of almost two hundred ships. But the decision to replace soldiers with guns . . ." I shook my head. It had never been tried, and what if it did not work? Using ships themselves as weapons, rather than using them to convey soldiers to do the fighting, seemed risky. Nonetheless, we were committed to it now. Hawkins's design, substituting gun decks for poop decks, meant that there was no turning back.

"It is no mistake, my gracious Queen," he said, reading my thoughts. "Our ships are much faster and more maneuverable. We can sail closer to the wind and turn quicker. We have dedicated gunners for the cannon and twice as many big guns as the Armada per ship. We have four times the firing rate and four times the accuracy. Windy conditions will favor us; calm conditions will favor them. But the Channel is never calm. Everything is on our side."

I smiled at him. It was hard not to smile at him. "Well, that is what Pharaoh thought when he set out chasing Moses across the Red Sea. God loves to bring a prideful nation down."

"Then he should love to bring *them* down. Your Majesty, from what I've heard, the officers and the ships are bedecked as if they were attending a banquet. The noblemen dress according to rank, with gold-decorated armor, jewels, gold insignia, and velvet cloaks. The musketeers wear plumed hats—for battle as well, I presume—and decorated powder flasks. The ships are painted red and gold and have flags flying from every possible mast and yard. It must look like laundry day at a housewife's cottage."

I could not help laughing. "More like a cathedral, I would think, with all the saints and Wounds of Christ and Virgin Mary banners flapping."

He knelt, suddenly, and took my hands. "I assure you, upon my life, we are prepared. Have no fear."

I raised him up, drawing him back to his feet and looking into his eyes. "I have never been afraid of any man, woman, or foreign foe. My heart does not know what fear is. I am Queen of a brave people. Should I be less brave than they?"

He smiled. "You must be—and are—bravest of all."

---

June turned into July, and intelligence about the Armada—so large that it took an entire day to pass any point on land—revealed that although it had left Lisbon the first week of May, severe storms had crippled it so it had taken shelter at Corunna, a port on the north shore of Spain. Drake and his fleet of a hundred armed ships aimed to strike at it there as it lay wounded and vulnerable at anchor in harbor. But when they were within sixty miles of Corunna, they were betrayed by the wind, which turned on them and blew northwest, toward England—perfect for the Spanish to resume their deadly journey. Afraid that the Spanish would slip right past them and get to England before they could, they had no choice but to turn and head for home. It turned out to be the same day the Spanish left Corunna, so they arrived back at Plymouth just in time. The winds that had so severely hurt the Spanish had done little damage to our ships—a good omen.

I had packed away my finery, ordered the jewels locked in the guarded Tower of London, retreated to Richmond, farther up the Thames. And waited.

From my palace window I could see the river, its ripples showing the ebbing tide current. The waxing moon played on its surface, making bright patches that broke and rearranged themselves as the water rolled past. On the opposite bank the reeds and willows were painted silver by the moonlight, the swans resting among them standing out as stark white. A night for lovers.

And then, a red glare through the silver moonlight. A beacon, twinkling from miles away. Then another. The Armada had been sighted. The local militia was called to assemble.

"Light! Light!" I called for candles. There would be no sleep tonight. I heard the commotion in the palace as messengers arrived, and then one was brought before me. He knelt, trembling.

"Well?" I said. "Tell me all." I motioned him up.

He was only a lad, perhaps fifteen. "I tended the beacon on Upshaw Hill. I lighted it when I saw the one on Adcock Ridge. It would have taken twenty-four or thirty-six hours since the first one was lit to the west."

"I see." I had my guard pay him. "You have done well."

But in truth I knew no more than I had just by seeing the beacon myself. Only when knowledgeable witnesses arrived would the truth be revealed. "Prepare yourselves," I told my guard. Raleigh, the head of them, was away in the west counties. He must have seen the Armada. How far along the coast had it gotten?

---

It was three full days before the details could reach us in London. The Armada had first been sighted on July 29 by the captain of the *Golden Hind*, guarding and scouting the entrance to the Channel. He spotted some fifty Spanish sails near the Scilly Isles and made straightway to Plymouth a hundred miles away to warn Drake.

The next day, July 30, the Armada had entered the Channel.

It was now August 1. "Tell me exactly what has happened," I said to the messenger. My tone was cool, though my heart raced.

"I do not know. I think the Spanish caught our western squadron in harbor at Plymouth, bottled up by the wind so they could not get out. They made an easy target for the Spanish to attack, if they sighted them."

"And then?"

"I was dispatched before we knew what happened," he said.

My heart sank. This was only partial news. Had our fleet been disabled by the wind and then destroyed by the Spaniards? Did all of England now lie open before them?

---

No one knew. We waited at Richmond as the days ticked by—August 2, 3, 4. The guards never left me, and all the entrances to the palace were sealed. We kept our trunks packed and slept little.

We feared the worst—that the Spaniards were even now marching toward London. "But," I told Marjorie, "we can comfort ourselves that all of England will not be conquered, no matter if they capture us and overrun London. There is more to the realm than the south counties and London. In Wales and in the north, the terrain is rough and the people rougher. The east is full of marshes and fens. If the Spanish cannot subdue the Netherlands after thirty years, they could never pacify us. New leaders would rise if I and my entire government disappeared."

"We breed fierce fighters," she said. "We would make their lives hell if they occupied us."

"And if they tried to station enough soldiers here to quiet us, they would leave the Netherlands empty and lose them," said Catherine.

I looked at them. They did not even pretend to be calm. Both their husbands were out fighting the invaders, and they had no word of them.

"Ah, ladies," I said. "We stand and fall as one."

But what *was* happening?

---

Late that night, Lord Hunsdon came to Richmond. I welcomed him with both dread—to hear what he had to say—and relief—to know the worst, if worst it was.

Although over sixty now, he was still a towering commander. I bade him rise. He drew himself up and said, "Your Majesty, I am here to convey you to a place of safety. You must leave London."

"Why?" I said. "I do not move an inch unless I know what is happening."

Catherine could not help herself; she stepped forward and embraced her father, murmuring, "Oh, thank God you are uninjured."

He patted her shoulder but talked over her head to me. "Even my news is old, though I have been kept abreast of it. But this I know: The Armada has reached the area of the Solent and the Isle of Wight. There have been two clashes already, the first at Plymouth—where we managed to escape being trapped at anchor and got the wind gauge on them—the next at Portland Bill. Neither was conclusive. Drake captured *Nuestra Señora del Rosario*, laden with treasure. It did not even put up a fight. When the Spanish captain heard who confronted him, he immediately surrendered, saying that Drake was one 'whose valor and felicity was so great that Mars and Neptune seemed to attend him.'"

Drake. It did seem that, at sea at least, he was unconquerable. "Then what?" I asked.

Hunsdon ran his hands through his thick hair. "The Armada kept going, and the English kept pursuing. So far the enemy have not been able to land. But the Isle of Wight will offer ideal conditions to do so."

"We have strengthened it," I said. "There's a huge defensive ditch, and Governor George Carew has three thousand men at the ready. We have another nine thousand militia guarding Southampton."

"Our navy will do all in its power to keep them from getting into the Solent waters and thus gaining access to Wight. It will depend on whether they can thwart the Spanish from using the flood tide to their advantage."

"And all this is happening—now?"

"I would guess at dawn. That is why it is crucial that you come with me and my soldiers to a place where the enemy cannot find you."

"What are you trying to say? That you are certain the Spanish will land, that we are helpless to prevent them?"

"I am only saying that *if* they land, the road to London is easy from there."

"But they have not landed. Not yet."

"For the love of God, Ma'am, by the time we know they have landed you will look out your window and see Spanish helmets! I beg you, protect yourself. Do not let your soldiers and sailors risk their lives to protect yours, if you have so little care for it yourself."

How dare he make such an accusation? "I have more care for England than for my own life," I retorted. "I will lay that down if it stirs up the courage of the people to resist." I could not sit on the sidelines, removed from action. "I want to see the naval action," I insisted. "I want to go to the south coast, where I can look out and see what is happening, rather than cower in a bunker in the Midlands!" Yes, I would go see it all for myself. This waiting, this second- and thirdhand news, was unbearable.

"That is not bravery but recklessness."

"I can be there in a day."

"No, no! The council will never permit it." He looked anguished. "You cannot, you must not, hazard your person. What a prize for the Spanish! If they killed you, they could display your head to all the troops. If they captured you, off to the Vatican you would go, in chains. How does this help your people?"

"William Wallace's dismemberment seems to have had no ill effect on his legacy in Scotland. Quite the opposite." I sighed. "I go nowhere tonight, in the dark. I send you back to your troops at Windsor—without me."

He could not order me or force me. No one had it in his or her power to command me. He set his mouth in a hard line of frustration and bowed.

"Dear cousin, I trust you," I said. "Keep vigilant at Windsor. And it is time the Earl of Leicester's army assembled itself at Tilbury. I shall give the orders."

# 7

fter he had left, Catherine all but wrung her hands. "If he was this grim, it is worse than he told us. My father does not like to cause undue alarm."

"I know that," I said. "I knew it when he didn't resort to his usual oaths and curses." Hunsdon liked to sprinkle his speech with rough soldiers' words and didn't care what the rest of the company thought of it. But today he had been too shocked to speak in his normal coarse fashion. "Who can know what is really happening? That is the cruel part." Thirty years a queen, and in this hour of supreme test, I was in the dark and could not lead. I looked out the window. The beacons had burned out. They had done their job.

---

The next morning a strange sight greeted us: Sir Francis Walsingham in armor. He clanked into the privy chamber, walking stiffly. He carried the helmet under his arm. Approaching us, he attempted to bow but could only bend halfway. "Your Majesty," he said, "you must transfer to St. James's in London. It can be guarded better than Richmond. Hunsdon told us of your refusal to take refuge in the countryside. But it is imperative that you move to St. James's. Hunsdon's army of thirty thousand can secure the city."

"My Moor, why are you got up like this?" I asked.

"I am prepared to fight," he said.

It was all I could do not to laugh. "Have you ever fought in armor?"

"No. But there are many things we have not done before that we must be prepared to do now," he said.

I was touched that he would even attempt such a thing—he, the consummate indoor councillor.

Behind him Burghley and his son Robert Cecil came into the chamber.

"So, my good Cecils, where is your armor?" I asked.

"My gout won't let me into armor," said Burghley.

"And my back—" Robert Cecil demurred.

Of course. How thoughtless of me. Young Cecil had a twisted back, although he was not hunchbacked, as his political enemies claimed. The story was that he had been dropped on his head as a baby. But that was manifestly untrue, for his head not only was uninjured but contained a brilliant mind.

Suddenly I had an idea. "Can a breastplate and helmet be made for me, quickly?"

"Why—I suppose so," said Robert Cecil. "The Greenwich armory can turn things out fast."

"Good. I want them by tomorrow evening. And a sword, the right length for me."

"What are you thinking of?" Burghley's voice rose in worry.

"I want to go to the south coast, head up the levies there, and see for myself what is happening on the water."

Walsingham sighed. "Hunsdon has already explained why that is not feasible."

"I insist I go out among my troops. If not the southern levies, then at Tilbury when the main army assembles."

"In the meantime, Ma'am, you must remove to St. James's," Burghley said. "Please!"

"I brought you a white horse," said Robert Cecil.

"A bribe?" I laughed. How odd that I could find anything to laugh about now. "You know I cannot resist a white horse. Very well. Is he—or she—ready?"

"Indeed. And with a new silver-ornamented bridle and saddle."

"Like the ones that the Duke of Parma ordered for his ceremonial entry into London?" Walsingham's agents had discovered that fact.

"Better," said Cecil.

Across the river in small boats, then the ten-mile ride into London. Along the road crowds of bewildered, frightened people clustered. I rode as calmly as I could, waving, smiling, to reassure them. If only I could reassure myself as easily. I saw no disturbances other than the milling people. The sky was overcast and it was chilly for mid-July. As we approached London, I did not see any smoke rising or hear any artillery fire.

St. James's was a redbrick palace used as a hunting lodge by my father. In its woodland park, it was far enough back from the river to be safer than Whitehall or Greenwich or Richmond. But as we approached, I saw that the meadows of the park, formerly home to pheasants, deer, and fox, had become a military campground. Tents spread across the grounds and columns of soldiers were drilling.

Hunsdon met us at the gates of the palace. Relief showed on his face. He had counted on my doing the right thing. "Thank God you have arrived safely," he said.

I dismounted, and patted my horse's neck. "Young Cecil here knows how to bribe me," I said. "For a queen, better a gift than a threat."

---

I passed the afternoon watching the men marching and writing to my commanders, stressing my demand to be out with the troops, confronting Parma, rather than hidden away. Hunsdon was immovable, but the commanders of the main army, Leicester and Norris, might feel differently. While I was writing the letters, Walter Raleigh arrived.

Never had a visitor been more welcome. "Tell me, tell me!" I commanded him before he was fully through the door.

His fine riding clothes were covered in dust and his boots mud-caked. There was even dust in his beard. I could not read his expression, but he did not look desperate. "It is safe in the West Counties," he said. "The Spanish were prevented from landing at Wight. Our fleet divided itself into four squadrons, led by Frobisher in *Triumph*, Drake in *Revenge*, Howard in *Ark*, and Hawkins in *Victory*, and forced them to sail past it, edging them toward the sandbars and shallows, which they barely escaped. Now they are heading toward Calais."

"Thanks, thanks be to God!" I almost fell on my knees in gratitude. God noted such appreciation. But I restrained myself. "But when they reach Calais . . . ?"

"Presumably there, or at Dunkirk on the Flanders coast, they will attempt to coordinate with Parma. But is he aware of the whereabouts of the Armada, and is he prepared to embark his troops immediately? Such a thing takes weeks of preparation."

"Parma is known for his preparation," I reminded him.

"When he has all the facts, yes," said Raleigh. "But does he?"

"If God is on our side, no," I said.

"The West County militias are traveling east to help the other counties," said Raleigh.

"It would seem your task is done, and done well," I said. "I release you to do what you have wanted to do all along—join the fleet. If you can catch them at this point."

He grinned. "I will catch them, if I have to mortgage my soul to hell to do it."

"Beware what you promise, Walter," I said. "Remember the old saying 'He who sups with the devil must use a long spoon.'"

He bowed. "I hear," he said.

---

That night my newly fashioned breastplate, helmet, and sword were delivered to me. I fancied I could still feel the heat in them from the forge. I ran my hands over the exquisitely designed pieces, then gingerly tried them on. If something of metal did not fit, there was no help for it. But they did. They fit perfectly.

"You look like an Amazon," said Marjorie in admiration.

"That was my intent," I said. I felt different with them on—not braver, but more invincible.

---

The next morning I got my response from Leicester at Tilbury. The fort was some twenty miles downstream on the Thames, where Parma's ships were sure to pass en route to the conquest of London. By massing the main army there, we meant to block his access to London, and we had put up a blockade of boats across the river as well.

I ripped it open, sending the seal flying.

"My most dear and gracious Lady, I rejoice to find, in your letter, your most noble disposition, in gathering your forces and in venturing your own person in dangerous action."

There. He understood better than old Hunsdon!

"And because it pleased Your Majesty to ask my advice concerning your army, and to tell me of your secret determination, I will plainly and according to my knowledge give you my opinion."

Yes, yes.

"As to your proposal to join the troops drawn up at Dover, I cannot, most dear Queen, consent to that. But instead I ask that you come to Tilbury, to comfort your army there, as goodly, as loyal, and as able men as any prince could command. I myself will vouchsafe the safety of your person, the most dainty and sacred thing we have in this world to care for, so that a man must tremble when he thinks of it."

Oh. But the way he put it . . . Perhaps it was best to let the main army see me. My presence should be used to strengthen others, rather than to satisfy my own curiosity about seeing the battle.

---

The Privy Councillors were aghast. Burghley all but stamped his gouted foot, Cecil tut-tutted and stroked his beard, Walsingham rolled his eyes. The others—Archbishop Whitgift and Francis Knollys—murmured and shook their heads. "This is a foolish, dangerous fixation you have," said Burghley. "And how like my Lord Leicester to encourage it!"

"It is too close to the expected invasion," said Walsingham. "And worse than that—the danger of going out among the people. Have you forgotten that the Papal Bull says anyone who kills you is performing a noble deed? How do we know who is hidden in the troops? It only takes one!"

"I am not a Roman emperor, to fear assassination by my subjects," I said. "So far the Catholics have proven themselves loyal. I do not want to start mistrusting them now."

"Even good emperors and kings get assassinated," he said.

"God has brought me this far, and it is up to him to protect me." I turned to them. "Gentlemen, I am going. I honor your care for me, but I must go. I cannot miss the highest moment of crisis of my reign. I must be there."

I wrote Leicester that I accepted his invitation, and he replied, "Good, sweet Queen, alter not your purpose if God give you good health." I did not intend to alter my purpose.

That night I ordered the Spanish riding whip, long since put away, to be brought to me. I would use it now, and the very feel of it in my hand would harden my resolve. We would not lose!

---

I stepped onto the state barge from the water steps of Whitehall at dawn to travel to Tilbury. This time the red hangings, the velvet cushions, and the gilded interior of the cabin seemed to be mocking me. I was surrounded by the trappings of majesty, but I was on my way to defend my realm. As we slid past the London waterfront, then on past Greenwich, and finally toward the sea, I sent out blessings on these places and upon all the people dwelling there, even though I could not see them.

Preceding me was a boat of trumpeters playing loudly, calling the curious out to watch from the riverbanks. Behind us came barges with my Gentlemen Pensioners and Queen's Guard, bravely attired in armor and plumes, and councillors and courtiers.

We arrived at midday, pulling up to the blockhouse of the fort. Lining the banks were rows of soldiers standing smartly, the sun glinting off their helmets. As the barge tied up at the dock, a blast of trumpets welcomed me, and then the captain general of the land army, my Earl of Leicester, flanked by Army Lord Marshal "Black Jack" Norris, walked solemnly to the end of the pier to receive me.

Seeing Leicester, dear Robert, so handsomely attired and waiting made me catch my breath. Just so he had waited at all the crucial junctures of my life; just so he had always been my chief supporter.

"Your Majesty." He bowed.

"All hail and welcome," said Norris, lowering his head.

I looked at the formidable rows of soldiers stretching in ceremonial lines up the hill.

"We have over twenty thousand here," said Leicester. He gestured up the lines. "I have arranged for you to inspect the camp and the river blockade first. Then, after dinner, you can review the troops and address them."

"I am pleased to do so," I said. I gestured to the next barge after mine, bringing my horse. He was being led down the ramp.

Leicester's eyebrow lifted. "A fine gelding," he said. "New?" Leicester prided himself on providing me with the showiest and best horses.

"A gift from Robert Cecil," I said.

He made the slightest of faces before saying, "Very good taste. Now, my most precious Queen, shall it please you to come with me to the camp?" He indicated the raised causeway we should walk up.

I was already attired in the white velvet gown I wished to be seen in, and would put on the armor before mounting my horse. This was such a momentous, almost a sacred, occasion that no ordinary costume was worthy. But white velvet, with all its evocation of virginity and majesty, came closest.

As we passed, each soldier bowed and the officers dipped their pikes and ensigns in respect. I looked into their faces, broad, sunburned, and frightened, and felt their courage in having left their farms and homes to come here and take their stand.

As we reached the crest of the hill, the camp spread out before us. Hundreds of tents, some of the finest workmanship, others of rough canvas, were pitched in tidy rows. There were large pavilions for the officers and green-painted booths for the lower-rank soldiers. Bright pennants and flags fluttered over them. Upon seeing us, pipers and drummers struck up their welcoming tunes. Then a royal salute was fired from the blockhouse cannons.

"Behold your legions!" said Leicester, sweeping his hand over them. "Stout Englishmen ready to defend our shores."

For one awful moment I felt that I might cry. So brave and so fragile, these men: the most precious gift my people had ever offered up to me.

"Yes," I murmured.

I walked up and down the companies of soldiers standing at attention, speaking a word to some, giving a smile to another, thinking how like a tall fence they were, or a line of saplings planted alongside a road.

"God bless you all!" I cried, and in response they fell, to a man, to their knees, calling, "Lord preserve our Queen!"

I also inspected the ranks of the cavalry, some two thousand strong. One company, decked out in tawny livery, was headed by Leicester's young stepson, Robert Devereux, Earl of Essex. He grinned as I approached and waited an instant too long to lower his head.

"Your Majesty," said Leicester, "young Essex here has raised a fine company of two hundred horsemen at his own expense." He tilted his chin toward the young man, proudly.

I looked at the richly attired company and mentally computed the cost. Young Essex had spared no expense. But the overall effect, rather than being stunning, was surfeit. "Umm," I said, nodding shortly, and passed on to the next.

---

We retired to Leicester's pavilion for the midday dinner. Only a select few were to join us; therefore the table did not stretch very far down the length of the room. For myself, I had included Marjorie and Catherine, as well as Walsingham, as guests. Leicester sat down with a flourish and said, "Your Majesty, all this is yours to command."

"I am here to commend, not to command," I said.

Leicester raised his goblet. "French wine. May we drink it in security, trusting that the French maintain their neutrality in this war."

We all sipped. "The Armada has anchored near Calais," said Walsingham. He was wearing the lower part of his armor but had left off the upper for comfort's sake. "Some fifty miles from Dunkirk where Parma is waiting. Or is he?"

"No one knows," Leicester admitted. "It is entirely possible that he does not even know the Armada has sailed."

"My reports say there is a great deal of activity in the Calais harbor," said Walsingham. "Many boats going to and from the Armada, which cannot anchor there without violating the French neutrality. But rather too much exchange going on. I think the Armada is refitting and repairing itself, with French help." He banged his goblet down, pushed it aside. "Plain English ale for me, please!" he called out.

The Norris men chimed in. "Our job isn't to worry about the French but to be ready for whoever lands here," said Sir Henry, Marjorie's husband. He had a wide face and youthful wheat-colored hair—in spite of his sixty-plus years—that made him seem open and guileless even when he was not.

"Father, an army is only as good as its weapons and training," said Black Jack. He came by the name because of his saturnine coloring, inherited from his mother. "You know what the local militias are made of."

"A lot of boys, carousers, and old dreamers," said a strapping, dark-eyed man at Leicester's left.

"'Your old men shall dream dreams and your young men see visions,'" murmured Walsingham.

"Forget the Bible," growled Black Jack. "The Spanish sail with a papal-blessed standard. That won't win the war for them, and quoting Scripture verses won't for us."

I turned to the man who had mentioned the carousers. "You, sir," I said. "Do you claim that the local militias and trained bands are made up of incompetents?"

He looked startled to be singled out, as if he were used to being ignored. "I meant only, Majesty, that we have no professional army, nothing but citizens roused out of their homes and hastily trained. Not like Parma and his German, Italian, and Walloon mercenaries. We do the best we can with the material at hand. I meant no disrespect."

"I told you my master of the horse was an up-and-coming young man," said Leicester hastily. "Someone to watch. May I present Sir Christopher Blount?"

A winsome young man. Drowsy eyes and a shapely mouth. Wide shoulders. Muscular arms visible by the swelling seams of his coat. "Are you related to Charles Blount?" I asked—one of my favorites at court, now commanding the *Rainbow* under Sir Henry Seymour.

"A distant cousin, Your Majesty."

"Looks run in the family, then," I said.

Others would have blushed and demurred. He just looked calmly back at me. Not a poseur, then, nor a pleaser.

Robert Devereux had been uncharacteristically quiet. He was drawing circles on the table with spilled wine.

"Robert." Two heads jerked around—Robert Dudley's and Robert Devereux's. "A lovely name, 'Robert,'" I said. "But I was calling for the younger one. Cousin." Robert Devereux and I were second cousins; he was the great-great-grandson of Thomas Boleyn, and I the granddaughter.

"Yes, Your Majesty?"

"You are quiet today."

"Forgive me. All this weighs on my mind." His gaze was as wide and clear as an angel's. And indeed, his features were like those in a delicate painting of Italian angels—limpid blue eyes, gold-brushed curls.

"Indeed, as it does on us all. Let us finish our meal and return to the business of the day."

Quietly we ate, speaking softly to the people on either side of us. I asked Marjorie how the father and the son differed in their military philosophy.

"Henry is more subtle," she said. "He believes in holding back, waiting to see what the enemy does. Jack believes in striking first and asking questions later."

"A bit like Drake, then."

"Yes, and—"

Just then there was a commotion at the door, and someone was admitted. Pulling his helmet off, George Clifford, Earl of Cumberland, strode toward us and stopped before me. Observing proprieties, he bowed before saying, "I've just got word, Your Majesty. Two nights ago Sir Henry Seymour's fleet stationed at Dover joined up with Admiral Howard's, following the Armada. Our entire fleet was suddenly a couple of miles from the Armada, cozily anchored at Calais Roads, and Admiral Howard decided the opportunity to strike was too tempting to ignore, in spite of the danger. So they rigged up fireships, those weapons of terror, and launched eight hell burners—ships aflame and loaded with cannon to explode in the inferno—at the very heart of the Armada. It succeeded, where all our broadsides and guns failed. The Armada's tight defensive formation is broken. In their panic to avoid the hell burners, they cut their cables, lost their anchors, and were scattered over the area. Now they are desperately trying to reassemble opposite Gravelines. Our fleet is going to attack them in their confused state. At last they have a chance to destroy them rather than merely harrying them."

"God's death!" I cried. "Fall upon them, rend them!" But the men who could carry out this action were far from hearing me.

In the meantime, I was here, at Tilbury, and I could speak directly only to the land defenses. That was the only power I had to affect the outcome of this war now.

I rose. As I did so, Leicester gestured to the fellow diners. "Your Majesty," he said, "please allow your devoted officers and soldiers to show their dedication. They wish to honor your fair and powerful hand."

A long line of strong young men filed forward and, one at a time, took my hand and kissed it.

# 8

I withdrew to attire myself for the coming ceremony. Catherine and Marjorie would prepare me, like acolytes vesting a priest. First there was my hair. I would wear my finest and highest wig, the better to hold the pearls and diamonds, symbols of virginity, and to be seen from afar. Then the silver breastplate must be carefully strapped on, its ties loosely fastened to accommodate the bulky white velvet bodice beneath it.

They stepped back. "Ma'am, you look like Pallas Athena, and not an earthly queen at all." The look on their faces showed me that I had utterly transformed myself from the woman, albeit Queen, they served every day into something higher. On this occasion I was more than myself. I had to be.

Outside, I mounted the magnificent white horse. Leicester handed me my silver and gold general's truncheon and the black Spanish whip and took the bridle of the horse to lead me.

Essex walked alongside, and behind him came Jack Norris, followed by a standard-bearer with the arms of England embroidered in gold on crimson velvet. A nobleman carried the sword of state before me, and a page my silver helmet on a white cushion. It was a very small group of footmen, but I did not want to be swallowed up in a ceremonial parade. I wanted all eyes to be on me, not my accompaniment.

The entire camp was gathered, waiting. As I rode into view, the roar from the crowd and the boom of cannon salute mimicked a battlefield's thunder. When I approached the crest of the hill where I would deliver my address, a company of scarlet-coated trumpeters suddenly sounded forth, cutting through the human voices with the high, commanding blast of brass. A hush descended, rippling through the ranks, from the closest to the farthest.

At the top of the hill, I wheeled my horse around to face the men spread out as far as I could see. My people. My soldiers. I prayed the wind could carry my words to them all.

"My loving people!" I cried. I waited for the words to float away. The crowd grew even quieter. "We have been persuaded by some that are careful of our safety to take heed how we committed ourselves to armed multitudes, for fear of treachery."

Yes, Walsingham and Burghley gave prudent advice, but ultimately self-defeating for this unique situation. To hide now would be to admit defeat. "But we tell you that we would not desire to live to distrust our faithful and loving people. Let tyrants fear! We have always so behaved ourselves that under God we have placed our chieftest strength and safeguard in the loyal hearts and goodwill of our subjects."

I took a deep breath, and the words rushed out, pushed by trembling emotion, changing from royal "we" to personal "I." "And therefore I am come amongst you, as you see at this time, not for my recreation and disport, but being resolved in the midst and heat of the battle to live or die amongst you all, to lay down for my God and my kingdom and for my people my honor and my blood even in the dust."

English monarchs before me had ridden into battle. Richard the Lionheart, Henry V, my own grandfather Henry VII had fought and risked their lives. I took a deep breath, filled my lungs with strength. "I know I have the body but of a weak and feeble woman, but I have the heart and stomach of a king and of a king of England, too—and think it foul scorn that Parma or any prince of Europe should dare to invade the borders of my realm."

Now a shout arose, growing like a roll of thunder. When it died, I continued, "And further, I declare that I myself will take up arms; I myself will be your general, judge, and rewarder of your virtue in the field."

Now the roar grew so loud my next words, exhorting them to trust in their reward and in Leicester, my lieutenant general, were drowned. Only the final words of the sentence, "we shall shortly have a famous victory over these enemies of my God, of my kingdom, and of my people," were audible. And with them, inexplicably, the crowd grew utterly silent.

I descended the hill with the stillness and hush wrapped protectively around me, my heart thudding, the sea of men a blur before me.

---

I kept my armor on even after the soldiers had been dismissed back to their quarters. In the officers' pavilion, a mumbling group of leaders circled nervously around me, dropping one by one to their knees to do obeisance. Their usual hearty demeanor was subdued, and some had tears in their eyes.

Would no one break this spell? For I felt I could not breathe again as a mortal until someone did.

Jack Norris, the plain speaker, did. "Three cheers for Her Majesty, a prince and better than a king!" he cried. The cheers resounded, the glasses clinked, and we were on earth again.

Leicester stood by my side, his eyes beholding me like a stranger. "I have known you since childhood," he said in a low voice. "But now I know I never shall know all of you. What I heard today I never could have imagined." He reached out for my hand, bent, and kissed it. "No one who was there will ever forget it. And I shall have copies made so all can savor it in all its meaning."

"It is your day as well, my friend, my brother. I am grateful beyond words that this supreme moment was our moment together." God, who had not permitted us to have any other life together but a public one, had crowned it with today's glory and let us share it as one. Our eyes locked together and said more than our inadequate words ever could. This unique and irreplaceable moment had sealed our lifelong bond.

Refreshments were spread out on a long table, but I had no appetite. Would I ever feel hunger again? Had the adoration and utter trust of my people satisfied all lacks within me? The rest of the company, however, fell on the meats, cakes, and flagons with unbridled gusto.

While the men were busy eating, the Earl of Cumberland sought me out. But at the sight of him, people flocked to hear the latest.

"At the height of your address, Your Majesty, I received a dispatch. The Armada succeeded in reassembling itself—"

A groan went up.

"—but they were shaken by the experience with the fireships the night before, and the fiercest battle of the war so far is even now being fought at Gravelines, off the Flanders coast. Word is that we have the upper hand and are pressing them hard. The main problem we have is the very real possibility of running out of ammunition. Some of the Spanish ships have already been blown into the North Sea and out of the Channel altogether. The rest are still fighting but drifting closer to the sandbanks. It looks as if they are a spent force."

"Is it too soon to declare victory?" asked Henry Norris.

"Yes. They might regroup and return. It depends on the wind. If it continues blowing north, they cannot."

"What of Parma?"

Cumberland shook his head. "I was told that, even if the Armada has passed him by, he plans to embark his army on the flat-bottomed transports he already has and float them over to England on the coming high tide. He can't get out of the estuaries in low water, but a high tide will answer that problem."

Walsingham hung over me. "You must return immediately to London," he said. "You must not be here when he arrives with his fifty thousand men!"

Did the man not understand? I fixed him with a sharp look. "My dear secretary, how can I leave? Did I not just promise, less than two hours ago, that I would lay down my life in the dust? Did I not claim to have the courage and resolve of a king of England? What would it say of my word if I turned tail and ran at even a hint of danger? I think foul scorn of *you*, sir!"

I meant it. Better to die here, standing firm, than to run away, than to betray my own words almost as soon as I had uttered them. The world respected the Trojans, the Spartans at Thermopylae, the Jews at Masada, Cleopatra facing the Romans. It did not respect cowards.

His sallow face grew even darker and, muttering to himself, he turned back to the food table.

"We stand here with you," said Leicester, and Essex, who had joined him.

"As do we," said the Norrises, father and son.

"We do, too," said Marjorie and Catherine. "We women are no cowards."

# 9

e watched. We waited. A thousand rumors flew over the whole of Europe. The Armada had won. Parma had landed. Drake was dead—or captured, or had his leg blown off. Hawkins and the *Victory* had gone to the bottom of the sea. Across England, too, the rumors flew. But Parma never rode over on that spring tide; it came and went without him.

No one knew what had happened to the Armada. Admiral Howard and the English fleet had chased it as far north as the Firth of Forth in Scotland, near Edinburgh. When it kept going, our ships turned back. They knew what awaited the Armada when it attempted to loop over the top of Scotland and then head south to Spain, skirting Ireland. The fierce seas and rocks in that inhospitable sea would destroy it. It destroyed even ships whose captains knew the waters, and these did not.

That is exactly what happened. While the Spanish were ordering Masses of thanksgiving in their cathedrals for the glorious victory of the Armada, it was being wrecked, ship by ship, on the rocky western coast of Ireland. Almost thirty ships met their doom there, and the few sailors who managed to struggle ashore were killed by either native Irish or English agents. All told, seventy or so ships did not return to Spain, and those that did were in such ruinous state they were worthless. By contrast, we did not lose a single ship.

It was September before the first bits of this information reached King Philip, who was puzzled. "I hope God has not permitted such evil, for everything has been done for his service," was all he said.

But God had sent his winds to aid England instead.

We celebrated. Church bells rang for days. Ballads were composed. Commemorative medals were struck. Services of thanksgiving were held all across the land.

In Lisbon, a street cry gloated over the Spanish defeat:

*Which ships got home?*
*The ones the English missed.*
*And where are the rest?*
*The waves will tell you.*
*What happened to them?*
*It is said they are lost.*
*Do we know their names?*
*They know them in London.*

Oh, we did. And we knew the names of all our own ships, and all our heroes. We even had an eighty-nine-year-old captain who had commanded his ship in Howard's squadron so well that he was knighted for bravery on the deck by the admiral himself. Such was the stuff *our* men were made of.

For the first month, I was lifted high on a cloud of exhilaration. It was beyond normal time, something extraordinary. It was as if I had only just now been born, learned to see, hear, taste and smell and feel. All my senses were heightened, to an almost painful degree. There are places far to the north in Norway and Sweden where in the summer it never grows dark. They say that during those weeks the people don't need sleep, that they exist in an extreme state of animation. Such were the weeks for me just after the threat of the Armada lifted.

We were preparing for a service of national thanksgiving at St. Paul's Cathedral. The banners Drake had captured from the *Nuestra Señora del Rosario* flagship would be dedicated, a mirror image of the service when the pope had blessed the Armada's flagship banner. I wondered if it even survived and, if so, where they would hide it away in shame.

The pope, however, in keeping with his vigorous peasant mind, seemed to delight in the outcome, as if he had never opposed it. In Rome, he declared, "Elizabeth is certainly a great queen, and were she only a Catholic, she would be our dearly beloved daughter. Just look how well she governs! She is only a woman, only mistress of half an island, yet she makes herself feared by Spain, by France, by the Empire, by all!" When his assistant chided him for his endorsement, he cried, "If only I was free to marry her. What a wife she would make! What children we would have! They would have ruled the whole world." He sighed.

"Your Holiness," the priest objected, "you are speaking of the archenemy of the church!"

"Ummm." Then he blurted out, "Drake—what a great captain!"

I suspected it was a case of one pirate respecting another.

When Robert Dudley related this story to me, we laughed together.

"He seems to have forgotten his principles, if ever he had any," said Dudley. "Of course, he is probably relieved not to have to make good on his promise of a million ducats to Philip. I trust you are not tempted to become Mrs. Sixtus?"

"Well . . . you know I fancy adventurers," I said. Then I slid into seriousness. There were things that must be said. "Robert, the question of marriage—it has always been there between us. The big questions have all been answered, and we have learned to live with those answers." I looked straight into his eyes. "Nothing can separate us now."

Our bond had survived the ghost of his first wife, Amy, the strong earthly presence of his second wife, Lettice, and my dedicated virginity.

He took my hand. "No. Nothing can."

I clasped his hand in both of mine. "Friend, brother, heart of my heart," I said.

Then we dropped our hands. Someone had entered the work chamber.

Burghley limped in. "Has he told you about Sixtus's comments?"

Dudley nodded, and I said, "They are amusing."

"Most likely not to Philip," Burghley said. "He is brooding and this will sour him further. But these dispatches"—he waved several letters—"confirm what I have heard. Your Majesty, you are now the most respected ruler in Europe. The King of France praises you and says"—he opened one of the letters and stabbed at it with his finger—"that your victory 'would compare with the greatest feats of the most illustrious men of past times.' Even the Ottoman sultan has sent congratulations."

"Perhaps he'll send a eunuch as a gift?" I laughed.

"And the Venetian ambassador in Paris"—another letter—"writes that the queen did not 'lose her presence of mind for a single moment, nor neglected aught that was necessary for the occasion. Her acuteness in resolving the action, her courage in carrying it out, show her high-spirited desire for glory and her resolve to save her country and herself.'"

"I did not do it alone," I said. "Without my sailors, without my army, without my councillors, I would now be chained before Sixtus, not joking about his marriage proposal."

My head was ringing with all the praise bestowed upon me. Take care, I told myself, that the head grows not larger than the crown. It was time to put compliments aside. "My dear senior councillor," I said to Burghley, "I trust you will join us at Whitehall for the celebratory military review?"

He demurred. "I have seen enough soldiers the last few months."

"Ah, but there will be jousting as well."

"Spare me." He winced. "It's a big bore."

"You are wise but not always diplomatic. Very well, then. We shall not look for you. But Leicester and I will be in the gallery, if you change your mind."

---

The afternoon was the best an English summer could offer. The sky was not pitilessly bright but was softened by the fluffy clouds of August. The air held us in a warm embrace. Seated in the gallery overlooking the tiltyard, Leicester and I waited to see the military review of the company that the Earl of Essex had raised for Tilbury. He had done it at his own expense, and now was adding more expense by sponsoring this display.

Settling himself, Leicester gave a violent shiver. Even on this warm day, he reached for a cloak to wrap around himself. Seeing me eyeing him, he said, "I fear my old tertian fever has returned. It is making me quite miserable. I missed going to Buxton for the waters at my normal time because King Philip made another appointment for me."

"As soon as this is over, you must go," I said. "The national thanksgiving service will not be held until November, at the thirty-year anniversary of my accession. You must be cured by then."

"If that is an order, I must obey," he said. "But I am loath to leave London now, with all the joy and celebration."

"It is an order." I had noticed that he seemed unwell, sometimes unsteady on his feet. I was relieved to have an explanation for it.

"Oh, look! Here he is!" Leicester pointed to Essex coming out into the tiltyard, followed by his men, all wearing the tawny and white Devereux livery. They marched over to the window of the gallery and all saluted me, Essex with the grandest flourish.

Then the tilting began, and Essex led off, jousting with the Earl of Cumberland. I looked over at Leicester. It had been many years since he had ridden likewise, but my mind supplied the image of it. Young, straight, strong, with gleaming red glints in his hair—this is what I saw. But the man beside me today was white haired, wheezing, and shivering. He needed the healing waters of Buxton.

"He's skilled for twenty years old, don't you think?" Leicester said.

Twenty—life's sweet time. "Yes," I agreed.

"When I go to Buxton, let him have my rooms at St. James's. He will use them well. I would like you to get to know him better."

"Very well," I said. "We'll play cards, dance—and wait for your return."

He took both my hands and kissed them, lingering over them. "We have been through much together, my love," he said softly. "But this last was best of all."

—

He left three days later. He would, of course, have to take his wife, Lettice, with him. He would travel to Buxton, some hundred miles from London, in slow stages, stopping off to see Sir Henry Norris at Rycote en route. I sent a little token to him there, a cordial made by one of my ladies from mint-flavored honey.

I felt nothing ominous. Quite the opposite. I imagined him receiving the gift. I imagined his spirits rising as he traveled through the countryside, away from duties, and then his body restoring itself as he took the course of treatment. The exultation, the relief at England's victory, and his performance as commander, all would buoy his recovery.

—

Then Burghley called on me and asked for privacy. He moved slowly into the room and sank down. His face was twisted in pain and he gripped the arms of the chair.

"You should have sent a messenger," I chided him. "You must take care of yourself. Do not undertake any unnecessary meetings."

"This one is necessary."

"A secretary would have sufficed." I shook my head. "Diligence is one thing, but . . ." The look on his face stopped my chattering.

"Oh, would that someone else could have come in my stead!"

"What is it?" Now a cold feeling was stealing through me.

"Robert Dudley has died," he said.

"No." That was the first thing I could think. It could not be. It must not be.

"He died eight days after leaving London," he said. "He reached Rycote, then went a day's journey beyond that, to Cornbury Park. After that he worsened and could not leave his bed. Six days later, he died, of a continual burning fever. In the ranger's lodge. I am sorry." He looked down at the floor as if he could not bear to see my face. "They say the trees in the park are visible from his bed. His last sight would have been—pretty."

Pretty. Trees. Were the leaves turning there? Or were they still green?

"Trees . . . ," I said. "Trees." Then I began to weep.

I stayed shut up in my chambers for two days. No one was allowed in—not Marjorie, not Catherine, not Blanche, not the lowest chamber servant to attend even to necessities. I did not refrain from showing happiness in public, but I would not show the face of grief. And so I waited for it to pass, knowing that only its sharp edge would pass, never the body of grief itself.

Timid knocks indicated food outside the door. I never opened it to see. Then more knocks, and a letter was slid under the door. I recognized the handwriting immediately: Robert Dudley's.

There is something mysterious and frightening about receiving a letter from someone just deceased, as if he or she is speaking to you from the grave, a wavering voice. Deep sadness and foreboding filled me as I opened it with shaking hands and read.

*At Rycote, August 29.*

*I most humbly beseech your Majesty to pardon your poor old servant to be thus bold in sending to know how my gracious lady doth, and what ease of her late pain she finds, being the chieftest thing in this world I do pray for, for her to have good health and long life. For mine own poor case, I continue still your medicine, and find it amends much better than any other thing that hath been given me. Thus, hoping to find perfect cure at the bath, with the continuance of my wonted prayer for your Majesty's most happy preservation, I humbly kiss your foot, from your old lodging at Rycote, this Thursday morning, ready to take on my journey. By your Majesty's most faithful, obedient servant,*

*R. Leicester*

*Even as I had writ thus much I received your Majesty's token by young Tracey.*

There was no secret, special message. It was an ordinary letter, teasing, affectionate, hopeful of the future, concerned with tokens. He had no suspicion that death was near. *In the midst of life we are in death*, says the burial service. But its opposite is true: In the midst of death we are very much in life.

We had been wrong. Something cruel had, indeed, separated us.

---

A day later Burghley ordered the door broken open. He found me sitting calmly. I would rise now, and carry on.

"He is to be buried at Warwick Chapel," he said. "Near his son."

His young son with Lettice, who had died at age six. "I see." But I would never go there, never see it.

"There is gossip—" he said delicately.

"What sort of gossip?" Was Robert Dudley never to be free of ugly gossip? Would it pursue him even into the grave?

"That his wife, Lettice, poisoned him. That she had to, because he planned to poison her."

"Those old lies!" Leicester's enemies had long called him a poisoner, with any sudden death being laid to his machinations. Then: "Why would he plan to poison Lettice?"

"There was talk that he had discovered her infidelity with Christopher Blount, the young man he had made master of the horse. Some twenty years her junior."

"Absurd," I shot back. Surely she would not dare to betray Leicester, the man she had used every wile to get.

"The story goes that she poisoned him with the flagon of poison he had prepared for her." Burghley looked apologetic. "That is only what people are murmuring."

"They won't stop until they blacken his name forever. Even in death he can't escape their venom."

"This one blackens the widow Lettice most of all," he said.

"So it does. So it does." But surely even Lettice would not stoop to that. But . . . her first husband had conveniently died when her liaison with Robert Dudley had been discovered. People credited Robert with it. But who stood to gain most? Lettice, not Robert. Lettice would gain an amorous and wealthy husband, better than the failure she already had. Robert would lose even the glimmer of hope of marrying me, and court influence as well. Yes, who stood to gain most?

I thrust these ugly thoughts from my mind. They were not worthy of me.

# 10

he next three months were a round of joy for my country and my subjects. There had been no other time in our history that had given us such widespread rejoicing. Agincourt had taken place in another country, and while a great victory, it did not ensure our very survival. While my spirits soared with gratitude and relief, my heart was heavy at my personal loss. It was a perfect reflection of life itself, the sweet and the bitter commingled in one drink.

But all things must end, even celebrations. In November I set forth to put the cap on our observances with a ceremony rivaling my coronation.

The procession began at Somerset House, the grand mansion I lent to Lord Hunsdon on the Strand midway between Whitehall and the Temple. We had an understanding that he allow foreign ambassadors to lodge there and to stage grand events. Today he welcomed me as more than Queen and cousin—he welcomed me as a fellow combatant in the defense against the Armada.

"What, dear cousin—no armor today?" he joked.

"It is not meet to wear it into church," I said.

"Oh, I didn't know that," he said. "It is regular clothes that don't feel right to me." He was eager, no doubt, to get back to the north, where he was warden.

This day I was wearing a gown with an enormously long train that would be borne by Helena Ulfsdotter van Snakenborg, Marchioness of Northampton, the highest-ranking noblewoman in the land. I had made her so—or rather, allowed her to retain her title after she was widowed and remarried a lesser-ranking man. I thought of her as my own possession, for I had persuaded her to stay in England long after her official embassy in the retinue of Princess Cecilia of Sweden twenty years ago. Cecilia was long gone, her mission quite forgotten, but her charming countrywoman was now part of our court and a favorite server in my private chamber.

"It is quite heavy, Helena," I warned her.

She merely shook her head. "I am strong. Am I not an Ulfsdotter?"

"You don't look like a wolf," I said. "But I always admired the Scandinavian animal names—wolf, bear, eagle—Ulf, Bjorn, Arne. They *mean* something."

"They can be hard to live up to," she said, picking up the train to practice. "Better to be John or William."

Somerset House and its courtyard were filling with the four hundred people who would make up the procession. Indoors the councillors, nobles, bishops, French ambassador, ladies of honor, household officials, judges, and law officers took their assigned places; outside a vast throng of clerks, chaplains, sergeants at arms, Gentlemen Pensioners, harbingers and gentlemen ushers, and footmen waited to line up in the correct position.

My chariot, pulled by two white horses, was covered with a canopy, topped with a replica of my actual imperial crown. I got into it, and Helena followed, gathering up my train to keep it off the street. At a signal the procession began to move, with the harbingers, gentlemen ushers, and heralds walking in front. Nearly all the rest followed in their wake, and then I set out in the chariot. The Earl of Essex walked behind me, leading my palfrey. It was the place Leicester should have had.

Behind him came the ladies of honor, then the yeomen of the guard.

Slowly, slowly, we made our way down the Strand, past Arundel House, past Leicester House—another sharp reminder of him, it stood dark and deserted now. Then to the entrance of the city, where musicians played atop the gate and I was welcomed by the mayor and alderman in scarlet robes. All the way to St. Paul's the streets were lined with the city companies dressed in blue liveries. The buildings and railings were all hung with blue as well, rippling softly in the breeze. Wild cheers greeted me at every corner. In many ways it was like my coronation day; but in other ways very different.

Besides the obvious contrast in weather—a cold January day, the sun sparkling off the snow, and this warm, overcast November one—the mood was different. Then I was a promise, a hope, an unknown. Now I had made good my promise, and a promise fulfilled is better than a hope. Together my people and I would celebrate that satisfaction.

We reached St. Paul's, and the chariot halted before the west door, where the Bishop of London received us, flanked by the dean and a mass of other clergymen. After a brief prayer, they led us in procession down the aisle of the nave, chanting a litany. On each side of the aisle hung the eleven banners captured from the Armada. All were ragged and stained, a silent testimony to what they had undergone. All had some religious emblem or symbol. But what else could one expect from a fleet that had crosses on its sails?

They drooped sadly and looked forlorn, as if asking where their ships were.

---

I was seated near the pulpit. The Bishop of Salisbury preached, and then I addressed a few words to my people. After so many words already, there were only a few basic ones to be repeated: Thankfulness. Wonder. Humility. Joy. Then I motioned for the choristers to sing verses from the song I had written about the Armada. Many more gifted poets than I had already written of the victory, but the words of a queen must mean something. The boys and men stood and sang, in their perfect, matched voices:

*"Look and bow down thine ear, O Lord.*
*From thy bright sphere behold and see*
*Thy handmaid and thy handiwork,*
*Amongst thy priests, offering to thee*
*Zeal for incense, reaching the skies;*
*Myself and scepter, sacrifice.*
*He hath done wonders in my days,*
*He made the winds and waters rise*
*To scatter all my enemies. . . ."*

The Armada medals I had commissioned bore the motto "God breathed and they were scattered." Indeed he had, and they were.

Afterward I and a small company dined at the bishop's home, returning to Somerset House after dark, with a torchlit procession. They saw us safely home and closed this extraordinary day.

---

There remained only one thing needed to honor the event. I sat for a portrait that depicted the two fleets in the background. Ours was sailing upon a clear sea, theirs being wrecked against the rocks on stormy waters. I wore the rope of six hundred pearls that Leicester had bequeathed me in his will. In this way I could include him in the commemoration, and in a form that would endure forever.

# 11

*February 1590*

ome, my ladies!" I called as two large crates were deposited in the guard room. "Something to brighten our dreary day, from the land where the sun always shines." I was very excited about this—unexpected presents from Sultan Murad III of the Ottomans.

Sultan Murad and I had been approaching each other for years. Walsingham had hoped to draw him into a military allegiance with us against Spain, and although he had not committed himself, he had sent congratulations upon the defeat of the Armada. We exchanged a number of fulsome letters, and I had sent him such English gifts as bulldogs and bloodhounds. Now he was sending us something in reply.

Marjorie eyed the crates suspiciously. "They look large enough to house an animal—a big one."

"I doubt there is a camel inside," I told her. "I'd love an Arabian horse, but I know that's not in there, either."

The crates turned out to contain sacks of dark beans, boxes of sticky, colored squares of jelly, and bags of spices. Some I could identify—cardamom, turmeric, hibiscus leaves, saffron. Others I could not. There was also an assortment of choice dried currants, apricots, dates, and figs. Featherlight scarves of rainbow colors were in an embroidered bag, and wooden cases contained two gleaming steel scimitars. Most magnificent of all, a huge carpet was folded on the bottom of one crate. When it was unrolled, an intricate design of colors and patterns revealed itself.

"They say the Turks make gardens to look like paradise," said Helena. "Here they have captured a paradise garden in thread for those of us who cannot go there."

The accompanying letter addressed me as "Most sacred queen and noble princess, cloud of most precious rain and sweetest fountain of nobleness and virtue." I liked that. None of my fawning courtiers had come up with these phrases—not yet.

The dark beans were identified as *kahve.* A merchant sailor who was familiar with them explained that in Turkey these beans were ground to a fine powder and boiled in a small amount of water, then drunk with honey or sugar. Islam forbade alcohol, and so they turned to this. Rather than stupefying the senses, it heightened them, he claimed.

And what were those sticky little cubes?

Something called *loukoum*, he said. Nothing to be afraid of, it was merely sugar, starch, and rose or jasmine flavoring.

After he left, I helped myself to one. I had a weakness for sweet things. "This is paradise to go with the garden-of-paradise carpet," I said, savoring it. "We should invite others to join us, else I will make myself sick by eating it all."

I issued a formal invitation to some thirty people—some I had not seen lately, and this would serve as a good excuse—to come to the privy chamber the next afternoon and "sample the delights of the East." We would spread the carpet out and arrange the foods on a long table. The cooks would experiment with the *kahve* beans. But as a precaution, we would have ale and wine ready.

---

The Cecils, father and son, were the first to arrive. They circled the table, examining the things on it, and finally took one *loukoum* each and made for the fireplace. In their wake my great protector, Secretary Walsingham, came forward.

I had not seen him in weeks. He had not been present at the Christmas festivities. Rumor had it he was ill, but his daughter Frances had insisted on continuing to serve me and I believed she would have stayed home to nurse him if he had been in a bad way.

"Francis!" I greeted him. "Your diplomacy is bearing fruit—literally. See what the sultan has sent us." But as he approached, the words died in my mouth.

"Oh, Francis!" As soon as I saw his drawn, yellowish face, I knew his illness had reached a critical stage; there was no hiding it. He was always swarthy, my Moor, but no Moor ever had a complexion like Francis's today. Instantly I regretted the note of alarm in my voice. "Are you not taking care of yourself?" I said soothingly. "I must dispatch Frances back to your household. It is selfish of me to keep her here to wait upon me when her father needs her so much more." I attempted to sound a note of lighthearted chiding. "You should have stayed home; it was not necessary to drag yourself out in such foul weather."

"Foul weather brings out foul spirits," he said. "And I am neglecting my duty of protecting Your Majesty from her enemies if I let such an opportunity pass to try to spot them."

"You have agents to do that," I reminded him.

"None as good as I," he said. It was a statement, not a brag.

"Your agents have done fine duty up until now. You should learn to trust them, as I trust mine. Such as you! If it were not for you, I would toss and turn and worry constantly about my safety, but as it is, I can forget it."

"You should never forget it," he said. As he spoke, I saw him clenching his teeth. It was hard for him to carry on a conversation.

"Go home, Sir Francis. Mr. Secretary. That is a command." God, I would not lose him, too! No more deaths, not now. My dear companion and keeper from my nursery days, Blanche Parry, had passed away just after the thanksgiving at Westminster Abbey, as if she had willed herself to live to see that day.

She had taken a chill and not been able to shake it off. This happens with the elderly, as if death sends his cold emissary to announce himself. She had sat by my side at the service, shivering and trembling. But still she murmured, "I do not need my sight to behold this day. I can hear it in the voices."

After we returned to the palace, she had taken to her bed and never left it. I tried to cajole her into rallying, but it was not to be. She had worn out the body that had faithfully served her for over eighty years.

"Now let thy servant depart in peace," she had murmured, asking permission with the formal biblical phrase.

"I must, then," I said, clasping her withered hands. "I must. But I would not, had I the power."

She smiled, that whimsical smile that I loved so well. "Ah, but you do not, my lady. So submit you must, and I as well."

She stole away that night. For me, to have lost both her and Leicester in close succession threw a pall of deep personal sorrow over the national rejoicing.

Dragging himself, Walsingham turned away to obey me and go home.

Next came Lord Hunsdon. Not much younger than Cecil, he was still vigorous in spite of his stiff legs. The only deference he gave to his age and joints was to leave the north during the stinging, bitter winter months and come back here to London.

Just behind him came the other branch of my family—he had married Hunsdon's sister—that had served me so well, the proper Puritan councillor Sir Francis Knollys. I tolerated his views because he was family, but I never let his religion impede his service. Francis produced a huge brood of children, some seven sons and four daughters. Odd in such a worthy father, none of the sons are worth mentioning here, and only one of the daughters, Lettice. And the things she is mentioned for—slyness, cuckoldry, adultery—would hardly make a father proud. I greeted Francis, trying not to hold his daughter against him.

Not reading my mind, Francis smiled and greeted me. Then he passed on to the table, eager to try the exotic fare.

I moved to the head of the table and announced, "Good Englishmen all! We have received gifts from the east. One you are walking upon—a fine Turkish carpet. Others are for you to handle and admire. Ladies, you may select a scarf. Men, you may handle the scimitars. But no dueling!" Lately there had been several attempted duels at court, in spite of their being strictly forbidden. "And most intriguing of all, there is a drink in the flagons—a heated drink, most welcome on this bone-chilling day—that warms your stomach and makes your head buzz, but not as ale does." I had not tried it yet myself, but I would later—in private. "There are superlative dried fruits, and a special sweet that, I am told, the eunuchs love." There, that should pique their interest.

Dark was falling so early on this winter's day. I ordered lamps and tapers to be lit, but the dark held sway in the corners and in the high roof. I had built this banqueting hall at Whitehall as a temporary structure, but I would never have the money to convert it into anything permanent.

The war with Spain on all its fronts was bankrupting me. The defeat of the Armada had not ended the conflict. It was merely one stage of it.

Recently our erstwhile ally France had been once again torn apart, this time by "the war of the three Henris"—the Catholic Henri, Duc de Guise, head of the Catholic League; the heir to the throne, Henri of Navarre, a Bourbon and a Protestant; and King Henri III, a Catholic and a Valois. But this was simplified when the Duc de Guise was assassinated, and so was Henri III. The French king, brave in his ribbons, perfume, and makeup, was removed from the stage of life, to be succeeded by his cousin from a different house and a different religion. The death of his meddling mother, Queen Catherine de' Medici, helped matters out immensely, from my point of view.

"My most gracious and beautiful sovereign." Standing by me was Robert Devereux, the young Earl of Essex. I snapped out of my musings on England's financial straits. He bent low, kissing my hand and then raising his eyes to look directly into mine, letting a slow smile tease his lips. "I do confess that, as a man, I have been more subject to your natural beauty than as a subject to the power of the Queen."

Such beauty as his, in words and face, should not be allowed to roam free. It was too distracting.

Standing beside him was a lovely woman. "May I present," he began, "my friend Henry Wriothesley, the Earl of Southampton."

"Am I meeting the ghost of Henri III?" I had just been thinking about him, and here was this apparition before me: colored lips, rouged cheeks, tumbling cascades of virginal hair, a double earring.

Southampton gave a tinkling laugh and laid his long, slender fingers on Essex's sleeve. He did not have the decency to blush, but then his rouge would have disguised it. "It is my honor to serve you, my sovereign lady," he said, falling to his knees.

I let him remain there for a moment, examining the top of his head. It did not appear to be a wig. I could always tell by the part. They never look natural.

"Arise," I ordered him. "So you have come to London. How old are you?"

"Seventeen, Your Most Glorious Majesty."

Seventeen. Perhaps he would grow out of it. "Do not keep overmuch company with Essex here. He has a bad influence on young lads like you."

"Oh, now that I am in my twenties, I am a bad influence on youth?" Essex teased. "You should keep us far from court, then. Send me out on another mission. I have the armor, and I am longing to go."

I had put him under Drake in Portugal in the so-called Counterarmada, meant to follow up our defensive victory with an offensive one. Essex's role had been swashbuckling and, in the end, ineffectual. My investment was squandered.

"Then you pay for it!" I snapped.

Just then Sir Francis Drake appeared, as if we had conjured him up by speaking of naval operations. The former hero of the Armada was not my favorite sight just now. But with characteristic sangfroid, he pushed his way over to me and fell on his knees.

"Your Gracious Majesty!" he said, kissing my hand.

He had not dared to show his face at court since the bungled Portugal venture. The sultan's generosity was providing him an opportunity.

"Do not forget so soon all the services I have done you, all the jewels, the gold, the hidden passageways in the sea, and singeing the King of Spain's beard. Let me prove myself again."

But I must hold fast to what financial reserves I had. There would be no missions for Francis Drake this year.

---

My ladies were clumped together near one end of the table, hovering over a plate of the *loukoum*, as well as an artfully arranged tray of pistachios, almonds, and hazelnuts. I motioned to Frances Walsingham to come to me.

"Frances, I have spoken to your father. He is very ill. You must leave court to go and attend him."

She bowed but I noticed her eyes straying to Essex. Everyone's eyes strayed to Essex. She had a special relationship to him, though, as her late husband, Sir Philip Sidney, had bequeathed his sword to Essex, as though passing on his noble reputation. As yet, beyond looking noble, Essex had done little to earn it.

Frances lingered a moment by his side, and then—did my eyes deceive me?—she touched her fingers to his. He hastily pulled them away, refraining from looking at me. Southampton pulled on his sleeve, his high voice distressed. "Come, sir," he said.

With one look back, Essex said plaintively, "If you might receive my mother—"

I shot him a withering look and did not dignify his request with an answer. Lately he had pestered me about it, as if that would change my mind. My mind did not bend under advocacy. If it was right, it needed none. If it was wrong, no amount of wheedling would soften me. Lettice was in the latter category.

Among my own ladies I tried to avoid the false and foolish, but often political considerations dictated that I take someone's daughter or niece, and, pity has it, we cannot always know what will come from our loins. Thus solemn councillors had daughters like Bess Throckmorton. So even here, there were two sorts: the true, such as Helena, Marjorie, Catherine, and her sister Philadelphia, and the flighty—Bess Throckmorton, Mary Fitton, Elizabeth Southwell, and Elizabeth Vernon. As one might expect, the frivolous ones were prettier than the reliable ones. Still, as Solomon said, "As a jewel of gold in a swine's snout, so is a fair woman which is without discretion." Just as I was imagining a golden ring in Bess Throckmorton's elegant nose, Sir Walter Raleigh's broad shoulders hid her from view.

He had been lingering overmuch in the privy chamber when Bess was about, I had noticed. He, as captain of the Queen's Guard, was charged with protecting the virtue of my ladies, even holding a key to the chamber of the maids of honor. Thus far nothing improper had occurred that I could detect, but my suspicions were up. He seemed lately to have singled Bess out for his attentions. I made it my business to interrupt them.

Bess immediately bowed her head and stepped back. She was always polite and subservient—on the surface. Raleigh turned around and, as always, the sheer presence of him was a marvel. Over six feet tall, solidly muscular, and now in his late thirties, he was a man in his prime.

"Your Majesty," he said. "I have tasted the *kahve*, and poetry is singing in my head."

Now he was about to present one of his verses. They were well wrought but I was not in the mood for any. I turned away, but he—without actually touching my arm—stayed me. As I looked over his shoulder, I saw Edmund Spenser, whom I had not seen for nine years, since he departed for Ireland. Raleigh all but pulled him over to me.

"My Irish neighbor," he said, grinning.

"I am come to London to present you with my humble offering," said Spenser. "It is dedicated in its entirety to you and presents your glittering and magic court in its epic grandeur. May I leave a copy with you?"

"If you please," I said. "What is the name of this wonder?"

"*The Faerie Queene*," he said. "It is only the first three books, of which there will be nine. The others will follow." In the fast-deepening gloom I studied his face. He was all thin blades and angles. I hoped he had not been stricken with the Irish dysentery that weakened so many of our men there. "I shall have a presentation copy delivered to you," he was saying.

But already he was fading from my mind as Raleigh murmured, "I have a great concern for the colony. I beg you, let a relief ship sail right away. It has been almost three years." He smiled that dazzling smile. "Let the Faerie Queen succor her child, Virginia."

"Is not my child thriving?"

"Not having seen her myself," he said heavily, "I cannot swear it." He was referring to my allowing him to name the New World colony Virginia in my honor but forbidding him to go there himself. It had been set up five years ago, but no one had visited it for the past two. The coming of the Spanish Armada in 1588 meant that I could not spare ships to sail to the New World and that danger was still there. There was an embargo on ships leaving English ports.

"There has been no word?"

"None," he said. "No one has seen the colony since the ships sailed back from Roanoke Island in November of 1587." He paused. "The little girl born that first summer will be three years old soon. Virginia Dare. The colony needs supplies. It needed them two years ago. It may be desperate by now."

He was right. Something had to be done. "Very well," I said. "I shall authorize a small fleet." Our footing in the New World was but a toehold compared to that of the Spanish, but by staking out territory in the north, beyond their grasp, we could, in time, offset their advantage. The Spanish held the southernmost parts of that coast, a place they called Florida, but we could contain them there and prevent their spread.

Was not the entire continent of South America enough for them? The riches of the Incas and Aztecs feeding their treasuries? As the landmass narrowed toward the wasp-waisted isthmus, the Spanish processed their loot before shipping it back to Spain. Twenty years ago Drake had realized that was their soft spot, where they could be surprised and raided. It had worked for a while, but then the element of surprise was lost and the Spanish raised their guard. Drake then moved his surprise to the west coast of South America, attacking them in Peru before they could transfer the goods to the isthmus. Drake. His genius was undeniable.

But the Spanish had learned from their mistakes and fortified themselves; they were rebuilding the Armada with more modern ships copied from our designs. A ship falling into enemy hands is a disaster, for its secrets will be revealed. We captured and destroyed so many of their ships, but, sadly, they had no secrets to yield, nothing to tell us we did not already know.

# 12

# LETTICE

*March 1590*

Did you achieve nothing at the sultan gathering?" I was looking at my foolish son, so gifted, so unable to use those gifts, so it would appear. "She noticed that you were there, did she not? Did you mention me? Did you mention another command? What *did* you mention?" Oh, my patience!

"I introduced Southampton to Her Majesty."

"What an achievement! You know she cannot abide fops. Now when she thinks of you, she will think of him."

"Stop baiting me!" Suddenly Robert swirled around, a graceful turn that made his fashionable, and useless, short cloak fly out. The sweetness and charm I had always associated with my oldest son had disappeared—all that remained was the impetuous soldier and slick courtier that others saw. "I'll not endure it!"

"You endure it from her, you'll endure it from me, your mother."

"She gives greater rewards. Her rewards are yet to come; you've spent all yours."

"You ungrateful bastard!"

"No bastard, unless what the rumors say is true—that Robert Dudley was your lover long before he became your husband, and that I'm his son."

"If I told you I did not know, would you believe me?" I could hardly believe I was speaking those words.

"I'd rather not. I'd rather think that I inherited the earlship of Essex by rightful descent. Mother, let's forget this. I spoke hastily."

Yes, let us forget these rash mutterings. I smiled and patted the place next to me on the cushioned window seat. "I am happy to have you here," I said. He visited me seldom these days, busy with his London dwelling. It had been Durham House, then it became Leicester House, now it was renamed Essex House. No matter its name, it was one of the grandest on the Strand. He had come by it through my marriage to Robert Dudley, Earl of Leicester, his stepfather. He would not have his blood, then, but was happy enough to inherit his house!

"You would rather we be at Essex House, I think," he said.

"Nonsense! Do you not find Drayton Bassett exhilarating?" I teased him. After my too-quick marriage to Christopher Blount, a man almost my son's age, following the death of Leicester, discretion had advised me to live far from court in the countryside of Staffordshire. If Her Majesty had never forgiven me for snatching her long-suffering love from under her nose and marrying him, the hint that perhaps I had amused myself with a young lover as well had earned her implacable hatred. To steal one's man was injurious; to betray or spurn him afterward was a crime. But I do not admit that I betrayed him. What was a lonely widow to do? I had many debts. The vindictive Queen had hounded me for Leicester's debts, stripping my home of all the movable goods. As if that would bring him back to life and return him to her. No, he sleeps in Warwick Chapel, and his marble monument completed my financial ruin. In his will, he lauded me as his "faithful and very loving and obedient careful wife." He also called me "my dear and poor disconsolate wife." Obviously I had to overcome my grief as best I could, with Christopher. So . . . as the Queen's own Knights of the Garter's motto says, *Honi soit qui mal y pense*—"Shame upon him who thinks evil of it." Leicester was pleased with my services as a wife, and there the matter should end. On his monument is engraved, in Latin, that I, his *moestissa uxor*—tenderest wife—out of my love and conjugal fidelity, caused this to be raised to the best and dearest of husbands. Of course, I wrote it myself.

To my surprise, my son smiled. "There's a part of me that would be content here," he said. "In truth, a part of me that longs for a quiet life in the country."

I laughed, but I could see that he was sincere. "My son, you don't know what you are saying!"

"I don't belong at court!" he burst out. "I'm not that sort of creature. To remember what to say to each person, the better to use them, and to hide my true feelings so they can't use me—Mother, I find it repugnant!"

"It is, indeed, hard work," I said cautiously.

"I am not a courtier! I am not the stuff of which they are made."

"Yet you do so well as one," I reminded him.

"For a little while. But I cannot keep it up. Every day I fear stumbling, falling from that place I have sweated so in climbing to. There are natural courtiers, like Robert Dudley—some say that was his main or only talent—and Philip Sidney. How easy it was for them!"

I turned his head so he could look out the window. "Take a long, slow look," I told him. Drayton Manor lay surrounded by an oak grove and, beyond that, fields. The village of Drayton Bassett nearby had barely an alehouse, a smithy, and a church and vacated convent. It was four days' ride from London under a sleepy sky. "After walking these grounds four or five times, riding across the meadows, and praying in the church, what would you do?"

"Well, Mother, what do you do?"

"I plan how to get back to court, and so would you, my dear. Solitude and rest are only craved by those whose lives are so hectic and demanding they cry out for surcease. For those of us who have nothing else, the quiet life is a dead life. I know you and your restless nature. You'd not last a month here." I would not allow him to throw his life away! "So let's have no more of that talk. Come here for respite, but not to retire."

He jerked his head back around. Now he was going to pout. I found his moodiness quite tedious.

"So, what is next for you? Do you not think it is time to choose a bride . . . the right bride? You are twenty-two and need an heir."

He just continued to sulk and tap his feet. "When I'm ready!"

"You're ready now. Perhaps if you were married, Her Majesty would see you as more stable, more fit for some high command. And if you married wisely, that could go a long way toward advancing the family."

"One sister married wisely, to a baron, and the other foolishly, to that Perrot fellow, and enraged the Queen."

"All the more reason why you must repair the damage."

"The damage to what? The Queen's temper?"

"The family's situation. You have a title with no treasury. Earl of Essex! High and fine sounding! It trails a thousand expenses but has no income from lands or houses, mines or ships of its own. Marry and correct this lack. You cannot live like an earl if you do not have the means of an earl. And if you would succeed at court—"

"I've told you, I don't belong there!"

What was I to do with him, my stubborn, wayward boy? I loosed my harshest barb. "What kind of soldier whines, cries, and sulks? Did Philip Sidney blunder when he bequeathed his sword to you, upon his deathbed? Sidney, the noblest soldier and chivalrous courtier who has lived in our times? You shame his gift!"

"I cannot be Sir Philip Sidney. There is only one!"

"He saw himself in you. Trust him. And . . . need I remind you of the other ways in which we have irritated Her Majesty—"

"Name them! None could compare with yours!"

"There was *your* refusal to let her use our manor at Chartley to house the Queen of Scots. Did you not realize a royal request is a royal command? And what did you do? You said no, because you were afraid the trees on the grounds would be cut down for firewood to warm her! Then you said you were afraid she would damage the interior out of spite because she disliked your father. Of course, the Queen just overruled you. The large moat there meant that they could monitor Mary's visitors more easily. That was all they wanted Chartley for."

"She *did* damage the fireplace!"

"She wasn't there long enough to damage much of anything. Walsingham and his spies caught her in their trap, and by that time next year she had been executed. Plenty of trees were still standing. And need I remind you of the insult to us, that your inheritance of Kenilworth has now gone to Robert Dudley's bastard son? That glorious estate, which should be *yours* . . . Oh, recapture the prestige we have lost. And the first step, the first step, is to marry!"

He jumped up, clapped his hat on his head, and made for the door. He almost collided with Christopher on his way in, barging past with no apology. Christopher, good-natured soul that he was, only turned and looked back in puzzlement. "*He's* in a hurry," he said. "But where is there to go?"

"Exactly what I was telling him," I said. "From here, the only beguiling road is the one leading back to court."

"Ah, now, you speak like you weren't born in the country."

"Those who are born in it are the ones most anxious to get away."

"My dear, we must just molder here," he said. "Molder away together." He began to kiss my neck.

Ah, but being almost twenty years younger, he could leave this country exile after I was truly moldering in my tomb. I did not know, could never have guessed, that I would outlive him by more than thirty years. Of course, his life span was not a natural one.

I returned his kisses, and soon we were up in the bedchamber, taking our pleasure in the still noontide. Christopher was a vigorous lover; what he lacked in nuanced skill he made up in enthusiasm. Youth is a marvelous thing. Not that I was old; I was forty-six, in my prime. Never had I felt more lusty, more desirable, more in command of my charm. How shall I compare my lovers? My first husband, Walter Devereux, Earl of Essex, was timid, unimaginative. I was not even twenty, and knew nothing. In fact, I was so ignorant I thought I did not like lovemaking! Only later did I discover it was Walter's lovemaking I did not like. I endured the nothing in the nights and we did have five children. Then Robert Dudley, Earl of Leicester, appeared and taught me—or did I already know but had not been able to practice?—passion. It made me think I loved him. Later, when we were married, he was older and tired. The splendid courtier with his gleaming chestnut hair, his sumptuous wardrobe, his straight-backed bearing, was replaced by a middle-aged man with a paunch, thinning hair, and a face that stayed red whether he was drinking or not. His long list of female conquests meant that his bed skills were finely honed, and they did not desert him. But he was no longer stunning to look upon; he no longer made a startling presence when he entered a room. Perhaps to the Queen he still did; perhaps she saw him only with the eyes of desire of her youth. Perhaps they both did: Since they had never consummated their attraction, it remained locked in perfect preservation. He did not see her thinning cheeks, her sharpening nose, her unnaturally tinted wigs; she did not see his puffy face, his balding pate, his stiff gait. Ah, love!

Christopher gave a great sigh of satisfaction and lay looking up at the sloping eaves of our chamber. Outside all was still, in the midday hush between work intervals. Soon the farmer would return to his fields, the smith to his anvil. But for us, no hasty repast, no mug of ale, just partaking of each other's bodies.

Christopher, plain Sir Blount, made me happy. He helped me forget my turbulent past and helped me bear the tedium of exile. He was good to molder with. If one must molder.

After he had left the chamber to return to his tasks, I lingered upstairs. The day was a fine one, the spring sunlight clear and sharp. I opened my wardrobe chest; a shining green square-necked dress called to me. It was March and the leaves were unfurling, the grass springing bright and piercingly emerald. I needed my gold and emerald necklace to go with the dress.

For an instant I felt an actual pain in my chest—what I imagine a stab to feel like, although I have never been stabbed—as I remembered that Christopher had sold it last year. Year by year he had sold off pieces of my jewelry to maintain us. At first he had let me choose which to sacrifice, but that was torture. Now he quietly took one, almost at random; it was less painful that way. There was also a lag before I discovered it was gone, so I got to possess it a little longer, in my mind at least. We were in even worse straits than I had told my son just now, because I did not want him to feel desperate, but we were. Leicester had left a heap of obligations for us to pay. His devoted Queen was not so devoted as to forgive him his debts to her, and relentlessly collected them. Being an earl brought its own expenses to my son, but little income. My jewelry kept us afloat for now. But Robert had to make his fortune with the Queen and save us all.

I would not end like my grandmother Mary Boleyn, poor and far from court. She, too, had married a man of no means and her junior in years, and was banished to the country, where she died young. Some say I inherited her easy virtue, her allure, and her looks, that I am more like her than anyone else in my family. She died just a few months before I was born. Perhaps her sad ghost entered me and said, "Do what I could not, my granddaughter. Use your eyes and laugh as your fortune." Well, I did not manage that. But my son can.

# 13

# ELIZABETH

*April 1590*

Today I had several audiences, so must attire myself suitably. Today I wanted tawny. Tawny, yes, the one with the gold embroidered sleeves. Not the one with the braiding at the neckline. As for the jewels: I had one of the finest collections of jewels in Europe, but that made choosing harder, not easier. Green today? I fingered the items with emeralds or jade in them. Knowing my fondness for emeralds, both Francis Drake and Robert Dudley had generously gifted me with them. But their gems were too large for this morning's audience. Then there was a badly designed necklace I had taken pleasure in buying (through a second party) from the estate of Lettice when her new boy-husband was hocking it. I would never wear it, as it did not come up to my standards of workmanship. But that was the point: to own it and not wear it.

Near it lay a tiny gold and emerald pin of a frog on a lily pad. Tenderly I took it out and examined it. François Valois, Duc d'Alençon, had given it to me, in the early days of our courtship. He had taken his nickname of "The Frog" in good sport, commemorating it with this jewel. I pinned it on, thinking how long it had been since I had worn it.

Alençon . . . As I passed through the gallery on the way to my audience, suddenly our old ghosts came shrieking toward me, pleading for a return to possibilities. Once we had stood here and I had kissed Alençon and placed a ring on his finger, before witnesses, and declared that I would marry him. That constituted a legal betrothal. And indeed, the order of service for our marriage ceremony had already been approved by the French commissioners and my prelates. The Virgin Queen had almost become a wife.

I paused and looked down. The wooden balustrade was the same, dark oak intricately carved. But the faces that had beamed up at us at our announcement faded away, as did Alençon's in the light of day. It was long over. At the time, the doctors had told me I likely had another six years of motherhood ahead of me. Now that window had shut. If I had married him, would I have six children by now? Three? One? And all the succession worry would not be plaguing me now.

I hurried past the haunted spot.

---

The audiences were dull, just the usual pleadings for money. (Is there, ultimately, any other kind?) The French Protestants wanted us to commit money and arms to shore up Henri IV, Prince of Navarre, in his fight to retain his crown; the military advisers wanted more ships and weapons and to invest in firearms to replace the old-fashioned longbow. "It was fine for Henry V but is outmoded now," they pointedly told me.

"Guns are inaccurate and clumsy," I reminded them. "And all the paraphernalia, the powder and the shot, are an ongoing expense, and delicate to boot." A little damp, and the powder gave up the ghost, leaving the gunman unprotected.

"Bows and arrows have their own drawbacks," said one man. "The gut stringing them, the feathers on the arrows—"

"God's death! Do you think I know nothing? Do you think I have never handled bow and arrow? Of course there are weaknesses, but less expensive ones than guns have." They call me pinch-purse and stingy, but it is not by choice. No, by God, if the realm were wealthy, we would have a warship for every citizen and shiny armor for every soldier! But we are not, and must turn our gowns and make a brave show. We have not done so badly for all that.

I was relieved to leave. It was enough to put a person in a bad mood all day. But as I reached the door, a messenger handed me a note, telling me that Walsingham was sinking fast.

I must go to him. He had dragged himself to council meetings all through March, despite his physician's warnings. "Nothing can save me," he had said. "I might as well be working, right up until the end." But had it hastened that end?

I changed my attire to the simplest I had and immediately set off in the royal barge to Barn Elms, where he lived surrounded by those trees at the bend of the Thames upstream from London. The journey was not a long one from Whitehall to his landing pier, and I was there by late afternoon.

My arrival caused a stir. I brushed the niceties aside. Then I brushed the objections aside.

He is not fit to receive you.

He does not want you to see him in this state.

You must not expose yourself to what afflicts him.

"I am here to minister to my friend, yea, to feed him with my own hand if need be," I told them.

Inside the house it was very dark; the late afternoon sun barely stabbed through the windows. Most were east facing, looking out toward the river. I smelled the unmistakable odor of illness, which grew stronger as I mounted the stairs to his sickroom.

Frances met me. "Your Majesty, it is not meet that you enter," she said. "My father has sunk very low."

"Should not those who love him be with him?" I answered. "When do we need them most?"

She looked surprised, as if she expected me to shrink from ugliness. "Now," she admitted, opening the door for me.

I could make out a large bed deep inside the room. One window did face west, providing rosy-tinted sunset light. Walsingham was lying motionless, barely discernible under the blankets and bedding. He did not waken when I approached.

Even in this flattering light, his face was yellow. All his features were shrunk and shriveled, as if his flesh had burned away. He had sunk fast since his last council meeting. The illness was swift and merciless.

"Francis," I whispered, finding his hand and taking it in mine, "how do you do?"

A foolish question. How could he answer it? But it was merely to arouse his attention.

"Not well," he groaned. "They will be here soon for me."

The angels? "Yes, to take you home to that spot in heaven you have earned."

"No one earns it," he croaked. Good Protestant to the end.

"Francis," I said, "you leave a mighty space gaping. No one can fill it. But I thank God for having had you all these years. You have saved me, and the throne, on more than one occasion." Oh, what would I do without him, his vigilance and his genius?

"Guard it well," he said. "And other forces will arise. Trust not the French. Oh, that I were here to wrestle with them!" He gave a weak cough. "But I must not question the wisdom of God in calling me now." Again, the good Protestant. Yet I questioned; I questioned all the time.

"Here, try to take some broth." There was a bowl of it by his bed, still warm, with the spoon beside it. I tried to give him some. But it could not pass between his clenched lips. His time had come, then.

"When they stop eating, that is the signal," a physician had once told me. "Everything begins to fail, and they no longer need earthly nourishment."

I would not weep. Not in his presence. It made it harder for them. Another wise person had told me that.

I settled myself by his side. I was prepared to wait, to wait with him. Frances crept into the room and took her place on the other side. We flanked him like church candles beside an altar.

Walsingham had served me twenty years, through the time of Alençon's wooing, through the tortuous journey the Queen of Scots made from luxurious imprisonment until she stood on the scaffold, caught by Walsingham's trap, through the supreme test of the Spanish Armada. William Cecil, Lord Burghley, had served me longer, but Walsingham had been my ultimate protection and the guardian of the realm. How could we survive without him?

It is a test, I thought wearily. Yet another test, to see how I can survive. There have been so many.

Frances was writing in a book. In the silence I could hear her pen scraping across the paper. What could be so important that she must write it at this moment? If it concerned her father's death, it was impertinent, invasive, now. If other, lesser, then insulting. When she left the room to order some fresh sweet herbs to be burned—to mask the choking odor of death—I picked it up.

It concerned her service with me. I quickly turned the pages. I had no wish to read how she regarded me. I knew I would brood upon it. Then there were pages and pages about the Earl of Essex. She noted what he wore on various days!

*My Lord of Essex wore today his copper-colored doublet.*

*My Lord of Essex, attired all in blue, which flatters him well, had his hose in a contrasting shade, the color of newborn lambs' fleece. . . .*

I clapped the book shut. She was in love with him! She was swooning like a green girl in the country. But he was far above her. She was sure to be disappointed. And she was no milkmaid but a widow with a child. I must warn her. What a fool she was to leave it there. I replaced it quickly on her chair.

I stood up, as if by so doing I could keep better guard over Walsingham. Fuzzy light was coming through the windows; the setting sun made the surface of the Thames gleam out the east window and enveloped the western, land, side in a golden haze. We were very near to Mortlake, where Dr. Dee, my astrologer, lived. Smoke from the burning herbs, curling up through the air, stung my nostrils and made my head swim. I swayed, felt unsteady. So I walked slowly to the east window and opened it a crack, hoping for fresh air.

Below me the river slid past, a sleek, winding snake. My head was spinning, and the blurry light made me feel I had entered a dream.

Sailing on the Thames, long ago . . . going to Mortlake . . . Trust not the French. . . .

The French . . . I remembered how foolish I had acted—as foolish as Frances about Essex—over the little Frenchman I had almost married. The little French prince who had so recently, and insistently, haunted me near the staircase at Whitehall sprang back to life again, as if I had opened a magical casement that transported me over time. So many things had ended then, with the Frenchman.

François had been my last, and in many ways my only, serious marriage possibility. I had been wooed by twenty-five foreign suitors over the years. I never intended to marry any of them, but it was my best tool of diplomacy. I had never met any of these men, never laid eyes on them. So they were suitors on paper only, not real, as I would never marry anyone I hadn't seen with my own eyes. (My father's example with Anne of Cleves was warning enough.) In any case I knew time was running out for this ploy. I was in my midforties and could not play this hand much longer. So when another round was started, this time with François Valois, Duc d'Alençon, the younger brother of King Henri III, I thought, why not? Even though he was seventeen years younger than I, reputedly ugly, and very short—what difference did it make? It was all a diplomatic sham. And so it might have remained, if my people had been more amenable even to the idea that I might at last marry.

But they hated the French and attacked François's envoy, saying he represented "an unmanlike, unprincelike, French kind of wooing." Someone even took a shot at him, frightening him mightily. And that shot changed my world. The French envoy blamed it on Robert Dudley, saying that he knew he was in back of it—since he had murdered once, why not again?

I was aghast. He accused my dearest friend and companion, the man I trusted so much that when I lay ill with smallpox I had named him Protector of the Realm, of being a murderer! I cried out that this was vile slander.

"Ma'am, there have been poisoning attempts as well," Simier, the envoy, said, "which I did not see fit to mention. It is well known that Leicester is a poisoner. He poisoned Walter Devereux, the Earl of Essex. He dosed him when he was on leave from Ireland, and it took effect once he was back in Dublin."

"This is not true! The earl died of natural causes! And why would he wish to poison the earl, in any case?"

Simier looked at me pityingly.

"I demand to know what you mean about the Earl of Essex!" I cried.

"Why, Ma'am, he poisoned him so that he could have his wife." He waited to see if I had heard him. "Lettice. They were lovers, and the earl was inconvenient. So Leicester poisoned him, just as he was about to open an investigation."

"Evil whispers!" I said. God knew they swirled around anyone of note.

He drew himself up, as if readying himself, reluctantly, for a coup de grâce. "It's no whisper, Your Majesty, that he and Lettice are married, and have been for a year." He paused. "Everyone knows this but you. While Leicester opposes your own marriage—even attacking me!—he is enjoying his own. He has a wife but begrudges you a husband."

I heard the words, but at first they were only that—words. But then I was forced to put them together, absorb them without letting Simier see how they rocked my world.

"I see," I said. "So the wayward shot has brought many things to light. I am thankful, sir, that you were not harmed, although other things have been."

---

A year. For a year Dudley had been lying to me, hiding the truth. And his wife still served me in my chambers, pretending to be a widow. It was impossible to say which hurt more: the betrayal, the loss, or feeling an absolute fool.

How she must have laughed at me, Lettice, my wayward cousin. With every step she took in my chambers, she mocked me. So she had had her way at last, triumphed over me, taken Dudley away? The merry widow, I had called her. No wonder she had been so merry. Man-hungry and aggressive, she had bagged her prey.

I dismissed her from my service, told her she was banished from court. I told her why. Instead of cringing or even being embarrassed, the hussy said, "You know now. And I am glad of it." The smug satisfaction on her face infuriated me. "It was a strain, keeping it from you."

When I am most angry, I am rigid. I was stone, clenching my fists, as I watched her leave my chambers, where she was never to set foot again.

---

So when Simier whispered to me that his master the prince, known affectionately in France as "Monsieur," had come secretly to England and was waiting in a hidden place to meet me, it was balm to my wounded vanity. No one had ever come courting in person before. Leicester had duped me, but here was another—a *prince*—who had come across the Channel to seek my hand.

I studied his miniature carefully in its oval frame. It showed a person with a pleasing enough face, dark, searching eyes, a wisp of a mustache, a pointed and weak chin. I wished I could say it was the portrait of a man, but it showed a boy. Of course, it had been painted some time ago. It also did not show the pockmarks that everyone mentioned, and it could not depict his height. People said, too, that his nose was bulbous, but it did not appear to be so here. Well, portraits say what we wish them to, or we do not pay the painter.

He was waiting, hidden in the summer pavilion where I had housed the French contingent away from the main palace buildings at Greenwich. I had joked to Simier that he must indeed be a frog, to have swum the Channel to come to me. I wondered how François would take the jest—that was my first test of him.

I was ready for the meeting. I wanted so much to like him. I wanted to seriously consider him; I needed to. For the first time there was no more Dudley in my landscape, blocking my view. Did I see more clearly because of that, or was my vision distorted?

I entered the summer house.

"Oh!" There was a French-accented gasp, and someone was clasping my hands and kneeling before me. Then my hands were being kissed, and the man was murmuring, "To clasp these hands at last. It is enough for me to touch them; but they are beautiful as ivory, slender and graceful as the Virgin in heaven. You, our Virgin on earth!"

I could not discount it as clumsy flattery, for I knew my hands were my finest feature. They *were* the color of ivory, and my fingers were long and smooth. I displayed them whenever I could, especially against dark gowns.

The person rose slowly, standing to his full height—which was not very high. My eyes, now growing accustomed to the dim light, looked down on a head of dark, thick hair. The top of his head only came up to my eyes.

Oh, he was tiny! A ripple of disappointment passed through me. The rest of the hearsay must be true as well. Now he was lifting his face and I beheld it. His nose *was* large, outsized for the rest of his face. His beard was patchy, his chin receding, and his face *did* have pockmarks. They were not the craterlike circles of gossip but were quite noticeable, and his poor excuse of a beard did little to hide them. Now he smiled. At least he had good teeth—white, even, and none missing.

"Your Majesty is disappointed," he said. "I can read it in your eyes. Ah, well, poor François is used to it. Why, my original name was Hercules, but after I took the pox and did not grow very big, I changed it to François. I did not deserve the glorious name of Hercules. And besides," he said cheerfully, "this way I was not expected to slay lions, clean disgusting stables, or battle a venomous Hydra—unless, of course, you count my mother!"

I let out a laugh at Catherine de' Medici's expense. A Hydra indeed, with her many-headed ambitions.

François was attired in a shiny green doublet, with green hose as well, and a patterned half-length cloak. "I only need a lily pad, Your Majesty," he said. "To be your true frog."

Had he worn this just so he could remind me of the frog nickname? He was so sweet, so disarming. He had passed the first test. "I am touched," I said, truthfully. "And I shall cherish my dear frog."

"I shall swim in your good graces," he said. "But I hope to be more than that."

---

And so ensued our curious courtship. There were secret picnics, outings, and dinners. The very furtiveness of it was part of its lure. He was gallant, amusing, and humble. In the soft predawn of those summer mornings, I could stretch under my covers and murmur to myself, "Elizabeth, betrothed to a French prince." The very words, "French prince," had a magic to them. *Once upon a time there was an English queen who loved a French prince. . . .*

I could still have children. It was not too late. I could embrace all those experiences of womanhood I had denied myself. What had begun as a cynical political gesture on my part—a protracted marriage negotiation between England and France would keep the French from signing a pact with Spain, and if Alençon would fight in the Netherlands at French expense, I then saved money and men—was turning into something more complicated.

I had not reckoned on his wooing in person, I had not reckoned on his being so personable, and I had not reckoned on losing my quasi-official consort to another woman at the same time. There were many things that were right about him. He was a prince, an heir of a royal house. His dignity and his credentials were equal to mine.

But my council, reflecting the feelings of my people, were not in favor of it. They did not know he was actually here, but they knew he was coming, having granted him a passport. After all these years of urging me to marry for the sake of the succession, suddenly they realized my wisdom in holding back and appreciated the advantages of having a Virgin Queen. Suddenly they could see nothing good about such a union. One of my subjects even had the temerity to write a pamphlet alleging that no young man without nefarious motives would be interested in a woman my age, and that if I had a child I would probably die, since I was too old. He also called Monsieur "an instrument of French uncleanness, a sorcerer by common vice and fame." Outside my palace walls I could hear taunting voices singing "The Most Strange Wedding of the Frog and the Mouse."

Before he arrived publicly, I had one thing I must do to settle my own mind. I must take him to see my astrologer, John Dee. Dee saw the future and cast horoscopes; he had selected my coronation day as the most favorable. I trusted him utterly.

So I enticed Simier and Monsieur out for what I pretended was a little sightseeing excursion on the river. Close-mouthed guards sat discreetly in back of the royal barge—indeed, they accompanied me most everywhere, silently and unobtrusively, but that is necessary for a ruler these days.

We plied our way upstream from Greenwich, past the wild Isle of Dogs, under London Bridge, past the mansions lined up between the city and Westminster.

"And now we leave the city for the country," I said, as we swept past Westminster, continuing upstream. By this point the river was narrowing, and it was easy to see both banks as the barge kept to the middle. Green riverside paths, old oaks with vast, spreading crowns, and half-timbered inns lined the shores, with swans paddling lazily in the shallows. On the left bank, Barn Elms, where Walsingham lived—lived in ignorance of my royal visitor. Just after it came Mortlake, Dee's home village.

"We'll stop here," I said suddenly. "There is someone I want you to meet."

"A hidden suitor?" asked Monsieur. "Do you have them everywhere?"

That was an amusing thought. "This is where my astrologer and adviser lives," I said. "He does not care to come to court." After we docked and alighted, Monsieur and Simier craned their necks, looking for a grand house, but saw nothing of that sort. "It must be a long walk for us," they said.

"No, it is just opposite the church." Already we had attracted a crowd of followers, mainly children. "He lives in his mother's house."

At that Monsieur burst out laughing, until Simier said, "So do you, my lord."

Having Catherine de' Medici for my mother-in-law was not an appealing thought.

As we reached his cottage, suddenly the door flung open and John Dee peered out. He did not seem surprised or flustered to see me, as most would. "Pray enter." He snapped the door shut behind us.

"Allow me to present my noble guests from France, envoys of François, Prince of Valois," I said. Best to continue the disguise. "John, you were not a tad surprised to see me here? I come seldom. Usually you come to me at court."

"I expected you," he said. "I would be a poor astrologer if I did not." He was tall, handsome, graceful—he would have made a perfect courtier, except that he lacked the slightest social instincts.

"I was treating my guests to the pleasures of a river excursion. Nothing is more lovely than a day here in high summer. Then, on a whim, I decided we should stop here, give them a glimpse of a small riverside village."

"What of the mysteries of the past that you can call up?" asked Simier. He was strangely subdued.

"It isn't the past men fear," said Monsieur, "but what is to come."

"Indeed," said Dee. He led us back through the cramped hall and then into an annex. I saw an array of skulls and stuffed animals crowded on shelves, as well as flasks filled with bilious green and angry red liquids and piles of rolled scrolls. But we did not stop here; he marched toward a murky chamber at the far end. Dee lit several candles. "This is better for what I wish to see," he said. "The crystals and mirrors do not like the bright light."

He unrolled some scrolls and began talking about how his studies showed that we English had rights to a world empire, and I could be queen of a British empire, and so on.

Hideously embarrassed that he should spout this in front of the French, I merely nodded. Dee and I must discuss this in private. Truly, the man had no sense of place and persons. "Let us leave the earthly realm for the stars," I said. "You, who traffic in the constellations, reveal our *immediate* destinies." Well he knew it was forbidden by law to cast my horoscope to predict my life span, but this was safe.

As did I, Dee turned to the topic with relief. "I always have yours at the ready," he said, laying hold of a scroll. "I do it every week. This week's"—he spread its crackling surface out beside a candle—"specifies that in the months to come you will be constrained by conflicting loyalties, very strong ones."

"Pish," I said. "That is a general state of affairs. Come, come, give us a novelty." Nodding toward Monsieur, I said quickly, "Now for my guest's horoscope."

"I was born on March 18, 1555," said Monsieur. "At Fontainebleau."

Dee spread out two more scrolls and studied them intently, then stopped and consulted the celestial globe.

"I was the eighth of ten children," said Monsieur helpfully. "I am of the royal house of France!" he blurted out.

Dee fastened his amber eyes on Monsieur. "Your birth date has told me well enough who you are," he said, then bent back over the charts. "Your birth was favorable and so were your early years. Then, I see, there was misfortune—a setback." He looked alarmed. "I—I see that you may be offered a kingdom ere long. I can tell you this, sir, you should grasp it, because it will make no difference in the end."

Enough of this. I motioned to Dee to stop. "This is not a good day for you," I said. "You are seeing little of matter. Show us some of your other toys." It had been a mistake to come here.

After a polite interval had passed, I thanked Dee for his hospitality in our impromptu visit. On the way out, his mother appeared and Monsieur and Simier bowed and flattered her, asking if she were Dee's younger sister rather than his mother.

While they were so engaged, Dee whispered urgently in my ear, "I did not tell you the worst," he said. "I saw in the duke's horoscope his miserable end. It is *biothanatos*, Your Majesty."

It was so dire he had not dared to put it in English. But I knew my Greek, and what it meant was "violent death by suicide."

---

With all these things before me, I knew it could not be. Part of me was relieved; the other part mourned. François arrived ceremoniously in a few days and was formally received at court. Our secret courtship was ours to remember and cherish, but under public scrutiny it was a different matter altogether. We were no longer our own selves but belonged to others.

Yet still I confounded even myself with the betrothal declaration before witnesses in the gallery at Whitehall. Why did I do it? There are those who see me as the master of all subtle games and political gestures, but in this case I was the slave of my own confusion. Perhaps I wanted to experience, just for a day, the emotions of a bride-to-be. For it lasted only a day. That night shrieks of fear and misgivings in my own mind kept me awake all night.

When the sun rose that morning, I knew I could not go through with it.

I told François that I could not pass such a night, ever again. I took the ring back. And closed the door on marriage forever.

Dee was right that François was doomed. He died a sad death from fever—not violence or suicide, unless it be suicide to venture onto a battlefield—only two years after leaving our shores—still fighting to claim some glory for himself in the ugly fields of the Netherlands. I wore mourning. I was mourning the death of my youth.

And Dudley? Eventually we resumed our relations, but always *she* was there between us. True, she stayed away from court, but that was small consolation. She was in the background, plotting and planning, like a spider. Their son died early, and they had no others. Dudley was heartbroken; besides his love for the boy, he was in desperate need of an heir. What good the granted title of Earl of Leicester, the vast estate and castle of Kenilworth, without a son to leave it to? And that had come true.

Both François and Dudley were gone, leaving no family trace, while Lettice and I remained, abiding.

A stirring, a strong burning smell wafted toward me. The sun had set on Mortlake, out the western window. Walsingham was groaning, turning. The past had flitted, full formed, all in only a moment; now it vanished. I was here once again. Frances had returned, her arms full of herbs, and she was putting some new ones on the fire. That had brought me back.

I smiled at her. The diary was gone off her chair. She had seen to that herself.

Walsingham died three days later. He was buried at night, for fear that his creditors would take advantage of his funeral to demand their payments. It was not fitting. As I said, if England had the money, a loyal servant would not meet such an end, but retire rich and fat. Those who served me paid a high price. I hoped heaven could reward them in the fashion I could not.

# 14

*May 1590*

I was concerned about Frances. My glimpse into her diary and her love-smitten sighs over Essex alarmed me. To be in love with Essex was a recipe for misery for someone like her. He held a high title and would doubtless make a marriage only from the ranks of his equals. And he was a womanizer, a man who enjoyed women's company overmuch. Like others of his sort, he was able to convince his quarry that his interest was genuine and singular. Obviously he had inherited this talent from his mother. It was no place for a girl like Frances to venture. The sooner she realized it, and, in self-preservation, stamped on her feelings for Essex, smothered them like a dangerous campfire, the better for her.

Was it my business to find a husband for the fatherless, dowryless girl? Did I owe my faithful Walsingham that? And was it my business to call Essex off, tell him to cease teasing Frances?

I disliked meddling in people's private lives. As Queen, I knew I had the prerogative, which is another reason I avoided it. It built up resentment, and to what end? It served no ultimate purpose.

I was debating this one fine May morning, sitting glumly at my desk, when Marjorie came to me and said, "Your Majesty, there is important news." She waited for me to look up, then said, "Frances Walsingham has married the Earl of Essex."

"What?" was all I could say. Then: "When?"

"Supposedly—although I don't know for certain—they married right after, or even before, Walsingham died."

"Secretly!" Oh, she was a clever girl, cleverer than I had given her credit for.

But my original feelings were not altered. He would not make her happy. She was no fit mate for Essex, who would need a fiery and strong woman to balance him. I had a chill thought: Had he married her because she was Sir Philip Sidney's widow, and Sidney had bequeathed his sword to Essex? Surely he did not feel duty bound, in an Old Testament sense, to take on his relict wife as well?

"This is a tragedy for them both," I said. "I need to speak to Essex. Summon him here."

---

We met in the privacy of my inmost chamber. I was sitting when he arrived. I did not rise. He knelt before me. I let him remain there a long time before granting him leave to stand.

"Well, Essex, what have you to say for yourself? Marriage is for life. I have heard of some yeomen having the same wife for fifty years. Is that what you want—to have Frances Walsingham your wife forever?" He had already made quite a name for himself among the ladies of the court. His amorous eyes roved everywhere. He far outdid his stepfather. "You must be faithful to her, if I allow this marriage. How like you that?"

His expression revealed that he had not expected this demand. So, he sought to both be chivalric and wed his dead hero's widow but to pleasure himself among more sensual, obliging ladies.

"I bow before Your Majesty's wisdom and request," he said, his head still bowed.

"Think carefully," I said. "I am the Virgin Queen and, regardless of rough humor in some quarters and abroad, I know I am what I claim to be. From that purity and that virginity I draw my power. I do not tolerate deviations in my court. Do you wish to remain in my service? For I am willing to grant you leave to retire to the country, along with your mother."

"Oh, I do wish to serve you!" he cried. "Oh, pray, do not cast me aside! I want to be the knight in your livery!"

He looked so earnest, standing there: straight and keen eyed.

"You are no longer Galahad, that purest of knights," I told him. "There was a time when I saw you as such."

"That was Sir Philip Sidney," he said.

"Bah!" Before I could stop myself, it was out. "His death was a waste!"

Essex went white. I had uttered a sacrilege. "It was noble! 'My need is greater than thine'—when he gave his water to another suffering knight!"

"Oh, you're a fool, Essex!" That came out, too, before I could stop it. "He had no business being there at all. The entire campaign to help the Dutch was mismanaged. He should never have left his leg armor off. He should not have given his water to another. It was all posturing!" There, I had said it.

"You strike at the foundation of my values," he said. "All that I believe in, you lay the ax to its roots."

"So you married Frances in order to feel noble? Very well then, feel noble. That will be your reward. Do not expect any other."

He bowed his head again. I could see that he was shocked. He had expected applause and reward for his chivalric duty. "Yes, Your Majesty."

"Absent yourself from court for a while," I said.

He opened his mouth to complain but shut it again.

He was gone. The foolish boy—his head all aswim with the flattery of having Frances swoon over his shirts, no doubt, and his perceived death duty to his dead friend. I shook my head; this jolt had certainly awakened me. But the lingering miasma of memories of Leicester now intertwined themselves, like smoke, around the living Robert Devereux, his stepson. Why did I care what he did? My own motives became suspect to me.

I needed to leave this stuffy chamber. A ride out in the countryside promised to be just the thing. No one could talk to me while I was galloping across fields.

Marjorie rode with me, as did my guards, but in essence I was alone. We left the environs of London behind swiftly once we had passed beyond Moorfields, those open fields lying outside the Moor Gate where laundresses stretched out their drying sheets on hooks and mischievous boys practiced archery.

This May the plowed fields were already springing with wheat. In wild meadows, the bluebells were in bloom, waving bravely. The air was clear and fresh, scented with flowering hawthorn from the hedgerows.

Robert Devereux's face as he pleaded his case floated before me as I galloped along. His big brown eyes, his newly sprung beard, his bluster and bravado all made him seem younger rather than the mature man he would claim to be. He was—how old? Twenty-two this past autumn. At twenty-two I had still been playing the dutiful subject of my tyrannical sister, subject to house arrest and constant vigilance that my slightest word might not be misinterpreted. By God! What luxury young Essex had. He did not have to worry that he would lose his life for a wrong answer!

We rushed under a low-hanging oak branch, and I ducked. Out on the other side, open fields beckoned. We emerged out of the shadows and into the bright sunshine.

---

Essex, Essex—what drove him? He was the last of an old breed of man—feudal, noble, seeking glory for its own sake. It stirred me in some ways, for I, too, was of an older time. My father had sought battlefield recognition on the fields of France, even when he was near to death, so incapacitated and swollen with his mortal illness he had to be lifted onto his horse with a hoist.

But the truth was that military commands, and heroes, had not held much political sway in a century in England. Essex had come too late. His time had passed him by.

My horse tired, and I felt his pace slackening. I would not urge him past his capacity, and so I pulled him up. I had finished thinking, in any case. What else was there to consider? Only what place I would give Essex. I would await his actions before deciding.

Marjorie reached me and halted by my side. She was panting, and her horse was lathered. "No one can keep up with you!" she said. Then our grooms pulled up as well, and we all rested.

The fields spread out around us. In the stillness of midday, only butterflies were stirring—small white ones flitting from row to row. In the distance a village nestled in a hollow, shaded by trees planted long ago. I could see a maypole sticking up like a finger on its outskirts. The old ways, the old customs. I felt a great pang at the rate at which they were disappearing.

"Come," I said to Marjorie and my companions. "A maypole. Let us go see!"

# 15

# LETTICE

*May 1590*

The rain kept falling, as it had for the past two days. Farmers were glad of it after our dry spell, I was sure, but their concerns were far from pressing to me. I wanted juicy pears and cherries as much as anyone else, but without the money to pay for them, I could not have them grace my table, for all that they grew in the orchards. Money. Money. What did my dear father like to quote from Proverbs? "The wealth of the rich is their fortified city." Puritans knew how to keep one eye on the practicalities of life, while keeping the other on the Scriptures.

Frances started to enter the room, then saw me and backed out. I could barely stand the sight of her, she who had wrecked the ship of our possible fortune. I was trying to master my feelings, but they must still show. It was not her fault, and I should not resent her. No, it was my son's!

He was, wisely, hiding from me. Ever since he had slunk back here with his bride, he had avoided being alone with me. A week now. They had been here a week, and then this wretched rain started. Turning away from the doorway, so Frances would not know I had seen her, I stared out at the dripping trees and the misty fields. The oak leaves had lost their bright new color and were halfway to their summer size; water ran off their scalloped edges and splattered on the ground.

Robert had made a gross misstep in marrying Frances Walsingham. Elizabeth was furious, sending them both from court. It was hideously like what had happened eleven years ago when I married Leicester. I thought all that would be put behind us, that Robert would work patiently to restore our fortunes. What if Elizabeth banished him forever? But no, that could not be. If he had betrayed her by marrying without her consent, I, his mother, was doubly betrayed. For he was meant to be our deliverance.

A particularly big gust of wind hit the trees, swaying them and slapping their branches against the window. Just then I saw Robert dashing between them, ducking down to protect himself. A moment later he stumbled into the hall, soaked. Thinking himself alone, he stamped the water off and shook out his hat.

"Don't spray water all over the chest!" I barked.

Startled, he dropped his hat to the floor.

"And not on the carpet, either!"

Sheepishly, he bent down to retrieve it. "I beg pardon," he said.

"And well you should," I replied. "When you have changed your clothes, you shall come to me in the solar."

He was caught at last.

---

Now he stood before me in the warmest room in the house, while the rain lashed outside. I stood looking at him for a moment, trying to see him not as a mother but as a stranger would. His physical presence was so commanding. He also had a sweetness of nature that revealed itself only after one had been in his presence for a while. On first and second impressions he won hearts. Oh, he had been gifted in all things, my son. The gods must be laughing at us.

"Mother?" he asked as I stood silently with my thoughts.

All my sharpness drained away. I had no rapier to thrust into him. I was overwhelmed with sadness and disappointment, with, yes—defeat. "Oh, Robert," I said. "Why?"

"That was *her* question," he said.

"Not for the first time, then, we think alike," I said. "And what answer did you give Her Majesty?"

"I could not give the true one," he said. "That having made her pregnant, I must now marry her."

"Must history always repeat itself in our family?"

"Your father looked after your virtue when you were in Frances's condition, and Walsingham, on his deathbed, glanced balefully at me—what was I to do? His widowed daughter was expecting—would be disgraced."

"Yes, we widows have a difficult time of it when our bellies swell, after our husbands have been in heaven a good long time already." I looked at my handsome son once again. "I am sure his looks were baleful, since his whole skin was yellow. But without belaboring the point, I must ask—why? Why did you seek her bed at all?"

"Do you mean, without belaboring the point that you were—are—beautiful and Frances is not? Your modesty was always one of your most becoming traits, Mother."

"Never mind my looks, that isn't what I meant—I meant her prospects, what she brings to the marriage."

"Her dowry, as it were?"

"If you must put it that way, yes. Everyone has a dowry, unspoken or not, invisible or not. And mine was not my face—there are girls here in Drayton Bassett with prettier faces, but you'll never see an earl pursuing them to the altar. In fairy fantasies, yes, but not in the world of the Tudor court."

"So it wasn't your face. Are you going to tell me what it was? Or would that be unseemly, to describe the lure of a courtesan to her son?"

What a naïf he was! I laughed. "First your line of sight is on the face, then it descends to the seat of Venus. Neither one is much of a dowry. Look elsewhere, to the practical—to lineage and fortune."

But of course a noble knight was not supposed to do that. He was supposed to think only of love, and of beauty. After that, of duty. Robert looked puzzled.

"I speak of bloodlines, power, and money. What else is there in a dowry?"

"I fail to see how you provided any of those in your own dowry."

"Then your education is faulty, for which I blame myself. Let me rectify that." I took a deep breath. Where common sense is present, this should not need explaining. "Bloodlines: I am at the very least the Queen's near cousin. . . . Some say more than a cousin; some say my mother was the Queen's half-sister. But that is gossip, impossible to prove. Power: My father is a trusted Privy Councillor, high in the Queen's esteem, and has been for almost her entire reign—over thirty years. My first husband, your father, was an earl, and his family had risen to prominence under the Tudors. The only thing I lacked was money. But court entrée or position can be used as earnest for money."

Was he following this? Did I have to draw it for him? He was jutting his chin out in the way he did when he wanted to be stubborn.

"Whereas Frances"—I hoped she was not listening anywhere—"has no notable family. Her father, rest his soul, achieved his position all by himself, by remarkable industry and cleverness. Admirable. But he came from nowhere and his family is back in nowhere. With his death, all power at court ended for them. And money! He was so in debt you know he had to be buried at night, for fear his creditors would swoop down upon his funeral procession if it were held in the daylight. So he could not even afford a simple funeral. In marrying his daughter, you have married only obligations and no future benefits. She's sweet and will be loyal. Had you had no money worries, that would be enough. A rich earl could afford her. The poorest earl in England—for that's what you are—cannot. And now you have thrown away your chance to improve your fortunes by that time-honored method, an advantageous marriage!"

"It seems to me that you are at least as disappointed that your own fortunes will not rise as you are that mine are stranded."

"We are a family, and our fortunes are one. But you are wrong. I am more distraught about you, because your life is just starting, and to start with angering the Queen makes for a poor prognosis. You could have risen high, higher than anyone else at court. Now—?"

"Then I'll content myself with the quiet life," he said. "Many virtuous men recommend it highly. As Henry Howard wrote,

*'Martial, the things that do attain*
*The happy life, be these, I find:*
*The riches left, not got with pain;*
*The fruitful ground, the quiet mind:*
*The faithful wife, without debate;*
*Such sleeps as may beguile the night.*
*Content thee with thine own estate;*
*No wish for Death, nor fear his might.'"*

"Where did you learn that? Cambridge? Well, Henry Howard was executed for treason. I would not trust his wisdom!"

# 16

# ELIZABETH

*November 1590*

our Glorious Majesty's Accession Day, ever may we hold it upon the highest altar of our thankfulness." Archbishop Whitgift bent low, so that the top of his miter was pointing at me like an accusatory finger.

"Oh, John." I sighed. "Pray straighten yourself up."

He seemed to unfurl himself, one vertebra at a time, until he was at full height, looking sternly at me. His new celebratory robes, ordered for the upcoming commemoration, glittered with embroidery and gold thread. "Your Majesty, I am not jesting. The words in the Book of Common Prayer, celebrating your coming to the throne, are not exaggerated. 'We yield thee unfeigned thanks, for that thou wast pleased, on this day, to set thy Servant our Sovereign Lady, Queen Elizabeth, upon the throne of this realm. Let her always possess the hearts of her people; let her reign be long and prosperous.'"

"It has been long, John, it has been long, and who could have foreseen that? As for prosperous, we do not do badly considering we are a little island with no gold. My gold is my people. The prayer is correct; I want always to possess that gold. And as it is not carried on ships, it is not liable to theft by the Spanish as is the other kind."

"Still, the Spanish will rob you of that love if they can," he warned.

"The way to keep my people's love is never to take it for granted," I said. "But tomorrow, as ritual and custom decree, you will preside over the service celebrating my Accession Day and recite that very prayer in St. Paul's. And the bells will toll, as they do every year, the trumpets and cornets will sound from the cathedral rooftop, cannons will boom from the Tower, and people all over England will light bonfires and take a holiday. You will come to the tilts here at Whitehall, will you not? They promise to be more spectacular than ever."

"I find the tilts too . . . pagan," he said.

"Oh, surely not pagan," I said. "King Arthur, after all, had knightly contests, and he was a most Christian king."

"I mean the extravagance, the vanity, the display. . . ." He shook his head. "The poor—"

"Ye have with ye always," I finished for him. "Even Jesus said, 'You can help them any time you wish. But not on Accession Day.'"

"I do not believe those were his exact words, Your Majesty."

I laughed. "What? Do you mean that Christ did not observe my day?"

He scowled, unable to jest. Whitgift's stiffness, his aloofness, made him unpopular. His theology suited me, but his personality was so dour.

"In any case," I continued, "your own raiment is so dazzling Essex would take second place to you. He would be crushed. Some might even accuse *you* of vain display—unfairly, of course."

Another sore point. Whitgift's high church trappings had earned him the nickname of "Pope," and he liked to be accompanied by a retinue. But I liked my clergy to look like clergy, my priests to look like priests. If that made me popish, so be it. Unfortunately, this only angered the plain-scrubbed Puritans and tantalized the crypto-Catholics.

It was almost impossible to balance these two contesting parties. Alone of all Protestants, the Church of England had come into being by royal decree, not by a popular movement. When my father broke from Rome, he never broke from his basic conservatism in ritual and formalities, and thus retained many of the old Catholic usages. It was an odd, tense marriage between inward Protestant theology and outward Catholic trappings. Much of my reign was troubled by these turbulent currents. My person, as Supreme Governor of the Church of England, held them together, but not easily. The compromise I had enacted at the beginning of my reign had not satisfied all.

"I shall absent myself," Whitgift said.

"You will miss a good show. Ah, well, then, ring the bells all the louder, and pray all the harder for me. I have needed prayers to sustain me all the thirty-two years I have sat on the throne, and will need them all the more from now on."

After he departed, I thought of those first moments when I had become Queen, the day so long ago now enshrined and encapsulated and turned into a holy day.

People were relieved when I became Queen. I had been popular with the people, but primarily because they disliked the reign of my sister. She was half Spanish and married to a foreigner. I was seen as "mere English," fully one of them, and my looks recalled my father's in his prime. In retrospect, his time was seen as a golden era. They wanted it back.

The rejoicings that first Accession Day were spontaneous; as the years went on, they grew increasingly more ritualistic and scripted. In the two years since the Armada, they had become rather disturbingly idolatrous. They had now been extended to St. Elizabeth's Day, two days later, and dedicated to Armada celebrations.

I did not instigate any of these things, but neither did I forbid them. Still, the excesses of the celebrations were making even me a bit uneasy.

---

At high noon on November 17 I and my honored guests walked to the tilt gallery, a long room at one end of the course, where we could see the whole tiltyard, its barrier cutting like a razor down its middle, its pennants fluttering in the brisk wind. Beyond the barricades were stands and scaffolds where the common people, for a fee, could watch. An immense roar rose as the people saw me passing through the open air, just before we mounted the stairs and entered the gallery. I stood and waved at them, letting them know I welcomed them.

I had my favorite ladies around me—Marjorie Norris, Catherine Carey and her sister Philadelphia, Helena van Snakenborg. They were all autumnal ladies, being of that mature age I liked to say bestows wisdom and others say bestows wrinkles. The younger ones—I despair of them. They seem lacking in character, flighty, obsessed with men. I need young ones about me, lest it be said that my court is no longer a magnet for the best in beauty, strength, and wit, but they irritate me. Today I made them sit farther back, behind the people of note. Flanking me on one side was the French ambassador, on the other, Robert Cecil.

The fanfare sounded, announcing the entry of the first pair of contestants. Like everything else at court, it was not simple. First a pageant car with its theme must make its way around the course, then the servants of the men mount the stairs and present their masters' decorated shields and read a poem proclaiming the theme—usually allegorical, of course. In this case, the first pair was Sir Henry Lee, my personal tilt champion, master of ceremony of the annual tilt, versus George Clifford, Earl of Cumberland. Henry had been my champion for twenty years now. I settled myself back as he came into the tiltyard, drawn in a cart decorated with crowns and wilting vines. Then he stepped out and made his way over to me, bowing low. He himself was covered in drooping, limp greenery. A buzz arose from the stands.

"Your Most Gracious Majesty," he said, "the time has come when I must yield up my tilt staff. I am a vine withered in age by royal service." He fingered one of the dying vines, evoking laughter. "Here, I present to you my successor, who I pray finds favor with you—the Earl of Cumberland." Just behind him came the pageant car of the earl, representing his family castle, with the earl dressed in dazzling white.

Sir Henry Lee was my age—fifty-seven! And was there a person in the arena who would not be aware of this? I stiffened.

"As you can see, I am bent and overtaken by age," he said. "The years have taken their toll, robbed me—"

I waved him to silence. "Go about your tilt," I said. "Now."

I was shaking with anger. The fool. If he had wearied of managing the tilts—which was a taxing job—why had he not come to me in private? Staging such a reminder of his age was impolitic. And if he was so old, why did he still indulge his lusts with the young women of my chamber? Yes, I knew about his little forays, his assignations with Anne Vavasour, among others. I'll warrant he did not remind *them* of his drooping vines, or drooping anything else.

I barely saw the tilt. I heard Lee's lance break, but then, he would have planned it that way.

The French ambassador . . . Who would have thought I would find the mess in France preferable to think about? I turned to him brightly and began to murmur about the distressing turn of events over there, what with the Spanish invasion in northern France. "Philip of Spain—the French king's enemy and mine." I sighed. "Can the man not leave a single Protestant prince to draw breath in peace?"

"That is why it is urgent that you aid him!" the ambassador said. "You have been delivered from the Spanish menace. Grant, in your mercy, the opportunity for others to be as well."

"Grant—ah, now, that is the problem." Robert Cecil leaned forward and joined in, as I had known he would. "'Grant' is another word for 'loan,' or 'gift.' Money. War is so *expensive*," he said petulantly.

"A good investment is never expensive," said the ambassador. "It often saves expense."

"I could bankrupt myself saving money," I retorted.

"Help us!" the ambassador said. "You will never regret it."

I would regret it before I released the first penny. "We ourselves are not free of the Spanish menace," I reminded him. "The humiliation of the defeat of the Armada stings Philip, and he is determined to send another and complete the mission. Preparing to defend ourselves is costly. Defense is always more dear than offense, as the enemy gets to choose the point of attack, whereas we must be prepared on all fronts."

"We need your troops," he begged. "I look around me here, see all these men thwarted in their military longings, able to do nothing but play in a tiltyard!" He waved toward the latest pair, strutting and preening before mounting their horses. Lord Strange was strange indeed with his forty squires and their azure tilting staves. A pageant car fitted up as a ship and bearing his eagle emblem rumbled behind. The ambassador had a point.

"We shall see," I said in my most lofty tone, the one that meant "No more now."

Shortly thereafter, the sad strains of funeral music pervaded the tiltyard, and then a funeral cortege appeared, driven by a gloomy figure of Time, drawn by a pair of coal black horses, black feather plumes waving. Within the funeral car sat a knight dressed in mourning—dark sables and black robes. His head was bent and he affected the pose of a penitent.

The funeral car stopped. The penitent got out and made his way to the gallery, where he stood before us. It was the Earl of Essex, who did not raise his eyes to mine but smote his chest and cried, "Forgive this heavy fault," and fell on his knees.

I let him kneel there for a long time before ordering him up.

We were still estranged over his hasty and secret marriage. My disappointment in him had been deepened when he refused to apologize or approach me again. And now he chose this showy, public manner of contrition—something that would win him attention and admiration. Always he sought to draw all eyes to himself.

I did not motion him to mount the steps to the gallery and address me. He stood many long moments, expecting that I would do so. I could almost hear the cessation of breathing by all the onlookers. The midafternoon sun caressed his reddish hair, exposed now that he had removed his helmet with its engraved pattern. The rest of the armor imprisoned him, making him stand stiffly.

"You and your opponent may commence the joust," I said.

His companion, Sir Fulke Greville, now emerged from the funeral car and motioned for their horses to be brought.

They mounted quickly and ran at each other at the barrier as quickly as possible. Greville did not flinch when he was unhorsed and his lance broken. He rolled a little way in the dust, got to his feet, and scrambled away, after bowing in our direction. Essex also beat a retreat.

"That boy is bold beyond words," said Helena, leaning toward me from her seat. Even after twenty-five years in England, I could hear her Swedish accent. I found it charming. "He needs a spanking."

"But who will give it to him?" Marjorie said. "His mother? She needs a spanking herself."

"A punishment. That's what he needs," insisted Helena.

But I *was* punishing him, keeping him from court. It had just made him more demanding.

"He is a plaything, Your Majesty," said Robert Cecil, from the other side. "Negligible. This is all he is fit for—dressing up and playing a knight at a staged tournament."

I was well aware that there was no love lost between the two Roberts, Cecil and Essex. For a time, in their childhoods, they had lived under the same roof, Essex being a ward of Burghley's. But the tall, gangly, aristocratic Essex had had nothing in common with small, scholarly, stooped Cecil. As they grew to manhood, their indifference had turned to rivalry. Essex could not comprehend that the indoor talents of Cecil might be more valuable to me than the outdoor ones he excelled at.

I shrugged and lifted my jeweled fan. The jousts went on, another nine pairs after Essex and Greville, thirteen in all. The sun was setting when the last pair broke their lances, ending the tournament.

Then, suddenly, another elaborate pageant car entered the field, lurching over the paths. A blare of music from players hidden near the barricades enveloped us, and the decorated car rumbled toward us before halting. It was draped in white taffeta, and a sign claimed it was the sacred Temple of the Virgins Vestal. It rested on pillars painted to look like porphyry, with lamps glowing inside. Three girls, in flowing, light gowns, emerged and dedicated themselves to me as Vestals, then sang out, "To you, the chief Vestal Virgin of the West, we dedicate our lives in service."

Then Sir Henry Lee stepped out of the temple, plucking a poem from one of the pillars. He proceeded to read it, praising me as a mighty empress whose empire now extended to the New World.

"She hath moved one of the very Pillars of Hercules," cried Lee. "And when she leaves this earth, she will be borne up to heaven to receive a celestial diadem!"

Had I known about this, I would have forbidden it. Instead, I was forced to endure it, knowing that people would assume I had ordered it.

---

There was, of course, a gathering afterward, to display the shields before they were formally hung in the riverside pavilion alongside the ones from former meets. The price of participation, as it were, was a pasteboard shield from each knight, especially designed for the tilt. There were many variations on the theme of knight: there had been enchanted knights, forlorn knights, forsaken knights, questing knights, and unknown knights. Sometimes they combined as forsaken unknown knights, and so on. There were also wild men, hermits, and the inhabitants of Mount Olympus. A man could be anything he wished for one of the tilts.

# 17

he jousters kept to their chosen personae in the Long Gallery, where the gathering was held, so the chamber swarmed with Charlemagnes, Robin Hoods, and King Arthurs. I liked moving among them, imagining I had been transported to another time and realm. Outside, clearly visible through the gallery windows, bonfires were blazing in the fields and along the riverbank, fiery necklaces of joy. Only two years ago signal fires across the land had announced the first sighting of the Armada, and now the memory of that victory added to tonight's celebration.

In the hills, at the signal stations, the brush and wood had been replaced, ready to be lit again if—when—the Spanish returned, as they had vowed to do.

But tonight, tonight, inside and out, fires meant only harmless play. Mid-November could be mild—as it had been the actual day I had become Queen—or it could be raw, as it was now. I was glad of the warming fires in the gallery, thankful to be indoors.

The gallery was so long there were two sets of musicians, one to play at each end. At the west end, lutenists and harpists played soft melodies and sang plaintive verses; at the east, sackbut players, drummers, and trumpeters made thumpingly good dance music. A bagpiper was to join them at the end of the evening for a rousing finale.

Unlike the jousters, I had changed my costume. I was now attired formally, as befitted this high national holiday. My ruff was so enormous, so pleated and starched, I could barely move my chin. My gown was stretched so widely across its hoops I was obliged to move sideways between people. I had chosen my tallest and reddest wig, piled high with curls and then made dazzling by jewels scattered throughout the tresses. Upon my bodice hung various emblematic tokens to please certain of my courtiers. I wore the replica of the glove of Cumberland, the eglantine pendant given me by

Burghley, the ropes of white pearls bequeathed to me by Leicester, and from my ears hung emeralds from one of Drake's voyages. I was a veritable trophy of commemoratives.

The younger people were dancing at one end of the chamber; others warmed themselves before the arching stone fireplaces. Burghley was gamely standing despite his gout. Such gatherings were a trial to him, but he did not want to give in to his infirmities. He relied on his son Robert to protect him from overzealous jostling or too-long standing. The two of them were huddled together, murmuring, but they broke off as I joined them.

"Another glorious celebration," said Burghley. "It is especially gratifying to have been present at the true moment."

"I said when I appointed you secretary of state that I judged you a man who would tell me the truth regardless of my personal wishes," I remembered. "And you certainly have fulfilled that mission."

"Not without some conflict, Your Majesty," he said.

"Truth telling is seldom pleasant, William," I said. "Only the brave dare to do it. By that rule, you are the bravest man in the realm."

A swirl of bright dresses passed by, young girls in the excitement of the moment, the eternal moment of youth. The faces change, the ladies pass off the dance floor and onto chairs, to be forever replaced by others. They were quickly surrounded by young men, the sons of courtiers and officials. I did not recognize some of them—I, who prided myself on knowing everyone. Who was that towheaded one? Who, indeed, the short one with the wide grin? Whom did they resemble? Who were their fathers and mothers?

One young woman whom I could name, an Elizabeth Cavendish, daughter of a minor courtier, was fending off the attentions of the towheaded boy, but not very strenuously. He looked vaguely familiar but not in an identifiable way. Now she turned her back on him and he grabbed her sleeve, spinning her around to face him again. While I was looking, he put his hand on the back of her head and forced her to kiss him.

"Sir!" I said.

He peeked out from behind Elizabeth's head and his eyes widened as he saw me. Hurriedly he pushed her away and bowed before me.

"Come here!" I ordered him.

"Yes, yes, Your Majesty." His legs shaking, he came over to me and sank down in obeisance until his forehead was almost touching the floor.

"Get up, you brazen creature," I said.

He stood erect but did not look me in the eyes.

"What is your name?" I asked. "We do not let anyone tarnish the reputation of a lady at court, no matter what her age. This is not France!"

"Yes, Your Majesty. No, Your Majesty." He was trembling. "My name is Robert Dudley."

Robert Dudley! What a cruel coincidence. But no—how could it be? Was he mocking me? "We do not find this pleasing," I said. "Answer us true."

"Your Majesty, most sovereign lady, I swear to you, that is my name."

Was there a resemblance? The blond hair had misled me. The eyes, the carriage—were familiar. "Are you the son of Douglass Sheffield?"

"Yes," he said.

Leicester's natural son, born of his dalliance with the married Douglass Sheffield! God forgive me, but a jolt of pleasure shot through me. He was Leicester's only living descendant, and this baseborn child would inherit all the Dudley estates when he came of age, while the Leicester title had passed to his brother Ambrose's house, leaving Lettice—nothing.

Suddenly he was pleasing in his forwardness and looks. "I see," I said. "And where are you now, what do you do?"

He stood a little straighter, and the tremor left his voice. "I am sixteen and I study at Oxford," he said.

"Very good, very good," I said. This lad pleased me. Nonetheless, standards must be kept. "You shall return there, and do not come back to court until you have learned better manners."

For an instant he was his father, the same exasperated expression of disappointment crossing his face. Then he smiled, an ingratiating smile. "In all things I obey you, Your Majesty," he said.

The girls were glancing over their shoulders to see our exchange; when Robert made his way out of the chamber, they turned their attention to others.

I glanced up and down the gallery, taking account of all those present. I saw Essex, taller than most, still affecting his forsaken knight persona. A shorter man kept him company, and he sported no costume. He had riveting, dark eyes that I could see even in the dim light.

Seeing me, Essex immediately left his friend and hurried toward me, but I turned away. I had no wish to speak to him at this moment.

To make my point, I motioned Raleigh, whom Essex hated, to my side. He was resplendently dressed, as usual—no one could fill out a brocade doublet like Walter Raleigh—but his smile was forced. It was he who was glum, for all that Essex wore the inky robes.

"Why, what is it, Walter?" I asked. "This is a happy night, but I see sadness in your eyes."

"As always, Your Majesty can see more than others," he said. "I thought I had hidden it well."

"What troubles you?"

"There is someone else who ought to be the one to tell you," he said. "Governor John White should do so."

John White! As soon as I heard that name, I knew. "Oh, Walter," I said. "The colony!"

"Sir John—"

"Is nowhere to be seen this moment. Tell me, quickly. The facts do not change, regardless of who presents them."

He closed his eyes, steeling himself. "With Your Majesty's gracious permission last spring, we were able to send relief ships to the colony in Virginia. But it has vanished."

"Vanished?"

"When White arrived, he found the island colony utterly deserted. The palisades and cabins were overgrown with creepers. They found chests broken open, books and maps and pictures all torn and ruined by weather, and Governor White's ceremonial armor eaten through with rust. There was not a sign of any of the hundred colonists, no clue but the word 'Croatoan' carved on a post at the fort, and 'Cro' on a tree."

"Indians? Did the Indians kill them?"

"No one knows. When White left them three years ago, they had promised that if they moved to another site, they would carve the name of that site at Roanoke, and that, if they had been attacked or forced to flee, they would carve a Maltese cross as well."

"What does 'Croatoan' mean?"

"It's another island some fifty miles from Roanoke."

"They must have moved there, then. What happened when White went there?"

"He was unable to land. The ships were driven out to sea, and thence back here. He has only just returned."

"Do you mean that no one knows whether the colonists survived?"

"I am sorry to say, yes, Ma'am—that is, no one knows."

"They have been abandoned? White abandoned his own family there, his daughter, his granddaughter?"

"He had no choice. He could not prevail against the elements. Ships are but wood and canvas, playthings of the currents and winds."

"Oh, God!" I thought of them cast away there, waiting for the ships that never came. Had the Indians helped them, befriended them, or had they massacred them? "I am grieved and shamed that the colony bearing my name of Virginia should have come to this."

"The New World is a dangerous place," said Raleigh. "Alluring, compelling, offering glittering prizes and gruesome death. For every reward, there seems to be a punishment. Inca gold in South America, arrows of Virginia savages in North America."

I felt tears stabbing at my eyes. There was a human face behind each victory and defeat, a personal price to be painfully paid.

All around me the music was tinkling and the dancers twirling. Voices rose above it, joking, laughing, happy in their moment. Outside, I could see the bonfires dying down, some flames still stabbing high into the night, others sunk into glowing mounds. The boats on the river were dwindling.

Raleigh was waiting to be either answered or dismissed. "Yet you are drawn to that New World," I said. "Had you been at the colony, you would now be lost as well."

"It is a chance every explorer must take, Ma'am," he said. "God willing, and with your gracious permission, I will set foot on that continent, sooner rather than later, I pray."

"Aye, and die for it," I snapped.

"A death I prefer," he said, "to withering away by a fireside." He glanced pointedly at Burghley, now huddled on a stool, his gouty leg thrust out.

I turned away and immediately saw Essex waiting his turn for my attention. As soon as he realized I had noticed him, he started forward, pushing others aside to reach me. In his wake trailed his companion, the man with penetrating dark eyes.

His costume was magnificent, I must give him that. The deep sable velvet of his sleeves, latticed with gold and jeweled ribbons, glistened as if he had just surfaced from a deep pool. I said so.

"If that is true, my own glorious mistress, it is from a deep pool of melancholy, where I have languished since losing your favor," he said, dropping to one knee, ostentatiously. "I break to the surface in beholding you."

"As part of your languishing concerned your lack of finances—for you have importuned me from a distance for months—I marvel that you could scrape together the means to pay for your devices and appearance here at the joust. Get up," I ordered him.

He rose. "Let me serve you again!" he said. "Send me to France, where I can lead your forces."

"You have no experience in command, and as yet there are no English forces in France," I said.

"But there will be," he said. "There must be! The Spanish menace—their boldness in landing in Brittany must be answered!"

"Why? Because King Henri IV has asked me to? My dear boy, if I had answered the begging call to arms of every king and kinglet and duke who has sought my help, there would not be a farthing left in our treasury by now. As it is, the war in the Netherlands has squeezed me dry. And that is known as a *little* war."

"As wars go, it is, Ma'am." The dark-eyed man spoke.

Who was this? Before I could demand an answer, Essex said, "My friend and adviser, Francis Bacon."

Bacon. Bacon. I peered at him. "Nicholas Bacon's son! My little Lord Keeper, aren't you?" His late father had been Lord Keeper of the Great Seal, and I had met his formidably intelligent son as a child.

"Indeed. You remember." He smiled.

"How could I forget? You made quite an impression on me when we first met, when you were—how old?" I had met him at his father's home—a house so tiny it had no garden. I had teased Nicholas, saying it was too small. Later he had brought Francis out, and when I asked how old he was, he chirped, "I am two years younger than Your Majesty's happy reign."

"Ten, Ma'am."

"Essex, leave this matter of France," I said, turning back to him. "I prefer to let the Continent bleed itself without our help. Now, to return to your finances—not only have you outfitted yourself extravagantly for this occasion, but you managed to repay the outstanding loan I had made you a while back by presenting me with one of your last unmortgaged pieces of property. A fine gesture. Ah, Essex, what am I to do with you? Now you are utterly destitute, having repaid me, and left your other debts to hang."

"I am at your mercy," he said.

"And I shall show mercy," I answered. "The monopoly for the tax on sweet wines, owned by your stepfather Leicester, expired with his death. I grant it to you. That gives you the custom fees for all the imported nectar wines from the Mediterranean—malmseys, muscatels, muscadines, vernages."

I had toyed with this idea in advance, but my sudden rush in decision took me by surprise. Even as I spoke the words to bestow the gift, I questioned myself. Should he be encouraged in his lack of self-restraint? But he shone so bright. . . . Should he be allowed to tarnish? God's breath, the luster of the court had dimmed so mightily in the past few years—was he its last glimmer? Should he be polished or covered up?

"Your Majesty!" This time his gasp was not feigned. "I am—I have no words, beyond a deep thanks."

I saw that even Francis Bacon's sharp little eyes had widened.

I pulled myself back, restrained my generosity. "The grant is for ten years only. It will expire in the year 1600."

He laughed wildly. "That is a whole age away!"

"It will pass quickly," I said. "Look to it."

Before he could gather his wits and begin effusive thanks, I motioned him away. Soon enough he would be pelting me with letters, poems, and gifts. Soon enough he would be strutting the halls of court.

The late hour changed the spirit of the evening. The older courtiers turned pleading eyes to me, as they wished to go to bed but had to be released by my permission. Burghley, Knollys, Admiral Howard, Hunsdon I sent home. Now the younger set could dance more freely on the boards, the musicians play more ribald music. I supposed, in the name of good humor, I myself should retire. Just as I prepared to announce my departure, I saw several of my ladies huddled together, bent over something, their backsides making a rainbow of colors—pale green satin, russet brocade, scarlet velvet. They were giggling, and it made the material of their dresses shimmer.

"What amuses you so?" I peered over their shoulders. "A book? Not the Holy Scriptures, I'll warrant," I said.

They tried to close it, but I grabbed it away, laughing as well. I felt giddy from my impulsive gift to Essex. I flipped the pages open and read a few passages. I blushed.

"Such language!" It was entirely ribald—a translation of the Italian epic poem *The Frenzy of Orlando* on the adventures—and misadventures—of the aforenamed hero.

They giggled all the more.

"Where did you get this?" I asked.

Mary Fitton, Frances Vavasour, and Bess Throckmorton simpered and bit their lips. Finally Mary said, "John Harington has been showing it about."

"My saucy godson," I said. "So this is how he directs his wit." I caught sight of him across the room, dancing heatedly with Elizabeth Cavendish. Mistress Cavendish, I noted, seemed not to miss Robert Dudley. I interrupted their frantic dance. John's handsome face lit up with genuine pleasure. "Your Majesty! My good mother!" he cried. His face changed when I waved the book before his eyes.

"John, this heats up the page," I said. "It is a wonder the book is not smoking. It is no fit reading for my maids of honor."

"I merely translate, I do not create," he said.

"Very well then," I said. "You must, by all means, finish your translation. I see that this is only the twenty-eighth canto, the part concerning the risqué tale of Giacomo. Stay home, away from merriment, until you have translated the *entire* poem, all forty-six cantos. Then you may present it to me."

"Your Majesty sets me a Herculean task," he said. "As an Italian scholar yourself, you know that well."

"As an Italian scholar, I shall be proud that my godson has produced the first complete English translation. After all, it was published in Italy in 1532. That was a long time ago." The year before I was born—a long time indeed.

"I shall dedicate myself to the task," he said.

He was always a good sport, my godson. I liked that about him. And he never asked me for preferments, grants, or favors. I liked that even better.

# 18

## *August 1591*

ssex had won. Henri IV had won. With great misgivings, I had sent one to help the other. Essex had pleaded on his knees for two hours—two hours!—in my chamber to send him to France. Henri IV had sent envoy after envoy, defensive treaty in hand. The Spanish had invaded northern France on two fronts, seeking to secure it as a Catholic ally by stamping out the heretic king and his Huguenots. From there they could funnel material into the Netherlands to launch a better attack on us. There was even the danger that all of northern Europe would be Spanish. So, for the safety of the realm, I was forced once again to send troops to the Continent. Always a sorry business, and one I did with a heavy heart.

In late July I had inspected Essex's troops, all fitted out in his tawny and white livery. There were some four thousand of them; three thousand more under commander "Black Jack" Norris had already crossed the Channel.

Essex was only twenty-three and had never commanded an expedition. He clutched Sidney's sword as Arthur had Excalibur, but it had no magic to confer valor or strength; it was merely a piece of metal. I was forced to rely on such a green boy as a general. The truth was that England had few seasoned land commanders. Our luck and our victories had come at sea.

He went with a fistful of instructions. He was not to lead any troops into action from his post at Dieppe until the French king had fulfilled his promises spelled out in the alliance treaty. He was, under no circumstances, to confer knighthoods on anyone except for deeds performed with exceptional bravery. I detested the idea of cheapening titles. I never handed them out promiscuously. To be a "Sir" in the court of Queen Elizabeth should *mean* something.

He had sailed off, taking my worries with him, in late July. I left London then to begin my year's Progress. During the troubled times of the 1580s, the Progresses had ceased. I had missed them sorely, as they had always served as a flowery and bucolic counterweight to the enclosed, airless, and intrigue-ridden palaces in the winter.

I knew it was an illusion. I knew that any venture that requires four hundred wagons and twenty-four hundred horses, that might require a subject to enlarge his house to accommodate the royal visitors, that harnesses the imaginations of every person living nearby to provide music, verse, and allegorical costumes, is hardly a lighthearted affair. Work, work is in back of it all. But when all that is done, how convincing the masque that emerges. And I like to think that in return I bestow something intangible on them, something they can keep in their memories. I hope a little of Elizabeth still lingers in each place and with each person I visit on Progress.

———

I would be going south this time, on a lengthy Progress. Eagerly I mapped out my route: leaving London, I would journey down through Sussex and pay a visit to the coastal cities of Portsmouth and Southampton before swinging back toward London. The two Cecils and I hunched over maps, dispatched letters to the prospective hosts en route, and discussed political benefits from the journey.

"I have a mind to wait in Southampton for a secret visit from Henri IV," I said. It would make perfect sense for him to cross over to Southampton and for us to put the final touches on our treaty. Besides, I was curious to see him, my mirror image and theological companion: a male Protestant ruler of a contentious country.

"As the common folk say, Ma'am, I would not hold my breath," said Burghley, wheezing himself. "Henri IV is a wily creature."

"His Protestantism may not be as firm as Your Majesty's," said Robert—*Sir* Robert Cecil. I had knighted him earlier this summer in recognition of his outstanding statecraft and loyalty. I had also appointed him, at the age of twenty-eight, to the Privy Council. His father was proud. But Robert had earned it, not inherited it. Thus began, this summer, what later became known as the war of the two Roberts: Cecil staying at home practicing politics, Essex abroad waving a sword.

"I don't care how firm it is, as long as he wears the label," I said. "Overdevoutness in a ruler is dangerous—it leads to the like of Philip II."

———

Oh! How glorious it was to mount up and ride away, out of the city and into the countryside. August is a heavy, rich month, the time when harvests are coming in and we can see the actual results of our labor. If it lacks the bustle and promise of spring, it can claim the fullness of completion.

Behind me stretched the rumbling wagonloads of things we would need on our journey. I carried all my own furniture—my bed and all its hangings, my wardrobe and writing desk, chairs, and cabinets—as well as my personal effects. Several more carts of trunks held my clothes. Most of the court was traveling with me, except for those lords who needed to attend to their estates. I was well aware that everyone did not regard the Progress as the holiday that I did; in fact, many courtiers considered it a hardship to traipse around the countryside and stay in accommodations that might not be up to the standards of comfort they craved.

I had selected Cowdray as our destination, the home of Sir Anthony Browne. He was old—well, perhaps not so old; he was only six years older than I. He was a Catholic, and open about it. Yet at Tilbury, when Philip was counting on my Catholic subjects to betray me and join his invasion, he had brought two hundred horsemen to me, declaring his intention "to live and die in defense of the Queen and my country." When the crisis came, he had sided with me rather than the pope. Now I would visit him in his home and show, personally, my appreciation of his loyalty.

On and on we trudged, churning up columns of dust. The wagon train stretched as far as I could see when I turned back to look. The novelty of it drew people out to stand by the paths and watch. I was weary and my face was stinging from the dust, but I smiled and waved, sitting erect in the saddle. This might be their only glimpse of me in their lifetimes. This is how they would remember their Queen.

We rounded a bend in the road, dipping down as we approached a stream spanned by an old stone bridge. As I rode across it, I heard a commotion upstream and then saw a flock of geese swimming toward the bridge. A group of boys chased them, waving sticks and yelling. One jumped into the water and swam after the birds, but they swiftly outdistanced him.

From the bridge I called out, laughing, "You'll never outswim a goose!"

The boys stopped and stared. It was clear I was no ordinary rider. But still they could not comprehend exactly who this woman was, surrounded by mounted men and followed by a huge retinue.

"They escaped! We'll be whipped if we can't catch them," one said.

"Escaped from your farm?" asked Cecil, pulling up beside me.

"No, from the goose fair!" said his companion. "Hundreds of geese for sale or swap, and ours got away!"

"Let them go," I said. "We will pay you for them." Already the geese were way past the bridge.

"But our parents will punish us for not minding them properly," said the first boy, standing waist deep.

"Oh, not after I explain to them. Can you take us to the goose fair? And let us meet your parents?"

The second and third boys on the river path now had that look on their faces that showed they suddenly realized who I was. They started nudging each other, whispering. Finally one stuttered, "Are you—are you our Queen?"

"None other," I assured them.

"But—here at Branston's Crossing? Here, with us?"

"Indeed I am. I am on a Progress to Cowdray, with all my friends. And after you bring me to the fair, I shall dismount and you can see for yourselves. I am eager to meet *your* friends."

Archbishop Whitgift was shaking his dark head, ominously. He glanced up at the sun, which was halfway down the sky.

"It's the Queen! The Queen!" the boys chorused.

"Now, quiet," I warned them. "Shall we not surprise your parents, and the fairgoers?"

They scampered away, motioning us, and we left the main road, telling the convoy of wagons to wait, and followed the dusty path along the riverbanks. We had not gone far when we heard the clamor of the crowd, and then we came upon the fair.

The noise had come not from people but from a multitude of geese, furiously honking. Spread out across both gentle, sloping banks of the river were flocks of them, their owners bargaining with eager buyers. Cages, feed, tents, and other paraphernalia related to goose keeping marked off each owner's proprietary area.

The boys ran ahead of us, clearing the way. But unable to keep a secret, they cried out, "The Queen! The Queen!"

Everyone but the geese froze. A hundred heads turned toward me. I held up my hand. "Please, my good people, I assure you, I come only to see firsthand what a goose fair is like. I trust you will show me."

The boys ran to get their parents, who hurried over to me. They stared, dumbfounded. "You—Your Majesty," they stammered.

"Be at ease," I told them. "I am your guest here, and I rely on you to show me what a goose fair is all about." I dismounted and my groom led my horse away. Then I turned to the parents. "And what are you called?"

"I am Meg," said the woman. "Meg Harrigan." She pushed her hair back, straightening her scarf. She was a stocky woman with a stained apron.

"I am Bart," her husband said. "Your Majesty, I—we—"

I hushed him. "It is *my* privilege to be here." I laughed, genuinely lightheartedly. "I am never invited to such things, only to dull diplomatic banquets and speeches. You cannot appreciate what you are spared. Now—show me your geese! And pray, do not punish your sons, for they were giving their all in trying to recover the lost ones."

Stunned, moving like sleepwalkers, Meg and Bart showed me their geese. It was the common response, and I am used to it. It was my task to make them relax, assure them that in my presence they need only be themselves.

"So every year at this time there is a goose fair here?" I asked.

"Yes. It has been going on since Norman times. We bring our best geese and look to acquire others to improve our flocks. We are very proud of our geese here. They provide some of the best feathers in the region, as well as prized meat."

"And they can honk to warn of invasion," said Cecil, attempting to be familiar.

But Meg and Bart did not know about the Capitoline geese who had honked and warned the ancient Romans about enemies sneaking into Rome. They looked blank and smiled uncertainly.

"Never mind," I said. "That was a long time ago. Now"—I drew them away—"tell me of your farm."

"We—we grow wheat and have an orchard. We . . . get by. We do not have much extra, but we fare well enough."

Suddenly the crowd lost its inhibition about the mysterious visitation, and now people were flocking toward me.

"My dear people!" I cried, holding up both my arms. "I am the guest of the good Meg and Bart here, and honored to be with you today." I turned to Bart. "What is the main prize here?"

When he looked blank, I said, "Fairs always have games, and games always have prizes, and one is the best of all. What is yours?"

"It is—it is—the hunt for the golden goose egg."

"Oh! There really is such a creature, laying such eggs?" I teased.

"No. It is just pretend. There's a gold-painted wooden egg hidden, and the child who finds it is rewarded with a new pair of shoes."

"Do you know where the egg is hidden?" I asked.

He laughed. "Of course. I hid it!"

"If I were to find it—?"

"I would have to direct you there, Your Majesty," he said solemnly.

"Then do so."

While everyone watched, spellbound, I followed Bart as he led me past a rock and a thick-trunked tree and then to a little dip in the field. A small rock, easily lifted, revealed the golden egg. I extracted it and held it up.

"I have found it!" I cried.

People dutifully clapped. Of course I had found it. I had been led right to it, by a captive subject. How could he have refused? Now the game was ruined. The Queen would leave and there would be nothing for the people at the fair.

"It is lovely," I said, rotating it. "Exquisitely painted. So beautiful that I will take it with me and treasure it always."

Again, wan smiles from the children. The Queen was all very well and good, but what of their game, spoiled?

"What do you think is fair value for this?" I asked. "A beautiful wooden egg, carved by my treasured subjects. To me it is beyond price."

They looked back at me, silent, unsure of what to say.

"I declare it is beyond valuation," I said. "But still, I should pay for it. What say you to—fifteen gold pieces? To be shared among you?"

Now people shrieked. "Oh, blessed Queen!" they cried.

"And for the loss of your geese," I said, turning to Meg and Bart, "here is—" I counted out coins that I was sure were way beyond the value of the escaped geese. "And now," I announced, "I would like to meet as many of you as can come forward. And please, teach me about geese—what makes a good one and what makes a bad one. I can only judge them by how they appear on my table."

They streamed toward me, and I had an afternoon, unsought, that meant more to me than any formal banquet or ceremony.

---

The dun, brush-filled fields stretched away on both sides; twilight fell. Then, suddenly, like an apparition, a glint of green. Cowdray Park hove into view, lush lawns studded with chestnuts, a long causeway lined by a double avenue of trees ushering us over the sunken River Rother and into the grounds. From the bridge I could see the great stone facade of the manor, with its noble gatehouse. Over it the family motto, "*Suivez raison*"—"Follow reason"—was mounted.

Sir Anthony was there to welcome us, almost pulling me from my horse.

"I am near speechless," he said. "I am honored beyond words that my sovereign comes here to me."

"It is I who am honored—to have subjects like you," I assured him. "And I bring a gift from some of your neighbors," I said, pointing toward a cage of honking geese, which the fairgoers had insisted we take. Not the usual royal gift, but I was curious to taste their famous birds.

It was growing dark. I was aching from the long hours in the saddle; I wanted to go to my chambers. Let there be no dinner, no entertainment, tonight!

We were whisked through the quadrangle and toward the principal lodgings, where Sir Anthony and his wife had vacated their quarters for me. I was to have at my disposal the withdrawing room, great chamber, and parlor, which backed onto the Great Hall. Even in the fading light, I could see the beauty of the great lantern atop the roof of the hall. But more beautiful were the oriel windows of my rooms, glowing with light, telling me that within there would be rest.

---

The beds were set up, reassembled from their pieces; the linens and pillows, beaten and fluffed to dispel the road dust and spread for me and the ladies in their adjoining chamber. Candles burned yellow in their sconces, throwing the wooden paneling behind them into shadowed relief. A warmed posset in a silver mug was handed to me to sip just before I lay down. The joy of taking to my bed at last, after a long day, was exquisite.

---

But I could not sleep. After all my longing to lie down, I remained wide awake. I could hear Marjorie, Helena, and Catherine breathing heavily in the next room.

Silently I rose from the bed, tucking my feet into slippers and finding a wrap. I grasped the candlestick by my bed and stole out of the room. I could guess the arrangement of the rooms; they always followed a similar pattern. The smallest, most private bedroom opened into a larger chamber—where my ladies now slept—and that would open into a larger chamber, and then into a larger. I passed through that first one as silently as I could. I would find the gallery and walk briskly; surely that would bring sleep to me. Perhaps I had been sitting too long in one position in the saddle en route here.

In the outer chambers it was deep dark; the large windows did no good when there was no moon. I stumbled on the uneven flooring but caught myself before falling.

I found the long gallery, a tunnel stretching into invisibility. One flickering torch at the far end served to show me its length. The great house slept as if under a spell.

A gaping door opened halfway down, its threshold a marble step. I stepped inside, expecting the same dead, dry smell as the stone gallery. But the unmistakable odor of incense and something else . . . something familiar . . . hit me.

I could see nothing. It was utterly black. I shuffled carefully, feeling the floor with my feet, extending my arms. I bumped into a pew, and realized I was in the chapel. That smell . . . It was the smell of old satin vestments. I heard a slight scurrying sound and instinctively shivered and pulled my feet back. Rats? But it came again, heavier, and belonged to a bigger animal. It belonged to a man.

Now a light showed itself, a candle held aloft. A group of men were huddled at the far end of the chapel, near the baptismal font. I could make out the shine of vestments draped over a back. A priest was officiating at something. A murmur of voices—the priest's asking questions and several others answering. Then the trickle of water, then more murmuring. This was a baptism. Someone was being baptized at midnight in a dark church.

I held myself absolutely still—not out of fear but out of a wish to be unseen, so that I could observe. I needed to see everything.

But the light was so dim. I could only make out the number of people—five—and that they were all men. Like wraiths they dissolved and dispersed, slipping quietly away from another door near the altar.

After a long time passed in dead silence, I crept up to the font. The smell of incense was strongest here; the rim of the font was still slippery with drops of water. On the floor lay a neglected square of paper. I could see that it featured a saint's face; I picked it up.

Someone had just turned Catholic, in utter secrecy.

# 19

he sun shone brightly on the long table stretching the length of Anthony Browne's orchard, set up for a picnic. The specters of the night before seemed a smoky dream. Had I not kept the paper with the saint's picture, I would have had no proof, even in my own mind, that it had ever occurred. But now I looked up and down the table, imagining rosaries in hands that held only spoons, hearing Latin when the accents were good, hearty Sussex, seeing Jesuits in every black-cloaked guest. As all the senior household officials wore black gowns, similar to those in a college, that made for a lot of Jesuits.

It was well known that Sussex harbored Catholics, and it had long been rumored that Cowdray was a center of conversions. The households of Catholic aristocrats served as religious havens. But the loyalty of Anthony Browne was equally well known, and I made him an example of how religion and treason must be kept separate. It was not treason to *be* a Catholic, only to heed the pope's call to turn me off my throne. The troubling question always was, Until the test came, whom would a Catholic choose to follow? The execution of Mary Queen of Scots, removing any Catholic alternative to me as queen, and the failure of the English Catholics to rise up during the Armada crisis, seemed to have answered the question. But their leaders, exiled Englishmen fomenting plots and plans across the Channel, did not give up so easily. They continued sending a stream of missionary priests to convert the country back to Catholicism. As a result, Catholicism had become a secret, household faith, with the great estates able to maintain chapels and hide priests on the grounds. When the inspectors came calling, the priests could live for days inside the secret rooms called "priest's holes." They had to be small to escape detection in the walls. It was impossible to catch them all, although several hundred had been arrested.

Now I looked at the smiling face of Anthony Browne, wondering if even he knew of the midnight happenings in his chapel. Perhaps they did not see fit to tell him, lest they endanger him.

The late-summer breeze was tickling the leaves in the orchard, and all around we could hear overripe apples thumping to the ground. Cowdray was an oasis of fertility and green in the barren countryside, but as the food was set before us—platters of the special geese from the fair, as well as local game, fish, cheeses, bowls of pears, fritters, and pitchers of beer and ale—I wondered how Anthony managed to feed us all.

The table stretched, so Anthony told me, almost fifty yards. They had spread a fair linen runner upon it, and wooden platters and goblets made us feel as informal as a traveling court ever could. I breathed in deeply, savoring the smell of the fallen apples. At a time like this, it was easy to feel that I was surrounded by honest, simple folk. But around me, for all that they had discarded their ruffs and padded breeches, the courtiers were as self-seeking as wolves.

On one side of me sat my host, and across from him, John Whitgift—an interesting juxtaposition. Old Burghley and old Hunsdon had remained at home, but their sons, Robert and George, respectively, were sitting, bright-eyed, farther down. My ladies, as always, sat together, wearing straw bonnets to protect their skin. Under the trees a group of musicians played country tunes, rollicking melodies that knew not of allegory and classical allusion. A maid was fair, not "the handmaid of Aphrodite," and a man was brave, not "like unto Hector." The people who knew and loved these songs, humming along with them, sat at the far end of the table.

"You have a loyal following, Sir Anthony," I said, nodding to them. I sipped my cider, fresh pressed, still sweet, and not yet heady.

"As Your Majesty knows," he said slowly, "loyalty is the most valuable trait in those we deal with."

*Did* he know of the secret ceremony in his chapel? Or was someone being disloyal to *him*? "And the hardest won," I said. If he did know, he was playing a dangerous game.

"I sought out the chapel for prayer this morning," said Whitgift suddenly, leaning forward.

"I had meant to show it to you after this," said Anthony. "I fear I was too slow in my duties as host." Did he look alarmed that Whitgift had examined it first?

"This old nose," said Whitgift, touching the long, thin ridge, "has smelled incense too many times to be mistaken in its scent. Sir, your chapel reeked of it this morning."

"Perhaps," replied Anthony, "your nose has lost its discernment. The years will do that. I speak as someone who shares the burden of time. Why, I know the apples here smelled much sharper in my youth."

"I can still smell a polecat, and the incense was almost as powerful." Whitgift had provoked our host, confirming my suspicions. Now I must tug his collar and call him to heel.

"There is nothing illegal about incense," I said loudly. "Do we not burn incense to drive away moths and cover up sickbed odors? Come, come, sir, you fret yourself. Enjoy the fresh country air, and think on the joys of being outside. Why, only a clergyman would seek out a cold, dark chapel on such a day."

"Ma'am, I *am* a clergyman, the foremost in the land."

"And showing it, John, and showing it." I waved my hand. "Dancers. Here come the dancers!" Trooping into the garden, dressed in wide flouncing skirts and homespun britches, the village boys and girls presented me with a bouquet and read a welcome speech, then clapped for their musicians to begin. To the sound of pipe and tabor, the dancers spread out under the trees, stately at first, then moving faster. Anthony and his wife got up to dance, then George Carey, rising with one of the maids of honor; soon the dappled sunshine under the trees was a swirl of movement. I looked around me; only I, Whitgift, and Robert Cecil were left. It was obvious why: Each of us was either too august, too holy, or too misshapen in some way.

The dancers under the trees . . . Oh, there had been a time when Leicester would have taken my hand and we would have risen together and danced until we were out of breath.

"If I may," a voice was saying. I saw a young man standing before me, his hand extended. "All ceremony is put aside, so my master said," he continued. "Rather like the master of misrule on Twelfth Night. And so I make bold to ask if you would dance with me."

He was tall, powerfully built, with reddish-brown hair. His accent was unmistakably Yorkshire.

I rose and gave him my hand, and he led me out to an open place, apart from the other dancers. He wasted no time but immediately began the steps of the dance, a simple country one, nothing like the dances Leicester had so excelled at. This required speed and strength, but no subtlety.

His dark eyes scrutinized me, and I hoped it did not show that I was pleased to have been rescued from my station and appointed place. "Everyone knows of your artful dancing," he said. "I was hoping to see it for myself."

His head bobbed down and then he straightened up again, as the step required. He was a compelling presence.

"Who are you, sir?" I asked.

"When all the rules are suspended, are we obligated to tell our true names?"

"When the Queen asks you, yes," I said. He knew I was the Queen; why should I not know him?

"I would like to say Gawain or Richard the Lionheart, but I am only Guy Fawkes of Farnley, footman to Sir Anthony Browne. Not even a sir."

"You are a long way from your home in the north," I said.

"And will go farther still," he said. "I am just come of age, and now need serve no man. I mean to go to the Continent, learn fighting."

What was it about young men, the Continent, and fighting? "Come to court instead," I said. I could use him in the Queen's Guard.

"I am called elsewhere," he said. "But I thank Your Majesty."

Yorkshire . . . the north, where the Catholics were so strong . . . serving in the household of Sir Anthony . . . "Which side will you fight on?" I asked suddenly.

"I—I—the English, of course."

Ah, but there were Englishmen fighting on both sides.

"Mind you choose the right English to fight with. I have forces in France now, under Sir John Norris and the Earl of Essex. I can place you there."

"Your Majesty is most kind," he said, bowing.

But he did not ask for any references or recommendations.

"We dine at Easebourne tomorrow," I said. "Come to me, and I shall have introduction papers ready for you."

"Easebourne?" he said slowly. "I would avoid it."

"Why?" I was surprised.

"It is cursed. And this place, too, Cowdray. I am glad to leave it before the curse comes true. Easebourne was once a priory, and consecrated ground. Dissolving the monasteries and turning over the property to courtiers did not undo their power and holiness. A monk pronounced a curse of fire and water against the despoilers. This place"—he waved toward the peaceful stones of Cowdray—"will perish in fire, and its owners in water. The buildings will melt and the owners drown." As he spoke, his northern accent grew stronger. "We do not know when. It might be tomorrow, it might be several generations."

"Everything ends after several generations," I said. "Even the things we try so hard to keep. We need resort to no curse to explain that."

"As you say, Ma'am." He bowed swiftly and was gone.

---

After the picnic ended, Sir Anthony and his wife made a point of showing me the walks and gardens of the house. He had the usual knot garden, quite an elaborate one, several fountains with gravel paths circling them, arbors heavy with vines, and a perfume garden with wallflowers, rosemary, lavender, and, of course, red and white roses.

"My gardeners are trying hard to breed a true Tudor rose," he said. "One with red and white petals. All we have got so far is striped ones."

"We Tudors have many stripes," I assured him. "I think I am the most striped of all, for I try to incorporate all the viewpoints I possibly can—short of treasonous ones. But my boundaries for treason are more lenient than most." I thought of mentioning the chapel and what I had witnessed there, but then remembered what I had chosen as my watchword: "*Video et taceo*"—"I see and say nothing."

"We have extensive fish ponds on the grounds," he said as we approached one. Several nets were strung across it, and an angler was seated at one end. As we came closer, he began reciting an obviously rehearsed soliloquy about treason. After enumerating its evils, he ended with, "There be some so muddy minded that they cannot live in a clear river, as camels will not drink till they have troubled the water with their feet, so they cannot stanch their thirst until they have disturbed the state with their treacheries." To be sure I did not miss it, he almost shouted the last words, an odd thing indeed for a private meditation.

"Too much incense can also muddy the air," I warned Sir Anthony. "Have a care, dear friend. *Verbum sapienti sat est.*" He should appreciate the Latin.

# 20

he breeze coming off the Channel was salty and made my lips sting. I was standing on the docks of Portsmouth, having made my way from Cowdray as far south as land would allow us. Across from us, some hundred miles or so, lay the northern coast of France. King Henri IV could easily slip across to meet me. I had given him a plain—for me—invitation to do so. As one sovereign to another, I could only invite, not command. But it would be in his interest to accept. I was sure he would.

I had had no word about my army and how it was faring. Essex and his men were to wait at Dieppe and join King Henri in taking Rouen from the Spanish. God's breath, if the French king valued his self-preservation, he would hie himself over here.

"Ma'am, let us betake ourselves of the hospitality of the mayor," said Robert Cecil, by my side.

I nodded, and he half closed his eyes, signaling that he understood. We both understood what was at stake here. Robert was as astute as his father but more willing to resort to secret or—should I say?—sneaky dealings. We must pretend we were here only to hear the recitation of the glories of the defeat of the Armada, to see the reenactment of the battle that had taken place right off Portsmouth, by the Isle of Wight.

The mayor had arranged a commemoration of that glorious summer day, the third battle of the Armada invasion. The Spanish had tried to land on the Isle of Wight, to secure a firm base only two miles off the mainland.

As we watched, small boats patrolled the waters just beyond the docks, flags identifying them as "Spanish" or "English" waving from their masts. They would demonstrate some of the naval tactics used in that battle.

Velvet-covered chairs were brought for the honored spectators, and we sank down to be entertained.

Out on the water, the exhibition boats, bearing long banners identifying their assigned roles, mimicked the action. On board the "Spanish" ship

*Duquesa Santa Ana*, an actor threw out armloads of rolled parchments, screaming, "The Bull! The Bull! The Holy Father has a whole shipload of Bulls!"

Ah, well, wily Pope Sixtus had gone to his reward last year and perhaps was amused by our little reenactment here, looking down from . . . Or was he looking up? *I* do not pretend to know a man's eternal destination. Let him rest in peace.

Another "Spanish" ship sailed past, this one identified as the flagship of supreme commander Medina-Sidonia himself, *San Martin*. The men on board were prancing and preening, wearing enormous feathers, dyed outrageous colors, that floated and flapped in their hats. "To parade in London!" they shouted. We all laughed heartily. The cocksure Duke of Parma had reportedly ordered his velvet suits for his triumphant state entry into London. Now, if they survived at all, they must hang in his quarters to mock his empty pride. More likely they had been torn and used to bind up wounds.

In the real battle, the wind—the English wind, we liked to call it—had picked up and begun to favor us. Everyone knew this part of the story by heart. No longer had our ships been dependent on the longboats to pull them, but were able to maneuver on their own. Frobisher's *Triumph*, the largest ship in our fleet, had hoisted sails from its trapped position and was pursued by *San Juan de Portugal*, their swiftest ship, but it barely moved in comparison. Over on the other side, Admiral Howard and Drake had attacked their seaward wing, pressing them toward the treacherous Owers Bank, an arm of rocky shallows that reached out toward the entrance of the Channel up to the Isle of Wight and on to Portsmouth and Southampton. If only they had been lured there! In wishful thinking, the "Spanish" ships in the enactment we were watching foundered and ran aground, but in real life they had seen the danger in time and steered away. However, in swerving to avoid the bank, they had missed the entrance they were seeking and been swept out and beyond that landing place. There had now been no place for them to anchor; they had been forced to continue down the Channel.

"We had been awake all night," said George Carey, "listening for any splashing oars that would mean the Spanish were landing. Oh, to see them sail away, their gilded rumps glowing in the afternoon sun, was the happiest sight I ever saw!"

"As they headed toward us in London," I reminded him. The defensive chain that had been strung across the Thames had been swept away at the first spring tide, and the fortifications defending the approaches to the city had not been completed. That left London with precious little protection as the beacon fires flared to warn us the Armada was coming toward us.

"Our only protection lay in our wooden walls, as the oracle at Delphi told the Athenians. In both cases, our ships," said George.

The play boats were coming in to shore now, their demonstration over, their oars raised in salute. They had given us a brave show. I waved at them, fluttering my handkerchief.

The mayor made his way over to us, grinning widely.

"You have pleased us well," I said.

"It is not over yet," he replied. "I have two more living mementos of that heroic occasion." Behind him, trumpets blasted. "First, the man who alerted us all." He ushered a stooped, unkempt man forward and led him to me.

"This is the hermit who lives in the ruins of St. Michael's Chapel at Rame Head—on the foreground beyond Plymouth—who kept a watch and was the first to light a beacon fire."

"Is it even so?" I leaned forward to look closely at him—the matted hair, the ragged cloak, the dusty feet. Was he an old monk, left over from the forbidden monasteries? Did he mumble his beads and walk in the tumbled-down ruins of his former cloister? Or was he just mildly mad?

"Indeed, yes," he said, in a voice as thin as frost. "I watch year round. But when I saw those ships, so thick and black on the water, sailing in a huge crescent, I knew them for what they were. The enemy. I lit the brush as quickly as I could."

He wasn't mad, unless so much solitude had warped him. "You did well," I assured him. Impulsively, I reached into my purse and pulled out a token from the victory—a square of cloth from one of the captured Armada banners. They were being treated almost as saints' relics, as far as holiness went. "This is from one of those proud ships. Proud no longer, but sunk!"

"I, then, shall be proud to fly it upon my shoulder," he said, smiling. His cracked lips parted to show yellowed teeth.

"And here is the other valiant protector," the mayor announced. "Sir George Beeston, brave commander of the *Dreadnought* and a great fighter in the action you have just witnessed."

He gestured to a tall man who had been waiting beside the trumpeters. His cloak snapped smartly in the wind, and he carried himself like a man who had never bowed under a burden. Only as he came closer did I see that his beard was totally white and his leathery face a mass of wrinkles, like a well-worn purse.

He was ancient! He bent one knee—not stiff, I noted—and said, "Your noble husband, lady"—looking at Catherine—"knighted me on the deck right out here after the battle. Me, at the age of eighty-nine."

Very few things make me cry, but I felt tears gathering in my eyes. This old man, defending the realm, made me proud to be Queen of the English people as never before.

"We have heard of you, sir," I said. "Let me give you something to commend you for that battle." I unpinned the Armada brooch I was wearing, a miniature of myself with the fleet in the background, encircled by pearls. "Your sovereign is grateful for such a subject."

Many other men would demur or make a show of refusing, but Sir Beeston took the gift and said only, "I shall treasure it as coming from your very person." He did not linger, looking fawningly at me, as a younger man might have, but stood up briskly and took his leave, which had the effect of my wishing he would come back. That which is most pleasing disappears too soon.

---

I awoke the next morning unsure of where I was—or should I say, *when* I was. I had so thoroughly gone back in time that it was with a start that I realized I was grappling with the still-ongoing war with Spain.

And I had come to Portsmouth not to be entertained with sweet remembrances of an old victory but to ascertain where we stood in the new confrontation. King Henri IV *must* come across to meet me. We *must* talk in person. He was a clever man and should know this. I had bankrolled him long enough for him not to be unaware of how critical it was for him to show himself in my court.

Robert Cecil understood the urgency of it, and he had outdone himself in the hinting letters he had sent the French king. I was coming to rely more and more on him, his sure touch and commonsense approach. His father had raised a worthy successor.

It was now a fortnight since Henri had received our softly worded summons. He knew the dates we would be in Portsmouth. Surely any day now we would spot his ship on the horizon. I felt it would be today.

Now, this morning, as I kept going to the window and peering out, Cecil shook his head. "Old women have a saying, 'A watched pot never boils,'" he said.

I laughed. "And a watched horizon always remains empty," I said. "You speak true." But somehow I felt I could will him to appear.

---

After four days we could wait no longer. There was nothing further to do in Portsmouth, and if we lingered another day it would become obvious we were waiting for something. I was deeply grateful for the Armada exhibition and hoped I expressed it sufficiently. But I stood looking forlornly out to sea while the mayor was orchestrating the leave-taking ceremonies. I felt deserted, abandoned by a false lover.

---

Soon enough I learned what was happening in France. No wonder the king did not want to face me. He had failed to make use of the troops I had sent, squandering their lives and my money. Of the four thousand men I had dispatched under Essex, the best and finest-equipped of any expeditionary force I had ever provided, only fifteen hundred remained. The other twenty-five hundred had given their lives up to disease while they waited in vain to join forces with the elusive French. Essex, easily duped, had led them hither and yon over hill and dale in France with no discernible purpose other than that he liked wearing his fine livery and commanding troops. As a reward for this foolishness, he knighted twenty-four men—for doing nothing. I was livid. I recalled him and published my declaration—in bold print, so even the French king could read it—to bring the troops home.

# 21

# LETTICE

*March 1592*

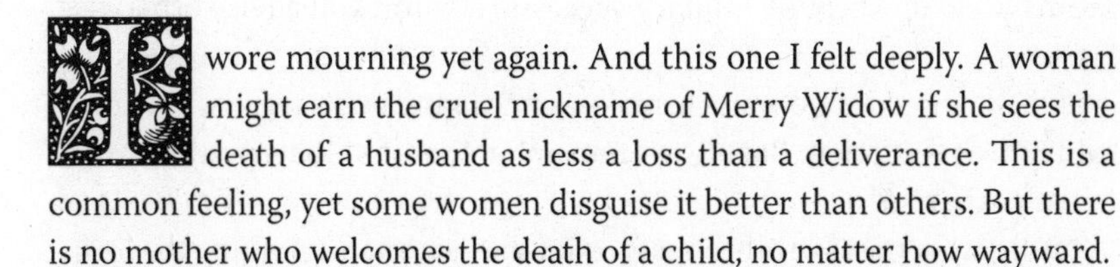

I wore mourning yet again. And this one I felt deeply. A woman might earn the cruel nickname of Merry Widow if she sees the death of a husband as less a loss than a deliverance. This is a common feeling, yet some women disguise it better than others. But there is no mother who welcomes the death of a child, no matter how wayward.

My youngest son, Walter, was dead, my sweet boy. And he was dead because of the fecklessness of his brother, Robert, and our prideful ambition. Of my four children, Walter alone never gave me sorrow. He was only twenty-two, killed in that inept war with the Spanish in France under the leadership of Robert.

How pleased we had been with Robert's appointment! How puffed up with what it signified: The Queen had bestowed a major command on Robert. He was on his way to distinguishing himself militarily and rising above the other courtiers who were confined to the halls of court.

Not that she had a great deal to choose from. Those fit to command land forces were few. There was Black Jack Norris and then there was . . . no one. The sea fighters had dispersed—Francis Drake and his cousin John Hawkins in disgrace from the failed Portugal venture, Richard Grenville dead after a heroic but suicidal one-man battle in his ship *Revenge* against fifty-three Spanish ships, Martin Frobisher retired to the country life in Yorkshire.

In earlier days, there would have been a host of fire-blooded young men qualified to take the field. Now there was only Robert.

Oh, how we had rejoiced over his elevation. His ascendancy over the scrabbling little Cecil now seemed assured. In vain his friend Francis Bacon had reminded us that military command was not the route to power in a Tudor court, and had not been even as far back as Henry VIII's.

"And is even less so when the ruler is a woman," he warned us. "It will serve only to threaten her. She may be a formidable woman, but even she cannot lead troops in the field, and any man she must rely on to do so will incur her resentment rather than her gratitude. She will not admire anyone who makes up for her own lacks."

I hated the way Francis came out with his smug observations. I wondered if he was a bad influence on Robert.

"How can she resent someone for doing her a good service?" Robert had asked, trying on various pieces of his armor to be adjusted. He bent his elbow up and down, testing its flexibility. The hinge creaked. "Will a simple dose of oil cure this, or do the parts need replacing?" he mused.

"Listen!" I ordered him. Francis's words were disturbing me. "The purpose of this command is to further your career and your ambitions. I see no other means to do it except by military success. How can you advise otherwise, Francis?"

"Oh, he should go to war. He makes a fine figure in his regalia, and it will gain him a reputation. But always remember that the Queen may have different goals."

"Why, what possible other goals could she have than smashing the Spanish?" Robert looked bewildered.

"Look in the Bible," said Francis. "'The heaven for height, and the earth for depth, and the heart of kings is unsearchable.'"

"When did you start reading Scripture, you atheist?" asked Robert.

"You do not have to be a believer in order to recognize wisdom there," said Francis. "And don't call me an atheist. It's dangerous!"

"No one's heart is unsearchable," I said. "The number of possible motives are usually very few."

"Very well then. I shall prepare a paper examining the Queen's choice of motives. But in the meantime, friend Robert, do as well as you like on the battlefield but do not court popularity here at home on its basis, or she will see you as a rival."

"The people *do* like me," he noted, delight creeping into his voice.

"It has been a long time since they had a popular hero," said Francis. "Leicester remained hated, for all that he was the Queen's favorite. There was Drake, of course, in his day—and Philip Sidney, who died in time to cement his hold on the imagination. They are hungry for another."

"It is your time," I assured him. "The place is empty. Seize it."

At last I could come into my own. My first husband, Walter, had bankrupted himself pursuing glory in that bog of ambition, Ireland, and only got debt and death for his efforts. My second husband, Leicester, had failed miserably in the Netherlands, when power and command were handed him. Now my eldest son would recoup all.

"Walter wants to come," Robert was saying.

"What better opportunity?" I said. "You can oversee him, guide him."

Remembering those words was God's torture for me now. I had urged it; I had encouraged it.

---

Walter was killed in September, only a few months after arriving on that fool's errand of a campaign. He fell into a French ambush when he was making a token sally before the walls of Rouen, hit in the head by a cursedly accurate French sniper. With difficulty his captain rescued the body and returned it to the English camp.

Having failed to achieve anything, having lost three-quarters of the men, Elizabeth issued her "Declaration of the Causes That Move Her Majesty to Revoke Her Forces in Normandy." Robert returned home, and together we interred Walter in his vault. That was only a few days ago, and now we passed each other like ghosts, trying to right ourselves as we fumbled along the corridors of the house.

I was laid low by grief in a way I had never been before. I should have been used to loss; my mother was gone, as well as my earlier husbands and my little son with Leicester. But losing a sickly child is not the same, for in one respect I had anticipated it from the moment I saw his puny frame and knew he was weak. But Walter had grown to manhood with none of the faults of my other children—missing the rashness of my daughters and the instability of Robert, he was closest to my heart. The future had looked glorious for him. Now he lay lapped in marble.

I told myself I should take comfort in my surviving children, should be plotting Robert's next moves now that he was back and had no clear path. While he was gone that little weasel Cecil had managed to get himself named to the Privy Council, where my aged father still sat. Next it should be Robert's turn, if he managed things well.

But my heart was not in my schemes. I did not even care if I ever went to London and felt no desire to leave Drayton Bassett. It even began to feel soothing to me. It no longer even felt like exile, and the court at London seemed a faraway and threatening place that no sensible person would want to frequent. Perhaps that was the worst part: to have been cast adrift from my former self.

---

It was a week since we had laid Walter in his tomb, and today we would return to say final prayers and offer flowers. I had asked both my daughters, Penelope and Dorothy, to come and honor their brother. They joined the family here: me, Robert, Frances and her two children—Elizabeth Sidney, age seven, and little Robert, a year old. As soon as the girls arrived, I felt even worse, for having all the surviving siblings together only emphasized the one that was missing.

Now, as we gathered in the hall, I looked hard at Penelope and Dorothy. Both were stunning beauties. Once I had taken great pride in that. Now I felt like Niobe, that foolish woman who bragged about her children only to have the envious gods strike them down one by one. Penelope was pushing her golden curls up under her hat, fussing with wayward strands. Her delicate, long fingers were pale and ornamented with only finely wrought rings. The dark fabric of her gown was in perfect taste for the somber occasion but fashionably cut. Her husband, Lord Rich, pampered her—with worldly goods, that is. Penelope had not wanted to marry him, but he could offer financial enticements as well as his title, and I am ashamed to say that her father and I insisted on the marriage. But they lived apart now, she calling him a violent man, and there were rumors she had taken up with my husband's distant cousin, Charles Blount. It felt slightly incestuous even to think about.

Dorothy had managed to incur the Queen's anger when she married Sir Thomas Perrot without royal permission. The years had not made the Queen relent. Dorothy accepted it and seemed content with Perrot, which was a good thing, after the price she had paid to marry him.

Less flamboyant in dress than her sister, she was just as striking. Her hair was a reddish blond and her features more regular than those of Penelope, who had a long, albeit elegant, nose.

Alas, new motherhood had not improved Frances Walsingham's looks—I would always call her that in my mind, never Frances Devereux. She was still so plain that it is difficult to describe her. How can one differentiate her from the thousands of other plain women in the realm? Her daughter by Philip Sidney was equally colorless; already any hope she had of growing into good looks had vanished. Like mother, like daughter. Her son with Robert, my grandson Robert, was a winning little thing, but he was only a year old, and at that age, all babies are winning. I hoped my son's good looks would drown out Frances's dullness as he grew up.

"It is time." The household chaplain, an earnest young man, appeared in the hall. We followed him out and walked silently to the chapel. The sky was overcast; the trees still bare. Mud oozed up between the bricks on the path, glistening as we trod upon it.

Beside me Christopher took my hand. He had been a bystander during this difficult time, not knowing how to comfort me for my loss of a part of my life before he had known me.

We entered the chapel, the gloomy day making it hard to see inside. The tomb was beckoning, its marble looking too raw, shouting out its new contents. The carvers had just finished with the epitaph and marble dust lay on the base, missed by the sweepers.

"Let us give thanks for the life of Walter Devereux," the priest intoned.

After he had finished mumbling his prayers, Robert stepped forward. "I wished to write a poem for my brother," he said. "When I was already laid low by the fever in France, they brought me word of his death, and I sickened so all thought I would join him, and two coffins be shipped home. I survived, but I could not find the words to frame a proper poem. So I will recite one written by another." He closed his eyes as if to read the words in his mind.

*"My tale was heard and yet it was not told,*
*My fruit is fallen and yet my leaves are green,*
*My youth is spent and yet I am not old,*
*I saw the world and yet I was not seen;*
*My thread is cut and yet it is not spun,*
*And now I live, and now my life is done."*

His voice had begun to tremble, and he reached out to the edge of the tomb to steady himself.

*"I sought my death and found it in my womb,*
*I looked for life and saw it was a shade,*
*I trod the earth and knew it was my tomb,*
*And now I die, and now I was but made;*
*My glass is full, and now my glass is run,*
*And now I live, and now my life is done."*

One by one we went up to the tomb and laid our wreaths and tributes upon it. Then the horrid moment was over, and we could leave this sunless chapel.

Dusk had come, and we were together for our supper, my scattered children under one roof again. As I looked at each of them, their present adult faces wavered and were replaced by the round ones I had known when they were small. There was, suddenly, a great peace about it.

"That poem," said Penelope. "Where did you get it, Robert?" She was cutting her meat carefully, and I remembered her daintiness as a child, refusing to eat anything with fat on it.

"Chidiock Tichborne," he said.

"The traitor?" said Christopher drily.

Robert looked up with consternation. "He was a poet. I know not of traitor."

"Don't play the innocent. He was executed as one of the conspirators in the Babington Plot," said Christopher.

"One that my father brought to justice! Robert, how could you speak his words at your own brother's tomb?" Frances had actually spoken out, and sharply. I was astounded.

"When he wrote of the tomb on the night before his execution, he knew whereof he spoke," insisted Robert. "I judge him only as a poet."

"Then you're a fool. Never do that again. What if the Queen hears that you quote a man who wanted to assassinate her?" said Penelope. "Do you want to ruin this family?"

"I do not think she would take offense," insisted Robert.

"She takes offense more easily than almost anyone I know," I said. Even as I spoke, I wondered if some spy might report my words. But I was still in the stage of not caring what happened to me. "She banished me from court and I remain banished, even though the cause of the offense is dead, and I am her near cousin. She remains angry at Dorothy. As for her other grudges and vendettas, the list is so long I could not name them all."

"Even if you could, I would not advise it," said Dorothy quietly.

"'Curse not the king, no not in thy thought; and curse not the rich in thy bedchamber: for a bird of the air shall carry the voice, and that which hath wings shall tell the matter,'" said Frances. "When my father was alive, he was the bird who flew to the Queen. Now we do not know who they are."

"Your father's loss was a great one to the Queen as well as to us," said Robert, reaching out to touch her hand. "Whoever fills that empty space will put the Queen in his debt."

Robert, making an astute political observation; Frances, speaking up—I was taken by surprise. Had I misjudged them, or had they changed?

---

After the meal, my girls—I kept calling them that, even though they were in their late twenties—drifted off together, leaving the men, Frances, and me to the fire in a privy chamber. Now that the family ceremony was over, Francis Bacon joined us, and another man I did not recognize.

"My brother Anthony," said Francis, pushing him forward.

The man almost hobbled as he approached me. "An honor, Lady Leicester." I had been allowed to retain my highest title, Countess of Leicester, rather than being demoted to plain Lady Blount, wife of a knight. His voice was thin and raspy at the same time, as if it had to travel a long way from his concave chest. He turned to Robert and nodded. "My lord," he said.

"Welcome," said Robert. He seemed more sure of himself, taking over the role of host from me.

"Anthony has just returned from France, as have you, dear Robert," said Francis. Unlike his brother's, Francis's voice was smooth, strong, and seductive. "You served the Queen on the battlefield and he served her in more shadowy venues," he said. "He had the good fortune to be . . . associated . . . with the work of your late father, Frances."

"So he was a spy?" Frances said. "Pray speak plainly. There are no birds here to fly to court."

What had got into her? Had she taken up the mantle of her father?

"Please, I do not merit that title," said Anthony, swaying on his feet.

I motioned for Robert to slide a chair over for him, and he sank down upon it, relief spreading across his face. He was clearly in bodily distress. "For ten years I gathered information for Secretary Walsingham. Not only from France, but from all over the Continent. France was a convenient collecting station. But changing conditions there, and my poor health—" He gave a hooting, raucous series of coughs and ended by mopping his mouth with a handkerchief.

"My brother is now in a position to transfer his services here," said Francis. "And we, if we are wise, will know how to use them."

"My wife says to speak plain," said Robert. "Pray do."

"Do I have your absolute word that the wood lining these walls"—He thumped the wall behind him—"is as far as my answer goes?"

"Of course, man! Speak up!" said Robert.

"Very well. It is so simple I am astounded you have not proposed it already. It is this: The great Secretary Walsingham is dead. He who protected the Queen for so long, who broke conspiracy after conspiracy and crowned his achievement with the challenge of ensnaring Mary Queen of Scots, in legally irrefutable proof, has left a great void. The Queen is naked—so to speak—before her enemies. There is no one who has been able to replace Walsingham."

"Nasty little crookback Cecil has tried to manage the network Walsingham left behind," said Christopher, who usually remained silent in political exchanges.

"It is in tatters," said Francis. "It is like a faithful hound that only obeyed one master. We must construct a new spy system and run our own intelligence service. In that way we will win not only Her Majesty's gratitude but power as well. Power to vanquish the Cecils and make our own fortune." He looked knowingly at Robert. "Will you authorize this? We will work for you. You will present the findings to Her Majesty."

Robert's face was blank. His eyes shifted from one face to another, as if asking permission. I nodded, locking my eyes with his. This was the way. This was where the battles would be fought. I felt a stirring of excitement in me at the challenge and, along with it, relief that I could feel anything again.

"My father had five hundred spies in fifty countries in his network, as far away as Constantinople," said Frances. "Can you ever match that?"

"Indeed, yes, I have been managing many of those very strings of informers," said Anthony. "I know how to do it."

"My father died horribly in debt," said Frances. "He paid for much of the service himself. The Queen wanted protection but was unwilling to pay for it. Father's motto was 'Knowledge is never too dear.' That was before the bills came due and his purse was empty." Her voice rose.

Robert attempted to put his arm around her to quiet her, but she pushed it away.

"Indeed, yes, that is the weak spot in my proposal," said Francis. "How to pay for it. We are all somewhat short of funds."

What an understatement. Christopher and I were reduced to pawning my jewelry, and the Bacon brothers were eking out livings as a lawyer at Gray's Inn and as a poorly paid secretary to a poorly paid secretary.

"Yes, there is that little matter," I could not help saying.

"But the Queen will surely be rewarding me after my service in France," said Robert.

"She awarded Cecil a place on the Privy Council while you were prancing before the walls of Rouen, issuing the governor a challenge to personal combat, claiming that the cause of King Henri was more just than that of the Catholic League and that your mistress was more beautiful than his," snapped Francis. "Silly posturing. Can't you see? You must give Her Majesty some service she needs—what *she* wants, not what *you* want." Francis Bacon was a relentless prosecutor, as he was known to be in the law court.

"I was the commander. I had to make a brave showing, else I would shame my Queen," said Robert.

"You shamed her when you disobeyed her orders and knighted men who had no merit to be knighted. Can you not see that it looks as if you are building up a body of men beholden to you?" said Francis.

I could see Robert thinking, weighing whether he had the stomach to press on with this. He might make his familiar I-want-to-retire-to-the-country statement. He sighed and then said, "Perhaps you are right."

"We will set up our intelligence network. Some of it will involve nasty characters, but you need not sully yourself with them. Scapegallows with names like Staring Robin and Welsh Dick and Roaring Girl—but you will never meet them. Others, like Kit Marlowe, I daresay you would not mind sharing an ale with at the tavern; he works clean, works for your cousin Thomas Walsingham, Frances." Francis nodded toward her.

"What about the Catholic priests?" said Robert. "The Jesuits who scurry from house to house, hiding from the law. Can we harness them? Christopher, you're known in Catholic circles."

He gave an uneasy laugh. "I was brought up Catholic, yes, and had entrée into that circle plotting for the Scots queen," he said.

"Work on your Catholic contacts," urged Robert. "They know a lot."

"I'm not sure it's safe to traffic that way," I said. I did not want to endanger my household. I glared at my son.

"The theater is another place crawling with men whose pasts—and presents—one does not want to delve into too deeply," said Christopher with a laugh. "But we can enjoy their plays. See villainy on the stage and not ask how they know the thinking of villains so well."

"Next, we must indeed build up a party," said Anthony. It was the first time he had spoken since his coughing fit. "And we must set up a line of communication with Scotland. That is where the succession is going. He will be our king before long, and those who have approached him and rendered him friendly service earlier will fare well in the new government."

For all my promise that nothing would go beyond this room, there were other ears in the house, and sounds carried. This was so close to treason I signaled for them to be quiet, and I tiptoed across the room and flung open the door. Nothing. The hallway was empty, dark. I shut the door again.

"We understand," I said. "No more needs to be said."

"A certain person is almost sixty," said Robert. The stubborn, reckless boy. "And we can count on those numbered days."

"Enough!" I said.

A mother always has the right to command her children to obey, no matter their ages.

# 22

# ELIZABETH

*May 1592*

Suddenly the ruff was choking me. I did not want to call attention to it, so I fingered it carefully, trying to pull it away from my neck in a manner that no one would notice. My neck was clammy, slippery, and then I felt my face start to pulsate and ripple with heat. God's curse! It was here again, when I thought I was quit of it. I had not been bothered thus for months.

I cranked the window open and leaned out of it, praying for a breeze. But there was none. The May sunshine shone upon a calm garden beneath my rooms at Windsor. I had stayed on here after this year's investiture of the new Knights of the Garter, thinking to enjoy this palace that was always too cold in winter. But this moment I would have welcomed a blast of winter wind.

"A fan, Your Majesty?" Someone had extended one where I could take hold of it discreetly. But no matter how smoothly I took it, the fact remained that someone had noticed, someone had seen my discomfort.

I turned to see the self-satisfied face of Bess Throckmorton. Embarrassed, I clutched at the fan.

"Perhaps a wetted handkerchief—" she began.

"No, thank you!" I said, while longing for one. I struggled to master myself. It would pass. It always did.

She bowed her head in mock servility. I did not like her, and I never had, for all that she was the daughter of my faithful ambassador Sir Nicholas Throckmorton. There was something sneaky and vain about her. Especially lately, when she had taken a sudden leave of court with a flimsy excuse. Now she was back, but there was something different about her, an extra haughtiness that shone through.

I had had to resort of late to writing notes to remind myself of things I could not always trust myself to have at my fingertips, and she had found one of the notes and brought it to me with a puzzled look. But that was a sham, as she knew very well what it was. Did she tell others—her young friends—that the Queen needed notes to remember things now? If I forbade her to say anything, that would call more attention to it, so I tried to make light of it, tearing up the note and saying it was of no moment, memorizing it before I did. As soon as I was alone, I wrote it out again, and this time I made sure to put it in the box where I properly kept them.

My older ladies understood well enough. Marjorie—my Crow—was far on the other side of it, being already in her sixties. The others, Helena and Catherine, were in their forties and beginning that passage that was so easy for some and so difficult for others. It is an unsettling thing when one's fertility begins to ebb and the window that opened in girlhood now begins to close. But now that mine was closed, let these torturous attacks of heat and sweat be gone! They were nothing but cruel reminders.

I would dismiss the ladies and send them out into the gardens to amuse themselves. Once they were gone, I would send for my physician and see if he had any remedy for this unpleasantness.

---

They took advantage of what they assumed was my generosity and left the chambers with telltale swiftness. I summoned Dr. Lopez from his home at Holborn, praying he would come quickly.

He was resourceful and reliable. And sure enough, before the river tide had turned or the ladies returned, Roderigo was announced in the outer chambers. If he was put out by having to rush here on such a fine day, he did not show it. Instead, his face lit up as he saw me. He exclaimed, "I am so relieved to see Your Majesty standing here in all her glory, not lying on a sickbed."

That was the wrong thing to say. "Why should I be?" I snapped. I felt that horrid heat starting to sweep over me again. Curse it!

He smiled. "The summons was so sudden," he said. He had a leathery face that reminded me of a sailor, a prominent nose, and a rather yellow complexion, like the slanting sunshine of late afternoon.

"Let us withdraw and I shall explain," I said.

Finally secluded behind closed doors, I told him of the return of my distressing symptoms. He kept nodding but said nothing. When I finished speaking, he remained silent.

"Is there no remedy?" I burst out. "You know me, you know everything about me." And it was true; he had fled the Inquisition in his native Portugal at the beginning of my reign and began to serve as my physician then. He had treated the young Elizabeth and now he treated the older one. He had seen me through the smallpox, the leg ulcer, headaches, and sleeplessness. He had been among the esteemed physicians who had examined me prior to Monsieur's suit to determine how many years of childbearing yet remained to me. There were no secrets from Roderigo Lopez.

"Time is the main remedy," he said finally.

"Time! I have granted it five years already. I suffered with it and then it subsided and now it is back, like—the Armada!" There were reports a new Armada was being built and would soon be dispatched to do what the first had failed to do. God's truth, I could deal with the Armada more easily.

"There are some herbs from our good English fields," he said. "They work—if you have willingness and a strong imagination. Then there are others, from the land of the Turks, that are stronger."

"I want those."

"They are not as easily to hand, but I can obtain them," he said. "There's broom root and caper buds and *sabine*. The stronger sun of the south makes for stronger medicine."

Something in the tone of his voice nagged at me. "Do you still miss your homeland, Roderigo?" I asked. I wondered how I would feel if I had to leave England and live elsewhere.

"One always misses one's homeland," he said. "But England has been good to me. I have had responsible positions in London, house physician at St. Bartholomew's, and a practice among the highest in the land, Walsingham and Leicester for instance."

Both of whom were dead—not the best examples.

He was a Jew but had converted to Christianity, which would not have saved him from the Inquisition there but permitted him freedom here. "Portugal's loss is England's gain," I said. "Now about these herbs . . . How quickly can I have them?"

He assured me he would get them within a month.

"How much longer will I have to endure this?" I asked.

"That is impossible to say," he admitted. "It varies so much for each woman. And so few reach this age—so many die in childbirth they never experience what happens when the body withdraws from childbearing. Look in the graveyards, see the dates on the tombstones. Think of the men who are with their third wives while their first and second, who provided them with children, sleep underground."

I shuddered. "The men die in war and the women in childbed," I said. "In any case life is short." Should I confide in him? "I am fifty-nine now,"

I said. "I feel as strong as ever, no different than at twenty-five." But there was that, that forgetting, misplacing things. So many more things to misplace, I reminded myself. So many people presented, so many names. And the old names were still in there, inside my head. No room for so many.

No, I would say nothing. Except in passing. "Is there any remedy for those old crones and smiths who bumble about and cannot remember where they left their hats?" I said lightly.

"Yes," he said. "The remedy is a son or daughter living with them who can keep track of these things." Then he laughed.

So did I. Until he left and I could stop the pretense.

---

There was too much giggling in the privy chamber. It was annoying me. Every time I swept into that room, a gaggle of the girls were hunched together, their backsides thrust out, as if to display the patterns on their fine satins. I myself had left off the heavier costumes, saying I wished to be more informal this summer. I thanked the summer sun for giving me the excuse. It would be more difficult in the winter. But by then Dr. Lopez's herbs would be in my hands.

They were an impressive collection of beauties. There was Elizabeth Cavendish, the lady the bastard Dudley had enjoyed kissing at the tilt. She was tall and skittish like a nervous horse. There was another Elizabeth, this one a Vernon, with reddish hair and soft-lidded eyes that promised many things. (She wore too much perfume.) Two more Elizabeths, opposites in coloring—Southwell, blond and round with plump lips, and Bridges, dark and often scornful. There was one Frances, a Vavasour, small and pert (who sang too early in the morning for my taste). Then there was Mary Fitton, with her oval face, black hair, and eyes that watched faces with rapt and breathless scrutiny, which most people found compelling. Her elderly "protector," Sir William Knollys, was evidently one of them. He was married but seemed determined to forget it when he was in her presence.

There was Mary Howard, whom I found rather stupid and tiresome, but her (dyed?) blond hair and huge brown eyes made her attractive to people who did not value conversation. (She liked to "borrow" other girls' clothes. Once she tried to "borrow" something of mine, claiming she thought I had discarded it.) Last there was brown-haired, voluptuous Bess Throckmorton, their leader. They seemed to consider her, the oldest at twenty-eight, their model.

Sure enough, they were clustered around Bess, whispering about something. I stood behind them and clapped loudly. They whirled around to face me, still tittering.

"As Pharaoh once said, if you are standing idle you must need more work," I said. "But never fear, I shall not take away your straw to make the bricks. However, I would like my dresses to be aired and pressed. The heavy winter ones, now, while I do not need them. Replace any lost pearls or gems; you can see the keeper of the jewels for extras."

Now they all bowed as obediently as little lambs. The last one to do so was Bess, and she only inclined her head slightly. I looked carefully at her. She had returned to court changed in some way. Certainly she was thinner; she had put on weight during the winter. Now it was gone, and her cheeks had lost their plumpness.

Everyone seemed to be holding her breath. Elizabeth Cavendish gave a nervous high laugh and Mary Howard turned her bulging brown eyes to the floor, studying her shoes. Mary Fitton adjusted her cuffs.

"What is it?" I demanded. "Have I turned into a monkey?"

Bess looked at me levelly. "I assure Your Majesty, I see no monkey here," she said soothingly.

Now the others burst into high-pitched laughter.

"I think you seek to make me one," I said. "But you do not fool me."

For suddenly I understood it all. "Although for a time, you did, and that is hard to forgive. I selected you to serve me in my private quarters—a position that many girls in the land would covet—not to dupe me. So where is he? Where is the father of your bastard?" Let them know, let them tremble—the Queen still saw all, observed all, even if she had to write notes to herself. Shame that that might be known increased my anger at her.

"At sea, Your Majesty." She looked almost relieved to be able to admit it.

"Raleigh?" He had taken leave to attack Spanish ships at Panama.

"Yes, Your Majesty," she said.

"The captain of the Queen's Guard, whose duty it is to guard the virtue of my ladies, who holds the key to the maidens' chamber, has used that key himself?" I was almost speechless at the audacity. Not only was he a seducer, but he was a liar. Before leaving for his venture, when there were rumors about him and Bess, he had sworn to Robert Cecil in a letter, "There is none on the face of the earth I would be fastened unto" and dismissed the rumor as "a malicious report."

"Yes, Your Majesty." Suddenly she looked ashamed. As well she should.

"He is a great seducer," I said. "But I never thought he would be the proverbial fox in the henhouse, with so much at stake. Courage, Bess. You are not the first to be deceived by such a man." I remembered his elegant poems to my charms and his great love of me, his calling me his Cynthia, his moon goddess. I shuddered with disgust.

"He is my husband."

A double betrayal! "And when did this take place?"

"Last autumn," she said.

When he was swearing there was no one he would be fastened unto.

"Well," I said, "you must leave court and go to your child, wherever he—or she—may be."

"He, Your Majesty. His name is Damerei."

"Peculiar name. On second thought, you will await your wayward husband in the Tower. I shall command him to return immediately. His crimes are threefold: deceiving his sovereign, seducing a virgin under his protection, and marrying without royal consent. I would add, lying when asked directly about a marriage."

Her composure crumbled and she said, "As you wish, Your Majesty. We did not undertake the marriage for any evil thought, but of necessity. It is well known that Your Majesty does not receive such requests gladly, and delays granting them, and time was urgent for us."

"How noble of Raleigh!" I laughed. "So eager to make you an honest wife."

As she bowed and left the chamber, I turned to the tongue-tied girls still forming a circle. "Stop staring, and learn your lesson from this."

"What lesson shall that be, Your Majesty?" asked Frances Vavasour. If it had been anyone else, it would have been mocking, but she was clear as water.

"There are several," I said. "The main one is, do not be deceived by a fancy man. Then, if you are—God forbid!—do not seek to hide it from me!"

---

Raleigh. I sat in my inner chamber and studied the miniature of him, which captured so well his arrogant charm. He was a volcanic spirit, restless at court, always wanting more. More than anyone else he seemed enthralled by the mystery and potential of the New World, as if the Old had grown stale for him or was too small to satisfy his appetite for adventure.

His appetite . . . his appetites . . . The carnal one was well known. I had spoken true to Bess; he was widely known as a seducer, and proudly so. There was a story abroad at court (which my rogue godson Harington had passed on to me) that he had backed a woman up against a tree in the woods. When she protested, "Nay, sweet Sir Walter! Oh, sweet Sir Walter!" he had ignored her and proceeded to that which they both desired, changing her cries into "Swisser Swatter! Swisser Swatter!" It made a good story, and if it was not true, as the saying goes, it should be. There are two kinds of tales: one accurate but not true, the other true but not accurate. Swisser Swatter was most likely the latter.

I sent for Robert Cecil, knowing he was always at hand. Not for him floating in a barge for a river party, afternoon matches on the tennis courts, long rides in the countryside. One wit had described him as always having "his hands full of papers and his head full of court matters," and that served me well.

In no time he was knocking upon the door, and I admitted him. Quickly I told him about Raleigh. He shook his head. "I questioned him on this very matter," he said. "You have seen my report. The man lied at every turn. If I may say so, Your Majesty, that is why he is so widely disliked, in spite of his looks and cleverness. Dishonesty stains his other virtues." He laughed, his little rounded shoulders shaking. "Now it makes sense," he said. "Some of the sayings I have heard. One, that he has been too inward with one of Her Majesty's maids."

"Clumsy wit," I said.

"The other, that 'all is alarm and confusion at the discovery of the discoverer, and not indeed of a new continent but of a new incontinent.'"

Now I laughed. "Clever," I admitted. I was still feeling cross, but it was subsiding. "Swisser Swatter must needs learn to control himself in the Tower."

Robert hooted. "You have heard that?"

"I do have a gown with eyes and ears on it," I reminded him.

But they did not hear and see everything, as they used to. I would have to try harder. This was, ultimately, of no matter. But what else might I overlook that was?

---

It was night. The usual gathering of card players and gossips filled the privy chamber; I could hear them from my own bedchamber but declined to go out there. They were all discussing the abrupt departure of Bess, I had no doubt. So many must have known of her marriage and the reason for it and only wondered how long the brazen game could go on before I became aware of it.

Catherine dragged a small chest across the floor to where I sat. The others had already gone to bed, and only a few candles were left burning in the chamber.

"In her haste, she forgot this," said Catherine, running her hands over the carvings on the rounded, ribbed lid. The initials "E.T." shone gold beneath the handle.

E.T. My initials. How amusing. Telling myself that I had the right to open it—as abandoned property, after all—I raised the lid and peeked in. A jumble of ribbons, pomades, and handkerchiefs greeted me. There was nothing of value here, which was a relief. I pulled a lacy handkerchief out and almost choked on the perfume. It was lily, a scent I dislike as it reminds me of death, in spite of its Easter association.

Catherine withdrew and left me to examine the contents of the chest in privacy. How well she knew me. What a treasure to have a friend who averted her eyes from my faults and opened them only to the good in me.

I felt beneath the rumpled mash of items and found some folded sheets of paper. Knowing I should not read them but unable to keep from it, I settled myself back and held the first paper up to the dim light.

It was a poem. Walter, along with everyone else at court, wrote poetry. He had presented me with many poems, usually heavy with allegorical and classical allusions. I was Diana, chaste huntress; I was Cynthia, radiant goddess of the moon, whom shepherds adored. What else had he called me? Athena, wise above all mortals, strong protectress of my realm. That exhausted the store of virgin goddesses, except for Hestia, but the imagery of a hearth-loving goddess did not fit me.

The ink was dark enough to read even in the poor light.

*Her eyes he would should be of light,*
*A violet breath and lips of jelly,*
*Her hair not black not over-bright,*
*And of the softest down her belly.*

The paper was shaking in my hands. I kept rereading the words, unable to believe what I was seeing. Violet breath . . . I had never been that close to her. As for the down and the belly . . . I gave a shudder. Vulgar.

No one ever had, or ever would, write such words to me. First, because my majesty would not permit such license, and second, because my person did not conjure them up.

I took out Leicester's last letter to me and reread its cozy, familiar greetings. *Pardon your poor old servant . . . my gracious lady . . . ease of her late pain . . . happy preservation . . . I humbly kiss your foot . . .*

Foot. Not lips of jelly.

I returned the papers to the chests—hers to the ribbed one, mine to my little bedside box.

I looked down at my slender but now veined fingers, with the coronation ring unchanged since that day I had first put it on. Its gold was not dimmed, its design only a little worn with the years. I had never removed it; it had been with me through every day of my reign. It guarded me, keeping me apart from all other women. Without it, what verses might I have received, what hot whispered vows in the night? Whose wife might I have been?

Instead, I was England's. The only husband who would not grow old, fail, or desert me.

# 23

*February 1593*

I fingered the jewel-encrusted miniature skull on its gold chain. Should I wear it today? Would it ward off the plague? I needed to attend the opening speech of Parliament; the official procession had been canceled due to the plague spreading in London, and I would go directly to the Parliament chambers by way of barge. Still, there would be crowds outside, not to mention the crowd in Parliament itself. No, it seemed popish and reeked of superstition. I left it off.

Essex had presented it to me just after I appointed him to the Privy Council. He was exuberantly grateful, making wild promises of his service. In truth, I had relented and named him a councillor despite his clumsy performance in France; since his return he had impressed me with his assiduous team of information gatherers at Essex House, headed by the Bacon brothers. Francis I already knew. There was not a cleverer man in England. His portrait painter had lamented, "If only one could paint his mind!" and written it in Latin around the miniature. Anthony was said to be equally intelligent but tormented by bad health—gout, stones, and failing eyesight. "A gentleman of impotent feet but a nimble head," someone described him.

Essex, turning his energy from foreign battlefields to domestic politics, procured election to Commons for at least eight of his followers. And besides Francis Bacon, his stepfather, Sir Christopher Blount, represented Staffordshire county. Was he was building up a party?

---

The surface of the river was dull pewter under the gray skies of February as my barge made its way to Parliament. Lent had not yet begun; this year Easter came late. But the bleakness and austerity of the weather called to mind fasting and rough shirts. Since I intended to ask for money, I dressed plainly, fitting the mood.

A crowd was waiting at the landing, their pinched faces and chapped, blotched cheeks showing the ravages of winter. How we all longed for an end to it. I smiled and waved to them, accepted their little notes and gifts, then hurried inside. The plague lurked in crowds.

The Speaker escorted me into the chamber. I had not called a parliament in four years. The subsidy the one of 1589 had granted me had just run out. The Crown was in desperate need of money. They must grant me more.

The members rose in respect, and the Lord Keeper of the Great Seal bade them be seated while he gave the opening oration. I took the throne beside him and listened.

Quickly he listed the urgencies before us. They could be summed up in one word: Spain.

Far from crawling back into his kennel after the ignominious defeat of his Armada, Philip had been emboldened by it. He had quickly rebuilt it, modeling his new ships on ours, so that his navy was twice as strong now as it had been in 1588, and of a more advanced design. He directly harried the Protestant world in France and the Netherlands. In Scotland, he intrigued with certain lords to land twenty-five thousand troops this coming summer, and the same thing in Ireland, attempting to gain a toehold in neighboring countries where he could launch an attack on us. In addition, he stirred up trouble in Germany and Poland, to cut off our trade with them. It was imperative that we have the means to counter him in his plans to conquer France, England, and Ireland.

"It is stunning that the revenues of England are now defending five countries!" the Lord Keeper cried. He pointed out that I had had to sell Crown lands to meet expenses, despite my ongoing frugality.

"In building, our Queen has consumed little or nothing," he said. "In her pleasures, not much. As for her apparel, it is royal and princely, as required for a sovereign, but not excessive. Her household expenses, being a solitary ruler, are small, yes, less than in any other king's time. In the past, Her Majesty, despite hardship in doing so, has always repaid her debts."

This was true. I had built no palaces and could not even afford to convert the temporary banqueting house at Whitehall into a permanent pavilion, something much remarked upon by foreign visitors. I had no consort's lodgings, nor children's, to support.

"And there is more!" he said. "When Her Majesty came to the throne, it was mired deep in debt. The navy had rotted. But she discharged the debt, and now she is able to match on sea any prince in Europe, which the Spaniards found out when they came to invade us." A purr of pride rumbled through the room. "She has compassed the world with her ships, whereby this land is made famous throughout all places!" The purr rose. "I trust that every good subject, seeing it concerns his own good and the preservation of his estate, will grant a generous subsidy. They are less than half that granted to her father, King Henry VIII."

He rumbled on about other matters, then called upon anyone who wished to speak. Suddenly an older man rose in the back. "I am Peter Wentworth, representative of Barnstable."

Not him! The fiery Puritan who had steadfastly opposed me in matters of religion, trying to force the Church of England to abolish priests, vestments, and music. But he could not be silenced now. The Keeper nodded.

"Besides the Spaniard, we have another enemy to address once and for all in this parliament. I mean the chaos that will descend upon us if Her Majesty does not settle the succession. We must frame it as a law and have her name the one to follow her."

The unmentionable topic, the one I had succeeded in silencing in the years since Parliament had ordered me to marry. How dare he?

The Keeper said, "Sir—"

"I have addressed these concerns in my pamphlet 'A Pithy Exhortation to Her Majesty for Establishing her Successor to the Crown.'" He waved a dark leather-bound book in his right hand. "I have presented it, yet I receive no answer!"

"Sir, this is not meet—"

"We have free speech here in Commons! I must present—"

"This is not the proper time; we are not framing law."

I stared at him, hoping by my stern gaze to silence him. But Puritans are not silenced by looks, not even from their Queen. Let the irritating man speak, then.

"Exercise that privilege of free speech, sir," I ordered him. "You may proceed."

He looked startled; now that he was told to speak, he stuttered. "I—I—" He thumbed the pages of the book.

"No, no book," I said. "You must speak from your own head and heart."

"Very well! You know I have urged this since 1562, when Your Majesty was smitten with the smallpox and we saw that if our captain perished, there was no one to take the wheel of the ship. Many, many shared my fear! But you did nothing to assuage that fear. After the Queen of Scots was . . . removed . . . I wrote my 'Pithy Exhortation,' urging you to act. Now, Parliament must act in your stead since you will not. Parliament must draft a law regarding the succession."

I felt the brush of heat spreading across the back of my neck like the palm of an overwarm hand. Dr. Lopez's herbs had helped quiet the attacks, like a flash of fire that crackled and struck, but had not altogether ended them. My collar grew damp, and the plain gown I was wearing suddenly felt like a hair shirt indeed.

"Parliament does not have that power," I said.

"Parliament determined the succession that brought Your Majesty to the throne," he said.

Now my face felt as if it were before a smithy's furnace. Parliament had passed a law of succession, but only according to my father's wishes—wishes that he changed quite often. I had been in, then out, then in the succession again. I did not care to be reminded of that.

"In compliance with the will of Henry VIII," I said.

Wentworth now whirled around and addressed his fellow parliamentarians, while not exactly turning his back on me. "History tells us what happens in a kingdom with no clear heir," he cried. "Each age is different; each age has its own particular horrors. Now, for us, should our gracious Queen die and no successor be known, fierce competition will break out for the crown. The realm will fracture into many pieces, making us easy prey for Spain." He raised his eyes to heaven. "Farmers will be slain in the field, children murdered in every town, women ravished, towns burned, and religion laid in the dust!"

"You paint a vivid picture," was all I said.

"Remember Rehoboam, Solomon's son! He lost his father's kingdom; it split in half. The eyes of all England are upon you!" he cried to me.

"Yes, they always are, and have been since my birth," I said calmly. There was a reassuring laugh from the chambers.

"My true and unfeigned love for you forces me to tell you, our most dear and natural sovereign, that if Your Majesty does not settle the succession in your lifetime, I greatly fear that you shall then have such a troubled soul and conscience, yea, ten thousand hells in your soul, when you die, as die you most certainly will—your noble person shall lie upon the earth unburied, a doleful spectacle to the world—"

"Representative Wentworth needs air," I said, motioning to the guards. "Remove him so that he may catch his breath."

"You shall leave behind you such a name of infamy—" He was hustled from the chamber, leaving a wake of silence.

It was up to me to break the silence, change the mood. Yet I was awash in sweat, and not from the prickling heat of my neck. *Lie unburied . . . die most certainly you shall . . .* I cleared my throat. "His words are wilder than

Christopher Marlowe's *Tamburlaine,* and I wonder he does not go on the stage."

That was what was needed. A peal of laughter rang throughout the chamber, and I had dodged the succession question once again. I would settle it my way, and in my own time.

---

The Parliament continued to meet all through Lent, paralleling the dreary weather of the season and the labored, penitential readings for services. Archbishop Whitgift loved Lent; it allowed him to indulge in his Old Church proclivities. Late dawns and early dusks called for flickering altar candles. Searching one's conscience lent itself to confession and abstention; fasting purified the soul. The time-honored wheel of the church year turned slowly, and the six weeks of Lent could seem very long indeed, depending on the privations one embraced.

There were no plays, few court festivities, no music, and no wedding solemnizations. The courtiers put away their gaudy clothes, and many returned to their homes in the country.

Though Puritans rejected the church year, holding a liturgical calendar to be popish, they seemed to keep Lent all year and wish the country would keep it along with them. Fortunately, political setbacks had curbed their power lately, and so their challenge to my government, and the threat of some sort of Calvinist-type reformed religion being imposed upon us was allayed.

I found solace in the old forms, although I did not flaunt them. I had, after all, grown up with them, and they were comfortingly familiar to me. I liked the whispered "Remember man you are dust and unto dust you shall return," followed by the flattened thumb smearing ashes on my forehead; I did not flinch from examining the list of transgressions I might have committed—lack of charity, lack of compassion, vanities, and self-delusion. In private I wore the memento mori that Essex had given me, sometimes drawing it out of my bosom and staring at the hollow eye sockets. When I looked in the mirror, my white face and the dark shadows of my eyes traced the same anatomy. The skull beneath my powdered cheeks was all too clear.

Death was very much on my mind, as this Lent plague still raged about us. Many had died in London, and the sound of the bells and the low, mournful cries of "Bring out your dead" did not abate. I sent what food and goods I could to help the survivors, but there was little anyone could do to stop the ravages. I ordered the theaters closed, as well as the concerts at the Royal Exchange, to keep crowds down and try to slow the spread of sickness.

"Queens have died young and fair," a poet said. I was no longer young, and Wentworth had just loudly reminded me I must die. I would die. Someone would sit on the throne after me. Who was that someone to be?

There were those who thought I could not bear the thought of death, seeking to avoid all mention of it, as if that would keep it at bay. But they were wrong about my motives. What I wished to keep at bay was attention turning to my successor and bypassing me. As soon as I named him, I would be creating an alternative government, someone to whom disgruntled persons could turn for redress. I would be rendering myself obsolete. I had said it plainly: "Think you I will set my winding-sheet before my eye?" From that, people thought it was the shroud I shunned, not being dead politically before my time.

It would have to be James VI of Scotland. We all knew that. But I would not formally name him. He was the only possible claimant who met England's needs. All the other candidates were either foreign, or Catholic, or more distant relatives. Since it was so obvious it would be James, why could they not stop harassing me about it?

I was not overly impressed with James, but he was the best to hand. As a thrifty monarch, I had nonetheless felt it a good investment to put James on an allowance, subject to his good behavior. As a result, he raised barely a murmur when his mother was executed.

James was said to be odd, but how could he be otherwise with such a mother and such a father? It was a miracle he was not insane. If he had a penchant for pedantry and favorites, it was a small price to pay for what he had been through. I hoped my people would welcome him . . . sometime in the far distant future.

---

Robert Cecil brought me reports of Parliament's debates. He sat in Commons, his father in Lords. Essex likewise sat in Lords, his retainers in Commons. I was shocked beyond words to learn that Francis Bacon, Essex's man in Commons, had objected to the subsidy to fight the Spanish, speaking out loudly against granting it in the time period we requested it.

Sir George Carey answered him robustly, saying that the Spanish had already sent 140,000 escudos of gold into England itself to corrupt the nobility, in addition to bribing the Scots.

"The Queen is determined to dispatch Sir Francis Drake to encounter them with a great navy!" he had cried. "Shall we deny her the means?"

Bacon rose and said the country could not afford the subsidy. "The gentlemen of the realm must sell their plate and the farmers their brass pots."

This disloyalty stunned me. Was he appealing to the masses over and above the peril of the country? Was Essex behind this? For Francis Bacon was his man and could have no justification on his own. Was his master seeking to undermine me, courting popularity directly with the people?

---

In the end he was overridden and I got my subsidy. But I would not forget his obstruction, and the seeds of my mistrust of Essex were planted.

I had now to address Parliament and thank them. I pondered much upon my words. Even though history ultimately judges our deeds, it is fair words that persuade people to allow these deeds and embellish them to make them glorious. I prayed that my words would be stirring.

When I returned to Parliament on its closing day, I was well satisfied with what I would say.

It was April, and Holy Week had begun. The air had softened and it was clear that spring was upon us. The still-unfurled leaves on the branches, seen from the river, were mistily green, and violets gave the grass a purple shadow. The oars dipped into the eddying water and seemed to propel us forward into warmth.

Standing before the Lords, with Commons listening outside the chamber, flanked by Hunsdon, the lord chancellor, on my right and Burghley, the lord treasurer, on my left, I waited while the Lord Keeper of the Great Seal assured them that "if the coffers of Her Majesty's treasure were not empty, or she could have replenished them by her own sacrifice, she would not have asked her subjects nor accepted this, even if they offered it freely."

I rose and addressed them. "I assure you that you do this so you may flourish; it is not for me. Many wiser princes than myself you have had, including my father, and to whom I am far shallow—but you have had none whose love and care can be greater."

Looking out at them, their honest faces turned to me, I felt inspired to continue and to warn them against fearmongering. "For my own part, I swear that my heart has never known what fear is. In ambition of glory I never sought to enlarge the territories of my land. If I have used my forces to keep the enemy from you, I have thereby done it for your safety, and to keep dangers at bay."

They were about to break into cheers, but I had important warnings for them. I silenced them with a look and continued. "I would not have you returning home into the countryside to strike fear into the minds of my people. Even our enemies hold our nature to be resolute and valiant. Only warn the people to be wary and not to be found sleeping. So shall they show their own valor and frustrate the hopes of the enemy."

The earnest faces before me were resolute. "To conclude," I said, "I assure you I will not incur any idle expense. Now must I give you all as great thanks as ever prince gave loving subjects, assuring you that my care for you has, and shall, exceed all my other cares of worldly causes."

I could feel the love in the chamber; it flowed between us, a bond as strong as an arm clasp. I would not fail them; they would not fail me. We were one.

# 24

## *July 1593*

t had been a delightful summer day. I had had an invigorating ride out from the stuffy confines of my apartments in Greenwich. After my return, I had enjoyed a picnic of sorts on the high grounds behind the palace. Ale, berries, cheese, and the thickest, sweetest bread—ah, perfection!

Then, awaiting me: the news. It came from France, through both Cecils, father and son, as though they feared to tell me singly.

Henri IV of France had embraced the Catholic faith. In order to ascend the throne, he had abandoned his conscience and bowed his knee to Rome. "Paris is well worth a Mass," he was reported to have said.

"He ascertained correctly," said Burghley, his tired voice barely above a whisper. These days he seldom came out; that he did so now spoke volumes. "Paris has steadfastly refused to admit him, and he cannot rule France without Paris." He looked sad, like an old hound. "That, Your Majesty, is the fact."

"The fact! The fact?" I burst out. "God's breath! Swithin's breeches! Cannot a person bend or alter facts? Could he not have persuaded Paris?" Even as I spoke, I weighed the likelihood—very poor.

"Paris is resolutely Catholic," said Robert. "To their folly!"

I thought of all the money I could ill afford poured out to maintain Henri IV as a Protestant claimant. I felt hot fury. I had drained the realm, my poor realm, to prop up this turncoat. Now it was all for nothing.

And I had lost my one major ally. There was no Protestant ruler in Europe now, apart from the Scandinavians. The Netherlands were still in revolt, but nothing resolved. A few German palatines and princes. As for the rest—Spain, Poland, Ireland, Italy, now France—all firmly in the papal grasp.

Oh! Damn the Parisians! Damn the French! Damn Henri! Was the defeat of the Armada all for nothing? Were we to stand alone forever?

"That traitor!" I cried. "After all his assurances to me!" For some reason, the useless death of Essex's brother came home to me. He had died for nothing, nothing, nothing. . . . I wanted to gouge out Henri's eyes for it, make him pay.

"He did what he felt he must," said Robert. "His heart was not in it."

"Damn his heart!" I cried. "I care not for his heart. Let them boil it in holy oil!"

Burghley laughed, a painful exhalation. "Now you sound like your father," he said.

"If I had the means—if I could—I would lead such an army, to punish that Judas. . . . He is worse than Philip!"

"Hardly, Your Majesty." Robert spoke. "He has not declared war on you. His Catholicism will be a matter of convenience only, not one of conscience. You may still count him as an ally."

"I cannot count a turncoat as an ally," I said. "I have no respect for such men."

"Which is better, an ally one does not respect or an outright enemy who is steadfast to his principles?"

"Oh!" I cried. "They should both burn in hell!"

"But in the meantime, which would do you the most good?" Robert pressed.

"They are useless, both of them."

---

But in the end, of course, I was to be forced to make a surface peace with Henri IV, after a few chiding letters and finger-waggings. I was powerless to do otherwise. His cynical politic conversion was another milestone on my journey to wisdom and disillusion.

---

The day of my birth was approaching, as it had sixty years ago. And just as it had been sixty years ago, when my mother had withdrawn into her chambers to await my birth, so I withdrew into the very same chambers at Greenwich. My parents had secretly married in January, my mother crowned Queen in June, and then, from August on, she had been confined to her apartments in Greenwich, as the old custom was. My father, too, had been born at Greenwich, and he wanted to honor it with the birth of his long-awaited son. Everyone was sure I would be that son, or pretended to be sure. Surely some must have had doubts, signs. But they dared not voice them—or perhaps my father did not hear them. When, on that seventh day of September, I was born cloven and not crested, he was stunned. But he put a good face on it, saying, "If it is a daughter this time, sweetheart, sons will follow!" And he kissed my mother.

He named me Elizabeth after his own mother, added "ss" to the proclamations announcing a prince, and sponsored a lavish baptism for me with all the dignitaries of the kingdom.

Beyond the boundaries of his kingdom, no one acknowledged me as legitimate, and the elaborate ceremony my father had arranged to emphasize otherwise had the opposite effect.

Sixty years ago . . . These September days were hot—had they been at the time? Was my mother sweltering as she paced from room to room in the locked apartments? Did she pray for a cool day when her labor began? I, too, wished for cooler weather. The stifling heat did little to assuage the occasional attacks I still had. I wandered the rooms, following in my mother's footsteps, trying to imagine what she had felt, as if somehow that would enable me to glimpse her.

I had no memory of her. Try as I would, I could not see her face, could not remember her voice. I had had a ring made that carried her portrait and mine, but looking at that ring was the only way I could ever see her as I went about my day. It was a very poor substitute. Just here she walked. . . . Just here she must have turned, and rested her elbows on the windowsill, and looked out at the wide river below, moving her face to catch the breeze. She eluded me like a shadow.

I had forbidden any celebration of this birthday. I did not wish to remind anyone of my age. Sixty—the very *sound* of it was old, conjuring up a host of other words: "graybeard," "Nestor," "elderly," "sage," "dotage," "walking stick," "gout," "impotent," "crone," "senile." I knew that was so, because long ago I had thought the same. Now I was supremely sensitive to those words, proof enough that I had arrived there . . . or was afraid others would think so.

I was still as erect and robust as ever, and my health was good. Under the wigs my hair had faded to sandy, red streaked with gray. I needed glasses to read, else the letters were just black squiggles to me. I tired more easily and my temper grew brittle earlier in the day. But those were small payments to old Chronos, and I was content enough. The years had fined me little.

No one else in my family had lived so long. Few kings of England had lived so long. I knew my history and I thought, after the Normans came, there had only been five who reached sixty, including the conqueror himself, who expired on the threshold of that birthday. I was grateful.

I would give myself a birthday gift and do my favorite thing: translate philosophy. And who should it be? Someone I had never tried before, someone difficult, to challenge me. I settled on Boethius's *Consolation of Philosophy*, composed more than a thousand years ago when the scholar was facing execution by the Emperor Theodoric. If he could find consolation in philosophy while in prison awaiting his death, I could surely find it when facing nothing more onerous than a sixtieth birthday.

Boethius wrote in Latin, which I always enjoyed translating. The economy of expression in Latin—quite marvelous. If a thought is six sentences long in English, it compresses into three in Latin. It is good we have the language of the ancient Romans to remind us of the elegance of their ways.

---

The afternoon sped by as I hunched over my desk, shuffling papers and searching for words. Reaching the level of the windows, the sinking sun poured directly into the room, making it hotter. I was about to put the papers aside and call for a cool drink when dear Helena came into the room.

She dropped a little curtsy. "My very best wishes to—"

I rose, put my finger across my lips. "No, my dear. This is a day like any other."

She understood. But this was not what she had come in for. "I am sent to inform you that you have an unexpected visitor. From Ireland."

Ireland! Had William Fitzwilliam, my lord deputy over there, returned? Was there very bad news? Had the Spanish made a landing? It could only be a crisis. We were nominal overlords of Ireland, and had been for centuries, but our grasp was shaky.

"She is waiting in the guard room."

"She?"

"The pirate. That pirate woman, the mother of all rebellions in Ireland."

"Grace O'Malley?" We had exchanged letters; she had appealed to me on behalf of her son, being held prisoner by my governor of Connaught, in Ireland. I had sent her a list of eighteen questions to be answered before I proceeded, and had not received them. If her answers had sounded right, I stood more than ready to help her. She had won me over by her first letter, in which she had asked me "to grant unto your said subject under your most gracious hand of signet, free liberty during her life to invade with sword and fire all your highness enemies, wheresoever they are or shall be, without any interruption of any person or persons whatsoever." I could certainly use her, and from what I knew, what she promised, she delivered. She sailed in her own ships, took musket and sword against her enemies—even, at one point, the Turks!

"Yes. She is anchored in the Thames at the palace landing steps. 'Tis said she is as fine a sailor as Drake himself."

That, of course, was impossible. She had not sailed around the world, fighting her way around the very tip of South America, finding a new passage through to the Pacific. Still, one could still be a superlative sailor without such heroics.

"I shall receive her with the rest of the court present." Whoever was here this afternoon could be present. "In the presence chamber."

Helena hurried away, and I stood pondering the Irish woman's real purpose in coming. She had provided me with an unexpected birthday commemoration, ensuring that this one would stand out in my memory.

---

I waited upon my throne in the presence chamber, its long wall of windows ensuring that I would be able to see Grace O'Malley very well. The hastily assembled courtiers lined both sides like choristers in choir stalls, everyone bursting with curiosity to behold this famous woman. And what did I expect? Someone with tangled hair, wearing a wolf skin? Or in pirate garb, men's breeches and high boots?

"Gráinne Ní Mháille!" the usher announced. "Grace O'Malley." The doors swung open to reveal a tall red-haired woman dressed in a fine gown. Two of my guards flanked her, and then the captain ordered a ceremonial search of her person. She held out her arms to make it easy for them. One of them cried out, "A dagger!" and snatched it from its sheath. The other guards drew their swords, holding her at blade point.

"You come into my presence with a dagger?" Surely she did not mean to attack me before all these witnesses. She stared back at me and did not reply. Then I realized she did not speak English, of course. I tried French and got an equally blank stare. Then Welsh, hoping I had found someone to speak it with. Nothing.

"Is there anyone here who speaks Irish?" I asked. "What about you, Francis?"

Bacon seemed to know everything, so perhaps he knew that language. He attempted to speak to her in a halting sentence or two. Then she spoke. Her voice was low and strong.

"Your Highness, she speaks Latin," said Bacon, relieved. "She asks if you do."

"Of course I do!" And had just spent the afternoon thinking in Latin. How fortuitous. "Francis, can you translate for the court?"

He nodded.

"Why, Mistress O'Malley, have you concealed a dagger on your person?" I asked.

"It was not concealed, Your Majesty. It was quite openly worn. I wear it for my own protection. There are many who would kill me."

"In Ireland, perhaps, but not here." I had heard of the attempts to kill her, but everyone in Ireland constantly attempted to kill his enemies. Grace had outsmarted and outfought all her would-be assassins.

She smiled at me, a dazzling smile, one that revealed a full set of teeth. "Here, there, everywhere."

I nodded. "You may approach the throne."

She walked toward me, but when she came to the spot where she should have bowed, she kept walking. The guards took her forearms and stopped her.

"You have forgotten the necessary submission," they reminded her.

"I have not forgotten," she said. "But I do not submit myself to you as Queen of Ireland, for I do not recognize you as such. I have submitted to your overlordship only as Queen of England."

"Then bow to the Queen of England as a guest, not a subject." God's wounds, but she was trying my patience!

She did so, and now was standing within ten feet of me.

"You may speak your piece," I said.

"With Your Gracious Highness's permission," she said, "I will tell it all." She laid out her case swiftly, with none of the storytelling the Irish were famous for. Perhaps she knew the stark facts would speak louder than any dressing upon them. She was twice married and twice widowed. Her first husband had been killed in battle. By him she had two sons; by the second, one son. Sir Richard Bingham, my governor of her region of Connaught, had killed one of her sons, Owen, and taken the other prisoner, where he was holding her half-brother as well. The third son he had tricked into declaring loyalty to him.

"He holds them against all law," she said. "He refuses to release them. He is a cruel and barbaric liar and torturer. Before he stole them, he stole my livestock and property."

"And you, mistress, have always followed the law?" I laughed. She followed no law but her own, and practiced bold piracy wherever she could. She had led many rebellions against the English before finally submitting, and I knew her submission was conditional.

"Except when others did not. I have found that when dealing with a lawbreaker, keeping the law myself puts me at a disadvantage in responding."

Her Latin was impressive. She reeled off those sentences, with their changes in tense and object, as easily as singing a ditty.

"And I understand that you responded rather vigorously."

She threw back her head and laughed loudly. "I harried his ships, used mine to ferry troops against him, and raided his seaport towns. He could not seize my ships, and they were as good as horses to me."

Perhaps she *was* another Drake, using her ships like an army.

"I would not want you for an enemy," I said.

"Nor would I!" she agreed. Then the smile faded. "Your Majesty, make that blackguard set my family free. Order him! He will have to obey you, even if he mocks God!"

"You should have waited for me to summon you," I said, "rather than thrusting yourself upon me like this."

"I had answered all the questions you put to me," she replied. "I had waited and waited for your response. While I waited, my son was suffering. You were a quick sail away. I had to come."

I was about to tell her I had never received her letter, but before I could reply, she suddenly shook with a violent sneeze, followed by another. It happens often here in Greenwich; they say the nearby fields make people cough. Marjorie Norris stepped forward and handed her a lace-edged handkerchief. She blew her nose in it loudly, then, turning on her heel, walked to the fireplace and threw it in.

"Madam!" Marjorie cried. "That was an expensive handkerchief, of French linen and lace!"

"But it has been soiled," said Grace, puzzled. "In Ireland we do not keep dirty clothes on our persons."

"Are you saying that you Irish are cleaner than we English?" I asked.

"In the matter of handkerchiefs, evidently," she replied.

The entire audience laughed.

"It is time that we continue this discussion in private," I said. "Come with me into the privy chamber."

Once inside, I offered her a seat, as well as some ale.

"The audience continues, but now we may sit," I said, taking a chair across from her. Several of my ladies would be present, but I thought the exchange would go better without the male Privy Councillors.

She remained sitting erect, and I realized that that was her natural posture. She was a handsome woman; now that I was closer, I could see that she was older than she looked from a distance. Perhaps it was her bearing and energy that belied her years.

"Tell me your story," I said. "From the beginning. I am told it is colorful. As colorful as those plaids you Irish wear."

"All Irish lives are colorful," she said. "And if they are not, we make them so in our minds. But mine truly was. My father was Owen 'Black Oak'

O'Malley, chieftain of the barony of Murrisk. Unusual for the Irish, we were always a seafaring family, and my father's ships sailed as far as Scotland, Portugal, and Spain. It was I who inherited the chieftain's vision of being able to look out to sea and know the coming weather, for all that my father took my brother out and hoped he had it."

Yes, I knew that feeling well. A father who wanted his son to carry certain traits, but found them in his daughter instead.

"Your father took you out to sea?" I could not help questioning.

"Aye, with a bit of persuading. You see, my mother did not think it seemly, not womanly, and said my hair would tangle in the rigging. So I cut it off!" She flipped her long hair over her shoulder. "And will again, if necessary." She looked at me and all but winked. "There are always wigs."

"Indeed there are." She did not need one, evidently. Her hair was still thick and mainly red, although silver was running through it, like threads on a fine fabric.

"Backing up a bit, when were you born?"

"I am not sure of the year, but your father was on the throne, and I remember when you were born. My father talked about it, about the king's fine daughter with the red hair, and said, 'See, my bonny one, all the daughters worth having have red hair.'"

She was older than I, then. To remain so vital and strong, the pirate's life was the secret. There were those who called me a pirate, but I could only finance and commission them, not sail myself. I was thus only a pirate once removed.

"I believe that is so. Your father was a wise man." Someone had once tried to assassinate me, barring my way in the palace garden and pointing a pistol straight at my bosom, but in the end he had wavered and dropped it. Later he told the guards he could not do it, as I looked the very image of the late king with his red hair. My red hair had saved me.

"I was married at sixteen to Donal 'Of the Battles' O'Flaherty. His name was fiercer than the man. It was not long before I was managing his fleet. His fleet of . . . um . . . merchant ships."

Pirate ships, she meant. But I just nodded.

"He was killed in battle. Next I married his nephew, Richard 'In Irons' Burke. He earned that name by always wearing his chain mail. Even when eating supper." She smiled indulgently. "We had one son, Tibbot, Tibbot 'Of the Ships,' called that because he was born on board ship." She sighed and leaned back at last, taking a long sip of her ale. "You may have heard the story. You most likely think it a tale. It is true."

"I am not sure what you mean," I said.

"The one about the Turks and me."

"I know you fought them on and off, fending off their pirate ships with your own."

"Very true. I had given birth to Tibbot the day before and was recovering in the cabin when the ship was attacked by Turkish pirates. I could hear shouts and clatter on the deck overhead, and then the captain appeared in the doorway saying things were going very badly for us. Was I to get no rest? I jumped up, swore at the inept captain, grabbed my musket, and rushed up on deck. The first man I encountered was a Turk, and I fired on him, felling him. Our ship rallied, and we captured the enemy, killed its crew, and added it to our fleet." She crossed her arms in satisfaction.

"Now about this time, I was coming to the attention of the English. You were increasing your control of western Ireland, and it was inevitable that we would clash. You were changing the ancient laws of our people, the way we inherited land, and we fought back. You can understand that, can you not?"

"I can respect it even though I must oppose it."

"Yes, I can see your need for the laws, but why did you have to forbid us our poetic bards, outlaw our long hair, our traditional mantles?"

Before I could answer, she went on.

"Nonetheless, I saw the futility of resistance and submitted to you in 1577—sixteen years ago. That was the time Sir Henry Sidney was lord deputy of Ireland, and I got to know his son, Philip. A sensitive boy. He was quite taken with my story, but then a poet would be. If you want to know more about me, read his letters. He recounts many incidents."

I had, in fact, read them. "The one that sticks in my mind is the one where you received ill at the hands of Lord Howth of Dublin, being denied hospitality at his castle because he was busy eating and did not wish to be disturbed. You had your revenge, kidnapping his son, and then you made him swear that he would never again turn away anyone asking for shelter, and that he would keep an extra place always set at his table for unexpected guests. I am told that he does."

"The rest of my story is more violent and less entertaining. Richard died and then followed struggles to retain my land and livestock. Then your man, Richard Bingham, appeared and entered into the fray. He became my enemy and has behaved in ways that do not honor his mistress, the Queen of England. No wonder we call him 'The Flail of Connaught.'" She thrust a sheaf of papers at me. "The particulars are all here."

I was wrung out from her story. "What shall we do about all this?" I finally said.

"I will serve you faithfully, as I promised, taking up the sword against your enemies. But in return, order Bingham to release my family."

That seemed right to me.

I was nodding to agree when she added, "And remove him from office. He is not fit for it!"

"So I shall, if you promise to stop aiding the rebels against me. For I know it is not just Bingham you fight but others of my agents as well. You are not called the mother of the Irish rebellion for nothing."

She looked caught out but shrugged graciously. "I promised to serve you," she said. "Is not the promise to stop opposing you implicit in that?"

"No, as you pick and choose what you will oppose."

She leaned forward. "Do I have your word?"

"Do I have yours?"

There was a long pause. "Yes," she finally said.

"The word of a pirate?" asked Marjorie Norris. "What is that worth?"

"When given to a friend, it is ironclad," she said.

"And when given to an enemy, worthless," I answered. "Am I your friend?"

"Yes," she said. "And I do not choose my friends lightly. They must pass certain tests. You have passed."

"And how is that?"

"I have met my match in courage," she said. "For that is the real reason I came—to see you and take your measure."

"You *are* bolder than Drake," I admitted, doubting my wisdom in openly bestowing such a compliment on her.

# 25

# LETTICE

*November 1593*

She has decreed that cloaks will be short next season at court," said my son. "No courtiers may appear in cloaks reaching past their knees. And we are not allowed to alter the old ones. Now there's another unnecessary expense added to our list!" He was sitting before the fire, wrapped in a deep green cloak of the sort now forbidden, staring moodily into the flames.

"What the Queen wants is necessary by definition," I said with a sigh. It did get tiring. Jump here, jump there, all on her whim. "Will you have to borrow to do it?"

"Not yet," Robert said. "The duties on the sweet wines during this cold time of year will suffice. But once it is warmer—" He spread his hands.

Yes, what was he to do next year? There was no military command for him in the offing, and, aside from regular attendance at the Privy Council, my son was unemployed. Francis and Anthony Bacon busied themselves with the new ring of spies, trying hard to bring in information that Robert could present to the Queen and earn her gratitude. But they had found little, and Francis's attempt to block the double subsidy bill in Parliament had earned the Queen's wrath. She now wanted nothing to do with him, so his stubborn stand on principle had injured all of us. For a man so intelligent, Francis seemed determined to act stupidly.

I was back in Leicester House, or rather, Essex House. What cared I for what it was called, as long as I was back in London? I was not welcome at court, but I could see Whitehall out one window and the Strand out another. All of London thronged past our gates, and a great deal of it entered the house, where we could hold our own little court.

This had once been a bishop's palace on the Strand, and some said the ghosts of old churchmen wafted through the halls of the rebuilt house. If so, they would scarcely recognize its maze of suites of bedrooms, picture gallery, gardens, and kitchens. Upon Leicester's death it had passed to me and then to Robert, who promptly renamed it Essex House. When I gave it to him, it was bare and empty. The Queen had forced me to auction off its furniture to pay Leicester's debts to her. Rumor had it she had bought our bed, just for spite. Refurnishing the house was taking a long time. Prices had risen since Leicester had furnished it. So the walls, which the Queen could not order stripped of their oak paneling and gilded paint, looked out onto nearly bare rooms.

"Warmer!" Here in England we longed for sun and warmth, but its impact on the Devereux income forced me to dread its arrival. "Yes, summer is our enemy. Unless you can turn the winter to your further advantage now." Oh, why could the Bacon brothers not come up with *something*? All their promises and fine talk had led nowhere.

"Christmas is coming," Robert said. "The court will be in close quarters. The Queen will crave my company, and then—"

I could not help laughing. "For another dance? Another whisper together at a performance? It is lovely she sometimes calls you Robin and sometimes lets you call her Bess, but words are cheap. She always prefers words; they cost her nothing."

"I feel like a stalled ox," muttered Robert. "I can go neither forward nor backward nor to the side. There is nothing for me to solve or rescue to make my name." He smacked at the cloak. "Nothing to do but dress up and prance, quarrel and chase women."

"You are too quick to do the last two," I warned him. "Stay away from duels, and do not womanize where the Queen will hear of it. To say she does not approve is hardly necessary. Look what happened to Raleigh. She is touchy about fidelity. And you are a married man." I feared Robert had inherited my amorous nature; little Frances was not keeping him purring by the hearth. But caution must be the watchword. Those who transgress had better be alert.

"Have I not pledged my loyalty to her time and again?" He sighed.

"Stay out of her circle of ladies," I said. "Go elsewhere in London. There is no shortage of women in the city." How I was to regret that advice.

I rose; it was growing dark already. Lamps must be lit. These November afternoons closed in dreary mist, and the sun set almost invisibly. The servants lit the wall sconces and brought in several table lanterns. Just as I was about to call for our supper, the Bacon brothers were announced, and Francis and Anthony entered the chamber, Anthony shuffling painfully across the floor and sinking onto the first bench he reached. He gave a plaintive hack or two, but Francis's eyes were shining.

"Welcome, friends," said Robert. "You brighten the chamber, just as gloom was clutching us."

"Our findings will brighten *you*," said Francis. "Oh, that they will!"

Robert drew up chairs around the table and moved two of the lanterns together to increase the light. He patted the tapestry on the table. "Something to show me?" he asked. "Here, or in Europe?"

"Lucky for us, right here," said Anthony. "Right in the Queen's own chamber!" He rubbed his long fingers together, seemingly out of triumph but really just to warm them.

Oh, this was marvelous. The closer to the Queen, the greater the threat, and the greater our reward for thwarting it.

"Where?" asked Robert.

"Her personal physician, Dr. Lopez!" cried Francis. "I have proof that he is intriguing with the Spanish."

"But what motive would he have?" Robert asked. "He isn't Spanish; the Portuguese hate the Spanish for taking their country."

"Perhaps he isn't a loyal Portuguese," said Francis. "Has Portugal treated him well? They have an Inquisition and he fled from it."

"But so does Spain." Robert was not convinced.

"Who knows why a man decides to dabble in the world of espionage? Perhaps for the simplest of reasons: money. The Spanish cannot help but pay better than the Queen."

"Lopez has a large family and is not rich," said Anthony, clearing his throat to speak. "So he had need. My agents in Spain have been tracking the spies that Philip is financing in England. One of them, Ferrera da Gama, is staying with Lopez in his Holborn house. That implicates Lopez. Lopez is trusted by the Queen and provides her medicines and drugs. Who better to poison her? Assassination is much cheaper than invasion and achieves the same end."

"Perhaps we should detain this Ferrera," said Francis.

"Yes, and in addition, alert the officials of Rye, Sandwich, and Dover to open and examine all letters from Portugal."

"Yes!" said Robert. "And easily explained, as I am the Privy Councillor responsible for Portuguese affairs."

Lopez . . . Roderigo Lopez . . . "Robert, has he not treated you?" I asked.

"Yes, I have consulted him on occasion," said Robert.

"Better not take his medicines!" Francis said with a laugh.

"He has had no reason to poison me," Robert said.

"Until now. If he finds out you are on his tracks, then—" Francis made a choking noise, grabbing his throat.

Lopez . . . There was more about him. Lopez. God in heaven, yes! People had accused him of supplying Leicester with the poison that supposedly killed my first husband, and Nicholas Throckmorton, and the Earl of Sheffield. As a result, when Leicester himself died suddenly, I was suspected of poisoning him in self-defense. Ultimately I had Lopez to thank for these calumnies.

"London is swarming with foreigners," said Robert. "Why they are tolerated I cannot fathom. They make a veritable nest where traitors can hide."

"There are foreigners, and then there are foreigners," said Anthony, his voice straining to be heard. "The diamond cutters who fled Antwerp, the starchers who starch our ruffs, we surely would not expel them. They pay double taxes as well."

"The Dutch, the Huguenots, the Swiss, very well. But how have these crafty Spanish crept in?"

"The Portuguese pretender Don Antonio has outstayed his welcome," said Francis. "Living upon Her Majesty's bounty and protection these fifteen years. He knows his cause is withering, so he and those surrounding him are taking desperate measures. I think they are transferring his birthright to the Spanish. That means Spanish agents, all sheltering under his wing."

"Isn't Lopez a Jew?" asked Robert.

"He converted, along with some hundred or so of his countrymen," answered Francis.

"There's a name for them. I can't remember it," I said.

"Marranos," supplied Anthony. "Of course, the conversion doesn't count in Spain. There had been Marranos for years, living happily, and then the Spanish expelled them in 1492."

"Stupid, stupid Spanish," said Francis. "There went all the brains in their court. They have been exhibiting stupid behavior ever since. Not that we should mind."

"Spain is only wealthy because she robs the Americas; otherwise she is the least productive nation in Europe. Can you name a single thing she makes? Everything is imported," said Robert. "For the Armada, she could not even make barrels that didn't leak. Pitiful. Francis is right. No brains."

"But this Lopez—" Anthony steered the subject back. "Is he really a Christian? I mean, Jesus himself was Jewish, which doesn't mean he wasn't a real Christian, if you follow me."

"How can we ever know? And what difference does it make?" asked Robert. "With *The Jew of Malta* playing continually to huge crowds here all year, he will already be suspect in people's eyes. Why, there's even a line in it about poison. Everyone knows they poison wells."

"'Everyone knows,'" scoffed Francis. "The lies that 'everyone knows' can fill a thousand scrolls."

"If only Kit could have seen this success," said Anthony. "The play was doing well when he died, but nothing like this."

"He drank too much," said Robert. "I know poets say it gives them insight, and perhaps it does up to point, but if he hadn't had a taste for the drink—"

"He couldn't have been lured to his death," said Francis. "A drinker is an easy mark. Easy to lure, and easy to smear. 'Christopher Marlowe, killed in a tavern brawl'—a nice cover story. He was silenced by someone higher up, someone made uncomfortable by his espionage activities. So have a care, Anthony."

"I don't go to taverns or meet with people at inns in Deptford," said Anthony. "I can barely get here to Essex House."

"There are slippery stones out in front of Essex House, where a weak man might stumble and hit his head," warned Francis.

"There are slippery places in court, and close to the Queen, where a proud man might stumble and end up in the Tower," retorted Anthony. "So have a care, Francis."

We all trod on slippery ground, it seemed. Our spy service empowered us to the Queen but entangled us with dangerous elements—disreputable Englishmen and enemy foreigners, who had no scruples. We must watch our steps indeed.

# 26

# ELIZABETH

*New Year's Day 1594*

I had been standing for hours, receiving the customary New Year's gifts. It was fortunate that I did not mind standing; in fact, I was noted for my ability to stand for very long times. Everyone at court gave me New Year's gifts, and I in turn presented a great number of them, although I myself did not hand them over. Instead, recipients were given a receipt and sent to my treasury, where they were allowed to select a gilt plate, tray, or cup.

Burghley had creaked forward and presented me with a writing set, while Robert Cecil had proffered a comfit box for sweetmeats. Archbishop Whitgift had obtained a prayer book with an olive-wood cover, carved in the Holy Land, and the Earl of Southampton gave me a bound copy of a poem.

"Not written by me," he hastened to add, "but by a poet I am proud to be patron of." He brushed his fine hair off one shoulder. I saw that he had left off the more flamboyant of his jewels, as well as his rouge. Perhaps he was becoming more restrained now that he had turned twenty.

I flicked open the packet. *Venus and Adonis.* "Frolicking of the immortals?" I asked.

"An immortal story," he said.

A William Shakespeare was the author. I knew the name. He had written plays about Henry VI.

"Do you compose verse yourself?" I asked Southampton.

"I try, but it is not fit to pass beyond my own chamber," he said.

"There are many others who ought to say that but do not have the good sense to do so," I said. "Thank you, and a blessed year for us all." I waved him on.

Might it be so. The one just past had had its troubles, but 1594 looked promising.

"Your Most Gracious Majesty." Dr. Lopez was holding out his gift, a latticed gold box. I opened it and looked inside, seeing two chambers with seeds and golden powder.

"Aniseed and saffron, which your generosity has granted me a monopoly in," he reminded me.

Monopolies—the way I could reward faithful servants without having to take money from the treasury. "I thank you, Roderigo. Your remedies have been most helpful," I said. His Turkish herbs had done their cooling duty and now I was seldom troubled by the heat attacks.

"I have a new shipment just in," he said. "I should like to bring them to you."

"Tomorrow, then," I said. I waved him on. I would have enjoyed speaking further to him—I always enjoyed his conversation—but the line was long behind him.

Young Essex now stepped up, resplendent in a white velvet outfit with pale blue trimmings. It was a good choice of color for him, setting off his wavy reddish hair. He wore no beard, making his sensuously full lips his most notable feature.

"Your most glorious Majesty, it is more than I deserve that I may kiss your fair hand." He bent low and took my hand, raising it to those plump, warm lips. I pulled it quickly away.

"What do you desire this year, Essex? Last year was a good one for you—Privy Councillor, settling yourself in your London household—what is left?"

"To desire and to deserve are not the same thing, Your Majesty," he said. "Well I know I deserve nothing, but I desire . . . everything." He raised his gaze to stare directly into my eyes.

He was a silly lad, transparent in his flattery, his naked hunger for recognition almost touching, his bids to counterfeit an amorous interest embarrassingly seductive. He almost made me believe it.

"What have you brought me?" I asked briskly. The line behind him was still very long.

He stepped still closer and lowered his voice. "If I were to give it now, and you laid it aside with the other gifts"—he glanced over at the table weighted with the ones that had come before—"the wrong person might see it. With your kind permission, I wish to present it in privacy."

He knew all the tricks. I sighed. "Very well. You may make an appointment through the vice chamberlain."

"Tomorrow?"

Tomorrow I was seeing Dr. Lopez, and I did not want to be rushed.

"No, perhaps the day after. The vice chamberlain knows my schedule."

As he took his leave, I saw that the line stretched even longer now. New Year's Day was a test of endurance here at court.

---

The soles of my feet were tender, but other than that I suffered no ill effects from the New Year's ritual. I could blame the foot soreness on the shoes I had chosen to wear; I should never subject new shoes to such an ordeal. So, at sixty I could still stand all day long and feel no worse than I had at thirty. That was a fine New Year's gift, that knowledge, better than all the bejeweled book covers and embroidered gloves and hanging pendants. I had given it to myself.

I awaited Dr. Lopez, a fine wool shawl about my shoulders. It was always cold in my chambers at Whitehall; even the bedchamber, small as it was in relation to its fireplace, remained chilly. That was what came of being so near the river, where the winter mists hung near the shore and crept into all the dwellings. It seemed a year since we had seen the sun. I shuddered as a chill swept over me. A little personal heat at this point would be welcome, but I did not wish it back again.

Where was Lopez? It was not like him to keep anyone waiting. He was always prompt and considerate. I paced a bit, kept company by Catherine and Marjorie. We all bemoaned the lack of exercise during these dreary months, but Christmas season at court was a compensation; their husbands, Charles and Henry, were here now. There were still four days left of Christmas, with plays, masques, and feasts, ending with the wild antics of Twelfth Night.

"I am grateful that your menfolk are keeping Christmas at court," I told Marjorie and Catherine. Well I knew that Henry would prefer to be at Rycote, where the hunting was good, and that Charles liked to use the winter months to inspect the harbor facilities up and down the coast. Neither man enjoyed court frivolities. Perhaps that was why I trusted them.

"Indeed, it is a gift to us as well," said Marjorie. "If I did not have him here at holidays, it would be easy to forget I am married. Our sons are always away fighting in some action or other, so there is no family life to speak of." She said it lightly, but I knew it grieved her that though she had four sons still living, she hardly ever saw any of them.

"My dear Crow," I said, teasing her with the old nickname, although her dark hair was fading. "At least they return to the nest every once in a while." Those of my own family had flown away, never to return.

All I had of family were from my mother's side, the closest being the children and grandchildren of Mary Boleyn, my aunt. Catherine was one of those, my first cousin once removed. She bore no resemblance to either her grandmother Mary or my mother. Where my mother's face was long, with a pointed chin, Catherine's was as round as a full moon. My mother's eyes were said to be dark and "invite to conversation." Catherine's were placid and comforting and never narrowed in anger. My mother was slim and Catherine was plump.

I remembered my aunt Mary Boleyn, who died when I was ten. She came little to court, for she had married a groom after her first husband died of sweating sickness. It was said to be a marriage of passion. If so, the passion was played out in private. The few times I was old enough to remember, she told me little stories about my mother, her fondness for apples and dried pears, how she liked telling Aesop's tortoise and hare story to her niece and nephew, her fumbling attempts to braid her hair the French way when she was young—anecdotes but nothing more. Now there were so many things I would ask her; then I did not know how.

Catherine had married into the Howard family—more distant cousins of mine. She and the admiral seemed well pleased with each other and were the parents of five children, grown now, with various lives in and out of court.

These women were the closest I came to having sisters, but between us was still a huge gap. As Queen, I stood alone, set apart.

Oh, where was he? How tedious it was to wait and wait; as I paced and ticked off the minutes, I reminded myself that my subjects were victims of waiting every day. They had no heralds to clear the way before them, no precedence in ceremonies or front place in lines.

A great clatter arose in the outer chambers, and in a moment one of the Queen's Guards strode in. "Your Majesty," he said, "grave tidings. Treason! Treason is afoot!"

A second guard joined him, grasping his sword. "Thanks be to the earl, you are saved!"

"What earl?" I demanded. "What treason?"

Essex appeared in the doorway behind the guards. "Treason against your very person, Your Gracious Majesty!" He all but leaped into the room, dodging around the guards, springing on his sprightly legs. He landed lightly and knelt at my feet, his wavy hair flopping over his forehead. "I have forestalled a dangerous plot to poison you."

He was waiting for me to say, "Arise." I did.

Drawing himself up, he took a deep breath. "Through diligence, constant watching, and secret information, I have uncovered this heinous evil. Evil that the others keeping guard over Your Sacred Majesty did not see."

Was it the Catholics? Had someone heeded the papal call? Had they risen up against me at last? Or was it a disgruntled subject, angry about a presumed slight? "Pray be specific," I said. "Who, what, where?"

"Look about your court; seek Roderigo Lopez. You shall not find him here, but locked up, where he can harm no one."

"Dr. Lopez? What do you mean?"

"Did you read the papers I gave you?" he demanded.

"No, not yet." I would read them when I got to them. "You were to come tomorrow."

"If you had read them, you would find the case against Dr. Lopez spelled out—the evidence against him tallied in full! He is in the pay of the Spanish, and his mission is to poison you."

"Pish!" Dr. Lopez had no dishonest corner within him. I knew people, I could sense things, and I knew him to be honest. And yet . . . is that not a trap the devil lays, another version of pride, to believe strongly that I had a special sensibility? Surely by now I had learned that treason could lurk in unlikely places? "Tell me of this plot," I said. "And where exactly is Dr. Lopez?"

"Lopez had a Ferrera da Gama staying with him, a Portuguese exile in touch with Spain. We were able to intercept his mail—"

"We?"

"The Bacon brothers and I, acting on my authority as Privy Councillor for Portuguese affairs, ordered all mail from Portugal arriving in Rye, Sandwich, and Dover be opened and examined. Behold! We netted Gomez d'Avila, a courier carrying letters to da Gama in code. In the meantime, we intercepted a letter from da Gama urging Lopez, for God's sake, to prevent d'Avila from coming to England. It said—these are the exact words—'for if he should be taken the Doctor will be undone without remedy.'"

"Pray continue."

"We were able to show the intercepted letter to da Gama and pretend that Lopez had betrayed him. That made him confess that they both were part of a larger plot to poison someone. But he insisted the victim of the plot was to be Don Antonio. When d'Avila was taken to the Tower and shown the rack, he, too, confessed."

"Confessed what? The exact confession?"

"That they planned to subvert the son of the pretender Portuguese king Don Antonio to the Spanish cause. The letters were written by a Spanish agent in Brussels, Manuel Luis Tinoco."

"And this is all you have uncovered? A plot among the Portuguese exiles? How is this treason against me?"

"Your Majesty, it is obvious that Don Antonio is but a code word for you.

The mysterious language about musk, pearls, and amber means something sinister relating to a woman's toilette."

"Is it obvious? It does not seem obvious to me. What does Cecil know about this Tinoco? He has agents in Brussels."

"Do not bring Robert Cecil into this."

"Do you dare to tell me what to do?" I stared at him. "It is imperative to widen the investigation," I told him. "I thank you for its beginnings, but now we need to call on other resources."

His face flushed. "What other resources? My agents—"

"Cannot be everywhere," I said. "You and Robert Cecil should coordinate your efforts. I shall tell him to pursue his contacts in Brussels. In the meantime, release Dr. Lopez."

"What?"

"Nothing has been proved against him. We have all grown weary of the parasitical Don Antonio. Is it any surprise his fellow exiles are deserting his cause?"

"But—poison!"

"You have failed to provide any proof or details about this poison. I say, release Dr. Lopez."

"You court danger," he said. "Do you not care about the safety of your person?"

"Yes, I care greatly. But I do not hide from shadows in the nursery, nor imprison innocent men."

"Innocent! We shall see how innocent he is!" Essex was almost shaking with frustration.

"You may take your leave," I told him. "I shall give instructions to Robert Cecil."

"Oh!" he muttered, bowing. I saw him biting his lip to keep from speaking further.

I turned to see Catherine and Marjorie standing mute in the corner, their faces white.

"Pish!" I said again, loudly, my favorite word of dismissal. "Fantasies! Why, Dr. Lopez has had so many opportunities to poison me, if he were going to, he . . ." My voice trailed off. People changed. People could be corrupted. People could be converted.

One would think that a physician who attended the Queen would be loyal, but . . .

"But just to be sure, should we test his herbs?" asked Catherine, in her smooth, soothing voice.

"I have already done so. I have tested them on myself."

"What of the new ones he gave you yesterday?"

I had not yet used the anise and saffron he had presented so grandly in the gold box. I asked for it to be brought, and when I held it in my hands I opened the lid and stared down at the contents. The sweet odor of the anise leaped from the box. I longed to put the seeds under my tongue and let their distinctive taste flood my mouth. But I did not.

"There is no person to test it on, and animals cannot be persuaded to eat these things," I said. So we would never know.

"Having failed in his invasion attempts, and failed in his call for your subjects to rise up against you," said Marjorie, "Spain's king now turns to the cheaper alternative—assassination. Did not the Duke of Alba himself say that it was pointless to invade unless you were dead?"

"Yes, I was told that," I said. "But you—and Essex—are linking Lopez and Spain and poison with no proof. Let us hear what Robert Cecil finds when he interrogates this Tinoco."

"You are reasoned and calm, as always," said Catherine.

As always, I kept my exterior self calm. But inwardly, I was shaking. I put the box down carefully to avoid jarring the contents.

# 27

*June 1594*

omething was wrong. Our glorious June had been corrupted, pelted by unseasonable deluges of rain and cold, followed by cruel blasts of heat. The natural world did not know how to respond. Flowers opened, then were stripped and frozen. The sweet Thames smelled foul.

To escape from the stench of the river I was at St. James's Palace, set by its hunting grounds. Beyond it stretched open fields, lanes, and pastures, ordinarily a delightful tapestry of waving grass and wildflowers but now waterlogged and empty of butterflies. This day was clear, for a change. That meant that citizens could emerge out of doors to do the things they had postponed—such as carry out, and watch, executions.

Only a mile away, across the fields, stood Tyburn, fast by the road leading out of London to Oxford, the place where convicted criminals were put to death. There was a gallows there, and a sort of table where the condemned could be laid and cut open, according to the sentence of being hanged, then drawn and quartered. On the way to the gallows, the prisoners were jounced along in a cart, hands bound behind them, jeered by onlookers. Often they would stop at a tavern for a last swig of ale; usually by this time the doomed were making jaunty jests. Not for them the long-faced repentance speeches of noblemen seeking to retain their property for their families. These poor souls had nothing to lose and so they went to their deaths in a jolly fashion, thumbing their noses at the gallows.

By the time they reached Tyburn, a huge crowd would have gathered. Parents pretended they brought their children to teach them the grim wages of crime, but in truth they went for entertainment. Sometimes, if they were lucky, the victims fought back (of course they always lost) or even managed to survive the first round of hanging.

The air was still, but I could hear, faintly smothered by distance but still too loud, the roar of a crowd at Tyburn. Dr. Lopez and his companions were being executed. Essex had had his way.

I leaned on the windowsill of my chamber, smelling the odd earthy smell of soaked bricks. St. James's had been a redbrick leper house before my father had evicted the monks and their wards, the lepers, and made it into a hunting palace. Now I felt the sorrow of those mistreated lepers rising up, accusing, wailing along with the crowd at Tyburn. After our meeting, Essex had written a hysterical note to Robert Cecil saying, "I have discovered a most dangerous and desperate treason. The point of the conspiracy was Her Majesty's death. The executioner should have been Dr. Lopez; the manner poison. This I have so followed that I will make it as clear as noonday." The tangle of confessions that followed, extracted by the rack, made it impossible to spare Dr. Lopez. Under torture he had admitted to spying for Spain, seeking to promote rebellion in England, and planning to poison the Queen. But under torture might not a man say anything? Cecil then claimed that no torture was used. No one could confirm its use—or would admit to it.

*The Jew of Malta* was playing to packed audiences in London, with its line "But to present the tragedy of a Jew, who smiles to see how full his bags are crammed" whipping them on to cry for Lopez's blood. Essex paraded through the streets shouting about the diabolical plot by the dastardly Jew, and soon the crowd howled for his death. Anti-Spanish and anti-Jewish hatred blended into hysteria.

The crowd was duly entertained. Dr. Lopez pleaded innocence on the scaffold, saying that he loved the Queen better than Jesus, and was met with howls of derision. Da Gama suffered the same fate, and then Tinoco provided novelty by surviving the hanging, jumping to his feet after being cut down and attacking the executioner. He had no chance, as two soldiers overpowered him and the grisly sentence proceeded.

Robert Cecil recounted all these details when he came to present me with a ring, taken from Dr. Lopez, that had been given him by King Philip himself, to carry out his deed. It was a dainty gold-encircled ruby.

"It looks like a woman's ring," I said. "Are we sure it is not his wife's?"

"We are sure, Your Majesty, of nothing," Cecil said, his face glum. "We just dared not take chances."

"The grotesque necessity of security," I said. "Or, as the common saying is, 'Better safe than sorry'? Except, Robert, we were dealing with a man's life. With *men's* lives."

"Where *your* life is concerned, there can be no leeway, no room for doubt."

The crowds were milling around outside the grounds of St. James's, still yelling, half of them drunk. I shuddered. Essex had used these people, had created a wave of public hysteria in order to force an issue. I felt instinctively that there was something else behind the entire case against Dr. Lopez, something self-serving for Essex. That he had been able to get this far with it proved to me that he now had a weapon to use against me as potent as poison—he had proved that he could harness popular opinion for his own ends and would not hesitate to do so.

# 28

*August 1594*

There could be no Progress this year. The icy rains fell day after day, far longer than they had fallen upon Noah. That the land did not turn to ocean and require an ark was only because the downpour soaked into our fields, swelled the rivers to rush the water to the ocean, turned ponds into lakes and lakes into inland seas. Unless a plant could grow underwater, the crops were doomed. Fruit trees had bloomed in what started as a normal spring, but the early fruit had rotted and fallen off.

In classical myths, seasons became disrupted because of some disturbance on Mount Olympus or a foolhardy action by an ignorant mortal. Demeter, in grieving for her vanished daughter Persephone, plunged the world into perpetual winter by withholding the crops. The Scriptures tell us that God will "shut up the heaven, that there be no rain, and that the land yield not her fruit" if we turn our back on him. I could discount rumblings on Mount Olympus, but was there some secret sin in the land that God was punishing?

No, no, I could not go that way. I could examine my own conscience, but I could not lift the covers of all the consciences in the realm. Dr. Lopez . . . I twisted the Spanish ring on my finger. I wore it next to the coronation ring, to remind myself that being the anointed ruler of England meant that I could take no loyalty for granted, and must be ever vigilant. But the question of his innocence continued to plague me.

In late June, north winds had plunged us into such cold that newly shorn sheep perished. In July, pellets of hail had fallen; now in August there were reports of snow in Yorkshire. And all the while, this incessant rain.

I decided to move to Nonsuch, my father's hunting palace some twelve miles south of London. It was still a novelty to me; it had been occupied by someone else and only come back into my hands two years ago. At my age, to acquire a palace where I did not know every corridor and every window was a rare delight. And this would afford me a glimpse of the country, let me see firsthand what was happening in the fields and orchards.

I had to ride beneath a swaying canopy erected around my saddle, as the royal carriage could not manage what remained of the roads. Likewise the household items had to be carried by mule and horseback. I would take as little as possible.

As we plodded along the sodden path, people stood watching us, calling out listlessly, bundled in cloaks. The dark skies and brown fields seemed to leech all color from the people as well, their faces blending into the dull hue of fallen leaves. The few animals still in the fields looked mournfully at us, suffering wordlessly.

I had not expected such enervation and defeat. It was the dull underpinning of what would later explode into anger and destruction, like the backing of a fragile Venetian glass mirror. As Queen, I would do what I could to help, but my means of doing so were limited. Had I known it was coming, we could have stored up food from last year's harvest. What use were the astrologers if they could not foresee this?

Shivering, we rode past the forlorn people and dripping orchards. Their faces haunted me.

---

And now we crested the hill that always gave a glorious view of the palace; from down through the alleyway of trees in sunny autumns you could see the glint of the gold-framed stucco panels on the inner courtyard walls, winking as if to say, *Nonsuch, Nonsuch, there is truly nonesuch in England.* Today it was enveloped in a gray mist, and winds were whipping the trees overhead, sending cold showers spraying across the path.

My father had built this palace to stun his countrymen with the extravagance of Renaissance design, and to match his hated rival, the French king François I, and his hunting palaces of Chambord and Fontainebleau. As if to press his claims to being king of both countries, he had built the outer courtyard in plain Tudor style, calling it "severity," and the inner one in an extravagance of French Renaissance design, calling it "exuberance." Exuberant it certainly was, with an enormous statue of himself on his throne to greet his visitors. He meant for the white and gold Italianate panels covering the entire inner courtyard—gods and goddesses, Roman emperors, and the labors of Hercules—to instruct his little son Edward in all he would need to know to be king.

My father had built this palace in 1538 to celebrate his thirty years of reign and the birth of his prince. Well. It was only a building. His prince had not lived. I had celebrated my thirty years of reign by the defeat of the Armada—something much more likely to last, and of import beyond my own family.

Not that I was comparing myself . . .

---

In spite of its opulence, Nonsuch was snug, designed to evoke a retreat, to celebrate the glories of the hunt. I appreciated that coziness now, as the rain drummed outside.

The ceiling in the presence chamber was dripping. Obviously the roof was in need of patching. If the roof of a mighty palace was leaking, what of roofs in cottages? My heart was heavy for those people.

---

My attendants wondered why I had come, but they were good-spirited about it. Catherine and Marjorie thought of sending for their husbands "to see if they were willing to suffer for us" but did not. The male courtiers would follow, grumbling, but for now we had the palace to ourselves.

We warmed ourselves around the sputtering fire in the privy chamber, throwing beans in the fire to tell our fortunes, reminiscing on our many years together. Sometimes, in the flickering firelight, I could see the younger faces beneath the aging ones: Marjorie in her days as the wife of the French ambassador, Catherine when the future Admiral Howard she married was dark haired and holding minor posts. Perhaps they could also see mine.

---

The rain finally stopped—or had we only been given a respite? Nevertheless, we took advantage of it, drying the bed linens in the sunshine, opening the windows to let the mustiness out, turning our faces to the light. The Privy Councillors came one at a time to pay their respects and inform me of any pressing business. Then one day, when fresh dark clouds started chasing across the sky, Francis Bacon was announced.

Francis Bacon: that man who had crossed my wishes in Parliament and then dared to apply for the post of attorney general. Essex, his patron, had pestered me about it until I had ordered him to desist and then given the place to Sir Edward Coke. That had angered Essex so much he began pressing for another post for Bacon. Partly it was to demonstrate his loyalty to a friend; partly it was to show that once he had sunk his teeth into a matter, mastifflike, he could be detached only by force.

Essex's fierce championing had made me suspicious of Francis Bacon; that and the fact that his uncle and his cousin, the Cecil father and son, did not extend patronage to him. Yes, it was possible that the elder Cecil did not want to raise up a rival to his own son, but perhaps it was more than that. In any case, I welcomed the opportunity to see Francis away from the court—and Essex—and judge for myself.

He presented himself in a dapper manner, bowing low and sweeping his hat off. "I am eternally grateful to Your Majesty for seeing me today," he said. His head was still down and I could not read his face to see if he was mocking.

"Eternity is a long time," I said. "I count myself lucky if gratitude extends beyond the day itself."

He straightened up. "You are wise as serpents," he said.

"But gentle as doves," I finished for him. "Well, Francis, what do you put before me for consideration?"

"Nothing, Your Majesty," he said. "I am sure Your Majesty is weary of perpetual consideration of things."

"Ah, there's that concept again," I said. "You are fond of speaking of perpetuities." I looked at him. "I prefer to speak of the immediate." He must stop the mincing now and present his case. I cocked my head. "You do not resemble your father in the slightest." His father had been rotund, with sleepy, half-lidded eyes. Nicholas Bacon had served me for the first two decades of my reign, but he had died suddenly. Mean-spirited people said that had he kept a leaner table, he might have lived longer. As if in reaction, his two sons were very thin, especially the elder one, Anthony.

"No, we take our looks from our mother's side," he said.

I waited.

"Your Majesty, I recently sent my uncle Cecil this letter, abasing myself in asking for his help." He handed me a paper. "He did not even answer."

"So you do have a petition?" I had known as much.

"My only petition is myself." He smiled, trying to make the mood light, but it must have been desperate for him to seek me out like this. I glanced down at the letter, skimming it. Phrases jumped out at me. "I wax somewhat ancient: one and thirty years is a great deal of sand in the hourglass. . . . I have writ unto Your Lordship rather thoughts than words, being set down without all art, disguising, or reservation. . . ."

"And you say he never answered you?"

"Yes, Ma'am. That is, no, he never answered."

I continued skimming it. It was hard to discern what post he was applying for. "You are vague," I said. "When you say, 'I have taken all knowledge to be my province,' that is all very well and good, but in what area is your expertise? It would seem you are most suited for the gown of academia." As a child, he had given such grave and adult answers to questions that I had dubbed him "The Young Lord Keeper." He had not changed.

"I have labored away as a lawyer in Gray's Inn, but the work is boring," he said.

"But, Francis, what is your specialty? You are not a soldier like Black Jack

Norris, nor a sailor like Drake, nor an astrologer like John Dee, nor a man born to keep the books like Robert Cecil. After all, you find the law boring."

"I could do any of those things!" he said. "If I set my mind to it, I could be a soldier, or a sailor, or an astrologer, or a secretary."

"But you would hate it. And what someone hates he does poorly."

"I hate being a . . . a servant most of all!" he burst out. "I have allied myself to Essex because Cecil would not help me."

"You are hardly Essex's servant," I said.

"Not his bodily one, but I am his minion! I am forced to be." His face was filled with self-loathing.

"You are less his minion than he is your dependent, I would venture to say. He needs your wit and your learning and your insights; he needs them badly." I held out the paper again. "So one and thirty years is a great deal of sand in the hourglass? God willing, it is not. You will have challenges aplenty. You may outlive Essex and find that your service to him recommends you to something more suitable to you."

His face sagged. "So you will offer me nothing?"

"Francis, I have no post for 'consultant.' Such a position does not exist. You would have to fill a more definite duty. 'Consultant' doesn't mean anything."

"I analyze situations. I have drawn up summaries for Essex, penetrating studies—"

"Which, doubtless, he ignores."

"But you, Your Majesty, would never ignore it. Or rather, if you did, it would be because you had read it and disagreed with it, not that you did not understand it."

I felt for him. "Francis," I said, "let me now give you *my* analysis of your situation. It is this: It is difficult for a man to serve his lesser, difficult for one so clever as you to be subservient to those who are dull in comparison. But the truly wise man can trim his sails to the wind and await his chance. Patience is a form of wisdom. And so is the sad knowledge that comes from Ecclesiastes: 'I saw under the sun that the race is not to the swift, nor the battle to the strong, neither yet bread to the wise, nor yet riches to men of understanding.'"

"What is the use, then?" he said.

He was toweringly intelligent, perhaps the cleverest brain in my realm. A person is born smart, but wisdom takes a longer time to acquire.

"Perhaps in the happy surprise that one day an unexpected favor comes your way, just as you have given up on it." I had a sudden thought. "Francis, I could appoint you Queen's Counsel Extraordinary, but you say you do not like the law."

"But if I must practice it, I would above all things prefer to practice it for you."

"It would not be a full-time position. I would only call on you when I needed you, in an occasional case . . . to consult. In that way you would be my consultant."

"I understand. I must continue with Essex for my bread. But be on call to you as needed."

"Yes. That describes it. You will accept?"

"May I call myself Queen's counsel publicly?"

"Of course."

"Your Majesty, I am eternally— I thank you."

So now I would have the quickest lawyer in the land at my beck and call, and all for the price of allowing him to call himself my counsel. My thrift at work.

# 29

# LETTICE

*November 1594*

Those wretched bells ringing everywhere! I yanked one of the thick tapestries over the window to muffle it further.

Elizabeth's glorious Accession Day. Thirty-six years ago. What in God's name would they do to celebrate the fortieth? Would the entire realm have to present gifts? My son was busying himself with last-minute preparations for the tilt, some ridiculous costume about a frozen knight. The expenditure. The waste. When we could be spending it furnishing Essex House as befitted his station.

I looked around the great room. I had restored much from the ordered-by-Elizabeth stripping; tapestries hung heavily from rods again; fat candles in sconces winked up and down the walls; and the long oak table gleamed with its gold Italian centerpiece, an intricate froth of statuary and embellishments. Yes, the import tax from the sweet wines had provided well for us. I had even been able to buy back some of the jewelry we had pawned, and my latest purchase was a coach with four white horses. I loved riding it through the streets; I loved it even better when the people mistook me for the Queen. And why not? We looked alike; we even had some of the same mannerisms. We could almost be twins, except that she loved the day and I the night.

Christopher disliked riding in the coach with me. There were times I found it irksome to be yoked to someone with such a determinedly commoner's viewpoint. He was so matter-of-fact about trappings, so uninterested in court climbing. He would rather be a soldier, spend his time out in the field. It was in his blood. At least I could console myself that he had the soldier's appetite for lovemaking.

Lovemaking . . . There was far too much of it lately in my family for our own good. My daughter Penelope had given herself over to the adulterous charms of Charles Blount and was now pregnant by him. Dorothy, released from her marriage to Perrot by his convenient death, had quickly married

Thomas Percy, an odd chap known as the Wizard Earl for his dabbling in science and alchemy. And Robert . . . His affair with the court lady Elizabeth Southwell was sure to reach the Queen's ears before long. What was I to do with these hot-blooded offspring of mine?

At least my own hot-bloodedness had netted me two titles. I could not see what theirs had netted them, aside from scandal. Lust should serve a purpose; lust should be used as bait. What fool just throws it away?

The Queen . . . The Queen knew how to use it as bait. She had been doing it her whole life. Now the bait had grown stale, but she did not seem to notice, and the young men at court were forced to pretend otherwise, to write sonnets about the fair wind caressing the pink cheeks of Diana, when the cheeks were in reality wrinkled and wan. Robert as much as anyone had to write such nonsense as "When Your Majesty thinks that heaven is too good for me, I will not fall like a star, but be consumed like a vapor by the same sun that drew me up to such a height. While Your Majesty gives me leave to say I love you, my fortune is as my affection, unmatchable." But when I laughed about it, he would huff and defend her. One part of him believed what he was writing; another part wanted to believe it; and the last part was ashamed of himself for having to do it. To assuage his anger and shame, he took young women to bed. Too many of them. I feared that he had brought something untoward upon himself and was suffering from it. And I do not mean his reputation.

Soon he would be reeling in, tipsy, with his companions from the tavern. They longed to spend their energies on a battlefield, but they were cooped up in the court, channeled into tamed, ritualistic war games like the tilts and not allowed to go farther away than a city tavern, lest *she* call them back at any moment on one of her whims. In these dark days of November the dusk, and the drinking time, started early.

I paced the room. It was deadly quiet. Nothing for me to do but wait. I went to my rooms and busied myself reading. If I had had anyone to go with, I would have gone to the theater. I wanted something to take my mind off what was happening all around me. I did not care to visit Frances in her rooms, or even to play with the grandchildren. They gave me a headache.

---

The light streaming in was thin, although it was nearly midday. I knew my son had come in late last night and was now reversing the days and nights, sleeping like a sloth. Frances and the children were up and gone; in any case, he slunk off by himself when he was on one of his tears. I would not have intruded in his marital chamber, but this was different.

Pushing the door open, I peered into the darkened room. I heard heavy breathing, on the verge of, but not quite, snoring. There was an odor of sour beer and soggy wool. It was time to get him up. I jerked the bed-curtains open and was hit with a wave of the beer and wool smell, much stronger for having been concentrated within the curtains. He let out a wheezing, blubbering gasp, then sat up, grabbing at his hair.

"So here's Great England's glory and the world's wide wonder," I said, quoting Spenser.

He groaned. "My head—"

"Is empty," I finished for him. "Purged utterly of anything, just as your bowels undoubtedly are. Get up. What if the Queen sent for you?"

"She won't," he said, shaking his head. "She never does, never does, never—"

"That simply is not true," I said, taking his hand to pull him out of bed. The years rolled away and he was a little boy again, until he stood upright and was a head taller than I.

"She's busy with Drake and Raleigh again," he muttered. "Listening to their grandiose plans, financing them, taken in by their brags."

"Their brags? Raleigh perhaps, but as I recall, Drake *did* sail around the world, discovered a passage below the tip of South America, claimed a coastline in North America for the Queen—little things like that."

"He hasn't done anything in five years. He's a has-been." Robert thrust his feet into warm slippers and made for the fireplace. "He's old. In his fifties. His seafaring feats were done fifteen, twenty years ago."

"Defeating the Armada doesn't count?"

"He didn't defeat it single-handedly." He groaned. "Oh, Mother, please! It's too early!" He huddled before the fireplace, rubbing his hands. "I need ale," he said. "To clear my head."

"First there's ale to muddy your head, then ale to clear it." Nonetheless, I asked a servant to bring a pitcher of it.

While we waited, I pulled back more curtains, to let as much of the thin light as possible in. Was it my imagination, or was his face blotchy? He was shivering as he stopped rubbing his hands and clasped his forearms.

"How will you be able to ride at the tilt tomorrow?" I wondered out loud. "You can barely sit on a three-legged stool."

"Tomorrow I will be well enough," he said.

At least he had been assigned the last day of the three-day celebration. The observance had crept from the actual day out into St. Elizabeth's Day. What a coincidence in nomenclature. Or was it just another example of the extraordinary hand of fortune that always favored her, in little things as well as big?

The ale did seem to restore him. Like a plant that reverses its wilt after a rain, he took on color and strength and was soon holding forth on his various schemes and how they would all return bounty a hundredfold. I told him to get dressed and come to my chambers; I had something to show him.

When he appeared, I had the midday dinner set before him, and he wolfed it down, smearing his napkin with the good cheese and custard.

"Now that you are restored, good son, I need you to look at this." I pushed the food tray aside and laid a book down before him, a thick-bound one that carried the scent of its newness. He stared at it, then shrugged.

"You are familiar with it?"

"Oh, yes," he said. "What of it?"

I stabbed the title with my index finger. *A Conference on the Next Succession to the Crown of England.* "It might as well be *How to Be Executed for Treason.* How do you come to be associated with it? Why, why, is it dedicated to *you*?" For the European author, "R. Doleman, from my chamber in Amsterdam," had thanked Robert for past favors to "friends" and said that after Elizabeth's death Robert Devereux, Earl of Essex, was the man in the realm who would have the power to decide between claimants to the throne.

"I have no idea," he said. "It is obviously Catholic propaganda, smuggled into England by Jesuits. Its style bears all the marks of Robert Parsons, Elizabeth's most determined foe from the ranks of Rome. Claiming it is from Amsterdam is so transparent it is laughable."

Parsons directed the Jesuits and their English mission from Spain. Ten years ago he had landed in England, but when his companions were captured, he fled, to continue his work from a safe perch. Counterfeit pamphlets, rumors, and false evidence were some of his favorite methods of bringing down leading Protestants.

"It's meant to damage *you*," I said. "Otherwise, why single you out and link you to things the Queen is most sensitive about—the succession and overpowerful subjects?"

"I don't know," he said. "I have many enemies. People who do not want to see me succeed, people who whisper against me, people close to the Queen who fill her ears with lies about me—"

"Oh, don't start on the Cecils again." He had become obsessed with the idea that they were dedicated to undermining him. "They didn't write it."

"No, but they will be sure to show it to the Queen."

"Therefore, you must show it to her first. Lament the shame of it. Commiserate with her about it. Steal the show from the Cecils."

He drew himself up, cocked his head to one side. "That is what I had planned to do. Right after the tilt. But first I need another fitting for my costume."

I should have asked him the particulars about it, but costumes and masques bored me. Let the Queen squeal over them. I looked as he turned his face and the light played over his cheek. Perhaps I had been wrong; his skin looked clear now. But we were so seldom utterly alone that I must speak, and not waste it on idle talk of costumes. "Robert, it seems to me—mothers notice these things—that your health of late, of late—" Should I hint, state, or accuse? "Are you feeling well?" I would begin with a hint.

"Except when I have too much at the tavern," he said. "I will try to avoid that from now on."

"I mean, not just last night, but for the whole past year. It seems—I think—you have changed. Your moods. Your rashes. Your sleeping. I fear you may have contracted the French disease."

"Because I've been in France, dear Mother?" He gave a winsome smile to warn me off.

"It is in England, too, dear Son. And you have had more opportunity to avail yourself of women here than in France."

"No! I haven't got it! Yes, there was a time when I feared . . . But no, it wasn't." He smacked his fist into his palm and suddenly his face contorted in rage. "I came to *him* as a patient, horror stricken, shaking with fear. Oh, he treated me, and then he blabbed it about when he was in his cups, laughing about me to his friends, saying I had *it*, was pox ridden. Well, I got my revenge!"

It took me a moment to realize what he was saying. No, surely he did not . . . He could not have . . . "Robert—is that why you trumped up those charges against Dr. Lopez, hounded him to death, raised the popular outcry when it seemed that legally he would escape you? For personal revenge?"

"No, of course not! What do you take me for?"

"I am not sure," I said slowly. "There are days when I don't recognize my son in you."

"That's nonsense. I don't know what you mean."

"Someday, when your own children are older, you will. You think they are part of you always, but that is not true." Let me get to the rest of the things concerning this stranger. "And speaking of children, is it true that you have been bedding Elizabeth Southwell and that she is with child?"

"Yes, it's true."

"I assume she will slink away from court when the time comes?"

"I assume so." He acted as if it were no concern of his.

"And your friend Southampton celebrated his coming of age by sheltering friends fresh from committing a murder. Why, why, do you persist in these dangerous alliances? A lady from the Queen's retinue, a man known for quarrels and violence?"

"Spirited people sometimes overstep the bounds," he said. "There is no life when a man or woman always has to keep within a circle. Southampton has many poets as friends as well as ruffians, and Mistress Southwell knows all the districts of pleasure that a woman can explore." He paused. "Now my cautious friend Francis Bacon can offset the others. He has managed to worm his way into a position as Queen's Counsel Extraordinary. *All* my friends are not in disgrace."

"Perhaps Bacon can do us some good in that position. Help the Queen incline her ear to us, so to speak." The Dr. Lopez episode, supposed to win her gratitude for her deliverance, had done nothing of the sort. The sordid affair, source of shame and horror, had been deemed unmentionable, as if to deny that it had ever happened. I heard that the Queen still wore the ring, though.

"He and his brother still work primarily for *me*," said Robert. "The royal appointment is case by case only."

"All will be well." I needed to tell myself that.

---

I left his chambers. It was early afternoon, and the house was empty. There was nothing to do. Oh, to be barred from court was so boring. I could only hear and see things secondhand, utterly at the mercy of the memory and descriptive power of others.

As long as I could have only secondhand excitement, I might as well go to the theater, I told myself. The new season was under way and there would surely be something amusing on. Even though he was dead, Marlowe was still being performed, but I hardly wanted to see *The Jew of Malta*. That friend of the enigmatic Southampton, Shakespeare, had some comedies and a bloody Roman play, but I was not in the mood for either. Kyd's *The Spanish Tragedy* would suit me best today. I grabbed my lacy face mask and summoned my coach.

# 30

# ELIZABETH

*Christmas 1594*

had given myself a Christmas gift. Two of them: Francis Drake and Walter Raleigh. I had beckoned them back to court; their exile had lasted long enough. I decided to forgive them for their human lapses—Drake for his misguided preemptive strike against Spain that had fizzled so spectacularly and expensively five years ago, Raleigh for his transgression with Bess Throckmorton two years ago. Drake had busied himself with a new wife and civic duties in his Devonshire home. Raleigh surely had had enough of being cooped up in Sherborne Castle in Dorset with Bess, where he had decamped after his release from the Tower. Both men had parliamentary grants for new ventures. They were ready to go again, and I was ready to send them.

In the meantime I had the pleasure of their company for the Christmas revels at Hampton Court, and of contrasting the smooth-tongued Raleigh with the plainspoken Drake, one a born courtier and the other best farthest from court. And all the while, the young Earl of Essex looking on, his envy piqued. Oh, it was all delicious. And I had earned the amusement, having been bedeviled by all three of them at various times.

The festivities were to follow their usual schedule: The court would move to Hampton just before Christmas, and once there, the twelve days would be a round of banquets, music, masques, and plays. The Lord Chamberlain's Men would put on the best of the season's new plays as well as one or two old favorites like *Doctor Faustus*. The master of misrule would preside in the closing feast; and in between there would be New Year's Day and the gift exchanges. My treasury had already weighed out the silver to be dispensed. It was a familiar routine, but there were always surprises—new people introduced, new styles unveiled, and, out of sight, new liaisons formed.

Hampton showed well at Christmas, lending itself to greenery and decorations; the Great Hall seemed to store up past merriment, releasing it anew each season. For days, lighted barges with liveried boatmen delivered their masters and mistresses to the water steps, where they mounted and approached the first gate, laughing, their hooded cloaks streaming out behind them.

Of course there were those few who preferred not to come, choosing to spend the holidays in their own houses; there were far more who wanted to come to court but were not invited. There were, after all, only so many rooms.

---

They began arriving: first the lowest-ranking courtiers, invited for the first time, with their curious and eager wives peeping into the halls and stairways; then the more important personages; and finally the highest, each trying to arrive later than his rival. Some announced their eminence by sending a token reminder of themselves from their estates, where they were spending the holidays. The royal larder overflowed with game pies, blackberry comfits, honey from prized hives, and even smoked swans from the country. The musicians got to practice on the first, less demanding audiences and polish their performances for the critical listeners who would follow. Players rehearsed in the Great Hall; the Lord Chamberlain's Men promised excellent drama chosen from the autumn's new plays. There had been an explosion of new material after the theaters reopened in London, after the plague, as if the playwrights had done nothing in the meantime but sit in their rooms writing while the theaters were shut.

There would, of course, be religious services, and Whitgift stood ready to preside, but business would continue right up until Christmas Eve. The French and Scots ambassadors dogged my every step, pretending to urge certain policies on me, in reality to spy for their masters. It was, as far as I was concerned, part of the festivities, and I would lead them into a merry maze. Hampton Court had a maze; that one was outside, and my diplomatic one would be inside.

On Christmas Eve, as Archbishop Whitgift intoned the closing prayers of the service, rows of candles were lit all down the great passageway leading from the chapel royal, and cornets announced the glad arrival of Christmas.

---

We held the Christmas banquet in the Great Watching Chamber, saving the Great Hall for the performance to come; its stage was being hastily erected while we ate; we could hear the banging and scraping over the sweet tunes of the lutes and harps. I had invited my forgiven adventurers to sit on either side of me; on their sides sat young Cecil and young Essex, making a parenthesis of rivalry around Raleigh and Drake. Farther down the table were Admiral Howard, Catherine, Whitgift, Charles Blount, old Cecil, Helena van Snakenborg. My godson John Harington and various Carey brothers filled out the length of the head table. The other tables were a swarm of courtiers of various degrees.

I shall not describe the food or the proceedings, for they follow an established pattern. What is memorable is what departs from the pattern. And now, like the Green Knight appearing at King Arthur's winter festivities, a savage strode into the room, nearly naked except for a loincloth, an elaborate many-stranded necklace, and a dazzling feathered headdress. Much like an animal taken directly from a forest, he looked around at us, his eyes darting everywhere, as if searching for an escape. In his wake a white man followed and took his place beside him.

Now Raleigh rose. "I bid you welcome, Captain Whiddon, and your guest from South America." The white man nodded, then bowed to me. "Your Majesty, and all the good parliamentarians who voted funds for my exploratory expedition, I present the first fruit of my preparation," continued Raleigh. "Jacob Whiddon, a captain who never hesitates to invade Spanish waters, reconnoitered an area on the South American coast near Trinidad for my proposed voyage there. He reports favorable conditions and brought this young man back to learn English so that he might act as our translator and guide."

"Speak, Ewaioma," prodded Whiddon.

The bronze man opened his mouth and said, in a surprisingly soft voice, "Ezrabeta Cassipuna Acarewana!"

"That means 'Elizabeth the Great Princess,'" said Raleigh. "I have explained to him that you are a great *cassique*, a chief of the north, who has many other *cassiques* at her command." He extended his hand to Ewaioma, who approached the table. "This great *cassique*, my mistress, has freed the whole northern coast of Europe from Spain and is a constant enemy of its tyranny. They fear her, and she will protect you from the depredations of that evil empire. You may trust your land and your people to her."

"I—give tanks," he said.

Drake now rose. "Perhaps you should explain to Ewaioma that *I* am the reason you are so feared by Spain," he said boldly to me. "It is I who struck terror into them, in Europe, in Panama, in Peru—in fact, the whole world over. I made it my mission from my early days to wreak vengeance on them. I pray my last deed will be to smite the Spaniard! Let me perish while thrusting a sword into one!"

"Amen!" yelled Essex, jumping up. The savage flinched at all the commotion. "Slay them here, there, everywhere!"

"Down!" I ordered my unruly hunting dogs. "Behave yourselves in a seemly fashion." That was the problem with warriors and adventurers; like mastiffs, they did not belong indoors. "Now, Ewaioma, I bid you welcome to Hampton Court and our festivities. You do not have a winter where you live, but here we pause at the darkest time to gather and celebrate. Eat, drink, dance, as you will."

Whiddon led the bewildered man out, and Raleigh leaned over confidentially. "I have more to show you, for your eyes only, if you would be so gracious as to come to my suite of chambers tomorrow. There is private information about gold that I wish to impart, as well as maps for you to inspect. Will you consent?"

My curiosity alone would lead me there, even if it were not my firm policy to test everything I sponsored.

---

St. Stephen's Day, December 26. As I made my way across the outer courtyard to Raleigh's chamber, I found it aswarm with people carrying curtains, costumes, and furniture into the Great Hall for tonight's performance. I could hear, dimly, the sound of furious hammering from inside the hall. I keenly anticipated the evening's entertainment, but now I was bound for a private performance. For I had no doubt he would put on a performance, my Walter.

I was not disappointed. He flung open the door, bending low, spreading out a cloak across the threshold. "We must seek to make what is just a story into a truth," he said.

"Then you should have put the mud beneath it, as the story goes, that you saved me from at Greenwich." I stepped carefully on the velvet. There was a tale that Raleigh had spread his best cloak on a mud puddle for me to tread upon, lest I sully my dainty slippers. People loved it. Unfortunately it had never happened.

He laughed. He had always had a warm, inviting laugh. "I must needs be more frugal now," he said. "I cannot sacrifice a good cape so easily. I have had hard times of late."

"Ah, Walter, when will you cease to be a beggar?" I asked. I was growing ever more weary of the continual requests—some more open and bold than others, but all a constant clawing—for money from all creatures about me.

"When Your Majesty ceases to be a benefactor!" He grinned, setting his hands on his hips—hips clad in fashionable breeches of slashed crimson satin. Then he ushered me into the chamber.

These chambers around the base courtyard had been built by Cardinal Wolsey for his guests, and as usual with the cardinal, he had spared no expense. Even though they were over seventy years old now, the rooms lacked no comfort. Just so is luxury immortal. The walls were covered in the finest linenfold paneling, and a frieze ran around all four walls. Wolsey's taste was for biblical scenes, and this one featured Samson and Delilah—most fitting. At least Bess had spared Raleigh's hair.

"Now I can impart the secrets to you," he said. "I must tell you of El Dorado." He clapped, and then opened a door leading to another chamber, motioning me in. Inside this smaller chamber, Ewaioma stood silently, almost naked, his body glistening with oil. Standing in a corner, one of Raleigh's servants leaned on a long, hollow cane, watching me warily. He dipped the bottom of the cane into a jug at his feet, raised it up, and blew a cloud of dust all over Ewaioma. He repeated this again and again, and slowly the Indian's body turned to gold. When he was a gleaming idol, Raleigh said, "This is what the Indians in Guiana do with their chief. On his birthday they coat him with gold dust. In some ceremonies, all the nobles do likewise, until everyone in the palace is covered in gold. Later they plunge into a sacred lake to wash it off, without trying to recover the precious dust. They have so much of it, they can throw it away." He rolled up his sleeve, smeared it with oil, then stuck his arm out to be dusted with gold. It was quickly transformed, the veins turning into raised threads, the hairs on his arm like golden slivers. He started to pull at his doublet.

"No need to go further," I said. I wondered what he would look like all coated in gold, shorn of his doublet and shirt, but did not pursue it. "I have seen enough."

He lowered his arm and motioned to the other two that the exhibition was over. "Let me tell you what Captain Whiddon has reported," he said, dragging a table over, and two chairs. He gave me the more comfortable one and put a pillow on it. He unrolled a parchment map and stabbed a thick finger on it. "There is an island just off the coast of South America, named Trinidad after the Holy Trinity. The Spanish have that. But they do not have the land beyond"—he stabbed again—"the land called Guiana. It is a jungle with many rivers cutting through. Somewhere in the highlands above the jungle and the basin of the Orinoco River lies the city of El Dorado, filled with gold. The Indian name for it is 'Manoa,' and it is so wealthy the chief has a garden of gold replicas of all the plants growing in his kingdom. We know this because a Spanish explorer, Juan Martínez, found it!"

"Then why does not Spain claim it?"

"She is trying to. The commander of the fort in Trinidad is an old man who is convinced of the truth of the story, and he has sent out his own explorers. But the Indians hate the Spanish and refuse to help them. As the enemies of the Spanish, we will be welcomed. Your Majesty, my good Queen, give me letters patent to explore, and a commission to seek El Dorado."

"Parliament has already granted you funds," I said.

"But without your gracious patronage, how can I claim the land on your behalf?" He leaned close, his voice low, as if to frame the words was dangerous. "The Spanish and Portuguese are not in possession of this coast. What matter if the pope granted it to them? He had not the right. Do we recognize the pope's authority in our own realm? Why, then, outside it? He is nothing but a deluded, corrupt old man, in thrall to the merchants of Italy and Spain." He shot a shrewd look at me. "Your father would never have hesitated."

"True," I admitted. "But this deluded old man, as you style him, has been most successful in rallying the Catholic faithful and stemming the tide of reformation."

"Yes, with the Inquisition!" Raleigh suddenly raised his voice. Eavesdroppers be damned. "That is why we must fight him on distant shores. This coast will serve as a base of privateering. And surely, my most dear Queen, you would not wish to see the cruel hand of Rome start to choke the noble natives of Guiana. Up until now they have managed to escape the fate of the Incas and the Aztecs, ruined by the Spanish. All that gold, going to Spain. But the Spanish have never found the source of that gold on the South American continent. It must have come from somewhere. I believe it is near this El Dorado. The Spanish have made off with the product, but we can secure the source itself!"

He was persuasion itself. But I needed little persuading. I longed to taste such adventure firsthand. Instead, I was forced to rely on others to live it for me. My blood sang at the thought of exploring this new land, discovering things we could only guess at in these snug rooms at Hampton Court.

"Very well," I said. "I appoint you to this and will have the commission papers drawn up. Let us hope the golden city of El Dorado is more real than the episode of your laying your cloak in the mud for me. As you said, we can seek to make the first story real. But in this case, either the gold is there or it is not, and we cannot conjure it up."

He dropped to one knee. "If it is there, I shall find it." He grasped my hand and kissed it urgently, so urgently my fingers stung. "I swear it."

# 31

I took my place in the Great Hall, now transformed into something else entirely. The carpenters and joiners had worked for two days to convert it into a theater, using the minstrels' gallery as the upper part of the set, fastening oil lamps onto wires to hang from the hammer beams and provide twinkling light. I was seated on a throne brought from the royal apartments, one I used when giving audiences. It elevated me so I had a fine view of the stage.

When all the rustling was over as the court took their places, the lord chamberlain, Lord Hunsdon, walked slowly out to the center of the stage. He looked like a white-haired bear, his big shoulders thrust forward as he shuffled one foot in front of the other. How deliberately he crept, my old cousin Henry Carey. Creeping time was creeping up on him. He would turn seventy this year, this dear relative.

In addition to his court, legal, and military duties, he was patron of the best acting company in the realm, which took its name from his title. Tonight he introduced their new presentation. It was impossible to mask the pride in his rough voice.

"Tonight, Your Majesty, Your Graces, the lords of the realm, all the company here present, the Lord Chamberlain's Men have the honor of presenting a new play, as yet unseen in any other venue. It is a fantasy about a night in high summer in which the fairies make mischief for themselves and mortals." He bowed low. "Here in the depths of winter, we can have a foretaste of June."

A new play! This was a surprise. Hunsdon took his place beside me, and I murmured, "What a treat for us. I daresay you can vouch for its quality?" It would not do to show what common people called a stink-pool.

"I have not seen it myself," he admitted.

"Not even in rehearsal?" This was alarming.

"No . . . but the writer is known to be good, and I have seen his *Henry VI*."

Oh, him. What was his name? Yes, Shakespeare. He also wrote poetry. I had skimmed over the *Venus and Adonis* that Southampton had presented to me last New Year. It was heavy for my taste, although his similes were good. "I hope his play is lighter than his verse," I said.

I saw Southampton's head in the front row, his aureole of hair making him unmistakable. Of course, he would be up close to see his protégé's play. Essex, too, was down in front, eagerly leaning forward, his lanky frame straining the velvet of his coat.

A filmy curtain veiled the stage, but it was slowly lifted, revealing a row of Greek columns and two actors holding hands, who quickly announced themselves to be the Duke of Athens and his betrothed, Queen of the Amazons. The lovers barely had time to lament the four long days until their nuptials before unhappy subjects of the duke appeared, asking him to enforce a father's right to have his daughter obey his choice of husband for her.

I sighed. This promised to be tedious. I disliked plays and poems about arranged marriages and all their variations, having escaped from them myself. Who wishes to see his own life dramatized? And besides, the stratagems the plays used to escape marriage were never as convoluted or clever as my own.

I had to admit, the lighting was very well done, and the suspended oil lamps brightened the stage perfectly. High in the reaches of the great arches above all was dark, but lower down the carvings, covered in gold leaf, were highlighted in stark relief.

"I remember when the whole hall was lit by tallow candles for the workmen," whispered Hunsdon by my side. "I was just about eight years old when my mother brought me here to watch. My uncle-in-law the King was so eager to have it finished he paid overtime for the workers to work all night. There were piles of lumber stacked outside where we stood, and the whole hall glowed from within like a lantern. It was magic—as we will find this play to be."

He was too tactful to mention that high in the timbers my mother's initials were still entwined with my father's. In the heat of love the building had commenced, and my father had put my mother's initials everywhere at Hampton Court, only to erase and destroy them later. But he had missed the ones in the roof of the Great Hall, or not wanted to spend the money to send workmen up there, and so this little token of their love remained. There were other places, too. One had to know they were there; one had to look for them. I searched the darkness above but saw nothing.

In the meantime, a painted scene of a wood had replaced the Greek columns, and potted trees were on the stage. The play's lovers had fled into a forest, and now there were fairies as well with their queen and king and a mischief-making spirit, Robin Goodfellow.

"Now comes the magic," said Hunsdon, "of a midsummer kind."

The land of faerie was evidently in confusion, their king and queen having fallen out. Their garments glistened and gleamed in the yellow light, iridescent like a snake's skin, and their voices waxed and waned as they spoke their poetry. I could follow the sense of it, but at the same time the words needed lingering over, and yet each rushed on each so quickly it was hard to savor them. Then suddenly the queen spoke of seasons out of joint. Her words were all too clear.

*. . . the green corn*
*Hath rotted ere his youth attained a beard.*
*The fold stands empty in the drowned field,*
*And crows are fatted with the murrion flock,*
*The nine men's morris is filled up with mud . . .*

She described perfectly the catastrophic summer rains we had had. No one had blamed it on a quarrel among the fairies, but it had made the entire realm anxious for the next summer to come, to set things right.

Her next lines—

*The seasons alter: hoary-headed frosts*
*Fall in the fresh lap of the crimson rose,*
*And on old Hiems' thin and icy crown*
*An odorous chaplet of sweet summer buds*
*Is, as in mockery, set . . . ,*

—frightened me. For as I had strolled about the winter grounds I had found roses budding and daffodils pushing through the frosty soil. One bad harvest, yes, that could be expected, but to have the seasons scrambled . . .

The play soon introduced a love potion so powerful that if it were smeared on the eyes, the victim was doomed to love whatever he or she next looked upon. There then ensued comical demonstrations of the potion's effects. But the hard edge of the humor was that in reality love caused disruptions almost that extreme. Again, there was my father's devouring passion for my mother, defying common sense or explanation. And the sad spectacle of my sister Mary, married to the indifferent Philip of Spain, against the interests of her country, and again, my cousin the Scots queen who had lost her throne for love-blindness. Within the circle of my own family there were enough examples that I did not need to search history and find Marc Antony or Paris to serve as warning.

The king of the fairies now said that once he had seen Cupid flying down to earth, and

*A certain aim he took*
*At a fair vestal throned by the west*
*And loosed his love-shaft smartly from his bow,*
*As it should pierce a hundred thousand hearts;*
*But I might see young Cupid's fiery shaft*
*Quenched in the chaste beams of the watery moon*
*And the imperial votaress passed on,*
*In maiden meditation, fancy-free.*

Suddenly the players halted, and Southampton rose, turned, and dipped his head to me in deference. Beside him, someone else stood and did likewise. Then the play resumed.

It was quickly explained that this shaft, which had missed the "imperial votaress," the "fair vestal," had pierced a flower and from thence derived the powerful love drug.

So I passed on, fancy-free? It had not been easily done, to earn those two words.

---

We retired to the Great Watching Chamber when the play ended. Here we would dance until the musicians tired and the youngest pages grew sleepy. I had, of late, had a pull in my knee that pinched when I lifted it, but that would not stop me. Tonight I felt like dancing; perhaps the play had that effect on me—all those fairies tripping about, and Robin Goodfellow speeding here, there, in an eyeblink.

While we had watched the play, the Watching Chamber had been transformed into a version of the faerie realm to match it. Bare tree branches were, by magic of paper and wire, made to bloom; the mists of midsummer were replicated by gossamer silk draped upon them and hanging from the ceiling; perfumed candles, twinkling from sconces, mocked stars.

"Why do we need nature? We can copy her well enough!" said the master of revels. "If we want midsummer in deep December, we have only to ask."

"If we have the money," said someone standing by me. "Money can transform one thing into another; it is the only true alchemist's stone."

Francis Bacon. I should have known. I greeted him. "Sir, you are looking well. How did you enjoy the play?"

"Well enough," he said. "Although I question whether even love juice could work so fast. Still, it was only to amuse us, and as such, it need not be true."

"Francis, you are too serious," I said. "I hope you plan to dance tonight."

"I have a sore toe," he said. "I would not want anyone to step on it."

"What a pity. Perhaps a stately measure, then?"

He smiled at last. "Perhaps."

I welcomed the gathering, and as I finished, the musicians struck up at one end of the chamber. They began softly, as if they wanted to capture the floating delicacy of the decorations. But as the guests talked and noise rose, they had to switch to livelier tunes.

I felt oddly bold tonight, as if someone had smeared a juice of audacity on my lids. I approached Francis Drake, who was standing stoutly against one of the tapestries, hands clasped behind his back, talking to Admiral Howard and John Hawkins. Beside them stood Catherine, trying to look interested.

"Ahoy!" I cried, startling them. They swung round to stare at me. "I say 'ahoy,' as I know you must be talking ships and the sea. What else would the admiral, Hawkins, and *El Draque* discuss?"

Recovering themselves, they bowed. Catherine laughed and said, "How well you know them! I was hoping that by joining them I could steer them in another direction—"

"Steer, woman?" said the admiral. "Now you speak as a helmsman, so what else shall we do?"

"Good Queen, the admiral envies the mission Hawkins and I are fitting ourselves for, with your generous patronage," said Drake. "We would he could accompany us."

"Drake, someone must remain here to guard us, while you cavort in the Caribbean."

He raised his eyebrows. "Cavort? This is serious business! Dangerous business, to sail into the Spanish maw."

"For you, danger is play," I said. "If you are too long deprived of it, you wither in despair. Even with your lovely new wife at your side in Devon." She did not seem to be at his side now, though. Perhaps she had stayed home.

He hung his head like a schoolboy caught out, then gave a roaring laugh.

But he was no schoolboy; his movements were slower and his figure stockier. He must be in his midfifties but looked older. Perhaps it was the sea air that had done it, weathering his face into hard lines. Beside him, his cousin John Hawkins, in his sixties, was thin and straight, but his years were upon him, no matter how lightly they sat. Was I foolish to let them embark on a treasure-hunting mission at their ages? They were the ablest seamen of the day, and Hawkins had designed the ships that gave England the victory in 1588, but they were . . . old.

They were . . . near my age. But dangerous voyages into inhospitable climes demanded more than my life at court, I assured myself.

"If I perish, I want to do so while firing at the Spanish," said Hawkins. "And besides all the gold we have brought England, we leave our charities—the one for relief of sick and elderly sailors, the Chatham Chest, and the two hospitals."

"Two?" I asked. "I knew of one, associated with the Chatham Chest."

"Just this year, I opened the Sir John Hawkins Hospital," he said proudly.

"Then I'll have to open a Sir Francis Drake Warehouse for Spanish Booty," Drake said. "But in all seriousness, our ships are being fitted, the supplies stored, and as soon as the Christmastide is over, we will set out." He looked at me, as if reading my thoughts. "We will not fail. We are in our prime, John and I, and there's not an enemy on land or sea that knows a trick we do not."

"I am just as glad you are not going, Charles," said Catherine to her husband, embarrassing him.

I left them still hugging the tapestries and turned to find Hunsdon waiting patiently for me.

He was beaming. "Did you like the play? Did you?"

"Indeed I did." I did not have to pretend. "It was . . . It is . . . odd, but I find it still captivating me. It seems to invade the senses."

"We were proud of it. Let me present William Kemp, the most important actor in the play." The man playing the rustic who had sported an ass's head bowed.

"Your performance charmed me," I said. "I will look forward to seeing you in other productions."

"I will never have another part like this one," he said. "Perhaps just as well. It was difficult to breathe inside that head." For emphasis, he brayed.

"I see you have met our ass," said Southampton, hurrying up. He was, as always, fashionably attired, and the faint perfume he favored announced his presence.

"Only one among many in a chamber of this size," said Hunsdon gruffly. "The court abounds with asses!"

Southampton smiled indulgently as if to signal, *Grumpy old men, what a bore they are.* "The ass in the play is a comic genius, and only an actor of your skill could have made him sympathetic as well as funny."

"I thank you, my lord," said Kemp.

"The man who wrote the play is to be congratulated. I am, you know, his patron," he said proudly. "And tonight I was as nervous as a parent, hoping his talent would resonate with the audience."

"I think, Southampton, you can relax now." Beside him a dark-haired man spoke, who had come up so quietly in the dim light I had not seen him. "For, if I am not mistaken, Her Majesty smiled throughout the play."

"May I present William Shakespeare, the man who gave us tonight's entertainment?"

The man bowed, his gold earring flashing as he bent his head.

"I am pleased to receive you," I told him. "And I am still emerging from the dream you created on the stage with your words. Pray, keep writing; give us more of your fantasies. What is next?"

"I am working on several things," he said. He had a soft voice that made me want to bend closer to him rather than asking him to speak up. "Another comedy set in Italy, a love story also set in Italy, and then good old English history."

"You have done Richard III and Henry VI. Are you working your way up to our times?"

"I have a long way to go," he said.

"Oh, but he works very fast," Southampton said. "He can turn out several in a year, if he's not distracted."

Shakespeare shot him a glance. "What man lives who is not distracted? The trick is to write through the distractions. Or to incorporate them into the work, so all is one."

"You are young," I said. "At this rate, you will reach my coronation in only a few years. Mind that you portray me flatteringly."

"In you, Ma'am, the truth needs no flattery, as it stands alone in its own glittering raiment."

"Oh, my, you cloak your own flattery in such glittering words," I replied. He was certainly nimble with them. I would have to read the *Venus and Adonis* more carefully to see what gems I had missed.

He and Southampton bowed and removed themselves.

"Poets! Playwrights!" snorted Hunsdon. "I'd hate to see either of them defending the marches up north."

"Then I am fortunate that I don't have to rely on them for anything but words," I assured him. "After all, I have you to direct the northern defenses."

Admiral Howard, having detached himself from the other seamen, came up behind Hunsdon. "I must salute you. Your acting company was superlative tonight. However, we are not beaten yet."

"Ah, you are a man who likes to fight a war on two fronts—the sea and the theater," I said. Howard was patron of the rival company the Admiral's Men.

"You should surrender now," said Hunsdon, "before you put on any more embarrassing spectacles like the last Marlowe revival."

"The more plays presented, the more likelihood one might be substandard. But it keeps our name before the public and buys my wife her jewels."

Catherine, who had followed her husband, fingered her ruby pendant. "Ah, what a hard choice it is, between the Lord Chamberlain's and the Admiral's Men, especially as one is my father's and the other my husband's." The admiral put his arm around her and Hunsdon grunted.

"Admiral, you have Edward Alleyn as your chief actor, whereas you, Henry, have Richard Burbage." I turned to Hunsdon. "It would be illuminating to have them play the same part in succession so I could compare them."

Hunsdon grunted again, dismissing the idea. "We have Shakespeare, and your Marlowe is dead," he taunted the admiral.

"But not his plays," said the admiral. "We can continue performing *Doctor Faustus, Tamburlaine, Dido, The Massacre at Paris,* and I need not remind you that *The Jew of Malta* has been revived, to great success."

"Pity you can't revive Marlowe himself, for his repertoire is so limited people will soon tire of it."

"Your Shakespeare is still an unknown, as far as what he will be able to produce, and for how long."

"Gentlemen, gentlemen, that is the glory of the theater—the suspense!" I wanted to bring this friendly squabbling to a close. I felt keenly the loss of Marlowe, both on the stage and in the shadows for the work Walsingham had trusted to him. I did not accept the story that he had died in a brawl, accidentally stabbed. His companions, all involved in spy work for various masters, were not gathered by chance in Deptford, where he was killed. I was convinced they were given a mission to kill Marlowe. But by whom? Walsingham would have been able to ascertain the truth of it. But Walsingham was gone and his replacements poor shades of himself. I shuddered in remembering the debacle of the so-called Lopez Plot, exposed by inept and biased agents.

The slow music stopped, and the musicians began to play a coranto, a lively beat that required quick steps. By all the gods, I would dance tonight! No more conversation!

Where was Essex? He had yet to speak to me tonight. I had seen him down in front at the play, but now he hung back in the dim corner of the chamber, his back to everyone, but recognizable by the very way he stood, draping his tall frame in a graceful slight *S* curve of the spine. It made his short cloak hang provocatively over his right hip, thrust out.

He was deep in conversation with two of my maids, both Elizabeths: Southwell and Vernon. One was tall and light haired, the other small, dark, and intense. I suddenly realized they could have perfectly filled the parts of tonight's play, Southwell being the tall and stately Helena, Vernon the emotional Hermia, "a vixen when she went to school," as she was described.

"Now there shall be three Elizabeths," I said, startling Essex, who had not seen me approach. He whirled around.

"There is only one Elizabeth, ever," he said, dropping to one knee and taking my hand to kiss.

"Nay, you insult these fair ladies, lovely and young Elizabeths," I said, nodding to them.

Now they both bowed, but as they rose there were messages in their eyes: Southwell tried to avert her gaze, but Vernon's was bold and direct, like the assertive perfume she wore. Her large eyes, which an unkind person might describe as bulging, were erotic, suggesting illicit pleasure to be found in her.

"May I borrow your company?" I asked them. "I would like to lead Lord Essex out in a dance."

His face flushed with pleasure, as I liked to see it. He gave me his hand and together we went to the center of the room. All the others fell away, leaving us in a circle of our own making.

The music for the coranto was loud and thumping. I had not danced it for a long time, but tonight I longed to. Had the play infused me with hunger that I thought myself past? The merry lovers trooping through the moonlit woods, seeking their partners, made me feel more alone. The lines they spoke echoed in my head. "Swift as a shadow, short as any dream, brief as the lightning in the collied night" . . . "So quick bright things come to confusion." We must snatch what dangles before us, before it flies away.

Essex, my boy, here before me, a man now. A boy changed into a man, swift as a shadow, to be sure. Myself, once a maid as young as Southwell or Vernon, now "withering on the virgin thorn," as the play would have it? No! I was a virgin, but not withered, not yet. I looked into his eyes, searching for recognition that I was a woman still, not a queenly nun. I saw that confirmation, that assurance, in them, in a gaze of such hunger it could not have been false.

I spun, I saw the winking lamps mimic stars all around me, I reveled in his adoration and the knowledge that I could still inspire unabashed passion in a man.

The dancing went on and on, until the musicians tired and the sky faintly lightened. I was determined not to show fatigue, and indeed, I did not feel any, for the excitement supplied all the stamina I needed. We drifted away to the royal apartments, and I led him through the ever-more-intimate chambers, from the large audience chamber to the presence chamber to the privy chamber and hence, finally, to the innermost one, where my bed and desk and private dining table were. We halted. He leaned forward to kiss me, as he had in dimly remembered dreams I had. But as in the dreams, I pulled away, lest he discover the pretend youth of my real flesh. I did not wish to reveal it. Let all be moonlight and artifice, as in the play, fantasies and fairies.

Thus it has been, and thus it must remain. Always I was Gloriana, the Faerie Queen, Imperial Votaress.

# 32

# LETTICE

*January 1595*

welfth Night, and I had to spend it drearily sorting through my correspondence, although I did eat the traditional cake—or a piece of it. I did not find the bean, the token of license and good luck. I hoped that did not presage what the rest of the year held in store for me.

Twelfth Night, and soon my son would be returning from Hampton Court, where he had danced attendance on the Queen, literally. I hoped he had scored some successes there. I knew Southampton and he had gone in high spirits.

That had left me all alone here to rattle around in Essex House. Christopher had gone to inspect the shipyards for his commander, the admiral, who was also enjoying himself at Hampton Court. I was just as glad to have him gone. The two of us alone together was no longer the thrill it had been.

Was it marriage? Why, oh why, when I had panted to be with him when I was still married to Robert Dudley, was I so indifferent now? And the same for Dudley—when I was still married to Walter Devereux, I had rushed to Dudley's bed in hot haste. All this cooled as quickly as a cake set out on the counter straight from the oven. Was it the everydayness of living together? Was it that the same hands, throat, lips, hips grew stale like the cake if it sat out too long? I did not know what it was, but it worried me that I preferred Christopher's absence to his presence lately.

And lately . . . Oh, had it really happened? Had I actually gone to bed with Southampton, my son's friend? For several days afterward I had pretended it never occurred; or rather, I refused to think about it. It was not the age gap—for, after all, Christopher is some sixteen years my junior—but the fact that it was my son's companion. What if Southampton told him?

The thing with Southampton must end. It must not be repeated . . . well, except for this next appointment. He was at Hampton Court and I could not cancel it, not without attracting attention to myself for writing to him. I would have to go through with the assignation. And then, no more.

Henry Wriothesley, Earl of Southampton. I licked my lips in remembering some of his precocious techniques. He was a daring person and that translated into his physical actions. I laughed softly to myself that there were those who thought him girlish, or that he preferred men. This misconception allowed him unlimited access to women. Perhaps that was why he cultivated it.

He had of late taken up with one of the Queen's maids, Elizabeth Vernon, whisking her to his apartments right under the Virgin Queen's nose. Sometimes he and Robert entertained both ladies, the Southwell one and the Vernon one, together. I had tried to warn Robert off Southwell but in vain, although her pregnancy would send her away soon enough. As for Southampton, his involvement with Vernon served to mask whomever else he romped with.

So young, and yet so dissipated. Ah, well. One person's dissipation is another's opportunity, and in our last time together I would take every opportunity to extract such pleasure that I would long remember it. Then . . . farewell, Southampton.

It was set for tomorrow night. Robert would linger at court for a few days after most had departed, hoping to have some quiet time with the Queen. Southampton would come to Essex House in the early evening on the pretext of finding Robert there, and affect surprise when he was not. I had already told the servants they were not needed for tomorrow night.

---

There was a soft knocking at the door. I let it repeat itself to make sure no doorkeeper was still on duty. All was in readiness. The candles were burning brightly in the hall and in all the rooms, and potpourri of sweet roses and marjoram was scattered about in silver bowls. I had set out several kinds of wines, including a selection of the ones Robert had the tax concession on—muscadines, malmseys, and vernages. The best cheeses from Staffordshire and dried fruit were arranged on platters on a polished table in the library.

I had chosen a red velvet gown with a low neckline. Those who think people with red hair should avoid red are dullards. The hair has an orange glow that is different from crimson. The Queen knows that well enough—there is a famous portrait of her as a child wearing a red gown. Well, we are cousins and share the same coloring, and the same sense of style. Around my neck I had fastened a ruby necklace—more red. I was ready. I took a deep breath, ran my tongue over my lips to moisten them, parted them, and opened the door.

A stranger stood there.

I stared at him, momentarily speechless. I was both disappointed and nervous. What if Southampton arrived now, and this stranger spotted him?

"Yes?" I finally said.

He looked puzzled that I had opened the door myself. He could see something was amiss. His dark eyes seemed supremely intelligent, the sort that would miss nothing. Damn!

"Lady Leicester?" he asked.

"Yes," I said.

"It could have been no other," he said. "Your beauty, for all that it is legendary, is singular and recognizable."

Well. He knew how to give a compliment. But what did he want? I must get rid of him.

"I have a manuscript for the Earl of Southampton, my patron," he said. "But the Earl of Essex wanted to read it first, so I promised to bring it here."

Patron. Southampton. "You must be that Shakespeare fellow. The one who wrote"—let my memory not fail me—"the long poem *Venus and Adonis*?"

"The same." He kept standing there, and did not hand over the package tucked under his arm.

"Won't you come in?" I was forced to ask.

Quickly he stepped in, shaking a light dusting of snow off his shoulders. Now he presented the leather case. "It is only a first draft," he said. "But he insisted on reading it."

I led him in to the first chamber and put the manuscript down on the nearest table. What was the least amount of time I could politely spend before sending him on his way? Oh, Southampton, be slow in arriving!

"I came directly from court. I was to tell you that neither Southampton nor Essex can leave just yet. They have appointments that cannot be broken. But your son will be here day after tomorrow, and Southampton the day after that."

I felt as if I had just been kicked in the stomach. I actually almost lost my breath. So it was not to be. If Southampton had to follow Robert, we would have no opportunity to be alone again.

"I see." Suddenly the red gown made me feel like a dressed monkey, the kind fools use in their antics. Well, I might as well entertain this fellow. Now that I thought of it . . . I had read snatches of his poem and it concerned the goddess Venus throwing herself at a young shepherd who would have none of it.

Was that what I had done with Southampton? Was this his way of telling me that I was unwanted, like Adonis told Venus? And how symbolic, to dispatch this poet who wrote about it. How like Southampton, to do it in this literary fashion.

"—well received at court," Shakespeare was saying. "I plan to make changes in it before presenting it again."

"I beg your pardon?" I must force myself to pay attention. And no point in sending him away. No one else was coming. Why waste the wine, the cheese, and the candles?

"I was saying," he said slowly, "that my play *A Midsummer Night's Dream* was well received at court." He was studying me, well aware that I was distracted. He was trying to ascertain why.

"Robert mentioned it," I assured him. "He was proud of the way it was played. Congratulations to you. If it made a good impression at court, you are well on your way."

He looked amused at what I said, as if he wanted to correct me but was too polite. "I go back and forth between pure poetry and plays," he said. "And lately I have written sonnets for Southampton, urging him to marry and pass on his beauty to another generation. I rather like those. They allow me to ruminate on time and eternity and such like." He grinned. "Poets enjoy that."

"It is a theme that never itself grows old." Grows old. Was I imagining it, or was he looking at me knowledgeably? Had Southampton told him? Was I a curiosity to him, an aged Messalina? "Would you care to see our library? You can inspect our selection of poets, and perhaps tell us what we lack." I led him up the stairs, down the polished and silent hallway, and into the magnificent paneled library.

If he was surprised to see a table laden with wine and food, he did not show it. It was obvious I had been expecting someone; now it was equally obvious I expected that person no longer. "Would you care for malmsey? Or perhaps vernage?" I asked.

"I always favored vernage," he said.

I poured out two goblets of it and handed his to him slowly. I touched the rim of mine to his. "Drink well," I said, taking a sip.

His stillness unnerved me. He seemed to be in complete command of himself, not needing to chatter. He turned away and began to inspect the books lining the shelves, nodding now and then. He seemed utterly absorbed in examining the collection. The bust of Augustus looked on from his pedestal.

"What is this?" he suddenly said, picking up a marble fragment from a shelf. He ran his fingers over it.

"It is what remains of a face," I said. "A friend brought it to us from Rome, where such pieces of antiquity are lying about for the finding. The best ones, of course, are taken by the pope for his collection. But I rather like this, for all its flaws."

He turned it so the candlelight showed its contours, more strongly than if direct light had shone on it. "All the features are still here, in vestigial form, softly suggesting, letting us supply what is missing from our own imagination. In that way we become part of it ourselves."

"Vestigial! I would not have expected that word, but yes, you are right." He was making me increasingly nervous. He saw too much. I felt as naked as Eve in the Garden when God went looking for her. "More wine?" I hurried over to the table to get the flask.

"Outworn buried age," he said fondly, still cradling the carving. "Yes, more wine."

I refilled his glass, and mine as well. A pleasant lightness was stealing into my head.

He was not exactly handsome, but he was pleasing. His dark hair was thick and had a natural curl; through it winked a gold earring. He had unusually red lips. I tried to avoid looking into his eyes because they made me nervous. Instead I looked at his collar, his cheeks, the lips, the hair. "So you are pleased with your patron?" I asked. Even as I said it, I knew it sounded silly.

"Oh, very," he said. "He is most generous, and appreciative. What more could a poet want?"

"To be free of a patron," I blurted out. "Even the best is a yoke!"

"No poet can be free of a patron, not even one as successful as I after *Venus and Adonis,*" he said matter-of-factly. "But a playwright can be, and that is my intention."

"I've no doubt you shall be successful."

"Perhaps there is a chance of success in your . . . friendship as well, Lady Leicester?" He looked boldly at me.

I stared back at him. He was tantalizing, that was the only word for it. He teased just by his presence and the eyes that saw through me. "Perhaps," I heard myself saying. "I am always open to new friendships."

"Indeed?" He put his glass down carefully, and laid the marble carving beside it. "Do you have many close friends, Lady Leicester?"

"I believe you know several of my friends," I said. "And you may call me Lettice if you like."

"I prefer 'Laetitia,'" he said. "That must be your real name? So much more elegant and classical."

"Like the marble carving?" I could not help laughing. What an odd conversation this was!

"Just like the marble carving."

It had never happened like this to me, a seduction with a stranger who did not bother to seduce, just drifted into it with classical references. I found it more exciting than compliments, verses, music, and innuendos, for it was so unusual.

The couches scattered around the library served us well; we migrated from one to another, as if each experiment had to be conducted on a different couch. Once I looked up to see Augustus, illustrious emperor and busy adulterer, sternly eyeing us, and I laughed. Perhaps that old reprobate was learning something. This one was.

---

Afterward—it was nearly growing light—he mentioned that I should take a look at the manuscript he had brought.

"You might recognize something in it," he said. "It concerns a man who comes to another's wife, and the welcome he receives."

Disappointment flooded me. How cold-blooded of him to tell me that.

"Not such a one as we have given each other, Laetitia," he quickly assured me. "Ours is different." He fastened his cloak and put on his hat. "It grows light. I must leave."

Just then a thud announced the arrival of a servant. "Hurry!" I said.

He dashed down the steps and was out the door before old Timothy dragged his broom to the hall to begin sweeping.

# 33

# ELIZABETH

*August 1595*

his summer had been cold and rainy, like last year's, and I could see the stunted crops in the featureless fields as Essex and I rode west across the country to Shrewsbury. We were on a pilgrimage of sorts, a visit to an oracle.

Robert had told me one spring night of a man living near Shrewsbury who was the oldest man in England.

"His name is Thomas Parr, and he was born in 1483," he said. "That makes him one hundred and twelve years old."

"When will you cease to be a liar, Robert?" I had giggled. We had been up late playing cards, and I was light-headed.

His face had gone rigid, insulted. "I am not lying! I have heard of him since I was a child. My sisters visited him once. You don't believe me? I'll take you there!"

"I had planned a Progress in the opposite direction."

"Change your plans. Better yet, forget the Progress and come alone with me." He put down his cards and leaned toward me. "Aren't you bored with Progresses? They are always the same. How can you stand another speech, another bad drama, another off-key choir?"

I could stand it because I had to, and because it was expected of me. And seeing their eagerness to perform, their desire to please, was important to me.

"Stop tempting me to neglect my duty," I chided him, picking up his hand and stroking it. Such a fine hand.

"I *am* temptation," he whispered. "I'll act as your guide, I'll show you my ancestral lands, on the border of Wales. Yours, too—your grandfather was Welsh, and we are cousins," he reminded me. "Your child-uncle Arthur lies buried at Ludlow, and my father is buried at Carmarthen, near Merlin's cave. It is in our blood. You must see it!"

I let his hand go. No. I should go on a Progress to assure my people. It was my duty. But—

"Very well," I said, raising my eyes quickly, hoping to catch his honest expression.

He looked delighted. Nothing else, no flitting triumph or consternation in his face.

"Oh, thanks be to the gods! I had not dared to hope my poor appeal would be heard. But I truly meant it. We will journey to an enchanted land. Together."

---

And here we were, the sun finally dipping toward the west on this long summer day, halfway to our destination. Far behind us, the necessary guards trailed. I did not take any ladies. The ones my age would have creaked and complained about a journey of this duration, and the younger ones would not have been interested.

"Tomorrow we will push on to Shrewsbury and Old Parr," he said cheerfully, although it was quite far. His vigor and strength would eat up the distance. And I would pretend mine would.

That night, spent in a simple Devereux holding in Evesham, I was so tired I could have slept on boulders. But I had awakened rested with the morning's light, ready for another hard day.

---

Westward through the countryside the landscape changed. This part of England caught more of the wind and rain coming from the sea, and it was wilder and greener than the eastern counties. As we got closer to Wales, this would become even more marked.

Shrewsbury, a market town on the river Severn, lay only ten miles from the beginning of Wales proper. Much wool came through here; I was familiar with the name on tax rolls. But Old Parr lived in the nearby hamlet of Wollaston, easily found by asking. Old Parr was famous, more famous than anyone else who had ever lived there.

"He's a hundred and fifty!" one boy cried. "He's so old, he looks like a piece of leather!"

"No, he's two hundred!" a little girl said. "My great-great-great-grandmother knew him. He looks like a locust shell!"

Their father put his arms around their shoulders. "He isn't quite that old," he said. "But—you know what the Scripture says about Moses? That he was a hundred and twenty years old and he was still a . . . a vigorous man? Well, Old Parr had to do public penance for adultery when he was a hundred!" He chortled with admiration.

"We must see this for ourselves," I said. "My thanks for the kind directions."

They bowed, thanking me for speaking to them. I handed them a fan for a memento. It was all I had, having deliberately come away with very few trappings.

---

Old Parr's dwelling turned out to be a small stone cottage on the crest of a hill, encircled with a fence. The latched gate was not guarded, and we were free to walk in.

It was dim inside and it took a moment for my eyes to adjust. When they did, I saw a small figure sitting on a stool in the corner. He leaped up, startling us.

"Who's that? Who's that?" he called, grabbing a stave propped by his stool and flailing about with it.

"It is the Queen," I told him. "Come a far way to see you."

He spat. "Go on, liar!"

There was someone else in the room, and she rushed over to him, wrenching the stave away. "Father! Father!" she said. "What if it *is* the Queen?" She turned to me, wiping her hands on her apron, squinting to see me. "I—I cannot believe it—but no one would dare such an impersonation!" She sank down on her knees. "Forgive us, Your Majesty. We are—I am—speechless."

"Rise, mistress. I hope you will not remain speechless, for I am here to learn from this most unusual subject of mine. I am sure he has wisdom to impart, for the years whisper it in our ears, whether we will or no."

Essex was standing awkwardly in the doorway. "This is the Earl of Essex, whose family is from these regions. Indeed, it was from him I learned of your father."

"What does she want?" Parr said querulously.

"That is no way to address your sovereign!" said Essex. "Apologize. Years do not confer immunity from manners."

"Quite so, Father," said his daughter. "Think of all the Englishmen who would faint away with this honor—the Queen in his own house!"

I laughed. "Well, my oldest subject—I think I am safe in calling you that—I am the eighth monarch you have had. How many do you remember?"

He settled back onto his stool, wiping his clouded eyes with the back of his hand. "Forgive me, my Queen. I meant no disrespect. My memory comes in with the first Tudor, King Henry VII, your grandfather. I was only two when he claimed his crown, and he remained King until I was twenty-six. He was the King of my strength, as the Scriptures say. Then the great King Harry, your father, that was from twenty-six to sixty-four, yes. And I was already seventy-five when you, his daughter, became Queen. But that was not so old, no! Moses was that old when he was called back to Egypt. And look at all *he* did!"

"So you have lived here all this time?" I looked around the little room. There was nothing extraordinary about it; it was a room like thousands of others.

"Not all the time," he said. "I joined the army when I was seventeen, joined your Welsh grandfather Henry Tudor's army. That is the only time I have left here, and after that stint in the army I had no desire ever again to leave, I can tell you that! Nasty business, no matter who's fighting. No matter what their cause, good or bad. Wounds and rotten food—no thanks."

As my eyes had adjusted to the light, I could see his daughter better. She was younger than my maids of honor.

"What of your family?" I asked. His wife must be long gone. What of the rest?

He gave one of his bursts of wheezing laughter. "No! Only my daughter here! Born of my sin." He sounded immensely proud of it. He crossed himself. "And I've done penance for it!" he almost shrieked.

His daughter spoke up. "Calm yourself, Father." She put her hands on his shoulder and turned to me. "I am the daughter of Katherine Milton, the woman he took up with. I think my father would not have been known outside our village except that his public penance revealed his age."

"I betrayed my wife!" he announced gleefully. "With a younger woman! And in these parts they still believe in public penance for adultery. I had to stand draped in a white sheet in the parish church for it."

"That is quite a feat for a man a hundred years old," I allowed. "And that was twelve years ago!"

"It killed my wife," he confided. "The shock, the scandal. But I am thinking of marrying again."

Essex burst out laughing. "Is that so?" he asked.

"Yes. A man needs a wife." He nodded vigorously.

"No doubt *you* do," I said. I peered at him. He had shaggy white eyebrows that overhung his lids, like a magus's, and bright brown eyes. For a man of his years, his skin was not too wrinkled, and I noticed he was sitting straight on his backless stool. Around the room were crude portraits of all the monarchs he had lived under—Edward IV, Richard III, Henry VII, Henry VIII, Edward VI, Mary, and myself. The one of me showed me at my coronation. I liked that.

"I have brought you a velvet cloak," I said, now doubting the appropriateness of it. "What do you have for me? I want only words, no gift." As if he had any objects to give. "Tell me what you credit with your long life."

"It's all in the diet!" he said. "I believe that eating mainly green onions, cheese, coarse bread—none of that dainty fare!—ale and buttermilk is what did it."

"It can't be just the food," said Essex, "for all your neighbors eat the same."

"No, there's more," he said slyly. "And I could tell you if—"

Essex slapped a half groat down in his palm so swiftly his words were not even interrupted.

"—you were so kind as you have just been. It's not only what goes in the belly, but what comes out of the head. My motto has always been to keep your head cool by temperance and your feet warm by exercise."

"Is that all?" I asked.

"It's enough," he grunted. "If you think it's easy, why then do so many fail to do it?"

"True, most people manage one but not both."

"Now, there's a little something else . . ."

Essex pressed another coin in his palm. "Do tell."

"The rest of my secret is this: Rise early, go to bed likewise, and if you want to prosper, keep your eyes open and your mouth shut." He clamped his lips together. "There, that's all I know."

"It has preserved him all these years," his daughter said.

"God bless him," I said.

"Will you be sending me a wedding gift?" he asked as we took our leave.

"You incorrigible old rogue!" I called back at him. "Yes. You have earned it!"

# 34

e were still laughing as we mounted our horses and rode away; my guards, having overheard what had passed inside the house, were guffawing, too.

"I forgot to ask him how old his intended is," I said.

"They say there is no man so foul, or so old, that some woman won't have him," said Essex. "And he is famous, too."

"But he hasn't any money for all his fame, to offset the drawback of being over a hundred," I said. I drew abreast of him. "Do you agree with him? That a man must be married?"

He smiled warily. "Ah, my Queen," he said, "you'll not trap me into speaking of marriage. I know the subject easily affronts you."

"I asked about men," I said, "in regard to marriage."

"Very well then. Yes, I think marriage is necessary for a man. Through it come alliances, inheritances, and legacies. An unmarried man is suspicious. I cannot help but feel that if Francis or Anthony Bacon were married, you would have more confidence in them. Their bachelorhood hinders their advancement."

"Francis Bacon again," I said. "You are determined to push his career. I almost think you fancy him yourself."

He reined in his horse. "Ma'am!" He looked horrified.

I laughed. "Such indignation! You have made your point. However, there are those who say—"

"Who? Who?" he cried.

"—that Francis is of that persuasion. Perhaps it is because he is so intelligent. You, on the other hand, pursue women willy-nilly, a trait of the brainless."

My maid of honor Elizabeth Southwell had left court to have his baby. For once I had said nothing on the subject. I felt pity for the silly creature, pity for Essex's wife and other children. He had promised me to honor his marriage, but a shameful tangle of lust and lies trapped him. He was not that different from Old Parr—they shared the same appetites and indiscretions. Men!

We had reached the place where the little road to Wollaston joined the main road. "Which way?" I asked. The guards drew up beside us.

"Turn right, go into Wales proper," said one of them. "Turn left, go back toward London through Wolverhampton."

"Let us go right," I said, "to Wales."

---

As we rode, the land became rougher and more hilly; the road deteriorated into a twisty, uneven path. Ahead we could see the beginning of the mountains, hazy in the western sun. Beyond that lay the sea, and beyond that—America. We passed people along the path speaking Welsh. I could understand only a few words; the child's Welsh that Blanche had taught me sounded different when spoken hurriedly by adults.

"We still have a far way to go," said Essex. "I have sent ahead to find a place where we can spend tonight. It is just in the village over the next hill. They say it has a fine view of the Berwyn Mountains."

Ah, this was so different from a Progress. So haphazard, so free. I wondered who our hosts would be, but it hardly mattered.

They turned out to be distant—very—Devereux cousins. They were the path Essex's branch of the family had not chosen—obscurity and peace. They had a small manor, sheep, and grazing fields. They seemed more excited to meet their exalted cousin than the Queen. That pleased me. Let someone else have the fawning and the—what had Essex called it?—the bad verses and the dull speeches.

After a simple supper of mutton stew and coarse brown bread, we strolled outside while they prepared our bedchambers. Sunset had almost come, and the burst of yellow light from the west illuminated all the hills and valleys and wrapped them in a golden glow.

"Standing here," I said, "I can believe that Merlin came from this land. It does not look real. Tell me, Robert, when we actually get there, does it look more real?"

He smiled. "No. It is magic all the way through." He paused a long time. "*Dwi yu dy garu di.*"

I shook my head. "I have to admit it—I cannot understand your words."

"I said"—he took my hands—"that I love you." He leaned forward and kissed my cheek.

I stiffened. He had said it, the straight statement, not wrapped in disguised courtier's words, albeit in another tongue. How should I respond?

His whispered "I love you" raced through my head, sweet as a delicate melody. I kept looking straight ahead, not daring to see his face.

A few seconds passed. Forever passed. I heard my own foot scraping the gravel on the path, heard him clear his throat, say, "I once lived near the sea on the coast, at Lamphey. After I left Cambridge. We have a family house there—"

"Oh, Robert, where do you *not* have a family house?" My voice sounded oddly high, but at least he had given me something to respond politely to.

"My uncle George still lives there," he said. "It's an old religious house, and your father gave it to our family when the monasteries were dissolved. It's in a lovely spot.

"Look down there," he said, pointing. "Far into those valleys. The green is so bright it looks like malachite. My father sleeps down there in his tomb. It's difficult to get there," he said, his voice rising. "When he died in Ireland and they brought him back here for his funeral, I wanted to go as chief mourner. But they wouldn't let me. Said I was too frail. So I never got to bid him farewell."

"How old were you?"

"Nine. Truth be told, I don't remember much about him. He was away so much, always gone to Ireland. But he once wrote me a letter telling me that Devereux men did not live long, and I should be daring in the pursuit of fame. As if to prove the early death curse, he died at thirty-seven."

"Ah, well, you have a long way to go, my lad. What are you now—twenty-what?"

"Soon to be twenty-eight."

"Oh, only another eighty-five years to go until you match Old Parr."

Twenty-seven. And I almost sixty-two. Only a fool could believe . . . But "*Dwi yu dy garu di*" danced itself through my mind, fleeting like a Greek chorus.

"Somewhere there's Llangorse Lake," I said. "Blanche Parry owned land around one shore. It was famous for eels, I believe."

"It was also famous for a lake monster, *afanc* in Welsh," he said. "As a child, I was told about it. I sat watching once for hours, but didn't see anything except the reeds along the bank and the men minding the eel traps."

"Was someone teasing you about it?" It was the sort of thing one told a child, then laughed to see him wait and watch.

"Oh, no! One of the old bards had a poem about it. It goes:

*'Anfanc I am,*
*Hiding always at water's edge,*

*Of Syfaddon Mere,*
*Any man or beast*
*Who dares contend with me today*
*Shall never depart*
*These shores.'"*

"No word on what it looks like?"

"Just a regular monster, I assume. Long neck, scales, breathes fire—Syfaddon is the Welsh name for the lake, by the way." He looked very excited just talking about the *afanc.*

"Do you wish to slay a dragon, as one of Arthur's knights?"

"I was born too late, and I admit it," he said. "But that does not stop the longing."

"To be Welsh is to long, to yearn," I assured him. "Always for that thing in a haze down the valley, or too far to sight."

"*Hiraeth,*" he said. "A longing for unnameable things." He reached for his little finger, pulled off a small ring. "Welsh gold," he said. "To keep Wales near you wherever you go."

---

The room they gave me to sleep in was a square one, its single window facing the mountains. They had heaped the straight, narrow bed with covers, pillows, and a worn tapestry. An elaborate iron lantern rested on a table, already lit, and a small vase of flowers stood on the windowsill. From the sweet scent of the reeds underfoot I knew they had just changed them and sprinkled them with summer herbs.

"Ma'am—Your Majesty," one of the daughters said, pushing open the door slowly to peek in. "Is there anything else you desire for your comfort?"

Her face was pure summer—tanned, glowing, blue-eyed as the flowers of the field. Two long blond braids fell over her shoulders.

"What is your name, child?" I asked.

"Eurwen," she said.

"Do you know what it means?" I asked.

"My mother says it means 'gold and fair.'" Her voice was tremulous. I realized that I must frighten her.

*Welsh gold.* "She was right to name you that," I assured her. I held out my arms. "Here, take hold of my hands." Cautiously she approached, then held her palms out, but kept her elbows close to her body. I took her little hands and squeezed them. "I thank you for your hospitality," I said. "Please do not be afraid of me. For I assure you, I am more afraid of you than you are of me."

She hung her head and giggled.

"Oh, it's true," I said. "When you think of me, remember how hard it is for me to meet strangers all the time. You do it so seldom. And I hope now we are friends and not strangers." I released her hands. "You have made me feel so welcome. Did you gather those flowers yourself?"

She nodded solemnly. "I tried to find yellow ones but I could only get white and blue."

"My favorite colors!" I told her. "I will love looking at them." I wished I had something to give her, but what little I had come away with had already been dispensed. "You asked me if I needed anything else. No, I have all I want here. But if you want to give me a gift, and let me give you one in exchange, could you allow me to become your godmother? I have many godchildren, and I can assure you they are all special to me."

"Oh . . . yes," she said, her blue eyes widening. She did not know what to make of it. That amused me, since everyone at court constantly jockeyed to see if I would consent to be their children's godmother.

"Very well then," I said. "From now on you shall call me Godmother Elizabeth, or if you want to be very grand, Godmother Queen. And I shall add Elizabeth to your name. . . . Oh, but it should be the Welsh Elizabeth. What is that?"

"Bethan," she said.

"Then Eurwen Bethan you shall be to me," I promised her.

After she slipped out, closing the door as quietly as she could, I made ready for bed. I needed no attendant to undress or prepare me; this was simplicity itself. How much of my life was layered in extraneous wrappings? It was head-spinning to be free of them, like a moth escaping from a cumbersome, confining cocoon.

I crawled into the rigid bed, as strict and straight as a nun's pallet. The daylight was fading into a deep blue, and night creeping up like a mist. I could hear Essex laughing and talking with his relatives in the other room. Doubtless he would go on until midnight. I had pretended they needed time together, but the truth was I needed to sleep.

Let him regale his hosts with his feats and tales until the nightingales sang.

Gradually the room darkened, and through the window I could see the first stars pop out in the sky. His feats and tales . . . What were they? Time was passing. He was twenty-seven, soon to be twenty-eight.

At twenty-eight I had been Queen for three years already. My father had been King for ten years. Of course, there were people who came into prominence later—Burghley was thirty-seven before I appointed him my secretary of state. My father did very little of lasting fame for the first twenty years of his reign, until he was in his thirties. But Essex was impatient, fretting like a horse kept in a stall.

A horse. Henri IV had described Robert as one needing a bridle more than a spur. He was correct. Essex was eager to gallop off to glory, but he had no destination.

# 35

he morning light came early here, and the simple room had no curtains. I awoke to see the clouds separate their milky white from the colorless sky that came just before dawn. Then, gradually, the sky became infused with blue tint, and day was here.

I had slept better than I did on my palace bed, but that may have been due to extreme fatigue. After each of his labors, Hercules undoubtedly slept very soundly. And now another long but exciting day awaited me. We would venture into Wales itself, and I would behold the land where the Tudors originated. We traced our lineage back to a twelfth-century prince, Rhys ap Gruffydd, but the family entered English history when my great-great-grandfather Owen Tudor took up with Henry V's French widow, Catherine Valois. Owen had been lurking as her valet, and at some point they became lovers and married secretly, or the other way around. It was in Wales that my grandfather landed to assert his right to the throne after being exiled in Brittany, risking all on one throw of the stone. That was ever our way. So far we had won every throw.

I arose and went to the window, looking out at the mist enveloping the valleys and mountains, swirling like smoke. The Devereux family, on the other hand, seemed to have lost every throw. All the more reason for them to keep rolling the dice. It brought to mind something Suetonius had written about Octavius Caesar—that he kept losing naval battles but figured someday he would win, so he kept betting on himself. And he had, too, finally defeating Antony and Cleopatra at Actium.

The noise in the house signaled that everyone was up. Our hosts graciously provided us with tart ale, fresh green cheese, and hard biscuits to send us on our way. I thanked them effusively and embraced little Eurwen, whispering, "Be sure to send me messages of how you do. I expect all my godchildren to give me reports." And to her mother I said, "I am privileged to share your daughter with you," when she tried saying they were not worthy and so on.

Essex was impatient to be gone, and they were probably also impatient to have us gone. A royal visit is always a strain, I knew, much as I would have it otherwise. The guards mounted up behind us and we set out, the rising sun behind us, down into the mist in the waiting valley.

The sun would burn it off later, but for now the dew made the green even more intense, almost glowing in its brightness. The path was slow going; I did not mind, as it gave me a chance to truly see the flowers dotting the meadows and the butterflies fluttering slowly above them. Very few people were about, only some shepherds, visible from a distance.

Suddenly from behind me a horn sounded, and the cry "Your Majesty! Your Majesty!" One of the guards rushed forward, spurring his horse on the tricky terrain. "There's a message!" I halted and waited for him; close behind him was the other guard, and a rider on a froth-streaked horse.

The startling suddenness of it made my heart race. How had they found me? Where had the man ridden from?

He pulled up and swept off his hat in the customary obeisance, then cried, "There's been an attack! The Spanish have landed!"

Essex had turned around, and he reined his horse up beside us. "What? What?" he said.

"The Spanish have made a landing in Cornwall," the man panted. "At least four ships, and many troops. They've burned Penzance, sacked some other towns—I rode here as fast as I could to find you. Robert Cecil only knew that you were heading toward Shrewsbury."

I had left him a sealed letter with my itinerary, vague though it was. I had to be reachable. It was a fantasy that I could be free.

"You have done well." I thanked God that I had left the itinerary and that the man had tracked me down. "Have more ships been sighted? Have there been other landings?"

"There are more ships, but as to other landings, I do not know. The beacon fires have been lit along the coast, and troops are mobilizing."

"I will return to London immediately." For an instant I looked across the beckoning hills of Wales, feeling all that the country meant to me, that now I could not visit. But I was a queen again, a warrior whose land was under attack, not a pilgrim, and I must make haste.

The Spanish! Their boots had tramped on English soil, something they had not managed to do even with the mighty Armada. How many of them were there? Four ships full of soldiers—that could be hundreds.

They had struck while my back was turned. Had they known? But no, that was impossible. My journey had been undertaken on a whim, and the ships had left Spain some time ago.

"To London!" I cried.

---

We were a long way from London, too far to get back in a day, or even three days. After the first fast gallop, we had to slow our pace. Our leisurely journey now ran backward; we rushed over the same paths without stopping to savor our surroundings. Past Wollaston and the redoubtable Old Parr; past Shrewsbury, unable to linger at the site where Henry "Hotspur" Percy had been defeated by Henry IV; quickly through Wolverhampton, where another decisive battle, this one between Saxons and Danes five hundred years earlier than Hotspur, had taken place, with the Saxons winning. Our land was dotted with such turning points. Let not someone later point to Penzance as one!

At length Essex halted and said, "It will soon be dark, and we have been traveling at a killing pace for what seems forever. We need a good rest, better than what we've gotten on the road the last two days, and so do our horses. We should stop at Drayton Bassett, only a few miles ahead." He paused. "The house is empty now."

At first I shook my head. I had no wish to spend a night under Lettice's roof no matter how far away she was.

"Please reconsider," he said. "It is the most sensible thing to do. There are stables, food, and care for the horses, and an entire house at our disposal. I promise no disturbances."

The thought of availing myself of any of her hospitality was repulsive. But the house was also Essex's. And he was right—we badly needed a good place to stop, a place with resources and no fluttering family to ask questions. We were in no mood to entertain or be entertained. Finally I agreed.

"I'll go ahead and be waiting at the house," he said. "Open it up and air it out, send the skeleton staff out for supplies." Without waiting for my reply, he wheeled around and cantered off.

The light was already failing, and the weak bodily part of me welcomed the knowledge that there would be a comfortable place to rest; the Queen resented the place itself. My attendants and I picked our way there, having to ask directions in the unfamiliar surroundings. By the time we reached it, it was full dark, and the long driveway leading to the house was ominous with its dense alley of trees, making it impossible to glimpse the house itself until you were almost upon it.

It was mostly darkened, but a few windows showed the faint glow of candles. We dismounted, and true to his word, Essex had stable hands to take the horses, and he himself stood in the doorway of the house to welcome us, his tall frame filling the entrance.

"Welcome to Drayton Bassett," he said.

We stepped inside, finding ourselves in a stone entrance hallway. Even in high summer, it was chilly. He led us into the winter parlor, through the entrance porch. In spite of the fine Turkish carpets, the house had a fortress-like atmosphere.

"Most of the furniture is put away," he said. "The house is not much used now. But I'll uncover these chairs, and the bedchambers are ready. You"—he nodded to the guards—"will stay in the adjoining wing with the rest of the staff. That part of the house, at least, is never closed up. As for you, my dear Majesty, I have allotted you the finest room in the house. It was my father's, and kept as it was ever since."

How diplomatic of him, knowing that I would never sleep in his mother's chamber. I nodded.

"I myself will occupy my usual chamber."

And where was that? I wondered. But I did not ask in front of the guards.

---

The supper laid out for us was plain but abundant, exactly what we needed. Thick loaves of bread, hearty hunks of Staffordshire cheese, pears and apples from the estate orchards, gooseberry sauce, and smoked venison filled our grumbling bellies, and the French claret soothed our troubled heads.

The guards politely withdrew, leaving Essex and me utterly alone at the long table. The candelabra between our places made a blaze of light in an otherwise dark surrounding. The candles had burned halfway down and were dripping on the table.

Oppressed with anxiety, I said, "Philip said he would spend every coin he had, down to the last socket of his candlestick, to defeat me. He is a man true to his word."

"Yes, unfortunately. Or 'fixated' would be a better description. He is obsessed with conquering England. And he will not admit defeat."

"He seems to have infinite resources to commit to our ruin."

"Most of them he has wasted, and they lie at the bottom of the sea."

I shivered. It was not just the odd cold in the room. "I pray we get back to London in time to direct our defense." I paused. "Although there are trustworthy and competent men already there—Admiral Howard, for one." I was deeply sorry now that Drake, Hawkins, and Raleigh were so far away.

He gave a grunt of dismissal. "The man has no vision," he said.

"He has common sense, something of great value in battle."

"Ummm." He dabbed at his mouth with his napkin, preoccupied.

I thought enviously of my father's reign. He had only had to fend off paper attacks from the pope; no foreigner had dared to actually invade the realm. But now this wretched Spaniard kept us perpetually in his sights; everywhere I looked he tried to thwart me. He, of course, could say the same about me.

I rose. "I am going to bed," I said.

He rose as well. "I will follow soon." He came around the table. "Let me show you back to your room." He guided me up the main staircase and to the third door on my left. Reverently he pushed it open. Inside several candles flickered on their stand, and the bed-curtains were pulled back. "If you need a fire, it is laid already. I must tell you that there is no one else in this wing, but I know you will have no trouble lighting it. I myself will be just next door." He let that sink in. No people. Himself with only a wall between us.

"Thank you," I said. "You are always my good host."

He nodded. "And you always my honored guest." He took my hand, raised it to his lips.

He left me. I closed the door softly behind him, enclosing myself within. He had tried to allow for my comfort, setting out washing water, a tray of sweetmeats, a bottle of sweet wine. I picked it up and looked at its label—*vino vernaccia*. One of the wines for which I had granted him the monopoly. I poured out a small glass and savored its deep, honeyed taste. I sipped it in front of the fireplace, with its applewood logs crisscrossed over kindling, waiting to be lit.

I took one of the candles and went about the room, looking. Looking to keep myself from thinking, as if action would blot out the strong, disturbing urges stealing around the corners of my consciousness. Here, on the wall: a portrait. I peered closer. It was Walter Devereux, Essex's late father, staring back at me. It must have been painted when he was very young. His eyes were direct and his high brow shining, as if he looked into the future hoping for good fortune. But Ireland had destroyed him, as it had so many other good men.

Ireland . . . What would Grace O'Malley do if she were I? How would she deal with the Spanish? How would she deal with the young man in the next room?

She would fight one and ravish the other. Or was that just my fancy?

Ireland. I turned again to the portrait of poor, doomed Walter. And next to it I saw the telltale nail, and shadowed spot, where the matching portrait of Lettice had been removed.

Essex was seeing to my comfort, indeed.

Lettice. I had not allowed myself to dwell on her or think about her. The thought of the promiscuous woman and her two promiscuous daughters outraged me. She cut a swath through the men of her station and, like the proverbial cat, kept landing on her feet. Or should I say in bed?

And her son is just two doors down. . . . A man thirty-three years my junior. Waiting in there. Waiting for me?

He can wait forever. He cannot expect any more from me than I have already given. I have spoiled him beyond reason. But never have I bestowed anything inappropriate.

*No one else here, no one nearby. No one to see what you do. Privacy beyond anything you ever imagined. You will never have another opportunity like this. Never again.*

God be thanked. We ask him not to lead us into temptation. I am human, and do not know my own weaknesses. I do not want to find their limits.

*Ah, but you are past the marriage game, past the point where you can be touched by scandal. The Catholics have always called you an incestuous bastard, child of a notorious courtesan, and your enemies have said you were unchaste. They can think no worse of you and will continue to make up lies. And your supporters will refuse to believe any scandal about the Virgin Queen.*

The Virgin Queen. The curious Virgin Queen. Do I truly want to go to my grave never even knowing what it is I have turned my back on? Do I not feel cheated in the deepest sense?

*Especially if no one would ever know.*

But Essex talks. He is a gossip.

*I can deny it. Whom will they believe?*

If only something could be done and then immediately erased, made not to exist. As we can taste a piece of pastry and then spit it out without swallowing it. But this is not like that. Once done it is done forever.

I stood trembling before the candlestand, breathing deeply. Which took more courage—to open the door and seek him out or to keep it shut? For many long minutes I stood. Then I walked slowly toward the door. I reached out, touched the cold latch. It was just a simple thing to lift it and walk through the door. I raised my wrist, and at the feel of the weight of the latch I dropped it. It was too great a deed.

I stepped back. The door would stay shut.

---

I slept as one drugged, and perhaps I was—by the scare of the Spanish, by the days of hard riding outdoors, by the last decision. But in the darkest hour of night, I awoke.

It took a moment for me to remember where I was, the bed I was lying in. I pulled back the bed-curtains. The air in the chamber was cold, and there was no hint of light from the windows. All time was suspended; whatever happened now, in this place, for the next few hours, before day came and re-created the real world, was as a dream, insubstantial and unsubstantiated.

Just then I heard a noise through the wall. He was moving about in there. He, too, was awake. I had been given another chance to decide, better now than if I had gone earlier. I could knock gently on the wall and he would come to me in silence. By mutual consent, we would not speak. Speaking would make it real, and this must not be allowed to be real. It would be no more real than the monster in Llangorse Lake, than Merlin's cave. In the morning it would cease to exist, would evaporate like the Welsh mist. Robert Devereux, my Robin, the Earl of Essex, was himself made of Welsh mist.

Another slight noise from the other side of the wall. He was listening, waiting for a signal from me. I could feel it. I tensed, knowing that if I made any noise myself, he would come in. I held my breath, holding myself rigid, lest I move and send a mistaken message. But what message was the mistaken one? The thought of the moment passing unfulfilled was so sad I did not think I could bear it. Surely, surely—I let out a sigh. Immediately I heard him change his posture, become alert. He had picked up the scent, like a hunting animal.

It was a scent he had undoubtedly picked up many times in his life.

No, I could not be one of many. I would not become just one of his women.

I was unique in his life, and thus it must remain.

I sank back down into the pillows, and let the flap of the bed-curtain fall. The rings made soft clicking noises, and he must have heard them.

---

The next morning, dressed and ready, I emerged from the room. He was standing before his door, pulling on his gloves. He looked at me piercingly. "Good morrow," he said. "I trust you rested well? Were you comfortable?"

"Entirely so," I assured him. "Knowing you were right next door was so reassuring I slept soundly all night through."

"I kept awake in case you needed anything," he said.

"That was thoughtful of you," I said. "But you had foreseen all my needs so carefully that there was nothing left unfulfilled."

"Well, one can never be sure," he said. "I did not wish to take any chances."

"Or miss any," I said.

I was ever the realist, sometimes to my sorrow. But seldom to my regret.

# 36

I expected London to be in an uproar. We finally reached it late at night; all the gates were closed fast and guarded. The watchmen cried out joyfully when they saw it was I, saying, "God be praised! The Queen is here!" We passed through quickly, I to Whitehall, Robert to Essex House. The streets were eerily quiet.

My first wild thought was to order the Cecils to attend upon me immediately. But the palace was asleep; it was long past midnight. Soon it would be dawn, and I could summon them. If I could manage a few hours' rest before then, my thinking would be clearer.

As soon as it was light, I sent for them, and for Knollys and Hunsdon as well. They did not fail me, appearing within the hour. I ordered ale and bread for them, as well as cushions for their seats. Only one of the four still had brown hair; the other three heads were as white as ermine.

"I returned as quickly as I could," I said. "Thanks be to your resourcefulness, Robert, in sending a messenger who found me."

Robert Cecil smiled and passed a hand over his trim beard. He never gave the impression that he looked for praise, but he brooded, so I was told, if he felt passed over. I wondered, not for the first time, how difficult life was for him with his short stature.

"It was prudent of Your Majesty to leave us your whereabouts," said his father. "Of course, finding you was like searching for one grouse in the heather all over Scotland." His voice was faint, as if the muscles in his chest did not have the strength to force it out. His gouty leg was propped up on a stool, and every time he moved, he winced, his breath whistling out into his wispy beard.

"I see it is all quiet here," I said. "I thought to find it otherwise, so I am relieved. Give me your reports of the action in Cornwall. I assume that men and arms have been dispatched, and the Channel patrolled?"

"Yes, we took that liberty, the Privy Council acting on its legal authority," said Hunsdon. "They report that the Spanish, who had sailed over from their stronghold in Brittany, departed quickly, although they caused great damage during the time they trampled on our land, burning and pillaging up and down the tip of Cornwall. Mousehole was destroyed, its people homeless now, and Newlyn and Penzance were sacked. No ships were sighted beyond the four that landed. But some of the householders, outraged at the attack, managed to capture a lone Spanish soldier. They trussed him up and delivered him to our officers. He's here now in London, and a little gentle persuasion has convinced him to tell us the bigger Spanish plans."

"Richard Topcliffe's persuasion?" I asked. The chief interrogator who operated his torture machinery at the Tower was known as an unfailing source of information. The Privy Council had the authority to approve torture if necessary.

"Possibly," said Knollys, his face red. As a good Puritan, he must have found ordering torture difficult to align with his conscience.

"Well, what did he tell us?" I burst out. "Do not be so coy!"

"He claims that his master the Spanish king is outfitting his new Armada, readying it to sail next summer. This one will be much more formidable than the first. They can now match us in firepower and gunner's skill."

"God curse that man!" I cried. "His money is endless, whereas ours—" I felt helpless anger tear through me. He was rich, rich, rich, drowning in gold and silver from his looted native mines in America, a never-ending well of it. An entire lost Armada had only caused him to thank God that he could afford to build another, whereas it would have bankrupted my entire kingdom. He could keep coming at us, and coming at us, and we could never bleed him dry. Thrift and skill and bravery and advanced ship design and better training availed us nothing; outperforming the Spanish still did not put us ahead, as they could always outspend us. I had started selling my inherited lands and even some Crown jewels, but that was a feather in the scales compared to what we really needed.

The door flung open, banging on each side, and Essex stood there, legs spread wide. "Why was I not sent for?" he cried.

"Essex! Hold your temper! This is not a full council meeting," I said. "I am only being given the first report of what has happened in my absence. Seat yourself."

"The Spanish made a brief landing," said Robert Cecil, sitting as tall as he could, glaring at Essex, distaste written all over his face. "Short but destructive. They caused great damage on the southwestern tip of Cornwall. A captured soldier has revealed that a new Armada is well advanced in its planning."

"I knew it!" Essex said, leaping up again and slapping his hands together. "I knew it. They are lurking in Cádiz or Lisbon like a spider, building their ships, plotting."

"The Spanish are always plotting, my boy," said old Burghley. "That alone means nothing. We have to look at their actions."

Essex's eyes narrowed. "Do not call me boy, old man!"

Now I turned on him. "My Lord Essex, have you not slept enough since your return? For you are as tetchy as a bear just out of hibernation."

"I've slept well enough," he muttered.

"Raleigh is back," said Hunsdon. "We should call him in."

"What did he find?" Oh, if only it *were* El Dorado. If only we had our own source of gold to match Spain's.

"Some ores—perhaps gold—no one is sure," said Hunsdon.

"But it wasn't refined gold," said Knollys. "The Indians have kept their source secret."

"Has there been any word of Drake and Hawkins?" I asked.

"We all invested in that venture and are eager for its success, but so far there's been no word," said Robert Cecil.

"The days when the Spanish outposts in America were easy pickings are gone. Drake and Hawkins, unfortunately, taught them how to protect their assets, and they took the lesson," said Hunsdon. "And there's something else, too, the obliging Spanish gentleman told us. This Armada will be different. They will use the Irish against us, as we used the Dutch against them. They would say it is yet another tactic they learned from us."

"They'll land there with troops and men, as well as harrying our coasts. Ireland is our back door, and they mean to come in that way," said Knollys.

"Oh, God!" Not Ireland, where I already had an unrest on my hands, led by a native hero. Was *I* cursed?

"So the rebellion of O'Neill is part of it?" asked Essex. "The Earl of Tyrone, that blackguard!"

I had proclaimed the Earl of Tyrone, a false ally, a serpent who had turned on us, a traitor earlier this summer. Hugh O'Neill, a man who had been brought up in English households, who had received his title from me, had reverted to his wild Irish roots, been anointed as high chieftain of the O'Neill clan, taking the formal, forbidden title of The O'Neill in ancient rites in an old stone chair in an open field at Tullaghoge in Ulster, and joined forces with another rebel and sworn enemy of England, Hugh Roe O'Donnell.

"Our lord deputy in Ireland, Sir William Russell, seems at a loss as to how to combat these slippery chieftains," said old Burghley.

"Ireland!" cried Essex. "That sinkhole of treachery, that land of bogs and rebels, that robbed me of my father!"

"They did not ask to be English," said Robert Cecil pointedly. "Nor do they want to be English, so they would call themselves patriots rather than rebels. We, after all, would fight to the last man if the Spanish attempted the same to us. In fact, that is what this meeting is about—making sure that does not happen to us."

I thought of Grace O'Malley and her list of grievances against us, many of them well founded. Cecil spoke true. Was Grace a "traitor"? In fairness I could hardly brand her so.

"You speak as if you sympathize with them," growled Essex. "Anyone who takes their side is a traitor to Her Majesty's government!"

"If your father had not died there, would you be so adamant about that? Your personal loss—"

"I owe them a death! I owe them many deaths!"

"Make sure it is not your own," said Hunsdon. "We want as few deaths as possible."

"Back to the Spanish," said Knollys impatiently, "the wellspring of our troubles. Without them, the Irish would not be dangerous to us. O'Neill is appealing to Spain on religious grounds, for, among their other failings, the Irish cling to the popish superstition."

"When they aren't practicing their native superstitions," said Hunsdon. "A lot of moonlit rites, fairies, and such." He shuddered.

"Call Raleigh here. We want a full report about his expedition, and what he's found. Tell him to bring his ores, or whatever they are," said Robert Cecil. "We need to consult with him about this new Armada, and how we can counter it."

"Why are his ideas any better than ours?" asked Essex.

"Because he's an adventurer and has had lots of firsthand experience with Spaniards. He's just come from their territory," said Robert Cecil.

"And because you are dazzled by him," snorted Essex.

"As you, without the goods, wish us to be by you," muttered Hunsdon. Only I was near enough to hear him.

---

My head was spinning. Everything seemed to be moving so quickly I had the sensation of standing on a tilting board. I sent for Raleigh straightway and prepared to hear his tale and, when that was done, to plumb his mind for our next step against Spain. We would meet privately in my inner chamber. While I waited, I forced myself to read the dispatches and petitions that had accumulated during my brief absence.

While I was shuffling through the papers, a message arrived from Raleigh. Could I possibly come to him? He had objects to show me privately that he could not transport to Whitehall. I was just as relieved to get out of the palace.

His residence, Durham House, lay near Whitehall, a bit downstream. They were so close I need not bother with a boat but could walk, flanked by my guards. It was a fine residence, a mansion whose turrets rose almost out of the water.

The spacious ground floor was gleaming but empty, and I was shown up to his turret room, climbing a winding staircase to reach at last the door that opened into his secluded study. Inside, he was waiting, a native of Guiana beside him.

"Welcome home, Sir Walter," I said, taking him in. He looked ravaged—his face gaunt and sun blasted, his body thinner by half, or so it seemed. His voluminous breeches could not hide the shrunken frame within them. "It was a hard voyage?" I asked, saving him the trouble of explaining.

He knelt, his movements still agile. "Indeed it was, but it was the voyage of a lifetime."

"Rise," I said. "What did you find? You went looking for El Dorado."

"I found a country as virgin as the Garden of Eden," he said. "Utterly untouched. It is a thing of fragile splendor, filled with plants and animals unknown to us, growing peacefully. Waiting for us, as it were."

"Waiting for us?"

"Waiting for us to reach out and pluck them. I have brought some home to show, for no one would believe me otherwise."

"I gather there are people there as well? Is he one?" I indicated the motionless man.

"Yes, he is the son of a chief, a *cassique*. His father was eager for him to return with us. At the same time, two of our boys were so taken with the New World that they decided to stay."

"Not Dudley's boy?" Robert Dudley's son and namesake was among those who had signed up for the voyage. The thought of his remaining there was displeasing to me.

"No." Raleigh shook his head. "He is much like his father, interested only in the world he already knows." His tone managed to convey his disdain for such people.

The world we already knew. From Raleigh's high turret window I could see the river shining in the sun as it rounded its bend for Westminster. Across it the gentle green hills of Surrey rose in the distance. Fluffy clouds floated over the fields. The world we knew was sweet enough, and I must preserve it.

"Did you find gold?" I blurted out. "I need not ask, for had you done so, you would have presented it first thing."

He coughed. Clearly he was still recovering. "We found a place where gold can be mined, along with abandoned metalworking tools," he said. "We did not want to start digging, as the river was rising fearfully and would have trapped us. But we marked where it was. And we've brought back ores." He presented a box brimming with rough rocks. "And here, look at these stones." He hoisted another box, this one filled with dull stones of various shapes and hues. "We found these lying in open fields, waiting to be picked up. We think they are sapphires and diamonds, but they and the ores will have to be examined here by assayers."

Neither of these samples might prove worth anything. Certainly they would not repay the cost of having sent the expedition. The stockholders, including the Cecils, would howl at being cheated.

All this time the Indian was standing stiffly. "Are you going to let him move?" I said. "Tell me of his tribe."

"Let me tell you how I found him." He moved to a table and unrolled a map.

"Pray be brief," I said. "You can explain at length to the other holders in the company."

He looked disappointed. "First, I must say this fine virgin land should be claimed by England."

"I already have one Virginia. Persuade me I need another."

"This region abounds in beauty and resources. The flatlands are covered in jungle, crisscrossed by rivers in the delta, lush beyond words. Let me show you one of the birds—the forest is full of these creatures, with vivid plumage such as we have never seen here." He picked up a cage from the floor and held it aloft. Inside were several small birds with an array of feather colors—turquoise, elixir green, sulfur yellow. "There are much larger ones. Imagine the trees filled with them! And growing directly on the ground near the riverbanks are these fruits." He showed me a shrunken one, an oblong object covered in hexagonal segments, with a bristly crown of spiky leaves. In picking it up, I pricked my finger. "Here, taste the dried flesh," he urged me, handing me a plate of yellowish chunks. I bit into one and it was very sweet. "Better than sugar," he said. "And the fresh ones, juicy and tender. I regret I can only present this mummified specimen."

"Have you named it?"

"Yes, the name 'pineapple' seems most fitting, as it looks like a huge pinecone."

Something stirred in a corner, too slow for a mouse.

"Allow me to present another denizen of this exotic country," he said, scooping up a grayish creature that looked like a huge locust. He put it on a table, where it rolled up into a ball. Proudly he tapped on it, and it made a metallic ring. "The Spanish call them *armadillos*—'little armored ones.'"

"I know what *armada*, and all its derivatives, means," I snapped. "I suppose they serve Philip?"

"If you claim this area of Guiana, they shall serve *you*," he responded. "Perhaps we can train them to attack."

I laughed. "An army that rolls up into balls? What would that do?"

"Roll underfoot and cause the enemy to trip?"

I could not help being amused. "Very well, Walter, you have entertained me more mightily than any play or concert. But tell me more specifically of your exploration." I nodded to the chair. "We may sit." I could see he needed to.

Gratefully he sank down onto it. "We spent a month on shore. The Orinoco delta is very wide, but none of the rivers flowing through it are deep, so we had to leave the largest ship behind and proceed in barges and wherries. I took about a hundred men. It was in the delta that we found the mine equipment, abandoned by Spanish workers whom we surprised."

"So the Spanish know of it?"

"Yes, they are also looking for gold. The natives hate them," he added quickly. "They welcomed us as enemies of the Spanish."

"The Indians were friendly and helpful?"

"Indeed they were, acting as guides and taking us to villages where we could get food. For as rich as the jungle was, it was hard to feed ourselves from it. The animals are swift and well hidden in the foliage and shadows, and unless you want to eat leaves, there is little on the trees to sustain you." He paused. "As lovely as it is, it is not a healthy place, and festers in heat and damp. Many became ill, and we were glad to leave the jungle behind for the uplands. We followed the Orinoco—sometimes it was thirty miles wide—until it joined the Caroní. There we found the abandoned Spanish anchor my informant in Trinidad had described, confirming his story. We were elated. Once we were on the Caroní, we were told there were silver mines nearby, so we broke up into reconnaissance parties. One group surveyed the river, another set out to find the mines and any minerals, and my group sought the source of a pall of smoke hanging over the land. It turned out to be a series of dazzlingly high waterfalls. And all around them, what I can only describe as heavenly country—the Garden of Eden I told you about. Altogether we penetrated some three hundred miles into the heart of Spain's colonial empire."

"What about the silver mines?" I persisted.

"We pinpointed their whereabouts," he said.

"But you did not actually find them?"

"No," he admitted.

"What about El Dorado?"

"The chief of the village, Cassique Topiawari, knew of it. Did I tell you he is over a hundred years old, and has seen much? He said it lay at the foot of the highlands, many days' journey hence. The inhabitants were fierce warriors; it would need a huge army to conquer them, certainly more than we had. On our next voyage, we can take adequate forces, and of course our guns will give us the advantage, but—"

"You haven't found El Dorado," I said flatly. "You haven't even seen it. All you have is an old chief's word for it." I held up my hands, silencing him as he prepared to argue. "I am resigned to the disappointing news. But you had best practice delivering it to the shareholders, who were expecting better return on their investment."

"Just owning the country would repay us a hundred, a thousandfold."

"In what? Armadillos and pineapples? Interesting curiosities, but they do not finance wars against Spain."

"Allow me to present Topiawari's son, who has been waiting patiently." He turned quickly and put his arm across the man's shoulder. "He is eager to meet the great *cassique* of the north, Ezrabeta Cassipuna Acarewana, in whose name I made my voyage."

The man stepped forward. Clearly he could understand the words. He bowed his head. He had the darkest, straightest hair I had ever seen, which even in the dim light shone like polished stone. It was bound with a headband woven with feathers bright as jewels. He was wrapped in a cloak also patterned in the feathers and looked as majestic as any European prince.

"Welcome, prince of Guiana," I said. "Small wonder you do not search for gems, when you can pluck such beauty freely from birds of the air to adorn yourselves."

He bowed again. "I come, I see great *cassique*." A grin spread across his handsome face.

"Are all the tribesmen this fetching?" I asked Raleigh.

"In the villages we visited, yes. In the delta they retreat into tree houses when the water rises; on higher ground they have huts and cabins. They are a jolly people, always laughing, and seem content. But then, as I have said—"

"Yes, they live in the Garden of Eden."

"Other tribes, though, they say are different. On a farther branch of the Caroní there is a tribe called the Ewaipanoma with eyes in their shoulders and mouths in their chests."

I laughed. "And you believe this?" I looked at the native visitor to see if the tribal name had sparked his interest. "True? Ewaipanoma?" I encircled my eyes and then indicated my shoulders. He nodded vigorously. But perhaps he had been trained to entertain Europeans with such tales. And Raleigh, like all adventurers, had enough of the boy still in him to credit the possibility. "What of the Amazons? Aren't they supposed to live along the river named after them?"

The man said, "Yes. Women. Strong. Once a year, warriors go. The women choose. Spend time of one moon. Men give jade, then leave. Baby boys, women send back to warriors. Girls keep, make strong. Grow up, also warriors. Next year, come again. More babies."

"Have you gone to the Amazons?" I asked him.

"No. Never seen."

Once again, a marvel that no one could verify. Perhaps the whole land was that way, a Garden of Eden indeed, vanishing upon closer inspection.

"You should have brought me an Amazon, Walter," I teased him. "I should like to see this wonder."

"*You* are the great woman warrior, our Amazon," he said, diplomatically. "It is you who smashed the Armada."

"Only acting through my admirals and my sailors," I said tartly. That was a truth that hurt.

"Your admirals and your sailors *are* you," he insisted.

"Alas, Walter, you have returned only to find the shadow of another Armada hanging over us. Rest now, and this afternoon come to Whitehall for our emergency meeting concerning this." I smiled, to make it seem less grim and pressing. "Welcome back to England."

# 37

Late afternoon, and we had convened in the council chamber. I looked up and down the table. The row of men on either side had divided themselves not according to age but according to politics. The bold ones—Howard, Raleigh, Essex, and Hunsdon—sat on the right; the cautious ones—the Cecils, Knollys, and Whitgift—on the left.

"The report, if you please," I said crisply. I remained standing at the head of the table.

Admiral Howard duly read what everyone already knew about the quick Spanish raid and departure. His sober expression made his already long face look stretched by invisible weights.

Old Burghley announced the confession of the Spanish prisoner and the specific plans of Philip for yet another attempt on us next summer.

"Does anyone have any other intelligence?" I asked.

Young Cecil stood up to unfold a map. Even standing, he seemed smaller than the seated men. "The shipyards are located here"—he touched a spot on the Spanish coast—"as well as here"—he touched another. "Our informants tell us that construction is proceeding on schedule and the ships are half built already."

"*My* informants tell me the Spanish are having difficulty procuring enough seasoned timbers," said Essex.

The two rival Roberts could compete in their intelligence services. Whatever one said, the other would contradict. The truth probably lay somewhere in between.

"Thank you, gentlemen," I said. "Now, as to our strategy, I would like everyone's recommendation." I nodded to Raleigh. "You may begin, Sir Walter, having just come from Spanish territories."

Raleigh now stood, and young Cecil quickly sat down rather than stand. I noticed that he avoided height comparisons whenever possible, preferring his contests to be on memos and documents, which could be equal size.

"I shall present my full report in a separate meeting, in respect to you investors," he said. In other words, he would postpone the bad news. We were not here to judge his voyage, so he was spared. "I have seen the Spanish improvements firsthand," he said. "I encountered their ships in Trinidad, and fought against the fortifications of Port of Spain and Fort San Joseph. I can tell you that they are now our equals in engineering and strength."

The faces up and down the table were set in glum acceptance. Several nodded.

"But that does not mean we must sit placidly and wait to be attacked," he continued. "When we see a snake hatching, we do not wait for it to emerge, but kill it in the egg. We should swoop down and attack the Spanish before they have a chance to sail here."

"We need Drake and Hawkins for that," said Burghley.

"The last time Drake led one of his raids, it was a dismal failure," snapped Essex. "Remember Lisbon in 1589?"

"Yes, but I also remember Cádiz in 1587 and the Armada in 1588. He is the most experienced in this type of action."

"He isn't here!" cried Essex. "And that's that! What, shall we sit on our hands and wait for him? When he sailed away in 1577 he was gone for almost three years! We can do without him!"

"Young Essex is right," said Admiral Howard. "We do not have the luxury of waiting. I suggest we attack as soon as possible, striking Cádiz again. It is their premier ocean port, and injuring it will hurt them both commercially and militarily."

"We will have to exercise extreme secrecy," said Hunsdon. "Not a word of this can leak out. Drake"—he glared at Essex—"was superb in being able to surprise the enemy. The Spanish did not know he was approaching until they saw his sails. But if we advertise ourselves . . ." His voice trailed off with the warning.

"The larger our fleet, the harder it will be to disguise ourselves," said the admiral. "But we need the strength of numbers if we are to damage the enemy. Sometimes Drake did not have enough men," he admitted. "Often strength and stealth are incompatible."

Raleigh stood. "When we get close in hand-to-hand fighting, there is a new weapon we can use that will shock them."

"Guns with improved aim?" asked Hunsdon. "None of them now are worth a piss. Half the time they explode in your face rather than the enemy's."

"Just as deadly, and utterly silent." He took a small jar and put it on the table, then pulled a quill from his pouch and dipped it in the jar. Last he removed a trembling mouse from a wrapping in the pouch, held it, and stuck the quill into its rump. The mouse squealed. "Now watch," said Raleigh. He put the mouse on the floor.

"Sir, do not loose a mouse in here, to run off and breed!" I said. Had the man no sense?

"He won't get far," said Raleigh.

Everyone turned his chair to watch. The mouse ran a few steps and then quivered. Next it halted and then fell over on its side. Raleigh picked it up. It was still breathing but paralyzed. "The Indians call it arrow poison. They get it from frogs and certain plants. It is deadly poison, and is most economical to use, as only a minute amount is required to fell the enemy. The paralysis soon turns to death." He flipped the now-dead mouse back to the floor. "I brought back barrels of it. It can take care of a whole Spanish garrison."

"But of course, as always in such things, the danger is in wounding yourself with it. How can we keep it utterly safe?" asked Cecil.

"Guns and cannons explode, too. War is full of accidents. But this would strike terror into the enemy, as it is such a gruesome way to die."

"We can add it to the arsenal, but I would not make it the first line of defense," said the admiral. "Now, as to the planning, is everyone agreed that we must take the fight to Spain? Is there anyone who wants to be defensive only, rather than offensive?"

"If we strengthened ourselves at home, improved our own fortifications, and expanded our fleet, there is little chance they could harm us, no matter how big their Armada," said Burghley. "An Armada must find a landing place, and those on our south coast we can defend, as we did in 1588."

"But they do have a landing place," said Hunsdon. "Ireland."

Ireland. The use of Ireland changed everything.

"True, and that could be our undoing," admitted Knollys.

"Then . . . it is to Spain we go?" cried Essex. "Down the Atlantic coast, then turn and hit the soft southern underbelly of the enemy?"

"Aye, and we'll turn Philip back into the king of figs and oranges, like the old-time kings of Spain!" cried Raleigh.

---

Preparing for the combined military and naval expedition, the largest such venture of the age, took a long time. The Crown could not bear all the expenses, so it was to be largely privately financed. I would supply eighteen warships from the Royal Navy, food and wages for the seamen. But the cost of levying the soldiers and sailors was the responsibility of Admiral Howard and Essex. Others would provide ships, both men-of-war and supply ships.

We were to have 150, of which 50 would be fighting vessels, and ten thousand men, divided between land troops and sailors. I wrote to the King of Denmark asking him to lend me eight ships and to forbid his subjects to furnish any to Spain. But he demurred, saying he needed all his ships to defend his own land. I had better luck with the Dutch, who were eager to strike at Spain in revenge for all they had suffered. They agreed to send a fleet to join us, along with two thousand infantrymen.

The fleet's four squadrons were to be commanded by the lord admiral in *Ark Royal*, the ship he had sailed as *Ark* against the Armada, Essex in *Due Repulse*, Thomas Howard in *Mere Honour*, and Raleigh in *Warspite*. The Dutch were under Van Duyvenvoord in *Neptune*. *Mere Honour*, *Warspite*, and *Neptune* were brand-new ships. The land regiments would be led by Francis Vere and Conyers Clifford—the two military men on the Privy Council—Christopher Blount, Thomas Gerard, and John and Anthony Wingfield.

The aim of the mission was precise: first, to attack and destroy ships and supplies in Spanish harbors; second, to capture and ruin towns on the coast; and third, to bring back booty from the towns and catch returning treasure ships. Nowhere did we state the word "Cádiz." That destination was a secret.

Although he was against war in general, as was I, Burghley drew up a proclamation that was for all intents and purposes a formal declaration of war against Spain. Part of me trembled to have it finally announced—after fifteen years!—but it was necessary. Its title was "Declaration of the Causes Moving the Queen's Majesty to Prepare and Send a Navy to the Seas for the Defense of Her Realms Against the King of Spain's Forces." It said I was acting only in self-defense. I was on peaceful terms with all other realms and we would not injury any—except if they aided the Spanish. Those we would treat as enemies. The commanders all signed, and it was printed in French, English, Dutch, Italian, and Spanish and distributed in all ports.

In addition, I composed a prayer for the expedition, and it was also printed and distributed widely. I sought to explain to God himself that our motives were pure—when in fact they were murky. I told him that he could surely discern "how no malice or revenge, nor quittance of injuries, nor desire of bloodshed, nor greediness of lucre has moved us to dispatch our new-set army." I begged him for good winds, "beseeching on bended knees to prosper the work, and with the best forewinds guide the journey, and make the return the advancement of Thy glory, with the least loss of English blood." I truly hoped he would grant the last.

Burghley was quite taken with it and declared that it "was divinely conceived by Her Majesty in the depths of her sacred heart."

So. They were to go, mounting a raid fifteen hundred miles away, using sea power to get there. It was daring and imaginative. True, Drake had done it once, and they would be following in his wake, but he had not had the resources of this expedition.

I was blessed to be served by such bold men. I had to remember that when their quarreling, preening, and posturing grew irksome. Audacity and courage, the two indispensable traits in men of battle, were arrayed before me in such profusion, I caught my breath and sent a prayer up to the Lord in thanksgiving.

# 38

## LETTICE

*March 1596*

It was here at last. Finally, power was devolving onto my son's head, drifting gently through the sunbeams to crown him with glory. Now he would have the long-sought opportunity to prove himself and vanquish all his rivals. I could hardly believe that the stingy, cautious Queen had authorized the flamboyant long-distance attack on Spain, and done it openly. She had even allowed a proclamation about it to go forth and circulate on the Continent.

Essex House had become a military headquarters, with Robert's companions gathering there daily. He was pleased beyond words to be surrounded by his fellows planning the voyage. Planning is the most satisfying part of any venture, when words stand in for goods and money, and there are never storms at sea or weevil-infested biscuits.

The only things clouding his happiness were sharing his command with Admiral Howard and his rival Walter Raleigh having a new ship. Raleigh had never quite regained his favor of old with the Queen, but with his usual skill at self-aggrandizing, he had turned his South American venture into a hugely popular book, *The Discovery of the Large, Rich and Beautiful Empire of Guiana with a Relation of the Great and Golden City of Manoa.* Now the Cádiz operation might complete the reparation of his fortune and turn him into the people's hero.

But he was in his midforties, although (I had to admit) still a man to make you speculate on what was under his breeches. His chest was often enough on public display. And it was a fine one. But Robert's fifteen years less in age were at this point an advantage. He could outwait him, if nothing else. And people always preferred a younger man. That was the way of things.

That assumed that the competition, and the men, would carry over into the next reign. How much longer could the Queen go on? Everyone who saw her commented on how young and healthy she appeared, how strong and full of purpose, but the woman was over sixty. Even the mighty Elizabeth,

Gloriana, Faerie Queen, et cetera, was made of flesh, not gossamer. She would crumble, wither, and die. That day would surely come.

My father was already crumbling, leading the way. I had first noticed how his face had changed after Christmas. His usual florid coloring faded, and something within him seemed to be melting.

I had rebelled against him all my life. He had been a bulwark I could push against. His Puritan rectitude, demanding our exile in Basel and Frankfurt during the reign of Mary Tudor, had been hard to bear. His lecturing and his seeming immunity against most temptations were even harder to bear. (Was that why I gave in to mine so easily?) But the erosion of the mighty walls was frightening beyond words to me. He had always been there. Even opposition can be comforting in its stability. After my mother died, so long ago, he made it difficult to feel compassion or pity for him, because he did not allow it of himself. But now my heart went out to him.

Ah, Lettice, I thought. You grow soft and sentimental in your later years.

No, I answered myself. I have only just now started allowing myself to feel.

And as for my later years . . . I was in my midfifties now. I could hardly believe it, and I was told (and chose to believe) that no one else could believe it, either. My hair was still red, with barely any gray, and still thick. My body was still slim and supple. My recommendation to anyone seeking my secret recipe: Forget the oil of hyacinth, the musk from Morocco, and make sure your lovers are at least a decade younger. Or better yet, two decades. Shakespeare and Southampton fit that criterion.

I had been unable to give either of them up. Oh, I had had fine resolutions about it. I had even rehearsed my speeches. To one I would say it was unseemly to have my son's friend as a lover. To the other I would say it was unseemly to have a friend of my lover for a lover. But somehow it had not come to pass. Each time I would tell myself, *This must be the last.* But it never was. For the longest time I managed to keep all four men—my husband, my son, and the two lovers—from knowing about one another. My husband and my son still did not know, but Southampton and Shakespeare had become aware of whom they shared. At first they professed not to care. In fact, they professed to find it erotic, and insisted sophisticated men were not possessive. But that did not last, and now there was bad feeling between them. Shakespeare had started to write unpleasant sonnets about my character, which Southampton made sure I saw, pretending it was accidental.

This expedition would take Christopher, Robert, and Southampton away, leaving only Shakespeare. I anticipated a lush time of playing to my heart's content with him, before letting him go. For once I would not be watched.

Essex House would be mine in its entirety, top to bottom—as would he. The fact that he disapproved of me, slightly, only lent a frisson of challenge to me.

In the meantime the preparations for the voyage would go forward, with the swarms of young men thronging our halls. My son had to supply their colors—his livery of tawny gold—although they were responsible for their own weapons. He also ordered his badge, *Virtutis Comes Invidia*—Envy is the Companion of Virtue—to adorn the liveries. I did not think the motto suited his situation, but I held my tongue. Lately I was having to do much of that. I was dying to know what had passed between him and the Queen on their private trip. But I could not ask.

Now we were keeping quiet company in the inner hall in the hour before supper.

I reached over and patted Robert's arm. I felt entirely content—except for my father's illness. (Why must there always be an "except for . . ."?) "Your preparations seem to be well in hand," I said. "You have given the tailors plenty of time. Everything should be ready."

He shook his head. "I dread getting the bill."

The bill. The reckoning. "If you can just hold them off until your return," I said, "you will have riches enough."

"The Queen expects booty—in addition to all the other goals of this mission. I can only pray that a Spanish treasure ship comes along at the right time."

"That is truly out of your hands," I reminded him. "But God is known to rain his favors down." I thought of all the men going. "Everyone is joining you. My husband—how will it feel to outrank and command your own father-in-law? And Charles Blount, your sister's lover."

"It is something I must accept," he said. "My inherited rank places me in high command. Christopher is a good soldier and I will rely on him."

"That's a diplomatic answer," I said.

I hated knowing that Christopher had been an underling to Leicester first, and now to my own son. It lessened him a little in my eyes, though I would never show it.

"You know that I am not noted for my diplomacy," he said. "I meant what I said. I will rely on Christopher, as I have for many years. Loyalty is the highest virtue of all. What good are any of the other virtues without loyalty?"

Did he know about Southampton and Shakespeare? I looked quickly at his face, but it seemed ingenuous. "Indeed," I said. "And are you being loyal to your wife these days? I worry about Frances." *Change the subject, Lettice!*

He looked surprised. "The Queen made no fuss about Elizabeth

Southwell," he said. "Odd. I expected her usual temper tantrum. Perhaps her vision is going bad. Or her acute senses are failing her. She seems not to notice that Southampton has been creeping around with Elizabeth Vernon, another of her ladies."

Southampton! "I have heard she is almost as pretty as he." I laughed lightly.

"Children should romp together, don't you think?" he said. "Why, they are six or so years younger than I am, and, as everyone keeps reminding me, I'm not even thirty yet."

"You did not answer me about Frances."

"We are very happy these days. And, Mother, Frances is a resilient woman. She survived the loss of Philip Sidney and she will survive my loss, should it come to that."

"Oh, do not speak of it!" I did not think I could bear it.

He shrugged. Perhaps that is the only way to go into battle. "I have a plan that will ensure my fame and success long beyond this mission. I want to hold Cádiz, turn it into a military outpost so we can harass Spain and maintain a foothold in her very guts."

"Replacing the lost Calais?"

"Yes," he said.

"Your vision is bold."

"The Spanish crisis needs such far thinking. Those men on the Queen's Privy Council—they scurry around trying to secure only what they see in front of their shortsighted eyes."

"God knows you have been stifled on the council and stalking the halls of court. Perhaps you belong in the field after all, for there have been few heroes there for two generations. May you make your name there, and come back with something that will endure. The jewels and gold and spices from a plundered ship will soon be spent; the strike against the Spanish will injure but not kill them. But a permanent outpost—yes, that can be your gift to England."

"I want to do something that will outlive me," he said. "Some notable act, some unique gift. Perhaps Cádiz can be that, for me."

"You are so many men, Robert," I said. "May they all become one."

---

While Essex House filled with tailors, boot makers, armorers, heraldry purveyors, banner makers, nautical instrument engineers, and map illustrators—a veritable manufacturing city gathered on our grounds—I slipped away, as often as I could, to visit my ailing father. I never took the ostentatious coach, and I wore plain gowns and left my jewelry at home. The other high-ranking officers at court had fine mansions along the Thames and the Strand, but Father, who had served the Queen during her entire reign and as her lord treasurer for the past twenty years, chose to live near St. Paul's, within the old walls of the City. Even in his decline, he came to Privy Council meetings every day, sometimes using a litter. But I never found him lying down when I came to see him. No, he was always sitting, usually at his desk, rustling through papers.

I had always been too busy, too involved in my own comings and goings, to give much thought to his situation. Now I was drawn to this house, and to him. I did not deceive myself that he was in need of me. I had many brothers and sisters. But what comfort they gave him I did not know. They, too, were busy with their own comings and goings. Suddenly, quite unexpectedly, my life had quieted down. There was little to strive for. My husband was not a courtier and would rise no higher. My son must make his own way, and no longer listened to me. He had his own family now and seemed on the very brink of power. My daughters, beauties though they were, had not used that beauty to further their positions. I had my lovers, but perhaps they were just a mask for the lack of any grand purpose in my life.

"Hello, Father!" I called to him. He was, as I expected, at his desk. He turned slowly to see me.

"Good afternoon, Laetitia," he said. He always called me by my formal name. Like someone else did.

"It's a glorious day," I said. "Will you show me what the garden is doing?" Spring was far advanced now.

"I haven't been out there today," he said, pulling himself stiffly to his feet. "But I daresay it would do me good."

Together we descended the stairs into the walled garden, with its bricks baking in the sun. There was an old cherry tree in the middle with a bench underneath. Several sleek cats lay dozing in the shade and stretched and yawned when we approached.

"Lazy rascals," said Father. "Why aren't they out catching mice? They're not worth their keep!"

I leaned down and stroked the one closest to me. It answered me with a rumbling purr. "Perhaps their mouse-catching days are over," I said, then could have smacked myself. "Or perhaps they know it is better to enjoy this garden. Tell me, Father, what is coming up?"

"I'm not sure. Your sister Anne took charge of the garden last autumn."

"Look, here's lily of the valley, and white violets," I said. "And sweet Williams coming up here. You will have a fragrant border."

"My roses survived the winter well," he said, making for the fence where they were staked. "All reds," he noted.

"No Tudor red and white?" I was teasing. Such roses were an artist's creation but did not grow in nature.

"No, red in memory of the first manor we were granted, by Jasper Tudor, Henry VII's uncle, for the annual rent of one red rose every midsummer." He fondled the stems lovingly.

"When was that?" His stories used to bore me. Now I wanted to hear them.

"In 1514. I was three years old. I swear I remember it, because my parents put red roses all over the house to celebrate. In any case, the unmistakable scent of the red rose always brings to mind wonderful gifts. I love to smell it through the open windows in June."

Three years old in 1514 made him eighty-five now. I marveled at him.

"I don't approve of perfumes, but if they must be worn, let it be rose!" He smiled.

I preferred the heavier musk scents from the east, but I merely nodded. My mother had always refrained from perfumes, in keeping with her Puritan beliefs. My mother . . . gone now for almost thirty years. Suddenly I wondered how lonely my father had been all this time, and felt ashamed that I had only just now thought of it. Tears sprang to my eyes. I had seen so little beyond myself. Now I was seeing wider and it was blinding me.

My father's dimming eyesight meant that he did not notice the beginning of my tears, and I checked them quickly.

"Well, you've got what you want," he said suddenly.

I did not know to what he referred. "Is that so?"

"I mean the counterattack against Spain. My grandson will distinguish himself and be happy at last."

"The command is split between him and the lord admiral," I reminded him. "And then there's Raleigh with one squadron, eager to prove himself again. It will not be easy."

"Nothing ever is," he said. "Surely you did not think otherwise?"

"Father—how have you lived all these years without Mother, as a bachelor? Has it been difficult?" That was what I wanted to talk about, not the Cádiz expedition.

"Didn't I just say that nothing is easy? I don't hold with Catholics, but Thomas More was right when he said we mustn't expect to get to heaven on feather beds."

Yes. Of course. He had his religion to sustain him. And now he was looking at me, disappointed. I had betrayed myself in asking the question. "Laetitia, if you could just understand the consolations of true faith, you would find that contentment you've always searched for. You were an unruly child, but I know that was because you were missing the most important thing in life. We brought you up in the faith, but . . . God has no spiritual grandchildren. Faith is not handed down; it must be grasped by your own hand. Just as Jacob had to wrestle with God himself in order to know him. It wasn't any good just being Abraham's grandson."

He had now lost my attention. My ears and mind closed. I didn't care about Abraham or Jacob. I never had. I never would. Those stories that sustained him meant nothing to me. I preferred the popular history plays that showed real people in recent times making decisions, and where those decisions led. That was immediate; that described my own world.

"Your own grandson, my son, seems to have a strong tie to God." One of his many sides that surfaced every so often was that of a religious devotee, given to fasting and extravagant displays of contrition. It did not last long.

"Seems to have? 'Seems' is a lukewarm word. It means one can't detect it." He shook his head, then made his way over to the bench, where he sank down gratefully.

"Father, we cannot see into another's soul," I said, sounding pious.

"True, but we can get a good idea from the outside reflection. Still, that's what *she* says. She'll make no windows into men's souls. Would have been better if she had!"

"You weren't so pleased when her sister did," I reminded him. "It meant you had to leave the country."

He sighed. "Yes. But whenever the Lord leads you somewhere, it is a blessing. I got to meet Peter Martyr and correspond with Calvin himself. Me, Francis Knollys!" He turned to me and took my hands. "Laetitia, I hope you are well. I mean, in your heart. I see that you are over fifty now. That time of life for a woman can be difficult, if she does not accept her . . . her station."

He meant I was getting old and I must recognize that and not make a fool of myself trying to overcome it. It would always win.

"Why, Father, I am only the age you were when you were just starting to serve under the new Queen. Life was beginning for you!"

"That was a unique occurrence," he said. "Do not think it can be repeated. No, you should look inward and be prepared, as we all must be—"

I was looking inward, too much so. I patted his arm, then stood up. "I'll come again soon. I want to see those flowers bloom."

He had lived so long. He had so much wisdom. Why could he not impart it, not even a little bit of it?

Shakespeare was fifty years younger, but he seemed to have thought more deeply about such things. All my father could do was cast his thoughts in a rigid religious template. Perhaps I was only using Shakespeare's body as a means to learn how to think. That was an unsettling idea.

# 39

# ELIZABETH

*July 1596*

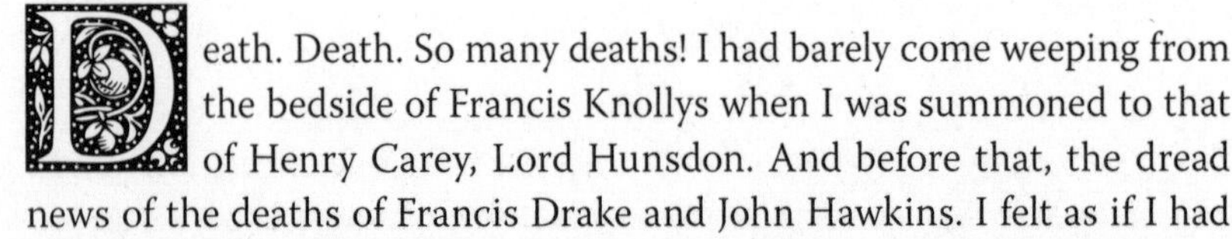

Death. Death. So many deaths! I had barely come weeping from the bedside of Francis Knollys when I was summoned to that of Henry Carey, Lord Hunsdon. And before that, the dread news of the deaths of Francis Drake and John Hawkins. I felt as if I had taken body blow after body blow. Knollys and Carey not only were strong supporting pillars of my council but were dear to me. I did not think I could bear their loss, strange as it sounds, after losing so many others. But this was different—they were not only my most trustworthy servants but also dear kinsmen.

It was hot. July had been brutal, with a sun seemingly bent on withering and drying everything under it, alternating with torrential rains. For the third year, there would be a bad harvest. The river stank; its foul odor permeated all the riverside palaces and homes. Inside my bedchamber it smelled like rotten fish. I found myself pacing, fanning myself, tears forcing themselves upon me at unexpected moments. Sitting on my desk was a coconut Drake had brought me long ago, which I had had mounted in a gold stand. This time he had brought nothing. He had never returned, dying of dysentery on his ship *Defiance* off Central America. He had done none of the things he set out to do. He had not taken any Spanish treasure or towns, and he had not carried out his lifelong dream of capturing Panama City on the isthmus. Instead, his party had been ignominiously ambushed and beaten back. He had lost his magic touch and must, tragically, have been aware of it. On his last night he had asked to be dressed in his armor so he could meet God like a soldier. He heaved himself up so that he would not die in bed, defiant to the end, like the name of his ship.

He was buried at sea off the coast of Panama, in the warm blue waters where he had made his name. They brought back his drum and presented it to me. It was sitting on a cabinet. I would give it to his widow. It was red, utterly silent, never to sound an alarm again, although some claimed that

Drake had vowed that if England was in trouble and needed him, someone should beat the drum to summon him and he would descend from heaven and defend us.

We mourned him, but the news overjoyed the Spanish, and they danced and celebrated knowing that *El Draque* would never trouble them again. Oh, the fleet on its way, I prayed, would be so infused with his spirit that the old sea dog would smile upon it and the Spanish swear that he commanded one of the warships.

His fellow captain and cousin Sir John Hawkins had succumbed before Drake and was likewise buried at sea. A sad and feeble ending their expedition had been, after so many glories.

And now Knollys was going, lying weakly in bed, mumbling Scriptures. He was surrounded by his many children and grandchildren. But his most illustrious one, Essex, was far away. The rest tried to comfort him, and I bent over his pillow, too, encouraging him to rally. But his years were too many for him, and they weighed him down and were carrying him off. I did not see Lettice among those clustered around. Perhaps they warned her when I was coming. But in truth, I would not have cared. And I could not begrudge her mourning her father—even though she had never mourned her husbands. I had not been allowed to be present at my father's deathbed, nor be anywhere around him. Instead, I had heard the news from a distance.

Knollys had been declining for years, but it was a slow withdrawal, so it was hard to notice. He was the oldest of my active councillors, having been born only two years after my father had come to the throne. Like Old Parr, he had witnessed the change of many guards, the rise and fall of so many. Were they passing like shadows now across a wall as he lay on his back in that upper chamber? The young Henry VIII; the joyous Anne Boleyn with her motto "The Most Happy"; the placid Anne of Cleves, whom he had met and escorted to London; his ward and fatally charming prisoner Mary Queen of Scots. He had witnessed a parade of religious creeds as well. As a fervent reformer, he had never come home to his new Jerusalem, although he was going to it now. I persisted in holding back the flood of the Puritanism he championed, and he would die with unfulfilled yearning for its triumph.

Opening his eyes, he fastened them on me, lifted his arm, and tugged weakly on my sleeve. I leaned far down to hear his whisper.

"What is it, old friend, old cousin?" I murmured.

He gave a slow, rattling laugh. "I have some words of good counsel for you," he wheezed.

"You have ever given me good counsel, Francis, and I treasure your wisdom."

"The first is—eighty-five years goes by very fast. But they are not all equal years. So if you are planning something for your eighties, look to do it now!" He laughed again, softly because he had no strength. "And the next is—beware of Robert, my grandson. Remember that he is descended from Richard, Earl of Cambridge, who turned traitor to Henry V. Remember also that you are descended from King Arthur, who was betrayed by a beautiful young man, Mordred. I have watched him grow up. We called the Scots Queen the Bosom Serpent, but I warn you, this boy also is a serpent you should not take to your bosom."

His wits were wandering. Nothing else would cause him to slander his own grandson so. "I can manage him," I assured him. "My father and I have controlled more difficult subjects than Robert Devereux."

"All it takes is one," he whispers. "One failure to be vigilant."

"Do not trouble yourself with these cares," I said, wiping his brow, which was sweaty and yet cold. "You have borne them long enough."

One of his daughters brought a wet cloth to soothe his face. I knew I should leave them. I looked down at him, saying farewell in my mind. His eyes were already closed.

---

He died a few days later, surrounded by all his kin—such a crowd of them they could not all fit into the chamber, I was told. He had been the father of twelve children, and most of them were still living. He was to be buried in his family tomb at Rotherfield Greys in Oxfordshire. So, on a scorching July day, his funeral carriage rumbled away and he left London forever.

But I had little time to mourn, for then Henry Carey took to his sickbed as well. Unlike Knollys, he had been vigorous until he was suddenly felled. True, his hair was white and his bulk more clumsy, but his oaths and appetites were robust as ever. It was as though a ruthless knight had unseated him in the joust, sending him flying through the air and crashing onto the ground.

There was no one to comfort me, as the one who could have—Catherine—was crushed. Her husband, Charles, was away on the Cádiz mission. Of course, she had her old mother, her brothers and sisters—Carey, too, had had many children, some dozen of them, not counting the natural ones. But Catherine felt his loss keenly, perhaps more so than her siblings. Her sweet and gentle heart was always open, and therefore easily touched.

Hunsdon lived not in a simple house like Knollys but in Somerset House, a grand mansion between Arundel House and Durham House on the river. His chamber smelled worse than mine because the sickbed odors mixed with the river stench, and his attendants tried to mask both with burning herbs. The result was enough to make you sick even if you entered the chamber healthy.

He was propped up in a luxurious carved bed with light summer hangings—so thin they floated and let most of the light in. His hair was whiter than the linen pillows he lay against, and his ruddy face had turned white, too. He was having difficulty breathing; with each intake of breath his chest rumbled.

He cracked one eye open and peered at me. "A Queen at my bedside," he said. "That's an achievement of sorts. But my family can't frame it."

"Here's something they can frame," I said. I motioned to the servant who had accompanied me to open a small trunk he had brought. Inside lay the robes and patent creating him an earl, which I had hastily had made for him. I spread them out on the foot of his bed. "My dear cousin, I create you an earl—the Earl of Wiltshire."

He grunted, in that way I knew so well. I expected an oath to follow. But he merely shook his head. "Ma'am, as you did not count me worthy of this honor in life, then I shall not count myself worthy of it in death."

"What?" I said. I had not expected that.

"Just what I said. Earlier it would have been welcome, but now 'tis too late."

*So if you are planning something for your eighties, look to do it now.* Knollys was right. Deathbed wisdom. Was he also right about the second thing he had said? "I am sorry, dear cousin. You were always worthy. It was I who did not see."

"Sometimes, yes, you have blinded yourself," he said. "Seldom about people. Usually about money or defense. And that, dear Queen, is not a subject for deathbeds. I should be praying. Fetch me a priest. Or at least someone to read to me!"

"I will take that duty," I said. "Will someone bring me a Bible?"

Catherine, her hand trembling, placed her own Psalter in my hand.

I took it, found it already marked for Psalm 90. I began reading, slowly, the words as much to me as to him.

*"For a thousand years in thy sight are but as yesterday when it is past, and as a watch in the night.*

*Thou carriest them away as with a flood; they are as a sleep: in the morning they are like grass which groweth up.*

*In the morning it flourisheth, and groweth up; in the evening it is cut down, and withereth.*

*We spend our years as a tale that is told.*
*The days of our years are threescore years and ten; and if by reason of strength they be fourscore years, yet is their strength labor and sorrow; for it is soon cut off, and we fly away."*

I gave a violent shudder, and saw Hunsdon eyeing me. "You are worse than a priest. Read me something good, or leave me."

The next psalm, 91, was more suitable.

*"He shall call upon me, and I will answer him: I will be with him in trouble; I will deliver him, and honor him.*
*With long life shall I satisfy him, and show him my salvation."*

"That's better," he grunted. "Even a long life is not long enough. But he's kept his bargain as well as he can, since we cannot live forever."

The door creaked open and his soon-to-be widow tiptoed in. She was a little, wraithlike old woman, delicate as a result of having borne so many children and ethereal in contrast to her husband's earthiness. She embraced Catherine, bowed to me, then glided over to her husband. Behind her was their oldest son, George, of the sleepy eyes and amorous disposition that ran in all the Boleyns. He would soon be Baron Hunsdon in his father's place. He joined his mother by the bedside. It was time for me to leave the family to themselves. I bent over and touched his forehead, knowing it was the last time those wise, skeptical eyes would look back at me. "Farewell," was all I could say, "faithful friend and servant."

Farewell to the man who as a boy had lived with my mother, one of the few still living who had known her; farewell to the man who had guarded my realm so well.

---

I gave him a full state funeral in Westminster Abbey. I did not attend, but it was all described to me. All the trappings were there—a black-hung hearse, trumpeters, standard-bearers, and officials in mourning cloaks—although the streets were oddly empty as the procession wound its way from Somerset House down the Strand. The heat, the debilitation, the still-stinking river had driven many away to their country estates. Those still in town attended, of course, but their ranks were thin, especially with so many away on the Cádiz venture.

The Cecils, father and son, were there, the elder making his way painstakingly to his seat, leaning on his tiny son, almost toppling him over from the side. It was obvious that before long old Cecil would come here again, but this time he would not be walking. The Bacons were there, and pointedly did not sit near the Cecils. John Dee and the young Wizard Earl, his protégé, attended. So did my distant cousin Thomas Sackville, Lord Buckhurst, who had the unpleasant nickname of "Lord Fillsack" because he was thought avaricious.

The coffin bore only the arms of a baron; he could have gone to his grave as an earl but, stubborn to the end, had had the robe and patent taken away so he would not even have to look at them and be tempted.

Archbishop Whitgift performed the service, and the coffin was then borne to the chapel of St. John the Baptist, where Hunsdon had already had his monument and tomb set up. Following the coffin the players of the Lord Chamberlain's Men walked in, swaying double file, carrying copies of their plays to place in the tomb of their patron. *A Midsummer Night's Dream* would be in the pile, to molder in the darkness of the tomb. I hoped it might live on in performance, for it belonged in the open air it celebrated so vividly.

---

The funerals over, the work closets of Knollys and Hunsdon cleared and empty, I felt alone in work as well as in person. I tried to keep this mood from Catherine and be a strong presence for her; Marjorie's crisp, forthright sense of reason provided a needed balance as well.

All was not gone, all had not slipped away into the dark, I kept reminding myself. All the more reason to treasure them while they were still here. Old William Cecil was fading, but I insisted he continue working for me, as if that would miraculously preserve him. Or was it to preserve me? When my ladies were gone and I was alone, I held up the mirror to my face in the gentle light from a northern window and saw what my portraits did not allow to be depicted. The face alone, shorn of its softening frame of hair, or hat, or jewels, was lined, with sharp folds on either side of my nose and my mouth. My lips, always thin, had small constrictions around the edges, as if they were straining to shut. My teeth—I tried not to show them. I had learned a way of smiling that more or less kept them covered. I had always had fair skin; it was still light, but its color was flat. Pink had to be supplied from a rouge pot, not from blood pulsing just beneath.

I was in my Grand Climacteric, my sixty-third year. It was supposedly fraught with peril. When I reached my actual sixty-third birthday in the autumn and thus began my sixty-fourth year, I would have survived a dangerous passage. I could not expect my face not to reflect that. Nor would I wish to be young again. But to be old! No!

This was an ugly summer, the third in a row. Scorching, oppressive sunshine continued to alternate with floods and downpours. The crops no sooner started to flourish than they were drowned. Food supplies would be crucial this autumn; any leftover stores would, after three years, be depleted. I must, somehow, secure extra rations. But from where? The entire Catholic world would be delighted to see us starve. So I could only hope to buy grain from fellow Protestant lands like Germany and Sweden, and word was that they had little to sell. I sent requests, even offering to supply the transport ships, but so far had had no response.

---

Awaking one morning and hearing the rain drumming—again—outside, I felt despair. The faces of the dying Knollys and Hunsdon kept playing in my mind, weighing me down with a sense of hopelessness. Leicester, Walsingham, Drake, Hawkins—they who had helped shoulder the cares of the kingdom with me had departed, and I was staggering beneath the weight.

Then, suddenly, words from the Book of Samuel whispered in my mind. "How long wilt thou mourn for Saul, seeing I have rejected him from reigning over Israel? Fill thine horn with oil, and go, I will send thee to Jesse the Bethlehemite: for I have provided me a king among his sons."

How long would I mourn those names? I must stop. God always provided another from among someone's sons. There was always another king, hence the shout "The king is dead. Long live the king." Today I would move. It was time, long past time, to fill Walsingham's place, empty these six years. I would have a new principal secretary.

---

Robert Cecil strode into the room, his short legs requiring many steps. He made up for his lack of stature by always being exquisitely groomed. His dark, pointed beard fairly shone, and his cloaks and doublets were cut to disguise the twist in his back. All in all he was a completely respectable representative; if foreign ambassadors had to look at the top of his head, soon enough they would be impressed by what was inside it. And there was an advantage in having your adversary underestimate you. I knew that only too well—although it had been years since I had had that experience. There was no one left who did not understand what they dealt with when they dealt with me.

"Ah, Robert, thank you for coming so quickly." He always did, but the habits I wanted to continue I made sure to praise. "You always answer my calls so diligently."

"It is my privilege to *be* called," he said.

"How is your dear father?"

"Tired," he said. "His gout is particularly bothersome this summer, and it tries his patience."

"May God send him relief. The pressing business of the realm has slackened of late, during the summer lull, which must be of some comfort." The niceties over—although I could have bantered with him all morning, enjoying as always his smooth, modulated voice and sharp wit—I said, "Essex and his boys are upon the seas, doing what they do best. You are here, doing what you do better than anyone else, save your father. It is time you captained your own ship, as Essex and Raleigh captain theirs. The name of yours is: principal secretary."

He looked first puzzled, then hesitant. God's breath, was he going to refuse it, as Hunsdon had refused the earlship? Were my gifts to be so spurned?

"I am honored," he finally said. "But I would not be the cause of anyone's breaking of a vow, even for my own advancement."

"What are you talking about?"

"I know that you promised Essex that in his absence you would not make any major appointments, and especially none to me."

"That is not true! No, it is more than not true: It is a self-serving lie. How dare he? Do you swear that he claimed that?"

"I swear it, upon all that I hold dear. The man said it twice, in case I was hard of hearing."

"What were his exact words?" I was stunned at the assumption of power and the duplicity on Essex's part.

Cecil put his hand on his chin, as always when he was pondering. Then he took on the bearing and the posture of Essex—he had a wicked sense of mimicry. "'I must inform you, little man, that there will be no important appointments without my knowledge, so while I am away do not look for any advancement. I have it on Her Majesty's own word. She has assured me I may set my mind at ease while I am away on that behalf.'"

"He said 'without my knowledge'?"

"Or consent, perhaps. I do not recall the precise word."

"God's wounds! So he thinks he must consent to my appointments? That I must inform him of my decisions, so he can approve or disapprove of them? Does he make himself Parliament, yea, more than Parliament?"

"I must confess, I was most surprised to hear it, for it did not sound like you."

"It did not sound like me because I never said, nor ever would say, such a thing! My words to Robert Dudley long ago still stand, and have grown stronger through the years: We shall have here but one mistress and no master."

"Well I am aware of that, Your Majesty."

"And because you are aware of it, and accept it, you will be my principal secretary, and we shall work well together. As for him, when he returns, he'll have a surprise."

"I would not be the cause of a quarrel between you," he said, politely, happy to be just that.

"Oh, in that case, I must withdraw my offer of the position." I watched the horror on his face. "For that, after all, is the only way to avoid it."

"As Your Majesty wishes. My only desire is to be of service to you, either by filling a position, or, in this case, by not filling it."

How quickly he had recovered his stride. How well he smothered his feelings. "Enough jesting, dear Robert. The place is yours. It could belong to no one else. It has been waiting for you to grow into it. The time is here." He had just proved it.

I had been hasty when I told myself that there was nobody left who did not know what they dealt with in dealing with me. Someone too young to have learned the lessons of his elders did not know. But Essex would find out. Oh, that he would.

# 40

Having seen John Dee at Hunsdon's funeral, I thought more and more of paying him a visit. He was mostly in Manchester these days, filling the position I had obtained for him—warden of Christ's College, an old college of priests converted to a Protestant institution. It was not ideal for him, but it was the best I could provide. He had ruined himself by his years on the Continent, engaging in bizarre spiritual quests that involved talking to angels and dabbling in the supernatural and ended, as often with these things, in an all-too-earthly, sordid wife exchange with his partner, supposedly ordered by the angel Uriel. Disillusioned, discouraged, and poor, he had returned to England to find his reputation as low as a turtle's underside.

But he was not the first man to follow a foolish quest, and he should not be treated like a criminal. He had hurt only himself and his own family. He had not squandered the public purse or stolen from the treasury. Surely he deserved credit for his wide knowledge and prior service to me. And so I would continue to support him as best I could.

I ordered the royal barge to make for Mortlake, after sending a message ahead to warn him. I knew surprise royal visits were unwelcome, however much people later treasured the honor, preserving the chair I had sat on and the cup I had held. None of us likes to be taken unawares.

As the barge made its way upstream, parting the water, I saw the debris and scum in the wake behind us. The smell from the dead fish was as bad as ever, and I kept my pomander close under my nose. A few swans were circling near one shore, their pure white feathers smudged with the green scum. There were far fewer of them than usual; I wondered if the rest had died, or flown elsewhere.

There were also fewer boats out upon the river. Business had slowed with the ongoing conflict in the Netherlands and slowed further with the turmoil in northern France and the Spanish attempt to capture Calais. The Spanish did not accept Henri IV's conversion and continued to besiege France. Wars were ruinous for business. When I thought of Antwerp, the former banking and mercantile center of Europe and the vital Continental wool trade, all disrupted and destroyed by these conflicts, I was furious. When would it end, and we could resume normal life? The sheep farmers who could not export their wool, the tailors who could not import finished cloth, the merchants who could not get European loans, all this weakened England.

The Cádiz mission must have been completed by now. It was no sure thing, but if it had succeeded, I would sing its praises. We needed a victory, something to celebrate. It had been almost a decade since the Armada. Memories were short, and the mood of the country was morose.

The boat bumped against the landing, and we were at Mortlake. I stepped out, onto the familiar ground of the little village, the church with its little cluster of houses around it, the big oaks shading the lanes. As I walked, though, I saw green leaves littering the ground and, looking up, noticed how sparse the leaf canopy was. The trees were dropping their leaves well before time, damaged by all the rain.

John Dee was waiting for me in his doorway, a tender smile on his face.

"You are back where you belong, I see," I said, noting his long beard, as white as milk, and his magus's gown with voluminous hanging sleeves and celestial symbols embroidered on it. "Here, in Mortlake."

He bowed and kissed my hand. "I know now where I belong. Sometimes one finds out only by living elsewhere."

Behind him his wife peered out. Unlike Dee, she had changed, looking older and fretful. No wonder, after her experience with enforced unchastity. She was probably more grateful to be back than her husband.

I stepped into the library and saw immediately that it was different. The walls were bare and the sagging shelves of books stripped. The shelves still sagged, but only in memory of the lost books.

"I returned to Mortlake to find my library ransacked and plundered, with many of my most precious volumes stolen," he said. "I once had the largest library in England—over four thousand books. Now"—he spread his hands—"this is what remains."

He had had rare scientific books, gathered from the suppressed monasteries before they were destroyed. "And what remains in your head," I said.

"That is only a fraction of the knowledge that was on these shelves," he lamented. "Many instruments were taken as well."

"Oh, John," I said. He had had navigational instruments, globes, and maps, as well as his alchemy equipment and astrological and astronomical charts.

"All is not gone," he assured me. "They were not interested in my charts, maps, or globes. Their appetite was for the alchemy equipment. I was rumored to have discovered how to transform tin into gold, so they took what they thought would do that. How stupid can someone be? If I had known how to make tin into gold, would I have been in the state I am in?"

"People believe what they wish to, John." God knows I had found that out. I smiled, remembering the day I had brought François here. The Frog . . . How we had laughed and played. Long ago, until Dee's reading of his future had silenced my laughter.

Suddenly I realized why I had come. "Do you still have your seeing crystal?"

"My shew stone? Yes, it's still here." He lifted a tasseled cover, revealing a round crystal about the size of an orange resting on a wax seal. He blew on it, clouding it over and waiting for it to clear. "You want to know about Cádiz," he said. It was not a question.

"Yes. They have been gone weeks now. The action is complete. I cannot bear not knowing what has happened! And—if it is bad, I need to know before they return, *if* they return."

"A complicated campaign is hard to discern in this little glass."

"Look for the town! See if it still stands!"

He tried to coax the image of Cádiz out of the depths of the ball. "I see smoke and blackness," he finally said. "It looks as if . . . Many piles of stones. The defenses are thrown down."

Excitement coursed through me, but caution reined me in. "What of the harbor? What ships do you see?"

He sighed. "Ma'am, that is almost impossible to make out."

"Try! Try!"

"The city, as you know, is like a fingernail at the end of a six-mile piece of land that curls up like a beckoning finger from the mainland into the sea. At the place where the finger joins the palm is a smaller city and another harbor. It looks as though there is a fire in the inner city's harbor. A big one. But I cannot tell what is burning."

"Are there ships outside the harbor?"

"I think so."

"Big ones? Unharmed?"

"Yes."

"Our ships! We had fifty men-of-war."

"I am not sure I see fifty. But this is a small glass."

"What men do you see?"

"I will have to coax the ball," he said, blowing on it again. Squinting, he peered at it from several angles. "Now . . ." He gazed intently for several moments. "I see men, but I do not know who they are. It has been a long time since I was at court."

"Let me try." I moved over and stood in his place. The depths of the ball showed colors and some wavy lines, but I could make out nothing. "I have not the skill in reading it," I had to admit. I was frustrated beyond words. He could see, but not identify, and I could identify but not see. "God's wounds! What a plight is this!"

"We saw the completed event," he said, "so the fleet must be on its way home. We will know soon enough. At least we know that they succeeded in sacking Cádiz, and that everyone has survived. Is that not what you sought to learn?"

"I'd like to know about the treasure. Was there any? Did they capture it?"

"I cannot imagine that they did not, Your Majesty. And . . . if I may so humbly request, would you remember your old servant when you come into it?"

"John, I have already provided a living for you with the position in Manchester, and do not forget, I gave you two thousand pounds when first I heard of the theft here." Did the man think I had money to spare?

"Yes, Ma'am, yes, I do not forget and am grateful, so grateful. But the post at Manchester—although I am grateful!—has unpleasant aspects. The other Fellows there do not like me. In fact, they make my life hell!"

"Small people always do, John. You must learn to make your peace with them. Not everyone can have your intellect; you must forgive them for that. Perhaps if you forgave them for their lacks, they would forgive you your talents. Envy can only be defanged; it does not die on its own."

"Yes, yes, of course." He straightened up, embarrassed by his begging. "I understand that your ventures to the New World, while I was away, have been unsuccessful?"

"Both were Raleigh's, and both failed," I said. "The colony in Virginia did not survive. His expedition to the Orinoco in South America discovered nothing of value. He returned empty-handed, except for a few souvenirs, including a most personable savage and some ores that turned out to be worthless—fool's gold." His part in the Cádiz venture should have gone better, or, by God, he would never set sail under my patronage again.

"Do not abandon the New World," Dee said. "That is where your future lies, not in Europe. To the devil with Cádiz, the Spanish, the French, the Dutch. Your destiny is to rule a British empire, stretching all across North America. Look that way, not to tired old Europe."

"Two failures do not encourage me."

"Two failures! And how many have you had in Europe?"

"My dear Dee, your vision is too big for reality. I daresay I supported the two missions *because* of your beguiling vision. But I cannot see that it is going anywhere."

"Patience! Keep sending out explorers. Let them plant the English flag. Drake did it on the west coast of America, Raleigh on the east. Send more!"

"I cannot afford it," I said flatly. "If this Cádiz mission does not bring back lots of treasure, it must be my last."

"Never. Never! I tell you, I see the scepter of Britain from shore to shore there. I see your seal, as empress!"

"Since I can see none of them, I suspect that sometimes your inner vision paints over what you actually see in that ball." I pointed to it. "Let us draw the cover over it and let it be, old friend."

---

I moved to Windsor for the remainder of the summer to escape the stinking city and river. Here the Thames had shrunk to a country stream, pleasant and sweetly rippling. In any case, the castle of Windsor was high enough above it, some hundred feet, to protect us from any wayward scents or noise. Looking out across the fields and meadows from its heights made me feel like the commander of a great battleship. Below me was the ribbon of river, and stretching as far as the eye could see were hedgerows, rolling fields, and woodlands. Not far away was the water meadow of Runnymede, where King John had been forced to sign the Magna Carta by stubborn barons. Ah, well, I must guard against being forced to sign away any of my Crown's rights. One Magna Carta was enough.

I always enjoyed Windsor in the summer; in the winter it was too drafty, and no wonder. Anything dating from the time of William the Conqueror would hardly be snug and modern. He had selected the site for its strategic location on a cliff and at the edge of a Saxon forest, to guard the western approach to London, as the Tower guarded the eastern.

As I said these words to myself, I suddenly realized how strange it was that my mother's grave was at one site and my father's at the other—as if they were guarding London, protecting it. My mother lay in the chapel of St. Peter ad Vincula in the Tower, and my father in the chapel of St. George here.

I was anxiously awaiting confirmed news about the Cádiz expedition. The placid countryside soothed me but did not calm me. Oh, when would they come? When would we know?

Young Cecil attended me every day, and in the quiet and privacy of the lull we were able to get much business done—the neglected sort, the things one always sets aside because they are not urgent, but left untended pile up and choke like unruly vines. Plans for the town of Deptford as it encroached upon Greenwich. Improved lists for mustering local militias. Testing of the weights and measures used in the markets. Repair to some stretches of the Wall of London. The unglamorous work of a monarch, which must go on when the robes and crowns are set aside, and woe to the monarch who omits it.

Did he feel passed over, one of the few young men not away at present? He had never ridden in the jousts, commanded a ship, or led troops. He did not sing or join in the dances. Did it eat at him? His wide green eyes gave away nothing; his courteous and gentle manner never betrayed any sense of yearning for that which he could not have. Yet I did not sense true contentment, but rather a resignation to limitations and a determination to excel wherever he was not hampered.

I liked to walk along the breezy upper ward, down the winding paved way where the Knights of the Garter walked every St. George's Day to the celebration in his namesake chapel here, their blue velvet cloaks trailing them, their order's garter insignia resplendent on their legs. For the newly elected, it was a high day in their lives. Only twenty-four men could serve as Knights of the Garter, and only I could select them. It was the highest order of chivalry in England. It always tugged at me that I could preside over this order of knights and yet could not be a true warrior. Like Robert Cecil, I could not lead troops or joust or command a ship. Both of us disqualified—I by my sex, he by his back. But by God, we could make them dance to our tabor!

One particularly hot day as I was emerging from the chapel, I saw an eager young man running downhill toward the green of the middle ward, waving his arms like a boy flying a kite. It was John Harington, who skidded to a halt right in front of me, gasping for breath.

"My dear godmother!" he said, bowing and then boldly kissing my cheek.

Here was another young man who had not gone off to sea, and he was able-bodied enough. "What mischief are you up to, John?" I asked. Today I was ready for it. I was ready for anything bold to amuse me, and I could usually count on John to provide it.

"I have brought you an invention, something so marvelous, so modern, so farsighted, that, being associated with your reign, it shall bring you more renown than the Armada in the annals of history." He was out of breath with excitement, his eyes dancing, suppressed laughter seeping out from around the corners of his lips.

Well, he *was* clever, I knew that. He had once engineered an ingenious mole trap that the gardeners at Hampton swore by. He had also designed a pipe conduit that could carry more water than the old kind. Perhaps now he invented an improved weapon that would give us an edge in war—a gun of some sort that was lighter and could fire accurately with less time in between each shot. That would certainly give our armies an advantage. "What can this be?" I asked.

"Come, and I shall show you. I have it set up. Mere words cannot do it justice! It must be seen in action." He pulled on my hand.

"Is it a military weapon?" I asked. "Will it be helpful in war?"

"Well . . . not exactly."

"Is it some sort of luxury?"

"Today a luxury, but tomorrow a necessity!"

"Is it expensive?"

"Not so much, when you figure it can service many."

"Will it improve the appetite?"

"Which ones?"

"Any of them, you saucy wretch!"

"Definitely. I swear to it." He laughed. "I told you, words cannot begin to convey a true picture of it. You must see for yourself!" He kept leading me uphill, toward the upper ward, where the royal apartments lay.

As we passed into the building, the guards seemed to snicker. When I looked at them questioningly, they dropped their gaze. John hustled me past them quickly.

We skirted the presence chamber, then went straight through the apartments into ever smaller rooms. My curiosity was rising. It would seem, if the gift were to serve many people, it would have to be in a large public space. Yet we were passing them. When we reached my privy chamber, I was utterly baffled.

I looked around the chamber and saw nothing out of place. The chair where Elizabeth Southwell usually sat remained empty; she was gone from court forever after bearing Essex's bastard. So much unsavory business seemed to cluster around Essex, for all of his glowing beauty. Pregnant girls, lascivious uncles, promiscuous mothers and sisters, turbulent, profligate companions.

Now John bowed and, with a flourish of his hand, indicated that I must go into my bedchamber. I did. Catherine and Marjorie were there, sewing placidly.

"Well?" I demanded. Oh, let it not be a pet—a monkey, a hedgehog, or a squawking bird. The "invention" was most likely a cage of some sort.

Now he was gesturing toward my small withdrawing private chamber, where I attended to the most personal toilet needs. No one went in there. I was irritated; this game had gone on too long.

"John, we have gone far enough," I said.

"Just within, it awaits!"

Marjorie and Catherine crowded up behind us, laughing.

I stepped in to confront a big, square chair with a privy seat and a barrel suspended on struts over it. If one were to sit upon the seat, the barrel would make a sort of canopy over the head. A chain hung down from the barrel.

The whole contraption was ugly and downright menacing.

"John, what *is* this? Why have you wrecked my most private room with this monstrosity?"

"Here, my dear sovereign. This will answer all your questions. Pray read, and then I will hold a demonstration. Your distaste will turn to awe." He thrust a pamphlet into my hands entitled "A New Discourse on a Stale Subject: Called the Metamorphosis of Ajax."

I flipped through it, finding details for how to construct the machine I was now standing before. Sprinkled throughout it were allusions to classical heroes, alternating with engineering diagrams.

"A jakes!" he cried. "A jakes! *Ajax!*" When he finished laughing at his own wit, he looked plaintively at me. "Do you grasp the pun? The jakes has undergone a change, a metamorphosis!"

"In what way?"

"Why, it will no longer be stale, or reek, or force people from their homes when the stench overpowers them. This newfangled jakes is a sweet-natured fellow."

"Enough puns! Tell me straight, what *is* this?"

"Why, it is a water closet," he said. "Let me demonstrate." He stepped up to the barrel and turned a faucet attached to a pipe leading down to the chair. Then he bent and turned another screw on its underside. "Ready now!" A great rush and gurgle of water ensued, followed by a belch. It was so loud it could be heard out in the presence chamber. "It is—oh, surely I need not actually employ it for its true purpose. You can see, you—er, one—sits here, at one's toilet, and then, rather than leave it—uh—standing, this water from the barrel will flush it away, into a covered chamber. Do you—um—understand?"

"Yes, John." I felt myself blushing. I was not sure whether it was because he referred to these personal things, or because of the picture in my mind of a royal flush being heard by the guards outside every time it happened.

"You will want to install them in every palace," he said. "It will transform them. And all I ask—"

"Is that they be named after you? From this time forward, change 'jakes' to 'johns'?"

"Oh! Now that would be jolly!" He cocked his head. "How many shall I order made to satisfy you?"

"Satisfy me . . . now that is an odd choice of word."

"I do believe it is immensely suitable," he said. "And all your ladies . . . They will surely find it pleasing, and it will allow them to feel more dainty."

"I think your invention shows ingenuity, but I am not sure it is practical enough to have a future."

He looked crushed.

"It is unwieldy, expensive, and devilishly loud, advertising one's business for a hundred yards in every direction. No, John, I do not think it will take the realm by storm. Nonetheless, because you are my very favorite godchild, I'll order one for the apartments in Richmond Palace. There!"

The ladies, young and old—they had all crowded in—tittered.

"You see how eager they are to avail themselves of it? Why restrict it just to Richmond?" John's handsome face was open and innocent.

"I believe in testing something for a bit before committing to it," I said.

"As you did in regards to marriage?" he asked, raising his eyebrows.

That man! The boldness of him! "Quite so," I said. "And it proved to be a most wise course."

"Your most glorious father, the King, embraced the new and jettisoned the old with gusto," he said. "I know he would have installed these everywhere."

"He had more money than I," I said flatly. "So he could afford more mistakes. Ah, John, it is a hard thing to have to grasp every penny until the copper oozes out." Now the unpleasant reality of the day intruded on the frivolity we were enjoying so much.

His face grew sober. "Indeed it is," he said. "And we appreciate the value you get for each penny. You have bought us a safe realm with it."

"Thank you. My extravagant, self-indulgent purchase this year, then, will be the ajax. No jewels, no gowns, no kidskin gloves. Ajax it is! I shall be the envy of Henri IV and Philip, no doubt. For all the glamour of the French and the wealth of the Spaniards, they must struggle along with the old way of tending to their business. The only thing I ask of you, John—"

He looked alarmed.

"—is that you keep the engineering design absolutely secret. No leaking it to the enemy." Too late I caught myself. "Now I am infected with your puns," I said. "Go to." I cuffed his head lightly.

---

Wanting to leave the dark empire of the ajax behind, I walked briskly out of the royal apartments and across the open courtyard of the upper ward. It was the highest point of the castle grounds and felt closest to the sky, which today was leaden with impending rain. I made my way down, past the old, squat, round tower that dominated the castle's profile. Down farther was the jewel of the castle, St. George's Chapel, rebuilt in what a hundred years ago was the latest fashion. My great-grandfather Edward IV had been determined to be buried here. His building program did not keep pace with his hectic life, and he died before it was finished. Nonetheless, his magnificent tomb was erected afterward, and the building grew up around him.

I stepped in, and it took a moment for my eyes to adjust. It was called a chapel but was almost the size of a cathedral, stretching a length of 250 feet from front to back. Behind me the huge western window with its stained glass threw ruby, sapphire, and emerald shadows on the stone floor, turning it into a tapestry. The odor of old stone, carried on the damp air, wrapped itself around me like a shawl.

I walked slowly down the nave, drawn to my father's tomb at the far end. On either side were the chantry chapels, silent now. Once wealthy families had endowed private chapels where their souls could be prayed for, day and night, to ease their passage through purgatory. A bequest, set up in perpetuity, paid a priest to devote himself exclusively to that duty. But, deemed popish superstition, chantries were outlawed, purgatory declared nil. Now the souls of all these people must fend for themselves. They left behind magnificent tombs and statuary in the forsaken chapels.

I reached the choir, the home of the Order of the Garter. The back row of stalls was reserved for those knights, and above each stall hung the knight's heraldic plate, his banner, and his sword. Upon his death, the banner and the sword were taken down, but the plate remained, a record of all the knights who had ever occupied that stall, going back to 1390.

If a knight proved unworthy, a reverse ceremony was held, stripping him of the honor of the Garter. During my reign only two such "degradations," as they were called, had taken place. The first was for Thomas Percy, Earl of Northumberland, who had joined the rebellion of the northern earls, the only uprising against me so far. The second was my cousin Thomas Howard, Duke of Norfolk, who had tried to marry Mary Queen of Scots, when she was a prisoner here in England, to support her against me. The degrading procedure was most solemn. The Garter King at Arms, flanked by the officers at arms and the Black Rod, announced the knight's degradation. Then the herald removed the plate, banner, and sword, but not quietly. They were torn down and flung to the floor, then dragged and kicked out the far western door and thence from the castle grounds and finally into the river.

I sat down in one of the dark, carved choir stalls. There was a plaque on the floor, midway down the chapel, marking my father's grave. In his will he had requested to be laid at rest "in the choir, midway between the stalls and the high altar," and there he had been brought on a cold February day.

It was almost exactly fifty years since then. Fifty years without him, yet he guided my thoughts every day. How I wished I could speak with him, for only five minutes, about the decisions I faced for England. But no, I would need more time. I would need fifteen minutes at least, the first five to tell him everything that had happened since his death, then five to sketch out the present crisis, and then, and only then, to speak of what to do next.

Time! You are so cruel. Why can we not take out the fifteen minutes in the past and hoard it until now, until needed? Fifteen minutes. That is all I ask. So little. So impossible.

# 41

# LETTICE

*August 1596*

ossip was in the air. It flew ahead of the returning forces, winging its way straight to us unhindered by national borders, by ravines or mountains. It whispered that we had been dazzlingly victorious in Cádiz. The town was ours; we had captured both the city and its fleet. And my son was the hero of the action, the first to charge through the walls and into Cádiz. What it did not tell us was anything beyond these few wild outlines, and how much treasure had been seized.

It would have to be a great deal. Cádiz was a rich city and would offer much booty, even if no treasure ships from America were in the harbor. There were rumored to have been fifty merchant ships awaiting the plundering.

"Let us celebrate!" I poured two goblets of sweet sack. "Let us drink their own best wine to salute their downfall! From the very port of Jerez!" I handed one to Shakespeare, who was sprawled out in the bed. He raised himself up on one elbow and took it, lifting it for a moment to his eyes, then sipping it.

"The best," he agreed. "You are indulgent, countess."

I hated it when he called me that. "In many ways, as well you know." These two months, with my three watchdog men away, would have qualified even in Nero's Rome as an orgy. Of course it was not possible to have an orgy with only two people, but Shakespeare seemed more than one person. He was never the same, from night to night, from day to day. I wondered if he was testing different roles. He was an actor, after all.

"You spoil me," he said. "It is hard to revert back to being just plain Will, as I must do regularly." He set the goblet down on a bedside stool and got up. "As I must do now." He walked across the room to fetch his clothes. "You see? Having my clothes put in a chest rather than in a heap on the floor is way above my station."

"Where are you going now?"

"Performance this afternoon. I'll have to hurry." He peeked out the window to guess the time.

"I haven't noticed you learning your lines."

"I don't need to. I wrote them."

"What's this play?"

"Come and see."

I wanted to, but I had purposely stayed away from the theater this summer. It might be too obvious if I was seen there. Above all, I wanted to keep this secret.

"You know I can't." I wanted to. I wanted to see him acting, becoming yet another person. "Stay here. Don't go." I did not know why I said such a thing. To test him?

"No." He put on his shoes. "You should know better than that, Laetitia."

"I was only jesting," I said lightly. "I know you esteem the theater above my company."

"It is my living," he said.

"It is your love," I said.

He kissed my cheek and then dashed down the stairs, his eagerness informing every motion.

"Come back afterward! I want to hear it all!"

He did not answer, and I hated myself for saying it. The door slammed.

---

I fought with temptation all afternoon to keep away from the theater. Usually I am not very successful against temptation, but today I was. I simply could not go there, could not be seen. I envied him his other life, the company of his fellow actors, the freedom of becoming someone else entirely, even if only for a few hours through his characters. He made whole new worlds; he did not have actually to sail to them.

"My mind to me a kingdom is . . ." Shakespeare had quoted Sir Edward Dyer's entire poem to me, but all I remembered was that first line. And oh, yes, "Such present joys therein I find that it excels all other bliss." He might as well have been describing himself. But perhaps all poets were like that and it was a common feeling among them.

What did I know about Will Shakespeare, anyway? He came from Warwickshire, a country man, a nobody in aristocratic circles. He was thirty-two years old. He had married at eighteen and had three children. His wife was eight years older. Perhaps he was always drawn to older women? She stayed behind in Warwickshire when he came to London to act and write. He had secured the young Earl of Southampton as his patron and published the wildly successful poem *Venus and Adonis,* following it up with

*The Rape of Lucrece* a year later. He acted in the Lord Chamberlain's Men and wrote plays for them. He refused all gifts I tried to give him, as if accepting anything would compromise him. Anything material, that is. Words, lovemaking—he was free enough with them. He never wrote a note to me, nor a dedicated poem, but he wrote about me in his sonnets and in his plays, although he was careful never to identify me by name. I had read enough of them to feel sure of it, although he never admitted it. He was as guarded as a Spanish bastion.

Spanish bastion . . . Soon the official news would come to us about Cádiz. And the arrival of my son in person, and . . . Southampton. And my husband. It would all be over for me, my interval of play. But something new would begin for my son, I hoped. His hour would have come at last.

---

The sun dipped toward the west. These summer days were long and oppressive, the heat unrelenting. The play would be over. I knew the actors would have been miserable in their heavy costumes. This summer had been difficult for them; if they were not sweating under the sun they were soaked from the intermittent downpours. But Will never complained.

Now he would be at the tavern with his friends, after the ticket sales had been tallied up. They would be discussing the performance, how it had been received, how it could be improved, and what was on the boards for the next day. He would have forgotten all about coming back here.

His world was so much richer than mine! A wave of angry envy washed over me. What had I said earlier? He was a nobody from Stratford. But it was I who was the nobody. I had no world outside the narrow confines of Essex House. I had lost my position at court long ago—and court itself was confining, limited—and yet, as a woman, I was not free to roam elsewhere at will. He, on the other hand, was the freest creature in the world. His wife did not confine him, and in any case, she was far away in Stratford. He could invade realms, countries, the past, all at his whim in his own mind. Here in London, he could frequent any tavern or any place he wished. And above all, he could exercise his mind, hone it against other wits, stretch himself as far as he could. His days were never dull repetitions, obligations, duty.

*Oh, Lettice,* I told myself. *There is not a person living upon this earth who does not have dull stretches of his life. The everydayness of life is parceled out to us alike.*

But I wanted to be able to go to the tavern and talk about my play—or someone else's. Did I yearn for Will, desire him, for the portal he provided into that forbidden world of freedom? He was my only glimpse, my only entrée, into it.

*Stop it*, I told myself. *You are sinking in self-pity.*

There was a soft knock on the door. He was here! He *had* come back! Flying to it, I flung it open, and saw a stranger standing there.

He pulled off his hat and bowed. "I am Sir Anthony Ashley, sent by the Earl of Essex." His clothes were gray with traveler's dust. "It is most urgent."

"Pray come in."

He followed me as I led him past the public rooms and into the withdrawing room. The door to the bedroom was discreetly closed. I poured him some ale and motioned for him to sit. "Where is my son?" I asked him.

"He is still at sea but will be arriving within the next few days," he said. "He wanted this report to be published before he got here." He thrust a packet of papers into my hands.

I opened it and saw the title: "A True Relation of the Action at Cádiz the 21st June, Under the Earl of Essex and Lord Admiral, Sent to a Gentleman in Court from One That Served There in Good Place."

"But why? Why not present it himself?"

"Because there are rival reports that seek to undermine his achievements."

"I thought we were victorious, and the earl had led the action." I could stand no more of this. "Tell me! What truly happened? We know almost nothing."

He smacked his lips, reminding me that he had ridden hard and was still thirsty. I refilled his glass, and he downed it gratefully. "Ah, that's better. Let me just tell you briefly, for to do otherwise is to drown in details. Yes, what you heard was true. But there is more. We were successful in surprising the town, although Medina-Sidonia—the former commander of the Armada and now stationed in Andalusia—spotted us when we were getting close, about twelve hours away, and tried to warn them. We did sack the town, after stripping it of its goods. But there was such rivalry between the sea and the land forces that they became their own enemies. The land forces, led by Essex, were determined to go first, and delayed the sea attack on the cluster of merchant ships. Those withdrew to the farther town of Puerto Real at the base of the peninsula, where Sidonia offered a ransom of two million ducats for them. Admiral Howard held out for four million, and while he was haggling, Sidonia ordered all thirty-six of them to be burned. The total loss we reckon as twelve million ducats. Had not Essex and Raleigh been rivals for glory in the campaign, and Essex not sought to thwart his sea action, we would have realized that twelve million. In addition, another small fleet of galleys escaped completely."

I felt cold. The Queen would be furious.

"There was talk about retaining Cádiz as a permanent base. Essex urged it. I know he had left a letter behind for the Privy Council about it. But he was overruled. He also wanted to stop in Lisbon on the way back, to see if we could take it, but he was overruled then, too, by an exhausted army." He scratched his head. "Your husband, Sir Christopher, did well, leading a ten-mile land attack on Faro before we reached Lisbon."

"Well? What did Faro yield?"

"Only a lot of books," he admitted. "From the archbishop's library. The town was deserted. They had been warned."

"Damn them!"

"Unfortunately, only two days after we sailed past Lisbon, a treasure fleet from America arrived there."

Now I felt sick; the coldness was replaced by nausea. The Queen would be more than furious. I could not picture how incensed she would be at this blundering and loss of her investment, and the punishments she would inflict.

"So it is vitally important that Essex proclaim his intention to attack Lisbon, and stress that he was impeded and prevented from it by others. He should not be blamed for the loss of that treasure, estimated at twenty million ducats. His judgment was sound; it was the others who failed. Already Raleigh is trying to circulate his own version of events. You know how clever that man is at promoting himself through his writing. He is a devilish good penman. First he transformed his cousin Richard Grenville's suicidal fight against the Spanish into legendary heroism in his pamphlet 'Report of the Truth of the Fight About the Isles of Azores This Last Summer,' and then he made his own fruitless expedition to Guiana into a matchless adventure in 'The Discovery of the Empire of Guiana and Manoa'—which he never even got to!—which was translated into Dutch, Latin, and German. We cannot let that happen to us!"

"No. We cannot," I agreed. "What do you propose to do?"

"I'll get this printed quickly, so it can be in circulation before Essex arrives. It must truly look as if it were written by a soldier. I know a printer who can do it."

"Good." I felt numb.

"The venture will rank alongside Crécy, Agincourt, and the Armada. It truly was a spectacular long-range expedition, and it succeeded. We must make sure everyone realizes it. For there is another problem."

How could there be? What else could possibly plague it?

"The precious stones, gold, and coin that were taken have not—oh, let me just state it! The looted goods have in turn been looted! The men have helped themselves, instead of reserving it for the Crown. I have a double commission, a secret one of publishing the letter and a public one of tracking down the missing booty."

"Excuse me." I got up and walked as quickly as I could into my private rooms, then ran for the basin, where I was sick. The goods gone. The Queen cheated—no, robbed—by her own countrymen. What did this mean for Robert, the leader of the expedition? I wiped my mouth and leaned weakly against the table to steady myself. A few minutes later I confronted Ashley again.

"You must hurry," I said. "Do not linger here. When may I expect my son?"

"Within a week." He cocked his head. "Are you not curious about when your husband will arrive?"

"Yes, yes, of course, but I assumed they would be together."

He looked amused. "I daresay. Actually, Sir Christopher will probably arrive first. He was on a different ship."

"Thank you," I said with as much dignity as I could muster. He acted as if he *knew*.

---

I paced the room. For an hour I had walked nervously up and down, unable to sit. I was distraught, thinking of my son's triumph turned to disgrace. *Were* the Devereuxes cursed? Why did these disasters keeping stalking us, poisoning our successes? He would have to mount a second campaign to redeem his role in the first campaign. Publication of the letter was a good start. When he arrived, he would have to trumpet the splendid, chivalrous escapades on the ramparts for the public. The common people loved daring deeds and brave knights. Since they were never to share the booty, they would not mourn its loss. Instead, they would sing the praises of the brave men in arms, banners flying, surmounting the ramparts in the name of England.

Finally I was able to sit without trembling. The candles were burning low, throwing oblique shadows on the walls, and the servants had long since gone to bed. Outside, a few drunken carousers were singing as they stumbled along the Strand, and on the other side, the faint sound of oars on the river. I opened the windows wider, to let in what little breeze there was, and was rewarded by puffs of air as heavy as a basket of wet laundry.

I would sleep in my lightest linen tonight, and even that would most likely be too stifling. I laid my dress aside and made ready for bed, wondering if I would sleep at all.

The bed was as we had left it earlier. I had not tidied it. As I smoothed out the rumples, I was disgruntled with myself. *Is this your way of keeping a memento, Lettice?* I asked myself. *Other women keep flowers or verses; you preserve a disordered bed. Fool!* I smacked at the covers.

"Are you angry at it?" a quiet voice from behind me asked. I whirled around to see Will in the doorway, a black outline against the candlelit outer room.

"How did you get in?" I cried. He had entered so silently.

"You gave me a key. Do you not remember?"

"Yes, yes . . ." The Cádiz crisis had driven all else from my mind. "Forgive me, my mind is roiling. I have had news about the expedition, not entirely welcome news."

"I heard as well. The news is everywhere, although I gather the ships are not back yet. It was the talk of the tavern. It quite drowned out the critics of my play, so I should be thankful."

"Good for you. I have less to be thankful about. Is that why you have come?" I realized how very late it was.

"I left my satchel here," he said.

"As long as you did not leave your purse," I said, I hoped lightly.

"What is in the satchel is of more worth to me than gold," he said. "I have the outline of the plots of my next play as well as several drafts of poems." He went around the bed, feeling behind the curtains. "Ah." He held up a leather satchel triumphantly. "Disaster averted!"

"You could, I suppose, have reconstructed them," I said. Just as my son would have to "reconstruct" his voyage for the public.

"Probably not," he said. "My first ideas are the clearest. After that they fade and become commonplace, losing all their originality." He patted the satchel possessively. "I also"—he looked toward the adjoining room—"wished to speak to you." Before I could move, he slipped out into the other room, and I had no choice but to follow.

In this large, empty chamber, I suddenly felt at a great disadvantage, clad only in a thin nightgown, while he was wearing his doublet, trunk, and hose. He stood a few feet away, watching me. Then he said, "I must not come here again. It must be over."

I had been expecting this, sometime, yet now that it had come, I could only ask dejectedly, "Why?"

"Must I list all the reasons? Surely you know them." He did not sound in the least regretful. That stung.

"Yes, I know them," I said. "And I concur. It must end. It never should have started."

"No. It never should."

"Are you sorry?" Again, the question I should not ask.

"No," he said. "If I said I did not enjoy it, I would be lying. I enjoy it all too much. Like those poor drunkards we see, still longing for that which is destroying them."

"That is not very flattering," I managed to say, thinking all the while that he was describing me, not himself.

"On the contrary, it is an extreme compliment. In any case, your husband is returning, and so is my friend Southampton. Sharing you with all those men taints my appetite, and what was fair becomes festering foulness. You owe your fidelity to your husband, and I owe mine to my friend."

"You speak true."

"Thus, I will say farewell. When we meet again, it must be in public."

He stood there in the middle of the room, his poise enviable.

No man had ever rejected me. I had been the one to call a halt, to say all the tired old phrases, no less true for being tired.

*I must do this for your own good.*

*You will find a woman better suited to you.*

*The fault lies in me, not in you.*

*If the world were different, we could be together.*

"There is someone else," I said, the tiredest phrase of all.

He shrugged. "There is always someone else, in a general sense, but at the same time, for me, there is never anyone else."

"What do you mean by that?"

"Only that, as far as my heart goes, I allow no one to penetrate it, but you have managed. Perhaps you succeeded because you are forbidden. But at the same time, that is why it must end."

I had never felt so humiliated by a man before. I nursed the wound, even as I finally said, "Of course."

He looked pityingly at me. "If I told you that I carry you with me always, that you inform my writing, that you will live in my plays and verse, would you believe me?"

I had to wipe that pity off his face. "Why should that matter to me?" I answered flippantly. "It isn't your writing I'm interested in." There. I hoped that hit home.

It had. For an instant a hurt expression crossed his face, but it was quickly replaced by indifference. Better that than pity.

Wordlessly he turned and left, and I lost him forever.

# 42

# ELIZABETH

*August 1596*

hat man! That nerve!" I flung the paper down in front of me, a pretend letter giving me the earliest report of the Cádiz venture, featuring the derring-do of the Earl of Essex, entitled "A True Relation of the Action at Cádiz." The adventurers were back. They had ventured into port at twilight, as if ashamed to face folks in the honest light of day.

"Patience, Your Majesty," said Robert Cecil. "More will be forthcoming, and have we not received, by hearsay, glowing reports of their success in Cádiz?" He strove to give an impression of calm, to offset me.

"I cannot trust any of them," I lamented. "They alter the telling to glorify themselves."

"All men do, Your Majesty. I fear that is just the human condition. That does not mean we must discount all of it." Robert Cecil shook his head as he shuffled the papers from hand to hand. The most impudent one was this account of the Earl of Essex, which he had tried to have printed secretly and distributed before his arrival. But his messenger, Sir Anthony Ashley, had also been commissioned to track down the treasure that had disappeared once the ships docked. A busy man, Sir Anthony. For as it turned out, he had helped himself to the very treasure he was charged with locating. Trunks of it had been sent to his London house, and he had sold to city merchants an enormous diamond that was earmarked for me. Neither the diamond nor the payment for it had been recovered. The man was an out-and-out thief. I sent him to Fleet Prison and relieved him of the so-called "True Relation of the Action at Cádiz" he was having printed. I then forbade all publications relating to the voyage, on pain of death.

"Where is Essex now?" I asked.

"I just received a request from him to call upon Your Majesty privately. He is, I believe, here in London."

I drummed my fingers on the desk. They echoed the drumming rain outside. Gusts of wind blew spray through the windows, but to close them was to feel as if we were in a tomb. Oh, it was so hard to think in this damp oven! "No," I said. "We shall receive him here in front of the entire court, in the most formal manner. Look to it."

In the meantime I pored over other sketchy reports about the mission, the most factual so far. The fleet had made good speed down to Spain, rounding the corner of Cape St. Vincent before striking Cádiz. The citizens were taken by surprise on that Sunday morning in June. One moment they were strolling in the great square, admiring tumblers and comedians, and the next, 150 warships and galleys, white sails filling the sea, were bearing down upon them. Panicked, they ran for safety to the old citadel on the highest point of land. And then the English commanders—particularly Essex and Raleigh—began to fight among themselves as to who would lead the charge, whether they should first pursue the merchant ships in the harbor or attack the town. Essex had his way, and the naval action was deferred. By the time it was joined, Sidonia had managed to jettison the treasure-laden ships and send them to the bottom of the sea. We had a certain satisfaction in capturing two of their newly built warships named for the apostles, *St. Andrew* and *St. Matthew*, but the other two, *St. Thomas* and *St. Philip*, were burned by the Spanish.

*St. Philip*! King Philip must have been gleeful about his namesake escaping our grasp, that is, if it lay in his nature to be gleeful.

The fighting took only two days. Then it took two weeks for the usual capture and counting of goods and burning of the town. Essex put on a chivalrous show in carrying out my instructions that there be no violence to anyone. He stood, unarmed, talking to Spaniards. He escorted Spanish ladies to the safety of boats to convey them out of the city, allowing them to wear their jewelry and carry trunks of fine clothes. The elderly were put in special boats. He gave his protection to all the religious orders and let the Bishop of Cuzco go free. He was courteous and respectful to nuns, virgins, and other honorable ladies. He gave his hand to the populace and let them kiss it.

I kept rereading the last two sentences, feeling anger rising in me like spring sap. So he was respectful, in public, of honorable Spanish ladies, but did his utmost, in private, to deflower the ones in our court? And as for giving his hand to the people of Cádiz to kiss—what brazen posturing and bid for popularity!

---

I set the day for his reception at court for ten days hence and ordered everyone to be present, on pain of incurring my displeasure. In the meantime, reports of his behavior here reached my ears. He visited Archbishop Whitgift and persuaded him to announce a day of thanksgiving throughout all the realm for the exploits of the mission. Attempting to circumvent my orders forbidding publication of his "True Relation," he had handwritten copies made to circulate among his friends and had it translated into French, Dutch, and Italian to be printed abroad. He commissioned an engraved map of Cádiz, with himself and his actions there, as another way of advertising himself without actual publication of the text. He presented a Great Psalter, taken in the plunder from Cádiz, to King's College at Cambridge, with a poem praising himself added to its frontispiece. This went:

*. . . what man never heard tell of that fearful grappling with Spain,*
*That famed Peninsular raid, which, under the command of a hero—*
*Greater than Hercules he—came right to Hercules' Pillars!*
*He (and in proverbs now, his name personifies valour)*
*Who is the friend and beloved of the common people of England,*
*Head and shoulders above the rest in height and honours,*
*Who held all menacing Spain in check, at the sack of Cadiz . . .*

So! He was greater than Hercules? Head and shoulders above the rest in height and honors? Anyone who doubted he was building up a party for himself, with the goal of seizing power, was as blind as Samson after his eyes were put out. The only saving grace was that he was not clever enough to do it secretly, so his intentions were plain to see. His need to appeal to the public meant everything he did was visible.

I must control him, before he grew too strong to manage. He was still vulnerable, his rivals more numerous and more powerful than he, despite his claim that he was head and shoulders above them in height and honor. Height yes, honor no. It was characteristic of him to think those two were inextricably tied together, as if to be tall were always to be singular. Craving power, he had become everyone's plaything.

The most ominous part of the poem was "Who is the friend and beloved of the common people of England." It was *I* who was the friend and beloved of the people of England. It was I who was their mother, their bride, their protectress. Not he. Never would I allow another to usurp my place in the hearts of my people. I had married England at my coronation, and as with any other marriage, no man must put it asunder.

---

For the reception I returned to Whitehall as the most convenient place for everyone to convene, even though the city was a dreary place this summer.

The rains had turned all the unpaved streets into muddy quagmires, and even the graveled ones were sinking and reverting to mud. The smell from the river had abated somewhat, as so many fish had died and been swept away. Englishmen being Englishmen, things went on gamely. The theaters put on plays; the markets, with their dwindling, sodden produce, stayed open; churches had their rush-strewing ceremonies; river swans were counted and marked. A dogged and determined lot, my people. The taverns did an increased business, spewing drunken people out into the night streets to roam, fight, and sing.

Lying in my bed, the small window open for what little air could come in, I would hear them shouting and singing below, on the street. Sometimes the songs were obscene, making me laugh in spite of myself. Sometimes they were pretty, with melodies that lingered in my mind. But more and more what I heard were songs praising the Earl of Essex, heralding him as the people's darling and their hope.

*"Sweet England's pride,*
*He is, he is,*
*Whose mighty deeds,*
*Are of old,*
*To keep us safe,*
*He's ever bold. . . ."*

He was indeed ever bold. I remembered *"Dwi yu dy garu di,"* "I love you." He had said it on that private journey, far, far away from court. But what did he mean? And why had he said it? There was nothing certain about him, nothing you could rely on, and he could turn against you in an instant.

---

All the court assembled to receive the Earl of Essex in the audience chamber. I wore the gold chain of state bequeathed me by my father. It hung heavily on my breast, the weight of the gold pulling at my neck. But *he* had worn it and never bowed his neck. Neither would I, and may his statecraft be with me now, with the chain to remind me of his presence.

Old Burghley and young Robert Cecil were seated on either side of me, and the rest of the Privy Council on benches flanking us. A long carpet stretched from the door to the base of the throne. Down at the far end a tall figure appeared, long legs outlined against the dark blue of the carpet.

"The Earl of Essex," a herald announced.

"He may approach," I said.

Walking slowly, his elegant figure exquisitely dressed in blue and white, the puffy feathers of his hat waving with every step, he came to me. For an instant, while he was still far away, he seemed every handsome courtier I had ever known. But as he came closer, he could only have been himself, the most elusive of them all. My child, my gallant, my adversary.

He fell to one knee, sweeping off his hat. The plumes trembled. The top of his head, with its wealth of hair, gleamed.

"You may rise," I said, and he did. "Welcome back to England, my lord," I said. "We have heard reports of your doings but prefer that you tell us all, now."

He looked around at the arena of his rivals and partisans. The swaggering Raleigh was standing to one side, arms crossed. Admiral Howard sat on the Privy Council bench, and his brother Thomas nearby. Francis Bacon stood quietly, his sharp eyes fixed on him. George and John Carey waited patiently.

"May I begin by the ending, which is, that it was a glorious success! Let me read a list of our achievements." He unrolled a small parchment. "First, all Philip's war vessels were destroyed, disabled, or driven away. Second, we took all the stores of naval supplies in the warehouses into our possession. Third, the city itself was captured. Fourth, the most prominent citizens are being held for ransom. Fifth, all the merchant ships and their cargoes have been intercepted, so that they will never reach the Indies or Spanish hands. Sixth, we took in a ransom of one hundred twenty thousand ducats for the city itself."

All eyes were now upon me, for my response. "Spanish loss is not our gain," I pointed out. "Treasure at the bottom of the ocean does us no good. Much of the plundered goods seem to have disappeared."

"We have achieved the primary purpose of the mission, which was to inflict insult, damage, and grief on the King of Spain. That we have done. We have thoroughly humiliated him. More is not possible, in the taking of only one city. And if I had had my way, there would have been a seventh prize. We would have held Cádiz instead of torching it, held it as an outpost of England to be a thorn in Spanish flanks, to have a permanent base to interfere with their treasure fleets."

"It was a foolish idea, and rightly overruled," I said. "It would have been outrageously expensive to man and maintain, and vulnerable, being fifteen hundred miles away."

"I humbly disagree, Your Majesty," he said. "And had my idea been followed about stopping in Lisbon rather than scurrying straight home, we would have been twenty million ducats richer. We missed the treasure fleet by only forty-eight hours, sailing right past it."

There was something different about him. I tried to make it out. Then I realized—the beard. It had an odd shape. "You have taken on a new fashion, sir," I said.

Just as I thought it would, the personal comment threw him off. He fingered the beard. "Yes. I grew it on the voyage and have decided to wear it evermore. I call it the Cádiz cut."

"It looks more like it was chopped off at the bottom," I said. "So you wish to be identified with Cádiz for the rest of your life? You may think better of that. For we tell you"—and now I rose—"we are most displeased! We invested fifty thousand pounds in this venture, and what do we have? Nothing! A Cádiz beard? Your vile servant Anthony Ashley has made more money than we! For he still has the cash from the stolen diamond, stolen from us, your Queen!"

"I swear to you, whatever money there is is yours!"

"We know well enough there is none left! We have heard about the streets of Cádiz running with wine and oil, the burst sacks of sugar, raisins, almonds, and olives, and the Spanish church bells, armor, hides, silks, carpets, and tapestries loaded onto our ships. But, sir, they have all disappeared!"

"It was a brave and noble venture. It was worthy of Drake," he insisted.

At the mention of Drake, heads bowed, briefly.

"Drake would never have returned so empty-handed. He never would have dared to come to us with *nothing*." I drew in a deep breath. "In addition, sir, you have sought in many ways to glorify yourself from this mission, and against our express orders about publication. How dare you disobey us? For as we have authority to rule, so do we look to be obeyed. There will be no general thanksgiving throughout the land"—I shot a look at Whitgift—"and we, ourselves, will publish an authorized version of the mission, drawing on several reports. There is to be none other. And last, we are outraged that, again disobeying our orders, you knighted sixty-seven men on this venture. You hold the office too cheaply, handing it out like ale at a country fair. To be a knight means worthy service and deeds, not simply being your friend. We shall unknight them, by God!"

Robert Cecil leaned over, asking permission to speak. I granted it.

"Your Majesty, I must speak on behalf of the new knights' wives. I think the men themselves would be content, but their wives will make their lives miserable if they must so soon give up being called 'lady.'"

A ripple of laughter flowed over the room, growing louder and louder.

"You have a good point, as usual," I said. "Very well. The ladies have done no wrong and should not suffer for the earl's misjudgment."

Essex's spade-shaped beard was trembling. "Him! Him!" He pointed to

Cecil. "While I was away, he beguiled Your Majesty into making him principal secretary, going behind my back."

Oh yes. There was that matter, as well. "We are astounded that you should accuse him of tricking us, implying that he is not worthy of the office. And, sir, we have heard that you claimed we needed your permission to bestow it." I was getting angrier and angrier. I touched the gold chain, to steady myself. My father had a temper, but he never let it blind him; he used it to manage others. "If this is untrue, then speak now."

"I understood that you would make no such appointment."

"Then it was your own fancy that led you to that understanding. *We* understood that you were to make no knights without merit. We are Queen here and free to choose whom we will to serve us. God's breath, we shall suffer no one ever to have it in his power to command us! And that, sir, is all. You are dismissed."

His face flushed, he bowed deeply, turned, and walked slowly down the long aisle. Behind him, the court was silent and stunned and then burst into a buzz of conversation. The courtiers spilled out across the carpet, closing his wake like waters refilling a trench.

"Was it necessary to berate him like that?" Old Burghley leaned over to me. "Public shame can make a man an enemy."

"He'll get over it," I said quickly, as if to convince myself. He did not seem the sort to hold on to anything—grudges or plans.

"I would not be too sure," he said. "Do not assume anything, about anyone."

"Now you sound like Walsingham. Did he not say, 'There is less danger in fearing too much than in fearing too little'?"

"A wise maxim. God rest him." Burghley wheezed. He pulled out a handkerchief and mopped his sweating face. I noticed, sticking out above his gown, how thin, wrinkled, and strained his neck was.

"I've a mind to make him surrender his part of the ransoms for the Spanish prisoners, as a way of restitution for his bungling of the spoils."

"I would advise against that, Ma'am," he said.

"He owes it to me!"

"I think in all fairness he did the best he could. The other commanders and he were at odds. Too many commanders is a recipe for failure, or, at the very least, for confusion."

"Are you questioning my judgment in appointing them? By God, my lord treasurer! Out of either fear or hope of favor you seem to regard my Lord of Essex more than myself!" He had even shaken Burghley's loyalty to me!

Without realizing it, I had raised my voice, and now the Privy Councillors were turning to listen. Burghley frowned, and that irritated me even more. "You are a miscreant! You are a coward!" I said, loud enough that they could hear.

"I am no coward," he said stoutly. "But there are those who fit that description, and we do well to ensure they fear us and not him."

---

In the end, there were two more satisfactions from the Cádiz mission. The aggressive participation of the Dutch in the campaign marked their complete sundering from Spain. I could feel that the money and troops I had committed to their struggle—the drain on my treasury that had begun over a decade ago—had finally paid dividends. It had achieved something, after all. The Protestant Netherlands were a fact now. Spain had lost them forever.

The other satisfaction was that, with the losses from Cádiz, Philip could not repay his loans from the Florentine bankers that autumn. They noted, "*Il re di Spagna è fallito*"—"The Spanish king is broke"—and a number of banks failed, causing them to say that 1596 was the year they and the King of Spain went bankrupt together.

# 43

It had happened. The third harvest in a row had failed, and now desolation stalked the land. Belatedly the sun shone, making a bright October, mocking us. It gave cheerful sunshine to the poor begging at city gates, to farmers, their own stores gone, scrabbling in the fields for food. Vagrants roamed the roads, threatening people. Discharged sailors and soldiers from the Cádiz mission loitered everywhere, looking for work and food. With Robert Cecil and George Carey's supervision, the government drew up a plan to provide food for the needy, but it was not nearly enough, for our attempts to buy grain from our Protestant allies had failed. We had no means of distributing it widely, nor enough of our own stored up to alleviate the crisis. Wednesdays and Fridays were declared fast days, but that affected only the rich. The poor were fasting already.

I was at Nonsuch. The days were magnificent, the sun shining as if through a golden glass, bathing the countryside in a mellow, tawny glow. The oaks stood proudly, rustling in their deep oxblood red leaves, not yet fallen, and beneath them darted an occasional fox, its coat matching the leaves. But where I was used to hearing the strains of harvest songs from the fields, there was silence, and the full October moon shone on empty fields.

I had not been there a week when Robert Cecil sought an urgent audience. He rode quickly from London and was there by late afternoon. I was waiting, knowing it could not be good news. I was not disappointed.

"Your Majesty, may it please God you are well," he said quickly, pulling off his hat, rattling off the formal address like a popish priest muttering his beads by rote.

"What is it, my good man?" He was becoming more and more indispensable to me as his father faded from the scene. He alone, of the young replacements in the Privy Council, was worthy of the one he was replacing. The others—pah. Little men.

"Two acute dangers! One at home, one abroad. Here, there has been an apprentice-led food riot in London. But more serious is a conspiracy of the hungry mobs in Oxfordshire to attack landowners who have enclosed their fields for sheep grazing. Our reports say that their grievances have made them reckless, crying that 'rather than they would starve, they would rise' and they will 'cut down the gentlemen rather than their hedges' and 'necessity hath no law.'"

"Where in Oxfordshire?"

"In midshire. They plan to gather on Enslow Hill, midway between Woodstock and Oxford, there to march on several landowners, robbing and killing them, burning their houses, and thence to Rycote to take Sir Henry Norris prisoner before beheading him. Then on to London, they say."

So it was beginning, the dreadful political harvest from the too-scant food harvests. "Enslow Hill, you say?" There had been another rebellion there, in 1549. Their choice of the same gathering spot meant they saw themselves as finishing what had gone awry the first time.

"Yes. And the day chosen is St. Hugh's Day."

November 17—my Accession Day. The symbolism could not have been more pointed.

"Do you have any intelligence about the numbers involved?"

"It is impossible to say how many will join when the hue and cry is raised. The ringleaders only number some fifty or so. Bartholomew Steer, a carpenter, is the leader and organizer; he comes from a village that once was a monastic estate and now has been enclosed for sheep. He also worked for Sir Henry Norris, so he has personal grievances against him as well."

"This is what we feared and were hoping would not happen." But this third year of bad harvest had pushed the people to desperation.

"We are working to infiltrate them. They meet and communicate at the various village fairs. In the meantime, we can quietly muster troops. Henry Norris has been alerted, and you know he can command supporters." Cecil spoke confidently, reassuringly.

"What else? You said two things."

"The Armada, Your Majesty. Philip has prematurely launched the Armada he was preparing for next spring. He was so incensed at the attack at Cádiz, he vowed immediate revenge. Our spies there have confirmed that the nobles thanked God on their knees for the coming of Essex and Admiral Howard because it catapulted Philip into action. The second Armada, planned and discussed for so many years, at last is launched."

"The particulars?"

"It is under the command of Don Martin de Padilla, admiral of Castile."

"Oh, God!" Padilla had been general of the oared galleys at the victory at Lepanto against the Turks and had defended the entrance of Lisbon against Drake in the ill-fated 1589 raid. "Unlike Sidonia, he is competent."

"There are about a hundred and fifty ships," said Cecil. "The same size as the first Armada, as our 1589 Portugal raid, and as the recent Cádiz mission. We cannot confirm how many soldiers are aboard."

"We would not expect them to sail so late in the year. They could count on that. And knowing that, they could also count on our having disbanded our fleet, so we would be totally unprotected. Where is their target? Where shall they make landing?"

He looked frustrated. "Our intelligence has not revealed it. It could be either Ireland, or, if England, the Isle of Wight, the Thames, or the west coast."

"In other words, anywhere!"

He tugged at his ear. "Yes, Your Majesty."

I clutched the arms of my chair, as if to draw strength and steadiness from the solid English oak. Attacked from within and from without. No standing army, and a disbanded fleet. What to do? What to do? I must decide, and quickly. Every hour counted.

Cecil was standing, waiting for me to speak, ready to carry out whatever I ordered.

"I must think," I said. "You may stay the night in your accustomed chambers and in the morning take my orders back to London." I had assigned Cecil permanent quarters in all the palaces so he could always be nearby if need be. I stood up. "Avail yourself of any of the fresh horses in the stable," I said. "The autumn has never been lovelier, and you may find it soothing. I daresay you did not linger to look at the fields and meadows on your way here."

He smiled. "I did not," he admitted. "But it would be a balm to do so now. I spend too many hours indoors at the council table."

"It will sap you," I said. As it had me. "Beware of constant council tables and no exercise. A man needs to see the sky at least once a day."

After he departed, I should have taken my own advice and gone outside. I thought better in fresh air. But I had to tell Marjorie of the danger at Rycote. I hurried to my apartments and found her reading quietly, head bent into her book.

Her hair was smoke gray at the part now, although the ends were still black, as befitted my Crow.

"Marjorie." I bent over and took her book gently. "Does this give you pleasure?"

She looked up, her eyes still dark and clear. "Oh, indeed. I am learning about the fall of Constantinople."

"There is solace in history," I said. "But now we must speak of the present, and its dangers." I drew her up. "I have just had word that there is a threat against Rycote, and Sir Henry." I told her what I knew.

"Bartholomew!" she cried. "To think that sweet child would wish us harm. He was always following us about; his father had been a carpenter as well, and brought little Bart along on jobs. While his father worked building stalls and stairs, Bart would hang at my knee, asking questions. I gave him a pup once, from a litter we had."

"Marjorie, he is no longer a child but an angry man who bristles with violence. Cecil said Henry had been warned, but perhaps I should send troops to protect him."

"Oh, no. That would shame him. We have four surviving sons, soldiers all, and that is protection enough. I should go!"

"Your sons are not here; they are in Ireland and the Netherlands. You must not go anywhere near. It would only give Bart a target. Should he capture you, he would have Henry in his hand as well."

"I am sure he would never harm me."

"Because you were kind to him as a child? The lion is not the same as the cub. No, you must not go!"

Marjorie paced the room, her heavy footsteps sounding on the worn floorboards. She was a big-boned woman, broad and tall, as befitted the mother of six sons, all military men, one of them the ablest soldier in England: Black Jack Norris. I always found her as stalwart as a soldier herself, and she had calmed me in many a crisis. But now she was trembling. I touched her shoulder and she jumped.

"I think troops would be prudent," I said. "At least until Henry can rally his own." Both he and Marjorie were in their midseventies. He was still vigorous, or liked to maintain that he was, being on horseback every morning before others were up on foot. But I appreciated how much of that might be posturing. He would need help; he would have needed it even if he were forty. The evil of those rebels, seeking to maim and kill, must be scotched, and quickly. That they would think of visiting such cruelty on my subjects was an insult to me, and they would answer for it. They must be met with force before they could do harm.

She shook herself to gain control. "I always thought danger lay in foreign battlefields," she said. "Home was the place you retired to in safety."

"In my land, that should be true. This is an aberration." We had been spared the hideous wars of religion that tore apart Europe. "A short-lived one, I hope." Then I told her about Spain's Armada.

"Oh, my dear lady," she said. "Troubles from within and without."

I pinched her cheek. "Now do your duty of cheering me about the Spanish, as you always do."

She laughed, the old Marjorie again for a moment. Then the smile faded. "We must pray for another English wind to blow them to pieces," she said.

---

I sat glumly in my bedchamber, my face cupped between my hands. I had asked Catherine to bring me my jewels. I would have to pawn some; the painful selection must be made. Catherine had dutifully set down several coffers, all locked. She, as keeper of the Queen's jewels, carried the keys.

"This one has the historic Crown jewels," she said, pointing to an ebony-inlaid one with a rounded top. "This one contains the everyday jewels, if you can call them that." She touched a polished walnut one with gold fittings. "And this holds your personal ones." That box was covered in mother-of-pearl.

I would never sell the personal ones—the pearls from Leicester, the emerald pendant from Drake, the Three Brothers ruby pendant from my father and his heavy gold chain, the *B* initial necklace from my mother, the frog pin from François. No, never. So I pushed that one aside. No point in even opening it.

Neither would I sell the historic ones. It was not possible. They belonged to England and must be here for the next person who sat on the throne. There was the thin gold coronet of Richard the Lionheart, set with tiny lapis studs from the Holy Land. There was a globule-shaped dark ruby worn by Henry V at Agincourt, inherited from the Black Prince; the square sapphire coronation ring of Edward the Confessor; a gold cross of Alfred the Great. I liked to take them out and tell myself the stories connected to them, such as the tradition that in personal combat with the Duc d'Alençon, Henry V almost lost the ruby when Alençon smashed at it with a blow to the helm, barely missing. We monarchs like to dare all, exposing our precious things in battle.

Battle. It was because of battle I was having to sell these treasures. Battles on land, in the Netherlands, battles on sea, now battles at home. *But Henry V,* I promised him, *your ruby did not survive Agincourt to be squandered now on the pitiful King of Spain.*

The everyday jewels . . . I would have to start casting them out to keep myself afloat, like a sinking ship throwing off precious cargo to save itself. Drake had had to do so on his way home once, throwing overboard three tons of cloves worth a fortune, but worth nothing if he could not free his ship from the rocks where it was stuck. And so the spices floated away, and he floated free. Thus it must be for us, I thought, pulling out a delicate gold and pearl necklace with hanging droplets of sapphires—a gift from the ambassador of Denmark. Diplomatic gifts would be the first to go, the easiest to let go of. There were pendants with rubies and dull uncut diamonds, earrings with medium-sized pearls, nothing outstanding in either the workmanship or the gems. Those came from France, Sweden, and Russia. Then there were the onyx necklaces from Spain, presented when we still had Spanish ambassadors here. The Spanish like black, I thought. Black jewelry, black-robed priests, black deeds.

There were heavy gold bracelets, now out of style, presented by long-dead courtiers. They would yield a good price, though, for their gold, and the givers would never know their fate. Brooches that were so heavy they pulled embroidery, pins that did not fasten properly, rings that were too large and went round and round on my finger—those could go. I was getting a tidy little pile. But how many ships could they buy? How many soldiers could they provision? Nestled among them, incongruously, was the gold-painted wooden egg from the long-ago goose fair. I smiled. It, too, was a treasure—but only to me.

Well, I had begun. I would pawn these and see what the yield was before I cut any deeper. I also had more Crown lands I could sell, although that was a last resort.

Catherine did not make it easier. She stood behind me, looking sadly at the glittering heap. She leaned over and pulled out an amber necklace. "Oh, you aren't going to sell this, are you? I remember when Ivan IV sent this!"

"I never liked it," I said. "It was an ugly color."

"But it was highly prized in Russia, where they like their amber dark."

"They are entitled to their preferences," I said.

"It was a shame about Ivan," she said.

"That he ended up called 'the Terrible'?"

"Yes, because he had great ability and insights," she said. "Not the least, of course, courting your friendship."

"Well, rest him, wherever he now is." He had become even more insane in his last days. On his deathbed he had taken the habit of a strict monastic order of monks and renamed himself Jonah. "I think I still have his sables. You are welcome to them for the winter. I know the cold is more of a hardship for you than for me."

"The winters are becoming harder to get through," she said. "Every year, when spring arrives, I want to tell the trees not to hurry to leaf out, lest winter make another attack."

I laughed. "Like the Spanish," I said. I stood up, feeling almost enfeebled. It was because of all the worry and inactivity, I told myself. I pushed myself away from the table. It was still an hour or so until sunset. "We need a walk," I said. "Pray come with me. We'll get Marjorie. We three old crows will take some exercise."

Nonsuch was the hunting lodge par excellence; whenever we came, the master of the hounds brought packs of the royal hunting dogs. But rather than hunt myself this time, I told the people of the area to hunt freely on the royal estate during this time of need.

We headed for the grove of Diana, a paean to hunting. A gentle wood, it had a platform at its entrance where I normally would stand to shoot, but today we passed under it and into the woods proper. A thick carpet of fallen leaves crunched under our feet, releasing a pungent, spicy odor.

"That smell is so peculiar to the season, it always means autumn to me," said Catherine, from behind us. She was having trouble keeping up, and we slowed. Her plump body, swathed in mourning for her father, was not meant for fast walking.

"Some say cloves or cinnamon smell the same, but I disagree," said Marjorie.

The golden avenue shone before us, beckoning us to its central feature, the cavern with its statue of Actaeon before it, surrounded by rocks and splashing water. Linking arms, we walked the autumnal aisle, three abreast, keeping faith and pace with one another. A great wave of gratitude swept over me, making me weak. These two women were the sisters I had created out of my own solitariness. My real-life sister could never have been a sister to me, with our mothers enemies; in any case, she was long passed away. I had taken friends and made them, as the Bible says, closer than a brother. Should I speak of these feelings?

As we reached the great statue of Diana, shielding herself from the intrusive eyes of the hapless hunter Actaeon, the fleeting sunlight dappled her white shoulders, caressing them. Her eyes were narrowed, and she gazed mercilessly on the huddled form of Actaeon beneath her, just as he was changing into a stag so his own dogs would leap on him to tear him to pieces for seeing the naked goddess in her bath.

"A lovely piece of work," said Marjorie, "but the story always revolts me. The man saw her naked. He didn't mean to. Why should he be killed for it?" She stared at the statue, challenging it, her jaw jutting as it did when she was annoyed.

"Careful, or she'll get angry at you," said Catherine in her soothing voice, as sweet as the dying light falling in the grove. "She's a goddess and must never be insulted."

"Virgins are touchy," said Marjorie, slyly looking over at me. "We married women, well, it's hard to insult us."

"Both of you have husbands who would never insult you," I said. "Neither Sir Henry nor Lord Charles would do such a thing. It is, I think, more often *you* who try their patience." But I laughed as I said it. Sisters, after all, can tease.

"It isn't I who tries Charles's patience," said Catherine. "What did you think of the letter where he cut Essex's signature off?"

Marjorie gave an explosion of laughter. "The question is, what did Essex think?"

On the Cádiz mission, the rivalry between the two had exploded when Howard had enough of Essex's always signing his name first on documents, so high that no one could ever sign above him, so he took a knife and cut Essex's signature out.

"He probably challenged him to a duel, which Charles ignored," said Catherine with a sigh. "He's such a tiresome boy."

A crackling alerted us that a deer was nearby. We stopped talking and waited. In a moment I glimpsed the deer's nose, then his shoulders. He was wary, looking at the cavern. Shadows were fast growing, and he could not discern anything to alarm him. He ventured closer to drink, then he spotted us and bounded away, his tail flashing.

"This Actaeon will live," I said. "Caution has served him well." I turned to look at each woman. "You both are fearful for your husbands, I know. One is in danger on his own lands, and the other must defend us at sea again. Without such loyal subjects, this Diana would not be safe. Never think I do not value, or understand, their constant sacrifices. And yours—for the constant worry on their behalf, and for serving me all these years, even though it means absence from them."

Wordlessly, they embraced me, silent in the moment.

Then, as was her wont, Marjorie spoke. "Well, are you not the imperial votaress? We are your vestals, even though we are not virgins. And I daresay, the young ones you have tried to keep as virgins, you have had little success in doing so." She gave such a laugh that had there been any deer still nearby, they would have fled.

"The fair of face are often weak in resolve," said Catherine. "Only you, Your Majesty, had both beauty and strength of will. The younger ones now in the privy chamber . . . I don't want to speak behind their backs—"

"Oh, do!" said Marjorie. "It takes my mind off the things that are weighing on it. You are so kind, mild, and quiet, they let down their guard with you."

"They are exceptionally beautiful, but they seem so easily, well, seduced, like Bess Throckmorton was, and Elizabeth Southwell."

"That's over and done," I said. "Both of them."

"Mary Fitton is being pursued by that dirty-minded old uncle of Essex's—William Knollys," said Catherine. "He haunts our chambers, making excuses to seek her out. The man is married, yet pretends he isn't."

"Mistress Fitton has that look," snorted Marjorie. "A look that says yes, even when she is shaking her head no."

"And Elizabeth Vernon," said Catherine. "I think she has a secret suitor."

"Another beauty with inviting eyes and inviting perfume," said Marjorie. "But after all, they come to court to make their fortunes, as the men do. The men's fortunes are in offices and appointments, the women's in making a good marriage. We cannot blame them for doing what comes naturally."

Twilight was here, and chill was creeping through the grove. We must leave while we could still see. "Come, my ladies," I said.

Carefully we made our way back to the palace grounds, feeling our way. Darkness grew so rapidly that by the time we reached the topiary garden, I could no longer make out anyone's features. Ahead of us torches were already flaring in the courtyard. Stars appeared one by one in the sky; Venus glowed brightly near the horizon, as if she were taunting all the Actaeons of the world.

We ate a quiet supper in the privy chamber, the younger women joining us. I looked carefully at Mistress Fitton and Mistress Vernon, but their demeanor was perfectly proper. The usual gallants of the court had stayed behind, so I was reminded of the saying "All women are chaste when there are no men." After supper they entertained us with sweet melodies on the virginal and offered us wines they had flavored with herbs from Italy. A few sips would suffice, as the taste was strong.

The young ones slept in the outer chamber, Marjorie and Catherine near me in the inner one. As we had a thousand nights and more, we made ready for sleep, they attending me, handing me my nightclothes and taking my day clothes away to be aired and then folded. I slipped into the adjoining room to my altar and prayer seat, there to pause at the close of my day, a nun keeping her own compline. The altar was quite bare, as befitted a Protestant one, but candles winked and jumped upon it, flanking the little vase of late-blooming musk roses and meadow saffron where a crucifix would be.

It was now full dark. I could hear the sounds of night animals, especially the cries of owls. The barren fields must be full of hungry rodents; the hunting was good for raptors. The owls were full, even if the farmers were not.

I continued the thoughts that I had spoken aloud to Catherine and Marjorie in the grove. Since then I had remembered the entire Scripture quote, from Proverbs: "There is a friend that sticketh closer than a brother." Catherine was my cousin, shared my blood on my mother's side. Marjorie's husband's father had literally shed his blood for my mother, making him more than a relative. He was one of the men accused of adultery with her and executed. He had been a close friend and attendant in my father's privy chamber, supporting him in his marriage. But he was swept away in the trumped-up evidence that Cromwell gathered against her. Perhaps what put it into Cromwell's head was the May Day joust in which my mother dropped a handkerchief and Henry Norris picked it up and mopped his forehead with it before returning it. Arresting him, Cromwell promised to spare his life if he would confess to adultery and name the others who had indulged along with him. Instead, Norris offered to undergo trial by combat to defend my mother's honor. Later, on the scaffold, when the others had cried, prayed, and made farewell statements, Norris was quiet, saying little. He knew it would avail him nothing and possibly cost his family their inheritance.

Some twenty years later the roles were reversed and his son—the present Henry Norris—was my jailer. During my sister's reign, I was kept under house arrest at Woodstock, near Marjorie's family lands at Rycote. He and Marjorie were my keepers, but gentle and kind ones. We all knew that his father had died for loyalty to my mother, and as I said, that made us closer than brother and sister. The Catholics say there are three baptisms: the baptism of water—the usual means; the baptism of desire—a fierce, committed longing for it; and the baptism of blood—dying for one's faith. There are likewise many ways of becoming related.

Surrounded by such stout and loving loyalists, how could I ever feel the orphan I technically was?

# 44

## LETTICE

*November 1596*

he November skies were leaden—as leaden as my spirits—while the carriage jounced along the paved remnants of the old Roman road north from London. I was headed to the Bacon house at St. Albans, there to join my son and his advisers. I did not really care where I was, as long as I was out of London. Essex House resounded with too many memories. I should never have allowed myself to let Will loom so large there, but it had happened invisibly.

I had lost interest in Southampton; he reminded me too much of Will, although they were nothing alike in looks or manner, as if the absence of one had caused his ghost to affix to the other. How ironic, since it was to preserve his feelings that Will had called an end to us—or pretended that was the reason. Perhaps it was not. Southampton could now invest all his considerable youthful energies in Elizabeth Vernon, whom he pursued with vigor. Well, happiness to their sheets, as Will said in one of his plays. To my own shame, I had attended some of those plays surreptitiously, slinking away afterward in embarrassment and vowing not to attend one again.

---

Oh, I knew the remedy. Find another. Tut, man, one fire burns out another's burning. Will's words again. His words were proving permanent, like darts embedded in my mind. Take thou some new infection to thine eye, and the rank poison of the old will die.

I slid my eye to Christopher, slumped over, dozing, in a corner of the carriage. With each bounce, his head jolted, but it did not wake him. As a soldier, he was used to sleeping in worse conditions.

Christopher gave a murmur and settled himself more comfortably, crossing his arms. I felt a great affection, but no desire, for him. I was grateful he had returned safely from the Cádiz mission, where he had performed well, leading land forces at both Cádiz and Faro. His cousin Charles had earned his knighthood there. The entire venture had been good for our family. But oh! Their return had spelled the end to my secret sin.

Christopher pulled the collar of his cloak up around his neck, nestling into it against the chill. He was in his midthirties now, no longer boyish in looks but a man in his prime. His dark hair was still thick and had no gray, his face seemingly permanently tanned from his soldiering. An attractive man—more attractive than the boy who had served Leicester in the Netherlands. Many a woman would find him tempting. Why could I not? If I could not change my feelings, he would take up with someone else.

I reached out to stroke his hand just as the carriage hit a nasty bump and awoke him. He opened his eyes, saw my hand against his, and smiled that drowsy smile that had always excited me. Today, however, all it did was reassure me that I could still please him.

---

By the time we reached Gorhambury House, after almost twenty miles, I was more than ready to leave the coach. We tumbled out of it, glad to have the earth beneath our feet once more, and walked a bit unsteadily up the graveled path to the long, plain dwelling amid its oak grove. Wisps of fog, dancing in the autumn wind, blew across the white facade. My cloak filled with air, rounding out like a sail.

We knocked at the main entrance door, but Anthony Bacon appeared at another one and motioned us that way. It was a smaller door, farther from the path, and we scurried in, the wind chasing us.

"Welcome," he said, his cadaverous voice echoing from his black-clad chest. I saw instantly that he was no better, and that saddened me. "I apologize for routing you here. The other door is not to be used."

I shrugged off my cloak. "Oh, is it under repair? It is good to get it done before winter, despite the inconvenience."

"Noooo . . ." He looked embarrassed. "My father nailed it up after the Queen's visit here almost twenty years ago, so no lesser person could ever step over the same threshold."

"Your father has been dead almost that long. After so many years, the house ought truly to be yours. It is time to open that door," I said, without thinking.

"My father is dead but the Queen is not, and she knows about the door," said Anthony. "She might decide to visit us again."

"Well, then nail it up again quickly," said Christopher. "How would she know?"

Always the practical soldier. Perhaps it was better to be with such a man than a poet. At least for everyday life.

He led us back into the main area of the house. In spite of having been enlarged over the years to accommodate the Queen, its dimensions were still small. The Great Hall was not very great, being only about twenty feet wide and thirty-five long. My privy chamber at Essex House was larger. Now, with the new fashion of huge windows so that walls were more glass than stone, Gorhambury looked darkly out of date.

"I have some mulled wine," he said. "Here, let me warm it." He shuffled over to the fireplace and held a poker above the coals; when it glowed red, he thrust it into the pitcher, making a sizzle. Pouring some into goblets, he handed us each one. Cupping my hands around mine, I sipped the delicious, sweet, dark liquid. I had been chilled straight through.

"Francis will be here shortly," he said, sinking down onto a padded bench. "And Robert, he's on his way."

"How do you fare, Anthony?" I asked. Being the first comers gave us a short, unexpected private time together.

He smiled a wan smile. "Not well, but no worse," he said. "I cannot travel beyond the house, although the Queen keeps inviting me to court."

He was wanted at court and could not go. I could go but was not wanted: one of God's little teases.

"Is it your eyesight? Are you having trouble reading?" A severe handicap for a spymaster.

"I can do well enough in bright light, but in addition to my eyes, I have—nervous attacks." As if to prove it, he gave a skittish laugh. "I collapse at inopportune moments. That is really why I cannot go to court. I cannot risk it happening in public."

That would undo him utterly. "No, you cannot." I patted his arm. "Neither of us can go, then, but we make a life for ourselves outside of it. There is a whole world beyond court. Poets speak of it, at least." Even my son had written a plaintive sonnet about being happy living far from court, saying he would be "Content with hip, with haws, and brambleberry, / In contemplation passing still his days." Sometimes he even meant it.

"Court's a bore anyway, Anthony," said Christopher, draining his cup. He got up and refilled it himself.

A door slammed. In a moment Francis appeared, brushing the drops off his shoulders. "Bleak out there," he said. He looked at Christopher and me. "No one else here yet?"

Francis gladly took a cup of the wine and swallowed it quickly. "Did you come up the old Roman road?" he asked us. "I saw your carriage. It's torture in a vehicle."

"I slept," said Christopher, pouring another cup. How much was he going to drink?

"I am probably bruised," I said, rubbing my side.

"That road is the one Boudicca used fighting against the Roman legions. She must have gotten quite a few bumps in her two-wheeled chariot. Ouch."

"A red-haired queen fighting foreign invaders," said Anthony. "History repeats itself."

"I hope not," said Francis. "Boudicca was beaten, in spite of her early victories. The Romans were too disciplined, too strong, and too many for her." He smiled, but with no humor behind it. He opened a small cabinet and took out some sling stones and ax heads. "Tokens of war," he said. "I collect them. They are still lying where they fell, from the battle at Verulamium nearby—Roman arrows and spearheads and British swords and sickles. They tell the tale of the battles clearly for those with eyes to see. I've trained mine to read these signs." He caressed one arrow tip. "The battle over for fifteen hundred years, but you still sing your song," he said.

"I don't like what you said about discipline, strength, and numbers," said Christopher. "We English have no discipline—our armies are makeshift. Without discipline there is no strength. And as for numbers, Spain is a much bigger country than we are. If those are the determinants, we are doomed."

"It's only necessary for the enemy to be lacking those things as well, and then you are evenly matched. On paper the Spanish look better than they really are," said Francis. "Do not fret yourself. There's a saying: The French are wiser than they seem, and the Spaniards seem wiser than they are. I am incorporating that in the collection of pieces I am writing and plan to publish next year."

"You have been muttering about these pieces for months," said Anthony. "They don't make sense to me. They are just a collection of your opinions. Why would anybody pay for your opinions? They are nothing but secular sermons!"

"They will pay because I am who I am," he said grandly.

"And who's that?" asked Christopher. "The only title you have is Queen's Counsel Extraordinary, and I don't see her asking your counsel for much of anything. Now you are offering your counsel to others, hoping they will show more interest? What do you call these little things?"

"Essays," he said. "I call the book *The Essays or Counsels, Civil and Moral, of Francis Bacon.*"

"Francis Bacon, Conceit Extraordinary," wheezed Anthony. "Having had to endure your philosophizing and analyzing all my life, I wouldn't give a penny for it!"

"Well, I hope others will."

"I'll raise a cup to that!" Christopher bolted down another one. "May you become rich and need no one's patronage. Publishing is the way! Get yourself set up with a bookstall in St. Paul's, like the Raleighs and the Shakespeares, and you'll flourish."

"I plan to sell there, yes," said Francis. "I'll do anything necessary to raise money."

"There's a hot market for memoirs of the Cádiz trip, if only we could tap into it," said Christopher. "Everyone is dying to know the details, but the Queen won't let us publish. Poor Robert." He looked down into his empty cup. "Poor me. I had a good one written up, lots of swashbuckling bravado."

We settled ourselves on cushioned chairs in the wood-paneled room. The richness of the carved linenfold paneling and the patterned ceiling made it feel warm but dark. The many candles and the fire did little to brighten it, as though the wood itself absorbed the light. Barely visible against the wall was a large portrait of the father, Sir Nicholas Bacon. The Queen's Lord Keeper of the Great Seal, he was clutching his staff of office and looking suspiciously out at his audience.

He had been a huge man, and the portrait did nothing to disguise it. Supposedly once the Queen had visited him here and remarked that his house was too small for him. He took the hint and enlarged the house for her next visit. It was an unwise man who did not catch the Queen's hints.

He had been a large man in other ways, having so many children by his two marriages that he had been unable to provide for them all. Sir Nicholas had been intending to sell certain property to ensure an inheritance for his youngest and most gifted, Francis, but had died unexpectedly, making young Francis practically a pauper for all his brilliance. Anthony had inherited the house, and generously shared it with his brother, but that did not ease the worry of always being out of pocket.

There was, of course, on the other wall the obligatory portrait of the Queen, looking as if she were twenty-five. It was the official portrait. This year she had ordered all the unflattering ones that made her look old—in other words, the realistic ones—confiscated and destroyed. Only the palace-approved image must be displayed. And so a perpetual Persephone looked out from portraits where Demeter should be gazing. Or someone even older. I had never realized it before, but there were no elderly Greek gods or goddesses. Well, the Queen intended there should be no elderly-looking monarchs on the English throne, either.

Across from the Sir Nicholas portrait was one of his widow, Lady Anne. She wore an expression of aloofness, as if she disapproved of his portliness. The old term for widow, "relict," fitted her well.

The rest of the room was spare. It reflected its owner: A scholar. A bachelor. Neither brother ever married. This was suggestive in itself. Perhaps the Queen assumed they were . . . or that their peculiar natures hinted at something beyond just bachelorhood . . . ?

Francis turned and stared at me as if he could read my mind. I almost blushed. I had to say something, so I said, "Didn't you meet the Queen here once when you were a child?"

"Yes, she asked me questions in that manner we all know so well," he said. "I was about eight or nine. It was the time she made the remark about the house being too small. She asked me if I studied Greek and Latin, called me a little scholar, and then asked what I thought was the most important thing a man should learn. I said, to unlearn what he had been taught. She laughed about it and teased my tutor."

"Well, I met her at the same age, and she wasn't so pleased with what I did!" Robert flung open the door of the room and stood in the doorway. He tugged off his mantle, tossing it on a chair, and its flying drops went all over us. "She tried to kiss me and I pulled away. I thought she was a crazy old hag. Now, of course, I join with everyone in praising her beauty." He swept off his hat before the portrait, mockingly.

Anthony looked nervously about and shut the door.

"Greetings, Son," I said. He dutifully bent down and kissed my cheek. "It was not exactly as you describe it." What if a servant overheard and reported his insult? "You never liked being approached by strangers, and you weren't sure who she was."

"The French say there is always one who kisses and one who allows himself or herself to be kissed, and I say, that day the Queen was the one doing the kissing." He gave a loud laugh and grabbed one of the wine cups.

"Well, she isn't now," said Francis flatly. "Now, when it counts, not when you were nine years old."

Robert shrugged, but it looked rehearsed. "I care not," he said. "The crowds cheer me, and I'm hailed everywhere I go. That doesn't happen to her anymore. People blame her for all the troubles."

"There's to be a parliament to address the problems," said Francis. "It will meet in February. The Queen is not insensitive to her people, you know."

"Did you bring Frances?" I asked Robert. Lately he had taken a renewed interest in his wife, or perhaps it was part of his effort to bolster his reputation.

"Yes, she's with Lady Bacon. In the library."

I supposed I should excuse myself and go join them, but I preferred to stay with the men. Lady Bacon was as starched as one of her Puritan ruffs and as scholarly as her sons, and I saw enough of Frances every day. When Charles Blount arrived, if he brought Penelope, then I would go with the women.

"Well, man, what did you call us for?" Robert said, rubbing his cold hands together. "I've asked some of our Cádiz fellows to join us, and they'll be here soon, so get to it."

His arrogance and presumption had expanded greatly with the adulation he had received from the public since his return. Somewhere inside he must know that it is rude to invite a crowd to someone else's house. But he excused himself from the usual constraints.

Francis ran his hands over his hips, as if he were getting ready for an athletic contest. "You asked me to analyze your position and to make recommendations. I have done so. Here is my summary." He twisted around to pick up an envelope, which he handed to Robert.

A wide smile on his face, Robert broke the seal and shook the paper out grandly. He began reading, squinting at the small handwriting, and the smile gradually drained away. Finally he folded the paper up, replaced it in the envelope, and tucked it into his waistband. "Your recommendations are nonsense," he said.

"How so?" Francis asked.

"To begin with, you think I should drop my military career. It's the only thing that's ever rewarded me with honors and money. So that's like asking the pope to give up the Mass."

"If the pope had been more flexible about the Mass, he need not have lost all of northern Europe. Take a lesson from him." Francis was not going to back down. "Can you not see that a powerful subject who pursues military glory would be threatening to someone of the Queen's nature?"

Robert ignored the question. "Second, you say that I must stop appealing directly to the people."

"Obviously, that is a direct challenge to any ruler, male or female."

"Third, you say I demand high offices and honors but don't have the talent for them!"

"You are remarkably good at hiding them, if you possess them," said Francis.

"I thought you were my friend!" cried Robert.

"I am your friend; that's why I am being honest with you. I did not say you had no abilities equal to your ambition; I only said you need to prove it to the Queen. Instead of demonstrating your worthiness, you throw temper tantrums and expect her to appease you. That game grows old. The Queen will tire of it. The day will come when she puts you aside like an outworn toy. Before that day comes, you must prove you are no toy. Now, while you still have time."

"You say I should give up soldiership. But the moment I was away, the Queen promoted Robert Cecil, giving him the plum office. I cannot even get offices for my friends. I tried and tried for the attorney generalship and the general solicitorship for you, Francis. Without my military command, I have nothing!"

"You need to be more subtle. If you could do that, everything else would follow."

"How? How more subtle? You know so much, do you? Give me an example!"

"Well, for example, you might announce leaving court to visit your estates and then cancel the journey if the Queen objects. Or nominate a candidate for an office and withdraw him pleasantly if the Queen says she prefers someone else. Is that specific enough?"

"It's out of character. She'll suspect."

"If you continue to behave that way, it will soon be in character. Oh, and stop complaining and harping on injustices and slights. They are over, and the Queen won't change her appointments, so be gracious about them."

"Only a hypocrite changes to please someone," snorted Robert. "Now I'll quote Scripture to you: Can the Ethiopian change his skin, or the leopard change his spots? No, and neither can I change into another creature at will."

"Bah. You are not one person but many persons. We all are. We can choose which of our many selves to cultivate for any purpose. Don't be so dense!"

"I must be who I am."

"You must be who you are called to be. And cut off that silly beard that you have so coyly named the Cádiz style. Every time you speak it wags like a flag, crying, 'Notice me, applaud me.'"

"Good for you, Francis," I said. "I agree. It is hideous. Son, it makes you look like a billy goat." As soon as I spoke, I regretted it. He would have to keep it now to show he did not bend his knee to his mother.

"My chin is no concern of yours," he said quietly. "And I think you are wrong to advise me to abandon military campaigns. With the end of our involvement in French affairs, we are free to turn our attention to Spain. In fact, I will do everything in my power to lead another mission next summer, as big and as strong as the Cádiz one. Far from following your advice, I plan to take the opposite path." The square-cut beard trembled and then stayed still when he closed his mouth firmly.

"That is foolish," said Francis sadly.

"It's within my grasp," he said. "All I want. Why should I stop now?"

# 45

e stamped out, leaving the room as dramatically as he had entered it. He almost collided with Southampton and Charles Blount, who were just arriving. Shoving them inside, he muttered, "Keep them company, for I'll not linger with fools!"

The two men looked around as if they had been deposited on a strange sandbank on an uncharted river. "What ails him?" Charles asked, pulling off his hat.

"He has just received an unpalatable truth," said Anthony. "He chooses to attack it rather than embrace it."

"Ah, that." Southampton draped his cloak properly over a peg. He was wearing brown velvet, which always set off his delicate coloring. There was no denying it—he was a spectacularly handsome man, a faun in a sunlit clearing. Holding him had been like embracing classical art. "No one attacks truth and survives; he'll come to his senses." He went over to the fire and warmed his hands, spreading out his long, slender fingers. "It's good to gather here," he said. "Kind of you to invite us out to the famous Gorhambury." He was always exquisitely polite. His own Drury House could gobble all of Gorhambury in one swallow.

Christopher was following him with watchful eyes. When Southampton bent to adjust his shoe, Christopher looked down. When he straightened, he looked up. He was not smiling. Did he know? I had been so careful, or so I thought. And it had been over for months, and the men had been comrades-in-arms at Cádiz.

"Gorhambury being such a quiet retreat, we brought our ladies," said Charles. "It is hard always to be in hiding."

Christopher's expression did not change. Although he and I had once had to do the same, he gave no recognition of the memory.

"The fair lady Vernon," said Anthony, with no trace of envy. "How goes that with the Queen?"

Southampton shrugged. "She does not know."

"Are you sure?" asked Christopher gruffly. "Isn't her motto '*Video et taceo*,' 'I see but say nothing'?"

"I think we are safe," he said.

"We were to discuss other business before Essex so abruptly left," said Francis. "Accession Day this year—do you know if the Queen means to hold the usual celebrations, with the Oxfordshire rising set for that date, and the impending Spanish attack?"

"She would never call it off," said Charles.

"Then she must feel secure that these threats are checkmated," he said. "Who has been dispatched to deal with Oxfordshire?"

"One of the Norris soldiers," said Charles. "He and his father, old Sir Henry, will do well enough—thanks to your spy network in the Midlands. One clever spy is worth a hundred brave soldiers. He—or she—makes the soldiers unnecessary."

Anthony made a comic little bow. "I thank you, good sir."

"Were you hindered coming here? Were the beggars out on the roads?" asked Francis.

"A clump of them were at the crossroad by the village," said Charles. "They were not aggressive, although they looked rough."

"The towns are full of vagrants, and not all of them are peaceful. We will have a job to do in Parliament, dealing with this."

"I suppose we must give them money," said Charles. "I know not what other remedy there can be."

"Along with the money, laws to control them. We cannot let people wander about from town to town. Each town should be responsible for its own."

Southampton poured himself a drink and sipped it. "Easy to legislate, hard to enforce. Well, *sir*," he said, raising his cup to Charles. "Congratulations. You have joined the ranks of knights."

Charles beamed. "Indeed. The good Earl of Essex made me one at Cádiz. Just as the good Earl of Leicester made him one on the field at Zutphen. Lady"—he suddenly turned to me—"that makes you the grande dame of all the knights in this room, being wife of one and mother of the other, and then of his knightly offspring, the third generation of knights."

"That makes me venerable," I said, "if not wise."

A silence descended as we remembered that neither Francis nor Anthony had been knighted. Perhaps there was something to Robert's claim that advancement came faster on the battlefield than in council chambers.

"Leicester knighted me, too," said Christopher to me. "We are all in your lineage, so it seems."

He was irritated, but about what I could not tell. If it was not Southampton, what was it?

"How is the theater this season?" asked Christopher suddenly. "Anything of note?"

"Not much," said Southampton. "Rather a dull season. The play about the Italian youngsters who kill themselves has been a big hit; people are flocking to see it. They love it when beauty goes down to doom—especially if it is all due to a misunderstanding. But other than that, nothing exciting."

"Isn't that Shakespeare's play?"

"Yes. But he hasn't had much joy in its success. His son just died, and he went back to Stratford. He returned a different man."

His son! I had known only that he had three children, but not their names or ages. He had steadfastly refused to talk about them. "How old was he?" I asked, casually, I hoped. Christopher's eyes darted to me.

"Eleven. His name was Hamnet."

"What an odd name," said Francis.

"His daughters are Susanna and Judith. Much more ordinary."

Hamnet. Susanna. Judith. Now they were real to me. And I could do nothing, not even send him a letter expressing my condolences. Even if I were not worried that Christopher would catch me, Will would not accept anything from me.

"That is very sad," I said. I had lost both a young child—my son with Leicester—and a grown son. They each hurt in very individual ways, but the loss of any child is near unbearable. We are not meant to outlive our children.

"Oh, he'll turn it into poetry, or a character in a play," said Charles airily. "At least he can get some good from it."

"That is a heartless remark, and could only come from someone who has never lost a child," I said.

"I didn't mean it to be," he said. "I think a poet is lucky to be able to transform his grief into something that lasts and will speak to others. That's all."

"People give too much attention to poets," said Christopher, with a genuinely menacing undertone to his words. "Some people, that is."

"If you mean me," said Southampton, "I am proud to be the patron of poets. Just as rich, fat men like sponsoring tournaments, so I, who cannot write verse, support that which I admire and cannot do."

Oh, clever disarmament. Thank you, Southampton. You may not ride in the lists, but you do know how to defend a lady's honor.

Christopher laughed, but his eyes did not leave my face.

I excused myself by saying I would join the women. Not only did I want to escape Christopher's disconcerting scrutiny, but it was seldom that I got to see Penelope. For her sake I could endure old Lady Bacon, surely one of the haughtiest ladies in the land.

They were sitting primly in a withdrawing room, which was quite warm. Its fireplace was big in relation to the dimensions of the room and heated it nicely, guaranteeing warm fingers, ideal for sewing. They had all brought needlework, and Frances's dark head was bent over hers as she labored with her thread, her tongue between her lips. Lady Bacon held hers at arm's length, as her eyes were bad, and stabbed at it with her needle. Elizabeth Vernon held hers in a dainty way, its unfinished portion draping becomingly over her knees. My Penelope was staring at hers glumly. She had never been good with the so-called women's arts—needlework, lute playing, and dancing. The genuine women's arts—the sort men preferred—however, she excelled at.

Lady Bacon turned to me, swiveling her head on her scrawny neck like a vulture. "So you have decided to join us," she said, making it sound like a condemnation. "Had enough of the men, have you?"

"Of these particular men at this particular time, yes," I answered her. "Too much politics." The polite feminine demurral; I shook my head as if it were all too much for me. "I am afraid I have brought no sewing." I smiled and threw up my hands apologetically. I detested sewing.

"Here," she said, "you can work on this panel of mine." She thrust a stiff piece of material into my hands and piled several skeins of thread on top. "I could use some help."

"Of course," I murmured. I fingered the yellow, deep green, and cream threads. The design featured lilies. "Good evening, dears," I said, looking around at the seated circle. Here they were, the key women in my life: my own daughter, my son's wife, my replacement in the bed of an ex-lover.

"Good evening, Mother," said Penelope, a smile stealing across her plump lips. She looked more content than I had ever seen her. Clearly, living openly with Charles Blount agreed with her. She had left the abusive Lord Baron Rich—rich as his name—after six children to live with a man who at the time was not even a knight. That must be love, I thought. Now it looked to my practiced eye that she was pregnant. This one had been conceived in desire, not obligation.

"It's my privilege to see you, and see you looking so well," I said. I tried to keep any note of whining out of my voice. Mothers always long to see their children, even grown ones, but if we voice it, we frighten them away. "And you, Frances. We pass each other in Essex House, but seldom sit down together."

"Indeed that is so. London is so busy. This retreat is restorative." She always had a fondness for Wanstead and even liked Drayton Bassett—dullness itself—so it was no polite affectation.

"And you, Elizabeth? What can you tell us of court doings?" There ought to be a term for one's successor as a mistress. Perhaps "mistress once removed"?

"It has been quiet," she said. "The Queen has been so distracted and challenged by the rumors of attacks, and by the riots and incidents in the countryside, that most of the usual activities have ceased." She looked up at me, her velvety, dark eyes inviting me to speak more. It was the first time I truly understood what was meant about Anne Boleyn's eyes: They were said to "invite to conversation." With such eyes, conversation was just the beginning.

"You must be bored, then," I said.

"Anything but bored, for she gives me permission to leave, and that means I can spend more time with Henry." It took me a second to realize she meant Southampton. Henry. I never thought of him as Henry. He better fitted the name "Adonis," as in the poem dedicated to him. And here was his Venus. Soft, seductive, perfumed with youth. I blinked and bent over my needlework. There is a point at which no amount of experience can offset youth, no matter how unpracticed. The finest, crispest autumn cannot undercut the supremacy of spring. Deep crimson does not have the charm of delicate pink.

I willed the tears away and thanked the gods for the sewing that allowed me to avert my eyes without suspicion. When I raised them, I was myself again.

---

We were given a bedchamber in the west wing of the house, the part built for the Queen. It was tastefully, but not stylishly, furnished, a dowager of a room. A dark bed, its bulbous posts supporting a heavy canopy, squatted in one corner, with a writing table and two cushioned seats beneath a window. I noted that the lily pattern of the cushions matched the one I had worked on; Lady Bacon must be refurbishing all the rooms to match. A thick carpet, a surprising luxury, covered the floor between the window and the bed. A generous number of candles were set about. However much they were struggling for money, the Bacons did not wish to give the impression of cheapness.

Christopher opened the window and a blast of rainy wind blew in.

"Would you please close it?" I tried to sound pleasant. But I would rather be anywhere but here with him tonight. A nun's cell seemed more appealing. *Lettice, there are no more nuns in England,* I reminded myself. *Only Her Majesty.*

He slammed it loudly. He had kept drinking all through the supper, and now his clumsy movements and flushed face made me think he must be drunk. Well, let him sleep. Let him sleep and awake the good-natured Christopher I knew. I did not like this man here tonight.

"Did you enjoy yourself among the hens?" he said.

"Yes," I answered. "It is always good to see Penelope."

"The daughter most like her mother." His voice was thick and sneering.

"I was never as pretty."

"But your behavior was similar. Who will replace Charles, I wonder? My trusting cousin."

"No one will replace him. They are devoted to each other." Perhaps I should make an excuse and leave; when I returned, he would be asleep.

"As you are to me?" Instead of falling into bed, he came over to me and took my neck in his hands.

I stared back at him. His eyes were hard to read in this dim light. "Yes. As I am to you."

"Would it were so." He did not sound angry now, just tired.

"Why should you think otherwise?"

He let me go and made his way to the bed, pushing the heavy curtains aside, sitting on its edge with his legs dangling, like a little boy. "All the men at Cádiz wondered what their women were doing while they were away. The more lovely the wife, the greater the danger."

Relief tingled through me. He was speaking only in general terms, not out of suspicion. "Since all the men were away fighting, I'd say there was little danger at home. What man of any note was here? Only the old, the infirm, the incapable remained. They made us long all the more for our absent men." I walked over to him, almost dizzy with the sense of reprieve. He did not know. He must not know. I must never do that again. "I spent the nights with you, in my dreams and thoughts." His very vulnerability made me wish to reassure him. I bent over and kissed him. For the first time since his return, I actually desired his kiss. For the first time, his lips were only his own, not a reminder of anyone else's.

He was a good man, a man to cherish. I would. *I do,* I vowed. *I do not deserve you, Christopher, but I will try to.*

That was my heartfelt promise. But what were my promises worth?

---

The next morning, as we prepared to leave, we had to step over the scattered forms of men sleeping all over the floor, their cloaks pulled over them, their legs sprawled out as they snored and muttered. I recognized some of them—there were the campaign veterans Sir Charles Danvers, a hotheaded, quarrelsome friend of Southampton's, Sir John Davies, and Sir Ferdinando Gorges; wild noblemen such as the spendthrift Roger Manners, Earl of Rutland, his spiky hair sticking up, and Edward Russell, the Earl of Bedford, sleeping like an angel; Thomas Radcliffe, the Earl of Sussex; William Lord Sandys; the Catholic-leaning William Parker, Lord Monteagle; and Robert's secretary, the Greek scholar Henry Cuffe, and Gelli Meyrick the Welshman.

Cuffe did not look very scholarly, and the noblemen did not look very noble.

# 46

# ELIZABETH

*December 1596*

he nastier the weather, the more I relished being outdoors. I licked the stinging mist hitting my lips as I sat on horseback in Greenwich Park, looking across the river to the desolate brown and gray of the Isle of Dogs. Ghostly ribbons of fog wove a pattern in the air above the water, floating down to the sea. It was the time when every Joan and Ned huddled indoors before the fire, and this year with meager food supplies to face the cold months ahead. I was here watching, as I had for weeks, wondering when the first beacon would flare across the river. In these dull days the bright flame would be easy to see.

There had been no word on the whereabouts of the Armada, although we believed it would head first for the Isle of Wight and then up the Thames to London. We increased the garrison at Wight and readied the ordnance of all the coastal defenses; a militia of twenty-four thousand from the southern counties was called up to defend the seacoast. The navy was fitted out and stationed along the Channel. Near London, ships were dispatched to guard the entrance of the Thames by Tilbury. Others were positioned as watch vessels from Sheerness to Chatham navy yard; the nearby Upnor Castle was strengthened with an extra contingent of soldiers. In case of a Spanish reprisal against our fleet in revenge for Cádiz, Admiral Howard ordered Raleigh to safeguard the fleet at anchor.

We had heard of the Armada's setting out, of the prayers said in Spanish churches for its success, singing the psalm "Contra Paganos"—"Against the Pagans"—in churches throughout the land. I looked up at the swirling, blustery sky. We would see, literally, which way the winds blew. Would they be Protestant winds or Catholic ones? Would they sweep the Armada onto our shores or wreck it as they had before?

At least we were safe from the homegrown insurrection. The Oxfordshire rising had never risen. Steer and his followers had been unable to convince enough people to join them, despite their busy recruiting in the countryside.

On St. Hugh's Day, they had bungled their start and been easily rounded up and taken to London, where they were now being tried. In the end, although people griped and complained, they were not willing to risk their lives or to attack the landowners. Some said they were in it as long as it was property, not people, to be destroyed, but when the talk turned to murder they wanted no part of it. The men involved were mostly young, unemployed, and without families—in other words, with nothing to lose.

Nonetheless, my Accession Day, despite my putting on a brave outward show, was a sober one for me. Knowing that the day when people had rejoiced that I had come to the throne thirty-eight years ago had become the day chosen by malcontents to express themselves weighed on my spirits. For every person who had joined the rising, there must be thousands who sympathized with it. I knew we would have to address these deep-seated discontentments, so I called for a parliament to meet soon.

The clean, stinging wind was welcome after the stuffiness and forced phrases at court, and the roiling weather reminded me that our indoor tempests were small things. The mighty hand of God seemed to be raking his fingers through the sky.

My hands were numb inside my fur-lined gloves. Still I lingered on the hilltop, watching the great lazy bend of the river and the skyline of London beyond that, spread out along its banks.

Wait! Was that a flare? Did I see a flash of red from the distant hill? I held still and waited, but it did not come again. It must have been a reflection. As I turned to head back to Greenwich, I saw a rider approaching. He sat his horse squarely, neither hurrying nor dawdling, his flat hat pulled low.

"Francis!" It was my elusive counsel.

He swept off his hat and nodded, coming close. He had a fine bay horse. I wondered if he owned it, but more likely it was borrowed from Essex. "Your Majesty," he said.

"This is unexpected company," I said. Others would have cornered me at a banquet or Christmas festivity, but he found this private ground. He was always clever.

"I was out for a ride in the park and thought I saw you. Your carriage and the way you sit your saddle are unmistakable."

Like all successful flatterers, he knew that the best flattery is to exaggerate what is true. I was a good rider, and I did have a straight back. "Thank you, Francis," I said. "It has been a long time since I have seen you at court."

"It has been a long time since you have called upon my talents, modest as they are, for your service." He replaced his hat, pulling it down to cover his ears. The wind flapped the hem of his cloak.

"The things that have needed counsel, unfortunately, have not been in your area of knowledge."

He smiled. "Are you sure? Did I not tell you I have taken all knowledge to be my province?"

"Yes, you did, and I know you are conquering new territory every day, a veritable Alexander the Great of the mind, you are. But the dreary, sad matters I have had to deal with—discontented subjects, another attack from my perennial foe Philip—did not require analysis but simple action." Now I waited for him to recommend Essex, his employer, for the task. I had let Essex sulk and sit since his return from Cádiz and his fizzled hero's welcome. The people still sang of him, but it was dying down.

"I understand," he said. "I am grateful that the danger inside the realm is over and hope that the same will soon be said of the one outside." He looked toward the city. "Let this stand safe!"

"How are you, Francis?" I asked. He looked well but clearly had something on his mind. "And Anthony? I despair of ever seeing your brother. Sometimes I think he is a ghost—or an alias for you. Is there really an Anthony Bacon?"

Francis laughed. "He exists but is unwell. All of him, except his mind, is failing. He must protect the body in order to safeguard his mind. It is a jewel wrapped in weak flesh."

"As in us all." An unwelcome reminder. "What have you come for, my good man? For I know it was not to watch the river with me."

"I confess I did wish to see you alone, and in a place that has no mementos of times past. You say you value my counsel, and so I present it to you in a form you can consult any time you fancy and have it to hand." He opened his saddle pouch and drew out a book. "I have written down what I know."

I took the slim volume. "In so small a space? That is not possible."

"I strove to be succinct," he said. "I wrote it as instruction for persons who might need it, but beyond that, as an exercise for myself. It is hard to capture the essence of one's own beliefs and knowledge. I deal with one subject at a time."

I could not open the book in the high wind with my gloves on. "I look forward to studying it. You have invented a new product: an invisible counselor."

"Some would say the Scriptures function thus," he said. "But my advice is on practical matters, such as custom and education, youth and age, deformity, building, gardens, and negotiating. I treat followers and friends—and how to discern the difference—anger, factions. Oh, and apropos of the present disturbances, there is an essay on 'seditions and troubles.'"

"Do tell. Give me a summary. I need it."

"Here's a quote from it: 'The surest way to prevent seditions is to take away the matter of them. For if there be fuel prepared, it is hard to tell whence the spark shall come that shall set it on fire. The matter of seditions is of two kinds: much poverty and much discontentment.'"

He spoke clearly and true. I looked at him, at this dark enigmatic man who was wise in so many ways but had no sure place for applying that wisdom. "Well considered, and well said. That is why I have called a parliament for next year—to take away the cause that almost lit the fuel in Oxfordshire. I plan to introduce poor laws to address this directly. I assume you will be in Commons? I will need your help."

He smiled. "Yes, I plan to run, and expect to be elected. I have, of late, decided that Essex is not in constant need of my services. I can spend as much time as necessary in this upcoming parliament."

So this was the real announcement. He had cut ties with Essex. They had fallen out for some reason. "Cut ties" was too strong; he had loosened them and was looking for employment elsewhere. What was their disagreement? Had Francis tired of giving advice only to have it ignored? Was Essex planning something that Francis could not condone?

"I see. I can count on you, then, to support my measures?" Not like last time, I meant, when he had voted against my subsidy.

"Within my conscience, of course, Your Majesty," he said.

"I never betray my own conscience and would not require it of another," I said.

What had come between him and Essex? How could I find out? Asking Francis directly would not reveal it. I must find another way, another informant.

---

The Christmas season was particularly gloomy. Sometimes December can be bright and cold, but this year it was murky and wet. It fitted my spirits, which were likewise murky and wet. We kept the festivities at Richmond, and nothing was omitted to signal any diminution of the holiday. The choristers sang as clearly as ever, the boar's head was serenaded as raucously as normal, and the plays provoked as much laughter as any other year. But I felt all the while that I was pretending for the benefit of others, as a mother will be cheerful before her children, while desperate to get food on the table.

The one genuinely bright respite came when Raleigh's Indian was baptized and took an English name, Percival. Archbishop Whitgift presided in the royal chapel and Raleigh stood as godfather, and the new Percival, wearing English cloak and breeches, repeated his promises in clear but accented words. He had been studying all year, becoming more and more a fixture at court, and to welcome him into our company was a touching moment. Afterward I gave a reception to celebrate the occasion. Everyone crowded around to congratulate him and question him about his homeland. Raleigh's cohort Lawrence Keymis had just returned from the Orinoco and was pleased to provide more details of the land and the elusive gold, which he had come close to locating—or so he claimed.

"I'm just about to publish my findings in *Relation of the Second Voyage to Guiana*. It will be almost like being there," he assured us.

Raleigh stood proudly by, nodding. "I long to return," he said. "But first, there is the matter of the voyage to the Azores to undertake, there to finish what we started in Cádiz."

The Azores venture was a sore point with me. Raleigh spoke true. The adventurers, not content with one mission, were clamoring for another.

"You sustained an injury that has you still limping," I said. "Let that heal before you go seeking another."

"If we waited for all wounds to heal, none of us would ever walk again," he said. "'Tis nothing."

"Percival" joined us and bowed. "I thank you that you come," he said to me.

"It is my pleasure to welcome such a fine new Christian," I said. He stood straight, his bronze skin not faded from our sunless days. Beside him Raleigh looked pasty and middle-aged, despite his splendid new midnight blue velvet doublet. "I hope that you will ever feel that this land is your home."

"Someday I go back," he said. "See my old father. Show Raleigh the gold place. For now, I like England."

His hair was a shiny, straight black that we never saw among our own people, not even with the Spanish, and his nose as straight as a Roman emperor's. He towered over Robert Cecil and looked eye to eye with Raleigh. A fine race of men, the Orinoco Indians. Essex might have been taller, but Essex was not here, still hiding away from court this season.

It was while we were at Percival's celebration that the blessed news came to us: God had proved Protestant once again. He had blown the winds up into a gale just as the Armada was rounding Cape Finisterre—"the end of the world"—at the western bulge of the Spanish coastline, scattering the fleet, driving it onto the shore, and wrecking some forty of the best warships. The few that survived were not enough to mount another attack so late in the year. We embraced the messenger and feted him, and I ordered that more of the palace's wine stores be opened. Tonight everyone could drink as much as he or she wanted, with my blessing.

The fleet was wrecked! We were safe! I felt giddy with relief and danced with an abandon I had not mustered in months.

---

My feet hurt. Not dancing vigorously in so long had definitely caused them to forget the shape of my shoes. I pulled them off, and Marjorie held them up, rotating them. "These look small," she said tactfully.

"Perhaps when I wore them in the rain, they shrank," I said. I wanted to soak my feet in warm water before climbing into bed, so they could recover before morning. Sitting on a stool with the water lapping up around my calves, I told Marjorie once again how thankful I was that the Oxfordshire rising had collapsed and Henry was safe. He had come to court this Christmas, making Marjorie very happy. I had assigned him a chamber just next to the royal ones so she could easily slip away to spend time with him.

He was stout, and growing stouter. I wondered why that often happens—in the middle years people grow wider, and then when they become truly old they shrink. Perhaps it is a good sign if one is still corpulent.

"There have been so few disturbances during your entire reign," she said. "That is almost unique in English history. It means that by and large you satisfy the people."

Yes, it had meant that. But now when I rode abroad there were sullen silences and no cheers, and sometimes they still sang of Essex in the streets.

Catherine brought a thick towel. "When you are ready," she said, holding it up.

"Charles can join us at court now," I said. "He is free to dock his warship and come ashore. I know you will welcome that." I had in mind a promotion for Charles, but I did not wish to reveal it now. It was time he received a new title. I bestowed them so sparingly that it was sure to attract attention. I merely smiled, keeping my secret.

"God has been merciful to us once again," she said. "Surely Philip will give up now. And yes, I'm delighted to have my husband back again."

I gestured toward the maidens' chamber, where the younger girls were sleeping under lock and key. "Doubtless they will also be glad to have their suitors back," I said. I knew they had them. It was the sneaking and the secrecy I abhorred, not the suitors themselves. Why could they not understand that?

"I shall read a bit," I said. "You need not wait up for me." No point in their standing duty while I read quietly. I settled myself in my most comfortable chair and moved two candles to the side table, while Marjorie excused herself to join Henry, and Catherine pulled out her truckle bed and smoothed the covers. But first she tiptoed into the little room where the formidable ajax had been installed, availing herself of it. We were all pleased by the way it functioned, but its roaring noise made us limit our use of it. John Harington, at court this season, claimed victory for his invention and was busy trying to promote it.

Francis Bacon's essays, as he called them, resembled a tray of sweetmeats—small, bite-size, tempting the reader to consume one after another until they became a blur. I selected one at time, trying to limit myself, choosing by the title. There were over fifty of them. Tonight "Of Vicissitude of Things" caught my fancy.

"Certain it is, that the matter is in a perpetual flux, and never at a stay. The great winding-sheets, that bury all things in oblivion, are two: deluges and earthquakes." England was doubly blessed, then, in having neither. I read on. He wrote of the breakup of a great empire and said it was always accompanied by wars. He specifically mentioned Spain and wrote that if it fell, other countries would plunder its corpse, plucking its feathers. After many examples, he concluded, "But it is not good to look too long upon these turning wheels of vicissitude, lest we become giddy."

I shut the book. He was right. The turning wheels of vicissitude could crush me. And his image of a winding-sheet: Had I not used that very example to explain why I would not name my successor? "Think you I will spread my winding-sheet before my eyes?" I had warned. The moment I named someone to come after me, all eyes would turn that way. We worship the rising, not the setting, sun. It is in our nature. Lament it I would; ignore it I dared not.

# 47

hristmas Day was over, and after the happy news of the scattering of the Armada, the holidays had turned unexpectedly festive. The men guarding the realm had returned in time to join the court for Twelfth Night, which proved exceptionally boisterous and merry. We were safe. We were delivered, once again. God smiled on us. It was hard not to congratulate ourselves, and hard for me to remind myself that the cries of "The Protestant Princess, beloved of Providence" came not from heaven but from fickle men.

There was work to do in the realm, and I must tackle it. We must prepare for parliament, and I must address the clamoring for another venture of derring-do from the Essex faction. Essex himself had continued to absent himself from court, nursing his grievances to whip up sympathy for his misunderstood self. In his view, he was always misunderstood. The terror for him would be in realizing I understood him all too well.

That person . . . that boy . . . who had nakedly said he loved me, the temptation incarnate at Drayton Bassett . . . where was he? He had seemingly been replaced by a pouting and sulking courtier, holding out for recognition and petting. I let him sulk and simmer, all the while wondering what was going through his mind.

His mind was not a constant thing. He was violently inconsistent, unstable. I had thought I could tame him as I had his stepfather, Leicester, but I was beginning to grasp that Essex's unhappiness stemmed from frustration of his personal ambition rather than anything that could be addressed. No matter what rank and honors he possessed, he would always feel that they fell short and he was thereby insulted.

---

Lent began, slow, creeping Lent. In Catholic countries wild carnivals snaked their way through streets and bawdy clowns entertained crowds; masked men seduced young women who pretended not to know them. But here in

Protestant England, we contented ourselves with using up the butter and eggs that were forbidden during Lent, along with meat. On the Tuesday before Lent began, households ate pancakes all day. In some towns there were pancake races, housewives running with skillets, tossing pancakes. Then stretched the dreariest, drabbest days of the year, the sparkling cold of winter and snow gone, the green of spring not yet here. It was a time of quiet reflection. If anyone had a tendency to brood, Lent would bring it out. The religious said this was their favorite season.

Burghley had worsened over the winter and made many apologies for skipping council meetings. I worried about him, as one always does about the elderly. He had been failing, little by little, for a long time. But I would not allow myself to envision my government without him. I was not a brooder; had I been, I never could have survived so long. I needed Burghley. He must rally; he must go on. My right arm could not lose its strength.

After five weeks of Lent, Holy Week, leading up to Easter, arrived. I knew all the services by heart, but each year I heard something different in them. Palm Sunday: the day Jesus rode into Jerusalem and was hailed by ecstatic crowds. He was the people's hope, their Messiah. By Wednesday his disciple Judas was making arrangements to betray him. By Thursday he was having his farewell meal with his disciples. Here in England that day was called Maundy Thursday and there was a curious custom attached to it, a ceremony in which the monarch washed the feet of as many poor people as his or her age and distributed twenty shillings to each of them as well as gifts of food and clothing. As I was in my sixty-fourth year, there would be sixty-four candidates. It was like to be a long ceremony.

It was held in the afternoon in the chapel royal at Whitehall, Archbishop Whitgift presiding. I wore a suitably dark gown, with removable sleeves so that I could plunge my arms freely into the deep silver basin of warm, scented water. The sixty-four poor women were seated on stools before the altar steps, and all had removed their shoes. I looked them up and down—they were young, middle-aged, and old, to represent all the stages of life. To be chosen was a high honor; after all, there were many more than sixty-four poor in the realm, and this year in particular.

Whitgift read the Scripture that described the origin of the custom. Before the Last Supper, Jesus had washed his disciples' feet, over the protests of Peter, who had refused to let Jesus perform the rite. Jesus had said, "If I do not wash you, you have no part in me." At that the impulsive Peter had cried that he should wash not only his feet but all of him.

The ceremony was supposed to teach humility on both sides. I had to kneel before each woman, take her feet, wash them, and then kiss them. It was a very intimate act. The feet are oddly private. We shake hands, but no one touches our feet. One by one I took them in my hands. Some were sleek and calloused, others bony. Some felt like claws. Only one young girl had soft insoles, and I knew her hard life would soon change that. As I handled each foot, I could feel my coronation ring pressing against the flesh, like a kiss. Each touch sealed the vow I had made in wedding myself to my people, one at a time.

There was no sound but the splashing of the water and the words I spoke to each in turn, commending them to God and reminding them to obey the great commandment that Jesus had given on this occasion, to love one another. I dried each foot and then passed on to the next person. Afterward the gifts would be distributed and we would part. I would never forget them; even though I might never see or talk to them again, they would remain a part of me, as Jesus had said. It was a great mystery how that happened, but it did.

The next day, Good Friday, the most solemn of the year, was dark and overcast, fitting the occasion. I could remember the old customs of rigorous fasting, creeping to the cross, and children dragging figures of Judas through the streets to be thrown on a bonfire. No one would wash clothes, as blood might spot them, and blacksmiths would not shoe horses, because they refused to work with nails that day. Fishermen considered it bad luck to put to sea, and miners would not go down into the mines. Now the preachers tried to dispel all this as popish superstition, but it was not so easily cast off.

When I came to the throne, England had just gone through three wrenching religious changes in only a quarter century. First my father had brutally broken a thousand years of loyalty to Rome and founded his own national church. Then my brother had imposed a radical Protestantism on the land. Next my sister had sought to annul all these changes and restore Roman Catholicism. So when I became Queen, the nation was dizzy from this religious whirligig. My "Elizabethan Settlement," as it was called, was meant to be a compromise and stop these violent changes. Like all compromises, it left elements on both sides unsatisfied.

The most fervent Puritans sought to ban all church calendar observances, declaring each Sunday the same. Some of them refused to celebrate either Easter or Christmas and would spend Good Friday working as usual. But they had made little dent in popular practice. If every day were the same, life would quickly grow tedious. Even nature varied the seasons.

Their Catholic brethren, on the other hand, would spend today in prayer and meditation, counting their forbidden papal-blessed rosary beads, perhaps even suffering with a hair shirt. Come Easter morning, both Catholics and Puritans had all better be found at the services of the Church of England, or pay a stiff fine.

I did not worry about what a man or woman personally believed, but the nation's official religion should be outwardly practiced by all its citizens. A religion was a political statement. Being a Calvinist, a papist, a Presbyterian, an Anglican labeled a person's philosophy on education, taxes, poor relief, and other secular things. The nation needed an accepted position on such concerns. Hence the fines for not outwardly conforming to the national church.

Some of the richer Catholic families, the ancient, noble ones, were wealthy enough to pay the fines week after week, but the ordinary man was not. Gradually, through rote attendance, he began to adhere to the new faith and forget the old. There was another factor as well: Most people did not care to squander their money paying religious fines, so all but the most stubborn and devout spared themselves that unnecessary expense. The memories of religious practice before 1558 were fading, and only the rabid Puritans and most stubborn Catholics continued to resist the Church of England.

When I was a child, the city and countryside were dotted with the empty shells of the monasteries. They had been so recently closed that the nation had not had time to absorb them. Many were quickly sold for private use and converted into homes; some were turned into parish churches. But others lingered on the landscape, their roofs stripped of lead, their stones plundered, their walls fallen. Even today there were some whose ruined arches looked like ribs against the sky, skeletons left unburied.

There was no denying that with the disappearance of the monks and nuns, a font of charity had vanished. The poor were left to wander and fend for themselves; the welcoming monasteries were now as derelict as they. The alms boxes were gone, the wayfarers' dole ceased. The answer to this was not to bring back the monasteries, as some had suggested, but for the state to assume these duties. That was what the upcoming parliament must address.

Most of the monastic ruins in London had been cleared, but there still remained, near Aldgate, what was left of Holy Trinity Priory, once the grandest foundation in the city. I decided to have a prayer service there, as a reminder that the ruins had been neglected long enough. The land should be used, even if the buildings were beyond redemption.

We wended our way through the London streets, going up Cornhill and past the Royal Exchange building, thence along Leadenhall Street. The city was quiet and few were out, as if in deference to the awful remembrance of the day. No one crowded around crying out "God Save the Queen!" and "Our

Blessed Queen!" I saw a few curious eyes looking out the windows, a few tentative hand waves. Then we were there, at the great gray relic of the order of Augustinian canons.

The roof was long gone, and the floor of the nave had been stripped of its marbles and brasses. Water lay in puddles in the sinking, uneven stones, where weeds and seedlings sprouted between the cracks. The windows were gaping holes, no glass remaining. Birds nested in the high crevices, and straw and mess in corners bespoke both human and animal vagrants. I had brought my chaplain to lead the private prayers, as well as some of my women. As we walked between the stumps of pillars, the grayness of the day and the grayness of the flooring making for no shadows, our footfalls echoed.

Once this nave had reverberated with chants; now it was silenced.

"Please direct our prayers," I told the chaplain. "This is a fitting place to be on Good Friday. It reminds us that all our human plans may lead us to nothingness."

We could see traces of the base of the great altar, and my chaplain stood before it, opening his prayer book. He bowed his head and then read, "Almighty God, we beseech thee graciously to behold this thy family, for which our Lord Jesus Christ was contented to be betrayed. . . ."

---

The short but affecting service over, we left to make our way back through London. Rain was threatening, the roiling, dark clouds puckering in the sky over the unprotected nave. The darkness of noon in Galilee years ago was being reenacted.

I wished we had come in the royal barge; it would have been a quicker trip back. But I had wanted to give my bargemen a rest on this day. So we would have to ride back through the quiet streets and hope the rain held off. Turning out of the Holy Trinity grounds—and they were extensive, as the monastery had had cloisters and kitchens, bakehouses, brewhouses, workshops, dormitories, and refectories—we headed west toward St. Paul's. Abutting the priory grounds was the church of St. Katharine Cree, where my dear Lord Keeper Nicholas Bacon lay, as well as, reputedly, Hans Holbein, who had perished in the plague in 1543 and been hastily buried like so many others. So there lay the man who had given the world the image of my father with his hands on his hips and his legs spread wide, in an unmarked grave.

Had we hugged the wall to go west, we would have found the grounds of another former abbey, St. Augustine's. But this one had been thoroughly digested by the city and, keeping only the name "the Papey" as a memento, was a place where ordinary men made their homes. Walsingham had lived there, as well as Thomas Heneage of my Privy Council and Thomas Gresham, who founded the Royal Exchange.

Turning left on Cornhill Street, we passed the poultry, mercer's, and other markets, closed now. Swinging toward the sprawling grounds of St. Paul's, we saw the Eleanor Cross at Cheapside standing guardian over the crossroads. It was as tall as a two-story building and impossible to miss. I had always loved the Eleanor Crosses and hoped to one day see all twelve of them. King Edward I had set them up three hundred years ago to mark the overnight resting places of his queen's funeral cortege from Lincoln to London. I brushed aside the knowledge that if I truly meant to see all twelve, I had best start the journey soon; only two were in London. The crosses served as landmarks and gathering places wherever they were. Farmers brought sacks of food, hunters game, and dog breeders their dogs, hawking their wares from the cross's base. Today, of course, it was empty. But tattered notices still clung to the pillar, which served as a posting place. They flapped and fluttered like flags. I asked one of my guards to dismount and inspect them. I was curious about them. He read several, frowned, and returned, shaking his head.

"Just trash, Your Majesty," he said.

That meant he did not wish to disturb me about it. "What sort of trash?" I asked.

"Low, ruffian sort," he said.

Were prostitutes openly selling themselves? At this tender memorial to love? Or was it mercenaries, assassins? Smugglers? "Let me see," I ordered him.

He ripped a few off and brought them to me. Sure enough, there was a testimonial to the expertise and skill of one Jill, working out of Mother Fool's tavern; a soldier recently returned from Cádiz who would fight for anyone's quarrel, and a political one—calling for the Earl of Essex to be lauded and celebrated. It also wished him to be elevated, to be named my heir. There was a sketch of him with his new beard and a ballad lamenting that the Queen did not appreciate him.

"Take them all," I ordered him. I would examine them later. The Essex movement was gaining ground, so it seemed.

St. Paul's was the one place swarming with people, but it always was. Not only were services held inside but it was also a setting for many a business rendezvous. People who preyed on the hapless, such as pickpockets and beggars, gathered there. Outside, the bookstalls were discreetly closed, but the hawkers were still prowling about selling things less legal.

The people who saw me turned and gave subdued greetings, but there were none of the wild shrieks I usually incited. It was true, then: My popularity had sagged due to the economic troubles of the country. It was not my fault that there had been three bad harvests in a row, but somehow I was connected to it. It went back to a biblical pronouncement—and now that people were eagerly reading the once-forbidden Bible for themselves in their own language, they had rediscovered it—that stated that an unrighteous ruler was directly responsible for rain and harvests. If the weather was bad, it was because God was punishing him for some sin—known or unknown. The Book of Leviticus said, "If you will not yet for all this hearken unto me, then I will punish you seven times more for your sins. I will make your heaven as iron, and your earth as brass: For your land shall not yield her increase, neither shall the trees of the land yield their fruits."

I was glad to leave St. Paul's behind and go out the nearby Ludgate, the westernmost gate in the city wall. It had been rebuilt only a dozen years ago and was fair and stout, with a statue of me on the outer side and the legendary ancient King Lud on the inner. The gate housed a prison as well, and as we passed under it, I could see a few of the prisoners up on the roof for their air. These were the gentlemanly criminals, that is, ones whose transgressions were debt or poaching or printing forbidden tracts. Then up Ludgate Hill and thence to the Strand, the graveled road paralleling the Thames and passing the great riverside mansions. They began right after the Temple Inns of Court.

The first one we came to was Essex House, where Robert Devereux was malingering, hiding from court. As we rode past, unannounced, I looked closely to see if anything was stirring in the great courtyard behind the ornamental gates, but all was quiet. He kept enormous numbers of retainers, so many that it was said "his house was eating him," but they were invisible today.

The rain would not hold off much longer. A gust of wet wind swept over us, and a few drops fell. We were still a mile or so from Whitehall.

Next we passed Arundel House, with its tall, towered gateway, currently empty. Its owner, Philip Howard, Earl of Arundel, had just died in the Tower, where he had been kept for many years. He and his whole family had converted—or reverted?—to Catholicism, and Philip had even prayed and had a Mass said for the success of the Armada! He had been named for Philip of Spain, his godfather, and was true to him. I turned my head away, not wanting to look at the house. Once Philip had been a winsome boy, and I willed myself not to see him as he was then, high-spirited and joyful. Now the Catholics were calling him a martyr and petitioning Rome to declare him a saint. That boy was no saint. Just ask his wife how well he kept the sixth commandment.

Next door was Somerset House, where Henry Carey had died last summer. His son George, the new Lord Hunsdon, now inhabited it. I had not been back there since Henry died; it would not seem the same house to me. I hoped George was keeping up the extensive gardens on the river side of the house, but I suspected he had little interest in flowers or fountains. Across the way lay a produce market where an old convent had been, now called Convent Garden. He could avail himself of that if he did not want to bother growing things himself.

Another flurry of wind. We spurred our horses to go faster, passing quickly by Raleigh's Durham House, set way back and near the river.

Almost back. Now the road widened out into the crossroad at Charing Cross and the magnificent Eleanor Cross standing there on its stepped octagonal base. It was very high and slender, rising like an ancient prayer poem. No one was there today, but dozens of papers fluttered from its shaft. I asked that those be removed so I could look at them later. Bearing left, we swung into the grounds of Whitehall, entering from the court gate that straddled the public road. The bells of nearby Westminster Abbey were tolling in recognition of Christ's death, ringing the Nine Tailors—nine strokes for a man, then thirty-three for his age. The last was reverberating just as we got inside. Then the rain broke.

---

I spent Holy Saturday inside, confined, as Christ had lain in the tomb—not to put too fine a point on it. For penitence and sobering, I spread out the leaflets and notes torn off the two Eleanor Crosses and read them carefully. The ones advertising their wares, legal and moral or illegal and immoral, were not my main concern, although they were educational. I learned of rate wars between the illicit grain hoarders and of the availability of gemstones "taken from the late Spanish expedition"—a good explanation for what had become of my share. The style in prostitutes' names this season was mythological. There were many Aphrodites, Venuses, and Andromedas, along with, puzzlingly enough, a Medusa. But the notes concerning Essex were alarming. There were salutes to his heroism, poems recounting his adventures, ballads about his gallantry, and, most ominous of all, claims for his lineage and royal blood, one notice even saying that "he was most worthy of the succession of any man living."

Another note, crinkled from exposure to sun and rain, proclaimed, "Said e. of Essex is proud son of e. of Cambridge and should finish his task. Arise!"

I bent over it, smoothing out the paper to be sure of the words. Yes, that was what they said. They spoke, then, of Richard, Earl of Cambridge, who was executed for treason against Henry V—Robert Devereux's direct ancestor seven generations back.

I knew all the genealogies of everyone. If you were a Tudor, you learned them almost before your *ABC*s, as they governed your life. Robert Devereux counted Edward I and Edward III as his ancestors. His royal blood was so diluted it would not amount to more than a teaspoon if you could measure it, but it gave a tincture to everything he did. Mine united the bloodlines of York and Lancaster; his was primarily York. Those wars were not forgotten, nor the bloodlines running further back into the distant past. During my father's reign many with stronger blood claims than Robert Devereux had been executed until there were none left to challenge the Tudor claim. But there are always other descendants, cousins, to continue the line. That was what made Essex dangerous.

And now he was hiding himself away, daring me to continue to ignore him, while he fanned the murmurs and desires of the people.

I would not call him forth, nor go to him. "He has played long enough upon me, and now I mean to play upon him!" I cried aloud. "I will pull down his proud heart, as we pull down dangerous houses!"

I unrolled another faded piece of paper. "Remember Richard II my lord. See him do what should be done. At the playhouse, now."

Richard II. At the playhouse. Was there a play about the deposition of that foolish king? I must look into this. Who was performing it? And to what end?

---

I welcomed Easter as the dearly sought release from a long winter of heaviness of spirit. It did not fail me. It never did, in its yearly reassurance that all would be well. The sun streamed through the windows of the chapel royal, hitting Archbishop Whitgift's white and gold vestments, making them gleam in heavenly splendor. The lilies on the altar stood fair and slender, purity in an imperfect world.

# 48

# LETTICE

*May 1597*

hat a long and dreary winter it had been. Each short day seemed longer than a midsummer's one, for when the spirits are low one hour seems ten. My son's agitation about his political situation occupied me, as a crying baby will demand attention. No matter how old the child or the mother, the need, and the response, is the same on both sides.

He had hidden away all winter, absenting himself from court. The court had not missed him; he had never been popular there. They were all jealous of him. The Queen was still angry, punishing him for the failure—as she saw it—of the Cádiz voyage. The people, on the other hand, appreciated the sheer bravado of the mission, and certainly King Philip was incensed about it. The ghost of Drake himself was probably applauding the audacity of it. Only the Queen held aloof, caring solely about the missed booty, not the glory of striking into the very heart of our enemy.

Because the Queen refused to call the mission a success, the logical next step—a follow-up attack on another Spanish target—found few outright supporters. The council was divided between those who thought England should have an aggressive war policy and those who favored a defensive strategy. As in other areas, Robert and the Cecils were on opposite sides of the argument. The Queen favored the Cecil position but might be persuadable.

"But not if you hide yourself away," I had told Robert. "As leader of the war party, you have to be close to her ear."

But he remained obdurate, unconvinced. His wife and children, though, seemed to benefit from his absence at court. Frances was as unprepossessing as ever, so easily overlooked, with her quiet, accommodating manner and her undistinguished looks. She called to mind St. Paul's description of love: bears all things, endures all things. I suppose, for such a man as my son, those were essential qualities for a wife.

She was a good mother. Better than I, and I admired her for that. Her eldest daughter, Elizabeth, was eleven now and had the long face and delicate hands of her father, Philip Sidney, but not his good looks; her son by Robert, little Rob, was six. He was a dreamy child, often preferring to play indoors even when the weather was sunny. He did not like riding but forced himself to do it, which bespoke courage but not aptitude.

Until now Robert had seemed indifferent to them, but during these months they caught his affection and he spent much time with them. Children soothed wounded pride; they judged a person by a different yardstick than the world. Under their adoring gaze, Robert grew calmer.

I enjoyed spending time with them as well—it was something to share with Robert that was not freighted with political weight. They were my grandchildren, after all. I knew I should be more attentive, but I usually held that children are not interesting until they reach fourteen or so. By this time I had many grandchildren: six by Penelope and three by Dorothy, besides Robert's. His obliging ex-mistress Elizabeth Southwell had boldly named her son Walter Devereux, making a total of eleven. Both Penelope and Dorothy were expecting again. I marveled at the fecundity of our family.

Alone of the children, Elizabeth Sidney was a goddaughter of the Queen, and named for her. I hoped that might mean some special attention for her, but since the death of Walsingham and Frances's transition from Sidney's widow to Robert's wife, the Queen took no notice of her. And Frances, in her unpresuming way, did nothing to change that.

Suspended in inaction, life feels eternal. Then, abruptly, it ends. It did the day Cecil and Raleigh came to Essex House to meet with Robert and form a plan for working together.

It was a shock to have the outside world bursting in upon us, like throwing open the shutters after a long winter to reveal the dust and cobwebs. They made an odd pair, diminutive Cecil and the broad-shouldered Raleigh. But where political interests converge, men start to look alike.

Robert was wary around them, unsure whether to trust them. When one's enemies come a-calling, it is best to keep one's back to the wall. So he made much of welcoming them, so effusively that it smacked of pandering. I would have to wait until later to know what was said, as they spoke in private. But all along Southampton had managed to let bits of news trickle in to us, and we heard that frustration with the Queen's inability to embrace any definitive policy was stalemating everyone's plans. Did not Jesus himself say, "Let your yes be yes and your no be no"? Her Majesty was not following his command.

The three men went into the chamber and shut the door resolutely. They remained there for several hours. I sent trays of food and flasks of the finest wine in for them; they were returned empty, the plates heaped with peels and rinds and the flasks drained. Eventually they emerged, looking content and companionable. This was as rare a sight as a planetary convergence of Jupiter, Mars, and Venus, and I wished there was a way to capture the image. Cecil had his doublet undone, showing his rumpled shirt beneath; Raleigh's smile harbored no skepticism. And Robert? My son looked truly happy for the first time in months.

I tried to keep my curiosity in check. I merely said, "I trust you found the refreshments to your liking?" knowing very well that they had.

"Oh, indeed." Raleigh wiped his mouth as if remembering the taste, mischief in his eyes. But I did not respond. Dangerous amorous liaisons had lost their thrill for me.

"Come, summon Christopher!" said Robert. "We are going to the theater, to celebrate. Such a fine afternoon, and such a timely play!"

"Why, what is it?"

"*Richard II*," said Raleigh. "Damn appropriate!"

"I wouldn't go that far," cautioned Cecil. "But it will be instructive."

"Has it been successful?" I asked. I had stayed away from the theater for months.

"Very," said Raleigh. "Packing the playhouse. It seems to have struck a chord. It's the story of a foolish king who loses his throne and the clever subject who deposes him."

"I fail to see how it is timely," I said. Elizabeth was many things, but foolish was not one of them. Quite the opposite.

"You'll understand after you listen to the lines," said Robert.

"Oh, have you read it?" I asked.

"Yes, I have a copy. It spoke directly to me."

"And what did it say?"

"I cannot sum it up so simply." He turned to the others. "As soon as Christopher comes, we should leave."

I found Christopher in the courtyard inspecting his horse. He was not keen on the theater, but I told him this was no ordinary performance but held some special meaning for these men, and it behooved us to know what it was. Obligingly he joined me, and then the five of us set out for the theater.

We arrived just in time. I saw, to my dismay, the author on the playbills posted outside: William Shakespeare. If Richard Topcliffe, the notorious torturer in the Tower, had been ordered to punish me, he could have found no better implement. I wanted no reminders of my humiliator.

We settled ourselves. Christopher reached over and took my hand. "It has been a long time since we have attended," he said solicitously. "Even though I'm not much for the theater, if it makes you happy . . ."

The play commenced. At the first lines, spoken by King Richard, "Old John of Gaunt, time-honoured Lancaster," the crowd quieted. The king, a slender actor with a melodious voice, was first commanding, then wheedling, then conciliatory. Was this why the people saw a similarity between Elizabeth and Richard? "We were not born to sue, but to command," the king said, as Elizabeth had been known to. Not much further into the play he capriciously banished Gaunt's son Henry Bolingbroke for the transgression of "eagle-winged pride, of sky-aspiring and ambitious thoughts." Then he just as capriciously altered the sentence from ten years to six.

Elizabeth was renowned, and resented, for her vacillation on matters of state, especially in military affairs. She constantly sent orders countermanding her commands, and only when men were finally at sea were they free of her imperious changes. On land she was not much better; her notorious reluctance to sign necessary decrees was legendary, usually involving several rounds of papers.

I felt uneasy when I saw the actor playing Bolingbroke. Tall, reddish-haired—and with a spade-shaped beard. Richard mockingly described Bolingbroke's "courtship to the common people." Imitating his walk, he said, "How he did seem to dive into their hearts with humble and familiar courtesy." He turned. "What reverence he did throw away on slaves, wooing poor craftsmen with the craft of smiles." He made a face at the audience, a false grin. "Off goes his bonnet to an oyster-wench." He swept off his hat. "A brace of draymen bid God speed him well, and had the tribute of his supple knee." He knelt with a flourish. "With 'thanks, my countrymen, my loving friends,' as were our England in reversion his, and he our subjects' next degree in hope."

The audience had spotted Robert by this time, and they turned to look at him as those lines were recited. It could not have been more pointed. Instead of ignoring them, Robert bowed his head. The fool!

On went the play to its conclusion. The "plume-plucked Richard" was first deposed, then murdered. Bolingbroke lamented "that blood should sprinkle me to make me grow." He vowed a trip to the Holy Land to wash himself clean in repentance. However, he kept the crown on his head.

The audience went wild applauding. Then the manager announced that the fortunes of Bolingbroke would be explored in later plays about the result of his action: the bloody War of the Roses.

Thus we were invited to lament the horror of the evil deeds while thrilling to the gore and irrevocable decisions that led to doom. Such is the theater.

The likeness of Bolingbroke and Essex was unmistakable. I felt that Will had betrayed us. Under our roof he had had ample opportunity to observe and capture Robert's mannerisms. Now he reflected them back in this grotesque character.

Never trust a writer, he had warned me. All the world is ours to kidnap and transform as we will, to our own purpose.

# 49

ecil and Raleigh left the theater and returned to their homes of Salisbury and Durham House, respectively, parting cheerily. Clearly the sober subject of the play had not depressed their spirits—a sign they were so enamored of their new-laid plans they felt impervious to political threat. I waited until we were safely within doors finally to ask Robert what had passed between them.

He tossed his hat toward the bust of Augustus, where it settled squarely on his head, feathers quivering. "Fortune favors me today in small matters as well as large," he observed. He sat down on a padded chair, pleased with himself. "My political foes came to *me*," he said. "Did you ever think that would happen?" He reached over to a platter where dried fruit was always heaped, plucked a fig, and dropped it in his mouth. "We now have a common purpose—or rather, three separate purposes that twine together. By joining forces, we further all three. Cecil wishes to soothe the Queen's bad temper, caused in part by the outré status of me and Raleigh. Raleigh wants to be restored to his old post as captain of the Queen's Guard; I wish to be empowered to mount a Cádiz-style anti-Spanish attack. With Cecil to persuade her for us, we can succeed."

"But why would Cecil wish to help you? What is in it for him? He never does anything without a purpose."

Robert had to think a moment. "He cannot advance himself while the government is paralyzed. The Queen will—the Queen won't—the Queen will—and in the meantime nothing happens. Men of action—me and Raleigh—who can break the dam have been unwelcome at court lately."

"And while you are away on this mission? Have you forgotten that every time you leave, Cecil grabs another office?"

"I am aware of that. But while I am held prisoner here I can achieve nothing. And—Mother, I long to get away! If only I could never come back!"

"Like Drake? He always wished to get away, and now he lies beneath the blue waves off the coast of South America."

"Maybe I'd go ashore in the tropics and stay there. They say the Azores are beautiful—a string of islands a thousand miles from Portugal. Paradise. A man could be happy there—"

He was going to start that again. "Nonsense. Not your sort of man; perhaps that Indian Raleigh brought back. You are an Englishman, and a Welshman, going back generations. This is your soil; this is where you must grow."

"Grow to greatness—" Now he got that dreamy look on his face, the one he had as a child at Chartley. "But the sun itself, that should nourish me, is fading. Or should I say the sun herself?"

"What do you mean?"

"She's slipping, I think. Girls in her chamber tell me she misplaces things, cannot always remember a face or a name. She limps from a foot injury and tries to hide her lameness."

"Who says this?"

"Elizabeth Vernon. She tells Southampton everything she notes."

"Or everything she imagines. I have heard the like whispered for years."

"Mother, she is old."

"She is only in her midsixties. My father lived vigorously into his eighties. Old Burghley is still holding on, and he's almost eighty."

"She's grown more cantankerous, indecisive, and meddlesome."

"She was always cantankerous, indecisive, and meddlesome. You are just not old enough to remember."

"You haven't seen her in years. If you did, you'd note the difference."

"Then get me an audience. I am the mother of her foremost subject. Make her receive me."

"I cannot make her do anything. No one can. That's the frustration."

"Then charm her into it. She's susceptible to that, and you are the best in the world at it."

"Now you flatter *me*," he said. "Lately she has been immune to my charm."

"When you return from this next voyage, you will have a new lease on her favor. But . . ." I looked at his beard, which I never had learned to like. "Were you not offended by the caricature of you tonight? I think it criminal of Will to have done it."

He shrugged. "He plays to his audience. He knows what people want, what is on their minds. All the talk of the common people has been about me, so he wanted to tap into that."

Why was he so obtuse? "The play presents you as a scheming people pleaser," I said. "A malevolent man with wicked motives. Do you not think the Queen will hear of it? Will it not confirm her worst suspicions of you?"

He laughed. "A play is a play. They are just for entertainment. They don't mean anything." He stood up. "Since it disturbs you so much, do you want to see my copy?"

---

That night, by the poor yellow light of three candles, I pored over the play. It was hard to read, but I was determined. It was my duty as a mother to read every word of a work maligning my son.

There was so much in it that pointed to him. It was impossible to pass over. And there was a scene in it that had not been played in the theater, a scene where Richard resigns his crown, handing it over to Bolingbroke. Obviously it was considered too incendiary to be seen.

But why would the Queen think my son aimed at replacing her? In the play, King Richard had unfairly banished Bolingbroke—not just from court, but from the country—and confiscated his lands and property, giving him every excuse to take up arms against him. In Robert's case, the opposite was true. The Queen had favored him, bestowed gifts upon him that, Bacon said, were disproportionate to his deserts. She was the font of his fortunes. Robert had stood beneath its cascades and drenched himself in its shining drops.

As I continued reading, I got more and more angry. Will had deliberately written it to sow suspicions against Robert in the mind of the Queen. God knew it took little to agitate her. Why had he turned on his erstwhile friend? And didn't he realize that, next to the Queen, Robert was the most dangerous enemy to make?

I kept reading, unable to stop, until the eastern window grew gold and overpowered the feeble candles. At times the beauty of the words made me forget their poison, but I steeled myself to read past that. The fact that the poetry imprinted itself in the mind, without effort, made it all the more hopeless to combat, like a substance that will dye our fingers with one light touch.

I tingled with fire, the fire of righteous anger, and it blotted out the deep fatigue underneath. Otherwise I never would have set out as soon as the morning permitted to confront Will. I knew better than to commit anything to paper, and so I must go in person. Better rested, and upon reflection, I would have stifled my feelings and exercised the ultimate caution: not going at all.

He lived in the Bishopsgate section of the city. Oh, I had kept up with his whereabouts, unable to draw a curtain across his existence. I even knew where he lodged—in humble rooms above a tailor's shop. I congratulated myself on my foresight in having this information, which I had gleaned by asking the right offhanded questions of Southampton and Robert.

Wearing a light summer cloak that nonetheless had a deep hood, I set out with my most closemouthed footman to hurry through the streets of London. A litter would attract too much attention, so I had to pick my way through throngs of people, avoid stepping in litter and puddles, and take the shortest route. Unfortunately, Bishopsgate lay on the other side of the city, and that meant trudging through the crowded poultry and stock market streets at Cheapside and the milling around the Royal Exchange. Finally I was at Bishopsgate Street, with its shops and taverns. Now to find the right house. I prided myself that I had never sought it before, but now I wished I knew exactly where it was. I was loath to ask, but I had to. Soon I found the storefront: a forgettable shop like a thousand others. Inside, a tailor and apprentice were bent over a box of buttons. They looked up when I walked in and eyed my cloak. When I asked where I might find Master Shakespeare, their faces fell. They had hoped for a fine commission for another such cloak as the one I wore. Upstairs, they told me, on the third floor.

What a dark and confined space this was, like the inside of a snail shell. There was barely room to keep my elbows from hitting each side of the staircase as I ascended, holding my skirts. On the first landing a tiny window let in a shaft of light. On the second there was no window. On the third a slit allowed me to see the door to one side.

It was a little door, narrow and unpainted. He lived here? I took a deep breath and knocked before I could lose my resolve. No answer. A shiver of relief passed through me. My courage had not failed; I had come; I had knocked. Now I could go in peace.

The door flung open, and Will stood staring at me. His expression was blank, but his eyes widened as they looked at me and all around me.

"I am quite alone," I assured him.

Still he stood staring, then silently beckoned me in. I followed him into a dingy, poorly lit antechamber. He backed in, then sat on a bench. Still wordless, he indicated a chair for me, one with a back and a cushion: the most comfortable one, no doubt.

"Laetitia," he finally said. It was not a greeting but a question.

"Your *Richard II*!" I burst out. He must know, it was important that I set it straight, that I had come on business. Strictly business. "It castigates Robert! I am most distressed about it. Why have you done it?"

"It isn't about Robert Devereux," he said calmly. "It's about a king who lived two hundred years ago."

"Then why does everyone think otherwise?"

He shrugged in that way I had once found endearing and now found infuriating. "I cannot help what people think, what they choose to read into something. I told the tale as it came to me, trying to be as true to the facts as I could. These people are long dead; they do not walk the streets of London or sit on a throne. Richard, I believe, lies right here in Westminster Abbey, and Bolingbroke in Canterbury Cathedral. You can visit their tombs if you like, assure yourself that they are indeed gone."

"No, they live daily on the stage! Spouting your words! You have brought them back to life."

"Have you seen the play?"

"Yes, and read it, too, every word."

He looked pleased. I could tell he wanted to ask me what I thought about it—as a play. "And?"

"And what?"

"If you saw it with no prejudice, would you have assumed it was about Robert?"

"Yes! The beard alone would have told me."

"Laetitia, there were no stage directions about the actor's beard. That was a choice of the actor himself. If he had taken up a trident, would you have thought him to be Poseidon? If all the evidence you have is the beard, you can throw that out."

"The description of him as courting the people's good opinion pointed at Robert. You know he has been hailed by crowds everywhere, and how it annoys the Queen."

"It was a literary device. I needed to have a concrete act of Bolingbroke's to convince the audience he had plans to undermine King Richard even before he was banished. On the stage, we must demonstrate, not merely state."

"It is hurting Robert! Inflaming the Queen's worst suspicions about him. Since his return from Cádiz, he's had scant thanks from her but much applause from the common people."

"Yes, I heard." He paused. "That does not mean I used him in the play. This is just one portion of a whole cycle of plays I am doing on the subject."

"What is the next one?"

"One about Bolingbroke, after he becomes king," he said. "His troubles are just beginning. For a man who is dead, that is." Now he grinned.

Grudgingly, I smiled back. I did not want to stop being angry with him. It was easier that way. "When did you move here?" I asked.

"A few months ago," he said. His eyes were following mine as I looked at his quarters. "I admit it is shabby. I do not entertain countesses here, so it does well enough for me. I'm seldom here, and when I am, I am writing. Better meager surroundings to write. Nothing to tempt the eye away, such as fine tapestry or paintings or inlaid tables. Come, I'll show you." He stood and led me into an even smaller room where a desk, chair, lampstand, and trunk were the only items. Heaped on the desk were sheets of paper; there was another pile on the floor. A surprisingly large window let in reasonable light. It afforded a view of the open fields beyond the wall and Bishop's Gate, the great northern road slicing through them. "Here I sit, seeing only what is in my head." He took up one of the pages, filled with writing, and peered at it. "This is the continuation of Bolingbroke's story," he said. "After he becomes King Henry IV."

Will's kingdom was so small, but it embraced a wide past and a rich present. This tiny room gave birth to the works seen by thousands. It was a marvel. "I am glad that you are happy, Will," I conceded.

"Who says that I am happy?" he asked.

Immediately I remembered about his son's death, and felt a fool. "In your work," I corrected myself. "You are immensely successful."

"Well, I have survived. So many of the other playwrights have died—Greene, Marlowe, Kyd. Or run afoul of the authorities. I take care to represent all viewpoints in my work, so I cannot be accused of any one in particular." He smiled gently. "Except by you, of course. And that's a mother's prerogative—to protect her son. I forgive you your misunderstanding."

So we were to pretend it was only a misunderstanding. Very well. "I heard of the death of your young son," I said. "I am sorry for it."

"Thank you," he said. "It was a heavy loss. One I know now I shall never recover from. He will always be here, but never here." He bent down and opened a box that contained more sheets of paper, hunting for a particular one. He extracted it and handed it to me. "Writing is a poor consolation, but it gives shape to grief. This is from another play I am working on about King John."

I felt oddly privileged to be reading it before it was performed. He tapped the lines he meant me to see.

*Grief fills the room up of my absent child,*
*Lies in his bed, walks up and down with me,*
*Puts on his pretty looks, repeats his words,*
*Remembers me of all his gracious parts,*
*Stuffs out his vacant garments with his form.*

"Oh, Will," was all I could say. I knew about the vacant garments. Walter's were still in the trunk in his old room. "You put a present sorrow back almost four hundred years."

"That is the only way to tame it," he said. Taking the page back, he said, "Now you have seen my workshop. Smaller than a smith's or the tailor's below. But it is all the room I need. It does me well enough, and I have just bought a large property back in Stratford. A pity it took what it took for me to pay attention to home."

Did that mean he was reconciled with his wife? Was he making regular visits back there to see her? I could not ask.

"So you need not feel sorry for me in these little rooms. I have others elsewhere. Of course, that is what the devout Christian will always say as well." He sighed. He seemed older. "What of you? What, truly, does Robert want?"

It was not safe to tell him, even if I knew. So I said, "He wants to strike another blow against Spain but is having difficulty persuading the Queen to approve another fleet. In truth, he's happiest when on a simple mission. The court is too complex for him to navigate." That sounded disloyal. "I mean, it is always a strain at court."

"Well, that is where I get most of my dramatic material from—the slippery stones of the court pavement, where a man can fall and break his neck in one misstep. All hundreds of years ago, of course." He paused. "That's Robert. What of you?"

I affected a lighthearted response. "Oh, things go on. This and that."

"What sort of thises and thats?"

"I—I—"

*I am empty, bored, directionless. Diversions have lost their power to amuse.*

"I am glad you are happy, Laetitia."

"Who says that I am happy?" I shot back at him.

Together we laughed. "Caught you," he said.

Suddenly I felt awkward. I wanted to leave. I made a show of gathering up my cloak and pasting a smile as false as the actor's beard on my face.

"Blessings on you, Will," I said, hurrying out the door and down the stairs. He did not follow.

# 50

retreated to Wanstead after that meeting, unwilling to hear any more talk about how my son was represented onstage in *Richard II* (despite Will's protestations to the contrary) or listen to Robert's naive ideas about how his new "friendship" with Raleigh and Cecil was going to pave the way back into the Queen's good graces.

But he followed me, appearing one afternoon in his jaunty fashion to keep me apprised of what was happening in London.

"Robert," I said, "pray give me a respite from that talk. It is simply too dreary. Here I can pretend nothing is happening, that I am far away in Moscow . . . or someplace." Then I grew suspicious. "Is there something wrong at home with Frances?"

He looked indignant. "No, of course not. I just wanted a retreat, myself. I won't bother you!"

God knew he could use a quiet withdrawal, a rest. "Very well," I said.

"I brought only Meyrick with me to see to my needs. You need not stir yourself."

Gelli Meyrick, his steward! I had never liked him, ever since he had attached himself to Robert in their days at Cambridge. He was a lowly sort, a wild Welshman whose real first name, Gwyllyam, was unpronounceable, one of the ones Robert had so unwisely knighted at Cádiz, and who now called himself Sir. He had chosen a strange coat of arms involving porcupines.

"I appreciate that, but please do not hide yourself away." It would be a welcome change to see him free of his entourage, excepting the unlikeable Meyrick. "Let us talk only of pleasant things. It has been a long time since we had that luxury."

It was easy, here at Wanstead, to float above the rumors and troubles of the realm—the continuing dearth in the land, the constant worry about

Spain (would we ever be free of it?), the question of the Queen's temper and her longevity.

Night. I loved night, when all was quiet. As the sun set, I always felt a strange excitement, as if life only began once it was dark.

I had poured myself a glass of wine and fitted fresh candles into the sconces, ready to read and think, when suddenly I heard a rapping at one of the windows in the next room. It was a sharp, startling sound, and sinister. I put my book down and listened carefully. Perhaps it was only a branch hitting the windowpane. But there was no wind tonight, and no branches were near the windows.

Rap! Rap! There it was again. I could not pretend it was not real. I rose. Robert was in another wing of the house, and I could not call him without passing the window. I crept toward that room and peered around the doorway.

A white face was staring back at me. It looked like a corpse, and I gave a shriek. It disappeared, then rose up again and made wiping motions against the glass with swollen, misshapen hands.

"Robert!" I cried. "Gelli!" Now I would welcome the burly steward and his strong arms.

Instead of ducking, the man kept making plaintive gestures, as if he expected me to let him in, with his grotesque hands. Then another face appeared at the next window. Suddenly there was a commotion outside; Robert and Gelli had rushed out and tackled the two men. A loud scuffling ensued, then silence. I rushed to the window and threw it open, peering down to see what was happening.

Robert and Gelli had the two men in hammerlocks, pinning them down, pulling their arms behind them.

"For the love of Christ!" the first man cried. "Oh, spare my hands!"

"Who are you?" demanded Robert.

"Do you not remember me, Gelli?" the second man said. "And you, Robert?"

"I've never seen you before!" said Robert, bearing down harder on his captive's arms.

"Cambridge!" the younger man cried. "I'm Roger Aylward! Oh, please!"

"In the name of Jesus," the first man said, "have mercy! Shelter us!"

"Not until you identify yourselves. I know no Roger Aylward," said Robert.

"I do," said Gelli. "He was a tutor at Trinity, worked in the master's office."

"Yes! Yes!" said Aylward. "I swear it!"

"But what about you?" Robert turned to the other man.

"I am John Gerard," he said.

"That's impossible. Do you take us for simpletons? Gerard is in the Tower."

"I escaped," he said.

Robert laughed. "Do not insult me. That is impossible."

"Not impossible. Free me and I will tell all."

"What? If the notorious Jesuit Gerard ever came here—which *is* impossible—I could not shelter him. It would ruin me if I were caught. Harboring a Jesuit! An escaped prisoner? Not upon my life. It *would* be my life!"

"I ask only for overnight. It's only five hours till dawn. We have a safe house to go to. But we must rest. And throw them off our track. They expect us to go west, so we have come east."

Gradually Robert and Gelli released them. Shakily the men got to their feet.

"Bring them in here," I said. "Quickly."

I was trembling. Could this be true? Could anyone escape from the Tower? And why would they have sought us, a known Protestant household?

The two men shuffled in and sank down onto chairs. I could not call a servant; I would have to fetch something from the kitchen myself—cheese, ale, any food would do.

While I was gone the men had taken off their cloaks and now were looking mutely about. The first man's hands were so damaged he could not hold the food but had to be fed by his companion.

"These hands are courtesy of Topcliffe," he said. "I was tortured several times but did not break, although the bones in my hands did. They hung me by my wrists for hours."

"Believe us or no, we have been prisoners for three years," said Aylward. "Ever since the Easter raids of 1594."

I remembered those raids. The government had made a sweep of houses suspected of harboring missionary Jesuit priests, and had netted many. But the biggest catch of all was the famous John Gerard, their leader. He has successfully evaded them for years, able to pass as a courtier who liked hunting, gambling, card playing, and fashionable dress. When he was not hiding in plain sight like that, he could live for days in unbelievably small hiding places, including under a fireplace grate at one time. Another time he had stood in an underground sewer when a Catholic house was raided at five in the morning. If anyone could escape from the Tower, it would be Gerard. But what if he was an impostor, sent to trap us?

"Prove that you are who you say you are," said Robert.

The man gave a rueful laugh. "I am sorry, I cannot provide identification papers. I can only show my hands." He held them up, a gruesome sight.

"Your companion might have done that," said Gelli. "Unless Topcliffe branded you, we cannot know you suffered at his hands."

"That may have been coming, but I did not stay to avail myself of that," said the man. "Since you do not believe us—and understandably so—but have been charitable enough to give us some food, we will be on our way." He rose.

"Not so fast," said Gelli. "Explain how you got out of the Tower—if you did."

"Simple but not easy. We were lodged in the Salt Tower, which is one of the outer towers overlooking the moat on the river side. With the compliance of our keeper, who was sympathetic to our cause, we were able to arrange to have friends waiting on the wharf."

"Yes, but how did you get out of the Tower?"

"We threw a small line across the moat; our friends caught it and fastened a larger line to it, which we hauled up to the roof. Then we went hand over hand across. Gerard's hands could barely hold. That finished them off," said Aylward.

"They must have missed us by now, or they surely will by morning," said Gerard.

---

"Let them stay," I said. "I believe them."

"Bless you, lady," said Gerard. He sank back down.

"Lay out pallets here," I said. "They need to sleep." While the men went to get them, I said, "I am not of your faith but admire your courage—and those of you who still remain steadfast even though your country affords you little reward." Catholics could not sit in Parliament or hold university positions. There was no Catholic in any government circle. To persist in Catholicism meant no career in public service.

"Those are the people we come to minister to, my lady," said Gerard. "They have no one but us to sustain them. So we gladly risk our own lives if that can preserve their faith. The great households provide some shelter, but they still need priests. There has been trouble at Cowdray, one of the mainstays. The new heir there is more militant and has run afoul of the government authorities, more's the pity. Many a baptism was performed there until recently."

"I *did* know both Robert and Gelli at Cambridge," said Aylward. "And I knew they were Protestant. But I also knew . . . forgive me . . . that recently Robert has had a falling out with the Queen, so I was hoping that it might be safe to come here. I am sorry to presume, but we were desperate."

I smiled. "We *are* a Protestant house," I said. "My father, in fact, was so staunchly Protestant he left England when Queen Mary reconciled it to the church. But now . . . it is less a conviction than a political necessity," I admitted. Suddenly I felt ashamed. In the light of such pure faith—like that of my father, even if at the opposite end of the spectrum—I always felt soiled and compromised. But how many among us burn with a true religious flame? "I am glad you are here," I said. "Please rest well."

"We will," said Gerard. "And we promise to be gone before first light!" In the gentleness of his voice, in his quiet humor, I saw the charm that had won so many.

---

True to their word, before I was up, the men were gone. They had neatly folded the linens and blankets. Resting on one of the pillows was a saint's medal. I picked it up as if it were poisonous. In a way it was. I turned it over. It was St. Lucy.

St. Lucy . . . St. Lucy . . . What did I know about her, indifferent Protestant that I was? She had something to do with eyesight, and her day was the shortest of the year. That would make her a good patron saint for me, since I liked nighttime. But Protestants did not have patron saints. Perhaps I could ask Christopher. He had been brought up Catholic. He might know.

I folded it in my palm. It was their thank-you gift, the only proof they had been here, and I treasured it.

"They're gone?" Behind me Robert was standing, seeing the folded bedding. "Almost without a trace. Thank God!"

"I had never seen a Jesuit," I said. "I had been told they were demons with cloven hooves and tails. Instead I found a humane and intelligent man."

He laughed dismissively. "They say the devil himself can appear to be humane and intelligent."

"He's certainly intelligent, and good enough company that the Puritans fear the rivalry," I said. "Although they don't give him much competition in that regard."

"Nonetheless, I'm glad they're gone. I hope no one links them to us. That's all my enemies at court would need to use against me!"

# 51

## ELIZABETH

*August 1597*

ou must watch this play with me," I told Marjorie and Catherine. "I know you don't fancy plays but I need your opinion. But you," I turned to the younger ladies, "might enjoy it. They say the actor playing Richard is quite dreamy. He has to be, for his face to match his poetic words."

The Lord Chamberlain's Men were to present the controversial *Richard II* this afternoon at Windsor. London had talked of little else, and although I had sent observers to the theater to report back to me, I needed to see it for myself.

It should have been an easy summer, with all the quarrelsome and strutting men away. No Raleigh, no Blount, no Essex. But once again we had foul weather; this was the fourth bad summer in a row, the fourth ruined harvest. Now it was seeming truly unnatural, and the people were growing more desperate and there was more talk of violence in the countryside. Parliament would meet and we would try to find a remedy, or failing that, immediate help for the destitute. There were few rides out through the countryside, and, sensing my unpopularity and not wishing to inflame it further, I did not go on Progress.

This *Richard II* did fan the flames. The Puritans had tried to close the theaters again and I was determined not to let them. But what irony that my power to keep them open allowed a play to put questionable ideas in people's heads.

The Puritans, that thorn in my side! I must contend with the stiff-necked, self-righteous Puritans on one side and the recusant Catholics and their sneaky secret priests on the other. I had been sorrowed by the actions of the new heir at Cowdray. Dear Anthony Browne had died, passing on the title to his grandson, who had openly flouted my religious laws, daring me to move against him. There had even been a small, secret monastery on the grounds. Reluctantly I had done so, closing their chapel with its Catholic rites and shutting the monastery, barring it up. Someone had tried to burn it down, as if to make that prediction of Guy Fawkes's come true.

Out in the countryside, the escaped Jesuits from the Tower were still at large working their mischief.

The Puritans, for their part, especially hated the theater, because actors pretended to be what they were not. Men dressed as women, posed as Julius Caesar, and so on. They cited Scripture—"A woman must not wear men's clothing, nor a man wear women's clothing, for the Lord your God detests anyone who does this"—to prove these things were abominations. Their scrutiny of Scriptures meant they could find a verse to support just about anything—one of the dangers of letting the unlearned have free access to Scripture. But as someone said, not without truth, the Puritans were against bearbaiting not because it brought pain to the bear but because it brought pleasure to the spectators.

Taking our places in the Great Hall, we settled ourselves. Rain was drumming on the roof overhead. Another fair summer's day denied us. It was just as well to be indoors.

The handsome young actor playing Richard was the first out on the stage and the first to speak. "Old John of Gaunt, time-honoured Lancaster," he said with a flourish. The play then plunged straightway into the story, a story any Tudor child had written on his or her heart. It was the wellspring of our dynasty, the act that set in motion the bloody civil war that lasted a century. It began when King Richard II was forced to resign his crown to his cousin Henry of Bolingbroke. This deed was a great transgression. Could an anointed sovereign ever truly resign the crown? A coronation was a sacrament, the right of it conveyed by blood, and the act of anointing and crowning permanent and inviolable. Could anyone undo it?

I assumed that was what the play would explore, and in one sense I was not disappointed. The play's King Richard made his case for that, saying,

*Not all the water in the rough rude sea*
*Can wash the balm off from an anointed king;*
*The breath of worldly men cannot depose*
*The deputy elected by the Lord.*

But others made the point that a king forfeited his right to be king if he neglected his kingdom; that the king could sin by harming his own land. It sounded dangerously close to Puritan doctrine.

Richard himself admitted that "we are enforced to farm our royal realm," while John of Gaunt put it more bluntly, saying, "This dear dear land . . . is now leas'd out—I die pronouncing it—like to a tenement or pelting farm," and "Landlord of England art thou now, not king."

I felt great relief. No one could accuse me of that. I was criticized for being penny-pinching, but better that than mortgaging the country.

King Richard went off to Ireland, and while he was gone his disgruntled nobles defected to Bolingbroke. By the time he returned, the Crown was all but lost. However, he refused to fight for it and even offered to resign it before Bolingbroke asked.

*What must the King do now? Must he submit?*
*The King shall do it. Must he be deposed?*
*The King shall be contented. Must he lose*
*The name of king? O' God's name, let it go.*

What sort of king was this? Even my sister Mary, who people assumed was a soft, pious woman, fought for her crown, wrested it from Lady Jane Grey's illegal grasp.

Richard was dispatched to the Tower, then transferred to Pontefract Castle, where he was murdered, following a hint of Bolingbroke that someone needed to rid him of "this living fear."

The way Richard was presented in the play, one could only conclude that he was a poor sort of king, but that the man who usurped his place was a villain, albeit a competent one. I was descended from both of them. I liked to think I had Richard's artistic sensibility and Bolingbroke's realism and practicality, rather than their weaknesses.

The play seemed abnormally short. And the action moved too quickly from the crisis to the end. "Something is missing," I said. It did not feel right.

The master of revels, Edmund Tilney, stood up. "There is an injunction against performing the actual abdication scene. I have forbidden it to be seen."

"But it is written?" I asked.

"Indeed, yes."

"And the actors know it?"

"Yes."

"I command that it be performed here before me. Censor it for the mutable crowds, but let me judge it for myself."

The actors quickly reassembled and begged leave to study their lines.

In a short while the lead actor appeared. "We are ready, Your Majesty," he said, bowing.

It opened, this subversive scene, in Westminster Hall, which served as a venue for both celebration and state trials. My mother had been tried here, to her woe; so had Thomas More. If all the sad trials held here had weight, the carved roof beams would sag to the ground, kissing the stone floor.

Bolingbroke was ready to assume the crown in a legalistic manner before his accomplices, when the Bishop of Carlisle objected and said it was meaningless without Richard's presence. Richard himself then came onstage, where, after much posturing and wordplay, he was forced to hand his crown directly to Bolingbroke. Asked if he was contented to resign the crown, he hemmed and hawed, first yes, then no. Then he acquiesced, saying,

*Now mark me, how I will undo myself.*
*I give this heavy weight from off my head,*
*And this unwieldy scepter from my hand,*
*The pride of kingly sway from out my heart.*
*With mine own tears I wash away my balm,*
*With mine own hands I give away my crown,*
*With mine own tongue deny my sacred state,*
*With mine own breath release all duteous oaths;*
*All pomp and majesty I do forswear.*

The effect was shocking. There is no formula for an abdication, but we were hearing one. One by one he flung off the pieces of his kingly armor until he was totally unprotected.

But could he? Had he not himself said, earlier in the play, that not all the water in the rude, rough sea could wash off the balm from an anointed king? If not the whole ocean, even less his own tears.

I had taken solemn oaths at my coronation and nothing could undo them. A deposed or murdered sovereign was still an anointed sovereign. Mary Queen of Scots was still Queen of Scotland all those years in England, and remained so on the scaffold.

But if this play convinced people that it was possible to reverse a coronation? It was dangerous, and this scene was downright revolutionary, even though the events it depicted were two hundred years old.

"Come, my ladies," I said, rising. I twisted my coronation ring around my finger, as if to prove it was still snugly there.

---

Shortly thereafter I received a request for an audience from the Polish ambassador. Things being placid (although it was a placidity I welcomed), I thought the court—what remained of it these days—would enjoy the diversion. So I invited him, not for a private audience but for a full reception in the presence chamber with the whole court and officers of the realm attending.

I had a soft spot in my heart for the King of Poland, for he was actually Swedish, and one of my fondest memories was the oddly touching courtship of King Eric XIV of Sweden—before he went mad, that is. His brother, the elegant and sophisticated Duke John, had come a-courting in his brother's name. In any case, Duke John's son, who sat on the Polish throne as Sigismund III Vasa, had been *elected*. His country was now a commonwealth, whatever that was. The Poles had made this transition over twenty years ago. But it was obvious such an anomaly could never last. How could a king be elected, for all the reasons of majesty examined in *Richard II*? A king or queen was not merely someone holding an office, like a sheriff, but appointed by divine will.

The August day was heavy and lowering, threatening a downpour at any moment. Turbulent black clouds tumbled through the sky, rumbling ominously. Inside, the fluctuating light through the windows made winking patterns on the floor.

I stood beneath my canopy of state, with its rich embroidery and scalloped border, flanked by both Cecils. Burghley leaned on a cane but refused to sit; young Robert was attired in his most solemn, statesmanlike gown, even wearing a hat. Farther on the side were the other council members: Charles Howard, lord admiral; George Carey, the new lord chamberlain; Thomas Sackville, Lord Buckhurst; William Knollys; Archbishop Whitgift. Their ladies, along with other courtiers, stood on either side of the long aisle where the ambassador would walk. I saw Francis Bacon and John Harington among them, and young Robert Dudley, numerous Carey and Knollys brothers and sisters and cousins, my maids of honor and ladies of the privy chamber. This would be enjoyable—panoply without deeper meaning.

The ambassador was announced, and he made his way down the long aisle. He was a stout little man, dressed all in black velvet with a high buttoned collar and a jeweled chain, from which dangled a star-shaped insignia of some Polish order. As he passed the smiling faces, he gave a tight-lipped twitch in response.

He approached, took my hand, and kissed it with papery-dry lips. Then he stepped back, and I took my seat on the throne to hear his formal address.

He began in sonorous Latin reciting his master's titles. "*Sigismundus Tertius Dei gratia rex Poloniae, magnus dux Lithuaniae Russiae Prussiae Mascoviae Samogitiae Livoniaeque, necnon Suecorium Gothorum Vandalorumque hoeredicatrius rex.*"

My Latin secretary obligingly translated. "Sigismund III Vasa, by the grace of God King of Poland, grand Duke of Lithuania, Russia, Prussia, Masovia, Samogita, Livonia, and hereditary king of the Swedes, Goths, and Wends."

I nodded in approval and motioned him to proceed. He continued in Latin, but not in a polite address. Instead, standing truculently before me, he said that his king was angry that after numerous polite requests that we stop hindering their ships and merchants trading with Spain, we continued our outrageous conduct, against all international law and custom. We were prohibiting their free trade and assuming a sovereignty over other kings, which was intolerable. The King of Poland would trade with whom he pleased, Spain as well as anywhere else, and hereby warned the Queen of England that if she would not stop this behavior, he would make her stop.

There was a stunned silence. Such a breach of manners and protocol had never been witnessed between a representative ambassador and his sovereign host. I opened my mouth to reply, but realized he did not speak English. Latin it must be, then, although I had not spoken it in years.

Anger coursed through me, but I put my thoughts in orderly columns like well-trained soldiers and marshaled them out.

"*Expectavi legationem, mihi vero querelam adduxisti.*" "I expected an embassy, but you have brought me a quarrel."

He looked surprised and annoyed that I would respond. What did he expect, the fool? Did he think I had not understood his Latin? "Oh, how I have been deceived!" I continued. "Your letters assured me that you were an ambassador, but instead I find you a herald. Never in my lifetime have I heard such an oration. I marvel much at so insolent a boldness in open royal presence; neither do I believe if your king were present that he himself would deliver such speeches."

Would these words be correctly reported back to his master? "But if you have been commanded to use suchlike speeches—which I greatly doubt—we must lay the blame here: that since your king is a young man and newly chosen, not by right of blood but by right of election, he does not so perfectly know the protocol of managing diplomatic affairs with other princes as his elders do."

The man still stood smugly—or perhaps he was having trouble following my rapid speech. "And concerning yourself, you seem to have read many books, but the books of princes you have not so much as touched, but show yourself utterly ignorant what is proper between kings," I informed him—the little snail. "Know you that this is the law of nature and of nations: that when hostility arises between princes, it is lawful for either party to obstruct the other's provisions for war, no matter where they originate from, and to foresee that they be not converted to their own hurts."

Enough of him. "For other matters, which this time and place do not serve, you may expect to be questioned by some of our councillors. In the meantime, fare you well and repose yourself quietly."

I turned to my court and said, "God's death, my lords! I have been enforced this day to scour up my old Latin that hath lain long rusting." A burst of applause filled the chamber, and the ambassador backed out. It was a long way to walk backward.

If this performance was an indication of the competence of elected kings to fill royal shoes, it was damning.

---

As evening drew in, I invited guests to gather in the privy chamber for a music recital. The rain was still dripping, making a measured background to the virginal and the lutes. Our mood was mellow after the incident with the Polish ambassador, and John Harington challenged Francis Bacon to carry on a conversation with him entirely in Latin for five minutes.

"As our gracious Queen has proved she can do," he said, winking at me.

"The Queen has no rivals there," Bacon said. "And to follow in her footsteps would be embarrassing. Let us try another tongue. I challenge you in Greek."

"You sidestep the issue. You know I have not studied it."

"But I have," said Robert Cecil.

And off they went. I could follow it all, and truth be told, had to bite my tongue to keep from correcting one of Cecil's verb tenses.

We all had a repast then, where each person contributed something to our feast, Charles Howard fine Reine Claude pears preserved in sweet wine, Buckhurst sherry from Portugal, and Marjorie Norris a potent Irish drink called *uisce beatha*, of which we had thimblefuls only, on account of its being so strong.

At the mention of Ireland, a pall descended over our spirits. Ireland was still in turmoil; rebellious native Irish, under their new leader, The O'Neill, were still hostile and growing in number. Marjorie's son John, "Black Jack," our best soldier, had not prevailed against them, had tangled with Russell, our lord deputy, and had asked to be recalled. His wish was granted, but we needed time to find his replacement. In the meantime he clamored to be allowed home.

"May it be the last thing he has an opportunity to send from that godforsaken, stricken land!" Marjorie burst out.

"He will soon be home," I assured her. "In the meantime, let us enjoy his gift, as his farewell to Ireland."

Gingerly we all took a sip.

"It takes a man indeed to quaff this!" I cried, my mouth stinging.

---

Bedtime at last, the cards spent, the virginal covered, the lutes put away. Sticky cups and empty flasks sitting on trays throughout the chamber, candles burned down. It was safe now to open the windows and let fresh air in, the rain having stopped.

I was already in my nightclothes and preparing to go to bed when a nervous rap sounded on the chamber door. The guard opened it and a hand thrust itself in, clutching a letter.

"For you, Your Majesty," the messenger said. He stepped smartly outside the chamber to allow me to read it in private.

I disliked the very feel of the letter, heavy with moisture, as if weighted down with its news. It had to be something bad to be delivered so late at night, urgent for me to know before sunrise. It could, of course, equally have been good news that could not wait. But I did not think so.

Slowly I opened it, unfolding it on the table where a candle still burned. Marjorie and Catherine stood on either side of me like protecting angels. I could almost feel the feathers of their wings.

"Sir John Norris passed from this world in my arms," wrote his brother Thomas Norris. "While awaiting permission to leave, he—"

I felt like an intruder reading this. Slowly I turned to look up at Marjorie, seeing only her strong jaw at this angle. "My dear Crow," I said, "this is for you, not me." Rising, I handed her the letter, and we exchanged places.

She read, then burst into tears. "He's gone," she said. "My brave son!"

And our best soldier, I thought. England's loss as well as hers. "What has happened?" I asked.

"He died of gangrene from a thigh wound," she said.

"Like Sir Philip Sidney," said Catherine.

"Damn Ireland!" cried Marjorie. "I've already lost a son there! My oldest, William, died there, and now John! There's still Thomas and Henry on that wretched soil! And Maximilian died in the Brittany war!"

"You have bred six sons, all six of them soldiers," I said. "It is a dismal thing to lose three. But I fear it is in the nature of their profession." I reached out to comfort her, but she turned away.

"They were serving you," she said. "It was under your orders that they went to Brittany and to Ireland, that they are still serving there."

"At least he had his brother with him," ventured Catherine timidly. "He did not die alone, as so many must."

"We can be thankful it was swift," I said. He had not lingered for almost a month, like Sidney. "And, as Catherine said, to have his brother with him must have been a comfort. To him, and now to you." I reached out to her again and this time she let me embrace her.

In stepping out into the privy chamber to tell the messenger there was no reply tonight and to return in the morning, I saw the empty *uisce beatha* bottle. It was good we had drunk it. I threw it out. One less thing to cause Marjorie pain when she looked at it.

# 52

*October 1597*

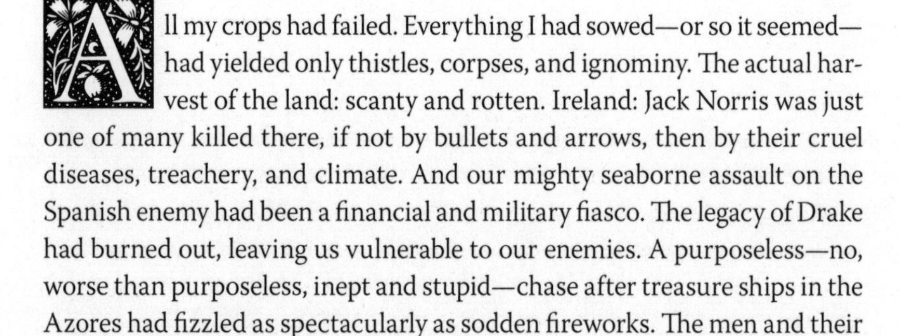

All my crops had failed. Everything I had sowed—or so it seemed—had yielded only thistles, corpses, and ignominy. The actual harvest of the land: scanty and rotten. Ireland: Jack Norris was just one of many killed there, if not by bullets and arrows, then by their cruel diseases, treachery, and climate. And our mighty seaborne assault on the Spanish enemy had been a financial and military fiasco. The legacy of Drake had burned out, leaving us vulnerable to our enemies. A purposeless—no, worse than purposeless, inept and stupid—chase after treasure ships in the Azores had fizzled as spectacularly as sodden fireworks. The men and their expensively outfitted ships had returned home in humiliation. The passing bell had tolled for England's adventures at sea.

---

Only Raleigh had the nerve to face me as if nothing had happened. The rest of the leaders slunk away—Essex and Christopher Blount to the country, Charles Blount to his London house. But Raleigh, ever ebullient, arrived at Hampton Court one fine October day to bring me his most precious and unusual gift, as he put it.

I had been taking my usual brisk morning walk in the gardens, angry at the clear, golden weather. *Now* it decided to be bright and clear, now when it was too late to do any good. The perfect crop-gathering weather was only a mockery when there were no crops to gather. When I was told he came to pay a visit, I burst out, "Oh, what can that man want now?" and whirled around to see him striding through the gap in the boxwood hedge.

"To greet you, fair Queen!" he said, rushing toward me.

"Ach!" I all but turned away. The sight of him annoyed me, although in truth he had behaved with more insight and resourcefulness than his master, Essex. I should never have permitted Essex to have overall command. He simply could not work with anyone else or coordinate his plans beyond himself.

"Does the sun hide its face?" cried Raleigh, already beside me. "Say not so!"

"I turn my face downward to search in my empty treasure chests," I said. But he knew our straits as well as anyone else. "What is it you bring me, Walter?"

"If I told you it was a pyramid of Inca gold, or the ruby from an Indian prince's scepter, it would not please you as much as what I offer!"

"Test me," I said. "Present those two things first."

He smiled his sun-melting smile. "Alas, I do not have them. I merely paint them with my words."

"As I thought. Well, then, for the third?"

He gestured to his manservant, who pulled a small, latticed cart over the graveled garden path. As he strained to tug it, it was obvious the cart contained something heavy. Perhaps it was ingots after all.

"Careful, careful, slow!" warned Walter as the cart lurched and was about to tip. He gave the man a hand and together they rolled it up to me.

The cart was actually a cage, with a barred door. It must be an animal, perhaps another armadillo. But that would not be novel.

I edged over to it. No odor. A clean animal, then. I knocked on the cage. Silence. No bark or hiss. A mute animal. I shoved the cage a bit. No movement. A placid animal.

"Oh, God's teeth, what is it?" I cried. "It does nothing!"

"Behold!" he cried, raising the cage door, so that light flooded in.

A enormous gray head with unblinking, round eyes stared back at me. It emerged, on a wrinkled neck, from what looked like a gigantic seashell or a suit of armor.

"Out, out you go," said Walter, opening the other end of the cage and prodding the creature from behind. He could not budge it. It just continued staring at me.

"Is this what you plundered?" I asked.

"Yes, I got it from a Portuguese ship just returning from Zanzibar. It seems the animal was a gift from a chief there."

"Why didn't you take their cloves instead?"

"The cloves had long been unloaded. Nothing remained in the hold but the delicious smell."

"And this creature." Now it was stirring, rearing itself up on its massive legs, causing its shell to hit the roof of the cage.

"Here you are, my beauty," said Raleigh. "Come out, come out."

But it could not descend from the wagon, and together the two men could barely lift it.

"Not here!" I said. Once they got it onto the ground there would be no more moving it. "It belongs in the New World garden." I led the way to the walled area I had designated for the plants people had brought from the Americas. There were rows of potatoes—both sweet and plain—more rows of tobacco (but they took up too much room with their broad, spreading leaves and I planned to move them), yucca plants and fleshy cactus plants with huge spikes, and plants with leaves like water lotuses and red or yellow flowers. There were ground-growing vines that produced orange-colored, ribbed gourds, called pumpkins, and tall, spindly plants that grew narrow, leaf-wrapped packages of golden kernels on a cob, called maize. There were bushes that grew beans. And these were just the ones that grew in our climate. Others had perished after the first summer.

"Let all the strangeness mingle together," I said. Straining themselves, they heaved the huge turtle from the cart and set it down between two rows of potatoes. Immediately it ducked its head into its shell, so it looked like a gray boulder.

"A giant turtle?" I exclaimed.

"It's properly known as a tortoise, Ma'am, as it lives entirely on land." He nodded gravely.

"How long will it stay like that?" I asked.

"It could be days," admitted Walter. "And she is probably shy and won't come out until she feels at home."

"You know it is a she?"

"The Portuguese were told it was. In any case, she has a woman's name. Constancia. It means 'constant, steadfast.'"

I looked at the immobile bulk. "Yes, I can see she fits her name."

"Every time you look at her—"

"I shall think of you, Walter. Now tell me, what does this remarkable creature eat?"

"The sailors told me she can go a long time without eating anything, but on Zanzibar she ate field grasses and fallen fruit."

"An inexpensive diet. We shall do our best to please her appetite." Constancia still had not moved, nor shown her head. I turned away. "Perhaps if we do not look at her—" I steered Raleigh away. "Now, Walter, what have you really come to tell me?"

We withdrew into the pond garden not so far away. "You are astute, as always. Nothing gets past you." We took a seat on a stone bench, across from the wall fountain that gurgled water from its grinning mouth.

"I do not have to be particularly astute to see past the gift to the giver. I assume you wish to tell your side of the ill-fated expedition."

"The voyage . . ." He began tentatively. Then, "Essex spoiled it! You put all of us under his command and gave orders we could do nothing without his consent. He used that mandate to tie us up in inaction. The man did not obey even the basic commander's rule to inform his subordinates of changes in plans. Because of him, we lost St. Michael's. I waited at our appointed meeting place, thereby announcing the English presence to the entire town, allowing them ample opportunity to remove their valuables and arm themselves. Knowing I would be severely reprimanded if I did anything without orders from Essex, I could take no action. Finally, after three days waiting, I decided to land the troops and try to capture what little remained."

"And where was Lord Essex all this while?"

"Eating, drinking, and enjoying himself with his men on the other side of the island. Yes! Instead of proceeding to St. Michael's garrison from the land side as he had promised, he remained in town, gorging himself and resting up."

"He sent not even a single messenger to you?"

"Nothing! And when we were reunited, he charged me with treason for landing 'without permission,' and his worthless cronies, the pretty boys Southampton and Christopher Blount, wanted to have a military trial right there and execute me."

"Well, you are alive," I said, trying to make light of it, but inside I was churning. I did not want to give him any words to quote from me secondhand. "What happened?"

"I forced myself to apologize to him, although the fault was all on his side. I was not going to give his supporters the excuse they were looking for to do away with me." He leaned forward, and if I had not been Queen, he would have clutched my shoulders and pulled my face up to his for emphasis. But he knew better. "My dear Cynthia, my moon, I fear that Essex is completely in thrall to these men—these boys—he surrounds himself with. They inflame him, fill his head with nonsense, or rather empty it, making it as empty as their own."

"He keeps a swarm of them at Essex House, I hear." They were young, violent, and without either achievements or hope of advancement: a combustible combination.

"*Swarm* is a good word, for they are like locusts—devouring his bounty and making up his army. They cut him off from the counsel of other people. The only levelheaded person in that house is his mother, Lettice. And he listens less and less to her. The same with Francis Bacon. The others sing the song he wants to hear, and he is dancing to it."

The song others sing . . . That is the true siren song, the one to lure us to the rocks.

"I am grieved to know this," I said. Raleigh's description of his behavior made him sound unbalanced as well as deluded.

"I am grieved to tell you," he said. "But it is imperative that you know. He, of course, will paint it a different color."

"Never hesitate to speak truth to me. That is the understanding that I have had with Burghley from the beginning."

"'The wrath of a prince is death,'" he quoted the warning given Thomas More. "It is dangerous to anger one's ruler."

"That adage does not fit me," I replied. "The two—the Duke of Norfolk and the Queen of Scots—I was forced to condemn to death I was never angry with, but sorrowful toward. And those I have been most angry with—as in the present company—have been quite safe. If to make me angry meant death, then you, Leicester, the Polish ambassador would all be dead. Even Lettice Knollys still breathes in peace—that she-wolf!"

"Point taken, my Cynthia. I shall never hesitate to speak truth, then."

---

The next morning I found that the tortoise had destroyed half the plants in my New World garden, flattening the beans, eating off the tops of the potatoes, stripping the pumpkin vines of their leaves, and squashing the flowers. Constancia had mowed through like an elephant and now dozed innocently in one corner, the sun warming her thick shell.

The naughty creature. I was of a mind to make Raleigh take it to Sherborne and let Bess mind it. But it was winsome, even though it wreaked havoc—like Essex and Raleigh.

---

The parliament of 1597 was a dreary affair, long awaited as an answer to the want and unrest stalking the land. The finest minds in the nation gathered to address the crisis; as will happen, the finest minds quarreled among themselves. There was a feeling of helplessness and confusion all around, knowing that the problem was caused by two things beyond our control—the weather and past history—and yet the solution could not wait for our wisdom to grow.

In the end, we passed a series of poor laws—legislation both to help and to control the population of needy. Some—like Francis Bacon—claimed that landowners fencing their tracts for sheep and evicting farmers had caused the shortage of cropland that was the root of the problem, and his supporters tried to make a case for limiting or even tearing out the enclosures. But like king Canute commanding the tide to stop, it was futile. The process had gone on too long to be rolled back now. Nonetheless, Bacon made an eloquent case, painting a picture of the future countryside, stripped of its villages and farmers, suffering the fate of abandoned Troy, nothing but weedy meadows.

The land issue having been taken care of—Bacon got two bills passed—Parliament moved on to the rogues and the honest poor, each requiring a different cure. The rogues were identified as begging scholars, fake shipwrecked sailors, fortune tellers, bearwards, false claims collectors, illegal workers, pretend charity workers, and actors—except those under a nobleman's patronage. These were all to be whipped and sent back to their home parishes, there to remain, with no more vagabondage on the roads.

Should any of these types be, in addition, an agitator or a leader of the lower classes, he should be banished to someplace abroad, never to return upon pain of death. Or, if a suitable place of permanent banishment was not available, he could be sent to the galleys instead, there to row for his own eternity.

As for the honest poor, a dole from their local parish was to replace begging. These were people unfit for work, through no fault of their own: the blind, the lame, the old, the frail. In addition, the parish would raise money for the raw materials for cottages for the poor, employing able-bodied poor to build them and providing apprenticeships for the children.

These laws were intended to put an end to all begging and wandering. Whether they succeeded or not, it was a noble effort. I did not know of any other country that had ever attempted it, and I was proud of our trying.

Jesus had said poor people were always among us, but he had not meant there was no obligation to help them. Up until now, helping the poor had meant that one person gave charity to another. Now, in England, we were saying that the government itself mandated relief for the poor. It was no longer enough to merely put a coin in an orphan's hand. Each village and hamlet had to be responsible for the poor souls who lived there.

As for the villains who mocked the poor by pretending poverty in order to claim false charity, they must be exposed and rooted out.

These were laws Parliament could be proud of.

---

All this while Essex was sulking in his house, refusing to take his place in the House of Lords or to come to Privy Council meetings. He had some thirty of his adherents in Parliament to carry out his bidding but did not grace the chamber with his appearance. He was insulted that I had created Lord Admiral Charles Howard Earl of Nottingham, and that Charles would preside over Parliament as lord steward, walking before everyone else. It had been my surprise, a well-earned reward to Charles. Essex also was driven into a fury by the wording in the patent that elevated Charles, giving him credit for his action against the Armada in 1588 and also for the Cádiz mission. Essex derided Howard's part in the Cádiz affair, thinking himself its one and only hero.

Through messages and messengers, he demanded that I reword the patent to omit the credit for the Cádiz mission. He hinted that "trouble" might happen if he and Howard were forced to appear in public together. He called for personal combat between himself and Howard, or one of Howard's relatives, Howard himself being obviously too old to put up an equal fight.

This bad behavior came at a most inopportune time, as King Henri IV of France had sent an ambassador, Andre Hurault, Sieur de Maisse, to ascertain our feelings toward him since his conversion to Catholicism and his inability—or disinclination—to repay the large loans we had made him. Henri was fond of Essex—as people were who knew him only from afar. His absence from court would raise questions. Somehow I would have to placate the tiresome boy, lure him back for appearances' sake. After the French had gone was time enough to decide what to do with him. I thought of him now as a problem to be solved; he had worn down almost all my affection for him. Only a thin veneer of it remained, like a ring whose coating has eroded from careless and rough wear.

It was also important that I put on a good show of appearance, so that when de Maisse reported back to his master he could tell him how healthy and young I looked. It was most unfortunate that I was troubled with a boil on my face that stubbornly refused to heal. I had to resort to thicker face makeup than usual—doubling the amount of crushed marble and eggshell to convey the requisite pearly whiteness. Catherine helped me; she was expert in mixing the right proportions of beeswax and powdered cinnabar to put on my lips and cheeks and knew how much water to use in making the face paste.

"I must look my best," I said, "for the French notice every little thing."

She was in high spirits; her husband's promotion had pleased her immensely, as I granted very few titles and seldom elevated anyone without good cause. Doubtless she felt his recognition was long overdue but would never nag about it. "'Tis said the French especially appreciate older women," she said.

I sighed. "They have that reputation. But the question is, how much older?" I turned the mirror this way and that, seeing how my face looked in different light. The boil was well camouflaged. I would draw eyes away from my face, in any case, with those old standbys, dazzling clothes and whopping jewels.

"I think the Italian gown for today," I said. "They will judge any French gown I wear with too practiced eyes, but I will get credit for my taste in selecting the latest from Italy." She helped dress me in a gown of silver gauze, with bands of gold lace, making me all ashimmer. I called for a ruby and pearl garland to drape across my bosom. As an unmarried woman, I was entitled to wear open-necked bodices. Of course, I always filled the gap with jewelry.

The ambassador was charming and urbane, but the French never sent any other kind. We spoke of many things, I attempting to discover exactly what Henri was thinking, de Maisse doing the same for me. The most urgent matter was the impending French peace treaty with Spain. They were anxious to have us join in, but how could we? King Philip, in spite of one wrecked Armada after another, kept sending them. It was true that our recent policy of attacking Spain overseas must now end—not from conviction, but from lack of effectiveness. But that did not mean we could afford to cease to arm ourselves against an invasion or to trust Spain.

Irritatingly, de Maisse kept inquiring about Essex. I gave one lighthearted answer after another, all the time conferring with the Cecil father and son about what to do to bring Essex in line before the ambassador departed.

"We cannot afford this," I told them, after the ambassador had gone. "Do you agree?"

Seldom had I seen both of them nod together. Young Cecil, Robert, had become more and more polished and self-assured as his responsibilities increased. Old Cecil, Burghley, had faded even in the few weeks I had not seen him. His mind was as alert as ever, but it was clear that his neck had less and less strength to hold that clever head up. As a team, the vigor was sliding toward the son.

"Yes, the puppy must be brought to heel," said Burghley, "before he spoils the hunt."

"Let us see—what brings a puppy to obedience?" asked Robert. "There are punishments. But he has already been punished—scolded and demoted. So what reward can we buy him with?" After a moment's thought, he had answered his own question.

"Offer something that costs you nothing and soothes his vanity," he said coldly. I was struck by his utter dispassion and his bald way of putting it.

"Something military, since he sets such store by that," said Burghley.

"We could offer him the lord admiralship," I said. "Howard is just as glad to retire from that post."

"No, it would be seen as taking Howard's leavings," said Burghley.

"What about Lord Keeper of the Privy Seal?" I asked.

"Not lofty enough," said Robert. "He likes something high sounding. What title is lying vacant? What about . . . Earl Marshal of England?"

"Horrible associations," I said. "It is vacant because its last holder, the Duke of Norfolk, was executed for treason."

"He won't care about that," predicted Burghley.

"Won't he realize that, since the post has been suspended for twenty-five years, it can hardly be vital to the realm's functioning?" I asked.

"He is too vain," said Robert. "He will look only on the outer trappings and not care how hollow they are."

"How harsh you are about his character," I said.

"He spent a few months living with us when he was nine," said Robert. "I came to know him well, and the grown man has not changed from that willful child who has ever relied on his looks and charm to carry him to the highest echelons of success." It was impossible to disguise the bitterness in his voice.

"My son is right," Burghley said. "Why do you think we never encouraged him to be part of our household?"

"Earl Marshal of England it shall be, then," I said. They were right: It was an honor that cost me nothing. In a sense he was already regarded as the military leader of the realm, so this added nothing beyond letting him walk in procession ahead of Nottingham, outranking him on formal occasions. A cheap price.

---

As I expected, Essex did not immediately accept the award with gratitude. He quibbled about the exact wording of the patent. When I met with him in private, he did not bother to flatter or please. Instead, he made his conditions known—the wording in the patent must be such and such and the ceremony conferring it on him held at such and such a place and time. He was not sure about returning to the Privy Council. Unless . . . I received his mother at court.

When he made this demand, I just stared at him. His face was in shadow, his arms crossed. I could not read his expression. Was it defiant? Hopeful? Nervous?

"Receive your mother?" I repeated.

"Yes. She longs to be reconciled to you. And I, hating to see the two women I love in opposition, am tortured by this state of affairs."

"The two women you love . . . your mother and your Queen? What of your wife? And I think there are certain ladies at court who believe you love them . . . or you have given them reason to believe so."

"I should have said three women. My wife is also troubled that you are so hardened toward the grandmother of her children. She is your cousin," he said. Now his voice had turned wheedling. "Your blood relative. As the years go on, they dwindle. Why be estranged from one of the few remaining?"

How dare he talk about my years, and the passing of generations? It was all I could do not to smack him. Instead, I pretended to ponder his words. *Everything for England,* I reminded myself.

"Yes, descended from my aunt," I said, playing for time while I thought. I would have to do it. But *how* I did it was for me to dictate. "Very well," I said.

He leaped forward, bent on his knee, grabbed my hand, and started covering it with kisses. "Oh, thank you! When may it be?"

"Sometime after the New Year," I said. In the deadest time of year, when court was empty.

"But—" he began, then thought better of it. He had wished her to come while the French were here and the court was brilliant with entertainment. *Not in a thousand years,* I thought.

I drew him up. "As to your own return to court . . ."

We had him now.

# 53

## LETTICE

*November 1597*

've won," Robert said proudly, his arms crossed and chin thrust forward. "She has capitulated, utterly surrendered." A document dangled from his hand spelling out the terms of his appointment as Earl Marshal of England. Robert Cecil had notified him that the final patent, on proper parchment, would be ready in a few days.

"In her entire life she has never capitulated or surrendered. Why would she do for you what she did not for Philip of Spain?" I took the paper from his hand and skimmed it. It was suspiciously innocent, naming Robert Devereux, second Earl of Essex, as Earl Marshal, the highest military commander in the realm. If I did not know the Queen as I did, I would have taken it at face value. But that was never safe with her.

He turned to another letter on the table that had just been delivered. Breaking the seal, he read it quickly. "Yes, my victory is complete! She can deny me nothing." He handed it to me, glee making his lips open in a wide smile.

I could hardly believe my eyes. She consented to receive me at court. I read further. After the holidays. Pity about that. But that was a small complaint.

"How did you manage that?" I had asked him to try, but it was a forlorn hope.

"Oh, I had only to mention it," he said breezily.

I doubted that. Something else must have happened. Suddenly the rise of excitement I had felt clouded over.

"Well, I thank you," I said. "It seems unbelievable. It has been almost twenty years since I have been allowed to come to court."

"Now that she has caved in, I will return to the Privy Council and to court. I understand that the council has been all at sixes and sevens without me. Now the suspension of business can end. My absence was highly inconvenient to them, so I hear."

He paced up and down the chamber, like a colt anxious to escape its stall and run. "A duel of wills, and I won," he said with wonder.

"That may be what she wishes you to think," I said. Knowing her since childhood, I remembered she had many ways of winning games, including the ploy of losing the first hand.

"It's what the rest of the court will think, as well," he said.

"She is willing to let people think anything they like if it serves her purpose," I said.

"Well, the title serves *my* purpose! So much for Francis Bacon's advice about eschewing a military role. I can hardly wait to see his face when I show him this." He smacked the paper affectionately. "I am the highest soldier in the land!"

I hid my misgivings. *Why, Lettice,* I asked myself, *can you not just receive this with gratitude?*

---

Robert returned to court like a Roman general to a triumph. His parade through the streets to cheering crowds proved that he was still the people's darling, and his absence had merely whetted their appetite for a glimpse of their hero.

I would be a liar if I said, even to myself, that hearing their cries and seeing him ride out, so handsome and fine, did not make my heart swell. When a mother holds her baby for the first time, does she not, in a secret place in herself, envision him a grown man, riding to splendor and acclaim? So few ever grow up to that. But mine had.

Robert returned to the swirl of court festivities for the French embassy, and he came home with tales of the dancing, the banquets, the music. The Queen, it seemed, had gone the distance in entertaining them, sparing nothing. Robert said she had even dusted off her flirtatious behavior for Monsieur de Maisse, wearing her lowest gowns and masses of pearls, fishing for compliments on her looks and wit.

"She even said, once, that she was never a great beauty but was accounted one in her youth," Robert recounted the morning after a fête. He laughed. "She gave him that sideways glance, leaving the poor man no response but to proclaim that indeed her beauty had been renowned in its day, and was still dazzling."

"He never should have said 'in its day,'" I said.

"She didn't care for that," he admitted. "She also teased him about her age, in one moment saying she stood on the brink of the grave and then, when he expressed concern, chiding him, saying, 'I don't think I shall die as soon as all that! I am not so old, Monsieur l'Ambassadeur, as you suppose.' It left him quite in a dither."

"As she intended."

"She *did* look quite fetching," he said.

"I wonder how long it took to make her so? Probably hours!"

Behind my laughter was the base of my own experience with that. I could still look the same from a distance, but . . . closer took an effort, and some time.

---

In the days that followed, and through Christmas, I beheld the glitter of the court from a distance, seeing it through Robert's eyes. I had been restricted to that for a long time, but now there was the tantalizing knowledge that soon I would be standing there seeing it for myself. Next to the wonder of miraculously seeing someone who did not live in our age—King Alfred or the Emperor Constantine—this was the greatest restoration I could imagine. I began planning my clothes, and what gift I would present to her. I was almost glad I had so long to think about it. It had to be just right.

Christopher was not particularly excited about it, but he had never had the experience of falling from favor. And these days he seemed more interested in spending his time with his seagoing companions than pining for court. There was also the delicate matter of Southampton and Elizabeth Vernon to worry him. They were going to approach the Queen and ask permission to marry but were waiting for the most opportune moment. Elizabeth was pregnant and they would have to marry, permission or no. Only the Queen's preoccupation with the French embassy had kept her keen eyes from noticing the girl's condition, which would soon be obvious to all. Christopher was jittery for his friend, fearful he might even be sent to the Tower. It all depended on what mood Elizabeth was in. But Southampton had never been a favorite, so he could hardly be accused of "disloyalty"—what she branded any of her male admirers who dared to take up with a woman who was actually available. So probably the worst they would have to endure would be a display of temper and some unpleasant names.

Anthony and Francis Bacon's spy service managed to intercept and copy Monsieur de Maisse's reports to his king. They regaled us with the ambassador's impressions of the Queen.

"'Here she says, "Alas, that you, who have met so many princes, have come all this way to see a foolish old woman,"'" read Francis.

"I hope he did not fall into that trap," said Robert. "The proper answer is to shower her with compliments."

"Yes, that is what he did. And then he notes, 'When anyone speaks of her beauty, she says that she was never beautiful, though she had that reputation thirty years ago.'" He paused. "Now hear his comment to his king: 'Nevertheless, she speaks of her beauty as often as she can.'"

I giggled and the men burst into gusts of laughter.

"His honest assessment of her looks: 'As far as she may she keeps her dignity, but her face is very aged: It is long and thin.'"

I had not really seen her in so long I was startled to hear her described thus. Twenty years is a long time, but like me, she still looked the same from a distance.

"He goes on about the fact that the English will not agree to a peace with Spain—"

"Of course we won't!" bellowed Robert. "That would be insane."

Francis sighed as he read more of the copied dispatch. "Even he ends as her admirer. 'It is not possible to see a woman of so fine and vigorous a disposition both in mind and in body. One can say nothing to her on which she will not make an apt comment. She is a great princess who knows everything.'"

Gloriana, the Faerie Queen, could still cast her spell, then.

---

The twelve days of Christmas ended, and a sleet-filled January descended. The distractions of the holidays finished, I could now give myself over to considering what gift I might present to her. The only appropriate thing would be a piece of jewelry. I hated it that Leicester had left her that magnificent six-hundred-pearl necklace, which should have gone to me. She had her portraits painted in it, clearly cherishing it and wearing it as proudly as a bride. So I would never give her pearls. She also had black ones from Mary Queen of Scots. No more pearls for her.

Emeralds? Rubies? Sapphires? She already had so many. Jade? That was more unusual. But I probably could not obtain it in time.

I must give her a jewel no one else ever had. Or ever could. Something to take her breath away, bind her to me. But I could not afford such a gem. Nor, even if I could, would it be unusual enough. Even the deepest red ruby, pulsating like a glob of blood, was seen on too many necklaces and rings at court.

We were of the same family. Was there anything, anything I had inherited that she might value? Mary Boleyn . . . I did have the Boleyn *B* necklace. She had given it to my mother; after my mother died I had kept it in memory of her but never worn it.

I had never known my grandmother Mary Boleyn. She had died the summer before I was born. I was said to be very like her in looks and temperament. I knew that, like me, she had married a younger man after her husband died, and it had caused a bit of a scandal—not because he was young but because he had no rank. Well, I knew all about that: two earls as husbands, then a plain gentleman, turned into a "Sir" only by my previous husband knighting him.

I remembered her young husband, though—William Stafford. He had come with us to Geneva when we fled England during Queen Mary's reign. There he had died, unfortunately just before it was safe to return. What an unhappy life my whole family had had. We seemed to be under some sort of indictment. It was only through my son that we had a chance at going down in history. The rest of us would be forgotten, lying in forgotten graves.

I kept my grandmother's necklace in a stout table chest with brass bindings. I had not opened the little box inside, containing the necklace, in many years. The hinge was stuck, and for a moment it refused to open. I did not want to break it, but I kept prying the tiny lids apart and slowly it gave way. Inside lay the initial *B* pendant with three pearls hanging from it, suspended on a gold chain. Carefully I drew it out, held it in the palm of my hand. The gold was undimmed, but the pearls had clouded a bit, their luster filmed over. It had been many years since it had hung on a woman's neck. Someone told me once that pearls should be worn next to the skin to keep them shining, and that the best way to do that was to have a kitchen maid wear them when she worked. That seemed a good way to lose them to thievery, so I had never tried it. But the pearls needed moisture. I would rub some olive oil on them.

A world lay in that necklace—the vanished hopes of the Boleyns. Truly, dull though they might be, these were pearls of great price. I had said no pearls, but these were different. They came trailing a lost world, the one from which we both sprang.

---

As the days wore on, we awaited the royal summons. Robert assured me that she would be issuing it shortly; she planned her schedule only a few days ahead.

"Assassins," he said. "They must not know her whereabouts in advance."

I carefully selected my clothes for the forthcoming occasion. I would dress plainly, soberly, and keep my red hair, still my best feature, neatly tucked under a cap. But most important, what would I say? And what would be the setting to say it in? She would receive me in a great public ceremony, as she did everyone she wished formally to recognize. That would be in the presence chamber, before the entire court. But afterward . . . would she invite me to supper? Or to sit beside her at a musical performance, where we could talk privately?

What would I tell her? Should I leap backward over the troubled years, back to our youth, when we were both Protestants under threat? Once we had been friends; I had looked up to her, my decade-older cousin, admired her, wished to be like her. She always seemed so sure of herself, so circumspect, so self-contained. I never saw her make a mistake, take a false step, whether in games or in speech. Later I came to resent it as a standard I could never attain. I made mistake after mistake, spoke when I should have kept silent, misread motives, wanted things too fiercely for my own good. It had taken me a lifetime to learn what Elizabeth was seemingly born knowing. But now that I had, wearily, come more or less to the same place, I was ready to make peace, yes, even to bow to her as the wise one, the victor.

I would tell her how grateful I was to be received again . . . how sad the years away had been . . . how fine she looked . . . how I had longed to embrace my dear cousin and to enter into her life again.

I would not ask her forgiveness because I had committed no crime—beyond wounding her vanity. Best to leave that unsaid. But what I wanted to say—and never could, of course—was that Leicester was not worth it. In the years since his death, it had become obvious that he left no memory or legacy; he had been all presence and no substance. Even his supposed friend, Edmund Spenser, wrote:

*He now is dead, and all his glories gone.*
*And all his greatness vapoured to nought.*
*His name is worn already out of thought,*
*Ne any poet seeks him to revive.*

"Vapoured to nought" . . . Yes, he had completely disappeared from memory, from history. There had been nothing there, or it could not have vanished so instantly and completely. Even a beloved hound lingers longer in the memory of its owner than Leicester had done in the country's consciousness.

Leicester should come between us no longer. Let him keep to his grave.

---

January gave way to February, and still no summons. More and more nervous, I kept questioning Robert about her mood, her health. Was she well? Keeping to her chamber?

Quite well, he said. Attending plays and enjoying them. Playing her virginals regularly, dancing with her ladies.

Could he not remind her of her promised invitation?

He laughed. "Mother, you have forgotten her nature. To remind her of anything is to rebuke her, and she does not take that kindly. Lately it is worse, as she actually does forget things and is fiercely sensitive about it. In the past, her 'forgetting' was politic, a way to make people dance to her tune. Now it is real."

What if she had truly forgotten? I had not reckoned on that. "Do you mean . . . Is she becoming senile?"

"Only selectively," he said. "With her, it is hard to tell."

"Can you not whisper a hint to her?"

"That might be dangerous," he said. "One does not want to anger the tyrant."

"I assume you mean that as a general principle, not that she *is* a tyrant?"

He shrugged. "What was the definition of a tyrant in ancient times? A ruler who behaved capriciously and unpredictably, with absolute power. She has long done so, excusing it by her 'sexly weakness'—blaming it on being a woman. But a tyrant in petticoats is just as much a tyrant as one in breeches."

"You should try to put those thoughts out of your mind and be in love with her again," I warned him. "For politics' sake."

---

At last the invitation was delivered. The Countess of Leicester was bidden to Whitehall on February 28, to come to Her Majesty's privy chamber.

I clasped the letter to my bosom. This was my deliverance; this was my reward for years of patient waiting and for the pain of recognizing my own part in our estrangement. A biblical phrase came to me (we never forget our childhood drills) that in its beauty and peace was like a caress from God: "And I will restore to you the years that the locust hath eaten." God can actually restore time, a Geneva preacher had said. Others can restore the goods, but only God can restore time.

My time would be restored, and Elizabeth and I would be young cousins again.

---

I waited nervously in the privy chamber, standing with a group of courtiers who were expecting her to emerge from her inner rooms at any moment. It was ten in the morning, and soon she would be going to dinner, passing through the chamber. Suddenly my dress felt too tight; I had trouble taking a good breath. Murmurs rippled through the crowd. She must be coming. But moments passed and nothing happened. At length a guard announced that Her Majesty would not be coming through the privy chamber; she had taken the private door from her apartments.

She had deliberately done this! I could hardly grasp her meanness in inviting me for a specific time and then avoiding it. I was insulted, shocked, disappointed beyond words. And more important: What should I do now?

---

Robert had a suggestion: He could ensure an invitation for me to a private banquet that she would attend.

An invitation to a great dinner party given by a rich noble, Lady Shandos, was procured, and I took myself to it, again wearing what I called my modesty outfit. Lady Shandos made a fuss about welcoming me and gave me a seat high in ranking.

And when would the Queen arrive? Her carriage was reportedly ready outside the royal apartments, waiting for her departure.

It waited and waited, and the voices at the banquet table grew tired and hushed. Then came a message for Lady Shandos: Her Majesty would not be coming.

---

I clutched at Robert's doublet, back in the privacy of Essex House. My fingers made welts on it, stigmata of desperation. "What is happening?" I cried. "Why is she doing this?"

"The woman's name is whimsy," he said. "It extends from something like a sudden change of dinner venue to aborting military plans at the last minute. Can you count the number of times she has sent me on a mission only to try to cancel it after I am on my way? I've lost count. That's why I always try to get far away from court as quickly as I can, before she changes her mind. Once she tried to pull me back from Plymouth as we were waiting to embark for the Lisbon raid. She even sent a ship after me!"

"It's too much to be a coincidence," I said. "It has happened twice now."

"Twice? Twice is nothing to her!"

"Do you hate her?" I suddenly asked. "For your words are venomous."

He seriously considered my question, as if he had never examined the possibility. "Hate her? Not her, but . . . what she is becoming. Her mind is growing as crooked as her carcass!"

"Robert!" What if someone heard? "Have a caution!"

"We've no spies here," he said. "I am sure of it."

"Do you truly think . . . ," I whispered, "that she is failing?"

"No, not failing, but growing more devious and obstructive. She goes less and less in a straight line to anywhere, that's what I meant by 'crooked.'"

"If so, then we must figure out a way to cross her path as she ducks and dodges." Even as I said it, I realized that meant I had let go of the hope we could come to a true meeting of the minds. That saddened me.

"We will waylay her outside her private chambers—'run into' her in the private passage outside the royal apartments. Remember, I have access to them," he said.

"I don't like the idea of it," I said. It would hardly be conducive to a pleasant meeting.

"It's this or nothing," he said. "She gives us no other choice. Now make yours."

---

With great misgivings, I decided to try it. I disliked everything about the method, but perhaps the surprise element would work in my favor. She would be caught off guard and might drop her hostility. Surely she had soft feelings for me somewhere in her memory.

The modesty outfit was getting a bit worn, considering it had never actually been seen by the Queen. I carried the beautifully wrapped Boleyn necklace, ready to present it and make my speech. *Your Majesty, I wish you to have this, which belonged to your aunt, my grandmother, in token of the ties between us.* Or something like that. I was careful not to rehearse it overmuch, fearing to rob it of spontaneity and sincerity.

It was midafternoon, and the Queen would be returning to her rooms after dinner and some conferences. Robert knew the way she took, coming in from the gardens to avoid traversing the suite of public rooms and the gallery. He stationed himself at one doorway and motioned me to stand directly in front of it. As we waited, at first I felt shaky with wondering what she would do when she saw us. Then that worry passed and changed to wondering if she might outwit us once again and avoid the private passageway. Finally it all dropped away and I just wanted to get it over with. I could not stand another moment of this.

Just then I heard voices down the passageway; several women swept down it together. Then the Queen, with two attendants, rounded the corner. She stopped when she saw me, hesitating. She was puzzling whether to proceed or turn abruptly and go back. But this passed through her mind in an instant and the hesitation was almost unnoticeable. Squaring her shoulders and drawing herself up—where was this crooked carcass Robert had described?—she came slowly toward us. Her face was blank, showing neither pleasure nor displeasure.

As she came closer, I saw that the French ambassador had been right: Her face had aged. I would not describe it as "very" aged, though. Her posture was perfect and the clothes she wore—a green afternoon dress with a tawny collar—flattered her and showed off her small waist.

Robert leaped out from behind the doorway and startled them. The other ladies I knew from our days in the royal chambers together: Marjorie Norris, gone gray now, and Catherine Carey Howard, my cousin. They looked timidly welcoming but awaited Elizabeth's reaction.

"Why, my Lord Essex," said Elizabeth. "You loiter inside on such a bracing day?"

"Once my feet resounded in these passageways at Your Majesty's bidding," he said, bowing and kissing her hand. "You have only to call again and I will fly to you for indoor amusements."

She raised him up and looked at me, showing no recognition. "And who have you brought?"

She knew very well! What was she doing?

"My most beloved mother, whom you said you would receive," he said.

Before she could demur, I stepped forward and curtsied so low my knee hit the floor. "I am Your Majesty's most loyal subject."

Silence. Then she said, "You may rise."

I did, and said, "And your most loyal cousin." I kissed her hand, and leaned forward to kiss her breast. Rotely, she returned the kiss on my cheek. I handed her the box. "I wish you to have this in token of the love between our families." I knew better than to say "between us."

She took it, then started to hand it to Marjorie, unopened. Robert grabbed it away and said, "Nay, but you and the ladies must see it. It is most rare!" He flipped the lid open and showed the *B* necklace lying on its velvet pad.

"It belonged to my grandmother, your aunt Mary Boleyn," I said. "It has always been my greatest treasure, and I want you to have it."

Her keen black eyes examined it. Was there a flicker of a smile on her thin lips? She handed the box back to me. "I already have one," she said. "An identical one that belonged to my mother."

Then she walked around us, leaving us standing in the passageway.

# 54

# ELIZABETH

*May 1598*

"I am touched," I told John Whitgift, and I was.

The archbishop merely nodded, but I could see in his dark eyes how pleased he was. "I was only hoping that Your Majesty would come here before the roses faded."

"Mine, or theirs?" I asked, but seeing that John took the jest as a true question, I quickly added, "Yours will bloom anew every year."

My Archbishop of Canterbury had planted a sunken rose garden, a tribute to my royal house and my own private taste in flowers, at his riverside episcopal palace. Its centerpiece was a trellis of entwined red and white bushes, since even his skilled gardeners could not re-create the actual Tudor badge of both red and white petals on one flower. Around the borders he had set masses of eglantine roses—my favorite. Musk roses filled in the spaces between them.

"You have created a rose heaven," I said. Their distinctive scent, made sharper by a morning rain, enveloped us. If only roses could bloom all summer instead of so fleetingly. Their quick vanishing makes us see them more keenly while they are still visible.

"When we go to heaven, there will be more than just roses to greet us," he said.

Heaven. There were now a great many people waiting there for me; more than were still here on earth with me. Perhaps life is like an hourglass, with dear ones the sand that slips from the upper glass—the earth—into the second—eternity. The bottom one is ever filling, the upper one forever draining.

"I still like to think of heaven as a garden," I said. "Pray, show me the rest of yours."

It had been a hard winter, making the sight of flowers doubly welcome. There had been times, when the sleet dashed and slid against my windows, that I thought warmth would never return. But this May had been exuberant, as if offering apologies for the long, cold months. Now I glided along as John led me up the stairs to the raised walkway above the long garden terrace that divided the privy garden from the orchard. On the left side were four neat quadrangles of flower beds, their plantings making a mosaic of color; on the right, the frothy white of a large orchard in full bloom. If I looked closely, I could discern variations in the white treetops, and even some pale pink.

"What trees are in your orchard?" I asked.

"Plum—but that's finished blooming now—cherry, pear, apple, apricot. I've had success with the apricots; you know how difficult they can be."

My father had first had them brought over from Italy. At the time, it was thought they would never survive here, but by catering to their delicate needs, some gardeners had been lucky with them.

---

Striding along the walkway, seeing the gentle flowers and swaying, flower-laden branches and beyond them the stately curve of the river, it was easy to think my realm a sun-lapped, well-tended garden. But the winter had been difficult not only weatherwise but also politically. The lord lieutenant of Ireland, Lord Burgh, Black Jack Norris's hated commander, had died suddenly, the victim, some said, of poisoning. The rebels had corrupted the inner circle of English command, it was rumored, so that they could do away with the leader. I had appointed deputies to temporary command, but for now my forces there were without a true commander, and the void was telling. The rebel forces, under The O'Neill and O'Donnell, were making steady gains, uniting traditionally quarreling Ulster, a deadly development. There were even reports that Grace O'Malley was joining them on the western side of the island. I had been remiss in recalling the repressive Richard Bingham from her area, and now I reaped the consequence. Grace was not a woman to brook insult or inaction any more than I was.

Ireland. I remembered when my father had first proclaimed himself King of Ireland, a formal declaration of liegeship after four hundred years of English invasion and occupation. I had been eight years old and wondered why he changed his title from "Lord" of Ireland to "King." I had even asked him, and he had said with a laugh, "It's tidier that way, making me king of everything—England, France, Wales, and Ireland—instead of lord here and king there." Of course, that had not been the reason, and I was not many years older before I knew that my father had tried to tame the Irish by making them Protestant, and he could not legally dictate their religion unless he was their king. The plan did not work, of course, and the Irish stayed Catholic—a dangerous outpost of southern Europe right at my back door.

During my reign, I had tried half measures with Ireland to save expenses. I had sent the smallest forces I could, and their mandate was limited: to keep the peace in the precariously held English areas of the island and try to domesticate the native Irish—by bribing them with English titles, instituting English law to replace theirs, introducing them to our customs.

It had not worked. The chieftains were willing enough to assume English titles, but they merely added them to their native ones. They resented our enforcing English law, and they found our customs repellent. We had been secure in our possession of Ireland only because they squabbled so much with one another that they could not pool forces to turn on us. That, apparently, was ending now, with the cooperation of the two Ulster chiefs.

There had been another reason we could keep them in check: Our armies were better trained and equipped and obeyed a chain of command. The Irish had individual warriors of great bravery but no logistical or strategic experience. That, too, was ending. The O'Neill had learned warfare on the Continent, the same great training field as young Englishmen.

What must I do now? Should I continue the same policy or increase our presence there? If it were not for the Spanish, the "Irish problem" would not be a pressing one.

"— Puritans are squalling again. They will never be quiet, but must disrupt good honest folk—"

What was he saying? I had not heard any of it. "John, I am sorry, my mind was wandering."

"The Puritans are starting their personal attacks again," he grumbled. "The other day, as I was walking to chapel, a group of them—I can always spot them by their dull clothing—set upon me, yelling, 'Get out of that woman's frock!' Imagine, insulting a priest's robes. They would have all ceremony gone, have the clergy wear farmers' breeches and pray in a stinking barnyard!"

"Some of them would have no clergy at all," I said. "There are dangerous ideas about. No clergy today, no king tomorrow. Everyone in the barnyard being equal." A dreadful thought. "But you, my black husband"—my nickname for him, for his old-fashioned robes and bachelor state—"serve the church well by guarding its traditions and its creed." It made him unpopular, but his "high church" theology suited me. In truth, it was not merely his beliefs people disliked but his haughty manners. Perhaps the princely prelates of the past had exhausted their tolerance for such behavior.

"You have a fine banqueting house," I said, stopping to admire the building. It was situated at the far end of the orchard itself, floating like a low ship in the sea of white blooms. The very words "banqueting house" meant summer to me, as they were airy, insubstantial structures where only sweets, drinks, and fruits were served as delicate music was played.

"Cranmer built it," he said, "along with his other improvements."

Cranmer. The man who had been my mother's chaplain and who rose along with her, attaining the highest religious rank in the realm. He had attended her in her last hours, hearing her confession, giving her communion. After my father's death he vowed not to shave his beard, in mourning. It was very long indeed when he went to the stake under my sister Mary. He lived on in my memory and in his exquisite words in the Book of Common Prayer.

"He always had an eye for beauty," I said, and let it go at that. But as a victim of rabid Catholicism, Cranmer was a reminder that the Puritans were not the only danger abroad in the land.

"In words and in service," Whitgift said.

"He left us some forty years ago, but there are still those who would wish me at the stake as well," I said. "The Catholics here in England may be quiescent, broken as a political force, but they are still strong in personal faith, and the Spanish are doing their best to restore them to political power as well. The missionaries—how many have we caught? Hundreds—and yet they keep coming." Father Gerard, escaped from the Tower, was still at large.

"I think we catch about half of the Jesuits," said Whitgift.

"I am besieged on both sides," I said. "The Church of England is too ceremonial for the Puritans and too heretical for the Catholics."

"It is in the nature of truth to have enemies," he said stiffly.

"Stand firm, stand firm!" I said, patting his cheek. "I know I can rely on you, my black husband."

We descended from the terrace and walked through the garden, taking care to stay on the path. Double violets framed each bed, with a ring of sweet Williams and primroses just behind them. In the middle were taller plants—daffodils, snapdragons, poppies, foxglove, hollyhocks.

"How is my Lord Burghley?" asked Whitgift, changing course.

"Poorly," I said. "It grieves me. But he still comes to council meetings by strength of will. And he still holds his own against the Earl of Essex and the faction breathing hot for war. A few days ago, when Essex was arguing about the necessity of attacking Spain again, Burghley reprimanded him and quoted the Fifty-Fifth Psalm to him: 'Bloody and deceitful men shall not live out half their days.'"

"What spirit! And what did Essex do?"

"Got angry, saying he was not deceitful. The overall meaning of the warning was wasted on him. In any case, since I do not wish it, there will be no further attacks on Spain. It is a waste of money better spent defending ourselves here at home." Essex could crow and demand, but in the end only I decided whether we went to war or not.

Afternoon shadows were lengthening. In the days of the monasteries, the monks would have been stopping for None prayers. It was time to leave. This was as close as I would get to a monastery, this old redbrick bishop's palace that went back five hundred years, to when Lambeth was just a marsh and the stones of Westminster Abbey were new.

---

We were at Greenwich for May, the best palace to be in springtime. I had been glad to leave wintry Whitehall behind. Besides, there were unpleasant memories of the last days there, and I wanted to efface them. I still shook with indignation when I remembered that encounter with Lettice Knollys. Yes, I had agreed to see her as a condition for Essex's return to court. But the more I thought of it, the more I resented it. I had bestowed the Earl Marshal title on him, and that should have been sufficient. That he kept bargaining and wheedling like a market vendor was distasteful and cheapened him—or rather, my opinion of him. We had had to trick him into thinking he had won a war of wills, when he should have realized it was a war that should never have been fought. A subject does not contend with his sovereign.

And when a sovereign makes his or her position clear, a subject should take note, not keep badgering. But no! That wooden-headed son, pushed on by his brazen mother, kept pursuing me, finally cornering me in my own private passageway like a hunted animal. If they thought thereby to have won some sort of victory, they were fools. Now I could only see her would-be gift, the Boleyn necklace, as a cheap attempt to stake familial claims in my heart.

# 55

he July sunshine was clear and bright, and beneath my windows the flowery border was filled with fluttering butterflies. One of the Greenwich gardeners had, in fact, created what he called a butterfly garden, filled with a jumble of plants that attracted them—rosemary, lavender, verbena, mede-sweet, and the charmingly named go-to-bed-at-noon. I loved to lean out the window and watch them, although at midday, when the sun was highest, everything lay still and even the butterflies rested.

It was too glorious a day to be indoors, but a matter of supreme importance had to be settled in council: the right man to replace Lord Burgh as lord lieutenant of Ireland. It was long overdue and crucial that we decide on our policy from here on. The O'Neill was becoming king of Ireland while we cowered in our outposts. He was starving out our fort at Yellow Ford, near Ulster.

There was a dearth of capable men to appoint. At length I had settled on Sir William Knollys. He was not brilliant, but he was experienced, sensible, and loyal. I would announce this decision today.

The councillors filed in, wearing their lightest shirts and breeches, no capes, no hats. I hoped to have the business over with quickly and release everyone out into the fine day. Only the inner circle was present: young Cecil, Essex, Admiral Howard, Archbishop Whitgift, old Lord Buckhurst, the young Lord Hunsdon.

I welcomed them and proceeded to nominate Sir William Knollys for the post, listing his previous appointments and qualifications. Around the council table there were nods.

Suddenly Essex stood up and said, "With your leave, Your Majesty, I must object. My uncle is not the right man for the post. I put forward Sir George Carew instead. He's had experience in Ireland, has served there in various capacities, and is a better fit."

I was surprised at his objection. Nonetheless, I said, "Does anyone here care to comment?"

Robert Cecil now stood up. "It is clear that my lord of Essex wishes to send Carew away from court to diminish his influence. He fears a rivalry and would vanquish all opposition."

"What a foolish idea!" said Essex loftily. "Why should I fear such a man as Carew?"

"Because he is growing in influence, having just returned from an embassy to King Henri IV with me. You seek to clip him before he grows any further."

"Why, what do you mean, man? The lord lieutenantship of Ireland is a much higher post than being second on an embassy to France. An embassy that achieved nothing, I might add. The French have determined to make peace with Spain, leaving us all alone to fight Philip. So you might as well have stayed home."

"You know Ireland is a graveyard of ambitions. It has chewed up many a man. Going there is like going to Hades—a man never returns, or if he does, he is just a shade. You want to send Carew there, send him into oblivion, so he can't oppose you."

"How dare you insult my father? He was one of those who died in Ireland, as well you know."

"Gentlemen," said Admiral Howard, rising to join them. "Pray, be calm."

"Cease the squabbling," I said. "It is pointless. I have decided that it is Sir William Knollys."

"You are making a mistake. That is a foolish choice." Essex jutted out his chin.

"My lord—" Whitgift reached out to Essex, making shushing gestures, wagging his finger furiously.

"I cannot let this pass!" Essex said, glaring at me. "I am being mocked and undermined. I will not tolerate it!" Abruptly, he turned his back on me.

Such a thing had never been done, nor seen, in all my years, that a subject upbraid his sovereign and then turn his back on her. I stared at his wide back, his shoulders at my eye level, his head a head higher. He was a large man, and his back looked as forbidding as a closed door.

"Go to the devil!" I cried, anger flooding through me at his effrontery. I smacked him on the ears from side to side, ordering, "Get you gone and be hanged!"

So swiftly that the eye could barely follow, he whirled around and grabbed the hilt of his sword, meaning to draw it on me. Quick-thinking Howard stepped between us and clamped his hand down over the pommel to prevent

Essex from actually following through on his gesture, which would have been instant treason.

"I neither can nor will put up with so great an affront, nor would I have borne it from your father's hands!" he cried. He stepped back, his eyes wild.

"If I were my father you would not walk a free man from this room," I reminded him. My voice was deadly cold, as it is when I am most angry. "You would go directly from council table to the Tower. And you would not linger long there, either. And as for affront, I have given you none, other than to refuse your suggestion. Hardly a cause for treason."

"I curse this room. I curse the day I was born, which I rue and will make everyone rue—" He rushed out the door, his feet clattering on the stairs and then dying away.

For an instant utter silence hung in the room. Then one of the guards said, "Your Majesty, shall we go after him and arrest him?"

Quickly I thought it out. His actions demanded that he should at least be detained, if not charged with treason. But I shook my head. "Let him go," I said.

He would most likely run back to Wanstead. He would take to his bed and sulk and fall ill. I would get messages that he was on his deathbed.

The noontime sun poured into the room, and the hot air, laden with the pungent smell of dust and drooping leaves, hung over us like a pall. The councillors remained where they were, some standing, some sitting.

"Gentlemen, you may go," I said. "Do not speak of this outside this chamber."

---

The day had been robbed of its beauty for me. The serenity of what saints called the blessed hour of noontide had been shattered. Walking down the grassy lawn to the riverside, I barely heard the cries of the wheeling gulls and lapwings. Before me several tall-masted ships rode at anchor, idle now, awaiting orders.

A subject had defied and threatened me in public. Not only that, he had implied I was not a true prince, that I was less because of my sex. "Nor would I have borne it from your father's hands," he had said. "In other words, he would bear more from a king than from a queen. A queen is less than a king." He questioned the very foundation of my power.

---

In the privacy of my inner chambers, I divulged to Catherine what had happened in council that morning. She would hear it from her husband in any case. Without the admiral's quick action, things might have turned out very differently. I still trembled to think about it. In recounting it, my voice shook. The more I thought about it, the larger it loomed, unlike other things that dwindle in perspective.

"I can still see his hand gripping the sword, with Charles's hand covering it, smothering his action," I said, my voice a whisper. "I think it was his father's sword. Or perhaps it was Sidney's."

Catherine's plump and usually serene face had assumed a masklike rigidity. "What difference whose sword it was?" she very sensibly said. "What matters is what he intended to do with it. What do you think that was?"

"I don't know. It could have just been a threatening gesture, like a stage prop. Or he could truly have meant to harm me. In his temper, perhaps he would have done so, unthinkingly. But regardless, by doing it in council, it was a true public challenge."

"What caused him to do it? Was he sitting down and suddenly leaped up? Did someone say something?"

"You make a good examiner, Catherine. Yes, let us trace the steps. I had boxed his ears for turning his back on me."

"As if he were an unruly schoolboy? You insulted him, then, as he saw it?"

"He did claim I had insulted him," I admitted.

She crossed the room and threw open the shutters. The hottest part of the day had passed, and the air was cooling. It made the room less confining. She poured out a goblet of summer wine—diluted with fresh water and flavored with mint—and handed me the slender glass. She knew I would find it soothing.

"Dear one, this is a most peculiar situation. You ask what subject would brook his prince so boldly, and in public? A telling question. But it has no answer that does not take into account another question: What other subject would you have felt free to smack in public?"

"I smacked that Bess Throckmorton," I said, "for her insolence and lies. And I'd have done the same with Elizabeth Vernon, if her liaison with Southampton were not punishment enough. He asked permission to marry her and I refused. Then he asked permission to go abroad. But he sneaked back home to marry her—with the connivance of Essex, I might add. Essex challenges me at every turn."

"I don't mean ladies in the privacy of your chamber, I mean statesmen in public," she said.

"I did throw a slipper at Walsingham once," I said.

"And you missed."

"Deliberately. I have a good aim."

"A slipper is one thing—it signals a comedy—a slap is another."

I did not like her leadings here. I was finding them painful. But I would not shrink from what they told me.

"Do you think I have behaved in an unnatural fashion toward him?" I asked.

"Everyone thinks so, although I know nothing untoward has happened between you."

"What do people say?"

"That you are lovers," she said.

"They said that about Leicester," I said. "It was not true."

"Since the age difference between you and Essex is so extreme, it makes for hotter gossip."

I had a dreadful thought. "Perhaps . . . *he* believes it in some fashion. He thinks I am in love with him and want to be his lover," I whispered. The night at Drayton Bassett . . . His assumptions had almost been proved true.

"Perhaps," Catherine agreed. "And your lovers' quarrels, with him playing sick and your humoring him, confirms it to him."

Never again. How had I been so blind and foolish?

I ended it, in my own mind. I would demote him from that exalted and special place in my affections where I had mistakenly placed him. Like John Knox yanking an idolatrous statue from a niche and smashing it on the floor, just so would I do to the young earl. Down from the crevice that protected him, down onto the floor to mix with ordinary men. Let him see clearly in harsh daylight exactly where he stood and what he was made of.

# 56

reland continued to fester. In the end I made William Knollys lord deputy of Ireland, a lower rank than lord lieutenant. That exalted post still needed filling. But this time its holder had to be a man capable of strength and resolution, someone to make the Irish tremble. I could not think of such a man, and until we had him, I would not send another weakling. The Irish problem needed someone like my father or, dare I say it, the Duke of Parma—someone ruthless and clearheaded.

In the meantime we hung on. The fort on the Blackwater River in Ulster was still in English hands but running low on supplies, and would be easily besieged and taken by O'Neill. Although it would be difficult to hold, we could not afford to lose it, so a relief convoy was to be dispatched from nearby Armagh.

The Privy Council continued meeting, in a hand-wringing way, minus its two polar anchors—Burghley and Essex. Until Essex apologized (the very least I demanded of him) he was not to set foot at court. Burghley was unable to, growing weaker at his London home on the Strand. The last meeting he had attended was the one in which he had quoted the psalm about violent men dying early.

Even so, I was unprepared for the news Robert Cecil brought me in late July. Requesting a private meeting, he told me that his father was no longer able to sit up in bed.

"No!" How had he gone down so far, and so quickly? "When last I saw him—"

"Forgive me, Your Majesty, but a month is a long time for him as he slides, against his will, away from us, and indeed, from life." He drew a deep breath. "I did not want it to progress any further without your knowledge," he said. "Misguided humility would have had Father keep it from you."

"I'll make ready and we shall go together," I said.

As I got ready, I could not permit myself to think the unthinkable. I would go to him. We would talk. I would send my own special physician to him. He would mend. Perhaps he would have to retire after all. Poor man, he had tried to, and I would not let him. But now, anything he wished. Anything. Anything to keep him with us, within calling distance.

Calling distance. I smiled in spite of myself. His hearing had grown so bad, I thought, I should rather say "within shouting distance." Certainly he had earned a rest. And relieved of his duties, he would grow strong again. He would flourish in retirement. He was only seventy-eight. Hunsdon had lived longer. "Come," I said. Suddenly it seemed urgent that we go.

Like many at court, he maintained a London residence. His lay on the Strand, a modest house with no river frontage. Considering his rank and station, it was remarkably self-effacing and humble. When I had visited him in the past, it had always been at his magnificent country homes, Theobalds and Burghley House. Indeed, his only nonpolitical preoccupation had been the building and furnishing of Burghley House, a project that went on for years.

The house was dark, its shutters drawn to keep out noise and dust. It had the peculiar, coffinlike feel of a closed house in warm weather. The servants showed us upstairs to the room where the fallen minister lay.

I was ill prepared for the shrunken wraith that lay in the bed. He had changed utterly from the frail but lively man in the council. There was so little left of him that he barely dented the mattress or made a mound under the covers.

*Oh!* I almost cried, then stopped myself. I saw Robert looking at me, observing how I reacted, hoping that I would not say anything unguarded. But saying unguarded things was a luxury I had never been permitted, and I would not begin now. "Why, William, we must make you strong again!" I said heartily, coming over to him. I bent down to kiss his cheek and saw his bright eyes, prisoners of his wizened face, beseeching me silently.

What was he thinking? Did my healthy form, moving briskly, make him feel weaker? Or did it restore him, if only briefly, to a lost connection to the larger world?

"The game broth you sent, Robert, appealed to him, but he was too weak to sit up and eat," one of the servants said.

"Heat it up," I said, "and I myself will feed you."

Now his eyes registered alarm. He mumbled and muttered protests.

"What medicines are you taking?" I asked. His servant obediently brought a box containing various bottles and vials. I pulled each out to examine. "I will send you others," I assured him. They would make him well. They had to.

The reheated broth was brought up, pleasantly warm in a serving bowl. I sniffed it. "It smells strong and nourishing," I said. One of the servants gently lifted him and, putting pillows behind him, propped him up.

He could barely sit straight, but kept slipping to one side, unable even to right himself. Then I knew. The strength was gone, utterly fled. It could not be called back; it had vanished forever.

Trying to keep my hand from shaking, I took a spoonful of the broth and slipped it between his lips. Only a little. He could not swallow much. I willed myself not to tremble, but once my hand wobbled and I spilled some broth on the covers.

He was eating to please me, as he had always tried to do my bidding. He was the bridge to my past, the support of my reign, the underpinning that made all the rest possible. It could not be over.

"Try, William," I told him. "I do not wish to live longer than I have you by my side." I felt that when he died, part of me would, too. How large a part, how vital a part, I could not know until it happened.

Tears sprang up in his eyes.

"You are, in all things to me, alpha and omega." I wept, his tears giving me permission to shed mine.

His hand scrabbled across the covers—he had strength only to move it that way, not to lift it—and he sought my hand and squeezed it.

"Thank you," he whispered.

---

The next morning Robert Cecil brought me a letter. "Father dictated it after you left. It will be his last letter. Your visit meant more to him than he could express, but even you cannot stay the inevitable."

"I have sent new medicines," I said helplessly.

"Knowing who the sender is is the best medicine for him," said Robert.

I opened the letter. It was advice to Robert from his father.

"I pray you, diligently and effectually let Her Majesty understand how her singular kindness doth overcome my power to acquit it, who, though she will not be a mother, yet she showeth herself, by feeding me with her own princely hand, as a careful nurse; and if I may be weaned to feed myself, I shall be more ready to serve her on the Earth. If not, I hope to be, in Heaven, a servitor for her and God's Church. And so I thank you for your porridges.

"P.S. Serve God by serving the Queen, for all other service is indeed bondage to the Devil."

The letter, light as it was, seemed as heavy as a piece of wood.

*His last letter.* There was already one with those doleful words scratched upon it. Now I would have two.

—

As twilight fell, I sat quietly in my inmost chamber. The sunbeams were picking out the very last contours and moldings on the wall as the day came to an end. Even in summer the sun sets. I hated to see it setting, knowing that Burghley's last day on earth was ending. As long as the sun stayed above the horizon, that last day was not over. Even as I watched, the sunbeams faded from the picture frames and lamps they were caressing, and the room grew dark.

Never had I felt more alone or more abandoned. One by one they had slipped away, the people from my youth.

There were the few, the very few, whose deaths caused deep wounds in my being. Burghley was one. And then there was my mother, Anne Boleyn.

It was not in my early days that I most keenly missed my mother, but later. Each year, as I grew in understanding, her vacancy seemed to expand until being motherless threatened to engulf me. Even today that gap is still there, when, if she still lived, she would be an elderly lady of ninety-one. But the dead never age, and a motherless child is always a child, even if she is a queen and sixty-four.

Then I had become a true orphan when my father died eleven years later. Well. We go on. We go on because we have to, and because the road is one way only, and there is no turning back to find these people, these people who have deserted us, as surely as a runaway soldier deserts his post. I know that is not fair to them, but that is what it feels like.

Burghley, how could you leave me?

—

After the death of a great one, there is silence and quiet. The palace felt as if it were under a spell, all movements suspended. The sun rose higher, and all of nature was stirring—bees droning from flower to flower, gulls soaring high above the wide river, gardeners clipping the bristly hedges—but within, it was closed and dark.

I must take charge. It was I who was muffled, I who was suspended. I had to take my first steps without Burghley. But at least they concerned him. I must order his funeral.

It would be as magnificent a one as I could command. Burghley was called the father of his country by both the common people and his fellow councillors, and he had surely earned this tribute.

Five hundred mourners, clad in black-cowled robes, attended the ceremony in Westminster Abbey. I hoped it was some comfort to Robert Cecil. It was small comfort to me.

# 57

wo weeks passed, and the drowsiness of high summer blended with my lassitude and low spirits over the death of Burghley. Since then, I had barely eaten much more than the sort of broth I had fed him. I had no appetite, so my women ordered only fruit, cheese, and bread brought to my chamber in the evening.

As I entered, Marjorie was waiting, not anxiously but calmly, along with Catherine. We would have another quiet night reading and sewing until I sought the oblivion of sleep. From outside the cries of night creatures came faintly to our ears—crickets, frogs, and owls. It was their turn now, while we rested. The heat of the day had lifted, and the air coming in was cool.

"Magical time," said Marjorie, standing by the window. "The balm of Gilead."

But from the gallery I heard footsteps, running footsteps. The tap-tap-tap sounded almost like a woodpecker. I rose, alert as a hunting dog.

In a moment my chamber guard admitted Robert Cecil, swathed in black. My first thought was, *Nothing could have happened today, as the terrible thing already happened many days ago.* That made us immune, did it not?

"Forgive me," he said, falling to his knees. His cloak spread out on the floor around him like a stain.

"No, forgive me," I said. "For no state business should intrude on you at this time."

"Only the highest of state business can do that, and this is urgent. Urgent!" He rose and handed me a dispatch, folded and wrinkled. "Oh, read it and add grief upon grief."

It was a notification of a massive military defeat in Ireland at the hands of The O'Neill. My marshal of the army, Sir Henry Bagenal, had taken four thousand foot soldiers and three hundred cavalry to relieve the fort on the

Blackwater, a key stronghold guarding the approach to Dublin and the south that O'Neill was trying to starve out. They had marched into a bloody ambush at Yellow Ford. Bagenal was killed, along with thirteen hundred of his soldiers; another seven hundred deserted. The English army was destroyed, and all over Ireland the English settlers fled. Our officials in Dublin begged O'Neill for an armistice in the most cowardly terms.

"The O'Neill rules," said Cecil. "They tremble before him. He can dictate his terms."

"Never!" I cried. How could my authorities have collapsed like that? "Upon my honor, this renegade Irishman shall not overthrow me!"

"Let us weigh the cost before making any pronouncements," he said. "It is likely to be very high. We have never yet found an answer to how to manage Ireland. It does not help that no one—soldier or official—wants to be assigned there. It is a thankless, futile task."

"Up until now," I said. "But I confess, I have not given it my full weight of attention in the past." I felt my eyes narrowing, as if I were entering an arena. "But when I do that, I will find a solution to the 'Irish problem,' as some call it."

I sent him on his way with instructions to make copies of the report and call the council first thing in the morning.

---

Hugh O'Neill. I had known him when he was in England, a ward in Leicester's household. We encouraged many of the highborn Irish to spend time here, thinking it would convert them to our ways. What fools we had been! All it did was give them a glimpse into our weaknesses.

Hugh was born about the same year as I took the throne. When I knew him he was in his early teens; he returned to Ireland when he was fifteen. He was short, stocky, and dark haired, with a large head, but with an ease of manner far older than his years. He came from one of the oldest Irish clans, a nobleman among them, and stood to become the next chieftain of the O'Neills, although the Irish did not go by strict primogeniture, as we did. There was always some confusion and suspense about who would succeed, often solved by a timely murder or riot.

He mastered our tongue and our ways; he could speak like a man from London, and when he returned to Ireland he helped quash—fighting alongside English troops—a rebellion in Munster fomented by the one of the clans. For that I rewarded him with an earldom, making him Earl of Tyrone. But it was never clear what side he was on. He had contacted the Spanish and invited their help. And now this triumph at Yellow Ford. It was the greatest military defeat the English had suffered since losing Calais almost exactly forty years ago. My sister Mary had said, "If you open my heart, you will find written on it 'Calais.'" I must not allow "Ireland" to be written upon mine!

I remembered Leicester standing with his arm around the boy's shoulders, saying, "He's a good lad," and ruffling his hair. Hugh had looked up at him (being so short, he looked up at most people) and smiled a guileless smile. A serpent's smile! And when I think of it, it was almost the same pose Leicester had used with young Essex. Another fetching lad, grown up to be dangerous. The shadow of these men fell across Leicester, as if to hang upon them was to hang upon poison.

---

The hastily assembled Privy Council met midmorning, and the disaster was laid before them. As I had been, they were stunned.

"More information has come in," said Cecil, spreading out his papers. "Thirty officers were killed at Yellow Ford, along with the loss of horses and cannon. Made bold by this, the Irish have risen in the other counties and overrun the English settlements. Our people are fleeing to Dublin, but there's no protection there, with only a five-hundred-man garrison. They are loading onto the first boats they can find to take them back here, abandoning the settlements. We stand to lose all of Ireland. And if the Spanish land, holding it against us, we can never get it back."

"Where are they now?" asked George Carey.

"The rebels have been burning and looting to within three miles of the walls of Dublin; they may capture it any day."

"Tell them about the way our brave authorities have sought to solve the problem," I said. As I had lain awake, thinking of it had heated me to a white-hot heat.

"They have sent offers to O'Neill for a truce," said Cecil.

"That's a pretty way to phrase it," I said. "Begged, you mean." I looked up and down the table. "Yes, we have begged to that man! My own Crown appointments, my deputies, the lord justices, have begged! I tell you, I will not let it be said that the Queen of England, who has faced down the might of Spain, ever bowed her knee to this base, born-in-a-thicket Irish rebel! I shall never endure such dishonor, nor let England endure it."

"What, then, shall we do?" asked Lord Cobham, warden of the Cinque Ports, mournfully.

I was incredulous. "We must conquer them. We must, at long last, commit enough men and troops to Ireland."

"But . . . where will we raise the money? Parliament has already voted the double subsidy. That only pays off past debts," said Buckhurst.

"And to raise the army?" cried Cobham. "No one wants to go there. There isn't an able commander available. Our troops can't operate there, in those bogs and wild terrain. The Irish don't fight fair in the open air like real armies; they attack and then melt back into the mists. The rain rots everything—the food, the ammunition, the weapons, even our papers and our clothes. We are felled by marsh fever. The Irish live off the land—or maybe they don't even eat! But we have to bring all the food with us. And where are we going to get it? Four disastrous harvests have left us with starvation in our own country. We are already having to import grain from Denmark and Danzig."

"Have you quite run out of breath now, Cobham?" I was upset. Everything he had said was true. But it did not change the fact that we had to fight in Ireland. "If you had been Noah, the ark would never have been built." I looked around at the panicked faces. "We will meet again tomorrow. Draw up a preliminary list of expenses and recruiting and victualing strategies. I expect no excuses." I turned and left the chamber.

Where was the Earl of Essex? Enough malingering and pouting. I would command his presence, and he had best present himself with no delay. I would pit one of Leicester's old wards against the other.

---

In the month since he had attempted to draw his sword on me, I had awaited some approach by him, some attempt at explanation. He should have been grateful that I let him run free rather than sending him to the Tower. Instead, he had written me insolent letters, as if I should apologize to *him*.

"The intolerable wrong you have done both me and yourself not only broke all the laws of affection, but was done against the honor of your sex. I cannot think your mind so dishonorable but that you punish yourself for it, how little soever you care for me. But I desire, whatsoever falls out, that Your Majesty should be without excuse, you knowing yourself to be the cause, and all the world wondering at the effect. I was never proud till Your Majesty sought to make me too base.

"And now my despair shall be as my love was, without repentance. Wishing Your Majesty all comforts and joys in the world, and no greater punishment for your wrongs to me than to know the faith of him you have lost, and the baseness of those you shall keep."

He was a child, and his missive would have been laughable were he not so dangerous. His very ability to recast events to construct an interpretation that no sane person could come to was frightening. That ability coupled with real power was lethal. He did not have the power yet. But his ability to invent and abjure himself of all blame was a skill to watch. My wariness toward him increased. And that wariness, tinged with fear, heightened my guard.

# 58

he morning made things clearer. The council meeting in the afternoon would be grim, but that was hours away. So I was startled when Sir Thomas Egerton, the Lord Keeper of the Great Seal, asked for an audience. I would see him in the afternoon—could it not wait?

He was a good and honest servant, and if he asked to see me, it was not for anything frivolous. I bade him come in. He entered the chamber, and as he did so, a puff of hay-scented air came through the window. His yellow, strawlike hair seemed to go with it. He was one of the few adults to keep the blond hair of a child.

"Have you received word from the Earl of Essex?" he asked, kneeling.

"No, nothing. Why? I summoned him to the council meeting. I expect to see him there."

"It is as I feared," he said. "I received this memorandum of advice from him regarding the Irish crisis. I had stressed in no uncertain terms that he must attend. Instead, he sent this." He handed me a sheet of paper with a long list of items.

"I did not ask for a list; I asked for his person." I flung the list onto my table.

"He is not coming," said Egerton. "He sent word that you should digest his ideas set forth here, and then he shall come."

"By God!" I cried. "He dares to disobey my summons?"

"He feels slighted." Egerton held up his hands as if to ward off blows. What, did he think I would strike him, too?

"He has lost his reason!" I shouted.

"If you would know his mind, you must read this. He wrote it to me. It is no treason to our friendship if I show it to you. If a man writes something down in black and white, he must be prepared for others to read it. It would be treason against my loyalty to you for me not to let you see it." He drew forth another letter, a much longer one.

With grave foreboding I took it and began to read.

*"If my country had at this time any need of my public service, Her Majesty would not have driven me into a private kind of life. I can never serve her as a villein or slave. When the vilest of all indignities are done to me, doth religion force me to sue? I can neither yield myself to be guilty, or this imputation laid on me to be just.*

*"What, cannot princes err? Cannot subjects receive wrong? Pardon me, pardon me, my good Lord, I can never subscribe to those principles. I have received wrong, and I feel it."*

First the sword, now this. He refused to submit to me. What other word was there for it but "treason"?

"I must think on this," I said carefully. "Thank you for bringing it to me."

Walking like one possessed back into my bedchamber, I found Marjorie and Catherine staring at me. "Has someone died?" Catherine asked, her soft voice even more soothing than usual.

"Yes," I said.

"Oh, who?" cried Marjorie, well acquainted with sudden news of death.

*My safety,* I wanted to say. *The unqualified love of my subjects.* "Many have died in Ireland," I murmured, not wanting to pour my heart out, even to her. If I waited a moment, perhaps the feelings would subside. It is never good to blurt things out.

She cocked her head knowingly. "This is not new tidings," she said. "The Lord Keeper did not rush here to tell you what you already knew."

"It's Essex," said Catherine. "The naughty boy has gone astray again."

"Why do you suppose that?"

"Only he seems to have this ability to trouble you," she said. "As my children do me."

"Oh, it is more than that!" I protested. "He is hardly my child." Both more than and less than that he was.

"You behave erratically toward him, and always have," said Catherine. "I know, as a mother, that to do so confuses children. They need to know what to expect."

"She speaks true," said Marjorie. "It is more like training a hunting hound than we would like to admit. A whistle, a clap, should mean one thing and one thing only. But you have given Essex so many signals it is little wonder he rotates like a weather vane."

"I have showered him with recognition and gifts. If anyone has been erratic, it has been him. He always wanted more and felt slighted." Her observation did not seem to fit.

"'That which is obtained too easily is esteemed too lightly,'" said Marjorie. "You know that saying. You never made him earn his rewards, so he did not link effort or merit with them."

I was incredulous. "If you saw this, why did you keep silent? I charged Burghley with the responsibility of pointing out truth to me, and he did. But you saw and said nothing?"

"Matters of state are different from matters of the heart. Besides, you *are* the Queen. We are friends, close friends, but there is a gulf between us. As Jesus' parable says, 'A great gulf fixed.'"

"That is between heaven and hell! It is hardly the same as between queen and friend, or subject."

"It may seem so to you, being on the upper level. But for us below, it is hard sometimes to reach across that gulf."

I had known this, of course, but thought the two here almost exempt from the stricture. I saw now that was not so. Oh, in how many ways had I been blind?

"Ecclesiastes says, 'Where the word of a king is, there is power: and who may say unto him, What doest thou?'" said Catherine. "I am sorry, dear friend, but you are also my Queen. A friend will always speak out; a subject must not. I must be a subject first and a friend second. You would not have it any other way."

She was right, but it was a cruel rule.

"So tell me now, and speak as friends: What do you make of the Essex situation? It is too late to undo what has gone before. When your hounds have not been trained properly but they are still good dogs, what do you do? You cannot make them pups again."

"You must bring them to heel immediately. There is no truth in the common saying—my, I am quoting so many today—that an old dog cannot learn new tricks. If he feels he has to, believe me, an old hound can change his ways," said Marjorie.

"Meet with him. Stick strictly to the business at hand. Treat him as a statesman and perhaps he can assume the mantle," said Catherine.

"Stop grooming him like a lapdog," said Marjorie. "First to be cuddled and then to be dumped on the floor. It is demeaning."

"When he nips and bites, I push him off my lap."

"Don't let him up there to begin with," said Marjorie. "He has no business there."

I looked from Marjorie's big-featured, plain face to Catherine's round, almost childish features, immensely grateful for these women. "Well," I finally said, "you have spoken boldly and told me a few things well overdue. I see now that country wisdom about hounds can be well applied at court." My jest faded. "Dear friends, do not keep your wisdom from me again."

---

The councillors were standing stiffly as suits of armor around the table. I told them to sit, and they did, equally stiffly. I could almost hear their joints creak. Everyone able to attend was there—with the exception of Essex. Even his uncle Sir William Knollys, fresh from the troubled island, had managed to come.

"Before we begin yapping like a pack of hounds, baying here and there, I would like a summary of the entire Irish situation, in simple terms. Sir William, you have just come from there. Tell us all. Feel free to go back as far as need be to paint a fuller picture." I would say nothing about the Essex absence.

Knollys, usually so jaunty and jolly, was white faced and drawn. The pallor of his cheeks made his odd three-colored beard—white at the roots, dun in the middle, brown at the bottom—even more noticeable. "First let me say, I did my best," he said. "But the situation is beyond control. The wild Irish are on the rampage, like a torrent overflowing its banks." He gave a nervous laugh. "Of course, in rainy Ireland, brooks are always overflowing."

"We know Ulster has rebelled, but what of the other regions?" asked Buckhurst, sitting up straighter.

"All in a boil," said Knollys. "Our deputies in Munster and Leinster cannot protect the settlers there, and all authority has collapsed. In the west, Connaught is making its usual nuisance of itself. The O'Malleys and the Burkes have been all but dancing with glee to see our downfall."

Grace O'Malley. Oddly enough, I wished she were here so we could talk. I wondered exactly what part, if any, she was playing in this rebellion. But she would claim it was no rebellion, merely an assertion of native rights.

"Ireland is not to be had on the cheap, and yet what is it worth?" said young Lord Cobham, scratching his head.

"Until now, little," said Admiral Howard. "She was so far off the main concerns of Europe she might as well have been in Africa. But when the Jesuits poured in in the 1580s, all that changed. Suddenly she got onto the Catholic bandwagon and sold herself to Spain."

"It is a given, then, that our policy there, of English settlements, a protected Pale of English authority, and a minimum military presence, is a failure," I said. "A second given is that Ireland's reinvigorated Catholicism means that there is now a Catholic presence in what had been a solidly Protestant line of demarcation in the north, an ally of our greatest enemy, Spain. Perhaps, as dreadful as this uprising is, it forces us to take action before the Spanish can secure their victim," I said.

"How are we going to afford a military capable of doing what needs to be done?" asked Knollys.

"We have stopped the raids into foreign territories," I replied. "We will not be having that expenditure again." The Essex policy had been as monumental a failure as the Ireland one. "Nor are we obligated in the Netherlands for much longer."

"We have other problems that hamper us besides direct war expenditures—the dismal quality of enlistments in the army and the corrupt officers overseeing them," said Egerton, the Lord Keeper. "They rob Your Majesty, pocketing the money allocated for clothes and weapons, recruiting men unfit for service, half of whom never muster at all."

"If you want to see such men in action, watch Falstaff onstage."

"At least Falstaff reports for duty," said Egerton. "In real life, the Falstaffs never go near a battlefield."

"We have had four failed harvests in a row," said Archbishop Whitgift. "I obeyed Your Majesty's instructions to have priests report grain hoarders and profiteers to me and preach that the better off voluntarily fast and give the saved money to the poor. I've had reports that in the north people have to travel twenty miles to buy bread. Where will the food come from to feed a large army? We have to supply it all. There's nothing to be had in Ireland."

"The Irish themselves live on reeds and moss," said Cobham. Titters went round the table.

"And who will lead such an army?" asked Carey. "No one has been successful. It calls for a great warrior, a nobleman who can attract followers rather than the motley Falstaff sort, and someone whom the Irish will fear."

"Where can such a man be found among us?" said Egerton.

The empty chair of Essex glared at us.

# 59

# LETTICE

*September 1598*

I heard wild laughter coming from Robert's chamber. It screeched out into the gallery, sounding like a flock of agitated parrots. For days he had taken to his bed, drawing the curtains and refusing all food. He had also refused all medical attention, saying it was a fever sent from God and nothing could vanquish it. His wife had hovered just outside the door but, apart from timid knocks, had not dared to enter.

Earlier this morning a messenger had brought him a dispatch of some sort. He had slipped it under the door and departed. Now this.

The laughter was hideous, demented. I must see what was happening. If the door was locked, I would summon someone to break it down.

But the door pushed open with no resistance. The laughter was so loud now it hurt my ears. The midday sun was blasting full into the room, making a curtain of light it was difficult to see through.

Was he in the bed? I fumbled my way to it and yanked the curtains open. But there was nothing there. The laughter stopped as abruptly as it had started, as if a ghoul or hell creature had come into the room and then fled. I turned, letting my eyes grow accustomed to the harsh difference between the sunlight and the dark recesses. Then I saw his feet, long white things like roots ripped untimely from the earth, stretched out, his toes in the sunlight. The rest of him was in darkness.

"Why, Mother, you come to pay a visit?" His tone was light, detached, faint, perhaps, from the raucous laughter torn from his throat.

"I was alarmed," I said, squinting to see him. His nightshirt was open, soiled, its drawstrings hanging down. He was sprawled, sloping, in the chair, as if he had no spine. I bent over him. I did not smell any beer or wine on his breath.

"I'm quite sober," he said. "No need to sniff."

I felt relief flooding through me at the assurance that he was neither drunk, hysterical, nor deathly ill. "What were you laughing at?" I asked, as if this were a normal encounter, as if he had not been hiding away for days, prostrate with anger and frustration over the Queen.

"Huh, huh . . ." He started guffawing. I was afraid it would change back into that hyena howl. He said, "He's dead. He's dead. The old boy is dead."

"What are you talking about?" I asked. "Who is dead?"

"Ph—Ph—Philip!" He burst out with a spray of spittle as he tried to stifle his hoot. "You know, the king of Spain. Or—what did Raleigh call him?—the king of figs and oranges?" He waved airily toward the letter on the floor. "After all these years of tormenting us, of being the dark shadow directing our actions, poof! He's gone." He lurched forward to pick up a goblet perched on the windowsill, gulping down whatever was in it. "Not quickly, no, it took him fifty days. He had a coffin in his room, ready. It was made of timber from one of the Armada ships!" He hiccupped. "Fifty days—that's even before I was in disgrace with the Queen. A long time ago, that was."

"What did he die of?" I stooped to pick up the dispatch. I read it quickly, but it did not say.

"Whatever it was, it was horrible," he said. "He was in agony, they say. Something in his jaw was eating him up. Oh, that is a reversal—being eaten by a jaw."

"He was seventy-one," I said. "One by one they leave us, those oaks that served to hold up the ceiling of our world." Elizabeth was only six years younger. Her turn was coming. "I remember when he came to England to marry Mary Tudor. I saw his entourage passing; little boys pelted his carriage with garbage. He was unpopular even then among us, as a Spaniard and a Catholic. But he was in his twenties, an attractive man who flattered the older spinster princess. She was wild with love for him. Made a fool of herself." Had watching her sister warned Elizabeth never to do such a thing? She had certainly taken it to heart. And learned a lesson in the perfidy of men, when her devout brother-in-law had flirted with her, with an eye to marrying her and keeping his hand in England after his sickly wife died.

"Well, Elizabeth is making a fool of herself now," snorted Robert, showing more liveliness.

"In what way?"

"Dressing up like a virgin and wearing those low-cut gowns that show her wrinkled old bosom."

"I thought she was a virgin."

"Yes, yes, she is . . . but just because a code of dress is prescribed for a certain station, if we have grown far beyond it, we should take heed. It's assumed most virgins are young and therefore flattered by loose hair and open bosoms. An old woman who dresses that way looks like a witch."

"Robert!" Such words were dangerous. "Have a care."

"I have no care. I have no station. I am nobody. I can say what I like."

"You are a fool," I said. "Shut your mouth. Get dressed. Act according to *your* station. The most famous noble in the land, sitting in the dark, wallowing in his nightshirt, is more ridiculous than anything the aging Queen has ever done. She is always a queen. At this minute, you are less an earl than anything I have ever yet seen."

---

Chastened, he emerged from his darkened chamber within the hour, dressed appropriately, seemingly alert and engaged. I sent him off to eat while I sat, shaken, at his reckless words. He had already almost taken an irretrievable step, a step too far. The dreadful folly of having tried to draw his sword on her, his hotheaded words comparing her to her father—and saying she was lesser than he and commanded less respect—and then his refusal to apologize, put his career, if not his life, in jeopardy. As she had reminded him, had she been her father, he would not have gone free from that room. And now she looked for some gesture on his part to show contrition. But he refused to take even the smallest step toward her, shooting out angry letters to others (which undoubtedly had been shown to her) and then staying away from the council, even for emergency sessions in the wake of the disaster in Ireland. The greatest military defeat the English had ever suffered there, and when the hour had come to make decisions, he had absented himself.

The Queen. I was still smarting from her insulting rejection of me and my gift, when she had invited me to court. It was a mean-spirited little drama, meant to humiliate me. It was unworthy even of her. Well. I would never see her again, except at a distance. But my son still must make his fortune by pleasing her. Perhaps he was so hostile to her on account of me. But it was too dangerous. She could be spiteful, but we could not afford it. Robert must make his peace with her.

---

The next few days passed uneventfully enough, as Robert regained his bearings and his health. After one of these bouts he always needed a recovery period. He never did explain why he laughed so much at Philip's death—perhaps now he did not remember. But Anthony Bacon brought information about Philip's last days, and they were no laughing matter.

It was sad to see a man in declining health describing another's similar situation. Anthony had grown even more frail and nervous and had attacks of shaking and heart pounding that came upon him suddenly. When that happened, he would jerk and sweat and have to cling to the arms of his chair.

His brother Francis seldom visited us now; Robert had made his disdain for his advice so blatant that his erstwhile friend stayed away.

"Philip had been suffering for some time," said Anthony. "He had a cancer of some sort, and his body was covered with sores. He lay in bed for at least fifty days, and brooded and brooded upon the loss of his last Armada. He feared it meant the end of his Enterprise of England, the one thing that had mattered to him. He felt a special responsibility for the English Catholics; after all, that is one reason he had married Mary Tudor. Now he had failed them."

"He must have felt that God deserted him," I said.

"So it seems," said Anthony. "He kept gazing at that waiting coffin. Did you know, he had over seven thousand saints' relics? They failed him, too."

"Pitiful." I thought of the bedridden old man, his body a putrefying mass of sores, with the coffin staring him in the face. He did not even have any teeth and had to exist on mush.

"Before you feel too sorry for him, let me tell you what the bastard did." Anthony's voice rose as he gathered his strength. "His last official business was to dictate a letter to The O'Neill congratulating him on his great victory at Yellow Ford and offering him support. Cheering on the Queen's enemy, he was passing his sword on to the next generation."

"Let him rot in hell!" No matter my own personal feelings for or against Elizabeth as a woman and a cousin, she was the Queen of my country and to insult her was to insult England.

"With all his saints' elbows and tongues and knucklebones," said Anthony. "I heard he had a square inch from the skinned St. Bartholomew and one of St. Lucia's eyeballs."

"Popish rubbish, and let him fester in it. They probably buried him chin deep in such stolen body parts."

"His heir, Philip III, is only twenty and does not seem as devout. He will probably auction off the relics to raise money."

"Well, don't buy any!" I said. There would be scant market for them in England in any case.

"I don't know; I've always wanted one of those pieces of the true cross. Although I'd settle for a vial of the Virgin's milk." He gave a great snorting laugh that soon turned into a painful cough.

"Call upon St. Blaise," I said. "That's the cure for sore throats."

Robert strode into the room, looking puzzled. "Whatever are you laughing at?"

"Philip again," I said. "Anthony was just talking about his collection of saints—parts of them, anyway."

Robert shivered. "Such a gruesome hobby," he said. His own piety, which came upon him in fits and starts, was of the Protestant variety—inherited from my father, most likely.

"I brought intelligence about Philip's last hours," said Anthony.

"Doubtless they were impeccably Catholic and involved a vision of some sort," said Robert.

"Yes, indeed, a vision. It wore an Irish cloak and had long hair and a bloodthirsty yell. Philip commissioned it—against us."

"A ghost? He called upon a ghost?"

"Would that it were. This one is alive enough—The O'Neill. Philip gave him his dying blessing, as it were. Said Yellow Ford was a great thing, and for him to go forth and do more, at Spain's expense."

Now Robert's face went pale, pale as it had been in his sequestered room where he had hidden from the sun. "He did that?" he murmured.

"If we doubted the battle lines were drawn, we now have our proof," said Anthony. "Ireland is Spain's surrogate, and it has won a mighty victory against us."

Robert let out a mournful sigh, as if all the deaths there, including his father's, entered into him. For once, he had no words ready.

---

Early the next morning a summons came from Greenwich. Her Majesty commanded the presence of the Earl of Essex at court, immediately, upon pain of severe punishment if disobeyed.

# 60

# ELIZABETH

*September 1598*

he candles flickered in unison. When one leaped up, the other mirrored it, as if they were competing to illuminate Philip's face. He would have liked that, I thought. He would have felt it an angelic tribute. He was comely and youthful in this miniature portrait, the one he had given my sister upon their betrothal. I had seen her look hungrily upon it before she had beheld him in person. He had a restrained smile in this picture, a teasing promise of high spirits—a promise he never fulfilled. After she died I had kept it; it served to remind me that the willful enemy plotting my demise had once been my friend in England and that no one is entirely a monster.

Now he was dead. Doubtless more candles were lit all over Spain, in little churches and in the great fortress of Escorial, where Philip spent his last years. They would not yet know of it in Peru or Panama, but next year requiem Masses would be said for him there. His obsequies would just go on and on, reverberating around the world.

I should feel some sort of triumph, or at least relief. Instead I felt naked. Losing my steadfast enemy felt oddly like losing a steadfast friend; both defined me. First Burghley, now Philip. They both had left sons to carry on after them, but the son is never the father.

I had the damning intelligence about Philip's message to The O'Neill. It saddened me, killing my stubborn belief that when our last moments on earth seize us, we become better than we have been in life and even the petty man becomes, briefly, noble. Instead, with his last breath, Philip had focused on his hatred of me and England.

*Once you were young,* I thought, looking again at the portrait. *But the only remnant of you that remained so was your intense ability to hate: malevolence burning bright in a withered old face.*

*Our duel continues, my old brother. It goes on, because you would have it so.*

---

They were all here, by God, including Essex. I had sent that wayward puppy a summons that even he dared not ignore. They were sitting glumly around the polished council table—the entire Privy Council, from the ancient Whitgift to the young, new Lord Cobham. The days since Yellow Ford had brought a flood of bad news, as well as a flood of fleeing settlers. Edmund Spenser had just barely escaped with his life from his burning house and barn; he was back in England, glad to be safe, and now composed verses re-creating the horrors—flames, looting, slaughter—he had witnessed in Ireland.

---

Today we would move forward, take command of the ship. We could drift no longer, or we would be dashed upon the rocks of Ireland, as the Armada had been.

Up and down the long table, fit for a monastery refectory, they looked to me to steer them. Essex sat alone at the farthest end, facing me, as if he were my antipode. I motioned him to move, take his place among the other councillors. Scowling, he did so, seating himself on Carey's side of the table, shunning the side with his enemies Cecil, Admiral Howard, and Cobham.

"Gentlemen, one might mistake this for a funeral," I said. "The only person to have died is Philip, and I would not expect such long faces on our side. Archbishop, it is fitting that you lead us in prayer before opening this momentous council."

His bushy black eyebrows rose, and he prayed in a sonorous voice.

"Amen," all chorused.

"Robert Cecil," I said, "as principal secretary, please summarize the choices facing us."

He stood, clutching the papers he had prepared—not because he knew he would have to present them but to order his own mind. I was sure that in his wardrobe all his shoes—polished and properly soled—were lined up according to season. "Very well," he said, nodding to all. "We have only three choices. One, withdraw and surrender Ireland to the Irish. Two, tread water and do the minimum to retain it. Three, throw our greatest force against it and subjugate it utterly. The first choice would be tempting were it not for the Spanish. It is thrift and common sense to rid oneself of a nuisance, unless someone is waiting to pick it up and turn it against you. The second choice has already been tried, and has failed. That leaves only the third."

"To my sorrow, I affirm that you are right," I said. "So we meet today to decide how to implement it, not whether to implement it. The die is cast—cast by Spain, not us."

"Very well, but how can we do this?" asked Lord Keeper Egerton.

"Money, money. It requires money we don't have," lamented Buckhurst.

"It will have to come from Parliament," said Lord Cobham, "and we just called a parliament. It is too soon to call another. They won't be in a giving mood."

"We still have the subsidies to collect from the last one," said Admiral Howard. "And in this time of danger, they may have to meet again."

"It's always 'this time of danger.' How long can I lay that burden on my people, extracting money from them out of fear?" I wondered. "But it has all been true, not a ploy on my part."

"All the money in the world won't help without someone to lead the attack," said John Herbert, the second secretary. He seldom attended council meetings but kept the notes from all of them. "We need a commander. A military genius."

"Perhaps we can get the witch of Endor to call up Caesar?" said Whitgift. "All our good ones are dead."

"Someone has to lead them. They can't be led by a ghost."

"Ireland has made ghosts out of scores of commanders," cried Essex, "including my father!"

"This time will have to be different," said Carey, beside him. "This time, the commander will have to be a man who will not be broken by Ireland, but will break Ireland. A man who can draw others to enlist and serve under him. Someone whose very appointment makes a statement."

"But who can that be?" asked Herbert, for all of us.

We all knew there was only one man now in the realm who could fit that description. Only one man who was both nobly born and a military commander. Only one man whom the people would demand be appointed. There was no choice.

Essex leaped up. His voice grew tremulous, as if he were speaking underwater. " 'Also I heard the voice of the Lord, saying, Whom shall I send, and who will go for us? Then I said, Here am I; send me.' Send me!" He rushed over to me, threw himself on the floor. "I am called! I am called!" he cried.

For what seemed several moments no one spoke or even moved.

"Are you certain of that?" I finally said.

" 'I heard the voice of the Lord saying'. . ."

"Did you actually hear it, or are you merely quoting the Bible?"

He raised his head like a naughty child, peeking out from under his hair, which had flopped down over his forehead. "The Lord speaks through Scripture," he said.

"Spoken like a good Puritan," I said. "But Catholics are right to warn that Scriptures can be read many different ways, and the devil wants to use our weaknesses to deceive us into false interpretations. Get up. You do not need a quote from the prophet Isaiah to justify your qualifications. The fact that you have served in overseas military operations is more persuasive."

He pulled himself up on his hands and knees and then stood upright, looking at me. His face was unreadable, blank.

"It seems that the position is yours," I said. "God have mercy on you, and on England."

---

I was sitting in the dark. Not that I meant to, but twilight and then full dark had crept up on me as I sat stiffly in my chair in my inner chamber. Supper had come and been sent back; I had no appetite.

I had had to appoint him. There was no one else. England had been weak on land for years, but never worse than now. Our larder of leaders was empty. But there was one thing Essex had that all the other failed commanders had not: a personal reason for wanting revenge on the Irish. Ireland had robbed him of his father, sending him to an untimely grave. I could only pray that somehow, in this crucible of need, he would convert his long-fallow potential into honorable action.

I was as bad as the Spanish—to have only prayer to rely on. What was it Philip had supposedly said as he launched the first Armada—"In confident hope of a miracle"? My hope was not even confident. In any case, no miracle had rescued them. Was it folly to think we would fare better?

---

The next day was my birthday. I was sixty-five. Was that anything to celebrate? Yes, something to be thankful for, but not to advertise. I had not planned any formal recognition of the day, knowing that to remind anyone of my age was not politically wise. Nonetheless, Marjorie and Catherine had small tokens for me, chosen with their usual thoughtfulness. Marjorie gave me a cordial flavored with meadow herbs from Rycote. A sip took me to the midsummer fields of that lovely part of the country. Catherine had secretly embroidered a pincushion showing our family connection. She and I were two flowers dangling from a very green and twining stalk. Her flower was lower than mine, one rung down on the genealogical ladder. But so skillful was she in the design that its asymmetry was pleasing. "I am three generations down from Thomas and Elizabeth Boleyn, and you are only two," she said.

"I was just old enough that I remember them, vaguely," I said. "They died when I was five or six. Not long after—after my mother. Your grandmother Mary outlived them all but still did not live long enough for you to know her."

"We are not a very long-lived family," said Catherine.

"That's a foolish thing to say! I am sixty-five now. And my mother hardly lived a natural life span. Thomas lived to be sixty-two and Elizabeth fifty-eight." How well I knew all these details.

"That still makes you older than any of them."

"Quiet!" I laughed. Then the laughter died. "You are right. And I am always thankful for each day."

"I must laugh at you children," said Marjorie. "For I am well into my seventies. I remember the Boleyns personally, and I saw King Henry as a young man. A sight never to be forgotten. He was glorious, shining like the sun. . . ." She stopped herself. "I don't feel old," she said. "But every day my body reminds me."

Seeing her every day, as I did, the changes had been subtle, and her younger self from past years shaded what I saw. But it was impossible to deny that she had grown old, even if she kept her strength and liveliness.

"Do you wish to retire?" I suddenly asked. "I kept my dear Burghley too long, and I vow not to make that mistake again. It is no friendship, no respect, to command service when the person no longer wishes to serve."

"When I am ready, I will freely tell you," she said. "Before long, Henry and I may wish to go to Rycote for good."

Before noon, gifts and tributes began to accumulate in the presence chamber, in spite of my trying not to emphasize the occasion. All the councillors had sent something, each oddly reflective of his personality. Cecil had sent a small portrait of his father, Whitgift a fourteenth-century Psalter, Buckhurst a bound copy of his early poems, Lord Cobham a map of the Cinque Ports, as befitted their warden. These mementos were more amusing than the formal gifts I received at New Year's. Then, a surprising box from Edmund Spenser. It contained a lengthy genealogy of King Arthur and my descent from him.

"Did he rescue this from his burning castle in Ireland?" I wondered. Poets were curious creatures. Yet if they were true poets, their work would be the thing they would rush to rescue above all else. It was impossible to ever write something again in exactly the same way.

"He is nearby," said my chamber usher. "He presented it early this morning."

He must have known his firsthand knowledge of Ireland—he had been there most of his adult life—would require him to testify at court. I decided to invite him to call upon me so I could thank him for his gift—and question him before the council did.

Essex did not send a gift, nor did his mother, Lettice. She would have been mad to have done so after the reception of her last one. The most unexpected token came from Wales, a small box of honey and cakes, with a letter from my goddaughter "Elizabeth." She wished me well and asked if she might come to court to learn English better. "And to see you, most gracious godmother," she wrote.

I was inordinately pleased. Here in this chamber of aging and politics, she would be a glimpse of the innocence we had all lost. And I was touched that she remembered and felt bold enough to test me to see if what began between us in Wales could grow.

---

My newly reinstated captain of the Queen's Guard, Raleigh, proudly led his friend Edmund Spenser into my presence. Coming behind them, uninvited, was Percival the Indian, wearing court clothes and holding his head high. Between two such tall and robust men, Spenser seemed shrunken and abject. But that was hardly surprising, given what he had been through.

Although only in his forties, he moved tentatively, like an elderly knight. "Pray you, be seated," I told him. I would not make this man stand any longer than necessary. I myself took a seat close by and motioned for food and drink to be brought, in case he needed them.

"You have suffered greatly," I said. "And your country grieves with you."

His eyes darted all over the room, like skittish little animals that were afraid to alight. "Thank you," he said in a faint voice.

"Can you tell me what you saw in Ireland?"

Raleigh was shaking his head vehemently. "If I may, I shall tell you, to spare him the repeating of it." Spenser gave a grateful nod. "His castle at Kilcolman in Cork was set ablaze; his infant son and his wife died there. He barely escaped, with his hair on fire. He had to stumble through the fields swarming with rebels to find his horse, and then rode blindly out into the night. He only found his way to safety when the sun rose and he could see where he was going. His castle home was smoldering behind him."

"I looked once and then could not look again," he said. "But I keep seeing it, over and over."

"The rebels saw him and pursued on foot, but they could not catch him. As he rode toward our garrison, he saw the devastation of the entire countryside. All gone. What we had worked years to cultivate, gone in the night."

"Gone, all gone," Spenser intoned.

"You are safe now," Raleigh assured him. Percival moved to touch his shoulder in reassurance, and Spenser jumped.

"Don't touch me!" he cried.

I wanted to hear more about Ireland, but it was cruel to him. "Thank you for the birthday gift," I said. "I am delighted to have my descent from King Arthur confirmed in such ironclad details." He sat stonelike. "And since the publication of all six books of *The Faerie Queene*, I have had the pleasure of reading it slowly and carefully, and I am dazzled by your genius." I did not flatter here; the man had wrought an intricate work of high art. And he had dedicated it to the Queen, "to live with the eternity of her fame."

"But as touching Ireland," said Raleigh gently to Spenser, "I believe you prescribed a remedy for that some years ago."

"Oh, oh, yes—" He nodded to Percival, who produced a manuscript-sized box. "Here it is. I know what should be done. I am more convinced now than ever that this is the answer." Struggling to his feet, he handed me the box with trembling hands.

I opened it, seeing the title: *A View of the Present State of Ireland*. "This should be of immediate use," I said. But obviously it had been written earlier; this poor creature, whose recent observations would be most pertinent now, could hardly hold a pen.

"The only way to rule Ireland is to destroy it and then build it up again, in our own image," he cried. "Burn it to the ground! Finish what they have started! Only by overriding all law, by stamping out every vestige of their language and customs and clans, can we turn it into a real country!"

The ugly face of violence now showed itself; spawned by the violence he had experienced, he was dyed in that color himself.

Unthinking violence was hideous no matter who was spouting it or who had been wronged. None of us could say we would not feel the same after seeing our families killed, but a gentle poet was such an unlikely avenging killer. If it could convert him, even in thought, it could convert anyone. Oh, what had the people of Ireland turned into, on both sides?

"I shall read your manuscript," I promised him. "Raleigh, let me tell you of Constancia the tortoise and how she fares," I said, changing the subject. "She went inert over the winter, and moving her indoors into a barn took four men, as she was so heavy and her shell did not afford any handholds. But she revived in the spring and now paces the Hampton Court garden. I think she is lonely. She seems to yearn. Can you bring her a mate?"

"Only if I can sail to where her kind lives," said Raleigh. "But the moment you give me leave, off I'll go. Percival, what do you say?"

"I am ready," he said.

We all laughed gently, and Percival and Raleigh helped Spenser to the door.

# 61

# LETTICE

*October 1598*

golden swirl of leaves danced outside my windows. October this year was a honey yellow succession of warm days. The harvest, again, was meager, making autumn like unto a beautiful woman who was barren. Still it was possible to appreciate the season's sterile beauty, to walk in the soft afternoons along brick garden pathways and take pleasure in it.

Essex House was now the center of the preparations for the Irish venture. I trembled to think about it. The Queen, for reasons known only to herself, had settled the fate of England in my son's hands. When he had burst out, "Her mind is as crooked as her carcass!" that day at home, I had hushed him immediately. The very birds of the air might be spies. But that phrase had stuck in my mind. I could not help thinking that perhaps her mind was faltering. She was sixty-five now and her behavior was erratic. She had forgone her Progress this year; the official reason was the death of Burghley, but I wondered if that was just an excuse because it was too demanding of her.

I had to admit that she had acted with uncharacteristic decisiveness in her response to the defeat at Yellow Ford and the uprising. But a Tudor can never accept rebellion or defeat, and her blood called forth her prideful response. It may have been the insult of the "bush-born kern," as she called him, besting her forces. With surprising speed she had determined to subdue Ireland and had chosen Robert as marshall of the army.

He would go where his father had gone and never returned. To the place that was the graveyard of one English commander after another. His most immediate predecessor, Lord Burgh, had perished last year, some said of poison. If malaria and treachery in Ireland did not do you in, poison finished the job.

This time the army was to be huge—the largest force ever sent to Ireland. They were talking of sixteen thousand foot soldiers and thirteen hundred cavalry. All under the leadership of my son, whose grasp of land warfare was tenuous at best. The only other sole command he had been given was in France seven years ago. Nothing was achieved there, except the death of his brother, my youngest child, Walter. Robert had become a military figure by fierce desire, showing how wishing for something can bring it about, but wishing does not bestow natural ability to go along with it.

Robert could make men follow him, but he did not know how to lead. That was the truth of it. Only luck could guarantee his success. But did not Caesar himself say luck played a large part in his battles? "The luck of Caesar" became a byword.

*Oh, ghost of Caesar, grant a little of it to my son!*

As I was framing these words, I rounded a corner and startled a flock of magpies quarreling over a heap of leaves and compost. Chattering, they rose up, wings astir. One . . . two . . . three . . . There were seven of them.

*One for sorrow, two for mirth,*
*Three for a wedding, four for a birth,*
*Five for Heaven, six for Hell,*
*Seven for the devil's own self.*

Quickly I made the sign to reverse the bad luck, crossing my two thumbs. The devil's own self was Ireland.

---

I hurriedly left the place where I had seen the magpies and soon heard the chattering of human voices, reminding me of the birds. It was Frances, arm in arm with an extremely pregnant Elizabeth Vernon, Southampton's disgraced wife. She had taken refuge under our roof—another thing for the Queen to hold against us. So infuriated was she that they had married in defiance of her forbidding it that she clapped Southampton in Fleet Prison. There he languished, while Robert brought him news of his wife's condition. *The Queen,* I thought bitterly. *She holds us all prisoner to her whims and prejudices.*

I greeted the lady who was now Countess of Southampton, whether the Queen would have it or no. At court she had been known as a beauty, with her sleepy eyes and tumbling curls, but now her face was puffy with the last stages of pregnancy and with weeping and worry. Her belly swelled out the front of her gown like the sails of a ship sailing before the wind.

"It's a boy," said Frances. "We have just held the wedding ring above her belly on a string, and it swung back and forth. That means it's a boy!"

I smiled. I had done the same with all my children, but I was wrong about three out of the five. "Wonderful!" I said.

She looked so uncomfortable she would doubtless be pleased no matter what the baby turned out to be. I was glad my childbearing days were over; it was a distinctly miserable state. I was also glad I had never revealed to anyone that Southampton and I had been lovers. Robert prided himself on knowing so much, but he was ignorant of this foray on my part. He also never knew about Will.

Southampton had been a good lover. I wondered, fleetingly, if he was different with Elizabeth. Men tended to be, I found, with women they respected. Of course, she had been his mistress for three years first. Ah, well, best not to think too hard about these things.

"All is in readiness for the birth," Frances said. "The midwife is waiting and the cradle lined with blankets and little mattress."

"May your time be easy," I wished her.

---

I left the gardens of Essex House and went out by the water gate. I was not ready to return to the house, where so many men were always loitering about. Robert seemed to have immense numbers of hangers-on, many of them elusive and troublesome characters, men who had not prospered at court or elsewhere and were looking to make their fortunes somehow, without straining themselves. These were younger sons of country families, adventurers who had staked all on piracy and impoverished themselves, disenfranchised religious zealots on both sides, ambitious scholars who found no appointments equal to their merits, and unemployed soldiers. Such were the flotsam and jetsam now sloshing around Essex House.

The Thames gleamed flat and broad in the sunlight, and I asked our boatmen to take me out.

"Where to, Countess?" the head boatman asked.

"To nowhere," I said. "Up and down."

"Tide is coming in, and we don't dare go under the bridge," he said. "But we'll go there and then turn back."

London was at its best this time of year. Boatmen out on the water were in a jolly mood, waving to and racing one another. The Queen's swans bobbed up and down, white spots covering the water. There were so many of them this year. The swan herders must have been busy this spring, marking all the new cygnets. I had missed the one day when they had to round up all the swans to count and mark them; it had been right after my nonreception by the Queen, and I was not in a mood to watch other creatures being added to her toll.

But today I did not begrudge her her swans. She had nodded once again to the house of Devereux, had gathered Robert under her wing. He had been given one more chance.

We turned before being caught in the gush of water between the pillars of the bridge and made our way back upstream. I watched the city thin and then die away as we passed Chelsea; the bank became lined with willows and reeds. Before long we came around the bend on the south bank with Barn Elms, the home of Frances, the place where old Walsingham had died.

Frances. Was she happy? Did Robert make her happy? Did she care? Did he? I could not read her at all. She was one of those creatures who always seem content, whose inner workings are never visible. Someone had whispered to me—was it Christopher?—that perhaps Robert had chosen her because she was the opposite of me. That after a mother of such storm and drama, he wanted a quiet wife who would make no demands. Well, he had gotten her.

Around another long loop of the river and we were abreast of Syon House on the north bank. The mansion was set far enough back that it was hard to see through the trees. That was the home of my Dorothy now, the new Countess of Northumberland. She had married the odd earl, Henry, not long ago, and entered into his strange way of life, enduring a husband who fancied alchemical experiments with men such as John Dee and Thomas Harriot, smoking tobacco, and stargazing. All my children seemed to have made peculiar marriages.

My daughter Penelope's lover was not as odd as the legal spouses of my other children. Charles Blount seemed a perfectly reasonable man, if one overlooked his and Penelope's flagrant adultery. They had a son already, a boy they had named Mountjoy. In the meantime, Penelope's legal husband, Lord Rich, seemed unperturbed by the situation and often dined with them.

The afternoon sun was glancing off the water and bothering my eyes. I was ready to return and ordered the boat back to Essex House. I took one last look at Syon House, standing like a sentinel, and sighed. If this was the life Dorothy wanted, then I would not question her choice.

By this time of day, more people had gathered at our home. The numbers swelled as the evening drew on, and we were expected to feed them all. Robert was considered a Great Man, and a Great Man had many retainers, all of whom he must provide for. But it was not in his means to do so, so we were heavily in debt and growing more so. Surely these men would go with him to Ireland and feed off the Queen's bounty, not ours!

---

After supper—once again stripping us bare, like a flock of crows—the men drifted off to wherever they roosted during the night, leaving us a semblance of privacy. Withdrawn into our chambers, there was only the family, and Edmund Spenser, who was staying with us. He was too shaken to return alone to his home of Petworth, and we wished to protect him here. He had forced himself to attend on the Queen, although it had taken all his reserves to do it. He would soon be called to the Privy Council, and that would be an ordeal. He was hardly sleeping, and when he did sleep, he was pursued by nightmares. He shivered and shook in his room because he could not bear for a fire to be lit. The flames, the crackle, the pop of wood—they sent him into a fit of fear. To warm himself he tried wrapping furs and blankets around his body; in truth it was not even cold outside yet, but his thin frame and shrunken spirit chilled him.

We tried broth, heated wine, and soups—anything to warm him from the inside. Irish spirits, of course, were the best, but the very smell of them made him scream.

"We'll have only good, warm Somerset cider, then," I assured him. Because of the bad harvests, cider was scarce this year, but what we had he was welcome to. If he fancied it, I would outspend myself to get more.

"Umm . . . yes." He sniffed it, as if to assure himself there was no whiff of Ireland. Then he gulped it thirstily. When he had drained the cup, he sank back, running his tongue along his narrow lips. Only then did he look around the room, noting the trunks and piles of clothes. "You are readying yourself," he commented.

"As best I can," said Robert. "But anything you could tell me to help me prepare I would gratefully hear. I have never been there."

"God has been merciful, then," said Spenser. "The first thing is, take waterproof clothes, as if you were going to sea. The damp is everywhere and will rot the shirt off your back."

Robert nodded, taking notes.

"Take twice as much artillery as you think you need. It has a way of disappearing. Most of the guns now arming the Irish have been stolen from us. And what doesn't disappear becomes nonfunctional from the damp—powder won't light; rust eats weapons up. Take a good supply of cats with you, good mousers, to protect the grain supply. Snakes would be better."

"I thought St. Patrick had rid Ireland of snakes."

"Then we should curse the Irish by importing them. Let them loose to overrun the island!"

"Sketch to me the general divisions of the land," Robert told him. "I know you were in Munster, at the bottom of the island."

"Yes, Raleigh and I and many others were given land confiscated after the Desmond rebellion there. But the thing to keep in mind is that rebellion can come from anywhere. No area is secure. If you want to think of Ireland as an oval clock face, then the top of it—from ten o'clock to two o'clock—is Ulster. We had never pacified that part, never even had the pretense of laying down English law there. That's where O'Neill is from, and his ally, Hugh O'Donnell. Then, at around three o'clock, the English have their stronghold—or should I say toehold?—at Dublin and the Pale. It's near to Ulster but until now had been the most secure.

"Going farther down, into County Leinster, we had a number of plantations, all overrun now. Then, farthest south, at five to seven o'clock, Munster, with more of our English settlers. In the west, at nine o'clock, Connaught County was never really pacified; the O'Malleys and the Burkes control that territory."

"That pirate woman, O'Malley," said Robert. "I remember when she came to court. She promised to fight for Elizabeth."

"A good demonstration of Irish reliability," said Spenser. "It was contingent on England doing certain things, such as removing Richard Bingham. Elizabeth followed through but then sent him back again. Grace O'Malley was not fooled by such transparent gestures, so she has repudiated her loyalty oath. One cannot blame her."

"Isn't she old?" Robert cried. "Even older than the Queen? How much of a threat can she be?"

"The pirate life keeps her young," said Spenser. "At least from what I hear. I wouldn't want to grapple with her. She commands a large fleet eager to do us damage."

"I don't plan to fight at sea," said Robert.

"She can help the Spanish, who necessarily will be arriving by sea."

"If I had my way, I'd choose the sea. But the Queen has dictated the terms of the war. It is by land."

"Who are you appointing as your commanders?" Spenser asked.

"I want Southampton to serve as my cavalry leader, master of the horse, if the Queen sets him free," he said. "And you, Christopher, as under commander, marshal of the army and a council member."

He looked surprised and pleased. "Raleigh?"

"No. He's head of the Queen's Guard here and wants to stay close to the Queen's petticoats."

"Or perhaps he's clever enough to stay away from that bog. After all, he's done much service there, going back twenty years."

"He was vicious, killing left and right without mercy."

"It doesn't seem to have done much good," said Christopher. "Perhaps he, of all people, sees firsthand how futile it is."

"This time it cannot be piecemeal, like our other efforts. This time the campaign must aim for no less than conquering the entire island, once and for all," said Robert.

"Good luck," said Spenser. "You set yourself an impossible task. No one has ever conquered Ireland, and no one ever will."

Robert drew himself up. "There is no such thing as an impossible campaign, if enough men and enough money are committed. And this time there will be. Sixteen thousand soldiers! Thirteen hundred cavalry! The Irish fear the cavalry; they'll quake when they see it."

"I've never seen the Irish quake, except with one of their agues," said Spenser. "Are you in sole command? Are you free to make your own decisions?"

"As far as I know. There will be no one over me."

"Except the Queen," I reminded him. "She is the supreme commander."

"Bah! She knows nothing of warfare. How could she? She's never been on the battlefield. Let's hope her meddling doesn't interfere with what needs to be done."

"She's paying for it, and she will want to have the last word," I said.

"Surely this time she will bow to the wisdom of those who know warfare," Robert said. "She wants to win."

"She has her own ideas," said Christopher. "One cannot say they are always wrong."

"They are always cautious, and here to be cautious is to lose," said Robert.

"You must not begin by antagonizing her," said Christopher. When had he gotten so analytical? "For example, by appointing Southampton. She will not permit it; she dislikes and distrusts him. She put him in prison! So do not waste your ammunition, so to speak. Do not get off on the wrong foot with her."

"Aren't you full of clichés today?"

"Clichés are often true," said Christopher. "Don't cross her. You'll lose."

"I need the freedom to choose my own officers."

"Anyone but Southampton, I would say. It is folly to nominate a candidate who is in prison for offending the Queen."

"But I want him," said Robert.

"Learn to want someone else," I said.

"That's not so easily done," he retorted.

Oh, that I knew. *Learn to want someone else.* I tried to follow my own dictum to some success. I had long ago ceased to want anything to do with Southampton. I could see him now and look upon him as merely the husband of Elizabeth Vernon and a friend of my son's. Will Shakespeare was more difficult. What I wanted most was to talk to him and hear his opinion on what was looming before Robert. He seemed to know everything that went on. Instead, I had to guess it secondhand through his plays.

His plays kept him in my mind. People talked about him; even the Queen called for him to present his dramas before her. She had liked the play featuring Sir John Falstaff so much she had requested one in which he was the main character, and Will had written *The Merry Wives of Windsor*, which was duly performed at Windsor during the Garter ceremonies. In his own way, he was as much a public figure as the Queen, even if he hid behind his characters. One could say that Sir John Falstaff was a public figure, that Shylock was a public figure, that Romeo was a public figure, while their creator kept his privacy.

The talk wound down. Spenser was yawning and needed his rest. Robert was restless in the chamber. I wished he would seek his wife's company instead of heading out into the night, but I no longer had any control over him.

Christopher and I retired to our chamber. Making ready for bed, Christopher was changing into his nightshirt.

"I hope he does not antagonize the Queen before he's even left," he said.

"Thank you for trying to speak common sense to him," I said.

"It is hard for you," he said. "For I know you would just as soon he stayed safely here. Danger seems to court him."

"You know me well, husband," I said. I was touched that he could understand how a parent would feel, since he was not one. I went over to him and embraced him. It was good to hold him; I had never ceased to appreciate the physical comfort of him. As I pressed him close to me, I felt both tenderness toward him and stirrings of desire. It had been a long time since I had felt that, for anyone.

He kissed me, reminding me of what I had once craved. I wanted it back again, the longing and the excitement.

*Lettice,* I told myself, *he has been right here all along. It is you who have abandoned him. Now reach out and reclaim him, and the joy of the marriage bed. It is your right—even the church preaches that. Does not the marriage vow say, "With my body I thee worship"? They do not mean kneeling and reciting verse!*

"Come, my marshall of the army," I whispered. It was exciting to address him thus.

# 62

# ELIZABETH

*January 1599*

welfth Night, and the torches were blazing high at Whitehall. We had had as festive a season as possible, thrusting troubling thoughts of the Irish out into the midwinter darkness. I called upon all the courtiers to attend me sometime during the Twelve Days, but especially upon this climax of the celebrations.

Tonight there was everything: a banquet with not one but three roasted swans, Raleigh serving as master of misrule, a full contingent of musicians and singers, and a new play, the continuation of *Henry IV*, the play that had introduced Falstaff to the world.

Essex, sitting beside me, leaned over and murmured, "This play is not as entertaining as the first part. All the interesting characters, like Hotspur, have been killed off, and Prince Hal is prissy."

What I wanted to say, and could not, was that the first part of the play seemed lusty and full of life, whereas this one dwelled on decay, disease, and age—subjects I shunned. There was even a moment when Falstaff was upbraided for having a white beard, a decreasing leg, an increasing belly, a broken voice, a double chin, and a single wit and told that every part of him was blasted with antiquity. Instead I said, "You might do better to choose such prissy fellows to have about you than the ones you choose." Southampton still lingered in prison, and his forbidden wife had been sheltered by Essex. She had just given birth to a daughter. His other ne'er-do-wells, the Earls of Rutland and of Sussex, were little better than Falstaff.

What neither of us would mention, but were both acutely aware of, was the publication of a book entitled *The Life and Reign of Henry IV* by John Hayward. Its title was misleading, for it covered the abdication of Richard II, and in its dedication Hayward compared Bolingbroke to Essex. Hayward would be questioned before the Star Chamber, but why speak of this now? It was Twelfth Night.

Sitting on my other side was Eurwen Bethan. At my invitation, she had come from Wales to spend Christmas with me, and her wonder at all she saw was the greatest holiday pleasure for me. To behold all this for the first time must be indescribable. Eurwen kept her words few, but her eyes shone.

She was now eleven, just on the brink of turning from a rosy-cheeked child into a slim maiden. As I had asked her, she called me Godmother Elizabeth and seemed content to do so, not reckoning it the startling honor a courtier's child would. At this time of heavy cares of state and growing bodily aches, she was April in my life.

As she was a distant cousin of Essex's, he was possessive of her, but I brushed off his attempts to intrude between us. I did not want this one pure thing in my life to be tainted by court politics or ambition.

I had over a hundred godchildren, and for amusement, I invited many of them to come together and meet her. They ranged from middle-aged people like John Harington to Catherine's twelve-year-old Howard niece. They made much of her, petting her and making her one of their company.

The play ended with an actor saying, "Our humble author will continue the story, with Sir John in it, and make you merry with fair Katherine of France; where, for anything I know, Sir John shall die of a sweat." He bowed. "My tongue is weary; when my legs are too, I will bid you good night; and so kneel down before you; but, indeed, to pray for the queen." He knelt on the floor and I stood, acknowledging him.

"Sirs, you all have pleased me well. I look for more of Sir John in France. And so, good night."

Now there would be dancing. The stage was cleared, the actors removed their belongings, and the musicians took their places. The burned-out candles were replaced, and the watching chamber lightened.

Essex bent down in exaggerated courtesy and said to Eurwen, "Cousin, shall we dance a measure?"

Although she had never danced before, she learned quickly, her eyes sparkling. Soon others joined them and the floor was filled with dancers treading this slow and stately tune. Essex's wife sat forlornly on one side. She was suffering from the early stage of pregnancy and kept her hand over her stomach.

Later the dancing would become more lively, but for now older people and children ruled the floor.

When Eurwen and old Lord Buckhurst and Sir Henry Norris and their like had retired, Essex and I finally danced. It was a galliard, a dance I had once excelled at. It involved a fair amount of leaping and feinting, requiring strong legs and good balance. I could still do it, but I grew hot more quickly than I used to.

"After all this time, we still dance together well," I told him as we passed each other in a step.

He looked back at me quizzically. "Still?" he said. "I would say 'always.'"

"Whether it is always or no, that depends on you," I said. "I am nothing if not constant. It is you who is mutable."

---

The holidays over, the decorations and accoutrements—masks, staves, bells, papier-mâché unicorns, curtains for the plays—carted off by the master of revels to be stored in Clerkenwell Green, it was back to the workaday world. Shorn of our resplendent costumes, plain-dressed Essex met with a somberly dressed me in the privy chamber. It was time to talk of Ireland.

"How soon do you reckon you will be ready?" I asked him.

"Recruiting takes time," he said. "And procuring the victuals, especially as it is now winter, and—"

"I did not ask for excuses, I asked for a timetable." I hated to be so short with him, but there were many aspects to be covered.

"March," he said. "I will be ready in March. But the expenses—I am running into problems—"

"You are deeply in debt to the Crown, in spite of your income from the sweet wine monopoly and all your lands. You seek to borrow more?"

"If I could be granted the mastership of the Court of Wards, vacant now that Burghley is gone . . ."

"A very lucrative post. I haven't decided yet how to award it. Essex, you are familiar with the Bible verse about being faithful in small things before you can be entrusted with large ones? Your continual need for more and more money to meet your expenses bespeaks a lack of thrift and management and hardly recommends you for more."

"I have grave responsibilities," he said. "I can hardly be expected to foot the entire bill for the war. Someday, the state itself will be seen to be responsible for that."

"The state is responsible. I have been selling off Crown lands. Do not tell me I am not the one financing the war!"

"I did not mean that. Only that someday—"

"I will not require the repayment of the ten thousand pounds you owe me, not yet. Will that help?"

"Yes, certainly."

"Very well then, but it will become due. I am not forgiving the debt, merely postponing it."

"Your Majesty forgives very little," he said.

"You have noted this? Then mark it well." It was time I spoke what I knew.

Nay, more than time. I stood up, aware of how he towered over me. No matter. "You have behaved toward me in a treasonous fashion before the Privy Council. You know to what I refer. I have also heard of the rebellious insults you have directed at me, both in writing and in speech. Behind my back you have mocked, challenged, and implied that I am less than I am. If you thought these words would never reach me, you are naive."

His face was a mask like the ones from the late revels. He stared back at me.

"Therefore, let me say it once, and take heed. I have borne these insults to my person. But I warn you, do not touch my scepter. The moment you do so, I must carry out the law against you, regardless of my own feelings in the matter. You will enter into dangerous terrain."

"I don't know what you mean," he said.

"I think that you do. Remember, I did not wish to execute Mary Queen of Scots. But the law required it. She tried to touch my scepter."

He gave a nervous laugh. "Is it my fault foolish people link me to Bolingbroke or put up placards about my lineage? Should I be punished for their actions?"

"No, nor have you been. I am not speaking of what others say or do, only what you say or do." Behind his narrowed eyes I could almost feel his mind churning. "Enough of this. We understand each other. Now, as to your appointments for Ireland, whom do you have in mind?"

A broad smile now spread across his face as the subject turned away from himself. "I propose my stepfather, Sir Christopher Blount, as marshal of the army and a member of the Irish Council of State."

"Why, what experience has he had?" The harlot Lettice's husband! His primary experience was in cuckolding Leicester, I suspected.

"He's a good soldier. He led a column of land forces at Cádiz and Faro and performed well in the Azores expedition. He's in his late thirties, old enough to command respect from the soldiers under him, young enough to fight alongside them in the field. And, although I can't be sure, I think he did some service for Walsingham. He was brought up Catholic and had an entrée into those circles, making him useful as an informant. Of course, he can't talk about it."

"No," I said. "No, he isn't suitable."

Essex frowned. "He seems very suitable to me. And *I* have seen him in the field myself."

"And I haven't, you are saying. No, I've not been there. But one doesn't need to actually be somewhere to comprehend it. He can serve as an officer, that's all. And not on the Irish Council, either."

"As you say." His words were submissive, but not his tone. "I propose Henry Wriothesley, the Earl of Southampton, as my master of the horse, in charge of the cavalry."

"No," I said. "I don't think we need to discuss the reasons. We both know them."

"You do not trust my judgment," he said.

"I trust my own better," I replied. "I must think of England's needs, not yours."

"Let us, then, discuss the terms of my service, since you place so little faith in me," he said petulantly. "What are my duties, what are my constraints—besides, that is, not being able to choose my own officers?"

"Ah, now, that attitude is precisely what I meant. You speak insultingly to me but I, out of fondness and our cousinship, will overlook it." I paused to emphasize my words. "I am prepared to give you great scope in your position. You shall serve as my viceregal envoy in Ireland. That means you have the power to proclaim and punish traitors, award knighthoods, levy troops, issue pardons under my Great Seal, and take on all royal rights except issuing coinage."

For the first time in the interview, a genuine smile spread across his face. "Thank you, Your Majesty."

"However, you must rule through the Irish Council of State, not on your own. You must submit to their judgment. And I warn you—no more making knights for scant service. It is a bad habit of yours and I will have an end to it. It denigrates the office and makes knaves into 'Sirs.' Let someone truly earn it in Ireland, by bravery and might of arms."

"I bow to your judgment and conditions," he said.

This was the time when I should call for refreshments, have someone play the virginals to celebrate our agreement. But I wanted to press on through all the business. "I am thinking that the army itself should be around sixteen thousand, the cavalry around thirteen hundred. That will be the largest army I have gathered and sent in all my reign. I will put you in command of six thousand infantry. For the rest, five thousand should be used to fortify Dublin and the Pale, two thousand to garrison Connaught, and another three thousand to secure the south, Leinster and Munster."

"I will have only six thousand?"

"That is enough for your purposes. A larger army would have trouble marching to Ulster. The terrain is boggy, uneven, and filled with fords and narrow passes. And it is to Ulster you must go, and straightway. Land, gather your supplies, and march. Hunt O'Neill down. That is your mission."

"He will be waiting."

"Of course he will be waiting! Surprise is out of the question as our tactic. He knows we have to ferry an army and supplies across the sea. But he can only prepare up to a point. Take him on as soon as you can, when your men and horses are freshest and your supplies greatest. Ireland will sap them all. So strike fast."

*This woman thinks she's a general,* he was doubtless thinking. *But she's just an old creature who's never gone to Scotland, let alone across the water to Ireland. She's never seen a rebel or a battlefield. She never even saw any ships from the Armada!*

"Yes, Ma'am," he said.

I had read much of battles both modern and ancient, and that can teach a person about war. But it was also in my blood. I was the daughter of Henry VIII; I was descended from the Conqueror, and before that Arthur himself. I belonged on a battlefield, and I would know my way around one by instinct.

Now was the time to call for the refreshments. At last we were finished with business, and I had spoken openly and honestly to him.

He sat back, relaxing in his chair. It was a relief to have this behind us. If his powers were less than he would have liked, they probably still exceeded his expectations.

Before the drink and tidbits could arrive, a messenger asked leave to come in and see Essex. I asked him to speak, and he said simply, "Edmund Spenser has died. He gave up the ghost shortly after you left, my lord."

Essex went as pale as a ghost himself. Then he did something very odd for a Protestant. He crossed himself.

"Ireland killed him!" he cried.

# 63

# LETTICE

*January 1599*

He had seemed well enough this morning. I had seen him sitting on his bench in his room, drinking warmed ale, hunched in his blanket. He had looked up as I passed and given a wistful smile.

"Essex is off to Whitehall this morning to see the Queen," I told him. "When he returns, we will know what his fate is to be."

"May his fate be good and Ireland's bad," Spenser said.

It was bitterly cold, with a damp that deepened its sting. Just after Christmas London had been blanketed with snow, and now icy shreds of it clung to windowsills and steps and exposed tree roots. January 13, St. Hilary's Day, by tradition the coldest day of the year, was trying to live up to its reputation. I wished with all my heart that Spenser could tolerate a fire in his room, for that was the only way to provide warmth.

Robert had gone to face the Queen and finally speak directly about his commission. I had begged him to keep his head cool and his tongue under control. I could only pray that he would.

I asked Frances to join me in my chamber, so we could sit and sew to calm our nerves. I hated needlework, but it was very soothing when the mind was jumpy. I did not see enough of Frances and scolded myself for that, but she was so easy to overlook. I was pleased that she was expecting again. Except for little Robert, born soon after their marriage, there had been no others. Perhaps he shunned her bed, but he owed her more children. She was having a difficult time with this pregnancy, and I assured her that that meant a trouble-free child.

"A child who troubles you in the womb will never trouble you afterward," I said. "Elizabeth Vernon, now, she had such an easy nine months, but the girl cries all night long, and also"—dare I say it?—"looks like a monkey."

In spite of herself, Frances giggled. "She does, doesn't she?" she agreed. "And both her parents so pretty."

We spoke of other things, court gossip mainly, who was sleeping with whom, fashions, and so on. Mindless subjects to beguile the time. Frances surprised me with her keen interest in these things and her near-perfect recall of dates, names, and details. Perhaps she was not such a prig as I had thought her, or, like some overlooked people, she made it her business to revel in others' doings. She was the daughter of a spymaster, after all.

"I'll ask Spenser to join us," I said, after we had exhausted all pending liaisons and divorces. It was time to elevate the conversation.

But when I went to his room, I found him sprawled on the floor, toppled from his bench. His cheek was pressed against the stone floor, the dry rushes partially covering his mouth. They did not move with his breath.

Gently I turned his head and held my hand before his nostrils, but I felt nothing. His feathered hat was perched on a chair post; I hurriedly pulled a feather out and put it by his nose, but not a tendril of the feathers stirred. He was dead.

I took his hand; it was cold, but then, it had been cold all along. The poor, poor wretch! How Robert would grieve.

His death shocked me but did not surprise me. He had arrived a dead man, only going through the outward semblance of living.

"Farewell, friend," I whispered. "You leave us too soon." He was only forty-six.

---

In three days' time there was to be a grand funeral for the man called England's greatest living poet. He would be interred in the south transept of Westminster Abbey to lie beside our greatest poet, living or dead, Chaucer. Robert was paying all expenses. In the sorrow and busyness of preparing for the funeral, he had no time to speak of his interview with the Queen, other than to assure me it had gone well and he had been given nearly everything he had hoped for.

January 16 was a nasty day, with spitting sleet and clouds hanging so low over London they nearly pressed on rooftops. Tiny sparkles of frost clung to fence tops and weather vanes. It was fortunate the coffin could be taken to Westminster Abbey on foot rather than having to use a funeral barge, for ice chunks were drifting on the Thames, remnants of the recent freeze.

It was to be a poet's funeral, as a soldier would have a military one. Instead of marchers, trumpets, and drums, he would be escorted to the grave by fellow writers. They had composed elegies and poems to be read at the graveside.

The mourners took their places in the abbey. My allotted place was near the grave site; behind me I could see that the great nave was filling up. Spenser was revered by many more people than he had realized.

The Queen would not come, but she never attended funerals. She had not attended Sir Philip Sidney's or Lord Burghley's. Apparently nothing would induce her to make an exception. Perhaps by her age she had lost so many people she could stomach no reminders of it.

If possible, the gray stones of the abbey seemed to squeeze the cold out of the air and concentrate it. It was colder inside than out, and I could hear dripping of Stygian water from a column behind the altar. All around me, effigies of long-dead knights and ladies slept on their tomb tops as if on pallets.

From down the nave, the long doors were pulled open and the procession entered. The coffin began to make its way down the aisle. Even the pallbearers were writers. I recognized the florid, beefy face of Ben Jonson and the lordly ones of Francis Beaumont and John Fletcher. George Chapman was there, and on the other side, the last one on the right, was Will Shakespeare. As he passed, he happened to look right at me. I was unable to look away; then he passed, and all I saw was the back of his black hat.

The pallbearers were followed by columns of other writers. I recognized Nicholas Breton and Henry Constable—who had written sonnets to my granddaughter, but really to her mother, Penelope—Michael Drayton, John Donne (Egerton's young secretary, who dabbled in verse), Thomas Dekker, and Thomas Campion. But there were many others I did not know. Slowly, swaying as they walked, the black double line made its way to where the coffin now rested on a bier. The stone floor had been opened to create a grave. Beside it, Chaucer's gravestone had not been disturbed, and his vault was not visible. So Spenser and he would lie side by side, but their coffins would not touch. The coffin was lowered into the grave.

"Here we consign to the earth the remains of Sir Edmund Spenser," intoned the priest. But rather than proceeding to the usual funeral service, he said, "His fellows will present their eulogies."

The first one merely said, "Here lies the prince of poets in his time, whose divine spirit needs no other witness than the works which he left behind him."

Another stepped forward and said, "Here next to Chaucer, Spenser lies; to whom in genius next he was, as now in tomb."

Another, his face indistinguishable beneath his black hood, said, "Whilst thou did live, lived English poetry; which fears now thou art dead, that she shall die."

I heard a clicking sound, followed by a soft thud. As each man spoke, he threw his scroll with its verse into the grave, followed by his pen. It was a parallel ceremony to the traditional one in which servants of the

Crown throw away and break their white rods of office when the sovereign dies.

Now the famous poets took their turn reciting hastily composed eulogies. Most, as one would expect, were forgettable. The ones that were not may have been written at some other time, lying fallow and awaiting their public voice.

Young John Donne stepped forward and recited, in a strong voice that carried well, "Death, be not proud, though some have called thee mighty and dreadful, for thou are not so. . . ." The poem then went on to reach a conclusion that death itself must die.

But words are not facts. Spenser lay dead, and nothing could change that.

Will stepped up. His eulogy would doubtless be high-flown and awash in classical references. But no. He said, "In death, simple is best. A song suffices. A baby needs a lullaby and a dead man needs a sweet melody, to offset the odor of decay." He cleared his throat. "Hear me, Edmund."

*"Fear no more the heat o' the sun,*
*Nor the furious winter's rages;*
*Thou thy worldly task has done,*
*Home art gone, and ta'en thy wages.*
*Golden lads and girls all must,*
*As chimney-sweepers, come to dust."*

He ended with

*"Quiet consummation have,*
*And renowned be thy grave."*

Then he tossed the poem into the grave and threw his pen after it.

Following him, Thomas Campion fumbled with several sheets of paper, finally selecting one to read.

*"The man of life upright,*
*Whose guileless heart is free*
*From all dishonest deeds*
*Or thought of vanity:*
*Good thoughts his only friends,*
*His wealth a well-spent age,*
*The earth his somber inn*
*And quiet pilgrimage."*

*The earth his somber inn.* I did not want a somber inn; I wanted a banquet hall. The earth offered too many riches to turn my back on them.

The tomb was closed, the earth thrown onto the coffin and the pile of pens and parchment. Spenser was gone.

---

As befitted the patron of the burial, Robert was to provide the funeral feast at Essex House. Tables had been set up in the hall, laden with the requisite funeral meats, cakes, and drink. We had also provided warm ale and wine to offset the cold that had crept into everyone's bones in the unheated abbey. The hall's huge stone fireplace did its best to banish winter from the room, but only those standing directly in front of it would benefit from the heat.

Everyone but the Queen was here. It gave me great pleasure to realize that although I was barred from court, court had come to me. Even Robert's political adversaries from the Privy Council were present: Cecil, Raleigh, Admiral Howard, Cobham. All were united in their tribute to Spenser this day, overlooking all other allegiances. Egerton was here with his secretary Donne, who was reaping praise for his "Death" poem; old Lord Buckhurst, leaning on his cane, was eager to talk to the young poets; George Carey, young Hunsdon, ambled about—although in his sixties he was young only in comparison with his long-lived father.

The room was becoming so full that the heat rose and we did not need a fireplace. It also sounded very noisy to me. I have noticed that following a funeral people tend to speak louder than usual, to eat more, and to become drunker, as if the specter of death can be thrown off his scent that way, like a baffled hound.

"I had a better line," a voice spoke into my ear. "But it was only a line, and not a poem."

It was Will. He had laid aside his black mourning cloak and now was wearing everyday clothes. I looked at him, seeing merely a man in his midthirties, a man with a pleasant face. How does a lover revert to being an acquaintance? It had happened. It happened because I did not dwell on, did not conjure up, any memories of him in any other setting. They were as interred as Spenser.

"What was that line? I need to hear it, as death frightens me so." An acquaintance who was once more occupies a peculiar place in which no confession is out of bounds. Normal reticence is exempt.

"It struck me that death is like a stern officer of the law," he said. "My line is 'This fell sergeant, death, is strict in his arrest.'"

At first it seemed simple, obvious. Then I thought about each of its words.

"Sergeant": An officer of the law, carrying out a superior's orders. "Fell": Evil, vile. "Strict": Following orders with no leeway. "Arrest": A double meaning. Arrest meant "stop." It also meant taking someone into custody. Suddenly I pictured a sanctimonious, uniformed lackey strong-arming those he oversaw, with no appeal.

Yes, that was what death was. A stern arresting officer. But there was no judge, no prison, no fine, no law. He himself subsumed them all.

I grasped my neck. "You almost make me feel his hand on me."

"Death is all about us," he said. "We just don't see him."

"Your words help me to do so," I said. "Death will always have a face, and a uniform, for me from now on."

"I hope you recognize him. He may not oblige by dressing that way. Remember, the French swordsman who dispatched Anne Boleyn tricked her into looking in the wrong direction, so she did not see the sword coming." He shook himself as if to cast off death. "But to speak of life: I hear that my Lord Essex will be leading the army into Ireland. May all go well."

"I thank you," I said. "His fortune rests in the outcome. But tell me, what of your theater? I heard it had been dismantled because of a property dispute."

"You heard correctly. We took the timbers away to reassemble them in Southwark, beyond the jurisdiction of the city."

"Down with the bear pits and the cockfights," I said.

"There are other theaters there," he answered, a bit testily. "It provides for people's pleasures. Something has to. Desires do not vanish because authorities would find it more convenient if they did."

As we spoke, I found my guard against him dissolving and old memories flooding in. The sound of his voice; the very naturalness in standing next to him and talking to him—they shifted the ground under me.

"What is your next play?" I primly asked.

"I hate that question," he said. "In fact, I despise it."

"I'm sorry," I said contritely. "It was merely—"

"A polite question, asked unthinkingly. Everyone does it. We all have rote polite questions flung at us. I did the same, asking you about Essex and Ireland. Then our task becomes to parry those questions. Someday, perhaps, we will be strong enough not to ask them in the first place and brave enough to refuse to answer."

I felt whipped by a schoolmaster. "I shall cease to be polite, then. If you wish to tell me what you are working on, I would be pleased to hear, so I may anticipate it. Otherwise, I shall wait and see it when it appears in the theater and be surprised."

"It's no surprise," he said. "I promised at the end of *Henry IV, Part II* that I would continue the story into the reign of Henry V."

"I haven't seen *Henry IV*."

"Pity."

"For you or for me?"

"Both. For me, that I cannot talk to you about it. And for you, because I hope you would have enjoyed it."

I did not want to talk about his plays. I could talk about them to anyone. I wanted to know what he was doing, where he was living, whether his two children still survived, whether he returned to Stratford often. He seemed different, more disillusioned, more focused on his livelihood. Playfulness had abandoned him, leaving a wary man in its wake.

Christopher joined us, putting an end to whatever might have grown in our pause, our silence. "I think Southampton is about to be let out of Fleet Prison," he said jubilantly. "I know you will be the first to welcome him."

"I shall be standing at the door," said Will.

"By the way, what are you working on now?" asked Christopher.

---

The end of March, but the days were warm like summer. The army was ready, and Robert would leave London and head north for Chester, where the troops would be ferried across to Ireland. I was immensely proud of him, and so worried as well that I would have kept him at Essex House forever, being outfitted, gathering supplies, planning his campaign. Christopher was going too, and I had the same pride and fear for him, with this difference: His fate was only personal, affecting his family, whereas Robert's was political, affecting not only his family but also the court and the entire realm.

There was a ceremonial gathering at the top of the Strand, and then Robert rode out on his great bay, followed by the nobility and gentry serving under him. The day was clear and the sky as blue as summer. How tall and fair he looked in the saddle! He swept his hat off as throngs of people cried, "God save your lordship!" and "God speed!" and "To the honor of England!" The crowds followed the army for four miles, cheering all the way—or so I was told. Frances and I had returned to Essex House after Frances had held his seven-year-old namesake up to see his father, telling him, "There goes your father, to save Ireland!"

We had not been inside long when the sky darkened, as if a witch had ordered the sunshine to be masked. Rumbles of thunder rolled over the city. Then the heavens opened, spewing out rain and hail, but only at Islington, just as Robert and Christopher and the army had reached that spot. Of course, people immediately took it for an omen—a bad one.

"He will start out fair but end in darkness and water," they muttered.

Looking out the window at the darkness that gave no rain for us, I reminded myself—over and over—of the reasons why Robert had accepted this task. He had put them, very succinctly, in a letter to Southampton.

"Into Ireland I go. The Queen has irrevocably decreed it. The council passionately urges it. And I am tied in my own reputation."

And now he was gone, for fair or ill, and Christopher with him. Having just been released from prison, Southampton would follow shortly.

Of the quartet of friends, only Will stayed in London. True to his promise, he finished his play about Henry V and, to my surprise and delight, put a reference to Robert in it, equating him with the great warrior king. The opening chorus said, "Were now the general of our gracious empress, as in good time he may, from Ireland coming, bringing rebellion broached on his sword. . ." Whenever audiences heard that, they cheered. All the nation's hopes were bound up in Robert.

# 64

# ELIZABETH

*March 1599*

I watched from Whitehall as Essex and his troops paraded past, glowing in their distinctive tawny liveries. If looks could win a war, then the Irish did not stand a chance. There was no doubt about it: He could muster a following. Men who would never have gone to Ireland joined him, partly drawn by the promise of rewards he was known to be (too) generous with, and partly to share in the glory they believed he was sure to reap. Row upon row of them passed down the Strand, heads high and plumes waving, before turning to head north out of the city and on to Chester. The sun hit the silver trappings on their saddles and ornamental bridles, and the biblical phrase "terrible as an army with banners" came to mind.

Crowds ran alongside the mounted men, crying "God save Your Lordship!" and "All for glory!" So they had cried when I rode out during the Armada attack. But that was more than a decade ago, and it was Essex they called for now.

Growling thunder muttered off in the distance, but the sun still shone here. I stood silently as the army passed away, out of sight. Later we learned that the heavens had opened up and drenched them with rain and hail the moment they were beyond the London walls. Omen? Some said so.

---

And now we were to wait. Wait for the troops to sail, to land, and to make their way to Dublin. There the lord justices would administer the oath of loyalty and present Essex with the ceremonial sword of state. Only then would business begin, the campaign be launched.

As soon as he could assemble his troops, Essex was to march north and confront The O'Neill. It would to be difficult to stay here, motionless, awaiting news. I had never felt more helpless.

---

Easter came, and with it a glorious English spring—daffodils, cuckoos, violets, and lily of the valley. No matter what surrounded me, it was impossible for my heart not to soar in such beauty, returned after a long absence. It acted as balm for my fretfulness.

But soon came word that the Earl of Rutland, whom I had expressly forbidden to join Essex, had gone secretly. Instead of sending him back, Essex had welcomed him and made him colonel of foot soldiers, knighting him in the bargain. In addition, the moment Essex had his commission giving him the power of appointments, he had made Southampton his master of the horse. I immediately sent orders countermanding this and called Rutland home. And as for Southampton, I demanded his immediate demotion.

I found this challenge to my authority so disturbing that my sleep fled. I had looked Essex right in the eye and told him that he must not do this; he had done it anyway, as if his obedience ceased to exist once he was out of sight. What was I to do? I could not recall him; O'Neill must be answered. I must use one disobedient subject to chasten another. But after it was over, Essex must be dealt with.

Those left behind were more tractable. There were Robert Cecil, Charles Blount, Walter Raleigh, and Admiral Howard. The latter three had all fought in their time but, in declining to go to Ireland, were all that remained to shield me should Essex make a threatening move. I hated thinking this way, but no Tudor who was blind to the possibility of betrayal had retained the throne.

I ordered the florid dedication in Hayward's *The History of Henry the Fourth* to Essex, which stated, "You are great indeed, both in present judgment and in expectation of future time," to be ripped from all the remaining copies of the book. I also granted Robert Cecil the mastership of the Wards of Court. He had earned it; he would use it wisely. Let Essex howl when he found it beyond his grasp.

There is always routine business to be attended to, even when great matters are at hand. Learned men have noted how, at a death, the widow will concern herself with minute aspects of the household, whether that cupboard door is aslant or that sack of flour tied well about the neck, when all the while her husband lies dead in the upper chamber. Just so it was with me. While all hung in the balance in Ireland, I busied myself with playing the virginals, attending concerts, taking little Eurwen on boat rides to show her London from the water, and inventorying my wardrobe.

I never discarded any gowns, although I often gave them away to the ladies who served me. Since my measurements never changed and I neither shrank nor expanded, being exactly the same height and breadth I was upon my accession, everything still fit. But I could never wear all of them again, even though they fit, for they were styled for a younger person. And I did not want to make sacred relics of them. I bestowed them on the startled Eurwen.

"Are you absolutely sure?" Marjorie asked. "I do remember when you first wore that green velvet, that day by the river."

I embraced Eurwen. "I am sure. It belongs on a girl, and that I am long past."

"Godmother, you are too generous," she said. "In Wales, when will I wear it?"

"It is not valuable," I lied. "Wear it when the sun rises one morning and you awake feeling special, for no reason at all. Wear it in the fields and at the supper table, and think of me."

All told, there were some three thousand gowns. "Enough for almost ten years, if I changed costumes every day," I said. Perhaps I should make a point of it. Perhaps if I did that, I would ensure my life for the next ten. There were tales about such things, a task that had to be completed before death could come. I seriously considered it, not for that reason but because I wished to wear all of them once more before . . . before I could not.

I looked at the piles of gowns. My horizon had changed. I had never thought of wearing, or doing, anything for the last time. No! I would not think of it now!

---

News began to trickle in from Ireland, and it was bad. Shocking. Several messengers arrived with posts of Essex's great victories. But there were no victories. He had taken what amounted to a Progress through the south and west of Ireland, instead of heading north to Ulster. The Irish Council had convinced him that it was too early to go north, that there would not be sufficient grass yet to sustain the horses. The cattle, to be used for food, were all in southern Ireland and could not be rounded up because that area was in the hands of the rebels and, besides, they were still thin from the winter. Therefore, before they could take on The O'Neill, they had to retake the south.

That was their argument. I suspected that some who had been part of the council for some time had their own vested interests in giving this advice. They all had property there! Essex listened to them, as it suited him to get his feet wet in this way before turning to his real task.

So he marched his men out, going through Leinster and then into Munster, making many futile attempts to engage the enemy but mainly being greeted as a hero in towns where nothing was achieved but empty ceremony.

His one victory, if you could call it that, was to take the castle of Cahir from some rebels. In the meantime, his officer Sir Henry Harrington was defeated at Wicklow, with half his troops deserting, and the governor of Connaught, Conyers Clifford, defeated and killed in the most gruesome way, with his head hacked off and sent to the Prince of Donegal. It was a loss almost as great as the one at Yellow Ford—three thousand soldiers gone.

It was now July, and Essex's forces had melted like snowmen, shrunk by desertions and disease. From the original number of foot soldiers, there remained only thirty-five hundred; of cavalry, three hundred. And he had the nerve to request two thousand more troops!

I may have been so angry before. It is possible. But I believe I was angrier now than I had ever been. This fool, having stripped the kingdom of money to support the expedition, was losing the war for England before it even began.

Oh, how The O'Neill must be laughing. How Hugh O'Donnell must be commissioning ballads about it. How the Prince of Donegal must be drinking toasts to Clifford's head, set up in his Great Hall. How England and its Queen must be mocked from Lough Foyle in the north to Kinsale in the south. That I, who had bested Philip and the might of Spain, was now the plaything of the wild Irish and of my own wayward subject!

Oh! The impotent fury I felt, when I could do nothing but clench my fists and curse at them, hundreds of miles away.

There were letters, of course. That was my only way of reaching them, and they were so slow and ineffective. But I poured all my scorn and invective into one. I hunched over my writing table, my glasses (which I needed now to read but did not like to admit to) perched on my nose, my pen digging into the paper with the force of my trembling hand.

I am known for my "answers answerless," my way of using subterfuge to both conceal and state my meaning. But not now. I could hardly find words blunt and strong enough to directly express myself.

No lavish greeting. Instead:

*From Her Majesty to the Lord Lieutenant.*

*We who have the eyes of foreign princes upon our actions and the hearts of our people to comfort and cherish—who groan under the burden of the cost of this war—can little please ourself with anything that has been achieved so far.*

*For what can be more true than that your two months' journey has brought in not a capital rebel against whom it would have been worthy to have adventured one thousand men? You would have scorned anyone else who claimed a great victory from taking such a castle as Cahir from a rabble of Irish rogues. And with all the cannon and materiel at your command!*

*If only you knew, and could hear, how The O'Neill has boasted to all the world of the defeats of your regiments, the deaths of your captains, and the loss of officers.*

*But are your losses so surprising? You have assigned strategy and regiments to inexperienced young men who want glory but have no idea of battle. Be assured, our hands are not tied, and we will undo these appointments and strip those honors you have inappropriately bestowed, against our express orders.*

*Your letter disgusts us. You baby yourself with all your troubles—that you have been defeated, that poor Ireland suffers because of you—blind to the fact that you are the cause of them.*

*And when we call to mind how far the sun has run its course, how much time has been lost, how much depends on this one thing, the defeat of The O'Neill, without which all the other things we have achieved in Ireland are like the wake of a boat in water, quickly vanishing without a trace, we order you, plainly, according to the duty you owe us, with all speed to march north. You must lay the ax to the root of this tree from which all the treacherous stock has sprung elsewhere in the country. Otherwise we have grave cause to regret our entrusting this task to you and will be condemned by the world for embarking on this enterprise without more care and forethought.*

*Although we formerly granted leave for you to return to England without prior permission—assuming that Ireland was quiet and you had duly appointed deputies to cover your duties—we now rescind this permission. On no account must you return until we grant you a new license, and that not until the northern action has been undertaken.*

*At the court of Greenwich, the nineteenth of July, 1599.*

There was more. I am reciting it from memory now, summarizing it. But I think I have captured its main meaning. I sent it as fast as mortal means could carry it.

I was adamant that he should not return, excusing himself, posturing before crowds, until he had carried out my orders. He was a deserter ever. I would not allow him to desert his post this time.

---

In the meantime we had a glorious summer in England. All the rain must be falling in Ireland, for we had fair weather and mild sunny days. After four failed, soaked harvests in a row, we were finally granted a reprieve. Flowers shot up in the royal gardens, hollyhocks and Canterbury bells taller than I, boxwood spreading thickly and robustly with glossy new leaves, spears of lavender waving in the gentle breezes. Boats plied the Thames, banners flying, and people thronged the river footpaths. In the open fields, archers practiced at the butts and falconers trained their birds.

"The last summer of this century," said Marjorie, as we strolled along the riverbanks at Greenwich, our guards discreetly following. Flocks of children came up to me, and I welcomed them. Their elders looked on, hesitating to approach, but I waved them over and spoke to each one. Overhead the soft clouds drifted, aimless as youths let out of school.

"It will be hard to write '16' instead of '15,'" said Catherine, hurrying along. Her short legs meant she had to use more steps to keep up with us. "My pen has a will of its own."

"It will be strange to think of its being 1600. I did not think I would ever see it," Marjorie said. "To live a long time is to taste of the tree of the knowledge of good and evil. A dubious blessing?"

---

In the lovely lull that is twilight, we returned to the palace, there to find our peace shattered. A messenger delivered a letter to Marjorie, straight from Ireland. With misgivings, she took it. News from Ireland is never good. Before opening it, she sat down. Then, slowly, cautiously, she broke the seal and read, quickly.

The letter fluttered to the floor and she stared dumbly across the room, seeing us no longer. She was silent, as we are after true devastation. Her arm hung limply, her hand suspended over the letter.

I bent and picked it up. She did not protest. Indeed, she seemed not to see me.

My eyes flicked over the writing. Without my glasses, it was hard to read. But I could make out the important things: Thomas Norris, governor of Munster, and his brother, Henry, had both died. They had both been wounded on August 16. Thomas had died quickly, but Henry had survived an amputation and lived another five days. Thomas had died in Henry's arms.

Six soldier sons, and now five of them gone, four claimed by Ireland.

Marjorie slumped in the chair, unmoving. I motioned to Catherine to help me move her to a place where she could lie down. Together we took her into my chamber and laid her upon my bed. There she could remain as long as she wished.

One son left. I would order him home from his post in the Netherlands. It was all I could do. Once again I was helpless when it mattered most. The tree of the knowledge of good and evil. Its fruit was bitter indeed.

# 65

Now the war had invaded my own chambers, felling Marjorie. She awoke from her sleep on my bed an altered woman—hesitant where she had been sure-footed, diffident where she had been outspoken. Even her voice changed. Her hearty laugh and booming timbre were replaced by a quiet, low tone. It is said that grief can turn someone's hair stark white overnight. That is, of course, impossible, since the ends cannot change. But from that night on, the part in her hair was white as a swan's wing, and as her hair grew, the white spread.

Sir Henry came in from the country to be with her. He, too, had changed. For the first time he looked like what he was—an old man. He was in his seventies, one of those men who kept his vigor and strength, but now it was drained away. He almost shuffled, and when he embraced his wife, they leaned on each other, sustained by their tragedy.

"Take her home, Sir Henry," I said. "Take her home."

I hoped she would recover, but in bidding them farewell I felt a great finality, the clanging of a door. I had not been able to tell my dear companion good-bye, for she had vanished in a trace, replaced by a broken stranger.

---

It is usually difficult to carry out duties with a heavy heart, but the challenge of the council chamber and the war served to rescue me, for in those hours I could not think of myself or of my dear Crow. I had to concentrate all my faculties on the desperate problems abroad. Word was that Philip III, the new Spanish king, was eager to continue his father's fight against England, and pursue it with considerably more vigor than that old, ailing monarch. He was readying yet another Armada (dear God, was there no end to the timber available for their shipbuilding?), first to strike at our shores and then to land in Ireland. That made it all the more imperative that Ireland be secured, and quickly.

But nothing was quick in Ireland, except excuses. I was told that Essex still had not set off for the north.

"By God's breath, if that man does not obey and go, I shall have him hanged!" I cried in council.

"Ireland is a great bog, in every way," said Cecil. "All reputation, honor, and action is swallowed up."

"I have received word that he has knighted eighty-one men!" I fumed. "Eighty-one, when I warned him against knighting without merit. The Irish are joking, 'He made more knights than he killed rebels.' There has been no fighting, nothing deserving the honor of knighthood. Essex awards it for strapping on a sword! Even my godson, John Harington, has been knighted, and he's done nothing so far. *I* had better bestowed it for his invention of the ajax! That contraption is more worthy!"

"Calm yourself, Your Majesty," said Admiral Howard. "You have the power to undo them all."

"I do not have the power to undo the blow to our reputation that Essex has rendered!"

Besides the admiral, Raleigh and Charles Blount were still in England, and they could serve as commanders to counter whatever Spain sent against us. Blount was a promising military man. It was ironic that Essex had vetoed the idea of my appointing him to lead the Irish campaign, on the grounds that he was too inexperienced, too low-ranking, and too "drowned in book learning." In an able man inexperience is soon remedied by action, a bullet does not know the difference between an earl and a yeoman, and one could do worse than study the battle tactics of Caesar.

"No, Essex will have to do that."

To think that England's fate was in his fumbling hands.

---

As if to underscore the stakes of our future, a crowd of unwelcome guests arrived and would not depart. By that I mean a host of weaknesses and decrepitudes to which I would not give diplomatic recognition and that I hid as best I could. I have already mentioned the glasses I needed to read. Without them print swam and turned into squiggling worms. Still, I kept them in a small purse and only pulled them out when absolutely necessary, and never in front of foreign envoys.

Practical people like my Catherine would tell me to be of good cheer, reminding me that great men who lived in an age before glasses had no help for the condition. "If Cicero had not been executed, he soon would have killed himself, as he would no longer have been able to read," she said.

"So he should have been thankful he was condemned to early death?" I asked.

"That is certainly one way to look at it," she answered. "And Marc Antony—he must have been almost blind."

I laughed, thinking of Antony groping like a mole. "He did not read much anyway, Catherine," I said. "And yes, I am thankful for this crutch, as any crippled man is, but I resent my lameness."

"At least you are not truly lame. You ride and hunt and dance well. Much better than . . ."

"Than others my age? Is that what you mean?"

"Well, yes." She looked down at her shoes.

Aha. That meant no one, not even Catherine, was aware of the sprain in my ankle that had bothered me for weeks and seemed never to mend. I felt as if I were hobbling but took great pains to force my steps briskly.

And then there were my looks. I have heard an absurd tale that I never allowed mirrors in my chambers and never saw myself in one past a certain age. It must have started because I banished portraits that were unflattering (some said realistic). It is wisdom to mask one's weaknesses from others, but only a fool masks them from herself. And I saw, all too clearly, how the color had left my face and the shadows—that in a younger person merely meant a sleepless night—never left the hollows under my eyes, no matter how rested I was. Oh, I saw, and did my best to disguise it, with the finest-ground pearls and talc mixture, with false roses made from ground carnelian. My hair, once glorious red-gold, had faded like my cheeks and was a ghost of its beauty, a wan reminder of what once was. So I never appeared in public without a wig, and I had many of them, in many different styles.

There were other things, not so easily disguised, that troubled me. More and more I felt currents were moving fast, moving beyond me, and that I had become old-fashioned, out of step. The clamor from the House of Commons, wanting to make legislation that had not been proposed by me, trying to tread on my prerogative. The notion, abroad in some countries, that they did not need a hereditary monarch with royal blood at all but could elect a commoner to serve as one just as well. (Look at Poland!) The religious sects that claimed no priest of any sort was needed, or other strange ideas about each person being his own priest, and even some that denied the Trinity. The explorations that were stretching us like a piece of leather, nailed to the far corners of the map—the Northwest Passage in the upper left corner, Drake's passage in the lower left, Muscovy in the upper right, the East Indies in the lower right. England must play her part in all these places, but how? We could not even manage Ireland close to home.

I found myself alert to what others denoted as signs of aging. Sleeping during the day. Walking into a room and forgetting what one has come in there to get. Reminiscing about the golden days of yore and how things have deteriorated since then—the manners of the young, the workmanship of craftsmen, the morals of women. Even if I agreed, I did not voice it.

One day I happened upon a letter in which someone wrote that "the giving over of long voyages is noted to be a sign of age," and it struck worry into my breast, as I had lately found Progresses to be too draining and time-consuming. Especially this year, I thought to stay at my post, ever watchful. But on the spot I decided that I would make an extended Progress after all. Perhaps it would be helpful if I rode out among the people again, those people who kept cheering for Essex, and remind them of who their ruler was and what a true sovereign looked like. I would go south, staying in the maritime counties that were threatened by sea, so that I would not lose sight of the danger and would be ready to respond.

The only concession I would make—and this could not be blamed on age—was to have a smaller train of people with me. So many men were away in Ireland, and there were fewer women attending on me these days, and Marjorie was gone. Logistically it would be an easier Progress because we could stay in smaller homes and move more quickly between them.

The plan called for me to travel south from London into Surrey, then turn eastward into Kent. This would allow me to inspect the defenses at the Cinque Ports—Sandwich, Dover, Hastings, Hythe, Romney—along the coast where the Channel was narrowest—and also the fortifications my father had built in Deal and Walmer when he was threatened by the French.

---

We were ready and set out on a fair day in late August. My usual number of carts had been cut to a fourth, and as we rode slowly across London Bridge people thronged us, crying out so joyfully that I never would have known their lips knew how to cry "Essex!" We passed under the Great Stone Gateway, the place where traitors' heads bristled like porcupine quills upon spikes. These were old enough to be unrecognizable.

From the gateway we passed onto the wide road that served as the high street for Southwark. It funneled all foot and animal traffic heading for London from the south up this way, and it was always crowded with carts, horses, herds of sheep, and people, although today they were held back for us.

As we rode slowly down the high street a boy with a placard came running out, holding it up and crying, "*Julius Caesar! Julius Caesar!* See it now at the Globe!"

I stopped and motioned him over. "Tell me, lad, who wrote it?"

"One of the company, Will Shakespeare," he said. "It's just opening. You should stop and see it!"

"Perhaps on my way back," I said. He must know full well I never attended public theaters, but what was the harm in asking if someone were ready to try something new? "Has he then left our glorious history?" I asked. His last play had been about King Henry V. Perhaps he felt it was dangerous to encroach any closer upon modern times. I must ask for a copy of *Henry V.* I wanted to comb it for references. I knew it mentioned both Essex's traitorous ancestor the Earl of Cambridge and Essex himself.

We left the environs of the Globe behind as we continued south past Southwark's markets spreading out on either side of the road. I was pleased to see that the vendors' baskets were brimming with apples, cabbages, leeks, carrots, pears, cheese, and eggs. At last the heavens had smiled upon my land and blessed her with plenty, after four lean years of biblical proportions. That warmed me as much as the sunlight pouring down on my head.

Farther off the road lay St. Thomas's hospital, once run by monks and nuns, now by lay doctors. It tended to the poor, homeless, and diseased. When the monasteries were dissolved there had been great fears about what would happen to the charitable institutions they left behind. But fifty years later, most of them had been taken up by others.

Still within sight of the river, this area was bucolic. Open fields, groves of trees, cottages, and greens made it feel a world away from London, although the Tower was visible across the water. Now we were out in the true countryside, and I felt myself lose the feeling of captivity I had in the city. We would head toward Croydon, stay with Sir Francis Carew at his manor of Beddington, then stop at Nonsuch on our way toward the coast.

Sir Francis had a medium-sized manor, and I was pleased that my smaller entourage could fit in there. Along with me was Catherine, of course, and my old friend Helena, whom I saw too seldom, Eurwen (whom I could not seem to send back home), Raleigh, and his ever-faithful Percival. Catherine's husband, the admiral, promised to join us at Nonsuch for a few days. It was as jolly an outing as I could make in these times.

Sir Francis Carew was one of those curious creatures, a lifelong bachelor. No more curious than a virgin queen, I suppose, but it is so rare it causes comment. Since we were about the same age, there was little chance either of us would change our state. He had been a faithful but unremarkable courtier much of his life, serving me on minor missions and staying clear of factions and politics, although his family ties were to the Throckmortons and hence to Raleigh, through Bess.

As we trotted down the lane, the clattering of our horses alerted our host, and he dispatched a line of servants, attired all in scarlet and black, to stand along the way and greet us. He himself waited at the entrance, his arms held wide like a welcoming father. When he saw us, he swept to the ground, his white head bent low.

"Up, Sir Francis," I said. "We are delighted to be here, to partake of your hospitality."

"The delight is mine, Your Majesty," he said, rising to his feet, his sunburned face cracking with his wide smile. "May this be your home for however long you choose to abide with us." It was a question, but a diplomatically asked one.

"It cannot be for more than three days, I am sad to say," I told him. No need to keep him in suspense or make him lay in unnecessary supplies. "But three days can be sweet enough."

"Indeed," he said.

He welcomed Raleigh with "Nephew!" and clapped him on the back. He stared at Percival until Raleigh introduced him. He bowed gravely to Catherine and to Helena, then, with exaggerated courtliness, bowed to Eurwen and said, "So you are the Queen's goddaughter. You look much as she did at your age. One would think you were of her own family." Eurwen blushed and lowered her eyes.

Seeing the great line of wagons following us, he gave brisk orders that they could park and unload in the barns at the edge of the park. "Although I think I have everything for your comfort," he said, "try us first, before you unpack."

I always insisted on my own bed, but perhaps tonight I would try to do without it. After all, is that not another notorious sign of aging—rigid, fixed habits? I must fight it. "Very well, but that might be dangerous. We may appropriate your things if they please us too much!" I warned him.

The chamber he had set aside for me and my ladies was unused. I saw no telltale signs of his having just vacated it himself. It was spacious and overlooked the extensive orchard on the east side of the house. A magnificent bed stood waiting, its layers of linen, blankets, and counterpanes swelling it like a woman near her time of delivery. The canopy was carved on its underside, and the curtains were of green and gold tapestry. It was not quite as fine as mine, but it came close. And there were regular beds for Helena and Catherine and Eurwen. They would not have to sleep in truckle beds.

He had provided a writing desk well stocked with ink, pens, wax, and paper. Another table, inlaid with ebony, stood waiting for jugs or pitchers of drink. A discreet adjoining chamber held the washing and privy implements.

A bit later he invited us to stroll with him in his garden.

"Twilight is the best time to visit a garden, and at this time of year, twilights are long," he said.

"Sir Francis," I said, "we like our chamber well."

He smiled. The man had the most winsome smile I had seen—it came from deep inside. "I have set it aside for you from the beginning," he said. "It was worth the wait." We were descending the stairs and he looked over at me—to make sure I did not stumble? "It has been waiting your entire reign, wearing the title 'The Queen's Room.'"

"It has stood empty all that time?"

"No, others have been allowed to use it. That is because I knew that when Your Glorious Majesty came, it would burn away the traces of the others as the sun burns away mist. However, after this, no one will be allowed to use it, lest it be sullied."

He was so serious I feared he meant it. "I am not sullied so easily as that, Sir Francis," I assured him. "It would be a waste of an exquisite room."

"Is a shrine a waste?" he asked, puzzled.

We had reached the main floor, and I decided not to pursue the subject further. If he wished to keep a shrine, so be it. I only hoped he would not enter the chamber after we departed with an open jar to capture my breath, as papists did for their Virgin. I looked back; my ladies were not laughing, but I knew it was difficult for them to suppress a giggle.

We swept out into the garden. The last rays of the sun were still slanting across the gravel paths with their boxwood borders, touching them with gold. I could hear the splashing of a fountain somewhere in the distance. The gravel crunched; Raleigh and Percival had joined us.

"When I began the gardens—which had gone to ruin when the property was in dispute—I thought very conventionally. It was only the middle of the century, after all, and I was hardly in the forefront of fashion. Hence, this knot design, which will make you yawn. Planted with the usual: dwarf box, black yew, and lavender."

I looked at them, and he was right. They were so predictable one did not need to look at them at all.

"But . . ." He turned and riveted his eyes on me. "My kinsman Walter has opened my eyes to wider vistas. Come!"

He led us out of the railed, neatly patterned garden and into an alley of trees that were shoulder high, lined up like soldiers. They resembled plums and cherries in their branch pattern, but their leaves were brighter green and waxier.

Raleigh smiled. "I jested about the king of Spain being the king of oranges and figs," he said. "Now he will be unique only in being king of figs. For soon Your Majesty will be Queen of oranges as well as apples, pears, plums, and apricots." He took one of the leaves and rubbed it hard. "This is an orange tree, and it has thrived here—with help from Sir Francis. I brought some orange seeds back from my Cádiz mission and persuaded him to plant them. That was three years ago, and thanks to his invention"—he pointed to a row of canopies on wheels—"they have survived our winters."

"When it gets cold, I cover them with these movable shelters," said Francis. "It has enabled them to take root here and grow. In a few years, God willing, they will flower and bring forth that joyous orange fruit."

"My subjects are ever inventive," I said. "But oranges in England? Who would have thought it possible?"

"I am calling this an orangerie. For obvious reasons," said Francis. "I hope you will return for the first picking. I will stew up a dish swimming with oranges for you."

"It would be an honor," I said. But how many years would that be? Would I even be traveling by then? Then, the forbidden thought: Would I even be alive?

"There is yet another invention," said Raleigh. "But it falls to our host to unveil it."

"Tomorrow, tomorrow," he said. "Enough marvels for today."

I agreed. The sun had fled the sky, turning the undersides of a bank of clouds pink-gold. I was ready for night's rest.

---

Our chamber proved just as comfortable in practice as it had seemed on first glance. Wearily I let Helena pull off my day clothes and dress me in my sleeping gown, setting my bed cap on my head. The low, patterned ceiling made us feel safe and snug. Several candles were burning, their flames steady in the quiet air.

"We are not so far from Hever Castle," said Catherine suddenly. "Have you ever visited it?"

Hever Castle: seat of the Boleyn family and the home of Mary and Anne Boleyn.

"No, that I have not," I admitted.

"Would you consider going there this time, together?" she asked. "I have seen it only once, from the outside, when I was still a child. The family was gone then."

Indeed they were. My grandparents had died soon after my mother, and the property became the Crown's. Anne of Cleves lived in it briefly. Since then it had acquired new owners.

"I don't know," I said. I did not know if I could stand it. Yet at the same time I longed to see the place where my mother had been young, before she had known the world. To make a sentimental journey, revisiting the past . . . another earmark of aging. Putting together the puzzle of the past, then, important only as one's own life closed down. "But as it would mean much to you . . ."

"It would. I never saw my grandmother Mary; she died before I was born, far away from her old life in east Essex. It seems the family was so smitten and scattered that we could never come together again. Now we can finally go back. Together. We'll hold hands and lay those ghosts to rest."

If only we could. They were restless, those spirits, cut off from any finality. Was the old castle overgrown, sleeping, like the enchanted ones in tales? Had the vines been growing since the Boleyns ceased to be? Had the moat dried up? What would we find?

There was no trace of the sensual Mary Boleyn in this granddaughter; at least none that I could see. Perhaps the admiral would differ in his opinion. As for me, they say I have my mother's eyes, dark and challenging. Our ancestors live on in us, calling us back to their territory, daring us to meet them on their ground.

"Very well," I said. "We'll alter our itinerary. Hever is only about twenty miles from here, and more or less on our way."

A little frisson of dread and excitement ran through me at the thought of this personal pilgrimage.

# 66

he day was brilliant with sun and radiating warmth. Sir Francis sent word that nothing was planned until early afternoon, when he would host a banquet in the orchard. Until then, we were free to do as we would.

"Ladies, to our country clothes!" I said. "No ruffs, no stays, no dark colors, and nothing that will tear on brambles—or if they tear, no matter." I felt giddy as a girl, able this morning to pretend I was not a queen but the country exile I had been as a child, living at Hatfield, Hunsdon, Eltham, and Woodstock, free to romp in meadows.

This day I did not even wish to hunt—too organized, too formal. Instead we would walk along the Wandle River, following its banks, and then into the woods of the deer park. I wore sturdy deerskin boots and a wide-brimmed sun hat, took a stick for walking, and bade everyone follow me.

At first Helena and Eurwen were right beside me, keeping up easily. Helena was fifty now, but her hardy Swedish stock meant she still retained her long-necked beauty, clear complexion, and vigor. I complimented her on her health, and she replied, "Even after all these years in England, I go by what my mother taught me in Sweden: A brisk walk before breakfast will add ten years to your life."

"I, too, swear by a walk before breakfast," I said. "I keep ambassadors waiting, but I am not myself until I've had my exercise. And I dare not face them without all my wits about me."

Helena smiled. "I doubt that you are ever separated from your wits."

"You have seen me in a fog or two," I reminded her. She had served me for many years. Now she was a quasi-relative. Soon after she was widowed she had married one of my Boleyn cousins, Thomas Gorges. Their first child, Elizabeth, was another of my godchildren.

"Did you bring Elizabeth?" I asked her. "It has been too long since I have seen your daughter, my namesake."

"Indeed I did," said Helena. "She is back there keeping company with some of the young men."

"Like her mother," I teased Helena. "Let's bring her up here. I want two of my goddaughters to meet." Turning to Eurwen, I said, "I told you I had many, and I look out for all of them."

A few minutes later Helena's daughter caught up with us, crashing through the brush alongside the path. She skidded to a halt and curtsied. Her hat flopped forward. "Your Majesty," she panted. She was the antithesis of her refined, stately mother. The only trait they shared was shiny golden hair.

"My Elizabeth," I said. "I have not had the pleasure of seeing you in a good while. Your godmother craves more attention, or she will feel forgotten. Here, I wish you to meet your sister in God, Eurwen. She is from Wales."

Eurwen smiled and bobbed her head. Elizabeth clapped an arm around her shoulder. "Do you speak English?" she asked.

"I am learning. . . ." The two of them meandered to one side of the path together.

"Just so were we once," said Helena.

"A hearty crop," I said. "You must come to court more often so I can know all your children." I had given Helena and her husband the old royal manor of Sheen, near Richmond Palace. "You are right close when we are at Richmond."

The footpath followed the riverbanks for a mile or two, curving with its curves, hugging the reedy shallows, alive with birds. From this angle Beddington Manor glowed a contented red, its roofs gleaming, its weather vanes catching the sun as they turned.

Soon we entered the woods of the deer park; oaks and alders closed over us, making a green shade. We were past the time of woodland flowers, and the forest floor held only green underbrush, some laden with berries. Creatures still scurried underfoot, vanishing with a flourish of their tails when they heard us. Instinctively we lowered our voices, hushed ourselves as if in a cathedral.

Suddenly I knew someone was right beside me; I felt breath on my neck. Jerking my head around, I found Percival only a few inches from my face. My heart leaped, then felt as if it stopped.

"Is he silent, or is he not?" Raleigh came up on my other side. "It's something the natives in America learn at an early age. They can stalk an animal so quietly it never has a chance to get away."

"Sides. Feet," said Percival, holding his foot aloft. He turned it at a slant and showed me how he walked on the edges of his feet, soundlessly.

"It works better with soft shoes, or barefoot," said Raleigh.

I would like to see Percival hunt the Indian way. I wondered how he tracked a deer or rabbit. They were so alert to motion. That is why we used beaters to frighten them and chase them toward us or into a blind. But to do it alone and on foot—remarkable.

"You long to return there," I said. "You are half in love with America." His expression told me I was right. "But we cannot spare you here. Not in these times."

"I know," he said.

"Do you think there is anything left of your holdings in Ireland?" I asked.

"There is not," he said. "I am virtually certain of it."

"You lived there and have seen the Irish better than most people. In your opinion, is there any remedy?"

"Only extreme measures," he said. "Annihilation. Bloodbaths. They respect nothing else."

"Are you saying, then, that they are indomitable? Unconquerable?"

"Any people can be conquered," he said. "There is no such thing as unconquerable. It depends on how many you are willing to kill. How high a price you are willing to pay."

His old bluster was gone, faded out of him. His handsome face was lined now, and early streaks of gray were threaded through his hair. He had grown up, my seafarer. "Bess. How is she?" I found myself asking.

A bit of his old smile curved his lips. "She is well, Your Majesty."

"And young Walter?"

"Six years old, and already a seaman. He'll fight in your navy one day."

"If he does well, I'll knight him for it," I said. It was time to put away my pique toward Bess. It had all happened many years ago. "I shall always need good sailors."

Out ahead the woods opened into fields where the deer, flushed out of their coverts, could be chased easily. Sunlight danced on the waving meadow grasses. But it was coming almost straight down, meaning that it was near noon, time to return to the manor.

When we arrived back, Francis greeted us heartily. "Only once a decade, no, once a lifetime, do the gods favor us with such exquisite weather. Even Solomon in all his wisdom, even Augustus in all his glory, could not have commanded a day like today! Oh, Your Majesty, how honored I am that you are here this day to share it with me!"

He then led us out past the house to the orchard, where long tables were set up in the shade, running almost its entire length. There was a seat of honor for me, but it was trimmed in meadow flowers rather than tapestry, and a crown of flowers waited at my place.

"I had hoped you would lay aside your regular crown and wear this instead, as our Faerie Queen presiding over her outdoor fête."

Blue cornflowers, violet windflowers, green columbines were twined together to make a circlet. Laughing, I put it on. But I knew it would become young Eurwen or Elizabeth Gorges better.

My closest attendants were seated on either side of me, near Francis. Raleigh, my official bodyguard, was closest to my person. On my other side, my closest relative, Catherine. I treasured our secret decision to seek out the Boleyn seat together, as descendants of the two sisters. I reached over and squeezed her hand briefly as if to signal, *I have not forgotten.*

We were seated in the apple area of the orchard; the leaves filtered out the fiercest rays of the sun, but dappled light fell on the table. Above us, branches dipped and swayed with their load of apples, wafting the musty, hot smell of autumn foliage toward us.

"I've had a first pressing!" said Francis, flourishing a pitcher. "Early cider. It's still apple juice at this point, but tasty nonetheless." He had his servers pour for us. The frothy, turbid brown liquid smelled of crushed fruit.

Raleigh rose. "Sir Francis is being modest. He will not tell us, but he is a fervid gardener and is experimenting with many types of plants. The oranges, for one. He has several varieties of pears—the midsummer kind that ripen early, and the 'watery' pears that are oozing with juice, and the wild hedge pear with its bitter juice for making perry. He grafts many different types onto one stock so he can compare the yield more accurately. And there are many other treasures in his gardens. I could not recount them all. I have a keen interest in foreign plants, and he has kindly agreed to cultivate some to see how they flourish here."

"It is never a chore to do what one loves," said Francis. "My plantings give me pleasure."

"Indeed, God himself walked in a garden and found it soothing. That was before there were thorns, weeds, and brambles," I said. "Sir Walter is correct. One may not boast of oneself, but it is no shame to boast of the deeds of another. It is my father who is also the father of England's present-day orchards, for in the same year as I was born he sent his fruitier to the Continent to bring back the best new varieties of apples, pears, and cherries, since the wars had so devastated our old stocks. He set up a farm at Teynham to serve as a model, and from there the stock that flourished was sent out. So if today Kent and Surrey are our prize gardens and the source of much of our produce, it is due to the foresight and investment of good King Henry VIII." I looked up and down the table. "Everyone knows he founded the Royal Navy, and the Church of England, and the Royal College of Surgeons, but how many recognize what he did for English agriculture?"

"To the King!" Francis drank to him, and we all followed suit.

"He would love this occasion," I said. "The good English air, and good English food, and good English people. Those were most precious to him."

Our banquet was a showcase of Francis's estate's bounty. There were venison and coneys from his hunting reserve, lamb from his fields, fish and waterfowl from his river, and fine bread from his wheat fields. Only the wine was imported, and he confessed that he had started a vineyard to begin making English wine.

"Now that would be a greater victory over the French than Agincourt," said Helena.

The day was perfect—almost. The meal was perfect—almost. I said so, thinking out loud.

"Why, what would Your Majesty change?"

"I would move the day back six weeks, to early July. We have missed the cherry time—my favorite fruit."

"That is not surprising, as the cherry is the emblem of virginity," said Francis. "And here in Surrey, it ripens at the very height of our fleeting summer."

"So much is cherry ripening a time of fairs and feasting that poets use it to suggest the brief time of merrymaking in our lives. Was it not Chaucer who wrote, 'This world is but a cherry fair'—passing quickly, soon withered away?" said Raleigh.

"But to control the seasons, even the masterful Sir Francis cannot do that," said Catherine. "What we have missed we have missed. We will have to come again next year, and come in time."

"Where Her Majesty is is always the right time. For she herself is time, and it must bow to her, as her loyal subject," said Francis. He gave a quick nod and his servers left the area. They soon returned with covered silver bowls and white serving napkins. One by one they placed them before us. Finally, when the last one was set down, Francis commanded mine to be uncovered. A server whisked the silver lid off, revealing a mound of huge, succulent, ripe cherries.

Oh, how cleverly they could fashion imitations in Venetian glass. I had heard of their work, which would fool even nature. I laughed. "And this fruit will keep forever. Thank you, good Francis."

"No, Your Majesty. It will soon perish. It is real."

That was impossible. "Have you some magic tree, then, that ripens late?"

"No," he said. "I have only the normal Kentish Red, which ripens in early July. It is what I have set before you."

Gingerly I picked one up. It was not even chilled. He had not packed it in ice (although how could it have kept for six weeks even on ice)? It was smooth skinned and its flesh was firm. I bit into it and its juice filled my mouth.

"It is real!" I said in wonder.

All up and down the table the other diners bit into theirs.

"Again, one is free to brag on another," said Raleigh. "My good friend Francis covered a cherry tree with a canvas to keep the sun from ripening the cherries at the usual time. He doused the canvas with water to keep it cool. Without the direct sun, the cherries kept growing until they were much larger than normal. Then, when it was within a week of Your Majesty's visit, he removed the tent and let the sun bring the fruit to perfection. He is the cleverest gardener who ever lived."

"I only prayed that Your Majesty would not change your mind, once the covering was off the tree," said Francis.

I had had gifts of rare jewels, fashioned into exquisite gold pendants and necklaces. I had been given exotic plants and animals from distant lands. I had had extravagant literary tributes. But this homely, simple gift brought tears to my eyes. "I think it is the rarest gift I have ever received," I said. "I thank you, Sir Francis."

---

We lingered under the trees all afternoon, with young musicians walking through the rows, playing and singing for us. At last we returned to the house, where lamps had already been lit, making it glow from the inside like a lantern. In the long gallery, we continued the musical evening. Sir Francis had two virginals, and I sat down to play on one, relishing the feel of the slender keys under my fingers. This instrument had a rich, mellow tone. The open windows invited in the heavy scent of night-blooming flowers, and I could see a late-rising moon just struggling to clear the garden wall. Quiet English countryside. Quiet English paradise.

---

We were to go hunting the next afternoon, and Sir Francis busied himself in the morning with the hounds and the beaters. Thus, he was not at home when Admiral Charles arrived from London, his boots crunching on the gravel of the entrance path.

Catherine, who could recognize his footsteps, flew out to meet him. I was always touched to see long-married couples eager to see each other. The white-haired Charles would not inspire faster heartbeats from most women, but he only needed it from one.

"We have been cosseted and entertained so lovingly by Sir Francis," said Catherine. "I thought you would never come! He's planned an afternoon of hunting—and the Queen and I are going to Hever the day after. It's so lovely here." She grabbed his hands and almost dragged him up the steps of the house.

"Welcome, Charles," I said. "Now Catherine can truly enjoy her stay."

He went down on one knee. "I fear your stay must end, and mine can never begin," he said. He rose. "Bad news. The Spanish have been sighted on their way to our coast."

The sun still shone on my face, but its warmth vanished. "I had feared this." I had not been to inspect the coastal towns yet, but it was too late. I would have to decamp to London.

I turned to Catherine. "No Hever Castle this time, my dearest." Suddenly I was sorry I had not taken the Mary Boleyn necklace from Lettice. I would now have given it to Catherine, her other granddaughter, as a consolation and a promise. "But we will go. I promise it as firmly as fate will permit a queen to plan for the next year."

My idyll was over.

# 67

Everything ran backward. Back along the road to Southwark, back through Southwark, the same vendors and the same advertisements for plays, back past the theaters and the bear pits—not leisurely now; we were in a great hurry. The faces looked up at me, the hands waved, and I felt myself to be a shield between them and disaster. They looked trustingly at me, secure in my keeping. My person was their protection, as it had been for forty years. I would not fail them now.

---

The council was waiting, ready to act. I looked out at their faces: Robert Cecil, narrow faced, unblinking. Henry Brooke, Lord Cobham, wild frizzy hair barely contained under his cap. George Carey, dark eyed like a Spaniard. The old workhorses: Lord Buckhurst, William Knollys, Archbishop Whitgift, sitting quietly, waiting.

"I came forthwith," I said. "I could discern no disturbance or action in the countryside I passed through, but that was a long way from the coast. What reports do you have?"

Admiral Howard stood and asked Cecil, "The report I brought to Her Majesty is a day old. What news do you have since then?"

"None, my lord," said Cecil. "Since the fleet was first sighted two weeks ago on the north coast of Spain, we have had no word. They may be far up the French coast by now." Anticipating my question, he said, "We have ordered the coastal militias to assemble and the beacons readied. We await your decision about what ships to deploy."

"I would deploy some on the west coast," said Cecil.

"Yes, the Armada is likely targeting Ireland for a landing," said Carey.

"I am thinking more of a force coming *from* Ireland," said Cecil.

William Knollys shook his head, making his three-colored beard tremble. "From Ireland? You think O'Neill will attack us? Or that Grace O'Malley?"

"The man I am thinking of has the same first name as I but a loftier title.

He has a spirit of disaffection and a large army. I have never thought he went to Ireland to subdue the Irish, but rather to reinstate himself in the Queen's favor. Since the Irish campaign has gone sour, he may try another route to imposing his will on the Queen."

Essex. Cecil had spoken the unspoken thought.

"We have forbidden his return," I said. "We withdrew that privilege. He cannot return until his task is done."

"When has he ever obeyed when it did not please him to obey?" said Cobham.

Both Cobham and Cecil were adversaries of Essex, Cobham having become one when I bestowed the Cinque Ports post on him rather than the importuning Essex. I had to keep that in mind. But their words could not be dismissed.

"Charles Blount—now Lord Mountjoy—has also said we should be wary, take precautions," said Cecil.

Mountjoy was the most experienced soldier left behind guarding England. His words carried weight.

"We consider ourselves warned," I said.

---

My nerves were on end. Each agonizing day there was no further word of the Spanish and no word from Ireland. I knew the fate of the realm was delicately balanced.

Finally something happened, but not what we were scanning the horizon for. Rather than rely on a letter, Essex sent his secretary, Henry Cuffe, to report to us.

I had met Cuffe before. He was formerly a scholar of Greek at Oxford and had welcomed me there with a poem on one of my official visits. At the time, I had been struck by his good looks and oratory; I had thought he would go far. But somewhere along the line he had left academia and cast his lot with politics. It had saddened me when I learned of it. Like many, I endowed the scholar's life with an aura it probably did not possess in daily living.

"Your Majesty," he said, dropping to one knee. "I am honored to be the one entrusted to present the correspondence of the earl to you." He held out a box.

I took it, motioning him to stand. Inside was a report from Essex. Quickly I read it, my eyes whipping through the formal phrases and postures, devouring the true contents. The earl's army was greatly weakened. He had lost many men. Nonetheless, he was going north to confront O'Neill, on my orders.

"I am even now putting my foot into the stirrup," he wrote, "and will do as much as duty will warrant and God enable me."

"So he has set out?" I asked Cuffe. "He has truly gone?"

Cuffe nodded.

"Where does he plan to engage O'Neill?"

"Our intelligence tells us he is in the vicinity of Navan. We will march there and confront him."

"Does your intelligence give you any reckoning of the size of his army?"

"It is difficult to gauge. The Irish army is not a solid body like ours. It assumes many shapes and numbers, contracting and expanding with the weather and its mood. But we think it is around six thousand men."

Twice the size of ours! "I see."

"But a stout fighting Englishman is worth five of—"

"Spare me this, Cuffe. You know it is nonsense. You are an intelligent man. Give me credit for being intelligent as well. So the earl goes out to confront his enemy, having squandered his strength and advantage, to meet him now from a position of weakness."

"That is too dark an assessment, Your Majesty," he said.

"Convince me otherwise," I countered.

He reeled off a list of excuses—the advice of the Irish Council, the unhealthiness of the land, the perfidy of our allies.

"Pish!" I said.

He laughed. Then he said, "It is not our mistakes up until now that will count. It is what will happen when the earl finally confronts The O'Neill."

He spoke true. "Surely he won't be such a fool as to challenge him to combat." Essex's favorite, meaningless, offer.

"The O'Neill is twenty years older," said Cuffe. "It might not be a bad strategy."

"Pish!" I said again. "As if he would gamble away his kingdom on such a thing. He's older, and as wily as they come. Even if Essex won, O'Neill would not honor it. He would only pretend to, using it to buy time. No, I utterly forbid such an action."

"As you wish, Your Majesty." He looked miserable—the dilemma of the intellectual man forced to serve, and excuse, his inferior.

"I will write my instructions to your master." How he must hate that phrase, and its truth. "But I count on you to convey them in all the force I have just used to you." I took a deep breath. "And now let us speak of other matters. You, sir, I remember from Oxford. What made you abandon that home to make a new one with the Earl of Essex?"

"Even scholars need to eat, Your Majesty," he said. "Service with the earl offered better worldly prospects." He stood, the remnants of his pride still visible in his posture.

"Worldly prospects, yes," I said. "But there is more. There is another world beyond that world."

"Do you mean heaven? That's too far away."

"No, I meant earth. A reputation. A body of work that lives on. Politics—it is a whiff of smoke, soon dissipated, soon forgotten."

"The higher reaches of both offer immortality," he said. "Not having the merit to attain either, I am better off to cast my lot with the one that pays highest."

"A Machiavelli."

"No, a practical man. Many must deny their ambitions or higher callings in order to put a plate on the table." *You would not understand that* was his unspoken comment.

"A man must do what he must," I admitted. "First we must survive."

"Unfortunately, yes. That is the great truth."

I looked carefully at him, at this young man who had veered off the path he was most suited for. His alert green eyes, his commanding height, his quick mind all bespoke his appeal and gifts. But they were compromised, devalued, in his service to the earl, where he would labor in obscurity.

---

Again, the waiting. Day after day tiptoed by, as if they, too, were holding their breath with the rest of us. Essex had gone north. Even at this very moment something was happening, but I could not know what.

A Captain Lawson arrived. Unlike Cuffe, he was sweaty and rough. It befitted his announcement: Rather than engaging O'Neill or vanquishing him, after going north and hunting for the elusive rebel, Essex had met with him in secret conference and concluded a treaty that essentially capitulated English interests.

"Outline them," I commanded this Lawson.

"He conferred with O'Neill in the midstream of the Lagan River between the two armies drawn up at the ford of Bellaclynth. First Essex challenged him to a duel, but the Irishman declined. Then he invited him to a parley, on neutral ground, where they could discuss their positions. The Irish army was stationed just behind the hills, out of sight, so we could not judge its size. Essex met with him, and after they parted, he announced that they had settled on a truce, renewable every six weeks, that guaranteed peace. The Irish are to keep possession of all their conquests until that moment, and the English promised to establish no new garrisons."

"There were no witnesses to this? The two men spoke alone?"

"That is correct, Your Majesty."

"Treason!" I cried. "To parley with a traitor, in secret, no witnesses present, against my express command to speak to him only if he sued for unconditional surrender or begged for his life. And then he has settled a truce with him, on terms entirely favorable to the Irish? It is nothing short of capitulation. To let them keep all their conquests. To hold back from manning new forts. A truce, renewable every six weeks, buying them time until the Spanish land to join forces with them." Oh, God! I had been betrayed. England had been betrayed. We were destroyed in Ireland.

The enormity of the blow quite took my breath away. Not only the money and men sacrificed, but the future. Ireland gone! An enemy, a rebel, at our back door, free to welcome the Spanish.

I excused myself, went into a private chamber, and tried to control myself. *Stop trembling. Think.* I closed my eyes and willed myself to become still. Moments passed, and then I reemerged.

"I shall write the earl," I said. "And you shall take the letter directly back, pausing not a whit."

I withdrew and composed a letter. It was dated September 17, 1599. I told him of my anger and distrust. "To trust this traitor upon oath is to trust a devil upon his religion." That was the crux of it. I ordered him to press on against The O'Neill. I refused to confirm any of the terms he had settled on with him. I declared them utterly null and void.

As I wrote, so furiously I can barely remember the wording of the letter, any more than a screaming victim can remember what he cried as he was set upon, I could not know he would never see it.

Thrusting it into Lawson's hands, I had a sudden question. "When did this illegal parley take place?"

"On September 7, Your Majesty."

Somehow I had known it. My sixty-sixth birthday. Was ever a monarch given a more odious gift?

"Ten days ago," I said. "Ten days! Leave tonight, to carry my orders to him. You should be there in three or four days."

"Your servant," he said.

---

Like a restive animal, I suddenly felt my quarters like a cage. Greenwich's wide green lawn seemed to shrink and imprison me. The view over the widening Thames only reminded me that Spanish ships might soon bob and float upon it. I wanted to await news safely away from London, in a more secluded and protected place. I would withdraw to Nonsuch, south of the city and in wooded hills.

I left hastily, taking only a small guard with me. For government councillors, I brought Cecil, Carey, and Knollys. The rest would stay behind, ready to receive news and alert us.

Once again, south over London Bridge, through Southwark, and then into Surrey. This time we headed west rather than east toward Beddington. The late-September sun was benevolent, evoking all the autumnal words that poets dwelled upon: "golden," "fruitful," "russet," "fallow," "fulfilled," "leaf-strewn," "mellow." A blaze of brilliant yellow surrounded us with falling, and fallen, leaves. The air seemed thick and rich, as if we were looking into a piece of amber, leaves, insects, and specks embedded in it. Spring had its delicate beauty, summer its somnolent murmurs, but autumn whispers its urgent messages to the soul. Hurry. Reap your harvest.

---

Nonsuch was musty. I had not visited it in several months. My father had always rejoiced in throwing open the windows and reclaiming his rooms. Would he have roared with joyous laughter now? Or would he have been too weighted down with cares of state to bellow as he loved to do?

Being here gave me a semblance of separation from the pressing matters of war. In the neat, stripped-down chambers I could try to strip the national situation down to its essentials. Ireland. We could not lose it. Essex was, in the most charitable interpretation, a fool. Or . . . he had sold England's interest to the enemy in exchange for some secret promise of reward. Which was it?

I did not want to think the worst. That was the way of tyrants, leaping to conclusions, condemning without evidence. I would await his response, and obedience, to my letter. This was a test, the supreme test, of his loyalty.

Only Catherine and Helena had accompanied me. Dear Eurwen I had sent home, for safety's sake. She should be far away should trouble strike. The Welsh borderlands had not seen turmoil since the days of my grandfather. She had wept at leaving, and I at losing her. I had heard no more from Marjorie in Oxfordshire, and I was glad to spare her more alarums.

Evenings were quiet: a balm to my spirits. We retired early, after partaking of the fresh perry from the surrounding orchards.

There is a great deal to be said for retiring early. I embraced a monk's daily hours and found myself in bed when, at court, I would have been still dancing or card playing. I kept the windows open and felt the cold-tinged air come into the chamber, soothing us, saying, *This is eternal. The seasons arrive and pass, but England abides.*

---

On the second-to-last day of September, I awoke slowly and naturally. No one roused me; no one shook me, whispered in my ear. No, I had the luxury and privilege—rare for a monarch—of arising when I would and moving as slowly as I liked.

I felt exceptionally groggy today. I stumbled out of my bed and asked for a tub of warm water to be brought where I might soak my feet—and wake up. It was placed in my innermost private chamber; I approached it gingerly and set my feet in it. The warmth spread up from my feet into my legs. But my mind was still dulled, floating. I must harness it. I was loath to do so. There was nothing but trouble to ponder.

I sat, arms draped, slumping, over the wooden tub. My nightgown was hiked up, allowing my legs to soak without wetting the gown. I felt like a dolt, someone who could not even add a column of figures. I kept shaking my head, as if that would awaken me.

The door flew open. Suddenly, before me, the Earl of Essex. He rushed in, then knelt before me. He was covered in muck.

My enervation was gone, vanished in an instant, fear bristling in every fiber of me.

"Your Majesty," he said, his voice shaking.

I sat, my legs in the tub of hot water, in my nightclothes, bereft of all trappings of majesty. Where was my guard? How had he gained entry to my inner chambers?

For an instant I could not speak. He was here, when he should have been far away in Ireland. I had forbidden him permission to return.

"I must plead my case before you," he said. "My enemies at court have poisoned your mind against me."

Here I was, almost naked—of clothes, of guard, of knowing what was what outside the palace—at his mercy. He stood before me, in his military garb. Had he surrounded the palace with his army? Had he brought it back from Ireland, all three thousand men of it? Why had I had no warning from London? Had he quite overpowered all the royal forces? I must play for time.

"And what case is that?" I asked, as naturally as if this had passed in a council chamber. I lifted my feet out of the tub and Catherine dried them off.

My wig was in my dressing chamber; likewise my clothes. There are those who, seeking simplistic answers, say that surprising me in my natural state gave Essex such an advantage over me that I never forgave him. That is nonsense. I am proud, and I do not wish my weaknesses to be paraded before the world, but my thinning hair and lack of proper clothes did not enter my mind when Essex barged in. My only concern was: Was I surrounded? Did he have the upper hand?

"Cecil—my enemies in council. They wish to see me destroyed and will spend every last ounce of their efforts to discredit me. I know while I have been gone, they have been busy, securing appointments for themselves and painting my actions as entirely black."

I drew myself up, as if I were in royal robes instead of a towel and a nightgown. "Why are you not at your post?" I asked him. "And why have you returned, against our express permission? Surely you have not abandoned your duty to come here to quarrel about minor matters?"

He looked at me, that glorious melting glance that had never failed to move me. He had the most beautiful, and persuasive, eyes I had ever seen.

"I gave you a commission. I required you to perform a high task. I forbade you to return until it was completed. Why are you here?" I demanded.

He dropped to one knee and took my hand. "To see you, my most gracious mistress."

"That had best waited until you had completed your mistress's task." My voice was sharp. I must temper it. Who was outside the door? Had his forces overcome my paltry guards? Was I even now in his power, his prisoner?

*Stall him,* I told myself. *Hold him off. Lull him. You have done it before, with others. You must do it again.* I stood as regally as possible draped in my nightshirt.

"I must explain everything to you. It is impossible to write everything in letters," he was saying.

"Did you receive my last one, dated September 17?"

"No, I had left before that."

"I see."

Whatever I had said in it was irrelevant at this point. It would only have been pertinent had it been read while he could still carry out his duties.

He, the supreme commander of the English forces in Ireland, had abandoned his post. He was a deserter. A traitor.

"What was it Your Majesty wished to tell me?" he asked hopefully.

I smiled at him. I hoped that, as an unadorned queen, I might still be commanding. That depended on whether I was at his mercy or he at mine. That would soon be revealed. "Shall we talk later? Let us meet for dinner in two hours' time. You can make yourself presentable, and I will dress. I welcome you to court, my lord."

The fool bowed and left my chamber.

As soon as he was gone, I rushed to the door and called for my guard. "How did he get in here? Were you sleeping?"

The five of them trooped to the doorway, hanging their heads. "He slipped past us. He had no guard and did not seem dangerous."

" 'Did not seem dangerous'?" I repeated. "He is as dangerous as an adder. They do not have guards either. Outside—is there anyone with him?"

In a few moments they returned, shaking their heads. "No army. Just a few of his retainers. No more than twenty."

We were safe. Now he was at my mercy. Mercy—there would be none. He had finally used up his allotment of it.

# 68

e would be back in only two hours. I had little time.

"Catherine. Helena. You heard it all. Now stand by me. Do not leave my side. And help me dress, quickly."

They handed me my fine cambric undergarments and my petticoat and slid one of my day dresses over my head. Then they brushed my hair back and fitted my wig over it. My face was so pale it would need more than the auburn frame of the wig to make me look alive again. "My rouge pot," I ordered. "Lip color. Leave off the white powder, by God, my skin is whiter than any concoction!" Last the jewels—a rope of gold and sapphires, pearls for my ears, and diamonds for my hair. I must look as I did every day, nothing unusual. "Hurry, hurry!" I urged them.

Prepared at last, I did not even bother to check my final reflection in the mirror. Instead, I summoned Cecil, Carey, and Knollys. They arrived, smiling and relaxed. Their smiles faded when they saw my agitation.

"Essex is here!" I hissed.

"But that's impossible," said William Knollys. "We know he was in Ireland just four days ago."

"Well, he's here now!"

"Where? Has he been sighted near Chester?" said Robert Cecil. "I knew he'd try to return. That's why we stationed the ships there. Why didn't they detain him?"

"He's been sighted, and right here in this chamber!" I pointed to the muddy shoe prints on the floor. "He stood right here, dripping mud and wet leaves!"

There was a collective intake of breath, the way comic actors gasp in unison onstage. But this was shock, and it was not funny. "Here, in your chamber! What of the guards? Were you utterly unarmed? No protection?"

"Nothing but me and my women," I said. "As for my guards, they were more useless than a paper sword. I had nothing but words to defend myself with."

"And your own majesty," said George Carey.

I gave a snort. "My wits served me better. He clearly did not find awe in majesty." This was the most chilling aspect of it. He respected neither my person nor my office.

"Whom does he have with him?" asked Cecil.

"When he burst in here, I thought he must have brought his army with him, to depose me. But my guards say he has only a small group of perhaps twenty men. Perhaps the army is following and this is only the advance party."

"Where is he now? How have you left it with him?"

"He has, I assume, gone to an empty set of rooms here at Nonsuch. And he is to return here at noon to talk. I told him we would dine together afterward."

"I'll call for the rest of the council to get here as soon as possible, and to bring enough guards and troops to overcome his retainers," said Carey. "We must trap him here."

"I shall speak sweetly to him until help arrives. He is so deluded it is easy to convince him I welcome him."

"Why is he here at all, if not to overthrow the throne?" said Knollys ominously.

"To rescue me from evil advisers, so he hints, who he assumes have poisoned my mind against him," I said. "He does not realize—he cannot grasp—that he is his own evil adviser."

"We will withdraw now and busy ourselves preparing a proper welcome for him," said Knollys grimly. "One in accordance with his importance."

"Is there anyone of note with him?" Carey asked.

"My guards recognized the Earls of Southampton, Rutland, and Bedford, Lord Rich, and Sir Christopher Blount, but nobody else." I took a deep breath. "Southampton again, to plague me! And the feckless Earls of Rutland and Bedford. And Lettice's husband. A pack of worthless hounds."

"No one of character would follow him, Your Majesty. He attracts only the wastrels and the malcontents," said Cecil.

"The common people exalt him," I said.

"That's because they only know him from afar. Up close, he draws only the court leavings."

"He will soon be back! Get you gone, and set the trap, ready to spring. I myself must be the bait, to lure and lull him."

Hurriedly they left the room.

"Catherine, you have an outstanding memory," I said. "Try to remember everything that passes between Essex and me, for later questioning."

"Your Majesty is renowned for her own memory," said Catherine.

"For something this important, we need two memories. You, Helena, study his face and expressions—you, who are so good at reading character."

"I think we know his character by now," she said.

"He is many characters," I said. "Which one, pray tell, will he be wearing when he returns?"

I would pass the time calmly with him until dinner. Then we would be joined by the rest of the people attending me. By the time the meal was done, help from London should have arrived. My siege would end.

There was a smart knock on the door. This time my head guard properly announced, "The Earl of Essex to see Her Majesty the Queen."

"Admit the earl."

The guard stepped back, and Essex strode in. He still wore the same clothes, but he had washed the mud off his face and hands and combed his hair and beard. He fell to his knees, almost sliding across the floor to where I stood.

"Forgive me for my wretched garb," he said, "but I was in such a hurry to reach you I took nothing with me, not even fresh clothes. Nothing mattered but getting here."

I fluttered my hand, signaling him to arise. "You have worn these clothes for—how many days?"

"I left Ireland on September 24. It is now the twenty-eighth."

I burned to say, *Three weeks after you parleyed with The O'Neill. What were you doing in the meantime?* But looking meaningfully at Helena and Catherine, I said, "Ah, you must be tired, my lord. Only Mercury himself could have traveled such distances so swiftly."

"If I became, temporarily, a god, it was only to fly to the feet of the great goddess herself, the Faerie Queen, there to serve her."

"We must refresh you," I said. "Here is some good English cider and fresh Kentish apples and cheese from Devon. It will welcome you back to your native land, after a half year of Irish fare. Pray you, have some." One of the chamberers poured him a cup and handed it to him; another held out a tray of the apples and cheese, cut and ready. He bolted the drink and gobbled the food. He was clearly famished. It reminded me of a lapping dog. My women and I stood politely by, abstaining.

"Now tell me, dear Robert, why you felt you must come now? What had troubled you so?" The syrupy words almost stuck in my throat.

Dabbing at his mouth with a napkin, he sighed. "When I received your last letter, so cruel, so hard, I knew it could not be truly yours."

"How did you discern that?"

"The stinging rebukes! This sentence alone: 'We know you cannot fail so much in judgment as not to understand that all the world sees how time is dallied.' And these: 'We must therefore let you know that, as it cannot be ignorance, so it cannot be want of means, for you had your asking. You had choice of times, you had power and authority more ample than any ever had or ever shall have.' "

"I am sorry that they wounded you. Perhaps I did not understand, fully, what you were going through." I kept my tone sweetly solicitous.

"Even so, such hard-heartedness has never been in my queenly mistress's nature. *They* have dictated the letter. It has their tone!"

"And which 'they,' my good man, do you mean?"

"The Privy Council! Cecil in particular! He is in back of all the maneuverings to discredit me. And since I left in March, he has had ample opportunity to plant the black poison of suspicion in your mind about me. While I have been risking my life in service to England, he has been lurking here, living warmly and comfortably. He's poised like a spider, spinning his webs to trap the innocent. He even looks like one, with his hunchback."

That was more than I could let pass. "He does not have a hunchback," I said. "And he has never yet entrapped an innocent man, like you did with Dr. Lopez!"

His face clouded and his eyes narrowed for an instant. "This just proves my point," he said. "He has utterly won you over. But"—he waved his hand expansively—"all the more reason why I needed to come posthaste to speak directly to you. The last letter said, 'We look to hear from you how you think the remainder of the year shall be employed—in what kind of war, and where, and with what numbers—which, being done and sent us hither in writing with all expedition, you shall then understand our pleasure in all things fit for our service.' And you ended with, 'And thus, expecting your answer, we end, at our manor of Nonsuch in the forty-first year of our reign, 1599.' Here is your answer, Glorious Majesty, in the flesh."

"I see that full well."

"It is too complicated to explain in a letter. You are right to expect to know everything, but if it were written it would take months. I can explain it all now."

And he proceeded to do so, in whining, self-exonerating tedium. He had suffered. He had been misled. The conditions in Ireland were inhuman. He felt unappreciated at home. Furthermore, he had achieved a glorious settlement from O'Neill. A truce!

"You were not sent to conclude a truce," I said, "but a victory. I did not finance this huge army, the largest I have sent anywhere in my reign, to make a truce."

He bristled. Yet agreeing with all his drivel was almost beyond me. I checked myself. "Well, time will tell if the truce will hold. In the meantime, have you word of whether you have a new son or daughter?" I knew Frances was expecting.

"No—no—I haven't been home yet. I came straight here. You—you are above everyone else in my life."

"That is touching, but do not tell your wife that."

"She knows. It is impossible not to know!"

"I hope all goes well with her delivery. Her daughter with Sir Philip Sidney is my goddaughter, you know. She is almost a young lady now."

"Fourteen, Your Majesty."

"A magic age."

"It depends on who you are."

True. I turned fourteen the year my father died, and there was little magic for me on that birthday. "Quite right. But I hope Elizabeth Sidney's life is touched with good things, including her new sibling."

Mercifully, I saw the table clock's hands almost at noon. This torture was over. Then the courtyard clock began chiming on the hour. Just then the steward announced, "Dinner, Your Majesty."

I beamed at Essex. "Shall we, my lord?"

---

The tables were laid in the watching chamber. The elaborate ceremony readying my place for me, which involved tasters and ceremonial rods, had already been performed. No poison had been found. I had invited Essex's companions to join us. He thought it was for courtesy. I meant it so I could have them under my eye. Now, stretching down the length of the table, were the greatest debtors in England: Roger Manners, the Earl of Rutland; Edward Russell, the Earl of Bedford; Henry Wriothesley, the Earl of Southampton. All had frolicked and gamboled, as well as gambled, across Europe and home. And then there was Christopher Blount. I watched him as much as I could without being obvious. What sort of a man was it who was content to take orders and follow in the wake of his stepson? He had served under him in Cádiz, done blind obeisance to him in the Azores, and now trotted after him, first to Ireland, and then back, straight into the eye of a certain storm. For that matter, what sort of man wanted to marry Lettice? The termagant must make his life hell. He was alluring, if your taste ran to dark looks and wide shoulders. Like Leicester before him, he could have been nicknamed "the Gypsy." Obviously Lettice liked that sort. Of course, she liked any sort.

Farther down the table were the rest of Essex's stalwart followers. I spotted Henry Cuffe, and there were several others who looked familiar. I must have seen them in passing at court, but none of them were talented enough to merit an appointment.

The courtiers who had accompanied me to Nonsuch were eager to press Essex and his companions for details of the Irish campaign, as if they were hearing exploits from the Trojan war.

Cecil, Knollys, and Hunsdon kept to themselves at one side of the table, eating quietly and only looking at the intruders from the corners of their eyes. The chatter rose; my relative silence did not call attention to itself.

"Ah, how blessed to taste English meat again!" said Southampton. "What they called lamb in Ireland was boiled army boots."

"What they called bread was stale coffin wood!"

"What they called ale was horse's piss!"

They laughed uproariously at their wit. All the while I was listening for the sound of horses and the tramp of feet in the courtyard, signaling the arrival of support from London.

"You met with Hugh O'Neill?" asked one of my lower-ranking chamberwomen. "What was he like? Is he handsome? Fearsome?"

Essex leaned back, lifting his chin as if he needed to think. "He's like an old hunting beast sporting many scars. Shaggy like a bear. But sweet spoken, full of that Irish charm. Fearsome? You wouldn't know to look at him he's killed so many."

"Would you want your daughter to marry him?" the questioner giggled.

"No, my daughter's to marry Roger here," said Essex, turning to Rutland. "We are to be brothers-in-law!"

I broke in. "Your stepdaughter Elizabeth Sidney? She's not yet fifteen. Why, my lord, did you keep this from me when we spoke of her?"

"It is—the details are not settled yet, so I thought it premature to make an announcement."

"Premature indeed," I said. "She's but a child." I fastened my glance on Rutland. "If you think to repair your debts by marrying a rich man's daughter, you are chasing the wrong quarry. A debtor's daughter married to a debtor will never have wherewithal to live."

Essex turned red at having his financial straits exposed. But he held his tongue. What else could he do? All his living came from my generosity, and if that did not stretch far enough, he had only himself to blame.

"Merrily, merrily," said Blount. "Anyone who marries for money earns it the hardest way."

"Anyone who marries for love will mostly likely wish to swap places after a year," said Bedford, laughing.

"What would the poets say?" asked one of the ladies. "You wrong them to belittle love."

"Poets are for sale like the rest of us. Else they would not hawk their books at St. Paul's bookstalls."

After more of this inane banter, at long last the meal ended. I rose and left the hall. As I passed through the gallery, I saw that the two courtyards were still empty.

I retired to my chamber, as if to rest in the midday. But inside, I paced. As every hour passed, it became clearer that Essex had not brought his army with him, or even part of it. He had drunk with his fellows at table and basked in the attention from the stay-at-homes, who he thought envied him. He had had his reward. Now I would call him back again and bring him to heel.

---

He came promptly, all smiles. But the time for smiles was over. I aimed hard questions at him and demanded direct answers. Why had he mangled his mission so badly in Ireland? Had he gone without the intention of carrying out my orders? Why had he obeyed the urgings of the Irish Council instead of me? Why had he deserted his post, disobeyed my explicit orders against returning, and flouted all authority?

He seemed stunned, and stammered something about my sweet majesty's temper being so changed toward her Robert.

"The Robert I knew is gone," I said. "The Robert who swore he loved me, as his sovereign and his cousin, would never have betrayed me this way. Now answer my charges."

The color flared across his face, red chasing white. "I am ever your Robert," he said. "But I like not this manner toward me."

"Like me no likings, but explain yourself or suffer the consequences. It is not for you to like or dislike what I do. It is the privilege of majesty to do as it will and for you to suffer it." I had dropped the false sweetness and now spoke plainly the disgust I felt.

"I—I had no thought of disobeying, I— The conditions there changed everything! All we had planned, here in England, was different in reality."

"Bah. How is sixteen thousand soldiers different on Irish soil than English? You seek lame excuses, when the reason for failure lies in your very person. I knew you were not the man for this task, for all your titles, plumes, and pompous display. Knollys would have been better. Mountjoy would have been better. Anyone would have been better!"

"Anyone?" he said. "Anyone?" he yelled. "I will not permit such an insult!"

"I decide what you will or will not permit. With the collapse of your Irish command, you have surrendered all power over your own person. I dismiss you, sir. You will be sent for later, to answer these questions, for, by God, you *will* answer them!"

His hand twitched, as if he would strike me. But he knew better this time. Instead, he drew himself up and bowed stiffly. "If my Queen commands, I must obey."

"You have learned this truth too late to help you."

An ache like a smarting slap spread from my chest to my shoulders and then through all of me. In absolute clarity, I saw him for what he was: a man without any of the qualities I had endowed him with—whose bluster and beauty had been convincing for a while. But no more. The door closed and he was gone. It was not only the Irish campaign that had collapsed.

# 69

hat evening, at my request, the three members of the Privy Council examined Essex for several hours. In answer to their questions, he repeated his excuses and self-justifications. They were not convinced and were deeply suspicious of his motives. At eleven that night they sent their recommendation to me that he be arrested. I gave orders that he be confined to his room. In the meantime, guards and soldiers had arrived from London.

Bidding Catherine and Helena a restful night, I knew there would be none for me. Between dawn and midnight the entire landscape of my court had changed, and in a monstrous way. I was left with an unfinished war, a leaderless army, and an empty place at the table of councillors.

I could not escape the thought that I was partly responsible for what Essex had become. He was a man of outsized charm and talent. Those dazzled my mind. Like a foolish parent, I had petted him and looked the other way when he disobeyed. Any punishment I gave him was light and passing, soon forgotten. And so, like a headstrong horse, he now ran unchecked.

---

The rest of the Privy Council arrived the next morning, having ridden almost all night. After learning that Essex was under house arrest and studying the notes from the initial questioning the day before, they ordered him brought before them for a formal hearing.

In the hall where hunters were wont to recount their exploits under the hewn-oak beams of the high ceiling, the Earl of Essex was brought out to stand bareheaded before all eight of his erstwhile peers in the Privy Council. He was ordered to answer six charges:

First, that he had been contemptuously disobedient to the Queen's instructions expressly forbidding his return to England.

Second, that many of his reports from Ireland had been presumptuous.

Third, that once he was in Ireland he had disregarded his instructions for his mission and substituted others of his own liking.

Fourth, that his sudden departure from Ireland was irresponsible and dangerous in light of the situation there.

Fifth, that he had broken all protocol in breaching Her Majesty's privacy.

Sixth, that he had abused his privilege of awarding knighthoods in Ireland by bestowing them on unworthy men.

The hearing went on for five hours. It took them only fifteen minutes to reach a conclusion, which they recorded and sent to me.

The Earl of Essex had transgressed in all six of these charges. His explanations were not satisfactory. They all awaited my verdict.

---

The next day was Sunday. Archbishop Whitgift conducted morning prayer in the chapel, and I was thankful to lose myself there. After the service I took a quiet dinner in my private rooms and asked Catherine and Helena to come on a walk with me.

---

We left the palace and walked across the inner courtyard, with its gleaming gold panels set in ivory white stucco and the huge statue of my father and my brother watching over it all.

*What would you do?* I asked them. *Father, would you ever have let Essex grow as big as he has? Edward, be thankful you did not live to detect the treachery that surrounded you.*

It was a perfect autumn day, the sort that Nonsuch was built to celebrate. Swirls of golden leaves drifted down, surrounding us. Some landed on the trimmed topiary like badges of honor, yellow against the green uniforms. Beyond the formal grounds, we walked toward the grove of Diana, its wooded lanes opening before us. There she still stood, creamy and white against the foliage, the splashing waters of her bath lapping at her feet. Her hands were crossed to shield herself from the eyes of the hapless Actaeon. He had come upon her in her nakedness, and for that he must die.

"A lovely piece of work," Marjorie had said when once we looked at it together, "but the story always revolts me. The man saw her naked. He didn't mean to. Why should he be killed for it?" At the time her question seemed sensible. But now I knew the reason.

Because mortals must not look upon the divine? Because a man intruding into the privacy of a woman's bath is assaulting her, in effect if not intent?

The eyes of the statue Actaeon were terrified and bewildered. He could barely comprehend his transgression. The eyes of Essex when he barged into my chamber had held no such uncertainty. He had acted as if he belonged there. That was his great trespass and his effrontery.

I knew there would be murmurs, people saying that in punishing him I acted out of vanity—that he had seen me without my regalia, seen me in my human and frail guise, that my pride could not permit that.

It was not true. But how could they know that? One has to be a queen or a goddess to understand. There *were* differences between us and ordinary people. I looked into Diana's eyes, eyes that had seemed heartless when I looked into them three years ago. But now they seemed to encompass both sorrow and anger, not heartlessness. They betrayed the dreadful knowledge of the gods that they are forever set apart.

*Diana, now I understand,* I thought. *But unlike you, I would not condemn a man even for such a shocking breach of conduct.* I had told Essex that he could insult my person but not my office. My scepter and crown must remain untouched and inviolate. It was for this that he must be punished, not for seeing me in my bath.

---

On our way back, I spotted Francis Bacon walking among the topiary animals, inspecting them. He looked up when he saw us and bowed. "I came to ask your permission to speak to the Earl of Essex but was told you had gone out. In the meantime, I amuse myself by looking at these toys."

"I am sure you have an opinion about them," I said. "You do about everything."

"Of course," he said. "You will find it set out in my essay about gardening."

"Is this a ploy to sell your books?" asked Helena playfully.

"Indeed, Lady Northampton, I would be pleased to *give* you a copy."

"I appreciate your generosity, sir," she said. "Unusual for an author."

"On what matter do you seek permission to speak to Essex?" I asked.

"I heard the news of his untimely arrival," he said. "Although I am not of the Privy Council"—for an instant his eyes lingered and his speech hesitated, for emphasis—"I rode along with them. I used to give Essex advice. I would like to do so now in his hour of need."

"It will do little good. He is past listening to advice, if ever he did."

"Let me visit him as a friend, then, paying a condolence call."

"I must insist that witnesses be present. If that fool had done the same when he spoke with O'Neill, half his troubles would not exist."

"Of course. I am not planning on helping him escape."

"If he tries to escape, his punishment will be worse. His days of merry escapes are over."

"It sounds as if, Your Majesty, everything is over for him."

"I have decided nothing yet. The Privy Council deliberated and recommended that he be arrested. Today is the Sabbath, and I am resting from decisions. Go to him. Give him some cheer, if you can."

He bowed again. "Thank you."

"It is good to have friends like you," I said. "He is a fortunate man that way."

After he left, Helena said, "He was coy about the topiary."

"As I recall from the essay, he dislikes them," I said. "He says they are fit only for children."

"That must be why they are so popular at court," said Catherine.

As we were crossing the courtyard, John Harington came out a door. He stopped in full stride and made a show of greeting us.

"What, did the fool bring you, too?" I cried. "Straight from Ireland?" Harington had followed Essex to Ireland and been knighted there. Now apparently he had followed him home. He dropped to both knees and bowed his head. I caught his belt and said, "By God's son, my godson, I am no queen. That *man* is above me!"

"No, no, Your Majesty. That is not so."

"By God's son again, you soldiers were all idle, useless knaves, and Essex the worst of the lot, for wasting your time and our army in such ways."

"There were so many difficulties, problems unique to Ireland—"

"That's a tune you all sing in unison, then?"

He lifted his face up. "No, do not judge me in accordance with him. I have kept a journal of my part in the campaigns, and it was not all in vain."

"Give me that journal, then. Let me read it."

"It is at home, not here."

"Then get you home and wait to be sent for."

He rose. "I do not have to be told twice, Your Majesty," he said, "truly."

He dashed away so quickly that Catherine and Helena burst into laughter. "He runs as if the Irish themselves were chasing him," Catherine said.

---

I must give my verdict tomorrow morning. It should be a wise one, not dictated by personal vindictiveness or desire to punish. I must segregate him from the rest of the world, that theater that had been his undoing. Segregate, but not deprive of life. Perhaps the enforced rest would restore him to sanity. In my deepest heart I had not given up hope that he could be redeemed.

---

Early the next morning I called the Privy Council. They stood at attention, looking nervous.

"We have reached a decision about the Earl of Essex," I said. "Does that surprise you? We have been accused of dithering and refusing to make decisions, but difficult matters require thought, and we dislike irrevocable measures. Therefore, it is our pleasure that the Earl of Essex be conveyed to York House, there to be kept under house arrest and supervision by Thomas Egerton, the Lord Keeper of the Great Seal. He is not to return to Essex House. He is allowed two servants. He may not walk abroad, not even in the gardens, and he is to be allowed no visitors."

All eyes turned to Egerton. He ran his hands through his hair, as if that would clear his doubts.

"As Your Majesty wishes," he said. The others looked pityingly at him.

"One of our court, the Earl of Worcester, has a coach at the ready. He can lend it to transport Essex to London. We want the shades drawn and Essex kept out of sight. You"—I nodded at Buckhurst, the admiral, and Cecil—"will ride behind and, upon arrival, escort Essex into his new quarters and settle him."

"What of his wife, children, and mother?" asked Cobham.

"We appoint Lord Hunsdon to tell them of the arraignment, the findings, and our decision."

"But can they not see him at least once? He has not seen them since he left for Ireland," said his uncle Knollys.

"That was his decision. He must learn that actions have consequences. If we pamper him now, he will take no lesson from it."

Any other man would certainly have had the right to see his family, but Essex would only construe it in the wrong way.

"Take him away, my lords. Take him away."

# 70

# LETTICE

*October 1599*

hat is that banging?" I cried. I feared it like a summons from hell. Banging was never good. It always meant an emergency. "Open the door!" I yelled down the stairs. Since my son's absence, the servants had grown lax and impertinent.

One of Frances's lady attendants rushed to the door. Where were the male servants? A pitiful lot! She tugged at the door and I could see a well-dressed man standing there. I had best go down.

Immediately I recognized him. It was George Carey, Lord Hunsdon, the Queen's cousin, and mine. This was state business.

"Cousin," I said. "We welcome you. Pray, come in."

He stepped across the threshold, removing his hat. "I thank you," he said.

But I could not contain myself, I could not wait. "My son!" I cried. "Is he safe? Does he live?" I had had no word in weeks.

Carey smiled tentatively. "He is safe. You need have no fear."

"Ireland—the dangers lurk everywhere. Oh, thank God, he is safe!"

"He is no longer in Ireland," said Carey. "He has returned to England."

It took me a moment to absorb these words. "In England? But where? And why?"

"As to the where, he landed and rode directly to the Queen at Nonsuch. As to why—that is the great question. Great enough that he has been placed under arrest, and is even now being installed at York House under the supervision of the Lord Keeper, Thomas Egerton."

"Oh, we must go to him!"

"Madam, you cannot. That is what I am charged with telling you. His arrest is strict. He is not allowed to walk outside. He is allowed no visitors."

"No visitors?"

"None."

"But his wife! His new daughter!"

"None, my lady."

I clapped my hand over my mouth. "But why?"

"He left his post in Ireland abruptly, in direct disobedience of his orders not to return, and threw himself at the Queen in person. He had concocted a scheme in his mind whereby the Queen had been deluded by false councillors—men like myself, my lady—and he needed to counteract this in person. He relied on his charm and desperation." He stopped and coughed discreetly. "But Her Majesty sets great store by obedience, and he had abandoned his post at a delicate time, throwing all into confusion. I must add that he had conducted an unauthorized interview with the enemy and, even by the most charitable interpretation, had surrendered English interests to him."

"Oh, God!" was all I could say. All was lost.

"He will be well treated," Hunsdon said. "Egerton is a most reluctant jailer."

"And my husband?" I only now thought to ask.

"He returned with my Lord of Essex. He is not under arrest. He will be home shortly. There are no restrictions on him or his movements."

"Her Majesty is gracious." I hoped that did not sound sarcastic.

"More than you know," he said. "Her father would have had the lot imprisoned and executed."

---

After he left, I sank down on a bench. My mind was whirling. Robert had risked all on a throw of the dice, and lost. Christopher was safe. What had happened in Ireland?

I must tell Frances. She had been waiting for every post, eager to hear of her husband's exploits. Her childbed had been difficult, and even now she had not fully recovered. Her little daughter Frances, her namesake, cried night and day and would not be comforted. She was eager to show her to her father, as if he would have some magic to quiet her. "Poor babe," she would say. "If your father could only hold you, your cries would vanish."

She was usually in her chambers, not having the strength to venture out, even in this mild weather. I knocked lightly, and she called out, "Please come in."

I stepped into her parlor and saw her sitting there, prettily attired. She was rocking the cradle at her feet, a beautifully carved one that had lulled her other two children.

"Mother Devereux," she said, smiling. "See how she kicks her feet today. She has not cried since last evening."

Dutifully I bent down and looked at the little face, framed with dark, straight hair. "Oh, that is good," I said. Then I straightened up and looked at her. "I come with surprising and unsettling news. Robert is here in England. He left his command in Ireland and rode here to see the Queen. Unfortunately she has had him arrested and put under the jurisdiction of the Lord Keeper. He is at York House. But he is allowed no visitors. We cannot see him."

Her little face did not register understanding. "For how long?" she asked.

"I do not know. It is for an indefinite period. Lord Hunsdon rode here to tell us."

"But I must see him!" she cried.

"The Queen is adamant. No visitors. Not even a walk outside."

"That is not healthy! How can he be denied fresh air?"

"I suppose she would say he can open his windows."

Frances slumped. "I have not seen him since March. I am his wife!"

"The Queen is well aware of that." I took a deep breath. "Did he intimate in any letters that he was thinking of returning?"

"No! He writes more letters to you and the Queen than he does to me!"

"Apparently no one was aware of it." He had acted on one of his sudden impulses, then. He was prone to that. But in this instance! How irresponsible!

"A number of people returned with him," I said. "She is letting all those go. Christopher will be allowed to come home."

"How fortunate that you are married to a lesser-ranking man, then," she said.

So the docile daughter-in-law had sting. "That is one compensation," I said. "But as the mother of the prime man in disgrace, I share all your worry."

I left her, trying to collect my thoughts. Soon Christopher would come, and surely he could tell me what had happened. I had heard little from him since he had gone to Ireland; he was not the sort to write letters. I knew that things had gone badly but, selfishly, I was only concerned that Christopher and Robert were safe. Each time a report arrived, I braced myself for bad news. As weeks passed and the names on the death rolls were those of others, I thanked God. Then I asked him to forgive me. I was afraid he would punish me for my selfishness by killing them in revenge.

At least they were out of Ireland, I thought. No matter what happened here, they were safe. Better to be disgraced and still draw breath than to perish honorably on the battlefield. Hardly very noble of me, but what mother can afford to be noble at her child's expense?

Was he ill? So often he had been ill, felled by his constitution. Perhaps he had despaired and thought his only hope of cure was to get out of the bogs. I sat before the fireplace, throwing another log on the fire, sending out bursts of sparks. I was chilled straight through, not from the weather but from fear.

I must have sat like this for an hour. Then I heard a commotion at the door, someone coming in. Christopher? I rose and looked down into the hall to see the top of that familiar head.

"Christopher!" I cried. "Christopher!" I rushed down the stairs.

He looked different. Thinner, darker. He put his bag down and stood wearily. "Wife, I am safely back," he said. I embraced him, putting my face up against his soiled and tattered coat. It had been stiff and bright with embroidery when he left. He took my chin and lifted my face toward his and kissed me. His lips were chapped and rough.

"And thank God for it," I said. He had escaped from Ireland, escaped the death that that land dealt out to anyone daring to spend time there.

"You know about Robert?" he asked.

"Hunsdon came here to tell me. He's confined at York House? And may have no visitors?"

"That's true."

"But why?"

"Let me sit. My leg is bothering me. It got smashed when a horse fell on it. Not broken, but it's not the same. And how about some ale? Wine? Anything, truth be told."

"Of course. Of course." I settled him in a comfortable chair before the fire and ordered some drinks brought, along with bread, pears, and walnuts. He took a long sip of the ale and relaxed back into the chair.

"I'll tell it as quickly as I can," he said, taking another sip. "Robert had nothing from the Queen but criticism and scolding. No matter what he did, she put the worst interpretation on it. He was convinced that his enemies back here were using every opportunity to turn the Queen against him. Her harsh tone told him they had succeeded. He felt he had to come in person, surprise her before Cecil and the rest knew he was here, and tell her his side of the story." He refilled his cup. "I thought it foolish. I thought he should take the entire army with him."

"Christopher, no! Think how it would look!"

"He was too cautious for that. Like you, he thought it would look bad. I argued that it didn't matter how it looked; at least that way he couldn't be taken prisoner. Well, now. That's what happened."

"But why?"

"Because he was foolhardy enough to come to England, without the Queen's permission, with only a small contingent of men, not enough to protect him. The Queen tricked him, made him think she welcomed him, when all the while she was making sure he didn't have the army with him. Once she knew that, she had him arrested. There was even a little mock trial before the Privy Council that condemned him for disobedience, and a few other things." He wiped his mouth. "The Queen's a wily one. She had us all to dinner and looking at her down the table, you'd never know that she wasn't delighted her dear Robert had returned. Then, bang! He's locked in his room to await the Queen's pleasure."

I remembered her cold eyes when she handed the Boleyn necklace back to me. Once she had loved me, but her change was absolute. How could I have forgotten what she was capable of?

"Why did she let you go?"

"He was the fish she wanted. The rest of us didn't count. Throw the minnows back in the water. And so, here I am, having swum back. Or rather, ridden back."

"What do we do now?"

"We wait. We wait."

---

Two weeks went by. London talked of nothing else but the arrest of Essex. Swarms of people gathered at our gates, and many more in front of York House. Ballads celebrating Essex's bravery and chivalry were brayed in taverns and outside his prison. Slurs against Cecil were painted on walls, calling him a mole, a miscreant, and a mouse. People muttered against the Queen, although they dared not do it so openly. Frances decked herself in mourning clothes and applied to the Queen for permission to visit her husband. She was turned away, so she went and took her place before the courtyard of York House and stood forlornly, attracting much attention, until the Queen ordered her out of sight. I was astounded at her audacity and rather applauded it.

Southampton, free to roam, moved into Essex House at Robert's invitation. He, his wife Elizabeth Vernon, Penelope, and Rutland took up theatergoing and lolled their days away in idleness, seeing a new play almost every day. No one had been punished, no one curtailed, for the injudicious gallop back from Ireland but Robert.

On the rare occasions we all dined together, I could not help looking at Southampton in wonder that I had ever involved myself with him. Had that truly happened? I could not imagine it now. He seemed a feather-pated child, laughing and playing while my son languished in prison. Rutland was no better. What pitiful material crept around court these days. No wonder Robert Cecil had no rivals.

"What's it to be this afternoon?" my own daughter Penelope—a companion to them in idleness—asked before dinner was over. Her paramour, Lord Mountjoy, to his credit, was attending to state business and seldom came with them.

"There's something new at the Swan," said Southampton. "But I understand it was just dashed off in a fortnight."

"Blah," said Rutland. "It's a comedy, too. I can't stand another romp with clever servants and fat masters. No!"

"Jonson's *Every Man Out of His Humour* is said to be amusing," said Elizabeth.

"I saw it. I don't mind sitting through it again," said Rutland.

They turned accusatory eyes at him. "When? You went without us?"

"You were riding," said Rutland.

Children: riding and plays and amusements. I was angry at all of them, as if it were their fault Robert was in disgrace.

"Essex! Essex!" wavering voices from outside carried into the chamber. I rose and looked out to see a group of at least twenty people, held back by the iron gates, shouting into the courtyard. "Brave honor graces him! Foul envy has struck him down! Set him free! Set him free!"

"He is not here! Shout your demands at York House!" Frances leaned out the window to answer them. "Shout them at Whitehall!"

"Frances," I said. "Sit back down. Do not shout such things in public."

She turned to me. "This is my home and I'll shout what I please. Let it come to the Queen's ears!"

"There is nothing that does not come to the Queen's ears," I hissed. "And do you think this"—I gestured to the gathering, murmuring crowd—"is helping Robert's cause?"

"Cause? His cause should be justice!" she said.

"Justice is a prostitute," said Southampton. "For sale to the best customer."

Then I remembered what I had liked about him. So young and so world-weary.

---

October turned into November. The crowds grew in front of the gates, and soon members of my household were inviting some into the courtyard and mingling with them. Christopher seldom missed an opportunity to go down and talk with them. Since his return from Ireland he seemed changed; once in a while I had even come across him in the chapel, sitting motionless and staring at the altar. I knew he had Catholic leanings, due to his upbringing, but he had always seemed cheerily indifferent to religion. Had his exposure to Irish Catholicism converted him? The wayside shrines, the Celtic crosses, the legends about saints and snakes and whatnot were said to be seductive. There is no one more vulnerable to the lure of religion than an uncommitted person, assuming he is not outright hostile to it. Christopher had never cared enough to be hostile. I hoped my suspicions were wrong. This was not the time to turn Catholic. We had enough trouble as it was.

Ever-larger crowds gathered in front of York House. Egerton, distressed at his role as jailer, ordered them away. But all his warnings had no effect. When his guards came out, the crowds melted away, but a few hours later they returned, like ants to a source of honey.

Suddenly Elizabeth Vernon and Penelope announced they could no longer stand the commotion around the house and left for the country. Once they were gone, the men felt free to indulge in all the tavern- and playgoing they wished, and to drink themselves silly. Frances, her daughter Elizabeth, and I remained sober and kept watch, while Christopher spent more time in the courtyard with the accusatory crowd.

Then the word came down: The Queen announced that the Court of Star Chamber was to issue a public pronouncement about Robert's misdeeds.

"She seeks to defend herself," said Christopher. "If we hear the murmurs and accusations in the streets, so does she. She cannot rest until the matter is settled."

"It will never be settled in any way detrimental to herself," I said. "Robert told me she plays with loaded dice, so as never to lose."

"That's Robert talking. Foolish of him not to see all along that if you are Queen you do not need loaded dice."

---

As the day neared for the hearing, I noticed Southampton suddenly curtailing his carousing and huddling with Christopher and Charles Blount, Lord Mountjoy, in my house. I asked Christopher several times what they were concerning themselves with, and he gave evasive answers. I disliked being shunted aside like that.

That they were plotting was obvious. What they were plotting was less obvious. Clearly it was in my own interest to be ignorant of whatever it was, so I would be innocent of any accusation of collusion. But the feeling of uselessness, of not mattering enough to anyone to be consulted, was painful.

---

If I had planned it, I could not have come into Southampton's empty rooms at a better time. But I had not planned it; I had merely come to deliver an invitation to a dinner at the Earl of Bedford's house nearby. I laid it on his writing table, and as I did so the unmistakable royal seal of James VI of Scotland glared up at me, affixed to a letter.

Before I even touched it I knew it was treasonous. Did I wish to keep my ignorance and my technical innocence? No, I was mistress of this household and I must know what went on here. Before I could read it, however, I saw beneath it a draft of the letter it must be an answer to. Quickly I took it up and read it.

Lord Mountjoy was continuing a correspondence with the Scots king that Robert had apparently started. He assured James that Robert entirely supported his succession after Elizabeth and had no designs on the throne himself. But he "suggested" that James might bring a Scottish force south to rescue Robert from his unfair imprisonment.

Oh, saints defend us! If Elizabeth got wind of this—! How could he be so rash as to commit this to writing?

I switched letters and saw that James, wisely, refused to commit himself or even name the thing he refused to embrace.

There were more papers on the table. Frantic with apprehension and fear, I took them up one by one and read them. They listed possible actions open to Robert. The first was that he should escape from Egerton and flee to France, where King Henri IV would be forced to shelter him. The second was that he raise a force of Welsh loyal to the Devereux name and foment a rebellion. The third was that he engineer a takeover of the court and hold the Queen hostage until she agreed to purge herself of evil advisers like Cecil, Howard, and Cobham.

Mountjoy was facilitating all this! Mountjoy, who had the Queen's confidence! Did Penelope know this? She must. They were all in on it together. Their playgoing and tavern drinking was just a screen, and I had not seen through it. My Essex House was a center of plotting and subversion.

We would all be turned out, at best, or imprisoned and executed, at worst. Christopher had joined them; my own husband was part of the plot.

Another letter in an envelope. Shamelessly, I took it out. If they had the right to endanger my life and my home, reading their private letters was certainly my right. It was from Robert, obviously smuggled out of York House. He said he rejected the idea of going to France, because he could not bear to live the life of a fugitive. But he did not repudiate the other two suggestions. What was he thinking? Did he seriously want to try one of them?

More letters. These were in a heap and were short, consisting of one or two paragraphs. Robert lamented his ill health. He was suffering from what he called "the Irish flux." He was like to die. But if he did not, he wished to retire into private life in the country. Evidently he had written to the Queen requesting just such a release. She must have ignored or refused it.

Others were lengthy exhortations to Southampton to repent and lead a good life, to turn from sin. They would have made John Knox proud. He told Southampton that they must honor the Sabbath. That they must spend all their time in prayer. He even wrote to his erstwhile boon companion, "You must say with me, 'There is no peace to the wicked and ungodly. I will make a covenant with my soul.'"

Had his wits quite turned? Had the strain driven him mad? Or was he so broken in body that he no longer had the strength to persevere? His friends still had energy and wits enough, it seemed, to endanger us all. Oh, if only I could go to him, see him! But I knew better than to ask the Queen. If she would not allow his wife to see him, she certainly would not allow me. Even to remind her of my existence now would harden her heart further against Robert.

---

That night as we made ready for bed, I looked over at Christopher, wearily pulling off his boots. At least he was home at a decent hour tonight. I tried to make myself as alluring as possible, wearing a sleeping gown that was made for beauty rather than comfort. I left off my nightcap and brushed out my hair. I even dabbed some violet perfume on my neck, something I had not done in a long time. Instead of getting into bed in the usual way, I slid in. Christopher did not seem to notice and threw back the covers and flopped down. This was going to take work. I had almost forgotten how.

I inched up to him and leaned on my elbow, looking down at him. His eyes were already closed; he was not even going to look at me. I leaned down and kissed him, and he opened his eyes, surprised.

"I have missed you, Christopher," I said.

"I was gone almost half a year," he admitted.

"I have missed you since you have been *back*," I said.

"I have been preoccupied, I know." He sighed. "Life is not normal. We all worry about Robert. As long as he is imprisoned, we are prisoners along with him."

"He would not want that," I said, parroting the phrase people use of the dead.

"I cannot help it. It is hard to lie here, warm and safe and beside you, when he is denied his own wife and a mind at peace."

How was I to get him to confide in me? "Do you think something might ever alter his situation?" I asked. I slipped my arm around him.

"In what way?"

"That someone—or something—might persuade the Queen to look at things in a different light?" I was so close to him now I could almost whisper in his ear.

"Only if Cecil stops blocking her light," he grunted. Still he made no move to turn toward me or kiss me.

"There is nothing you or I or anyone can do about that," I said, tempting him to follow that thought.

"I am not so sure."

I waited for him to elaborate but he did not.

Suddenly I was angry at his aloofness and made up my mind to end it, if only to prove something to myself. But I must not show my anger; no, I must be soothing and seductive. Surely I must remember how! I began caressing his hair and kissing his lips in a rain of swift, teasing pecks. Slowly, very slowly, he warmed to me. It was like rousing a bear from his den. So much work. But I prevailed. I still knew my business, *that* business. But I failed to achieve my goal—that he make me his confidante.

# 71

he bells were tolling again, as they did to mark every Accession Day. The city of London rang with them—deep-throated peals from St. Clement Danes, shriller ones from St. Helen's, mellow ones from Lambeth, doleful ones from Westminster Abbey. They blended together like a choir with voices ranging from the high purity of a boy's slender throat to the resounding bass of a barrel-chested man's. Elizabeth, Elizabeth, Elizabeth, they announced. Queen, Queen, Queen . . .

"Forty-one years the old harridan's been on the throne," said Southampton, buffing his nails as the sound poured relentlessly into the room.

"Shush. None of that talk. Someone might report it," said Christopher. As if to prove his point, there was a rustling in the curtains, and a servant entered with ale, bowing and pretending to be deaf.

"I was not born when she came to the throne," said Southampton. "I don't remember a time when she wasn't Queen. Sort of like God. Always there, looking and watching. Rewarding sometimes, punishing other times."

"Christopher asked you to stop that," I said. "If you cannot remember, I do. I can tell you that what she replaced was so dreadful even a child was aware of it. We like to think that England passed directly from the hands of King Henry to those of Elizabeth, but in truth we had to endure the rule of a child, and then the rule of an old bitter woman. Neither was able to lead the country. I tell you, when the word came that Mary Tudor was dead and Elizabeth was Queen, we rejoiced like a man let out of prison."

"And now she keeps *us* in prison."

"If you are in prison it is because you fancy yourself to be so. You insult Robert, who truly is in prison."

"I am in prison alongside him in sympathy."

I looked around him, at the finely polished table with its silver candlesticks on its tapestry runner that his arm was flung carelessly across. "A prison you can walk out of any time you choose," I said.

Robert, I had heard, was so ill he could not even stand to let his bedding be changed, and had to be moved in a sling. The Irish flux, they called it. But I suspected it was his crushed spirits that debilitated him. He had been summoned to attend the hearing at Star Chamber but replied that he was too ill to attend.

The Lord Keeper, by tradition, delivered a speech to the people from Star Chamber at the end of the legal term, and the pronouncement about Robert was yoked to this. The fact that the truce had expired in Ireland and O'Neill had rearmed made the government even more hostile toward Robert. The session was scheduled for November 29. But five days before that, a royal summons arrived for Charles Blount, Lord Mountjoy.

"What can it be?" cried Southampton. "Don't go! They will arrest you!"

"I've done nothing," he said.

The letters. The government had found out about the correspondence with King James. It was treason even to discuss the succession or Elizabeth's death. "Are you sure?" I asked him.

"I wasn't even in Ireland," he said. "I stayed here, manning the defenses against the Armada. Which, as it turns out, was wrecked once again on its way here. God is truly an Englishman. Or a Protestant. In any case, I must go. It is too late to run away."

"God protect you," I said, and it was more than just a polite phrase.

---

He returned at dusk, clutching a bulging sheath of papers. He was almost grinning. Stepping in and throwing off his mantle, he announced, "I am appointed lord deputy of Ireland in Robert's place." He seemed stunned, but not as stunned as the rest of us.

Was the Queen ignorant of what had gone on here? Had her vaunted ability to know all that passed within her kingdom declined? Or . . . did she know very well, and far from rewarding Mountjoy with this post, was offering him up as a sacrifice?

So Robert was to be replaced, never restored. The waters were closing in around him.

---

At the Privy Council hearing in Star Chamber—which Robert did not attend—before laymen and judges of the kingdom, the government read out its grievances. Lord Keeper Thomas Egerton began by lamenting the tide of rumors and false reports that were causing unrest in the kingdom. He mentioned the libels against court members, the cowardly writings on palace walls. Far from being spontaneous, these were orchestrated by a traitor somewhere, or a group of them. He did not accuse Robert directly, but he had no need to. Everyone understood whom he meant. He then went on to stress the gravity of the Irish situation and the shocking deportment of the commander in leaving his post abruptly and contrary to royal command.

Lord Buckhurst, the treasurer, followed with specific figures of the expense of this large, lavishly provisioned army, which could have mowed through Spain if it had been turned in that direction. Instead, it had dissipated all its advantages. The truce, dictated by The O'Neill, negating all the English achievements, or hope of them, mocked the Queen's honor. And Essex had agreed to them—and who knew what else, in the privacy of their unwitnessed talk.

Others chimed in, accusing Essex of wasting public money, disobedience, gross incompetence in the campaign, and making a dishonorable and unauthorized treaty with the enemy.

But there was no sentence from the Queen. No indication of what she intended to do with him. He was to remain at York House. And—almost as an afterthought—his household was to be dispersed. He had no need of retainers or servants now, and they were to quit Essex House immediately.

---

"We are stripped," I said, stunned. All around me the servants were taking their leave, finishing their last tasks. They dared not linger with the Queen's explicit orders that they vacate—had not their master come to his sorry pass by disobeying a direct order from her?—yet they did not wish to leave things in chaos. One hundred and sixty were to be dismissed. We were allowed to retain only the ones absolutely necessary to keep the household running—a very few cooks, groundsmen, stable hands, boatmen, and chamber scourers. I had no experience of living this way.

"I had little thought of becoming a dairymaid at my age," I said to Frances. "Yet I will have to learn to milk."

---

Southampton decided to decamp; he certainly would not remain in an echoing, empty space like the ruined Essex House.

"Back to Drury House for me," he said, airily. "It's in the fields, but who needs the river?"

"We women will stay until the Queen orders us to depart along with the last of the servants," I said. It was the nearest we could be to Robert.

"Thank you for your hospitality," he said, bowing, and taking my hand. He turned the palm up and caressed it an instant, too quickly for anyone to see, and looked me in the eyes. His face was blank but his eyes burned into mine. I remembered when those blue irises had filled my vision.

"You are welcome," I said, pulling my hand away.

"And where's the rehearsal to be?" A familiar, lost voice called into the room. Will stepped in, looking around in the gathering gloom. He stopped when he saw me.

"Not here, Will," said Southampton. "I'm moving. The servants have gone, and like a rat abandoning a sinking ship, I'm after them." He looked slyly at me. "I had offered the hall here as rehearsal space for his new play. Will wanted to recite his part privately to see how it flowed onstage, before getting anyone else's opinion."

"If I walk through it as an actor, it is far more revealing than reading drafts," he said. He seemed embarrassed to have come upon me. Undoubtedly Southampton, in telling him the house would be empty, had implied I was moving. It would have been ideal private rehearsal space.

"So you have returned to acting?" I asked. This stiff, impersonal conversation was awkward.

"Only in small parts," he said. "Nothing that would make a real difference in the performance."

"He gets tired of being himself," said Southampton. "Oh, don't we all?"

"You are welcome to use this space. God knows it is being wasted. Just don't mind the lack of attendants," I said.

"It is better without them," he said.

"You have had a hand in the politics of the day," I said. "Your plays about English kings have been linked to Robert, and not to his benefit, as you well know. The flattering mention of him in *Henry V* has, alas, not come true."

"He hardly returned home with the Irish rebellion broached on his sword, as you so charmingly phrased it," said Southampton.

"He broached himself on his own sword," I said. "If it makes me an unnatural mother to state it, then so be it. I am not blind to his faults."

"I have left English history as a subject," Will declared. "I have been in ancient Rome, most recently, and now am engaged in Denmark. My newest effort is set there, at Elsinore."

"Politics again!" cried Southampton. "Anne of Denmark—King James's wife—she's from Elsinore! That was one of her family castles. James spent time with her there on their honeymoon. Are you hinting at the succession? You know it's a hot topic."

Will smiled. "No, it has nothing to do with that. It's a reworking of an old play about a Danish prince, Hamlet, whose father has been murdered by his uncle. You would agree, there is no connection to the present royal family."

"What part are you playing?" I asked. "You don't look very Danish."

"I'm playing the ghost of Hamlet's father. Since I have to wear a helmet, no one can tell whether I look Danish or Italian or Scottish."

"That's good," said Southampton, "because you don't look any of those. You have the most boring, common English face I've ever seen."

"Why, what's wrong with looking English?" I asked.

"It's the 'boring, common' part he objects to," said Southampton. "Who of us wants to be that—although by definition that's exactly what most of us are."

"You are welcome to use this space whenever you like," I said, changing the subject. Robert had not wanted to be ordinary, and therein lay his doom. "I promise not to intrude."

---

The dreary business of dismantling proud Essex House continued. This was the second time I had witnessed it, and it wrung my heart. Both times were at *her* insistence. After Leicester died, she had ordered it stripped to repay his debts to her. (What sort of love was that?) Slowly and painstakingly, I had built it up again, only to have its contents vanish once more. At least this time I did not have to render the goods, only cover or store them to protect them from neglect. The rooms grew emptier, each chair removed or tapestry folded away a memory dismissed. Our living contracted down into a very few rooms, while the rest of the house was ghostly.

Will did return, to help Southampton move or, rather, to help him sort through his papers to make sure none of his own were mixed in.

"For someone so indifferent to publishing, you are very possessive about your scripts," Southampton said.

"I'm possessive so that they can't be published," said Will. "Why should the publisher make money that should be mine? If a stray copy should land in one of those men's hands, they'll print it and keep all the money for themselves. They'll include all the mistakes—they'll print any version, no matter how corrupt. Or, I should say, a version as corrupt as they are. So"—he hugged his manuscripts to his chest—"I will keep them close."

Southampton shrugged. "I don't have any. I gave them all back. Look all you like."

"That is one reason I like having rich friends," said Will. "I need never worry that they will rob me."

"I'll collect the last of this tomorrow," said Southampton. He turned to me. "Until next we meet, Lady Leicester," he said, bowing smartly.

May it not be at Robert's hanging, I prayed. But even to say the words was to call it into being, so I was silent.

Will continued poking through the pile of leftover papers on the floor. He knelt down, setting a candle to one side, looking carefully at each item he pulled forth. Finally, he held one up and said, "Aha! Here's one overlooked."

It was only a single sheet. "That cannot be a full play," I said. "It must be only one small revision."

"No, it's a sonnet I wrote when he was my patron. In it I urged him to marry and replicate himself. So, since he has obeyed, it would seem to have done its work." He waved it dismissively.

Without thinking, I reached over and grabbed his arm. "Don't destroy it!" I said.

"Keep it, then," he said. "I will always know where to find it, should I ever need to publish the sonnets. And perhaps, if his daughter grows up to be ugly, or, in any case, not as dazzling as he, he may need to consult them again."

He turned to look down at his hand, still clutching the paper, as he pressed it into mine. He moved quickly away and stood over the pile of papers, hands on hips. "That's all, then," he said.

"Shall I expect you for a rehearsal?" I asked. "You are welcome to use the space."

"Thank you," was all he said, turning to the door.

I was left looking around my abandoned home. Oh, would life ever return to it?

# 72

# ELIZABETH

*December 1599*

n the deepening twilight that is London in mid-December, church bells began to toll. The sound penetrated through the blue gloom with a sharpness not possible in warm weather, an ominous ring, like the keening of grieving women.

It meant that someone of great importance had died. But there was no one of that rank and stature near to death. Lord Burghley had gone, Sir Francis Drake had gone, Lord Leicester had gone, and now little men populated the court and the realm. Immediately I summoned Raleigh, stationed with his guards in the watching chamber.

"What is this?" I asked. "All the churches of London announce a death."

"I shall inquire and bring an answer upon the instant," he said, looking as puzzled as I.

While I waited, I stood with Catherine looking out at the darkening waters of the Thames rippling past. There were fewer boatmen out in these blustery days, but still I saw a number of craft diligently making their way up and down river. Londoners were a hardy lot.

"I hope people do not think it is I," I said, with a light tone that did not match what I felt inside. I knew that people were attuned for those bells, that all across the land there was speculation about what span of my life still remained. They had been wondering ever since I turned fifty.

Catherine knew better than to utter a platitude. She merely reached out and took my hand.

"Ma'am!" Raleigh strode through the doors. "They say it's the Earl of Essex. He sank low last night and now has died."

I had known he was ill, but he always collapsed with illness when things went badly for him. It was nervous prostration, not true disease. But this time he had succumbed. Still, it came as a shock.

"The Irish flux, then," I said. "Poor man. Send for Thomas Egerton. What a sad thing, to have the man in his charge die. I never meant to inflict this great a burden upon a man of such good conscience."

"The earl is gone," said Catherine, shaking her head. "It seems impossible. Such a man, larger than all around him, cannot just vanish."

"Others, just as large, have vanished before him. There is no man too large for death's jaws." But I could not believe it, either. The beautiful, wayward child gone, before he had attained whatever it was he had been seeking. Now, as I remembered him, he seemed to go backward in time, shrink, grow younger and happier, until I was gazing at that enigmatic boy at his mother's side who had refused to kiss me.

Full dark had fallen before Egerton arrived. He swept off his cloak, glittering with night mist, and knelt.

"Thomas, I am grieved for you and for him," I told him. "Please rise. When did it happen?"

He brushed his fair hair and said, "It did not happen. The earl is alive. Just barely, but alive."

"Then why—"

"A servant from the house must have spread the word, and no one thought to verify it. It was well known that the earl was sinking, and the people just assumed that the illness had followed its natural course."

"Will it?"

"I cannot say. He is weak, but he has been weak for some time. He does not seem to be losing ground."

"I shall send my physicians to him." I was momentarily elated that he was not dead. Then, the pressing problem of what to do with him came back.

"Send them to my wife as well," he said. "She is gravely ill, and I cannot tend to her as I need to. The earl usurps all my care and attention. It is not he who is the prisoner, but I. Find him another jailer! Set me free!" Egerton burst out.

"Why, Thomas, I did not know that your Elizabeth was not well," I said. "Certainly you must not neglect her to hover over the earl, who is never content, no matter how much attention he receives. And as for another jailer—if there were another man so honest, strong, reliable, and as kind a friend to the prisoner, I would appoint him in an instant and relieve you. But there is not. So you must endure a while longer. If the earl survives, we will have a proper trial for him and settle his situation."

After he left, I turned to Catherine. "Only royal deaths are announced by bells. So this is what the people think of him?"

"A state funeral can have such bells," she reminded me.

"Only with my permission," I said. "I did not give it. I was not even asked."

—

My physicians confirmed that Essex was indeed very ill but the outcome uncertain. He was not exactly at death's threshold, but any turn for the worse would push him over.

"His liver is stopped and perished," one of them reported.

"His entrails and guts are ulcerated," said another, shaking his head mournfully.

"I shall send him some of my game broth," I said.

"He may be past that," the physician said. "But knowing it came from your hand may prove healing."

It had not saved Burghley, but it was all I could offer.

—

Christmas was coming, and a new century: the year of our Lord 1600. We would celebrate at Richmond this year, and in mid-December the court moved. As I entered the royal barge, I looked back at York House, so near to Whitehall. It was quite dark. Only a few lighted windows reflected in the black, lapping water.

Richmond had been readied for us, and the palace was comfortably snug. The familiar boat-shaped bed with its sea-green hangings greeted me like an old friend.

"You have been waiting for me, have you?" I addressed it. It is easy to imagine that our beds, chairs, and tables miss us. Certainly knowing that when I returned to one of my palaces all would be unchanged was a comfort to me.

Catherine was with me, and the admiral would soon join us. Helena, living so nearby, would also come, bringing her family. The younger maids of honor and the ladies of the chamber were looking forward to the court festivities, hoping for a season of flirtation that might lead somewhere. Their trunks were full of new gowns and old family jewels.

The Great Hall would be the focus of dances, banquets, and new plays. I had ordered it hung with greens, garlands, and holly.

Although everyone was bubbly with excitement, and the palace glowed with decorations and anticipation, I could not shake a melancholy that had settled in my bones. This time last year Essex had been healthy and ready to embark to Ireland. We had danced together at Twelfth Night. But now I suspected that even then he had been corresponding with O'Neill, perhaps arranging their meeting. And I knew that he had also approached King James—secretly, he thought. If I wished we could somehow turn back a year, he must wish it even more.

And there was something else—an uneasy superstition about the turning of the century, leaving behind the one I was born in. It felt vaguely unlucky, as if the new century would cast me out as someone who did not belong.

As I stood in the bedchamber musing on this, Catherine knocked timidly.

When I bade her enter, I saw to my surprise that her husband was there with her.

"Why, Charles!" I said, ready to make a jest about his being in the bedchamber. But his somber face, and Catherine's tear-streaked cheeks, stopped me.

"He has brought sad news," said Catherine. "It seems—it seems—" Her choking tears made it impossible for her to continue.

"Marjorie Norris has died," he said. "I came here as soon as I heard."

My heart stopped. I swear it. There was a pause where nothing stirred within me, and I felt myself falling, a great swooping gasp. Then it started up again. Beat. Beat. I gripped my hands together tightly and said, "How?" My voice was just a squeak.

"It was grief for their sons," he said. "Sir Henry sent word from Rycote. She never rallied from the loss of the last three in Ireland in such quick succession, he said, and just dwindled away. He was powerless to stop it—although when I last saw him he was withering away, too. He will follow her soon."

"That is fitting," I said. They had been together for fifty-five years, a rarity for a marriage. But oh! I had been with them almost that long.

"She will be buried in the family tomb at Rycote chapel," said Charles.

I would never see her again. That enormity only just now settled on me. Whether or not we had said formal good-byes did not matter. I had grown accustomed to the truth that one seldom says them to the people one loves the most. But never to hear her laugh again, never to walk together through the autumn leaves, never to hear her astute comment about someone again . . . oh, this would be hard.

"We will pray for her," I said. And, sinking down on my chair, I did. But the prayer turned to one of thankfulness that God had given me such a faithful friend, and for so long. "The Lord giveth, and the Lord taketh away," I said aloud. "Blessed be the name of the Lord." In the end, what else can we believe, if we are to survive?

---

For the younger people, particularly those celebrating Christmas at court for the first time, I suppose it was a festive event. Certainly the fires blazed as brightly, the musicians played as sprightly, the snow flew as furiously, and the banquets were as sumptuous as of yore. If I had been seeing it through fresh eyes, it would have dazzled me. I got myself up in the richest gowns, draped my ropes of pearls over my bosom, affixed my jeweled hair ornaments, and sallied forth to my own tournament: a test of my skill in creating make-believe. I wanted the youngest to remember this when they were old, to be able to say, "I shall never forget Christmas in the old Queen's court." I owed it to them—and to myself.

Nonetheless, I had a shiver of foreboding when midnight came and the entire century that began with "fifteen" slid into "sixteen." To straddle two centuries is a fearsome thing; one does not have to be superstitious to tremble at the veiled years stretching out, disappearing in a fog of mystery. This century would outlive me; how many years would I be allowed to tread into it?

Raleigh was standing beside me when the last few moments of 1599 flitted away. His sturdy presence made the absence of Essex all the more noticeable. What a difference a year can make in our fortunes.

"Your Majesty looks glum," he said. "That is no way to welcome the new century. 'Tis said whatever you are doing in the first minutes or hours, you'll do all year. Whatever is troubling you, thrust it aside immediately, lest it stick!"

I laughed. "You are good medicine, Sir Walter," I said. "I was thinking only that I don't like the sound of 'sixteen' as well as 'fifteen.' But I must get used to it."

"You should take as your model our dear Constancia," he said.

Constancia? Who was that? A Portuguese lady? I did not want him to realize I did not know, so I smiled.

"The tortoise, Your Majesty," he said pointedly. "Remember?"

"Oh! I thought you meant a fair lady."

"She is fair—if you are a male tortoise. But there is none nearby. She must be lonely."

"All maiden ladies are not lonely, Sir Walter. And why should I take her as my model?"

He shrugged. "The centuries come, the centuries go—she lives through them all, hardly noticing."

"But hardly participating, either," I said. "I would not envy that." God knew I had plunged fully into the life surrounding me.

Peering down the long corridor of the new century, I knew that whoever followed me would inherit the problems I had failed to solve.

But already I could feel, like the delicate stirring of air in a sealed room, the longing for change in my people.

"The gloomy look again," said Raleigh. "Come, we must dance and chase that melancholy away."

---

I got through it. All the masques, the recitals, the master of misrule's uproarious Twelfth Night, even a comedy about courtly people hiding in the forest. It was yet another offering by that busy fellow, Shakespeare, who played a rustic in it. He must do nothing but write, or else he wrote very fast. Although I laughed and nodded, I paid little attention, putting on as good an act as the actors themselves.

Now at last it was over. The carts carrying the theatrical costumes and props rumbled away; the courtiers returned to their homes; the servants stripped the greens and the banners from the Great Hall, and we faced January with no adornments, no shields.

---

We crept along through the dreary, cold month, this year an especially dismal one. The weather, like a wayward child, swung back and forth between freezing sleet and drifts of snow and warmer spells that melted the ice and sent melancholy drips from every eave and down chimneys to make fires smolder and sizzle. I visited Westminster Abbey on the date of my father's death and made a melancholy circuit around the chapels, paying homage to the tombs of kings and nobles, my guards following me at a discreet distance. In the winter the building never really got light, but by early afternoon even that was fading and most of the illumination came from the candles and torches. In spite of constant roof repairs, I could hear dripping water everywhere and see puddles on the flagstones.

Westminster Abbey: home of our national triumphs, our coronations, and our thanksgiving celebrations, guardian of the past. Once a year I came and walked through my family's chapel at the far end of the nave. My grandfather Henry VII had torn down the old Lady Chapel to build his new mausoleum, and it was a graceful and soaring work of stone. He lay inside a magnificent fenced tomb, shockingly modern when it was first constructed, of Italian design. He had, uncharacteristically, spent a fortune on it. Now his effigy lay serenely on top of his tomb, beside his wife's, content with his expenditure.

My brother and sister lay nearby; Edward's grave was at the foot of his grandfather's. My sister's effigy rested upon her hearse in the north aisle. Her funeral was the last time the old Latin requiem Mass, which had rung out in the cathedral for centuries, had been heard. I walked slowly by it, looking at her shadowed face. It was a good likeness, her mouth clamped tight as it was when she was standing her ground—which had been most of the time.

The dank and the dripping made me shiver. So this was the best we could offer the eminent for their resting places? I left the chapel and made my way down the aisles past the other side chapels that were full of tombs and markers.

In the Chapel of St. Nicholas, closest to the royal chapel, lay Elizabeth Cecil, in an alabaster altar tomb with a black marble top adorned with poems written by her widower, Robert. She had died shortly before his father, Burghley. I had been so preoccupied with my own grief in losing my cousins Hunsdon and Knollys that I had failed to notice Robert's loss. I felt a sudden rush of understanding of what my little principal secretary was enduring—an early widowerhood, the loss of his father, which could not be compensated for by offices and honors. He had never mentioned it, never sought to bring it to my attention.

Almost across from it was the Chapel of St. John the Baptist, where that dear man Hunsdon rested. His family was busy erecting a monument that seemed to go all the way to the ceiling.

As I proceeded down the aisle, reaching the arm of the north transept, I turned to visit the Chapel of St. Andrew, right by the north entrance. Not to be outdone by the Careys, the Norris family was erecting a monument that would soar twenty-five feet and be festooned with figures kneeling and praying. Marjorie would be amused by its pretensions, no doubt. I could almost hear her ringing laugh if she beheld it.

# 73

It was strictly forbidden for anyone to predict my death or speculate about the succession, or even to discuss it in public. But it was on everyone's mind. I alone could break the rule and dare to probe my future, and it was for the good of my people that I must do so. I myself would rather not know. But ignorance is unforgivable and negligent in a ruler.

My old adviser and astrologer John Dee was back in London for a brief visit from Manchester. I asked him to see me.

He had noticeably aged. His shiny, dark eyes were still vital, but they stared out from a weathered, lined face, and his beard was white as a summer cloud.

He scrutinized me likewise. "Your Majesty is looking well, it pleases me to see. The years sit lightly upon you."

I laughed. "Quite the contrary. They weigh upon me, especially since we have entered a new century." I gripped his arm, a thin stick under his satin sleeve. "I am afraid, John. This time to come does not feel friendly to me." I held up my hands. "I know I must die in it. I will not outlive it. I shall not be Thomas Parr, who has seen three centuries—born in the 1400s, lived through the 1500s, and I pray he is still alive to see this 1600. But that is not given to anyone but him. And I am not sure I could bear the weight of a crown for all those years."

"So . . . I gather that is what I am here for? To part the curtain of the future for you?"

"Yes. I would rather glimpse what lurks there, no matter how threatening. So set up your equipment. I will wait. We will not be disturbed."

"Very well." He shuffled over to a little trunk he had brought. How slow his movements were. When we have not seen someone in a long time, all the changes are exaggerated. He extracted his mirror, his scrying glass, his charts.

"I need a table," he said.

I called for one.

He carefully spread out the implements of his trade, then leaned forward and said gently, "If Your Majesty is ready, we may begin."

Was I ready? I gripped my hands together and said, "Let us begin, then."

First he consulted meticulously with his astrological chart. Then he asked that the curtains be drawn so he could see the reflections in the mirror and the glass better. Muttering, he bent over them, squinting his eyes and moving the candlestick farther away. There were long silences as he seemed to hear other voices, see invisible beings. I almost held my breath but I could not wait long enough.

The moments ticked by, stretching out as I waited—first boringly, then nervously, and finally agonizingly. Why did he not speak? What was he seeing? I dared not speak and literally break the spell.

At length he covered his scrying glass with a black velvet cloth and put his convex mirror into a satin bag with embroidered symbols on it. He sank down on the cushioned bench that had been provided for him. His shoulders slumped as if an intolerable weight had been draped across them.

"Tell me! Do not spare me!" I cried, breaking the silence.

He raised his eyes to me, and the tortured look in them almost stilled my heart. "It has come at last," he finally said.

"What? What has come at last?"

"The last battle. The one that has been waiting for you."

"The last battle?"

"The supreme test," he said.

"But . . . the Armada? Was that not the supreme test? Did it not come during 1588, the year foretold as the annus mirabilis, the year of prodigies and wonders?"

"That was not it," he said apologetically. "Would that it were."

"Is Spain invading again? Is that it? Was the Armada year of 1588 but a rehearsal?"

"No. Spain will not come again, at least not in a form that is threatening."

"Ireland? Will the Irish unite under The O'Neill and invade us?"

"No. Ireland will be vanquished."

"France? Will France turn on us, revert to being our old enemy?"

"No," he said.

"What, then?" I cried. "I have named all our enemies. Is it another plague? Or religious convulsion?"

"None of those things, but you are getting closer."

"What do you mean?"

"You are now naming enemies that are already on our soil and can undermine us."

"Oh, John, torment me no longer! Name the thing!"

"Civil war," he said. "One Englishman against another."

The War of the Roses. The succession! "After my death—there will be fighting about who inherits the crown?"

"No. Not that. The crown will pass peacefully."

"Enough riddles! Speak plain!"

"I cannot see quite clearly enough to speak plain. There will be a battle, Englishman against Englishman. A battle not over who wears the crown but over whether there should be a crown at all. And before that, a rebellion against you. Mordred will arm, will challenge you. And as Arthur's heir, you must withstand him. *That* is your supreme test. There will be a great battle, and the outcome—I cannot see it here. The glass went murky, the mirror clouded. It was as if to say, *It has not been decided yet.*"

"Camelot must die," I said. "That is the story. It was too perfect to last. And so it went down in rebellion, disillusionment, and perfidy. Arthur was betrayed, and by those he loved and trusted most—Lancelot and Guinevere."

"It was not Lancelot who led the battle against him, but Mordred."

"But it was the betrayal of Lancelot that set it all in motion, that ruined the fellowship and code of the Round Table."

"Something always sets it in motion," he said. "In the Garden, it was the serpent. In Camelot, Lancelot. Here"—he paused—"you must identify it. But I daresay you recognize it."

Yes. I recognized it. "Must there be a true battle, or can it be staved off?"

"There will be an actual battle. What I see is not a symbol but an actual clash of arms."

How could that be? Essex was under arrest. But what of his followers? They gathered in his courtyard, milling and shouting. "And you cannot see who will prevail?"

"No, Your Majesty."

"Or do you see it and wish to spare me the knowledge that I will be defeated?"

"No, I honestly do not see it. Just the noise and smoke of battle."

"Who, then, do you see wearing the crown when the civil war starts?" Perhaps that was a way of finding out the winner.

"No one I recognize. A man."

"Not James?"

"No. Not James."

"His son, then?"

"Unfortunately he does not wear a sign, and I cannot recognize him. He has most likely not been born yet."

"Oh, God! Is there no end to this?" A cry wrung from my heart.

"What do you mean, Your Majesty?"

"I mean, will the crown never be safe and reside in peace?"

"Nothing is safe," he said. "But your rule will be remembered as Camelot, a golden age for England."

"Golden, and lost," I said. "I would rather have iron and endurance."

"That is what makes you a great monarch," he said. "You are not dazzled easily. If at all."

"Oh, I appreciate the value of what shines and scintillates. I have made shrewd use of it. But I am not deceived as to its essence, and its worth. There needs to be iron underneath."

"I have grieved you," he said.

"How can the truth grieve me? The truth is the truth."

"The truth can be ugly."

"Not as ugly as the Gorgon. She need not turn us to stone, render us unable to move. I shall be prepared. I shall watch for the arrival of Mordred. Now I know he is coming."

---

After he left, I sank down on my chair. Was I ready for this? There had been no battle for the crown since my grandfather met Richard on Bosworth Field. That was over a hundred years ago. But no one had forgotten it. The fence around Henry's tomb in Westminster, which I had just seen, showed the lost crown in the bush, waiting for him to retrieve it. Recent secret correspondence about the succession—captured by Robert Cecil—speculated on who might inherit my crown and said it was not likely to fall into a bush for want of claimants.

No one had forgotten what was presumed to be the last battle. But now Dee saw that it was not so; it was only the penultimate one.

# 74

## LETTICE

*March 1600*

he winter was unrelenting, gripping us in mastiff's teeth, tearing our cheeks and hands with piercing cold and icy wind. In spite of gloves and creams, I quite forgot that my hands were not rough, red, and scaly in their natural state. We continued to huddle in Essex House, conserving our fuel, lighting so few candles that it was perpetual night inside. Only when Will came to rehearse did I bring out all the lights, pretending that we lived this way all the time. But he did not come often, and the rest of the time we lived in gloom. Will was in high demand that season, performing for the Queen at Christmas, polishing several new plays, and struggling with his Hamlet drama. Perhaps that was how he kept moving forward. He was even embroiled in some lawsuits and quarrels among his acting company. They lost the leading man who played buffoonish comic parts, and his replacement called for a different type of script. An acting company is never stable, so it seems. A bit like court.

Robert recovered from his bad attack of flux, slowly gaining back strength. So I was told. I was not allowed to see him, and neither was Frances, in spite of her pleas. His brush with death had intensified his religious mania, and now he spent hours in prayer and ecstasies, just as he had once spent hours choosing clothes and drinking. He did nothing in moderation. The Queen, meanwhile, seemed to have stashed him at York House and quite forgotten him, carrying on one of her diplomatic endeavors with visiting Dutch envoys.

Then, suddenly, as was her wont, she issued orders that Sir Egerton was to be relieved of his duty as Robert's keeper, returning Robert to Essex House under the supervision of Sir Richard Berkeley. He was still forbidden to leave his house and not permitted visitors. We were all to vacate, immediately, and find other quarters.

"Where does she expect us to go?" I asked Frances. "I have no other lodging in London."

"She wants us out of London, I daresay," said Frances. "We can move to Barn Elms. It is not so far out of the city."

"Or go to Wanstead. But that is even farther." Forget Drayton Bassett! I might as well be in Cádiz there.

"Charles Blount has a house in the city," said Christopher. "It isn't grand, but at least it's within the city walls. He's in Ireland, after all. Since Penelope is living there, how can she deny her mother and family a place?"

"Very easily. She can say there's no room. And there probably isn't."

"Better a small house with some furniture than a big one that's bare," said Christopher.

"My, that sounds biblical," I said. I said it lightly, but lately Christopher had been carrying a rosary tucked in his sleeve. I was warning him that I had seen. "So, will we invite ourselves to move in with Penelope?"

"We have no choice, if we want to stay in London. Do we?" asked Christopher.

"Yes!" said Frances. "We must be near Robert!"

It had come, inevitably, that moment when appeals are made to one's children. I was in need now. And these, my children, would now have to bear my helplessness and my supplications.

---

Penelope lived in the northwestern part of the city, in a large house alongside the wall between Cripplegate and Aldersgate. It was a relatively quiet area, protected from street noise and traffic by its large walled garden.

"Penelope!" I called, rapping quickly on the thick wood door. The others lined up behind me, well-dressed beggars.

She herself opened the door, smiling. "My displaced clan gathers," she said. "A pity it is for this reason that you come under my roof."

Did she mean it was a pity that her scandalous liaison with Charles Blount meant that they entertained few official visitors, or that it was a pity we were in this plight? Both, perhaps. "It is long overdue," I said, stepping in and motioning to the others to follow. In came Frances; her elder daughter, Elizabeth; nine-year-old Robert; the nurse, clutching the new baby; and Christopher, ill at ease at having to ask for charity.

"I welcome you," said Penelope. "It has been lonely here since Charles went to Ireland. Elizabeth Vernon went to live with her husband at Drury House. Of course, a house full of children is never quiet, but they are hardly true company."

Since she now had nine children, ranging in age from thirteen to the crib, she knew whereof she spoke. Children filled one space while leaving others empty. "You are as fertile as the orchards of Normandy," I said. "And as perpetually lovely. No matter how many years an apple tree has borne fruit, its blossoms every spring rival the youngest trees. And so do you, my daughter."

I was proud of her, as confounded by her beauty as everyone else.

She looked impatient, annoyed at having her most noticeable feature remarked upon yet again. "Come, I'll show you your rooms."

The house was larger inside than it looked. The downstairs rooms stretched long and narrow back toward the private garden, light flooding in from the side windows; upstairs there were many chambers, some of them spacious and others snug under slanting eaves. It had an air of sunny contentment. Lord Rich's house was grander, but Penelope had lived in it without any contentment at all. I put my things down on the bed with a clean feeling of relief to be in a simple, ordered place, a place with no memories.

---

That night at dinner we spoke in hushed voices. All the children had finally been settled in their beds.

Penelope sighed and took a sip of her wine. "Ah. That first taste of wine, earned after a long day's watching of little ones, is the best vintage there is." She looked at me. "You know what I mean, Mother," she said, almost winking.

"You have left me far behind in that contest," I said. "Yet I do concur, the first few moments after a job well done are always the sweetest. Savor them."

An unknowing person would have envied the faces reflected in the gleaming dark wood of the table—the most beautiful woman in London, another woman who was twice countess and cousin to the Queen, a brave soldier, another woman, wife in turn to the two foremost men of her time. My long earrings caught the candlelight and twinkled in the mirrorlike surface of the table; Penelope's rich curls almost touched the wood. Yet we mimicked condemned prisoners, our faces grim.

"Have you any word from Charles?" asked Christopher.

"Only indirectly, from men returning. He has barely arrived there; it just seems long to us." Penelope tapped her fingers on the table, her long nails clicking.

"Well, what do they say?" pressed Christopher.

"That the morale was so low before he came, he raises it just by setting foot there."

"As long as that's all that's raised. No expectations."

"I don't think anyone has any expectations for Ireland now. We are quite threadbare of hopes," Frances said.

"What about—the Queen? Does she have hopes—expectations?" Penelope wondered.

"No one knows what she thinks," I said. "They never have. They never will. But I imagine she has a grim determination to trudge on. She never admits defeat."

"So far she has never had to. This may be different," said Christopher.

It might be. It might not be. I cared not. I cared only that Robert be spared and set free. God forgive me, I did not even care what happened to England. I was past that.

"*If* Charles can turn the tide in Ireland, she will be more amenable to forgiving Robert. If he cannot, then Robert will be held doubly responsible for the loss there. So we *must* hope. We *must*," said Penelope.

A strapping servant entered with a pewter platter heaped with slices of carved pork, followed by another with a mound of honeyed parsnips and carrots. A third refilled our wine goblets with claret. All talk ceased for those moments, but not our thoughts.

"Sir Richard Berkeley is to mind him," said Christopher, after they retreated back to the kitchen. "He'll keep a keen eye on him." He thrust a piece of meat into his mouth.

"At least we know he finds torture distasteful," said Penelope. "Or he did when he was warden of the Tower." She moved her food around on her plate but did not eat.

"It is torture for Robert to be imprisoned, kept solitary in our stripped house, held without a trial!" Frances cried.

"Do not long for a trial," cautioned Christopher. "Can you name any accused of high crimes who are pronounced 'not guilty' and let go? Better not to have a trial."

"Trials are nothing but a showcase where the judges pronounce what has already been decided," agreed Penelope. "His only hope of escape is to avoid a trial." She took a long drink of wine.

"What does that say about our celebrated English legal system?" I said bitterly.

"That it's as flawed as a three-armed octopus," said Christopher. "But three arms are better than no arms."

---

For those with no cares, it would have been lovely to live in this stone house with its leafy garden, on this gracious street of goldsmiths, cordwainers, and trade halls—barbers', embroiderers', haberdashers'—along with small publishers and alehouses. It was a lively area, and its refined trades did not spew forth foul smells and garbage.

But we did have cares, and the tranquil setting could not soothe us. It acted only as a frame to our torment.

---

The days passed as Robert was held incommunicado in Essex House. April came, then May. Frances wrote more plaintive letters to the Queen, which received no reply. We heard at last that Charles Blount had taken the sword of state in Dublin and immediately set about a fierce campaign in the south, where O'Neill had ventured. Although Charles had an army only two-thirds the size of Robert's, he had what Robert had never had—the unqualified support of the Queen and council. His requests for funds and supplies were promptly met, and as a result O'Neill quickly had to retreat north, abandoning his new conquests.

Penelope was elated, but at the same time she did not want to rub salt in our wounds, to remind us that Charles was succeeding where Robert had failed. Her loyalty to her brother and her lover pulled her first one way, then the other.

"Perhaps it means the Queen has learned from the mistakes she made with Robert," she said. "A victory in Ireland, brought about with this hard-won knowledge, will surely soften her toward him."

"If she wants to give him credit," said Christopher. "But she seemed determined to give him no praise for what he did there."

"Victory has a way of changing one's perspective," said Penelope.

"It is a little too early to speak of victory," said Christopher. "One battle is not a war."

---

As the days dragged by, I wandered the streets of London to distract myself and get away from my own family. We were so collectively miserable that we only reinforced one another's darkness. Out on the streets I could forget, if only for an hour or so, the thing that preyed like a demon on my mind.

As much as it was possible to lift my spirits, my walks through the streets helped me return to the house feeling better than when I had left. The hurly-burly of life was out there, and waiting to welcome us back. But on the third day of June, when I stepped into the hallway, I saw someone who made me feel worse: our erstwhile friend Francis Bacon. He was deep in conversation with Christopher and Frances, standing in that stiff way that was his hallmark. He turned when I walked in, forcing a smile.

"My dear Lady Leicester," he said, bowing, "I am so pleased you have returned in time for me to see you."

He looked older—but did not we all? These had been aging days for us.

"Welcome, Francis," I said. "How is the Queen's counsel?"

"I do have Her Majesty's ear," he said quietly. "That is why I am here. I was telling your husband and Frances that there is to be an inquiry and hearing in two days in which Robert will be examined. Four lawyers will specify his misdemeanors before a commission of eighteen."

Again! Before I could stop myself, I blurted out, "Eight months since he was first imprisoned! This is justice?"

"It is not a trial," said Bacon.

"Then what in God's name is it?" cried Christopher. "How long can you hold a man without trial? We've already had two mockeries of hearings—the first at Nonsuch and the second in the Court of Star Chamber. Nothing was resolved, and Robert was kept imprisoned."

"It is—it is—a deep inquiry as to the—the circumstances."

"What's the purpose of it?" said Frances.

"The purpose," said Christopher, "is to shush the murmurs against the Queen for holding him without reason."

Bacon shook his head. "I came in friendship, to let you know. If you take it another way, then I regret coming. Fend for yourselves." He turned to the door.

"We have been fending for ourselves," I said. "We need no admonitions from you to do so."

Christopher moved to block his way to the door. "Who are these lawyers who will lay out the case?"

"Sir Thomas Egerton, the Lord Keeper of the Great Seal, will chair the meeting. The sergeant at law and the attorney general will present the facts."

"You said four lawyers, Francis," I said.

"Four, yes, four. I am—I am—to speak last," he admitted, looking around Christopher for a way clear to the door.

"That which thou doest, do quickly," growled Christopher, stepping aside and almost thrusting him out.

"I am no Judas," said Bacon. "I came to prepare you. I am the only one who dares to come here openly. You have your slinking spies and informants, but never forget it was Francis Bacon who came here in daylight."

After the door shut behind him, I said, "Snake though he is, he spoke true. No one else wants to be seen with us." I was a long way from my Puritan childhood, but Scripture once learned is never forgotten, and the words from Isaiah, *Like one from whom men hide their faces, he was despised,* whispered in my mind. *By arrest and judgment he was taken away.*

"Once they trailed behind us, singing Robert's praises," said Christopher. "They waited hours for a glimpse of him."

"Yes, I remember." That golden day when he rode away to Ireland at the head of his troops . . . It would only cease to exist when my mind faded. "But now we must address what is coming. I am not sure people have forgotten him. Otherwise the Queen would not feel it necessary to justify herself in this public manner."

"There, now, you've said it. It is nothing but an exercise in self-justification," said Frances. "Her reputation is what she values above all, the love of her public, and she will defend that to the death, for she cannot reign without it."

"Then this hearing, or commission, or quasi trial, is nothing but a means to clear her own name," said Christopher. "The verdict is already decided. If she is to be right, then Robert has to be wrong."

# 75

# ELIZABETH

*June 1600*

ome of the most glorious summer days in memory passed, as if taunting us. May, celebrated in English poems and songs as a gladsome time but often in real life cold and rainy, in this year of 1600 lived up to its reputation, as if the new century wanted to set a standard. The trees in the palace orchard exploded in blossoms; every garden tree bristled with new leaves so bright they glowed like stained glass. Hedges bloomed in fragrance, and wildflowers in the fields outside the city walls carpeted the ground in color and scent. The first few days of June were even more beautiful, promising us a summer that would pass into legend for perfection. But as if in mockery of nature, what I must endure indoors was mean and ugly.

The Essex hearing had been forced upon me, and like anything forced upon me, I wanted to vomit it up. It was my paramount goal to avoid ever being in such a position. But once again Essex had led me where I did not want to go.

"I have you to thank for this," I told Francis Bacon, who had come to Whitehall to tender his respects before setting out for York House. He bowed low but, wisely, said nothing.

"Well, are you prepared?" I barked at him. "This had better be the last of these hearings. I still think a trial would have settled things better. But no, you and Cecil warned against it, and you are the cleverest heads available to me, so it gave me pause. You had better be right!"

He smiled that self-contained smile. "I know I am, Your Majesty. A public trial would have fanned the flames of popular support. Essex would have used it to showcase his strengths and make the people forget his transgressions. Then *you* would have been the one on trial. This way, in a closed session before commissioners and two hundred of our own select audience, we can control the information."

I grunted. I was sick of Essex and his dominating all public discourse.

Even locked away, he managed, as if he were a vapor, to waft out into the general air. People were demanding to know why the hero of Cádiz (how quickly they forgot Ireland!) was being held without charge and without trial. What they could not see, could not understand, was that without his irksome presence, the government was running better and the Irish campaign was showing success at last. In his absence from public life he had shown just how unneeded he was. So, in a bid to put an end to the murmuring, there was to be a hearing and an examination of all the facts. What there would not be was a pronouncement of "guilty" or "not guilty." What would happen to him was up to me, not a judge.

York House would serve as the setting. Francis, as one of the four lawyers to preside, adjusted his hat and made ready to leave.

"Take care in all things," I said.

---

Essex was brought in to kneel before the long table where the commissioners sat; later he was given a cushion, and after that a chair. The examination went on from eight in the morning until seven that evening. The entire Irish debacle was pawed over and Essex's manifest failings proclaimed. It had all been said before, at Nonsuch. Bacon read portions of the letter Essex had written after the episode in the Privy Council when he had tried to draw his sword on me. In it he had tried to throw the blame on me, saying, "What, cannot princes err? Cannot subjects receive wrong? Is an earthly power or authority infinite? Pardon me, pardon me, my good Lord, I can never subscribe to these principles." While that may have shed light on his attitude of grievance, it added little to the subject at hand.

In the end, while no sentence was pronounced, he was stripped of his offices—Earl Marshal of England, Privy Councillor, master of ordnance. Only the post of master of the horse, his earliest office, would remain, at the personal command of the Queen. He was ordered to return to custody in his house until Her Majesty made her pleasure known.

Exhausted by these proceedings and still weak from his recent illnesses, he took to his bed again to recover.

---

"You did well," I told Bacon.

"I hated doing it," he said. "It felt like stabbing a blindfolded child."

"Blindfolded?"

"He couldn't see what was coming," said Bacon. "He was helpless."

Now he made me feel ashamed, which was his intention. "It is true, he was in a vulnerable position," I agreed. "But a child cannot learn until he is humbled. Your friend has shown a stubborn reluctance to learn. Now perhaps, far from being blindfolded, his eyes will be opened."

"What do you mean to do with him?" he asked bluntly. "That is the only question remaining, and yet it could not be raised."

"I cannot set him at liberty until I know it is safe to do so. When I can trust him, we shall see."

"What does he have to do to set your mind at ease?"

"I am not sure, Francis. I will know when I feel it."

---

Things quieted down. Life went on, seemingly merrily, in the summer days. There were weddings, boat outings, and garden parties. The hearing at York House had served to discredit Essex with anyone of standing, so he no longer had a party at court, and the squabbling and factionalism that had plagued us dissipated. It was an immense relief, and a rest well earned for me.

In July I released Richard Berkeley from his duties as Essex's keeper, but I still did not allow Essex to leave his house. Gradually I was setting him free.

In late August I lifted the restrictions on his movements. He need no longer be confined to his house. He could go anywhere he liked—but not to court. He was not to set foot at court.

---

"In being kind, you are being cruel," said Catherine. "You set him loose but forbid him to come to the one place where he draws his strength."

"Exactly. He grew too strong, and at my expense. I fed a cub who turned on me. Let him find his food elsewhere."

I was worried about my own expenses. I could not ask Parliament for any more subsidies. I sold more Crown lands and jewels and was even reduced to having a sale of marketable items from the treasury.

I sat staring at the Great Seal of my father, one of my proud inheritances. Its design was old-fashioned now, but it was historic, and its silver would bring a good price. But oh! To surrender it was to lose part of him. His fingers had held it, his hands had carefully slid it into its velvet bag.

"Forgive me," I murmured, putting it out of sight lest I lose my determination. I must get money wherever I could find it. The exclusive right to duties on sweet wines held by Essex for ten years was due to expire in late September. I would take it back. I could not afford to let a fallen courtier reap its rewards any longer while I pawned my father's inheritance.

---

Essex announced that since he was no longer welcome at court, he was retiring into the country. He began pelting me with letters.

"Now, having heard the voice of Your Majesty's justice, I do humbly crave to hear your own natural voice, or else that Your Majesty in mercy will send me into another world. If Your Majesty will let me once prostrate myself at your feet and behold your fair and gracious eyes, yea, though afterwards Your Majesty punish me, imprison me, or pronounce the sentence of death against me, Your Majesty is most merciful, and I shall be most happy." This had the ring of a man who could not comprehend that he had had his last audience with me. He still thought he could charm his way into any arena he wished. I did not answer. Soon another letter followed.

"Haste paper to that happy presence, whence only unhappy I am banished. Kiss that fair correcting hand which lays new balms to my lighter hurts, but to my greatest wound applies nothing. Say thou come from shaming, languishing, despairing Essex."

The fair correcting hand set the letter aside and gave no answer.

Others arrived, each more groveling than the last. He was always a superb letter writer.

"This day the lease which I hold by Your Majesty's beneficence expires, and that excise of sweet wines is both my chief income and my only means of satisfying the merchants to whom I am indebted. If my creditors will take for payment as many ounces of my blood, Your Majesty should never hear of this suit."

Then, as the day passed when the lease on the wines expired, he ratcheted up his appeal.

"My soul cries out unto Your Majesty for grace, for access, and for an end to this exile. If Your Majesty grant this suit, you are most gracious, whatever else you deny or take away. If this cannot be obtained, I doubt whether that the means to preserve life, and the granted liberty, have been favors or punishments; for till I may appear in your gracious presence, and kiss Your Majesty's fair correcting hand, time itself is a perpetual night, and the whole world but a sepulcher unto Your Majesty's humblest vessel."

All told, he wrote over twenty letters. That he was in pain I believed, and regretted it. But what sort of pain? Was it the pain of public embarrassment or the pain of being denied the things he felt were his due? Or the fear of financial ruin? He owed huge amounts of money, all advanced to him on the security of his income from the sweet wines. While he had been imprisoned he had been out of his creditors' reach, but now that he was a free man he was at their mercy. But he had had his chance to enjoy the wine license, and now the time for that was past. England needed the money more than he did.

Francis Bacon, perhaps feeling guilty for his part in the hearing, pleaded for him and commented on his eloquent appeals. I merely said that I had been touched by them until I saw that they were just ploys to get his hands on the sweet wine license again.

"He warbles like a nightingale, but his song is only to trick me, Master Francis," I said.

"He is destitute," said Francis.

"I forgave him the debt of ten thousand pounds he owed the Crown when it was obvious he couldn't repay it. He should be grateful for that," I said. "I never forgave any other man's debt."

"Desperate men seek desperate remedies," he said.

I looked at him. His smooth brown eyes gave nothing away. "Is that a threat? And does it come from you or from him?"

"It is merely an observation, Your Majesty. There are certain animals that will not attack unless they have exhausted all other means. Some snakes are that way—they must be provoked and cornered before they strike. But their poison is deadly."

"He has missed his opportunity. If he had meant to strike, he should have done it when he had an army at his back. Now he has not the means." But even as I said it so certainly, I knew assassination did not require an army, just someone close at hand. "I know he has been in correspondence with James in Scotland," I said.

Francis's face registered his surprise. "He has?"

"Don't pretend you didn't know. If I do, so do you. He wanted James to send an ambassador here, along with troops, and set him free. Then, I suppose, he planned to ingratiate himself with James, having exhausted my bounty and my goodwill. Of course, I would have to have been removed first."

Now Francis looked truly horrified. "I am sure—I am sure he had no such thing in mind."

"Then why did he ask Lord Mountjoy to proclaim his case and then return from Ireland with troops to back him up?"

"I know nothing of this." His expression told me he was telling the truth. His falling-out with Essex was permanent, then, and he was barred from his confidence.

"Mountjoy has tasted his own success now and is not tempted to give it up to bolster his old friend. Away from England and the soft, subtle wheedlings of Essex and the strident ones of his mistress, he has become his own man. A man just as selfish and ambitious as any other. His way to power does not lie in being subservient to Essex but in bringing home peace—what was the phrase?—broached on his sword. Mountjoy is no fool. I always liked him."

"This is all very ugly," said Francis.

"This is what court is behind the masques and sonnets," I said. "I wonder that you did not write an essay about it."

"Even I did not comprehend the venality of it," he said. "But I will remedy that."

"No one will believe you," I said. "Generation after generation of young people will have to learn this lesson firsthand." I sighed. "Look you, Francis, I have not given up all hope that Essex might be redeemed. But first he must accept his situation and not seek to evade it. For once corruption has set in, in any entity, if it is fed, it grows. It must be purged out. Hence, I will not feed him with more corrupting income."

"I bow to your wisdom, Your Majesty," he said.

"Don't mock me, Francis."

"I do not. Perhaps you see what I cannot. I see only a broken man pursued by angry creditors. You see danger. You cannot afford to be wrong; I can."

"You understand my position."

"But you must understand his. He is not evil but an Icarus—he has flown recklessly too near the sun, melting his waxen wings, hurling him to earth."

"His life lends itself to such poetic interpretations. That may be his lasting legacy."

---

To fill Marjorie's empty place, Catherine's younger sister Philadelphia came to court. She had served me in the past and I welcomed her back. She was very different from Catherine, having spent about half of her life on the Scottish borders, where her father and then her husband commanded the western marches. They were the Barons Scrope of Bolton, whose castle had first housed Mary Queen of Scots. Philadelphia had taken on some of the rough talk and mannerisms of the north, but I always found them refreshing after the simpering niceties of court talk.

She took to pestering me to restore Essex, or at least grant him the sweet wine license so he could repay his debts.

"What a charming advocate he has," I said. "He is fortunate in that way. But you don't know him as I do. He is not broken yet. To rule an unruly horse, you must deprive him of his provender."

"But if he appears at the Accession Day tilts, will you look gently upon him?" she asked.

There had been rumors that he was planning a spectacular reappearance at the tilts, since they were not technically at court. Icarus would soar again, or try to. "I will certainly look upon him. In what manner I cannot say."

How like him it would be to swoop down at the tournament and act as if nothing had changed.

---

The day, November 17, drew near. We had had a warm, dry autumn, and the weather held, to everyone's relief. I received many letters and gifts of congratulation on my forty-second anniversary of accession. The French king sent a public letter of praise, along with two horses. The estates of the Netherlands sent a dark, carved cabinet with ivory insets. We had just won a joint victory over the Spanish at Nieuport, and the end of the seemingly endless war was in sight. Sixteen hundred had been a good year after all.

The court was swarming with visitors for the celebration. I had decided to order a new gown for the occasion, something that would seem more martial than usual. I wanted the bodice to imitate the decorated breastplates of ancient Rome, with the pattern outlined in beads and pearls. The theme of the tilts would be *victory.*

A few days beforehand I received another letter from Essex. He congratulated me on the day and begged once again to be forgiven. "I sometimes think of jousting in the tiltyard and then I remember what it would be to come into that presence, out of which both by your own voice I was commanded, and by your own hands thrust out," he hinted, inviting me to respond with an invitation. I did not.

It was the last letter he wrote me.

# 76

## LETTICE

*November 1600*

I walked between the lines of clothes flapping, drying in the brisk November wind. Since our return to Essex House, I had had to take on many of the former staff's duties. We simply could not afford to have all the servants back. This particular chore I did not mind. I liked feeling the stiff cleanliness of the linens and the shirts; it reminded me of my time in Holland when I had been in charge of that task for the family. Everyone in Holland seemed to wash all the time; the billowing laundry on a thousand lines mirrored the sails on their boats constantly plying the harbor. The sharp, fresh smell of the clothes as I pulled them off the line made me feel clean as well.

I tried not to think of other things, just pluck the laundry off and fold it into a large basket. There is a balm in mindless tasks. So from dawn to night I tried to keep my mind from wandering to our plight. That, of course, was impossible.

Hoisting the basket up onto one shoulder, I made my way back into the house. I was on the river side, where I heard no street noises, just the sound of the Thames flowing past. Inside the house I would scurry into the laundry quarters to deposit my basket. Thank God I did not have to iron. I had not the skill. We sent the ruffs out to be professionally starched and ironed, but the rest was done here.

As I came back through the main room, I saw Robert sitting in a throne-like chair, gripping its arms and looking morose. Christopher was hunched on a stool beside him, speaking in a low voice directly into his ear.

"A fine day," I said, attempting to sound cheerful.

They looked up, annoyed to be interrupted. "Yes, fine," Robert muttered. He was still thin from his ordeal; his strength had been broken. A spindly hand extended from his sleeve, fretfully peeling an apple.

"It is November 16," said Christopher. "We wait."

"Oh, Robert." My heart, which I had thought completely numb, was stabbed with pain for him. "It is too late for you to go, even if you heard from her. You have no costume, no pageant car, no presentation shield."

"If I heard, I could create something overnight. If I heard—"

"You must shut that window and stop watching out of it."

"He has crawled, humiliated himself, and been ground underfoot. I agree with you—if he is to be a man, he must stop." Christopher looked disgusted, scowling at Robert as he dropped the peeling knife. Christopher grabbed it up and with one swipe, cut the peel off. "Here." He thrust the apple back at Robert.

"You are right," said Robert, turning the apple over and over as if he did not know what to do with it. "I always hated the tilts anyway. The expense. The time wasted coming up with a theme. To hell with them. All I want is the renewal of the sweet wines license. Now that she's insulted me, she can turn around and give that to me. Perhaps that is *why* she has been so publicly unkind."

"You are a dreamer, Robert. You always have been. She's unkind because she's a mean woman and enjoys it," said Christopher.

"She's more complicated than that," I said. "Our best course is to keep silent."

"I have no choice. I cannot write her again."

"Damn right you cannot!" said Christopher.

Just then Robert's steward, Gelli Meyrick, appeared. He was scowling, as usual. He was intensely loyal but a hothead. "Why are you cowering indoors like a crone?" he said. Close behind him was Henry Cuffe, the scholarly secretary for foreign correspondence. He knelt and delivered a letter to Robert, who took it with trembling hands.

"Well?" demanded Christopher and Gelli.

"I shall open it in private," said Robert, pressing it against his chest.

"Don't you trust us?" they asked.

"I am entitled to read a private letter in privacy!" said Robert, rising and drawing his robe around him. He stalked off to his bedchamber.

I turned hopefully to Cuffe. If no invitation came from nearby, at least our foreign allies remembered our existence. "Can you tell me—" I began.

"I am sorry," he said. "I am not at liberty to tell you anything about the letter."

"It had a royal seal on it," said Gelli. "We are not fools. It is not from France, nor from Sweden, nor Russia. Where else but Scotland?"

"About time," grunted Christopher. "After Robert has had his little show of independence, he'll let us read it. Perhaps—perhaps—"

"Don't even say it," I warned him. The whole dalliance with James VI seemed pointless to me. It was so obvious that James would do nothing to jeopardize his standing with Elizabeth, and certainly not for a disgraced courtier. Yes, James was growing impatient, but Robert could not help his case.

I left them. Increasingly I was preferring the company of Frances and the grandchildren to these frustrated, petulant men. The siege of ill fortune had transformed her into a creature who showed sparks of fire. She had allowed the marriage of her daughter to Roger Manners, the Earl of Rutland, to go forward, but only because the headstrong girl fancied herself in love with him.

"It is very difficult to argue with a fifteen-year-old," I had agreed with her. It did not get any easier, I thought, but I did not tell her that. Penelope and Dorothy had hardly become docile and passive as the years passed.

"Perhaps I'll have another daughter to replace her," said Frances as we had commiserated over unmanageable daughters. That was her way of announcing that she and Robert were expecting again. They had consoled each other, then, in the ancient way after he had been allowed his freedom.

I was pleased to hear it. I trotted out the old phrase "Just as long as it is healthy—"

"Oh, yes, I am feeling quite well," she said. "God forgive me, I know it is selfish, but it has been my delight to have Robert home and not roaming."

Little Rob, his namesake, was nine now but seemed to prefer indoor pursuits to outdoor ones. Perhaps he would become a scholar or a churchman. I would not be sad to see the end of the martial ambitions of the Devereux men. Rob, with his mop of golden curls, was a dreamy boy who liked making up stories. He was the same age my Robert had been when his father died and he inherited the title of earl. Perhaps he would have the privilege of pursuing the things that suited his nature best, rather than being forced to make his way prematurely in the world.

Frances had laid aside her black clothes when Robert was freed but still dressed plainly. Since we were not invited anywhere, the lack of means to buy fancy clothes was not obvious. We passed the afternoon in quiet conversation, sipping heated wine and nibbling on little cakes. We both pretended we would have it no other way.

---

One always imagines that the days that change one's life must be marked with something extraordinary in nature—storms and lightning, darkness at noon, and so on. In truth they are indistinguishable from any other, which is one reason we feel mocked, as if the world is telling us we are inconsequential. The day that we got word of the Queen's decision about the sweet wines was a dull November day, cold but not overly so, drizzling but not pouring. She did not even deliver the verdict to us but let it trickle to Essex House by general gossip. The man delivering cabbages and onions to our kitchen said to the cook, "Pity about the sweet wines." She asked him what he meant and he said, "That the Queen is keeping them for herself. I heard it at the market."

Later a blacksmith confirmed it, having heard it on the street. Then, with darkness already falling, a bulletin from court, from Secretary John Herbert. He informed us of various decisions taken that week, regulations for the distribution of grain, a change in the day the swans were to be marked, increased fines for garbage in the city, and then, oh yes, Her Majesty was reserving the revenues of the duty on sweet wines for the Crown, as she wished to spare her loyal and beloved subjects any further taxation. I kept staring at the paper, rereading it, seeing words but rejecting their meaning. It could not be. But it was. The words remained on the page, not fading or changing no matter how many times I read them.

We were ruined. Ruined. We could not survive. We owed more than we could ever repay now. They would take us to Marshalsea Prison as debtors, and there we would die. I stumbled into my room and groped for a candle; suddenly I was afraid to sit in the dark.

Oh, there'll be dark enough in that cell, my terrified mind shouted. But you'll want it dark, so you can't see the filth and the rats in the straw. I was shaking all over. Until that moment, I had not known I had trusted the Queen to show mercy at the last minute, had never really allowed myself to live in any other alternative. "Oh, my God," I whispered. I was beyond tears, beyond any remedy to relieve the shock and fear.

"Damn her to hell and flames!" Christopher was standing in the doorway, a bottle in his right hand. He raised it and drank directly from it in long slurps. "Curse her evil bones!" He was drunk. He slouched into the room and knelt down beside me. "What're ya sitting here in the dark for?" His breath stank of ale. He was no help; was there no help anywhere?

"I'm afraid, Christopher," I said. "The darkness seemed kinder than the light."

He grabbed my sleeve. "Sittin' here like a snivelin' coward, that's not my wife. Here, have some." He thrust the bottle up to my mouth, but I turned away.

"You oughta be happy. It's all out in the open now. We donna have to pretend. She's our enemy, that's that."

Who was this coarse, simplistic stranger? When had he replaced my Christopher? "No, she's not our enemy," I said. "She is merely looking out for herself." I paused. "I doubt—I doubt we are even enough in her mind for her to call us enemies. We are negligible now, no one who needs to be considered." I was back where I had been as a child in exile, a nobody. But no, our family was important enough we had to go into exile. That meant something.

His only response was to take a swig of the liquor.

"Money, it's only money that matters," I said. "Blood, service, bravery, loyalty—without money, they don't matter." What good Robert's noble lineage and small amount of royal blood? The rats at Marshalsea would not heed them.

"You just now see that? Even a child knows that." He found another candle to help the feeble one I had lit, and suddenly the light was doubled. "Maybe it isn't her," he said. "Maybe her mind has been poisoned."

"Don't console yourself with that delusion," I said. "A weak king or queen can be the pawn of bad counselors and advisers, but this one is a pawn of no one. Never has been." Oh, she had been clever and self-possessed ever since I had known her, outwitting those in power with ease even as a young princess. I wished I had shared that trait. Instead, I saw now, I had been a good schemer but a poor strategist, unable to plan for contingencies. But what good did it do me to recognize that now? It was too late to help and only served to deepen my despair.

"We'll see," he said ominously. Then he reeled out of the room.

How long I sat there I do not know. I heard the street cries dying down as curfew was rung and the night deepened. Finally my shaking stopped. I should go to Robert. No, I should leave him his privacy. I should not barge in on him and Frances. Stumbling toward my bed, I lay down to obliterate the day and wake to another.

---

I awoke to dull light coming from a sun muffled in clouds. I had been dreaming of horses, riding slowly along a high cliff with the sea foaming far below. The air was syrupy with salt, but I loved the way it smelled, of seaweed and waves. I dismounted and stood at the edge of the cliff, watching the water roll in and dash against black rocks. Down below, between two jagged boulders, something was caught, bobbing. A body? Then I saw the sea strewn with timbers and debris and knew it was a shipwreck. Was it the Armada? Spaniards had washed up on shore in Ireland, they said. Ireland . . .

"Mother!" Someone was shaking my shoulder. "Oh, help!"

I was pulled from the surging sea back to Essex House. Frances was standing by my bed. In the dim light I could see tears on her cheeks. "What is it?"

"Robert. He won't rise. I think he's—he's unconscious."

I tumbled out of bed and pulled on a robe, then rushed with her to their room. A trail of discarded clothes led to the curtained bed. I pulled them back and saw Robert sprawled out, not sleeping but unresponsive.

"Drunk?" I asked, hoping it was true. Oh, let him merely be drunk. Christopher had been drunk. It was their way of shutting things out, things too painful to look at straight on. I smelled his breath, but it did not smell of ale or sack or wine. Instead, it had a strange, sweet odor.

"Robert!" I shook him but he did not stir. I turned to Frances. "What has he taken? Did you find anything in the room? By the bed?"

"I have not looked. When I could not rouse him, I came straight to you."

"Let us search. Everywhere." Trembling, I patted the sheets and blankets, feeling for a telltale bottle. Nothing. I got down and looked under the bed, then on the sill and behind all the chests. "What happened last night? Did he go to bed in a normal fashion?"

"He read the bulletin from Secretary Herbert. He read it over and over. Then he sat silent as a stone. Then Gelli came in, roaring. Then Christopher, drunk. They yelled and talked about revenge, but Robert just sat there. Finally they left us alone. Only then did Robert speak. He merely said, 'I am doomed.' I tried to tell him it was not so. We had our children, we had one another, we had our youth and our health, no one could deprive us of those things. He just shook his head. I went on, reminding him that those were prized above all else. 'Without them, riches and rank and public esteem are worthless. Remember Burghley and his gout. Every day was torture for him, regardless of his high office and the Queen's esteem.' "

"What did he say?"

"Nothing. He just kept shaking his head. So I did what I do with the children. I said gently, 'Come to bed now. Rest.' He obeyed, crawled in, and fell asleep in my arms." She gave a sigh. "Or so I thought. But while I slept, he must have left the bed and availed himself of something—some draft, some potion—perhaps to make him sleep sounder—but I did not know we had any such medicine."

"Call for a physician. We have to find the bottle!" I looked again at Robert, still and pale.

Left alone in the chamber, I was frantic. Where could it be? I took his silver-topped staff and poked along the tops of the cupboards, then rifled the insides. I felt on the underside of the mattress ropes, then stopped myself. This was foolish. A man does not go to such lengths to hide an empty bottle, only a full one. One of the windows was open a crack; I could feel the draft. Pulling aside the thick curtains, I opened the casement and looked down. Lying beneath the window, half under a bush, was a flask. I rushed down to retrieve it, pushing the branches aside and scrabbling to grab it. My fingers closed around it and I dragged it out.

It was empty, and it smelled sweet, like Robert's breath.

By the time I returned to the room, our physician was there, leaning over Robert, ear to his chest, listening.

"I have it!" I said, holding the flask.

The physician, Roger Powell, turned and held out his hand for it. He looked for a label, then shook it. "There is still some inside. Get a cup so we can pour it out." In a moment he had one, and he drained the flask of its small amount of greenish liquid.

"I know what that is," said Frances. "He brought it with him from York House. It was given him when he had the flux, to stop his vomiting."

"Who gave it to him?" Powell's voice was sharp. He sniffed the liquid.

"Whoever treated him. I was not allowed to see him. At one point the Queen sent her own physicians."

Accusation hung in the air. But that was foolish. The potion had helped him when it was used as prescribed.

"It is made from the deadly nightshade," said Powell.

"Is there an antidote?" I asked.

"A rare one—the Calabar bean. It comes from Africa."

"Is there anywhere in London where we can get it?"

He looked distressed. "It is popular for witchcraft. If you know anyone willing to admit to witchcraft, then you know more than I."

"There must be someone who supplies it. Perhaps down at the docks."

"Witchcraft isn't openly practiced. We would have to find someone who is trusted by that group." He looked over at Robert. "And find him or her fast."

Suddenly I was grateful for the disreputable characters who gathered out in our courtyard. I had told Robert to send them away, that they gave a bad impression of disloyalty, but he had ignored me.

---

It took only a few minutes to find a ragged Welsh boy eager to run such an errand. He would say he needed it for a love potion, as he was sick with love for one who spurned him. "Hurry, and there's an extra groat for you," I promised him. We might be poor, but we had money for this.

I returned to the chamber, where, under Powell's direction, we burned camphor under Robert's nose in an attempt to awaken him and propped him up on pillows in hopes that it would stimulate him. By now the word was out all over the household, and Cuffe, Meyrick, and Christopher tried to enter the chamber, but Powell told them to stay out and let Robert have enough air.

The boy returned in two hours, clutching a burlap bag with a smooth-skinned brown bean inside about the size of my thumbnail. It looked completely harmless as I held it up and turned it around.

"Yes, that's it," said Powell. "I'll grind it and then we can measure the powder. I will have to estimate the exact dosage, and that will be difficult since I do not know how much nightshade was in the potion. We want only enough to counteract the nightshade, not go beyond it and act as a separate poison."

He worked fast and all I could do was pray. There were so many unknowns. If we had guessed wrong about the potion—if the flask was not connected with Robert at all, or had been thrown out at an earlier time—if he overdosed on the antidote—

The strain of it made me burst into tears, and it was Frances now who had to comfort me. She was calm, but that was because she did not realize all the implications of our ignorance about the dosage.

It was noon before the draft was ready, and we had to spoon it into Robert's slack mouth, then hold his jaw shut and massage his throat. The liquid went down. Then, when the cup was empty, we settled down to wait.

I felt poisoned myself; I was dizzy and numb. Perhaps handling the bean had infected me. But no, it was only the powder that was active. I sat in a corner chair, reliving all the other times I had kept watch in his chamber. This was the worst.

It was dark before he stirred, very slowly. He moved his right arm up and brushed his forehead. Still he remained silent, with closed eyes. A flush spread across his cheeks, making red sprinkles. Then, another movement: He licked his lips with a pale pink tongue.

Powell was instantly beside him, bending over him. "A cloth," he ordered. "Cool water and distilled feverfew." It was brought and he wiped Robert's face, stroking it back into life. At last Robert's eyes opened and he looked around blankly.

"Thank God you are safe!" cried Frances, throwing herself across his covered legs. Powell jerked her away.

"No weight on him!" he barked. Then he flexed Robert's arms and massaged the hands. "Come back to us," he ordered him, like a magus.

Robert gave a faint smile. He lifted one hand and squeezed Powell's fingers.

———

He slept through the night and the next morning found his voice again. His first words would be crucial. Had he meant to end his life?

He held up one hand. "Where have I been? I am so weak."

"You don't remember?" I asked.

"I remember nothing, just going to bed."

"You took nothing?"

"I couldn't sleep, so I got up and took some of the medicine I had for the flux." He shook his head slowly.

"Does it help you sleep?" I asked.

"It calms the stomach and makes you drowsy," he said. "I was at my wits' end; I was wide awake. I was wide awake because . . ." He was remembering. Oh, let him not! But it was too late. ". . . the Queen . . ."

"Think not of the Queen now!" said Frances. "Forget all that came before. Rest, my dearest."

---

In two days he was eating again and his strength had returned. But his eyes looked different, as though they had seen too much and now belonged to someone else.

And if he had not meant to end his life, why had he thrown the flask out the window so no one would know what he had taken?

# 77

# ELIZABETH

*December 1600*

e had gotten through the harbinger year of 1600 and all was well; nay, better than well. In November, a resounding Anglo-Dutch victory against the Spanish at Nieuport meant that our fifteen-year military involvement on the Continent could end, and happily. In Ireland, Mountjoy had continued to turn the Irish tide back, and O'Neill, while not captured yet, commanded dwindling forces. To expand our trade, I granted a royal charter to the East India Company, competing with the Portuguese in Asia. It would make its first voyage next month. I also had in mind to reestablish a colony in the New World; the new edition of Richard Hakluyt's *The Principal Navigations, Voyages, and Discoveries of the English Nation* excited public interest in the venture. With the dawn of the new century, Dee's prediction of a British empire did not seem so impossible.

Essex had come and Essex had gone. His popular support, which at one time had seemed so threatening, had melted away. The songs about England's sweet pride had died out in the taverns. The scrawled insults to Cecil had ceased.

Yet even as the people forgot him, and as he faded from public consciousness, he grew in mine. Bacon's calling him Icarus had set that image in my mind and transformed him into Greek mythology. There had been something ancient and otherworldly in him. People said he was born out of his time, and perhaps he was. His beauty and attitude of expectation stayed with me always, reminding me of the potential in him that I had believed in once and, somewhere deep inside me, believed in still.

---

There was much to celebrate this Christmas, and I meant it to be a jolly one. Everyone was welcome at court, and I invited all the foreign envoys and secretaries and called for all my ladies to attend me. It was good to bring everyone under one roof. I would keep it at Whitehall this year. Eleven plays were slated to be performed for us in the Great Hall. I requested special musical compositions for the occasion and appointed John Harington to be master of ceremonies. I also ordered the kitchens to create a new dish of some sort—it could be meat, pastry, or even a drink. If it was successful, we would name it "1600" and it would stand as a remembrance of the first year of the new century.

The influx of ladies who did not keep regular attendance in the privy chamber meant we needed more beds and that the so-called maidens' chamber would be crowded. But that was all in keeping with the season.

The holy day was over. We had worshipped in seemly fashion in the royal chapel, relived the sacred night in Bethlehem when the shepherds gathered, the angels sang, and the lowly manger was transformed into a symbol of God's love. The sweet voices of the choir had floated in the chill air, recalling that angel chorus. With bent head I had given heartfelt thanks for the benefits that had devolved on England this past year and surrendered up my personal losses and pain—the death of Marjorie, the collapse of Essex.

Now the festivities would begin.

---

The next day the first, and grandest, banquet opened the celebrations. Everyone was invited, so we needed to employ the Great Hall to hold them all. True to their commission, the cooks had confected an elaborate pastry re-creating a walled city. It was wheeled in on a cart, displayed on papier-mâché "grounds" of rolling green with trees of sticks and green tissue. The pastry walls were a foot high, and the little buildings nestled within had roofs of red icing, half-timbers of cinnamon sticks, sweetmeat doors studded with raisins. The largest structure, a cathedral, had tour-de-force soaring steeples, flying buttresses, and a rose window made of colored sugar chips. Several taverns, with tiny painted signs swinging at their entrances, featured drunken patrons reeling out.

"Splendid!" I proclaimed, quite astounded at their creation. "But to destroy it will make us into barbarians, sacking a city."

"That is why we have concocted a drink to go along with it," the chief cook said. "You may call it '1600,' but we named it 'Attila.'" He poured a goblet from a tall pitcher and handed it to me. "Your Majesty, pray taste and tell us if this makes you feel like a destroyer of cities."

The heated drink warmed the goblet, radiating into my hands. I took a sip and found it unlike anything I had ever tasted—it was sweet, yes, and strong, but it had a bitter undernote, hinting at spices from below the equator.

They waited expectantly. I nodded and took another sip. "Very good, gentlemen. But what gives it the hint of bitterness?"

"Its base is sweet malmsey, but to that I added palm wine, which comes from the Levant, and then extract of dates. Then I ground a bit of manaca root from Guiana into it."

I took another taste. The sweet wine base called to mind Essex and the wretched sweet wine episode. "Yes, I see. I think you may safely call it Attila. He doubtless drank just such a concoction." I laughed, trying to thrust the Essex image from my mind. "Sir Walter, do we have you to thank for the manaca root?"

Raleigh bowed. "Indeed. The Indians set great store by it, adding it to their fruits and meat. For us, though, its bitterness means we need to temper it with sweetness."

I saw that Bess was in the shadows of a pillar, while her husband stood in the light. "Bess, do you use the root for other cooking?" I called out to her, to let her know it was time she came out of the shadows and took her rightful place beside Walter.

Startled at the recognition, she stammered, "Sometimes for baking, Your Majesty," she said.

"Good," I said. "You must send us a sample sometime."

The cooks managed to cut the city apart in deft fashion, slicing the walls, cathedral, shops, and taverns into neat portions. Large as the display had been, the throng quickly gobbled it up. Even the fastidious Robert Cecil ate a portion without getting a single crumb on his face.

"Your Majesty," he said, "have you met my children? Allow me to present them—William, age nine, and Frances, age seven." The little Cecils came forward and bowed. The new generation. It would not be long until they were making their way at court and in the world.

"They are lovely, Robert. You are undoubtedly a good father." He probably approached fatherhood the way he did everything else—prudently and methodically.

"I can only be father, not mother and father," he said. "I do my best."

There had been no hint of his remarrying since he had lost his wife three years earlier. He seemed quite a solitary figure. "Your best far excels that of anyone else," I assured him. At least anyone now living.

George Carey joined us, plate in hand. He was attacking the last bit of his pastry with gusto, smacking his lips. "A superlative start to the holiday," he said. "And I promise an ending just as impressive. Wait until you see what the Lord Chamberlain's Men are presenting for Twelfth Night. It's even called *Twelfth Night*."

"How obvious," I said.

"The title is the only obvious thing in it," he said. "Oh, it's quite confusing."

"I have to assume it involves mistaken identities?" I said.

George waved his fork. "How did you know?"

"It's such an old staple, it will be a challenge to do anything new with it. I hope I will not be disappointed. If I am, I shall forbid any more mistaken identity plays to be performed this season."

"We are doing some innovative work," he said. "It isn't all mistaken identities."

"For your sake, I hope that's true," I told him. Really, I was weary of them. How many times can sets of twins, or brothers and sisters, be separated and then reunited?

"Our main playwright is working on a revision of the Trojan war story," he said. "In it, Achilles is not noble, Troilus is a fool, and Helen is not worth fighting over, a silly giggling thing."

That sounded more promising. "When will that be ready?"

"Not in time for this season, unfortunately."

"Well, tell him to hurry it up."

Carey bowed and then took his leave.

I saw Southampton lurking in the back. I was surprised he dared come, but then, I had said it was open to all. I called him over. He came, showing no embarrassment or hesitation, bowing low with a flourish.

"So, my erstwhile master of the horse for Essex, how have you passed your time since returning so abruptly from Ireland? And how is your wife, my erstwhile attendant?"

He was dressed all in black. "I pass my time in sadness," he said.

"Over your marriage or your master?" I asked.

"Over my master," he said. "How could a loyal friend not?"

"You would do better to apply your efforts to repaying your debts," I said. "I understand you are some eight thousand pounds in debt."

He looked back at me with those clear blue eyes. "I am doing everything to remedy it. But I am obligated to support my widowed mother. I have just sold more of my lands, a third of my inheritance."

"A better way to remedy it is to stop your gambling," I said. "Those without funds should not bet."

Southampton was a die-hard gambler, seemingly unable to stop. He merely nodded.

"How is your master?" I could not help asking. "Is he keeping well?"

He looked incredulous. "Well? No, he is anything but well."

I wished I had not brought up the subject. I wanted to know, but as there was nothing I could do, it was better not to discuss it. "I am saddened to hear it."

Southampton's mouth dropped, and in truth, I should just have said nothing. "I shall tell him," he said.

I saw that Southampton was not the only disgraced Essex follower who had found his way here. Roger Manners, the Earl of Rutland, and his friend Edward Russell, the Earl of Bedford, were drinking near the musicians. Both these young men were as deeply in debt as their leader and doubtless had come for the free food and a chance to find someone gullible enough to lend them money. I hoped there was no one of that description in the hall tonight.

Youth, youth . . . Enough of them and their follies. My eyes went to an older man who was putting his plate down. He seemed to be alone, so I sought him out. "You look lost," I said.

"Never lost, Your Majesty," he said. "But alone, yes. My cousin brought me, but he's nowhere to be seen. 'The Queen invited everyone,' he said 'and that means *us*.' I hope he was not mistaken. I am William Lambarde, Your Majesty."

"No, not at all. It is a pleasure to meet my subjects. What do you do?" He looked like a scholar of some sort. "Are you at Cambridge? Oxford, perhaps?" I did not want to insult him by naming the wrong university. Teachers and students were notoriously partisan to their institution.

"Neither. I work alone, but I have compiled a book of Anglo-Saxon laws and written a history of the county of Kent. I would have done one of all England, but Camden got there first."

"Your work must be gratifying. I have heard of it."

"Kent, Your Majesty, has a rich history. Of course your own Hever is there. I found the original plans and deeds dating back several centuries."

Hever. Catherine and I must make our historic visit there this year. "Indeed?" I said. "Could you send me your findings?"

"I would be honored," he said.

John Harington came over and bowed smartly. I noticed that his doublet seemed to have expanded since the last time I saw him, and I was not surprised that he was having a second helping of the pastry.

"Greetings, John," I said. "I look forward to your rule on Twelfth Night," I said. "Your only constraint is to refrain from making any comments or jests about the Earl of Essex."

"That is not a constraint," he said. "There is nothing remotely funny about him or his situation."

—

Even though the nights were at their longest, by the time I returned to my chamber dawn was not far away. I marveled at how quickly the evening had flown.

"I think it was a success, Catherine," I said.

"You sound surprised," she said as she unfastened my necklace and gently loosened the ties of the great ruff around my neck. Oh, it felt good to get it off.

"I am. It has not been the merriest of times at court, since the business with Essex. I took the chance that an open invitation would heal wounds and bring the old factions in. The sooner court life returns to normal, the better for everyone."

Her sister Philadelphia came over to remove my wig. She lifted it off carefully, its tiara and ornaments still clinging to it, and put it on its stand. "I've got a fresher eye than my sister, having not been here for a while, but it seems that underneath the smiles there were blacker thoughts. The wastrels—Southampton and company—will go straight back to Essex and report everything."

"Of course they will. Does he think, because he is gone, all life will cease?" I said.

"No," said Philadelphia. "But I hope it does not stir him up."

"To what?"

She shrugged. "A jealous and disordered mind can always find something. I have heard that the atmosphere has changed at Essex House from one of mourning to one of militancy."

"I know that they have opened the courtyard to all and sundry, and anyone with a complaint or discontent is gathering there. Puritan preachers who are too radical for any regular congregation, disgruntled Catholics, and lately an infusion of Welsh borderers. A strange mixture. But we have our informants. Nothing passes that we are not aware of."

"That is good," said Catherine. "Otherwise it would be difficult to sleep soundly."

# 78

he twelve days of Christmas are the busiest time at court of all the year. From dawn, with morning prayer in the chapel royal sung by the voices of the Westminster choristers, to the tables laden with every conceivable form of fowl, fish, and meat, desserts of cream, ginger, and rose water, fruits in red wine, pitchers and flagons of drink for midday dinner, and on into the evening with masques, dances, plays, and entertainments, there was not an instant of stillness. In the late afternoon people could steal away for a nap before the evening's activities, but otherwise the time between the end of the night's play and the new day was so short it afforded little rest. The young did not need the afternoon pause, but the older courtiers relied on it.

On the third night there was to be a masque, and the eighth day was New Year's, which entailed its own long ritual of gift exchange. Then on to the grand finale, Twelfth Night itself. In between there were concerts, poetry recitals, games, and card playing. And always, of course, the parade of fashion in which each courtier tried to outdo his or her fellows in sartorial splendor; those who declined to enter the contest had the pleasure of rating and criticizing the others.

One of the rewards of the season for me was seeing the faces of those who had been absent from court for any number of reasons. To me, that was a better New Year's gift than any of the predictable offerings of lockboxes, gloves, ruffs, bejeweled combs, carved bracelets, lockets, poems, velvet-bound books. Robert Carey, Catherine's younger brother, was always delightful to see again; he was very unlike his portly, sensual brother George. Sir Henry Lee, my retired champion, turned up for the festivities, bringing with him my former maid of honor Anne Vavasour.

She was still beautiful in her wild, dark way. She bowed low before me as we found ourselves in the library together one afternoon. I told her so.

"I thank Your Majesty," she said, from beneath her spiky black lashes, which framed eyes as blue as an October sky. Lee stood protectively by.

Mary Fitton, another former maid of honor often pursued by men, was here. I chanced upon her gazing at the displays of Accession Day shields in the gallery. Even though her back was to me, I recognized her black hair, which shone with what seemed to be purple glints.

"Mistress Fitton," I said. She whirled around to see me and then sank low.

"Up, up," I said. "I am pleased to see you." She had been driven from court by the insistent pursuit of the married Sir William Knollys as surely as Daphne had been driven to extreme measures by the unwelcome chase of Apollo.

"Not as pleased as I am to be back, Your Majesty."

"It is quite safe," I assured her. "I think Knollys is off in another direction these days."

---

The next few days were a swirl of headdresses, ruffs, jewels, music, and feasts. In the short winter days some of the men went hunting in the fields beyond the palace, returning with red cheeks and chapped lips. New Year's Day came and found us all indoors while the ceremony of gift exchange commenced.

"What will be your colors today?" Philadelphia asked. "Remember, it sets the tone for the whole year."

I laughed. "That is but a superstition, that whatever is done on New Year's must repeat all year. I will wear black and white today, and I would like all my ladies to do the same. We will look like snow and ice and black tree branches—appropriate for winter."

As I had every New Year's for the past forty-two years, I stood and received gifts, then directed the giver to claim a receipt to exchange with the treasury for his or her gift from me.

The line progressed smoothly. I had a chance to linger for a moment or two with each of the guests individually, which was more meaningful than the gifts they handed me. I greeted Lord Keeper Egerton warmly. This past year his service to me had cost him dear. His wife had died shortly after he had begged me to release him from his jailer's role, and I still felt sad about that. Seeing him here, and seeing him smiling, was a great relief to me. His boyish face had aged and his blond hair now showed streaks of gray.

"I wish you a good year with all my heart, Thomas," I told him.

He smiled wistfully, as if to say, *Impossible, but thank you.* Then he turned to the young man just behind him and said, "May I present my secretary, Master John Donne? He is my faithful and industrious helper."

Donne had a saturnine complexion, a long, thin face, and the reddest natural lips I had ever seen. "Your Majesty," he said.

"Jack writes poetry to amuse himself in his off hours," said Egerton. "Nothing published yet. But you might enjoy one that I found excellent."

Oh, God. Not more poetry. I forced myself to smile. "Indeed?" I said, in a tone that should serve as a warning.

But Jack did not heed. He handed me a beribboned scroll and said, "My unworthy effort." I had to take it.

Shortly afterward William Lambarde came through and presented me a leather envelope. "Hever Castle, Your Majesty," he said.

"You are quick!" I said. I grasped it eagerly.

"These are not the historical records—I have those at home and must compile them for you—but what I know in my head. It can get you started, and the rest will follow."

"I thank you," I said. "I am curious to know everything about it."

---

At long last, the day of standing was over. In the privacy of my inmost chamber, I took off my satin shoes and sat down. I opened the leather envelope and pulled out the Hever papers. Lambarde had included drawings and local stories about the castle, as well as a brief description of its history.

Catherine peered over my shoulder. "Perhaps this year we can make that journey together," she said. She extracted one of the papers and studied it intently.

I handed her the entire packet of papers. "You can peruse all these, to prepare." I unrolled the poem from Master Donne. "I must do my homework," I said. "Reading the offerings of the would-be poets." I laughed.

The poem was entitled "The Bait" and it began, "Come live with me and be my love."

"Oh no," I groaned. "This is not only stale but copied!" He had stolen from Christopher Marlowe and even from Walter Raleigh's parody. Did he think I did not know the other poems . . . or, more ominous, that I would be unable to remember them?

But as I read further I saw it parted company from the others after a few lines and said something entirely different.

*Come live with me and be my love,*
*And we will some new pleasures prove*
*Of golden sands, and crystal brooks,*
*With silken lines and silver hooks.*

*There will the river whispering run*
*Warmed by thy eyes, more than the sun.*
*And there the enamored fish will stay,*
*Begging themselves they may betray.*

*When thou wilt swim in that live bath,*
*Each fish, which every channel hath,*
*Will amorously to thee swim,*
*Gladder to catch thee, than thou him . . .*

*Let coarse bold hands, from slimy nest*
*The bedded fish in banks out-wrest,*
*Or curious traitors, sleavesilke flies*
*Bewitch poor fishes' wandering eyes.*

*For thee, thou need'st no such deceit*
*For thou thyself art thine own bait;*
*That fish, that is not catch'd thereby,*
*Alas, is wiser far than I.*

"Odd imagery," said Philadelphia. "Slimy nests—fish swimming toward a person—" She shook her head.

"It is arresting," said Catherine. "Not the usual compliments."

"I have never been compared to someone wading in the water and attracting fish," I admitted. "I am not like to forget this one."

"Christopher Hatton once said you fished for men's souls with such sweet bait that no one could escape your net," said Catherine. "But that was so many years ago and was privately said. How could he have known about it?"

The red-lipped Mr. Donne was proving more intriguing than his quiet demeanor had suggested.

---

More days of merrymaking, until I swore that my guests would not wish to look upon a comfit or drink a cordial or dance a galliard until next Christmas. I know I felt that way. At last the end was in sight and we made ready to celebrate the last day. There was a communion service in the morning, at which I presented gold, frankincense, and myrrh at the altar, and the children of the chapel sang carols. There would be a play in the afternoon, followed by the long-awaited Bean King feast—and then, praise God, they would depart for home.

All morning the workers had been busily transforming the hall into a stage and arranging the chairs and benches for the audience. Upon arrival, I made sure I was seated between our distinguished visitors, Don Virginio Orsino,

Duke of Bracciano, and Grigori Ivanovitch Mikulin, ambassador from Czar Boris Godunov. George Carey, the patron of the acting company, sat directly behind me. All around us the buzz of anticipation rose; although other plays had been presented through the holidays, the best was always shown last.

George rose and took his place before the curtain. "My good friends, it is my great pleasure to present a new play called, in honor of its debut, *Twelfth Night*. I trust that it will bring enjoyment to all." Bowing, he sat back down. "I can only hope this is good," he whispered to me. "The costumes, at least, are rich, and we have both music and dancing."

"George," I said, "everyone's mood today is so happy that they will enjoy almost anything. Besides, has Shakespeare ever failed you?"

To the Russian envoy I said, "If there is anything you do not understand, please tell me and I shall make sure to translate."

He sighed. "I think my English is sufficient," he said.

The play began. As I had been told earlier, it involved separated twins. But since they were a man and a woman, only a blind man could have confused them. No, not even that. A blind man, in real life, would be the first to know they were not the same person because of their voices. The theater could be very silly, and this was one of these times.

There were two women, Olivia and Viola. One had taken a vow of chastity for seven years, and the other was the female twin, disguised as a man. One hardly needed to be a genius to know that they would mistakenly fall in love and problems would ensue. Nonetheless, the predictable tale was executed with skill and tidbits of poetry and song that were charming.

And then, onto the stage strode . . . Sir William Knollys. Not the actual man himself, but such a blatant mimic that he was instantly recognized, to the delight and howl of the audience. He sported the same multicolored beard, wore the willow green doublet that was Knollys's favorite, and had the same mannerism of crooking his little finger when he wanted to make a point. In this his name was Malvolio, the steward of the Lady Olivia, and he made a fool of himself chasing her.

I saw Mary Fitton doubled up with laughter and then realized that Lady Olivia looked like Mary.

Every word that Malvolio spoke was drowned out by the audience's laughter, to the extent that it was difficult to follow all the dialogue. In one scene, Malvolio was tricked into wearing an outlandish outfit with yellow cross-garters, making him look like a stork. I spotted Knollys sitting on the left side of the audience, hunched over, hands over his hat. But then I saw that he was laughing along with everyone else. The old goat was at least a good sport.

One of the actors in a small part, that of Olivia's servant, was darkly handsome, with deep-set eyes. I chided myself that my eyes were still drawn to such things.

The actors exited the stage and a clown came out to address us, singing a melancholy song out of keeping with the rest of the play. Its mournful, minor-key refrain of "The rain it raineth every day" was puzzling.

"What is this?" asked Duke Orsino. "I do not understand. He is a clown, but not funny."

"Neither do I," I assured him. "Perhaps it is from the wrong play."

---

While the stage was dismantled and the hall made ready for tonight's banquet, I discreetly retired to my bedchamber. I was tired; twelve days of merrymaking had quite worn me out. It would never do to droop during the long evening ahead; it would surely cause comments. I lay down on my bed, staring up at the carved canopy above me. Already it was lost in shadows; the short day had ended while we were at the play.

I hoped that both envoys would return to their masters with good reports. I had done all I could to make the palace shine with opulence for their visit, ordering all the windows washed (no mean task with so much glass and such foul weather), covering scratched tables with fine fabric, and stocking the rooms with extra candles and firewood, as if the cost were irrelevant. I took it as a favorable sign that an Italian duke, whose family politics were intertwined with the papacy, should see fit to visit this "daughter of heresy." As for the Russians, it was best to keep on good terms with them even as we competed for trade routes.

Tonight I would wear all white, intensified with diamonds and pearls. Likewise my officers and attendants would attire themselves. There is nothing more formal than white. I groaned a bit as I sat up and steeled myself for the long preparation. It was akin to a knight putting on his armor. But appearance is paramount.

My vast dress, heavy white satin brocaded with white silk and covered with rows of pearls, had its own attached cape that framed my back. A heart-shaped gossamer collar rose up behind my head, its edges twinkling with diamonds. Inside that was a stand-up collar of purest pale lace. My hair—or should I say, my towering wig—was dotted with pearls and fanciful white flowers of silk. My toes, peeking out from under my skirt, gleamed with white satin.

Draping a towel over my shoulders and neck, my ladies applied the face powder of ground alabaster, the rouge and lip color of fine cinnabar.

"You look like Diana herself," said Catherine, smoothing the makeup with her gentle fingers.

"From a distance," I said. "And candlelight is kind."

Philadelphia held out a vial of crushed violets and applied the perfume to my neck and wrists.

"Violet in deepest winter," I said. "A sort of magic." The same magic I was attempting: to be something out of season. It was a fitting choice, then.

---

The Great Hall was ablaze with torches and candles, the long tables covered with bright woven cloths, candelabra placed at intervals, their pale beeswax candles dripping already. The first part of the meal would be ordered and seemly, with servers bringing an endless stream of platters, the meat still steaming from the roasting fires. Nero himself could not have provided more choice and quantity. Showpieces, to be brought in and paraded around the hall before being eaten, were peacock, swan, and pastry fantasies sprinkled with sugar and nutmeg. Washing the food down, the guests had a choice of ale, malmsey, white burgundy, claret, beer, and sack.

Decorous music, provided by lutes, viols, harps, and the clear voices of young singers, filled the hall with delicate melody.

I took my place between the two envoys. Ambassador Mikulin told me that in Russia they constructed ice palaces in winter where they would hold such banquets.

"All made of ice," he said. "Each candle inside reflects a thousand times."

Duke Orsino shivered. "Uncivilized," he said. "No one should live where winter lasts more than a month."

"We Russians like our winter," Mikulin said. "If we have a short one, we become despondent."

I remembered the sables Czar Ivan had sent me. They must wear them year-round.

At length the servers brought in a huge cake; in truth, it was several cakes baked separately, and then fitted together, as no oven could hold such a monster. Trumpeters sounded their silvery notes, followed by a drumroll, and John Harington stepped forward, standing before the cake. "As master of ceremonies, I invite you to take a piece of this cake. Somewhere within this half there is a bean, and within this half, a pea. Let the men take pieces from the bean side and the ladies from the pea. You all know the rule: The man who finds the bean is the Bean King, and the lady the Pea Queen. This night, you are to do whatever they command you. All rules are gone. You may speak to whomever you please, swap stations so that the servant becomes the master, and vice versa. To our distinguished foreign guests, please enjoy this English custom. Now!" He gestured toward the cake, laying down two knives on each side. "Help yourselves!"

There was a mad scramble as people rushed to cut the cake. John brought me a piece. Although I bit carefully, I knew he would have made sure I did not get the pea. Let someone else be Queen for tonight.

For a few moments there was only the sound of chewing. Then Catherine gave a gasp. "I have it. I have the pea!" She held it up for all to see.

"So, Catherine, I am to obey you!" I said. "Give me a task!" The room grew quiet as everyone turned to see what would happen.

She hesitated. Clearly she had not thought anything out, never expecting the role to fall to her. "Recite the Lord's Prayer backward. In Latin."

"Am I allowed to write it out and then read it backward?"

Used to allowing me anything, she hesitated again. "No," she finally said. "That would be too easy."

All eyes turned to me as I tried to write the words out in my mind, picture them, and recite them. *"Malo—a—nos libera sed,"* I started. *"Tentationem in inducas nos ne et."* I got as far as *"nobis da quotidianum"*—"give us today our daily"—before I got hopelessly tangled up and stopped, laughing.

"That is not fair!" cried Harington. "It's been over forty years since we've had Latin in church here. Who could remember?"

"I would do better with Cicero," I admitted.

"Oh, but tonight you can't choose!" said Catherine, turning to give another victim his orders.

A few minutes later a cry went up on the other side of the hall. A young man was holding up the bean, looking surprised. He turned it around as if he could not believe it.

"So!" said Harington, rushing over to him. "Tonight you will rule over us all!" He knelt before him. "Your servant, sir," he said.

The young man said, "Which character in the play would you be?"

"The clown," he said. "His song closes the play."

"Then sing for us," the Bean King demanded.

If he had known Harington, he could not have chosen a worse task. He was a poor singer, unable to carry even as simple a tune as "Fair Annie." Turning red, he belted out an obscene ditty about a miller's daughter.

That brought the hall to clapping and yelling, and soon everyone was indulging in upside-down behavior: soldiers tripping a dainty measure, women shouting bawdy verses, servers helping themselves to the wine and refusing to pour for anyone, children, long past their bedtime, running wild, overturning tables, unscolded.

The Bean King was thoroughly enjoying himself, ordering people about while stuffing himself with sweetmeats and bolting cup after cup of different wines.

"They say it will make you sick," he said. "But tonight all rules are suspended, and that means I can overindulge and mix whatever I like."

"Don't be so sure of that," I told him. "I do not think the laws of nature are set aside quite yet."

He squinted at me. Clearly the wine was behaving in its normal fashion inside him. "Your hair is red as a rooster's comb," he blurted out. "Perhaps I should order you to crow." He hiccupped. "Crow!" he said.

I threw my head back and gave an imitation of a cock crow. People clapped. Then someone came up to the Bean King and asked him, "But what of your brother? Why is he not here? Did he not want to see it performed?"

"Busy writing. He has to finish something by next Wednesday."

I wondered who this boy was. He did look familiar, but I could not place him. I kept looking. Then I had it. He was one of the actors in the play, the dark one who had caught my eye.

"Who is your brother?" I asked him. "Who are you, for that matter? I see you had a part in the Lord Chamberlain's Men. Do you belong to that company?"

"No, I do not belong to any one company, but act with whatever one will have me. It is hard to find work."

"I would think you would be suited to many different roles," I said. It was true. He could play handsome, he could play plain, shy, bold, strong, or weak. He seemed a shape-shifter as far as his type went. "What did you say your name was?"

"Edmund. Edmund Shakespeare."

Now I understood. His brother was the author of today's play. "I have met your brother," I said. "He is quite the success here in the public theater and at court."

"Yes, I know. He has been generous to me, but I try not to presume. I was only seven when he left Stratford, so in many ways we were strangers."

"That can happen." As it had with me and my older sister.

"You don't know what it's like, having him be so famous, and in the same field. I'll never escape his shadow, but I am compelled to keep acting. There isn't anything else I want to do. But everywhere I look, there *he* is!"

"Envy is a corrosive thing," I said. "Try not to let it eat you, or you will cripple yourself."

"How would you know?" Truly, this night was a night of uncensored talk.

I laughed. "How young you are, or you would never ask such a question. I certainly know firsthand what it is to follow someone whose success was outsized, legendary. I am, after all, the daughter of King Henry VIII."

"Oh!" He clapped his hand over his mouth. "Oh, forgive me!"

"My dear Edmund, tonight everyone may speak freely. I am doing so in telling you that when I was your age, I never thought to attain one-tenth of the stature and wisdom of my father."

"And now they say you have eclipsed him, that you have achieved far more."

"They lie who say that. No one can eclipse or equal him. But it is possible to carve out a separate destiny and success, no matter who your father or brother is." I reached out and took his chin. "Believe me."

# 79

# LETTICE

*January 1601*

hey were everywhere—sprawled out in the hall, eating, complaining, the stink of their wet wool in the air nauseating. My house was not my own any longer, but a staging ground for disgruntled men—malcontents who looked to my son to lead them. To lead them where, and to what?

He had emerged from his collapse a different man. I had known it the moment I saw his eyes when they opened after his near death. And the distant look in them had never faded away, as if he had traveled to a land so dreadful he could never come all the way back. He seemed stronger, as if he had won immunity, but indifferent, too, to his newfound strength.

We had passed a dreary Christmas and New Year. We had no feast, no celebration. Our only guests, if you could call them that, were the men who milled in our courtyard lamenting their various grievances: the creditors who kept pressing them for payment, their lack of opportunities at court, and the failure of the world to value their services. There were pirates and failed courtiers and disinherited aristocrats, unemployed soldiers and sailors, rough retainers from our estates in Wales, whipped up by Gelli Meyrick.

There were probably spies among them reporting everything back to Elizabeth and the Privy Council, but it was impossible to detect them. The government had to be aware that the crowd was a mass of discontent, but discontent has to be molded into some shape in order to be dangerous. So far they had no direction.

Robert made a show of buying bottles of the same sweet wines he used to collect the duties from. He would pour out the golden liquid and stare at it like a lovelorn boy, then drink to the Queen's health. "Every drop I drink is a penny in her purse," he said, waving his glass about. "Am I not being a loyal subject to drink myself into oblivion, all in the Queen's name?"

"Here, here," said Meyrick, joining him. "Let us kill ourselves to enrich the Queen."

Christopher, who had absented himself from my bed and my company since Robert's collapse, sullenly drank with them but said not a word. Others—the Earls of Bedford and Rutland and Lords Monteagle and Sandys, Captain Thomas Lee and Robert's feckless uncle George Devereux—were more vocal in their opinions.

"Did you hear that Raleigh has been appointed governor of Jersey?" said Lord Sandys.

"We know why," said Henry Cuffe, filling another glass.

"Why?" asked Uncle George.

"It's all part of Cecil's plan," said Cuffe. "His scheme to let the Spanish into England. It's obvious. Raleigh is part of his faction, and now he will control the western defenses of the realm. Cobham, that other Cecil man, commands the Cinque Ports in the south. And who has the northern borders? Cecil's brother Thomas. If that isn't enough, Lord Buckhurst and Admiral Howard, Cecil's supporters, control the treasury and the navy. They all stand ready to deliver us into the hands of Spain."

"Good God, man!" cried Robert. "Can this be possible?"

"Think about it. Cecil has been pressing for peace with Spain. Was he not the leader of the group that persuaded the Queen to call a halt to our overseas attacks on Spain? He will be rewarded for that." He swallowed the rest of his drink in one gulp. "He wants the Infanta of Spain to succeed Elizabeth. He said her claim was as good as James's."

"He said this publicly?" demanded Christopher.

"Yes, of course, or I wouldn't have heard about it." He paused. "I must write to James. He has to persuade Elizabeth to declare him her successor, before it is too late and Cecil—" Robert gave a heaving cry. "She is entirely in his power. She listens to whatever he tells her. Oh, that this day has come!"

"And she was always so independent," said Cuffe. "In the old days, when her mind was—"

"Her mind is going," cried Robert. "Her body went a long time ago!"

I touched his arm and shook my head. He must not say such things, not in front of others. But Robert shook my hand off querulously.

"I'm concerned for her. If she is incompetent, unable to rule, then Cecil and his minions will get control," he said. "Her behavior toward me proves that she is not herself, that her mind is deteriorating. She locked me up, then held me without trial, then took away my livelihood on a whim—" He looked about to burst into tears. "Me, whom she loved!"

His version of events conveniently left out any provocation on his part. I must speak to him privately. But for now it was enough to hush his attacks on her.

"She has lately asked for more leniency for Catholics and even . . . Jesuits!" hissed Thomas Lee. I had always found him sneaky and violent, an ominous combination. "More proof that she is being persuaded to offer conciliation to Spain. That, from the Queen who braved the Armada."

"Each thing by itself might have an explanation, but taken all together, there's only one pattern: a Spanish one. Note whether she takes to wearing a mantilla. I wouldn't be surprised," murmured Bedford.

"Maybe she'll take up bullfighting!" cried Sandys.

This elicited a roar of laughter.

"She's a man in all other ways, so why not fight bulls?" said Meyrick.

I had to get them out of the house. This was dangerous talk. I spoke up. In case anyone was spying, I wanted him to report that I had defended the Queen. "Please. She is our Queen, and to speak thus of her is un-English."

"Scared you'll be reported?" sneered Meyrick.

I stared back at him. It was the first time he had openly challenged me, but I had sensed a duel between us for Robert's loyalty and attention. "You are the one in danger of that. You should watch your mouth."

"Spoken like a cowardly woman," he said. "But what else would you be?"

"I am the mistress of this house," I said. "Leave it. Speak your treason outside, with the faceless crowd."

Robert stood. "No. I am the master of this house. You may stay." He shot a look at me, robbing me of words. I had never thought to see this day. I had lost my son.

---

I left them to fulminate, shout, and denigrate the Queen. Robert had cause for resenting her, but most of the others could only blame their failure to achieve status at court on themselves. Elizabeth was astute, and through the years I had noticed that she used the aristocrats for window dressing at court, to dance and fulfill ceremonial positions, but the real power was held by clever commoners like the Cecils and Walsingham. She avoided anyone who reeked of personal trouble or instability, which let out most of the men in the next room. That they would hate her for it made sense. But now they would seek their redress through Robert. They would lead him into ruin, if he let them.

But in his present state of mind, he could not even think clearly. And now he had turned aside from me and cast his lot with them.

---

Nonetheless, at night they had to go home and Robert had to return to his own chambers to sleep. I prowled the hall waiting to catch him; I met him as he rounded the stairs, hurrying to his rooms.

"Robert." I blocked his way. "I must talk to you. In private."

"Not now, Mother." He tried to brush me aside, but I refused to budge. Strong man that he was, there has never been a man strong enough to dissuade a determined mother.

"Yes, now." I opened his door and was the one to usher him into his own room. Meekly he followed. It was a bad sign that his resistance could be so easily broken.

"Be quick about it," he said. "I still have work to do tonight."

"What sort of work?"

"In all due respect, Mother, it is none of your business."

"Your business is my business."

"Not any longer."

"Our fates are bound together. Nothing can happen to you that does not affect me, and the entire family. Think of your children before you embark on any rash ventures."

"The children will fare well enough. What I do does not matter, now that I cannot support them."

"The family still has its good name. I beg you, do nothing to tarnish it. Leave your children an unblemished legacy, even if they are poor. There is no disgrace in honest poverty."

He laughed. "Odd words coming from you. You have fled from poverty your whole life."

"I see more clearly now."

"Mother, please leave. I told you, I have work to do."

"And I asked you, what sort of work? What sort of work is done late at night, in secrecy?"

"Very well, then. I am going to write to King James as Cuffe suggested. He must be warned about Cecil and the Spanish."

"As Cuffe suggested. Why do you listen to him?"

"He makes sense. For the first time, someone speaks logically and with my own best interest at heart."

"Are you sure of that? What are his own interests in this?"

"He hasn't any. That's why I trust him. And now, Mother, I must get to my task." He sat down at his writing desk and pulled his ink and pen out of their container. He took a fair, blank piece of paper and began writing.

—

The next few days were difficult ones for me. In spite of my retort to Meyrick, I *was* frightened. The crowds of disreputable men grew in the courtyard, some of them so unsavory I wondered what wayside ditch they had crawled out of. At the same time, companies of radical Puritan preachers, forbidden a pulpit or a license to preach openly in parks or markets, held forth, standing on boxes to create their own makeshift platforms.

The Catholics, backed by international forces, presented an external danger to the realm. The Armadas were the supreme example of that. But the radical Puritans created a much more subtle one, for they corrupted and influenced the thinking of everyday citizens. The Puritan parliamentarian Peter Wentworth had gone to the Tower for questioning the royal prerogative. But these preachers went further.

From my window—for I dared not venture out in the midst of this unruly crowd—I could hear the ringing words of one of them. When he spoke, the men fell silent, spellbound.

"For is not a ruler appointed by the Lord?" he cried. "Thus it has been of old. The prophet Samuel was commanded by the Lord to seek out Saul to anoint him King of Israel. But"—and here he paused provocatively—"when Saul failed to obey the Lord, the Lord withdrew his favor and his royal appointment. He told Samuel, 'I am grieved that I have made Saul king, because he has turned away from me and has not carried out my instructions.' Samuel then informed Saul, 'You have rejected the word of the Lord, and the Lord has rejected you as king over Israel.'" He looked around, gauging his audience. "To drive the point home, Samuel tore the hem of Saul's robe and said, 'The Lord has torn the kingdom of Israel from you this day!'" He held up his own cloak and ripped it. "And thus the men of the Lord must do when the king . . . or queen . . . departs from the right path. Calvin taught us that we citizens have a right and responsibility to restrain and correct any sovereigns who have abused their duties to God and their own people. Yea, and if they will not submit to correction, to depose them!"

A cheer went up, growing until it enveloped the whole courtyard.

Then a clear voice asked, "But in what way may sovereigns abuse their duties?"

The preacher looked startled, as if he had not expected to answer from his lofty perch. "You will know it when you see it!" he said.

"Different men see different things in the same action. I pray you, be specific."

The preacher drew himself up like a brooding hen. "We cannot ask the Lord to be specific!"

"No, but we can ask men to be. I leave the realm of spiritual duties to God and someone's conscience, but when you speak of political matters, that should be specified. In what way, precisely, does a sovereign fail to fulfill coronation oaths? Not protecting the realm? Not enacting fair laws? Depriving men of rights? I am puzzled, sir."

"You are a devilish troublemaker!" cried the preacher. "Everyone knows what I mean!"

"No, not everyone!" Now other voices joined the dissenter. "Give us one example. If you have one, it should be easy."

"All right, then! Holding men without cause in the Tower, because they said something that angers the sovereign. Like our own Peter Wentworth, taken from Parliament in the midst of his speech and locked up!"

"Yes, yes!" the courtyard voices cried.

"And he died there!" someone yelled. "Died for speaking his mind about royal meddling!"

Now the yard erupted in cheers and shouts. It was true, all too true, about Wentworth. Elizabeth should not have done it. But that did not fit the description of a tyrant. Someone can be judged a tyrant or a bad ruler only on the basis of his or her entire reign, not one isolated incident.

But that subtlety was lost on them.

---

As the days of January wore on, Henry Cuffe and Gelli Meyrick found more "proof" that Cecil was subverting the government and planned to destroy Robert and his followers. Southampton was out riding along the Strand when Lord Grey, his enemy—and one of Cecil's adherents—attacked him. They had been at odds for years, forbidden by the Privy Council to duel. So they settled it this way. In the fray, Southampton's page had his hand hacked off.

Soon thereafter, Robert began frequenting Southampton's Drury House for long meetings. Once again I tried to confront him and get him to confess what he was doing. Once again he tried to elude me.

"You seek to interfere and meddle," he said. "So we will no longer meet here, where you can eavesdrop."

This was the first time I had had a chance to really look at him in days. He seemed healthier; he had put on a little weight, and his color was good. But his eyes were still not his own. They belonged to someone else. He had a black velvet pouch fastened around his neck, which he kept touching.

"What is that thing around your neck?" I asked. I feared he was now dabbling in the occult. I reached out toward it, but he shrank away.

"Nothing that need concern you," he said.

"Is it witchcraft? I must know!"

He laughed, a genuine laugh. "No, Mother. Such things hold no lure for me. It is— I've received an answer from King James, and I must keep it about my person at all times."

"What does he say?"

"If I told you that, there would be no need to keep it close to me. Rest assured, he means no trouble." He bent over and kissed the top of my head. "Now, dear Mother, I must go!"

"Please give my greetings to Southampton. Tell him I regret the incident on the Strand."

"It is proof that we have not imagined their malignity against us."

"Who? What malignity?"

"Grey is a creature of Cecil's. Clearly they think they can attack us with impunity. They plan violence against us. It has gone beyond conspiracy now. They are ready to act."

"But Grey was punished. The Queen put him in prison."

"That was just for show, to cover their real intent. He'll be out soon, mark my words."

---

A week later, Lord Buckhurst's son Robert Sackville called on us. I received him, realizing this was the first visitor we had had from what I increasingly thought of as "the real world" since December. It was a poignant reminder of what our life had once been.

"We welcome you," I said.

He was a lanky man with a nervous habit of smoothing his abundant hair. "Thank you," he said. "Is the earl at home?"

"Indeed," I said. "I shall call him."

Robert soon descended the stairs, fluffing his cuffs. He seldom dressed formally these days and was out of practice. He gave a stiff little smile. "Greetings," he said.

"My father, the lord treasurer, wished me to convey to you his friendship and good wishes."

Instead of saying "thank you," Robert snorted with laughter.

"I beg your pardon?" asked Sackville.

"His friendship," said Robert, as if it were a joke everyone would understand.

"My lord, he is indeed your friend, as many are at court. But it is difficult for those friends to defend you when your behavior invites sinister interpretation."

"Won't you sit?" asked Robert. "Let us go into a private room."

Was I invited? It would have been awkward to exclude me, so I slid in after them.

Robert called for refreshments, as he would have done in his past life. Ale, poppy-seed cakes, and currants were brought out.

"Now then," said Robert, popping a cake into his mouth. "Go on with your good wishes."

Sackville had been unnerved by Robert's demeanor, but he coughed and said, "These I have already expressed," he said. "But your friends wish you to know that the Queen is alarmed at the rough company and swordsmen who frequent your halls, the subversive preachers in the courtyard, and the lavish entertainments going on at Drury House in your name and by your partisans. It all seems very strange to us."

Robert gave that skittish laugh. "Strange? Strange? I assure you, it is no such thing."

"It alarms Her Majesty," Sackville repeated carefully and distinctly.

"Let the old bitch be alarmed!" said Robert. "What do I care?"

Sackville just stared. Slowly he put down his goblet and his half-eaten cake. "I see," he finally said. "Good day, then."

He turned and left the room. I heard the door open and close, then his footsteps on the path outside.

"Robert! Are you insane? Oh, what have you done?"

"I've told the truth. I stand by it. And it might interest you to know that they've already let Grey out of prison. That proves that even the law can't—or won't—protect us against *them*. The lines are drawn. We will meet their attacks with equal force."

---

Robert went to Drury House that night, but the next he stayed home, sitting before the fireplace and reading. He sat, wrapped in furs, and kept a flagon of ale close at hand.

Frances was sitting on the other side of the room, embroidering. Her time was near, and I hoped the new baby would bring them some joy in the midst of this unhappiness.

"You stay home tonight, Robert," I stated.

"Indeed," he said, reaching for his glass. He took a long sip of it.

"It is good to see you here."

"I have to be here," he said. "With all the suspicion, I cannot be seen at Drury House. I have to fool them!" He gave a laugh. "But my men will meet at Drury House, as always, to draw up a strategy for our resistance. There, I've told you. That makes you my accomplices!"

“Your resistance? What resistance? Against what?”

“I’ve said enough. Just know that many are with me in this. Some close to you—closer even than I. At least in the eyes of the law.”

“Do you mean Christopher?” Oh, God, let it not be so.

“Ask him where he’s been tonight,” said Robert. “When he finally gets in.”

# 80

I had not been back in the room for an hour when Christopher reeled in. His breath stank. I almost retched, and backed away. He stood swaying, looking at me warily.

"Why, wife, you shrink from me?" He lurched toward me, and I backed farther away.

"You are drunk," I said. "I will see you in the morning." I left the room. I would find someplace else to sleep tonight. God knew we had enough rooms in this huge house.

But when I settled myself in one of the empty guest rooms and ordered a fire to be kindled in the cold fireplace, I was shaking. I was lost in a thicket of secrets, feeling my way blindly. Robert was deep in plans, and Christopher was his accomplice. That these plans were dangerous no one need tell me. Every day Meyrick was marshaling more Welshmen, bedding them in stables and houses throughout the city. Every day messengers arrived, bearing sealed letters that Robert eagerly ripped open, then took up to his rooms. They were already under government scrutiny, and their disrespectful reception of Lord Buckhurst's son would reverberate in the palace. And when the Queen heard herself called "the old bitch," her fury would know no bounds.

What were the meetings in Drury House about? Perhaps I could pry it out of Christopher. In times past, when he had been my hungry admirer, he would have told me anything. Unfortunately, then he had had nothing to tell me. Now, when he had changed so much and left me—in thought if not in person—he was sealed in silence.

Tonight he was woozy with drink; tomorrow he would be sober and cold. If I returned to our bed . . . if I caught him just as drunkenness slid into sleep, then perhaps he would let slip what he knew. The thought of embracing him, coaxing him, was repellent, but it had to be done. I forced myself to leave my newfound sanctuary and return to our room.

He was sprawled across the bed, fully dressed, snoring. The ale fumes hung over his head like a fog, and I had to hold my breath to lean close to him. I gauged his depth of sleep; still too deep to rouse. Patiently, I stretched out beside him. I would wait, wait to catch him at a vulnerable moment. I must not allow myself to slumber even for an instant.

It was a long night. I was aware of every sound as time slowly passed. I heard the scurrying of mice behind the panels. This would have bothered me in another time; now mice were the least of my concerns. Far more alarming were the clankings and muffled voices from the courtyard where nearly two hundred men kept constant vigil. Sometimes I heard the splash of oars as a boat docked at our landing stairs, carrying more conspirators.

A faint light was showing around the drawn bed-curtains before Christopher groaned and rolled over. "Oh, God—" he muttered, in a normal voice, not slurred or papery thin.

Now! I slid close to him. "Oh, my poor dear," I murmured.

"Uh," he uttered.

I stroked his forehead. "What a night you must have had," I whispered. "All that ale—"

"Too much ale," he mumbled.

Each word was articulated clearly. His mind was hitched back to his tongue, then. "Tell me what you have decided," I said. "I need to know. I am in as much danger as you," I assured him. "But I need to know what sort of danger."

"Uhhh—" He winced as he opened his eyes and the dim light hit them. He put his forearm up over them to shield them.

"What have you decided at Drury House?" I pressed.

"Nothing yet. Three ways we can go . . ." His voice trailed off. ". . . argue . . . which is best."

He was going to tell me. He was still groggy enough to suspend his judgment and guard. "What three ways are those?"

He was silent for so long I feared he had gone back to sleep. I nudged him.

"Attack the court first . . . surprise them. Or march into the city to get more men. Or capture the Tower, to control the city?"

"How many men do you—we—have?"

"Over a hundred and twenty nobles, knights, gentlemen. The sheriff of London says he has another thousand for us. Others will join in as we march." His voice was becoming steadier as he awoke. "We have a plan for taking Whitehall. I'm to be posted near the great court gate and take control of that. Ferdinando Gorges thinks it won't work. He's a coward."

"What does he think you should do instead?"

He shook his head. "I don't know," he said.

"But he must have an opinion."

"There were a lot of opinions, most worthless."

"What did you settle on?"

"We didn't. There is no plan." Suddenly he was alert and would betray no more; his judgment and wariness had returned.

"No plan? But how can you proceed, if there is no plan?"

"I don't know. I know nothing. There is no plan."

As unbelievable as it sounded, this turned out to be true. But at the moment I only thought he had returned to himself, had brought down the portcullis that guarded his thoughts. At least I had found out a few things—too few.

"If you betray us, you will pay the highest price," he suddenly said.

"Why do you think I would betray you, my own husband?"

"You betrayed husbands one and two, why not husband three?"

Just so, I learned he had turned against me. Had the rebels stolen his wits and loyalties so completely? What did they offer him in return?

The secret meetings at Drury House continued. I made no effort to ask Christopher about them—it was hopeless—and watched Robert closely, but I learned nothing. The February days, dreary and bone-chillingly damp, stretched a pall of gloom over the house. Only Frances with her pregnancy provided a spot of happiness and normalcy, as we talked about what she might name the baby. She was willing to choose something from our family tradition, as if she wanted to please Robert and commend herself to him.

---

It was the evening of February 6. Nothing special in that date, no anniversary of momentous happenings. I was sitting before a low-burning fire and thinking of adding more logs—strange how one remembers such details—when a visitor was announced.

It was quiet in the house. Regular visitors did not come now; the clandestine ones sneaked in and the rowdy ones milled in the courtyard. I rose, ready to receive him or her. My mind was blank. I expected no one in particular.

Will walked into the small room. He took off his hat and said, "Laetitia."

The moment he spoke I knew he was here on dangerous business. His voice was higher than normal and his smile seemed artificial.

"Yes, Will," I said. "What troubles you?" I could see this visit was political, not personal.

"A risky thing has happened. Your husband and a group of men from a tavern dinner came over to Southwark tonight to request that my theater company perform *Richard II* tomorrow afternoon. They offered to pay us well. But what it means—I am leery of it. They want us to enact the abdication scene—the one forbidden to be printed."

"Who else made this request?"

"Gelli Meyrick, Lord Monteagle, Charles Danvers, and Christopher. Others I did not recognize. My company financial manager, Augustine Phillips, tried to put them off. He said such an old play was unlikely to attract much of an audience. But they then guaranteed payment equal to a full house. What objection could he then give?"

"None," I admitted.

What was there about him that made me want to confide in him? It was all I could do not to blurt out, "Will, help me! I am lost!" Instead I had to smile and say, "Pray stay a few moments. Let me just add another log to the fire and call for some ale."

I expected him to clutch his hat and say, "No, I must go. I cannot be seen." Instead he nodded and said, "I would like that."

We sat across from each other beside the fire. For the first time I could see him apart from my wants, a man with concerns of his own. "You would risk the Queen's displeasure if you were to do it. She would be alarmed. What do you think is the purpose of it?"

"Your husband stated it baldly. 'To rouse the populace,' he said. Evidently he and his fellows are hoping to overthrow the Queen, make her abdicate like Richard II. They want to rally supporters by showing this play."

Oh, God. Robert was in the thick of it. Christopher and Meyrick and Southampton and the others were not the beneficiaries. It was all for Robert. Did he hope to—was he planning to take the throne himself? Who else was a candidate? Would they go to all this trouble and danger for James of Scotland? What could he promise them that would make them want him instead of Elizabeth?

"This is dreadful," I finally said. Christopher's confession about their plans had confirmed a coup against Elizabeth. All I could do was sit and watch, relegated to the sidelines.

"It is more than dreadful," said Will. "It is the end of our world. My career will be ruined—I will be seen as the traitorous playwright. Your son is doomed. He cannot win. And Elizabeth is destroyed. She will not recover from this betrayal—I mean, her spirits and her trust. She lives by the love of her people."

"Don't perform the play!" I cried. "Stop it now."

"Phillips has already taken the money. In the theater, box office is all."

"We both stand to lose all," I said. There was a wonder in stating it so simply.

"All," he said. "It is a cruel reward for Elizabeth in the sunset of her reign, to be greeted with this. And for me! Would that I had never written that play!"

"You will survive this," I assured him. "I am not so sure about the house of Devereux."

He shook his head. "If Robert attempts this folly . . . yes, it will doom him, if not his house. There is no support for him. Why cannot he and his supporters see that?"

"They have blinded themselves with bitterness and wishful thinking. Will"—I reached my hand out to him—"I have tried everything to make them see clear. But I am ignored and shunted aside. I am helpless. All I can do is watch. Watch them go down to ruin."

"Save yourself," he said. "Distance yourself. That is what I will do." He stood up. He dropped my hand. "I plan to be in my rooms, writing my new play, when the day comes."

"Do you know the actual day?"

"No. I think they are past planning. I think they will just set out, willy-nilly, with no forethought. They will be quickly destroyed."

"We must rescue ourselves," I said, thinking even as I said it he must think me an unnatural mother. I quickly added, "We are, after all, not the main players. The leads go to others; the stage is commanded by them."

He smiled. "Laetitia, one would think you were to the theater born."

"Life is a play," I said. "Surely you of all people have noted that?"

I saw him make his way toward the door and recalled happier times, when both our moods were so different, "Yes, frighteningly so," he said, leaving my threshold.

# 81

# ELIZABETH

*February 1601*

t was still. Too still. Around Whitehall, the throngs that usually swept through our public right-of-way had melted away, leaving the buildings stranded in a sea of pavement and dead grass.

"I have never seen it so quiet," I said to Catherine, standing beside me as we looked out upon the empty grounds. "They say such silence comes just before an earthquake, that the animals sense it, the birds fly away."

"Or before an eclipse," she said. "The sky darkens, the air cools, and all is hushed."

For days the city had been agitated, with reports of fiery little Welshmen sleeping in attics and cellars, fresh horses being stabled in whatever makeshift stalls could be found, the movement of goods along the western roads from Wales and the northern ones from Scotland. Yet, like the faint trembling and wisps of smoke before a volcano erupts, it was impossible to know exactly what it portended.

"An eclipse is always a bad omen," I said. "And so is anything that mimics one."

Catherine shook her head. "We have lived through many of them, and we will live through more."

"Bless you, Cousin. You are my right arm."

"No, I am your left," she said. "Here is your right."

She had seen Robert Cecil enter before I did, followed by Raleigh. I turned to face them. "What is it?" They were clearly vexed.

"There's been a special performance of *Richard II* this afternoon at the Globe!" cried Cecil. "They are just getting out now—a mob of men, grinning and shouting."

"It was commissioned by Essex's men. They guaranteed a payment to cover it, no matter the size of the audience. It's an old play, and the actors didn't want to stage it," added Raleigh. "No actor wants to perform something passé."

"Did they show *the* scene?" I asked. But I already knew the answer. What was the point of staging it otherwise?

"Indeed they did," said Raleigh. "The Essex men insisted on it; it was part of the agreement."

I had the best spies in the realm. I appreciated that. But they could not know everything, be everywhere. I had someone who attended on Gelli Meyrick and another who served Frances Walsingham in her chamber. I had been less successful in placing anyone in Essex's private quarters. His movements, and his aims, were shrouded in obscurity.

Twilight was falling; it came early on these February days. The play had finished just in time to allow the audience to disperse before darkness enveloped them. A faint mist lay over the river already, and it would creep up out of its banks and envelop the city.

"It must end," I said. I suddenly knew this was the hour. The time to strike.

"Are you sure?" asked Cecil. "Perhaps we should wait, let the plot—whatever it is—come to a head."

"That is always the question," said Raleigh. "Do we leave the plotters unmolested, in hopes that they will unequivocally incriminate themselves? Or do we cut it off before it can reach dangerous fruition?"

"We have done both, in the past. The rising of the northern lords in 1569—we forced them into action before they were ready. The Scots queen—we had to let that develop far enough that we had enough evidence to proceed," I said.

"It is always a gamble," said Cecil.

"I think we must follow the pattern for the northern lords," I decided. "If unchecked, this fomenting rebellion may overwhelm us. We cannot afford to wait for more evidence."

I sounded more certain than I felt. There was no doubt that Essex, with his popularity, presented a dilemma like that of the Scots queen. My actions toward him must be decisive, and without ironclad evidence of his hostile intent, my motives would be suspect. God knew I could not afford to offend public opinion at this point.

"What shall I do? Arrest him?" asked Raleigh.

"Not yet," I said.

"Are you sure?" he asked. "Don't give him a chance to slip away."

"Send a messenger and command him to appear before the Privy Council tomorrow." He had turned away the friendly warning from Buckhurst's son, insulting me in the process. For my father, that would have been enough. He would have been in the Tower already. But calling me an old bitch, while it showed gross and shocking disrespect toward my person, was not treasonous. I reasoned carefully, keeping my scepter and my self distinct, trying to see where he had insulted one without injuring the other. To do otherwise would taint the brilliance of my reign by insinuations of the kind his followers put about, to risk losing the people's belief in me.

---

My messenger was turned away. He arrived at Essex House when Essex himself and his inner circle—Blount, Southampton, Meyrick, Cuffe, Rutland, and Danvers—were settling themselves down to a big meal, discussing *Richard II* with gusto while chewing their mutton and slurping their ale. Essex told the messenger he did not wish to speak with him and dismissed him into the night.

"Arrest him!" said Raleigh. "This is tantamount to throwing down his challenge."

I was torn. How many insults could I endure from this man? How many slaps, how many dares? "No. Let us try one more time. Let us provide the rope whereby he hangs himself."

"Do you want to be deposed?" cried Cecil.

"Is that his aim? I do not think anyone knows what the aim of this deluded, confused man is," I said. "Not even he himself."

"His aims may be separate from those of his followers," said Raleigh. "The point is, they should not be allowed to control the events. There should not *be* any events."

"Of course, you are right. And there will not be. But I must send one more messenger, give him one more chance. I will send Secretary Herbert."

"It is already late," said Cecil.

"Order him to report to the Privy Council first thing tomorrow morning, Sunday."

But Essex turned Secretary Herbert away. It was near midnight when Herbert returned to me.

"He refused to talk to me. He pleaded ill health, although he looked hearty enough to me," Herbert reported. "He was surrounded by his cronies, flushed with ale, wearing his best blue doublet. I have never seen him look more splendid."

"So." I took my time in responding. "Go home, John. You have done a good night's work. Now sleep. The rest is up to me."

---

The hour had come. The hour that Dee had prophesied, when he said a great final battle would shadow the latter years of my reign. Mordred, he had said.

Was Essex my Mordred? It was tempting to think so, but there is no such thing as exact repetitions, exact fulfillments of prophecy. I was a descendant of Arthur, but I had no Round Table, no Lancelot, no Guinevere, no Morgan Le Fay. I had only my own powers to sustain the realm.

---

The night was dark, no moon. Looking out my window at the river, I saw no reflection on the water, although I could hear its gentle lapping. The dead, dull hour held the city in its grasp.

Catherine slept on her bed near mine, breathing lightly. I envied her for a moment but put that aside. *I keep vigilant so you may sleep; so all of you in my kingdom may sleep.*

My father had entrusted it to me, his beloved England.

*I will preserve you, my people,* I vowed. *If for an instant I thought another could serve you better, I would make way for him or her. I have no desire to rule an instant past the time I may rule to your benefit, but to leave before that time is to desert you. And that I will never do.*

---

I did not really sleep. I lay down, true, but I did not draw my bed-curtains—those who would have drawn them slumbered peacefully—and so I saw the deep blue that signaled the winter dawn frame my windows.

February 8. It was the fourteenth anniversary of the execution of the Queen of Scots. A cursed day.

Whitehall was unprotected. We had only a scant guard, my two-hundred-strong Queen's Guard and the fifty Gentlemen Pensioners. Essex House was but a twenty-minute march away, and its courtyard was filled with eager soldiers and retainers. It was Sunday, when the apprentices—always a volatile group, and one that was taken with the likes of Essex—would be off work in the City. We were utterly vulnerable. As I lay watching the deep blue turn violet and then pale gray, I thought that perhaps Raleigh was right. We should have taken them last night. Now we had lost the advantage.

Up, up. I called for my clothes and dressed myself in serviceable garb to withstand a very long day. Raleigh was announced in the outer chamber. I went out to meet him and saw that he was in his soldier's uniform, clutching his helmet under his arm. I could see by his face that he, too, had not slept.

"Your Majesty, I propose to speak to my kinsman Sir Ferdinando Gorges this morning. He is with them at Essex House, but perhaps he will talk to me. It may still be possible to reach them, before . . ."

"Be careful," I said. "We cannot know what they might do."

After he left, still in the mist of dawn, I called Cecil and told him to send the councillors back to Essex House. "This time, it will be an official summons," I said. "Lord Egerton must take the Great Seal, and if they do not respond, command their obedience under its authority. In the meantime, send warnings to the lord mayor and aldermen of London; they'll be at St. Paul's Cross for the eight o'clock sermon. Those are the biggest crowds of the day, and the rebels may try to recruit them."

I stopped myself, realizing I had just formally anointed them "rebels."

"Yes, Your Majesty." Cecil did not contradict my choice of words. "I have already taken the liberty of alerting the lord mayor. I will also see what forces our supporters can command in the City, in case we need them."

Now I would wait. Wait, while the vast, sprawling palace seemed to be holding its breath. Although it was impossible to do anything else, to think of anything else, I must make a show of it. I called for my secretary and my correspondence box. There were diplomatic letters I should answer, local petitions to respond to. The foreign secretary of King Henri IV inquiring about a property dispute near Calais . . . a request for a royal portrait from the Merchant Adventurers . . . a proposal that captive bears be better fed by their wardens . . .

"Your Majesty!" There was a fierce knocking on the door, and the voice of Raleigh.

"Enter!" I bellowed. Oh, God. Whatever it was, this was the first report of the situation.

He strode in, brushing drops of water from his sleeves. "Essex insisted that Gorges and I talk only in the open, from boats in front of Essex House."

"Never mind the particulars, what did Gorges *say*?"

"He said, and I quote, 'You are like to have a bloody day of it.'"

So. Now all was clear. It was as bad as the worst we had imagined.

"Then he signaled his comrades, who rowed out from the water stairs aiming muskets at me. I did not stay." He laughed, as if at his simplicity in stating the obvious.

"I am sorry, Walter. It is sad to lose a kinsman who chooses a different path." As I had known time and again.

"Christopher Blount yelled from the shore that he should kill me."

"Then he's as big a fool as your cousin," I said. "It's a shameful thing when a man becomes enthralled to his own stepson." What did Lettice think of her son and husband leading a rebellion? Was she encouraging them? Or was she horrified and helpless? "Did you see how many men they have? Was there a large crowd?"

"I couldn't see into the courtyard. But it looked as if some of them had already gone. Most likely to the City."

I turned and looked out the window. I did not see any crowds approaching.

Every moment that they held off gave us more time to collect our counter-forces.

It was ten o'clock. The crowds at St. Paul's would have already dispersed. The rebels had lost their opportunity there. By this time the deputation of councillors must have reached Essex House. All depended on this. Perhaps they would be respectfully received and Essex politely swear to his peaceable intentions.

But no! That would be the worst result, for it would be a lie and serve only to buy him more time. We must flush him out now, not later.

"Thank you, Walter. You must see to your guardsmen now. They must be ready, all two hundred of them."

Bowing hurriedly, he swept out of the chamber. I stood rooted to that spot, as if nails fastened my feet to the floor. I would stay here, helpless, while the rebels poured into Whitehall, stormed into the chamber. I could see their faces, see Essex flushed and bright eyed, see Christopher Blount, open mouthed and yelling, see Southampton with his pretty curls flying. They would truss me up, convey me to a little room, force me to abdicate, as the Scots queen was forced, as Richard II was. They would treat me with exaggerated courtesy, bowing and mocking, wrench the coronation ring off my finger, try it on themselves. Then I would be transported to some place of "retirement," a place well guarded. Whom would they put in my place? Essex himself? Or would he proclaim himself lord protector and summon James of Scotland to come claim his crown?

They would capture Robert Cecil and the other Privy Councillors, have a trial, and execute them. The realm would be left without either monarch or wise councillors, for they had no one of any caliber to staff the government with. The leaders of this grim treason had all tried for court positions and failed to obtain them, due to lack of qualification.

My feet moved. I slid first one shoe, then the other, across the patterned floor. Movement gave relief; just doing something broke the spell of helpless waiting.

I walked through the connected rooms of the royal apartments, with a guard at each door, clutching his halberd, wondering if I were reviewing them in order to take my leave. Would I remember each table, each tapestry, the view out of each window, in my prison cell?

Whitehall was a massive palace, spread out over twenty-three acres. Some called it the largest in Christendom, but how could anyone know that? Nonetheless, it could take several hours just to pass through all its halls and its two thousand chambers. How far would I progress before I was apprehended? Like a silent wraith, Catherine kept pace with me. I kept stealing glances out the windows as we glided past. No movement; nothing stirring, either on land or on the river.

The brisk walking calmed me, and by the time we reached the shield gallery I felt strong again. This gallery, overlooking the river, was the place where the fanciful shields from the Accession Day tilts were displayed. They lined the walls and framed the windows; forty-one years' worth of them gleamed back at me. Had I held my last tilt celebrating my coming to the throne? Who would sit upon it this November when the seventeenth rolled around?

"I will," I said out loud. "God did not bring me to the throne and keep me here through all the dangers I have seen to desert me now."

"I believe that, dear Queen," said Catherine.

"He will keep me here where he has placed me," I insisted.

We turned and left that gallery. I walked swiftly through the adjoining rooms toward the wooden privy gallery that connected the palace to the upper story of the high Holbein Gate. The mist had lifted, and a thin, cold sunlight shone on the grounds. "Let us at least walk in the garden," I said to Catherine. "Surely that is safe."

Two of Raleigh's guards in their scarlet uniforms, ornamented front and back with the golden Tudor roses, fell in behind us. I was glad of it and did not try to elude them. They clutched their velvet-handled, gilded halberds tightly, and the heavy sound of their boots was reassuring. They were exceptionally tall and strong; in fact, they were selected for their physiques. I only hoped that their prowess equaled their stature. The privy garden was very large, with green and white painted rails bordering gravel walkways between squares of ornamental plantings. My father had set it out, and the wooden columns with gilded heraldic beasts in every square had not changed. The middle of the garden featured a large fountain and the elaborate sundial from Catherine de' Medici that indicated the time in thirty different ways. I looked up; the sun was not quite at its zenith—which would still be low in the sky these February days—but it was approaching it.

"I am guessing it is eleven o'clock," I said, turning to Catherine and the guards.

"Not quite, Your Majesty," said one of the guards.

"I am guessing it is past eleven," said Catherine.

"Now we will have our answer," I said, peeking at the device.

"You are correct," I told Catherine. "It is a little past eleven."

Oh, what had happened to my embassy? They should have returned by now, Essex in tow. Something had gone wrong, dreadfully wrong.

"We can wait no longer," I said. "I must send to know what has become of Lord Egerton and the others." The garden, the heraldic beasts, the fountain, all were invisible to me. All I could see was Essex House.

Back in the state apartments—well guarded with a double row of men—I sent for Cecil. He was nearby in his own court quarters and appeared almost instantly.

"Something has gone awry," I said. "They should have returned by now. We must send to know what has happened."

Still all was quiet. No mobs were descending on us.

"I have already done so, Your Majesty," said Cecil. "Forgive me if I was premature."

"No, it saves time." Time, time—it seemed to be barely moving. Was it my enemy or my friend?

# 82

ecil's men returned very quickly, shaken and out of breath. They brought the attendants of the original party with them. We received them all in the privy chamber. Behind me was the huge mural of my father and his Tudor dynasty.

"Tell me what you know, and tell all of it. Spare me nothing," I ordered them.

They looked at one another, as if trying to select a spokesman. "For God's sake, men, one of you speak!" I cried.

A small, balding man stepped forward, clutching his hat. "I was with Lord Egerton," he said. "When they reached Essex House, the deputation was surrounded by a sea of jeering men in the courtyard. I could not hear anything they said, but finally Essex himself came out. Over the tumult I could just hear Essex yelling that traitors planned to murder him in his bed and he would now defend himself. Then Lord Egerton put on his hat and read out a statement, and held up the Great Seal."

"He had to invoke his office, then," I said. "The document called for them to submit to my authority, lay down their arms, and state their intentions, on pain of treason. What happened next?"

The man looked tormented. "They—they shouted to kill Lord Egerton and to dash the Great Seal upon the ground."

I stared. For a moment I was unable to speak. "And then?"

"Essex escorted them into the house. All of them! Then he locked them up, and set a guard on them!"

"What? He is holding the Crown representatives hostage?"

"Yes, Your Majesty." He hung his head.

"Look at me. Stand up like a man. It was not you who did it. Where are they now?"

"They set out toward the City, followed by all their rabble from the courtyard. The men shouted that Sheriff Smythe of London was on their side and had a thousand men ready to rally. I think they mean to call out the citizens of London, try to recruit them to their cause."

"But what is their cause?" No, that was a foolish question. More accurate was, What is their pretended cause?

"I heard Essex yelling, 'For the Queen! For the Queen! The crown of England is sold to Spain! A plot is laid for my life!' "

Cecil smothered a laugh. "He has gone over the edge, then. The only one plotting is he himself."

"And as he entered the City through Ludgate he cried, 'England is sold to Spain! The Spanish Infanta is to rule here!'"

I turned to Cecil. "What of the men you assigned to follow him?"

Cecil coolly flicked his finger. "Roger—what did you find?"

A young man, thin and dark eyed, stepped forward. "I did follow them," he said. "They ran up to St. Paul's, evidently hoping to catch the big crowds there, but it was too late. The sermon was over and people had scattered. Then they rode farther into the City, toward Fenchurch Street, where Sheriff Smythe lives. But the sheriff had exited out his back door. So they have sat down to a meal at his expense!"

"I do not follow," I said.

"When they found him not at home, they invaded his quarters and helped themselves to his wares—beer, cheese, and beef. They are still there, guzzling."

"They are eating, when they are trying to raise a city to arms?" I asked. I wanted to make sure I understood.

"Yes, that seems to be the case," admitted the man.

"So we have time to secure the City?" I asked. "What of the sheriff?"

"He seems to have vanished," said the man.

"And his thousand men?"

"A fantasy," said the man.

"I have dispatched the Earl of Cumberland, with a small detachment of troops, and have ordered a chain to be drawn across Ludgate so they cannot escape by the route they came. We have also drawn up a barricade of coaches to block the Strand near Charing Cross and locked all seven gates of the City," said Cecil.

I turned to him. "Why, Robert Cecil, you have the mind of a soldier!" I said. "Good work."

"With your permission, I will send my elder brother, the Lord Burghley, out in the City to proclaim Essex a traitor and promise a pardon for anyone who deserts him now," said Cecil.

"You have it," I assured him.

---

I sat down to my midday dinner. I tried to eat as heartily as ever, but it was a ruse. I meant for people afterward to say, "She did not alter anything, not even her demeanor." Sometimes the outward aspect must be our all.

---

Once again, the waiting. News only slowly trickled back in.

Lord Burghley had read his proclamation. . . . The men sitting in the sheriff's house had sneered that a herald would proclaim anything he was paid to. . . . Some of Essex's titled followers had deserted, including the Earl of Bedford and Lord Cromwell. Essex had called for a clean shirt, as his present one was sweat soaked. . . . Christopher Blount had tried to secure more weapons. . . .

Essex rushed out into the street, his napkin still around his neck, and yelled that he was fighting against atheists and Spain (a strange combination) for the good of England. The sheriff approached Essex and told him that he, the lord mayor, and the Privy Council requested that he surrender and go to Mansion House. Essex ignored him, turned away, and made for Ludgate again, evidently seeking to return to Essex House. But there he ran into the chain barring his way, and the Earl of Cumberland with his pikemen. Essex tried various ruses to get through, including a lie about a free pass from the lord mayor and the sheriff. But bless him, the captain was an unimaginative fellow and kept repeating that his orders were to bar the way.

Then Essex's followers lost patience; one of them fired his pistol, yelling, "Shoot! Shoot!" and rushed the pikemen. But they were stalled, and the pikemen returned fire. A shot passed through Essex's hat; his page was shot dead. Christopher Blount attacked the pikemen with his sword; he was gored in the cheek then clubbed on the head and fell, unconscious, on the street. Essex fled, leaving his stepfather to the enemy. From there they rushed back into the City, then managed to make their way back into boats toward Essex House, where their hostages awaited. Lord Monteagle fell into the water, nearly drowned, and was captured.

It was dusk. Undoubtedly the sundial in the garden illustrated the exact passage of hours. But all I had to do was look out the window and see the gathering gloom to know what hour it was.

"Where are they?" I cried. It was not over.

"No one knows," Cecil said. "But it is assumed they have reached Essex House by now."

"By God!" I cried. "I am minded to go out into the streets this moment and see which of us rules! Let us have it out!"

Cecil looked horrified. "Your Majesty!" he cried.

"Are you afraid they will choose him? If so, let it be! Let us duel here and now, a clean choice!" I meant it.

"You cannot trust the rabble," he said.

"If I cannot trust the rabble, I am no longer Queen," I said. "Bring me my cloak. Call my guard!" I would face off with him, on the street outside.

"That is foolish," said Cecil. "Not because they would choose him over you—they would not—but because in the confusion of battle, which may yet come, God forbid you might be injured."

"I shrink not!"

"But you cannot risk it—not if you are to be a mother to your people. You cannot leave them unprotected."

He was right, of course. I would have faced Essex down, on any field he chose, but I must think of my people. They would be left with a fine legend of their fighting Queen, but abandoned into Essex's hands. "For now, I will wait," was all I allowed him.

Darkness would soon follow. There would be more to come. "Dear Catherine, now it is your husband who must save the day," I told her. I had ordered the admiral to coordinate the Crown's forces. They would surround Essex House on both the river side and the Strand side. I had also ordered that cannon be transported from the Tower and stand ready to demolish the house if resistance continued.

"He has ever served you and will acquit himself well again," she assured me. "In all the crises of your reign, he has been your stalwart."

"Would there had been no crises," I said. "But if they must come, what a blessing to have a man like Charles to deflect them." Essex had gone mad. "A pity to lose one's life due to delusion," I murmured.

"I beg your pardon?" asked Catherine.

"I grieve for Essex," I said.

"Then you are as mad as he!" she cried.

"Why? The loss of a once-fine young mind is a tragedy." I stopped.

"I beg you, do not grieve publicly for him."

"I have not, and I will not," I said stoutly. But oh! I was grieved beneath my anger and arousal.

The City had not risen. The people had not flocked to Essex's cause. His recent popularity had counted for nothing in the end, against their longtime loyalty to me. He had not stolen my people's hearts from me. I was deeply thankful and breathed a prayer.

Full darkness had fallen. The attendants came in to ready the bedchamber for sleep, but I ordered them away. "I shall not sleep until these foul rebels are under lock and key in the Tower. Away with you!"

A message from Cecil: The freed hostages were waiting in the presence chamber. "Come," I told Catherine, and we hurried there. Egerton, Knollys, Lord Chief Justice Popham, and the Earl of Worcester stood, surrounded by jabbering, questioning councillors. They fell silent as I entered.

"My loyal men," I said. "Did you have a hard day of it?"

Egerton stepped forward and knelt. "Unexpected, but not hard. Essex took us inside to protect us from the mob—there is no other word—in his courtyard. But they followed us up the stairs, calling for violence. He ushered us into the library, then turned the key on us, after promising to return swiftly."

William Knollys glanced over at him. "My own nephew! I never thought—but we were well provided for. In fact, we were sent entertainment in the form of Essex's wife, his sister Penelope, and his mother, Lettice."

"Those ladies did their best to help us pass the hours, although they were more anxious than we were," said Popham. "I had no doubt that our side would prevail and we would be rescued, whereas these poor women were victims. Their men would go down to doom, and they knew it."

"Nonetheless, they made a brave show of it, talking about the latest plays, offering us dainties and wine, and making merry," said the rotund Worcester. "It was bizarre."

"Gorges let us out," said Knollys. "He had gotten back ahead of Essex and pretended he had orders to release us. He is no fool. He knew their number was up."

"So Essex will get a surprise when he returns?" I asked.

"The sort of surprise he deserves," said Worcester grimly.

---

We had a supper for all the councillors and attendants in the privy chamber.

"My loyal friends!" I cried, rising. "I drink to all of you." I raised my goblet. "Without you, I would not be what I am. Never think I am not mindful of that."

They rose with me and solemnly drank. Then Cecil said, "This night will see us safe, with all danger passed."

"God be praised!" said Knollys. "God be praised for sustaining our glorious prince on her throne."

---

I heard all the details of what came to pass at Essex House that night. Essex and his few captains returned as dusk closed in and scurried safely into the house. After that the admiral's forces cut off their access to the river. On the other side, Lord Burghley and others forced their way into the courtyard.

The house was surrounded. They began sniping at the windows, and shattered glass flew everywhere.

Inside, Essex was frantically burning his incriminating correspondence; he sent his lieutenants out to keep firing long enough to hold the Crown forces at bay until he could complete his task. Then he and Southampton took to the roof in response to the demand that they surrender. Southampton yelled, "Only if we are given hostages to guarantee our safe return!"

"Yes! Yes!" Essex had cried, from the roof, his cloak flying, a silhouette of black desperation.

"Rebels cannot bargain with princes," shouted the admiral.

A cease-fire was arranged to allow the women to leave. Chivalrously, the admiral allowed them two hours. The ladies of the household poured out. When the time was over, the admiral drew up the cannon.

"We will demolish the house and everyone in it," he said. "Surrender now!"

More men joined Essex on the roof. "'Tis better to perish by cannon fire than the rope or the ax," cried old Lord Sandys.

But the younger men were of less fiery mettle. After much deliberation, Essex walked to the edge of the roof and cried, "We will surrender under three conditions!"

"What are those?" answered the admiral. "Her Majesty will not compromise herself."

"First, that only you shall arrest us, and that we are treated in a civil manner, not as criminals. Second, that we are granted a fair and impartial trial," he said.

"I can guarantee that," said the admiral. "And your third condition?"

"That I be permitted my personal chaplain, Abdyias Ashton, to attend me in prison."

"Granted!" cried the admiral. "Now surrender yourselves."

In a few moments the men came out and knelt before the admiral. Essex put his shining sword into the admiral's outstretched hands, and Southampton likewise. Slowly and deliberately, so did the others following behind them.

It was ten o'clock, a cold and windy night. The rebellion had lasted only twelve hours. Now the tide was against them, and they could not go downstream to the Tower. Instead, they were ferried across the river to Lambeth Palace. The oars dipped in and out of the fretful water, conveying them to their perpetual enclosure. Freedom was gone.

When Cecil told me, I sank down on my cushions in my inner chamber.

"It is over, then," I said.

"Yes, Your Majesty. God be thanked, it is over," he said.

"Go to your rooms; rest," I said. "What a long night. But they are not yet in the Tower."

"They will be soon," he said. "We are only waiting for the tide to turn. It should, by two o'clock."

"Until I know they are in the Tower and locked up, I shall stand vigilant," I said. "You may rest—your job is done—but I may not."

"Your Majesty, I think you can trust your servants to do the rest," he said.

I laughed. "It is no reflection on you if you sleep now. *Your* task is done; but I still must guard the gates and entrances to my realm."

He bowed. "As Your Majesty wishes," he said.

---

I was alone in my chamber. Catherine, at my request, had retired to another sleeping place. I wanted it that way. My windows overlooked the river, and I stood at one and kept my eyes fastened on the dark, rippling water, alert for any movement. Even in the moonless night, I could make out the towers and buildings of Lambeth slightly upstream. They were not so very far away; perhaps a half mile or so.

I could see, by the ripples in the water, exactly when the tide turned. The little clock on my table had just struck two.

A slight movement on the water from the faraway Lambeth dock. A boat had set out, its rowers heading downstream to the Tower. It was a swift one; the lesser rebels would follow. This one must hold only Essex.

The boat drew abreast of Whitehall. I pressed against the window glass, as if it would grant me enhanced vision to see inside the vessel. But it passed, shrouded in darkness.

# 83

ive more hours, and then the dawn brought in the new day. I felt purged of all emotions, as if they had been taken captive along with Essex. But that was an advantage: It meant I could act quickly, untroubled by clouded feelings.

I ordered details of the treason to be printed up and distributed throughout the City. I summoned lawyers to study the mountain of evidence and prepare for the trials. I posted over two thousand men levied from the home counties to keep order in London—some were stationed at Charing Cross, others to patrol the pleasure grounds of Southwark, with the theaters, cockpits, and bear gardens, and more around the Royal Exchange. I could take no chances.

In all, eighty-five men taken from Essex House were in custody. In truth, only a few of those warranted close examination or trial. Essex himself, of course, was the prime mover. After him, Southampton. Then the lesser ones: Rutland, Sandys, Monteagle, Bedford, and Blount. The commoners and servants of Essex—Danvers, Cuffe, and Meyrick—would also be held responsible for their actions.

---

It was four days since the uprising, and at last I was sleeping again, unwinding like a tightly coiled spring slowly loosening. My appetite had crept back and I was looking forward to my supper for the first time since the ordeal had begun. I even agreed to have it out in the privy chamber so more people could share it with me. To chase away the gloom, I chose a red gown. But before I could traverse from my inner chambers to the privy chamber, three of Raleigh's guards surrounded me. I tried to shake them off.

"Gentlemen, the danger is past," I said. "I merely go to sup with my attendants and friends."

"There is more danger," one of them said, his throat rumbling, "and it was heading for your chambers."

"What do you mean?" I asked. I looked around; the corridor was empty. "I am trying to calm the court, not agitate it."

"Do you know a Captain Thomas Lee?" another said.

"Yes, he served in Ireland and was Essex's messenger to O'Neill. But he was not part of the rebellion."

"He is now," said the first man. "He was caught just outside your door with a knife. He has already confessed that he meant to take you hostage and force you to release Essex."

"My God!" How had he gotten so close? "Where were you, then, when he sneaked into the apartments? What good your liveries, your embroidered golden roses, if you cannot guard me properly?"

"He said he had soldierly business with you."

"He said you knew him well. We would never have believed him, but one of us recognized him. 'He served in Ireland,' he said. 'And besides, he's cousin to the Queen's old master of the tilt.'"

"A questionable member of that family," I said. I was remembering something unpleasant about him. Oh yes. He had once sent me the severed head of an Irish chieftain, thinking it would please me. I shuddered. It had proved not only that he was uncouth but that he knew how to sever heads. "Where is he?"

"Bound and waiting for you out here," the tallest of the guards said, pointing to the privy chamber.

"Very well, then, let me see him."

This was not the quiet dinner I had envisioned. The tables were still set, and the crowd assembled, but on his knees on the floor was the captain. The courtiers made a wide semicircle around him, staring.

I walked over to where he knelt, two huge guards on either side, their hands on his shoulders.

"Captain Lee," I said. "This is the second time I have met you. There will not be a third."

He glared up at me. "Let him go! Set the Earl of Essex free!" he muttered.

"Why? Because you say so? He is a traitor. And now so are you." Suddenly I was weary of this. I did not even have the stomach for any further talk. "Take him away," I ordered the guards. "Try him ahead of the others. His case is clear-cut. It does not require much legal review."

As he was dragged out, I made a show of inviting everyone to take a place at table as if nothing had happened. But now I knew this would not be over until Essex was dead. Like the Scots queen, as long as he lived there would be plots on his behalf and I could not draw my breath in safety.

"My good friends, let us drink to health and peace!" I said, holding my goblet high. My hand did not shake.

———

Things moved swiftly in the next few days. I called peers of the realm to come posthaste to London to act as witnesses in the trial—nine earls and sixteen barons. The Privy Council selected the Queen's counsel to prosecute the trial—seven lawyers of the realm, including Francis Bacon. Lord Buckhurst would preside as lord high steward over eight judges. The trial would take place in Westminster Hall, where so many others had been held.

If by a trial one means a way to determine guilt or innocence, this was not a trial but a hearing to determine just how guilty these men were—not *if* they were guilty. They would be allowed to speak and defend themselves, but the hearing satisfied the need to have all the facts presented and recorded, and punishment meted out. In years to come someone could revisit the hearing and know what had passed. That was its purpose—to marshal the facts and enter them into the public record.

In preparation for the trial, it was necessary to prepare the minds of the public. The most efficient way of doing that was to order all the preachers in the realm to present the facts of the case in their sermons. Since attendance at church was mandatory, most people would hear the message.

That was Sunday, February 15. As a precaution, five hundred soldiers were sent to St. Paul's Cross, where the most important sermon would be heard.

On Monday, Captain Thomas Lee was tried at Newgate Prison; on Tuesday he was executed at Tyburn, the prescribed traitor's death of hanging, disembowelment, and quartering. At the same time, the Privy Council from Star Chamber published indictments of the men in the rebellion. These were that the Earl of Essex, the Earl of Southampton, the Earl of Rutland, and Lord Sandys had conspired to depose and slay the Queen and overthrow the government.

On Wednesday, the lawyers put the finishing touches on their case. I instructed Francis Bacon to leave out anything pertaining to the succession or *Richard II* or deposition.

"The rebellion speaks for itself," I said. "We need not go into these peripheral matters."

"But, Ma'am, we mentioned them in the sermons and in the indictment," he said.

I looked at him. I had not seen him in many months. The strain was showing on his face, in the lines and look around his eyes. "Francis, I know this is difficult for you. It is very rare that a man is called to prepare a case against his erstwhile friend. While you had forsworn his political path, friendship is a different matter. One can still love beyond politics. I believe my father always loved Thomas More, and I am sure you will always love Robert Devereux. God knows he is easy to love—that was his downfall."

Francis merely stood, clutching his hat. A slow smile played at the corners of his mouth. "Your Majesty is wise," he said. "But my loyalty is entirely yours, even as I grieve for my friend."

"I grieve alongside you," I said. "You understand why I wish to pass over the deposition part. Why allow people to picture something? An image burns itself into the mind. Likewise with *Richard II*. It gave a vision and script to something nebulous. Treason . . . abdication . . . Those are abstracts. But once you have seen it enacted before you . . . it becomes possible. In a sense it has already happened, and you have embraced it by watching it." I pulled myself up. "In any case, we have a trial to conduct. Your task is to prove that Essex's actions were premeditated. If he is mad . . . that absolves him. He may have tipped over into the realm of madness, but he was in complete command of his senses when he challenged me, parleyed with O'Neill, came back to England against my express orders, gathered his followers at Essex House, and encouraged them—" I caught my breath. Reciting these things enraged me. "You understand," I said, putting a stop to it.

"Yes. To my sorrow, I do."

"What of your brother?" I asked. "How is Anthony faring?"

"His illness progresses. I fear for him in this. He may not survive it."

"I am sorry to hear it. Essex's fortunes have touched many, and dragged many down with him." I looked at Francis. "You are not among them. Never castigate yourself for extricating yourself from that doomed man. It is no sin to survive."

He shook his head gently. "I thank Your Majesty for understanding. Many do not."

"They want to pin the Judas label on you, do they? That is simplistic. To accompany a traitor on his path is not loyalty but treason," I assured him.

I thought of Essex in the Tower. It would be easier if he were indeed mad. The mad see things differently than we do. He had refused to see any of his family. He refused to confess to the Dean of Norwich, who had been sent to attend him. He had waved him away, insisting on his innocence.

His innocence . . . perhaps in his own mind. But his mind was disordered.

---

Robert Cecil asked to see me, and I admitted him. "The earl's wife begs us to spare him," he said. "She has been on her knees before me."

"Frances Walsingham?"

"Yes. I had always thought her marriage a political one—after Sidney, how could it be otherwise? But she is distraught."

How naive men are. Philip Sidney! "Sidney may not have been as good a bedfellow as Essex," I said. "Men who write sonnets to women other than their wives often live entirely in their own poetic mind. A woman wants more." I laughed. "You blush? Oh, Robert, if you are to wed again, you must shed your exalted vision of women. We want a *man*."

"Uh"—he cleared his throat—"would you consent to receive her?"

This would be difficult. I could not spare her husband. Yet in charity I should hear her. "Yes, I will." Suddenly I wondered about Lettice. She had been quiet. No appeals, no letters, for all that her husband and son were prisoners and soon to be tried.

"Have you had any appeal from Essex's mother?" Perhaps Cecil had set it aside.

"No," he said. "There has not been a word from Essex House."

"Is she there?" Perhaps she had retired back to Wanstead or her estates in Drayton Bassett.

"From all my reports, she is there," he said.

---

I agreed to see Frances the next day. She came to the privy chamber and I ushered her into my private quarters. My attendant shut the door behind us and then discreetly disappeared.

Frances stood before me, dressed all in black. Her belly was enormous. But she looked directly at me, unflinching.

"When is your child due to be delivered?" I asked her.

"Yesterday," she said, then laughed. "It tarries."

"You should not be abroad," I said.

"When the pains begin, I know to start for home," she said. "This is my fourth."

"Let me help you, then. Ask me quickly what you wish to ask, and then I may send you safely home."

To my shock, she flung herself facedown on the floor.

"Frances!" I cried. "You must not."

She raised herself up on her arms. "I will do anything. I will sacrifice this baby; I crawl before you. Spare my husband! If he perishes, I cannot live, I cannot draw one breath afterward!" She burst into tears. "If the death warrant is signed, I will never live an hour past that!"

"Frances," I said, as gently as I could. "You know what he has done. It was heinous. The law does not permit him to live."

"He was misled—he did not know!"

"Alas, he did know," I said. "He was warned, over and over again. No one can deny that. Would that they could."

She sank back down and buried her head in her arms, sobbing. I bent down and embraced her. "Frances, Frances," I said. "It is a tragedy for England."

"It is a tragedy for me," she said. "England can endure. She has had many tragedies. But I shall not survive."

"You cannot know that." Neither of her husbands, for all their mighty reputations, was worthy of a simple, loving woman. They loved themselves—or honor—more. "We must steel ourselves. Often it is the women who show the most bravery and endurance." Oh, might the fates send her another husband, this one her equal.

She pulled herself away. "As you say." Already she had distanced herself. "You will not save him, then?" she said, standing up. "You, to whom he genuflected, whom he worshipped?"

"Except when he tried to capture and depose me?" I said. "I as a person could overlook that. I as a queen cannot, and I told him that. Long ago."

She dashed the tears away with the back of her hand. "I go, then."

"God be with you," was all I could say. She would need his sustaining hand.

"Since you will not be with me, I must make do," she shot back.

"God is not second best," I said. "Do not insult him. You will need him."

---

February 19, eleven days after the uprising, Essex and Southampton stood trial. I would not attend. But I received a full report from everyone involved.

At the near end of the hall, where the stairs led up into St. Stephen's Chapel, would sit the lord high steward, Buckhurst, under a canopy of estate, presiding in my stead. In front of him would be eight judges—Lord Chief Justice Popham leading them. Facing them were the Queen's counsel, lawyers who would prosecute the case. Attorney General Sir Edward Coke, Solicitor General Thomas Fleming, Queen's Sergeant Christopher Yelverton, the recorder of London, two sergeants at law, and Francis Bacon made up the seven.

Stretching between them on each side were the twenty-five peers who would act as jury. At the far end of the hall, a long bar stretched to divide the spectators from the trial.

Buckhurst entered the hall escorted by seven sergeants at arms and forty of Raleigh's guardsmen, led by Raleigh. The lieutenant of the Tower had had the prisoners rowed upriver for their trial, and at nine o'clock he was ordered to produce them. The gentleman porter of the Tower marched in, carrying an executioner's ax with its blade turned away, followed by Essex, dressed in black, and Southampton, dressed in a voluminous gown. They took their places in the middle of the square of their examiners, facing the judges.

The jurors were called and answered one by one. Then all sat.

The charges—plotting to deprive the Queen of her crown and life, imprisoning the councillors of the realm, inciting the people to rebellion with untruths, and resisting arrest—were read out, and both men declared themselves not guilty. Then Sergeant Yelverton opened the prosecution, accusing the prisoners of treason as heinous as Catiline's conspiracy in ancient Rome. Attorney General Coke followed, reminding the jury that merely resisting royal authority with force was treason; it was not necessary to prove premeditation. And furthermore, he orated, Essex's plan to call a parliament was subversive, and "a bloody parliament that would have been, where my Lord of Essex, that now stands all in black, would have worn a bloody robe!"

Next the witnesses were called. First was a statement by Henry Widdington, describing the events of the morning of February 8 at Essex House. Next, Chief Justice Popham, swapping places, was sworn in as a witness and recounted his treatment when his party had gone to Essex with the Great Seal. The Earl of Worcester backed him up in all the details. Raleigh told of his encounter with Gorges and being warned, "You are like to have a bloody day of it."

Sir Gorges himself testified about the conferences in Drury House planning the coup, and then claimed that he had urged Essex, the afternoon of the event, to submit to the Queen.

Essex asked for the right to question him, and it was granted. Essex warned him to answer truthfully. "Did you in fact advise me to surrender?"

"My lord, I think I did," was all Gorges was prepared to admit.

Essex almost yelped. "This is not the time to answer 'I think so'—you would not have forgotten."

Southampton, the other accused, rose to defend himself. He made a sorry showing. First he said that although he had plotted to capture the court and the City, these plans had come to nothing; therefore he was not guilty. He also said he had had no idea when he went to Essex House that Sunday morning that Essex had any fell intentions. Furthermore, he had not heard the herald in London proclaiming them traitors, nor had he drawn his sword the whole day.

"My lord, you were seen with a pistol," said Coke.

"Oh, that!" said Southampton. "I had taken it from someone in the street, and anyway, it didn't work."

"You were with Essex the entire day in the City. If you did not agree with his aim, you had many chances to separate yourself."

"I was carried away with love for him!" said Southampton sadly. "I am a victim."

As further evidence, the court produced the written confessions of Danvers, Rutland, Sandys, Monteagle, and Christopher Blount. The latter had said, "If we had failed in our ends, we should, rather than have been disappointed, even have drawn blood from the Queen herself."

Finally Francis Bacon rose, testifying against Essex. He likened Essex's false cries about his life being sought to when Peisistratus of Athens cut himself and then entered the city claiming his life was in danger. "But this does not excuse you. How did imprisoning the Queen's councillors protect you against these people—Raleigh and Cobham and Grey—you claim threatened you?"

Essex sputtered. "You! You false man! What about the bogus correspondence between myself and your brother that you arranged, so the Queen would be impressed?"

Bacon just smiled pityingly. "'Tis true. I did everything I could to help you win the Queen's goodwill. I cared more about you, and made more efforts for you, than I did for myself. But that was when you were still her loyal servant."

"I only wanted to petition the Queen to impeach Cecil."

"Did you need swords and violence to do that? Are petitioners armed? What man will be such a fool as to believe this was anything other than naked treason?"

Essex began to fall apart, as he did under pressure. "Cecil! You and Cecil! He's leading a Spanish conspiracy, and you are in on it! When I cried out in the streets that the Crown was sold to the Spaniard, it was not of my own imagination. A trusted councillor had told me that Cecil said the Infanta's claim was as good as any other's."

A great silence fell, and Essex smiled. Now he had said it. Stony faces of judges, jury, and prosecutors stared back at him. Then there was the sound of curtain rings sliding over a rod, and from behind a curtain at the top of the steps emerged Robert Cecil, who had not been present until now.

He limped down the stairs and took his place opposite Essex, staring him down. The tall, black-clad Essex faced Cecil, more than a head shorter.

Furious but, unlike Essex, able to speak coldly and calmly, Cecil let loose. "My Lord of Essex! The difference between you and me is great. For wit I give you preeminence—you have it absolutely. For nobility I also give you place. I am not noble, yet a gentleman. I am no swordsman—there you also have the odds; but I have innocence, conscience, truth, and honesty to defend me against the scandal and sting of slanderous tongues, and in this court I stand as an upright man, and Your Lordship as a delinquent." He paused to draw breath, then continued, "I protest, before God, I have loved your person and justified your virtues. And had I not seen your ambitious hunger inclined to usurpation, I would have gone on my knees to Her Majesty to have helped you, but you have a wolf's head in a sheep's garment. God be thanked, we know you now!" He shook his head. "Ah, my lord, were it but your own case, the loss had been less. But you have drawn a number of noble persons and gentlemen of birth and quality into your net of rebellion, and their bloods will cry vengeance against you."

Still standing on his height and nobility, Essex mocked, "Ah, Master Secretary, I thank God for my humiliation, that you in the ruff of all your bravery, have come hither to make your oration against me today."

But Cecil brushed the insult off and pressed him. "Which councillor was it who quoted me about the Infanta? Name him if you dare. If you do not name him, it must be believed to be a fiction."

"Aha!" crowed Essex. "Southampton here heard it as well."

"Who was it, then? Again I say, name him!"

"It was . . . the comptroller, Sir William Knollys."

"Summon him here," ordered Buckhurst. "I know he has absented himself out of family loyalty, so he would not have to testify against his nephew, but now he must come. And do not tell him what this is about. He must be utterly ignorant of the coming question."

The proceedings were suspended while Knollys was fetched from his home and escorted into the court. He stood before Buckhurst, who detailed Essex's accusation against Cecil and asked if he had ever heard the secretary express those thoughts.

Knollys took a deep breath and thought out loud. "Yes . . . he did speak of it. But . . . it had to do with something else. Something else . . . What was it?" He shook his head as if he could tumble his thoughts around inside. "Oh yes. It was when that Jesuit had written the tract 'Conference on the Next Succession.' Cecil said it was impudent of him to claim that the Infanta had the same rights in the succession as anyone else."

"That was what he said? That it was *wrong* of the Jesuit to make that claim?"

"I believe his exact words were 'a strange impudence,'" said Knollys.

Buckhurst wagged his head from side to side. "And so now we have it. You have lived under an illusion, Lord Essex. An illusion of your own making."

The court was adjourned while the jury members withdrew to make their verdict. When they assembled again, they stood and, one by one, placing their left hands on their right sides, made the pronouncement: “Guilty, my lord, of high treason, upon mine honor.”

Essex stood quietly, asking only for clemency for Southampton. Southampton whimpered and asked for mercy.

Buckhurst pronounced sentence. “You shall both be led from hence to the place from whence you came and there remain during Her Majesty’s pleasure: from thence to be drawn upon a hurdle through the midst of the city, and so to the place of execution, there to be hanged by the neck and taken down alive—your bodies to be opened, and your bowels taken out and burned before your face: your bodies to be quartered—your heads and quarters to be disposed of at Her Majesty’s pleasure, and so God have mercy on your souls.”

Essex looked around, his head held high. “I think it fitting that my poor quarters, which have done Her Majesty service in diverse parts of the world, should now at the last be sacrificed and disposed at Her Majesty’s pleasure.” Then he bowed, flipping his cape out.

The court was stunned at his arrogance and lack of contrition.

The prisoners were returned to the Tower with the executioner’s blade now turned toward them.

# 84

I was sitting in a high-backed chair, rigid like a Byzantine icon, as the day drew to its close. I had not eaten all day, fasting in order to feel more keenly what was happening in Westminster Hall. The hall's carved wooden ceiling had looked down alike on the joyous and the tormented, and that just within my own family. Today what did they see, what did they hear?

A knock; then a messenger entered. "They are pronounced guilty," he said.

I stood. "When?"

"Just now. I have run straight from the hall."

It was so nearby he was not even out of breath. "Both of them?"

"Yes, both Essex and Southampton. They are on their way back to the Tower."

I went to the window and peered out. There were enough boats on the river that it was hard to know which one carried the prisoners. I let the curtain fall. "They shall never leave it," I said. "They go upon the river for the last time." What must it be like to ride anywhere, knowingly, for the last time?

"Mr. Secretary Cecil clinched the day," he said. "He made a surprise appearance from behind a curtain, just as in a play. But he turned the tables so thoroughly against Essex that the earl had no recourse. Standing beside that strapping man, never did Cecil, in his small stature, play taller. He will be providing a transcript of all the happenings. The scribes are copying furiously this very moment. But it will take several hours."

"But you have brought me the meat of it," I said. "The rest is pastry decoration."

---

It was done, then. It was done. I felt immense relief to be delivered from the long-hovering threat, but no satisfaction. Just so I had felt when Walsingham had exposed the Scots queen unequivocally and the judges had pronounced sentence. My suspicions had been confirmed. But I would rather have had them turn out to be unfounded.

I gathered my women about me. These faithful companions of my chamber deserved to hear immediately what had happened. Then I withdrew with Catherine, and we were alone in the bedchamber.

"Once more I will be thanking Charles for his timely service to the realm," I told her.

"He still has Essex's sword," said Catherine. "What will you tell him to do with it?"

"It should be returned to the family," I said. "When all this is—over."

"When will that be?"

"As soon as the papers can be drawn up and arrangements made."

"Arrangements? The executioner, a grave plot? There is already a scaffold at Tower Hill. He will not be going to Tyburn, I assume?"

"No, nor to Tower Hill. He will have a private execution on Tower Green. A new scaffold must be built. It has been almost fifty years since there has been an execution there. Lady Jane Grey was the last one."

"Why send him there?"

"Because he requested a private execution."

"Or because it would be too dangerous to permit the public to witness it out on Tower Hill?"

"Both, Catherine. If the public makes a ruckus, then it reverses our victory. He must perish out of sight."

---

The trial had taken place on Thursday; over the weekend Essex agonized with his Puritan chaplain, Abdyias Ashton, whom he had asked for ere he surrendered. He had relapsed into a state of frenzied religiosity that focused entirely on his soul and excluded his grieving family. He would not see his wife, mother, sisters, or friends. Instead he confessed all to Ashton, who then insisted on bringing Privy Councillors to partake of these unburdenings. So on Saturday, only two days after the trial, a very different Essex writhed in front of the admiral and Cecil, breast beating and then writing out four pages of confessions, allegations, and blame.

"Well, men, you have witnessed his breakdown," I told them, as they presented me with the original papers—not a copy. His tiny handwriting, shrunk to get as much as possible on the pages, made it hard to read. "It is never a pretty sight."

Before me Charles and Cecil stood stiffly. The confession began with his admission that he was "the greatest, the vilest, and the most unthankful traitor that ever was born." He was exaggerating, as usual. But he named names of everyone associated with his plot, drawing in Lord Mountjoy and his mistress, Penelope. She had insulted him and egged him on by telling him that everyone thought him a coward, he said. "Look to her, for she has a proud spirit," he warned.

"It runs in the family," I grunted.

"In the midst of all this, he suddenly demanded that his attendant, Henry Cuffe, be brought in to face him," said Cecil. "And then he accused him to his face of leading him into it all."

"Ah, he is the same man despite his protestations of reform," I said. "He has ever sought to blame others for his misdeeds. It is always someone else's fault—in his eyes."

"But not the law's," said Cecil. "The law has spoken." He hesitated, then shot a glance at Charles. "There is one other thing . . ."

"You must tell it," said Charles.

"Essex admitted in our presence that, and I quote, 'the Queen will never be safe as long as I live.'"

"Those were his exact words?" I said.

"Indeed," said Charles, "though I hate hearing them repeated."

"He only admits what we already knew," I said, more lightly than I felt.

"As regarding the others—Cuffe, Meyrick, Blount, and the rest," Charles said, "they will stand trial after these first two are dispatched."

"What of Southampton?" asked Catherine. "You did not mention where he was . . . was to go."

"Not Tower Green," I said. In truth, I had thought little about him. He was so inconsequential.

"If he is to join Essex on his exit from this world, then you should decide," said Cecil.

That annoyed me. "Do not issue orders to princes," I said. "I shall decide when I decide. Have the papers been drawn up?"

"They will be ready tomorrow, and awaiting your royal signature," he said.

"Sunday. I would never sign an execution warrant on a Sunday!"

"Monday, then," said Cecil.

"Monday it shall be, then. And the execution can proceed on Tuesday. Ready everything."

---

He had said not one word about me in his confession, or to the councillors, or to his chaplain. This time there were no appeals, no tear-stained letters, no poems, and no protestations. At last the golden tongue and pen of the earl had fallen silent.

Nor was there to be any word from me. What could I possibly say? If I said all I felt, it would fill not four pages, as Essex had done, but a hundred. *Where have you gone?* I wanted to say. *What infected you, corrupted you? Was there anything I could have done to alter it? Did I play any part in it?*

But those questions were not ones a queen could ask a subject, and this subject would never have the self-knowledge to give an honest answer. So: silence on both sides.

Provision must be made for his body. It had to go somewhere after it fell on the scaffold. I gave orders that a grave be prepared in the little church of St. Peter ad Vincula, which stood only yards away. It served as the final resting place of many executed prisoners. The higher ranking were inside the church, and the lesser people were buried in the graveyard around it. I had never been able to force myself to go inside, for all that it had fine marble monuments. My mother lay there, and I could not bear to think so closely upon how she was taken there, still warm from the scaffold and not in a proper coffin. Others kept her company, a whole host of them: her brother George, and Thomas More, and Queen Catherine Howard, and Lady Jane Grey. But if I stood there and looked, there would be only one grave I would see: hers.

*I mean no disrespect,* I told her in my mind, as I had a thousand times. *But, Mother, I have made my peace with it all, as I have had to.*

Lent was about to begin. We always had a play at court on Shrove Tuesday. I must think of that. I must select something. Life must go on, flow smoothly, as it always had.

Although we did not observe the carnival excesses of Catholic countries, nonetheless we traditionally marked the last days before Ash Wednesday in our own distinctive manner. At court we had a "farewell to luxuries" banquet, and attended a play. The plays were usually lighthearted, but this year that would not do. Shakespeare had a new one. We would see that. It was the least he could do for us, after allowing his company to cooperate with Essex and stage *Richard II* with the forbidden scene.

---

Monday, as promised, the heavy parchment death warrant was placed reverently on my desk to be signed. I did so, not wishing it to linger in my possession, and dispatched it to the lieutenant of the Tower. A little later I realized that I had not specified what day the sentence was to be carried out, so I sent a message telling him to proceed Wednesday morning. I also ordered that there be two executioners, in case one was incapacitated at the last moment. It was to be a private execution, but there must be witnesses—the Queen's Guard, led by Raleigh, and nobles, aldermen, and councillors.

—

The banquet proceeded normally. The usual ceremonies were performed, the plates and dishes magnificently presented, the delicate glassware filled with the best wine. The chatter, however, was subdued. The only subject that must not be mentioned drowned all the others.

It was a relief to take our places to watch the play. Let the actors talk and act while we sat mute and motionless. The subject of the play was the Trojan war—nothing could have been further from the events around us.

"Shakespeare seems to have deserted our realm and our time for the ancient world," said Catherine, by my side. "First a play about Caesar, now this."

"A love story—*Troilus and Cressida*?" said Charles, making a face.

Catherine pretended to be offended. "And what is wrong with that?"

"I am too old," said the admiral. "Love affairs are not my main concern any longer."

"Charles!" She smacked him with her fan teasingly.

*Nor mine,* I thought. *Love affairs have ceased to have any meaning for me. Nonetheless, I can still tolerate them onstage or in a poem.*

I settled back, expecting heroic characters, combat scenes, and tragic lovers—all earmarks of the Trojan war—told in Shakespeare's haunting language.

Instead, the play featured two unsavory characters, one of whom had the most scurrilous view of life and people I had ever heard. Every time he came onstage—which was far too often—I winced. He opened the play and closed it, wishing diseases on his audience as his farewell to us. As for the famous names of Homer, they were transformed into unrecognizably mean little people. Hector chased Patroclus for his armor, coveting it. Instead of a duel between the noble Hector and the warrior Achilles, Achilles killed an unarmed Hector in cold blood. Helen was an empty-headed strumpet, Cressida a liar, Troilus a fool, Ajax an ox. There was not one character I would invite to my table. And Shakespeare's beautiful use of words had shrunk as small as his characters. Convoluted parallels, tortured usages, not a single line that sang in the mind. Only one passage, spoken by Odysseus, sent a chill through me and seemed to whisper, *This is what has just happened.* It was "Power into will, will into appetite, and appetite, a universal wolf, so doubly seconded with will and power, must make perforce a universal prey, and last eat up himself." Essex's wolf appetite had devoured him. Had the playwright thought of him when he had written it?

I wanted to apologize for inflicting the play on everyone. But the mood of it—disillusioned, hollow, sad—perhaps reflected what we were all feeling.

I said good night and brought the evening to a close. It had been a fitting penance for whatever part I had played in the downfall of Essex.

---

Dawn, and Essex would soon be led out to the block. I shut the doors of my inner chambers and did not admit any company, even my ladies. The day plodded on; the sun approached its highest point, ending the morning. I could not read, nor fasten my mind on anything. I sat down at the virginals and began to play from memory; it required no effort of the mind or will. The sweet, round notes floated around me, caressing like supple fingers. When thoughts flee and words are inadequate, music can act as timely balm.

There was a soft knock. No one would knock except for something—the one thing—that I must be told.

"Enter," I said.

The door swung open and Cecil entered, then walked softly over to me. I stopped playing.

"Your Majesty, it is over," he said. "Essex died this morning."

I nodded. I could not speak. In a moment, I continued playing. Cecil left.

---

The next day I ended my isolation and readied myself to hear the details. It was necessary that I hear them, although there was nothing I wanted less. Let him have vanished in a wisp of cloud, easily flying from life to death, an instant translation between the two worlds.

Raleigh, as official observer, recounted it all to me in private. Essex had been led out at eight o'clock by three clergymen. He was dressed all in black—satin doublet and breeches, velvet cloak, with a wide hat and startlingly white ruff.

"I was standing beside the block, as was my duty," he said. "But several people accused me of gloating at the fall of my enemy, so in order to ensure peace, I went up into the White Tower, where I could see everything but not be seen."

"Ah, Walter," I said. "Such petty rivalries should not have surfaced then."

"It was not Essex who objected, but others. In any case, he took off his hat and bowed, then proceeded to his farewell speech. He acknowledged that he deserved to die. But then he spoke wildly. Here." He fumbled in his cloak and extracted a paper. "I will read his words. I do not want to invent any. He said, 'My sins are more in number than the hairs on my head. I have bestowed my youth in wantonness, lust, and uncleanness; I have been puffed up with pride, vanity, and love of this wicked world's pleasures. For all which I humbly beseech my Savior, Christ, to be a mediator to the eternal Majesty for my pardon, especially for this, my last sin, this great, this bloody, this crying, this infectious sin, whereby so many for love of me have been drawn to offend God, to offend their sovereign, to offend the world. I beseech God to forgive it us, and to forgive it me—most wretched of all.'"

"He always had the gift of words," I said. These were in keeping with that genius; it had not deserted him. "May God have mercy on his soul."

"He ended by forgiving his enemies and asking God to preserve you."

"He made a good ending, then."

"After that, he removed his gown and his ruff. Then the executioner knelt and asked his forgiveness, which he gave. Next he removed his doublet and revealed a red waistcoat underneath."

Was that so the blood would not be so noticeable? Or did he mean it to signify martyrdom?

"He went obediently. He laid his head on the block and extended his arms to show he was ready."

"I hope it was done quickly."

"It took three blows of the ax, but I think the first did its work."

Thank God. "And he was—he is resting—"

"He was buried quietly and respectfully," said Raleigh. "But the executioner was attacked in the streets afterward and had to be rescued by the sheriff. People were—upset."

I had best keep the soldiers stationed in London for a while longer, then.

"I understand," I said.

"There is one more thing," he said. "Not everyone mourned his passing. I received this letter regarding Lord Sandys from his wife. He is still awaiting trial." He handed it to me.

It was short, and the pertinent lines had been marked. "Woe the day my lord was drawn into that plot. He was lured by that wild Essex's craft, who has been and is unlucky to many but never good to any. I would he had never been born!"

A fitting epitaph for Robert Devereux, although it would not appear on his tomb. *Who has been and is unlucky to many.* Above all to himself.

# 85

# LETTICE

*March 1601*

*weet England's pride is gone, welladay! welladay! / He did her fame advance, in Ireland, Spain, and France, / And now, by dismal chance, is from us taken. . . ."*

The faint strains of the voices drifted in to me as I lay trying to sleep. Earlier—I mean when Robert still lived—I would have found them tormenting. Now they served to keep him alive for me. As long as people were singing of him—ah, was that not a sort of life? A half life? Any tremor of life was better than none.

"They shall make ballads of us after our death," Helen of Troy had told Paris. And they still lived.

I arose and went to the windows, flinging them open. A blast of cold February air hit me, but I leaned out. A small group of people were huddled at our gates, grasping the bars, peering into the empty courtyard, where hundreds had thronged but such a short while ago.

"Abroad, and eke at home, gallantly, gallantly, for valor there was none like him before. . . ." I could hear them more clearly now, and my ears drank in every word. "In Ireland, France, and Spain, they feared great Essex's name, and England loved the same in every place. . . ."

I would send money and food out to them. They could not know the gift they brought me, confirming that Robert had been loved, and still was loved. I stood for the entire ballad, chilled through. Called "Sweet England's Pride Is Gone," it had appeared only hours after Robert's execution, as songs from the people will.

"Yet Her Princely Majesty—graciously! graciously!—hath pardon given free to many of them: She released them quite, and given them their right! They may pray, day and night, God to defend her."

Yes, they might pray, those eighty or so who had been arrested, questioned, and then let go. Lucky men. But Christopher was not among them.

He would stand trial around March 5, five days from now. There was no hope that he would be spared.

It was four days since Robert had been executed. I had kept vigil the entire night before. I knew the hour appointed for his death. As the time crept past it, I wondered why I did not feel a great stabbing, a riving, within my very self. How could I not? It was the last cruel surprise in all the cruel surprises of our lives together.

Now I had a message from Admiral Charles Howard, seeking a time to return Robert's sword. He had handed it over when he surrendered. I had been part of his life that day—my last time to be so—as Penelope, Frances, and I were forced to while away the hours with the imprisoned Privy Councillors while my son went out to raise a rebellion. The councillors were as embarrassed as we were. They were good men, gentle men, who had been forced into their roles and bore Robert no ill will.

All of it was painful, misconceived, and this final act with the councillors was a fitting close to the whole venture. The admiral had allowed us free passage out of the house, holding their fire for two hours. Now he had the last act in this misbegotten drama to get through: returning Sir Philip Sidney's sword.

Robert had refused to see any of us in his last days. Frances went into labor and delivered a daughter whom she named Dorothy, but Robert was never to know of her.

Robert had been buried in St. Peter ad Vincula within the Tower. Buried with the queens and martyrs, I told myself. At least his resting place would always be preserved. And someday, someday, long in the future, all the particulars of his case would melt away, and people remember only his gifts and beauty. Time erases details, and only outlines remain. Robert's outline was so singular the common people already felt called to make ballads about him.

I went back to bed. I would sleep. I would think of Christopher in the morning, when the light made it easier. Christopher still lived, nursed by a tailor into whose shop he had been carried, wounded, on that fateful day of uprising; two royal guards now stood watch over him. I had no access to him, and he had sent me no messages. If I could have only a quarter hour with him, perhaps I could understand what had happened. I knew only that the laughing, ebullient young man I had married had changed into another creature entirely, and I had no inkling why. I was soon to be a widow for the third time. But never before had I lost my husband before he actually died.

---

"The Earl of Nottingham, Lord Admiral Charles Howard." My servant announced our noble visitor. I was ready, wearing all the insignia I was entitled to as countess: my eight-rayed coronet, my ermine-trimmed robe with its prescribed length of train. Once these things had been vitally important to me.

"We welcome him," I said.

The white-haired admiral entered the hall and approached me, treading softly. I had not seen him in years and knew him only from Robert's animosity toward him. He had resented sharing command with him on naval ventures, insisting on signing his name above the admiral's, until Lord Howard had cut out Robert's signature in exasperation. Ah, well, that was one of the details fading away already.

"My Lady Leicester," he said, bowing. "I have the honor to return the sword of the Earl of Essex, surrendered to me." He held it out, a shining token.

"It is my honor to receive it," I said, taking it. "It will be kept for the earl's son. He is only ten years old now. May he always use it in defense of the realm."

I laid it on a cushion. In some ways it was a hateful thing. I wished little Rob could stay far away from anything requiring a sword. It ended in either death or dishonor, it seemed. At the very least it meant a man could not pursue anything worthwhile but must go chasing after the French or the Spanish or Irish or whatever enemy was in fashion at the time.

"So, my good earl, will you stay with us a bit?" I rang for refreshments before he could refuse.

We could speak of anything except my son. Or my husband. Very well, I understood that. "I trust Lady Catherine is well," I said: the polite, innocuous inquiry. "Is she still with the Queen?"

"Very much so," he said. "With the death of Marjorie Norris last autumn, she is her closest companion."

"It is good when blood relatives can also share our lives," I said. Mine were all distant or estranged, starting with the Queen.

"They may visit Hever Castle together," he said. "Perhaps you could join them."

Hardly. But he was trying to be polite, poor man. And it was a good sign that Catherine, my cousin, had not spoken openly against me. *Perhaps, perhaps . . . No, Lettice, that is foolish.* "Perhaps so. I have never been there, for all it was my grandmother's girlhood home."

"I have recently seen a newfound portrait of your grandfather William Carey," he said. "He was a handsome man."

If he *were* my grandfather, and the King were not . . . Again I smiled. "I would like to see it," I said.

But was it not possible that Mary Boleyn had found him more pleasing than the demanding King and had preferred him, and that all this speculation about the King being the father of her children was mere wishful thinking, because having royal blood—even if the royal from which the blood comes is not admirable—was preferable to being a commoner? Again, the outlines fade. . . . The great bulk of Henry VIII eclipses the slender one of William Carey.

"If they invite me, I shall surely come," I said. Polite talk.

He stood. I should have called Frances to receive the sword. I had meant to call her later in the visit, so as not to tire her. Now he was leaving. Too late. And I could not ask him about Christopher, nor the impending trial.

"I take my leave," he said. "I can only say, my heart is grieved."

"As you must know, I am grieved beyond words."

I accompanied him to the door.

"He was a son to be proud of," he said as he fastened his cloak. "Never forget that."

"It is a comfort," I said.

The door opened and closed, and he was gone.

But what of my husband? Would no one console me for him, speak kind words, write ballads? Christopher was nobody, nothing to the state. He had lived, and would die, unknown. And I, his wife, must grieve for him alone.

The trial would be held in the Tower, not Westminster Hall. Alongside him would be tried Sir John Davies, Sir Charles Danvers, Gelli Meyrick, and Henry Cuffe. Although I knew I would be turned away, I had to try to see Christopher. The authorities would not reveal the address of the tailor shop, but I did not need the authorities. I knew where Ludgate was; I knew where the fighting had taken place and where Christopher had fallen, unconscious. All I had to do was go there, and any obliging gossip on the street would point me to the nearby shop. So it proved.

It was a small, unprepossessing shop, little more than one room. I saw the bolts of wool and linen, saw the wooden worktable through the front door. But one large guard caught me staring and rushed out. "Begone! Do not loiter here!" he yelled.

"My husband lies within," I said. "I wish to speak to him."

"The traitor Blount?"

"There's been no trial yet, and until there is he cannot be labeled 'traitor.' "

"He's guilty as Judas and will go his way," said the man. "Now leave. The prisoner is allowed no visitors. That was the rule in letting him stay here to recover, rather than being clapped straightway in the Tower."

"He is recovering, then?" I asked.

"He's mending well," said the man. "He'll be well enough to stand up at his hanging."

"Please!" I begged him. "For the mercy of Christ!"

"If I let you in, I would be the next to stand trial. Now go."

It was no use.

---

Stumbling home, passing easily through Ludgate, where Christopher had fallen, I felt worse than if I had not gone. Knowing that I could do nothing to help him or even to help myself was torture. I resolved to be there when they took him out for his trial, to at least press close to him on the street.

---

I expected there would be secrecy surrounding the exact date of the trial, and starting the next day I returned early in the morning and stood watch across the street. Nothing that day. Nothing the next. Or the next. But then, on March 5, almost two months since the uprising, early in the morning (but I had come still earlier), a contingent of armed guards arrived at the house. Soon a litter emerged, with a prone figure lying on it. It had to be Christopher. The guards took their time shouldering the burden, arranging their grip, backing up. *Now!* I darted out from around the corner and grabbed the edge of the litter before the guards could react. I peered into it and saw Christopher's drawn, bandaged face, with a blanket muffling his neck and body.

He had trouble focusing his eyes and clearly did not recognize me. The jolt to the litter startled him, and then he knew what was happening. "Lettice!" he murmured.

"Damned wench!" A guard dug his fingers into my shoulder and yanked me away. The force of his pull tumbled me onto my knees. When I found my feet again, the litter was already halfway down the street. I ran after it, but the ring of guards around it meant I could not get close. I followed it past St. Paul's, down Cannon and Eastcheap, and then finally to the Tower itself. The ugly gray walls, which looked cold even in high summer, loomed ahead. I stopped, knowing I could follow it no farther. Solemnly, like a funeral cortege, it passed across the bridge spanning the moat and disappeared.

I stood, catching my breath. On my left side rose Tower Hill, where the scaffold awaited. I would not be back. I would not join the crowd at the execution.

I cast a last glance at the stone walls enclosing my dead son and now holding my living husband.

---

The day was interminable. I knew the verdict was already decided and the trial but a legal exercise. Still, I could not help picturing Christopher trying to answer the accusations. Did he have to do it from his litter? Or did they lift him onto a chair? Let it be a chair with a back support, not a stool. Surely they did not make him stand.

It was full dark when an official messenger from the Privy Council delivered an envelope to me with the pronouncement. He looked about furtively and made to leave the moment the envelope touched my hand. But I stopped him. The very least he could do was to formally tell me the verdict.

"Sir Christopher was found guilty," he said.

"And?"

"Sentenced to death, my lady."

"When?"

"A fortnight from now."

They were giving him longer than they had given Robert. Perhaps they wanted him to recover sufficiently. "And the others?"

"Sir Charles Danvers received the same sentence. He will suffer on the same day as Sir Blount, March 18. Gelli Meyrick and Henry Cuffe will go next week, March 13."

"And the last, Sir John Davies?"

"Not sure of that, my lady." He looked more furtive than ever, and I thought, *Oh, God, they may reprieve him. Why? Why?*

"Did Sir Christopher have any message for me?"

He shook his head. "I did not speak to the prisoner. They dispatched me straightway with this report."

"I thank you." I supposed I should reward him. Reward the messenger for evil news. But it was not his fault. "Here." I gave him some money and let him go.

Now Frances crept into the room. She had barely recovered from her difficult childbirth and was moving slowly. Why had I ever disliked her? She had turned out to be the most steadfast of my daughters. She sank down into a chair and waited, her large, dark eyes fastened on the fatal envelope.

My fingers trembled a bit, but I tore it open and started reading. Obligingly, she moved a candle closer to me on the table so I could read the hateful writing better. "We, the loyal servants and councillors of Her Gracious Majesty Queen Elizabeth, hereby record and testify to the proceedings of the trial of the rebels of the late uprising against Her Majesty. . . ." At least they had the decency not to call them traitors until the verdict had been announced. It went on, detailing the interrogation and Christopher's confession of intent to draw blood from the Queen. Their ends were to seize the Tower, hold the Queen hostage, call a parliament to force the removal of all the "evil councillors"—Cecil, Raleigh, Coke, Cobham. Who would rule in this interim they demurely avoided stipulating.

The councillors remarked that far from seizing the Tower, it was ironic that he was now being tried inside it.

The confessions of the others were included, but I did not concern myself with those. That was between themselves, the Queen, and God.

Frances and I sat quietly in the room, as if in a chapel keeping vigil. She was now twice a widow, and I would be thrice one. Our fates now linked us inexorably. As battle makes brothers out of men, widowhood forged a strong bond between us.

# 86

I had no desire to leave the house and kept as secluded as a desert monk. Indeed, the house was my own monastic cell and within it were all the memento mori I needed to contemplate mortality. I was suspended between two dates—every day was one further removed from Robert's death and one closer to Christopher's. Carefully Frances and I gathered and folded up Robert's clothes and possessions. Some she would keep for the children, others give to the poor, others keep for the memories. I asked only for one of his miniatures and an odd little Spanish church carving of a cherub he had brought back from Cádiz.

"Cádiz," I said, holding it, examining its gilded wings. "The last time he was happy." I stroked the angel's head.

"We all have a time that turns out to be our pinnacle of happiness," she said. "But at the time we think there is more to come."

"What was yours, Frances?"

She stopped smoothing the cloak she was ready to fold. "I think it was when Robert first made clear his intentions," she said. "I had had one noble knight in my life. I had not thought to have another. I was seventeen when Philip died and I thought my life was over. Truly, it just began when I married Robert."

"You said you would not draw a breath an hour after his death," I reminded her. "Yet here you are, still breathing."

"We surprise ourselves," she said. "Each breath I draw, I draw in pain. But I have to keep breathing so my children are not orphans."

Our pain was compounded when we learned that others had managed to buy their way out of execution. The Earl of Rutland got off for twenty thousand pounds, the Earl of Bedford for ten thousand, and Lords Sandys, Monteagle, and Cromwell for five thousand, four thousand, and three thousand, respectively. The Earl of Southampton, although condemned along with Robert, still lived in the Tower. His mother was said to be pleading powerfully for him, and I knew that she would end up paying a huge fine and he would go free. Technically these men were still prisoners and would be until the last penny was paid, but freedom loomed.

---

I petitioned the lieutenant of the Tower to be able to see Christopher or to write to him, but he said that was not possible. Then I inquired—oh, dreadful question—whether his body would be released to the family. The answer came back, no. The body of a convicted felon was the state's, and he would be buried in the churchyard of St. Peter ad Vincula—outside, as befitted a man of low rank. Only one glimmer of mercy shone through: The Queen had commuted his sentence to beheading. He would not suffer the horrors of hanging, disemboweling, and being drawn and quartered, as the unfortunate Meyrick and Cuffe did on March 13.

---

On the morning of March 18 I broke my word to myself. I would force myself to look on at Tower Hill. I, who had brought him into the world, had not witnessed Robert's exit from it. Perhaps the last duty I could perform as a wife was to accompany Christopher on the final steps of his journey. It was to be public, unlike Robert's.

But as I approached the area of Tower Hill, the thick crowds made me regret my decision. I had never attended a public execution, but they were supposed to serve a moral lesson, striking fear into the hearts of the onlookers. In practice, though, they treated it as an amusement, like bearbaiting and cockfighting, only better, since the victims were people and not animals. I tried to shut my ears to the jolly laughter and chatter of the crowd. All these people were free, free to waste their lives and substance, free to abuse their gifts, while Christopher was not even free to write a letter. I hated them.

Ahead of me loomed the slope of Tower Hill, with the scaffold perched upon it. So many had died here, so many sanctified it by their blood. Thomas More, who supposedly quipped as they steered him up the steps that he appreciated their help in mounting the scaffold, but as for the coming down, he would shift for himself. Cardinal John Fisher, whom Henry VIII had warned that if the pope sent him a cardinal's hat there would be no head to put it on. Henry Howard, the poet Earl of Surrey. Guildford Dudley. Thomas Cromwell. All of Anne Boleyn's supposed lovers, as well as Catherine Howard's genuine ones.

I threaded my way through the crowd, more tightly packed the closer I got to the scaffold. Finally I was jammed between two hulking men, but their size prevented anyone from pushing me aside. I was as close as I could get, and I could smell the hay strewn over the platform—fodder to absorb the blood. The headsman, with his black hood, was waiting, as was the block. Two clergymen stood by. At length there was a roar and I saw two men being brought out—Christopher and Charles Danvers. They would pass close to me as they mounted the steps, and I found myself paralyzed as I watched them approach. Christopher would come within an arm's length, but I could not move. Then, suddenly, I could, and reached out and grabbed his sleeve. He turned, unrecognizing, and the soldier guarding him hit my arm away. Then he mounted the steps, dragging his feet.

The bandage was gone but a livid scar ran down the right side of his face. He seemed dazed, unable to comprehend what was around him. The Crown representative read their crimes and their sentence. The clergymen stepped forward to speak in low tones to the men. Then the official asked if they wished to make a statement.

Christopher seemed to suddenly awaken. He spoke in a clear voice of his treason and said that he deserved to die. He said he forgave all his enemies, especially Sir Walter Raleigh. Then he cried, "I die a Catholic!" Looking wildly around, he saw me. "No, no!" he said. "Go!" Still I stood rooted, and he said, "Obey my last wish!"

He had given me permission. I could go, and not witness the horrible end. I obeyed. Turning my back on Tower Hill, I ran, my hands clapped to my ears. But I still could not drown out the shouts of glee that went up when the headsman struck.

# 87

# ELIZABETH

*April 1601*

Easter morning, April 12. The winter was over, all of it, gloriously over, and the pall that had descended on February 25, Ash Wednesday, the day of Essex's execution, lifted at last.

The gloom that had attended Lent this year—both in nature, with its bone-chilling mists and lingering frosts, and in my heart—now dissipated. I had thought the sound of birdsong and the bright yellow of new-sprung flowers would never come again, or if they did, would have lost the power to gladden me. But they still had the magic to make things new.

Throughout the land people gathered to watch the sun dance as it rose on Easter morning, an old belief. Here in the palace we put a bowl of water in the eastern window of the privy chamber to catch the phenomenon. Catherine, Helena, and I bent over it, watching eagle-eyed, but the sun only danced because of ripples in the water.

"I suppose one needs truly to believe," said Catherine. "One needs to look with the eyes of a child."

"Yes, we are all too old and have seen too much," agreed Helena. "Even little Eurwen will be acquiring the eyes of her elders now. Most likely this is her last Easter to see the sun dance."

"Most like," I said. "She will be thirteen now." The age I was when my father died. On that day I had stopped being a child. "I will bring her back to court." I needed to, for she had lost a kinsman and would forever associate me with the act of his death if I did not bring her close to me again.

We were still at Richmond, unusually late for this time of year. Usually we had transferred to Greenwich by now. But that had allowed Helena to stay with me longer, and I enjoyed that. Attired in our most sumptuous dress to honor the occasion, we, along with the entire household, attended the Easter service. The pale light from a hundred tapers in the chapel royal was lost in the blaze of sunlight streaming in the windows; only the thick Easter candle, meant to burn for forty days, held its own.

---

The wider world soon came calling in the persons of French and Scottish envoys. Both came on account of Essex—the French to ascertain what had happened, the Scots because he had called them. By the time James responded to Essex's plea that he send troops to assure that Cecil did not take over the government and give the succession to the Spanish, Essex was dead. Gamely James's envoys carried out their diplomatic mission, seeking to distance themselves from the fallen courtier. I entertained the Scots and assured them of our continued friendship and support. They almost trembled with eagerness to mention the succession but read the warning in my eyes.

As for the French, Henri IV had sent Marshal Biron as his envoy to express his condolences and thanks for my safety. It took all my willpower to arrange suitable entertainment to honor him. But I needed to be sure of French support, particularly in the coming months, when we wished to bring the dragging, draining, pointless war with Spain to a close.

So I smiled and teased and flattered Biron. When he touched on Essex, I assured him I would have spared him had I been able. I said this with a sigh of melancholy. If I had been able . . . so many things I would have done. Or not done.

"Ma'am," he said, leaning near me in affected confidentiality. "Do you know what my sovereign said upon hearing of your masterful handling of the uprising?"

"I am sure I cannot guess," I replied, and waited for him to tell me.

"He said, 'She is only a king! She only knows how to rule!'"

"Ah, well," I said, flattered against my own better judgment. But finally to have attained parity as a king—the competitive and meaner part of me danced a little dance and nodded upward toward my father. Son or no son, he had had what he sought in the succession to his reign.

---

After the French emissaries were dispatched, it was time to address some matters at home. The East India Company merchants planned to send four ships to the Far East. However, they wanted my blessing on their venture and asked me to write letters to the exotic rulers they expected to meet with, and to provide them with the proper gifts to present.

"For if we come in the name of our Queen," said the spokesman for the company, "they are like to pay us more heed."

"But they will have never heard of me," I said.

"Oh, that does not matter," he said. "The mere sight of the royal seal will impress them."

"How many do you expect to encounter?"

"Perhaps half a dozen. Could you provide letters for that many, just to be on the safe side?"

"I can draw them up, but leave the name blank, so you can fill it in," I said. "And as for gifts, what would catch the fancy of these rulers?"

"Something from England," he said. "But it must be waterproof and unbreakable and not subject to spoilage on the long voyage."

"You set me a hard task, gentlemen," I said. "It is difficult to find something uniquely English that will also fit those criteria."

"Oh, and it must be small as well. We do not have much space on board."

"I must think upon it," I said. "What lands do you hope to reach?"

"Sumatra, Java, the Moluccas," he said. "And whatever else we stumble on. Perhaps even China."

I could almost smell the spices, wafting across the warm water from the islands. "The tropics rot cloth, so I cannot make a gift of that. A delicate clock would rust in the sea air. Dogs are out of the question, although the sultan of the Turks was impressed with our native breeds, the bloodhounds and mastiffs."

"We can trust Your Glorious Majesty to provide exactly the right gift."

"I will do so," I said. "I am proud that we are sending English ships and merchants so far away. We have established many trading stations all over the East. In years to come they should pay off." Our failure to set up any permanent colonies or even trading posts in the New World was a pity, but it could be counterbalanced by those on the other side of the globe. At least we knew that was rich in spices, pearls, and silk. So far the New World had yielded only gold, unfortunately in the hands of Spain. "Do you have any thought, or hope, of finding Terra Australis Incognita? If it exists, that is."

"We are not equipped to go that far south," he said. "And in any case, it would be so cold there that the spices we seek would not grow."

"But it probably is a myth," said his companion. "So far no one has sighted any land that far south."

"That is for another generation, then," I said. "We must leave them something of their own to discover."

---

That afternoon I thought hard about what I could possibly send to the Far East with them. Their restrictions were so severe even a fairy could not find berth on their ships. Something small . . . something waterproof . . . something unbreakable . . . something impervious to salt . . . something unmistakably English . . .

"I have it!" said Helena. "It is so obvious."

"Is it? Then why is it not obvious to me?"

"When I came from Sweden with Princess Cecilia's embassy, King Gustav sent miniatures of himself to everyone—do you remember?"

"Yes, I do. I still have one—somewhere." More and more I had to say that, not having a precise recollection of where long-unused things were. "It was charming."

"Well, then—you could send a similar gift to the foreign rulers. They would never have seen an English queen. It would be a novelty for them. You can order duplicates of a portrait you have already approved."

"Yes . . . I suppose . . . Very clever of you."

"A little glass plate will allow it to withstand the salt air, and the size will be perfect. And imagine what they will think when they see what a ruler of Europe wears. They will covet the same!"

"Thank you, Helena. You have done me a great favor."

"Just one thing. As a reward, I want one for myself."

"You shall have it."

Over the years, my costumes had become even more elaborate. I gave the people an unchanged portrait of their Queen, a fixed element in their lives. All else might change, but your Queen does not. That is the message I wished to send them. But I was getting old, and I noted the telltale signs: how increasingly impatient I had become with repetitions, how rigid about carrying through with something. To others that looked like stubbornness, but I knew it was because if I did not do it immediately, it would slip my mind. And there was forgetfulness, which I had been living with for a while. The constant effort to disguise these things—these failings?—was worse than the failings themselves. Yet I knew the keen eyes and the whisperings, the wolves ready to pounce if they smelled weakness. I would not give them that opportunity.

---

The letters of introduction, illuminated in red and gold, presented to the captains went thus:

*To the most high and most mighty* ___________ *, of the* ___________ *,*
*most puissant, sole, and supreme lord and monarch.*

*Elizabeth of England, France, and Ireland by the grace of God queen, to the most high and mighty prince,* ___________ *, greetings.*

And then followed a letter setting forth our intentions and our well wishes, in English, Latin, Spanish, and Italian. I gave them the letters along with the completed miniatures and sent them on their way.

---

The summer passed pleasantly. The harvest was still not good, but neither was it disastrous. The Continent was quiet. The government ran smoothly with Essex gone, its chief irritant removed. I appointed the Earl of Worcester and the Earl of Shrewsbury to fill vacancies on the Privy Council and enjoyed the quiet balmy days of July and August.

Then came September, and the news I had hoped never to hear: The Spanish had landed in Ireland. Thirty-three ships, with five thousand troops, arms, and ammunition, had anchored at Kinsale on the southern part of the island. They were under the command of Don Juan de Águila, who had led the attack on Mousehole in 1595.

Our troops were primarily in the north, fighting O'Neill and his adherents, and these reinforcements were in the south. If the O'Neill forces could get south and join with the Spanish, we would be outnumbered.

Quickly I ordered reinforcements to Ireland and wrote Lord Deputy Mountjoy, "Tell our army from us, that every hundred of us will beat a thousand of them, and every thousand, ten thousand. I am the bolder to pronounce it in His name, that has ever protected my righteous cause. I end, scribbling in haste, Your loving sovereign, E.T."

If only it were true that our numbers counted disproportionately. But that was wishful thinking. We had been winning in Ireland. Now came the test. At last the Spanish had directly engaged us on land.

"Old Sixtus," I muttered. "It is too late for you to offer your reward of gold to Spanish boots on our soil." He had not lived to see it. Good.

It is satisfying to outlive one's enemies, and the schemes of one's enemies. One of the unheralded benefits of age.

# 88

Autumn, and the time of gathering in. My sixty-eighth birthday came and went, and I did not encourage anyone to mark it. I did not want to remind the world of my age. But I could not escape marking it myself.

I took a short Progress to Reading and Hampshire and was pleased to see farmers selling their produce along the road. The wagons were not heaped as high as they would have been in a good year, but at least there was something. That sharp smell of leaves crackling underfoot filled my nostrils and made me think—as that autumnal scent would always make me think—of Marjorie. I had just heard that Henry Norris had died and joined her in the family tomb. He had not endured long without her.

With a sigh, I turned my thoughts to more immediate and pressing concerns. The subsidies granted by Parliament in 1597 had run out this spring, and I had called another one to meet in October.

This one would be difficult. They grew ever more demanding and encroached more and more upon my royal prerogative. Traditionally, Parliament's role was to advise, and advise only. But they could introduce bills for me to approve. I could—and did—forbid them to put forward bills on the church, the succession, and monopolies.

I halted my horse and looked around the fields, the stubble in them like little picket fences. Like the farmers who tilled these fields, I must tend to Parliament. Both grew unruly without care. Both must be made to yield for our subsistence.

---

I conferred with Francis Bacon, who had become quite an accommodating servant of the Crown. His trenchant mind was at my service, as he had proved in the Essex trial. Afterward he had been vilified as a turncoat, so he wrote an apology to defend himself. I am not sure it convinced anyone.

He seemed sad eyed as he entered my consulting room, bowing solemnly.

"Come, come, sir, it is too fine a day to look so drear," I told him. "Soon the winter will give you cause enough." Outside the Greenwich windows, the autumn sun sparkled on the Thames.

"True, Ma'am, but clouds already hang upon me."

I had forgotten. Anthony had died. "Forgive me. I forgot that you mourn your brother."

"It was expected, of course. He had declined for years. Yet the scandal of the Essex affair hastened his end."

"There was no scandal in it for him, and it is no shame to faithfully serve a master. No one blamed him for any of it."

"He was devastated at the turn of events."

*Some survive better than others,* I thought. "Francis, the new parliament . . ." I must steer onto the real road I wished to travel. Talk of Essex was a dead end, literally.

"I will be sitting in it, as you know," he said. "And it is my highest wish to serve Your Majesty's concerns."

"I have many, as you are well aware, Master Bacon. Most of them, as with most of life, have to do with finances. Even the Bible says, 'Money answers everything.'"

He looked startled. "It does? Where?"

"Ah, Francis, you do not bury yourself in Scriptures?" I laughed to let him know I was teasing. "Ecclesiastes says, 'A feast is made for laughter and wine maketh merry, but money answers everything.'"

"It certainly pays for everything."

"In spite of frugality that would rival a desert father's, and selling Crown lands and jewels and even my father's Great Seal, the country is sinking toward bankruptcy," I said. "We must end this pointless war with Spain. Until then, I must call on Parliament once again for money. I hate it, and they hate it, and there is nothing I can do about it!" I felt my neck growing hot with anger at my helplessness. I had tried so hard, and yet England was as bad off as when I had come to the throne.

"I am sure they will grant whatever you request," he assured me. "As for expenses—I inherited Gorhambury House from my brother. It is a lovely place, but the burden of keeping it weighs on me."

"I have fond memories of visiting your father there," I said. "Tell me, is the door still sealed up? The one I walked through?"

"Indeed it is," he said. "You must return so that we can reopen it."

"When this is settled, I can make pleasure jaunts. But the . . . the recompense for your service at the Essex trial . . . Is it not sufficient to allay the expenses of Gorhambury?" How delicately we must tread around the payoff to Francis for so ably opposing Essex in the trial. I had given him the twelve-hundred-pound fine levied on Sir Robert Catesby. Many of the adherents of Essex had been fined and let go. I hated to part with even a penny of the money, but Francis had earned it.

"I am grateful," he said. "But the expenses at Gorhambury are ongoing. As I noted in my essay on wealth, better a one-time expense than a continual one."

"And what is a kingdom but that very thing? It must be continually nourished. Yet even as I nourish it, it nourishes me. We draw strength from each other."

He nodded. Then he said, "There is something that Parliament means to address, and that you may oppose. They will demand a reformation of the monopolies. They say that such reforms were promised in the last parliament and have not been carried through." He paused, as if waiting for me to explode. I think he even stepped back two feet.

"I am well aware of the problem, but the monopolies are necessary."

"With all respect, Your Majesty, why are they necessary?"

"How else can I reward people? Good God, I have no means otherwise! Oh, in the middle of my reign, before these ruinous war expenses, I had a surplus to distribute to worthy people. Titles, too, and lands; offices and appointments in the government. Even an honest man could make a windfall on the Court of Wards—Burghley did. But in the last decade, that has dried up. I have nothing extra to bestow. The monopolies fill the gap. I would like the income for the Crown, but it is cheaper to yield it than to pay loyal supporters nothing. The monopoly on sweet wines, though, I have kept. It enabled Essex to live like a king, and now it helps pay my creditors." I stopped for breath. What a tirade.

"The people resent them," he said. "Your reasons may be valid, but all they know is that they must pay unreasonable rates for common items like starch, playing cards, and salt."

"We all have irksome things in our lives. God knows, mine started with being a woman in a role cast for a man!"

He inclined his head. Never had a gesture of submission seemed less submissive.

"Oh, very well!" I said. "I know that subject is old. I have, I like to think, overcome it! But the monopolies—there are two kinds. Some are well earned by their discoverer, or their perfecter, someone who finds a better way to tan gloves, or to set type. Why should another profit from his labor? If anyone can come in and snatch, or share, the profits, what incentive do people have to invent something?"

"I do not think those are the ones in contention," he said. "The ones resented are the ones I named, common household products. There are dozens of them. Did Raleigh invent playing cards? No. Why, then, should he collect duties on them?" His eyes flashed. "Because he is a royal favorite? If so, the Crown takes from the poor to give to the wealthy. It is a reversal of what Robin Hood did, and he is celebrated as a hero."

"That was a long time ago," I said.

"I am only warning you," he said. "As a loyal servant should." He bowed deeply.

I wrestled with this after he departed. Everything he had said was true. But beyond that lay the question of royal prerogative. It should be within my rights to bestow monopolies on deserving subjects. At what point should I yield to public pressure?

---

I conferred with Cecil on the upcoming parliament. This would be the first one without his father to lead it, and he would be sorely missed. Even in Burghley's declining state he had ably managed the one that met in 1597.

"We are on our own, Robert," I told him. "It is always hard to step into a father's shoes. Particularly in our cases, when the shoes were so big."

"Sooner or later it comes," he said. "I think we are prepared. You have issued orders that the Parliament not waste time in idle talk, proposing vain measures, but tidy up ones already passed and speedily get to the subsidy bill."

"Yes," I said. "I want this parliament over by Christmas, not dragged out."

He nodded.

"And there is something else," I said. "I have had petitions thrust at me as I walk between chapel and palace, or to public ceremonies. They come from ordinary citizens, angry about the monopolies. I know this Parliament will take up the matter."

"And our response?"

"I will hear what they have to say and how strongly they press the matter," I said.

---

Parliament convened in October of 1601; I opened it at the House of Lords. I was ceremoniously attired in my robes of state, wearing my crown, moving slowly to allow everyone a glimpse of me. The orb and scepter were carried before me. People looked, but few offered the customary "God save Your Majesty." I felt a chill in the air, and not because it was October. The Essex affair had damaged my popularity.

Entering the chamber, mounting the steps to my throne, I suddenly buckled under the weight of the heavy robes and swayed. Several men rushed to steady me, but it was frightening. I took my seat and clutched the emblems of office, determined to regain my equilibrium. Sixty or so faces looked back at me, with over a hundred commoners standing at the back, and others at the threshold of the chamber.

Lord Keeper of the Great Seal, Sir Thomas Egerton, gave his opening speech. He announced that the reason for this parliament was twofold: the war with Ireland and Spain and the need to finance it. He told them to be confident of a good outcome, for "God hath ever, and I hope will ever, bless the Queen with successful fortune." He then went on to detail the perfidious plots of Philip II and the dangers I had overcome. Turning to me, he burst out, "I have seen Her Majesty wear on her belt the price of her blood, I mean a jewel that had been given to her physician to do that which, I hope, God will ever deliver her from!"

Dr. Lopez . . . I had kept his ring and often wore it, not on my finger now, but on a chain. I nodded vigorously, to show how well I had survived, and to emphasize my health.

The opening ceremony over, I rose to exit the chamber. Outside, the House members pressed tightly and I could barely make my way. I held up my hand to ask for more space, and someone called, "Back, masters, make room!" A loud voice from the rear answered, "Even if you will hang us we can make no more room!"

I pretended not to hear, but oh! I did. What was this surly mood among the members? I did not deserve this. Never had I passed into the House with no greeting or passed out of it with a taunt.

---

My misgivings about Parliament proved true. They refused to consider the subsidy until the matter of the monopolies was settled. Member after member railed against them, in spite of Bacon's and Cecil's attempts to present the Crown's case. Promises would not content them. A long list of the present monopolies was read out: currants, iron, ox shinbones, aniseed, vinegar, blubber oil, smoked pilchards, playing cards, salt, starch, drinking glasses, and many others.

"Where is bread?" cried one member. "I am sure that bread must be on this list. All the other necessities are!" He snorted. "If we don't take action now, it will be there by the next parliament!"

"Bloodsuckers of the commonwealth!" a member from Hertfordshire said. "The prices are outrageous and drive the prices of everything up. The increase on bundles of calfskin makes every pair of shoes for the poor cost more!"

"It is not to be borne!" another cried.

---

Clearly this was a crisis for me. Parliament members next began to consider what remedies they might take. Should they draft a bill, legislating the end to monopolies, examining existing ones for legality? Should they take a more conciliatory route and present me with a petition asking me to rescind them?

"I have done all I can," said Cecil, pacing nervously. "I fear we are losing control. So far they have not directly challenged your royal prerogative, but that is just a matter of semantics . . . and of time."

My position was that my right to grant monopolies was above the law, part of my royal right. Parliament did not have the power to encroach on that or limit my freedom on any prerogative. To grant them this power would be to say that they ultimately ruled England, not I.

And yet, and yet . . . I knew a fundamental change was afoot, and to resist it would damage the monarchy more than granting it. Granting it . . . Yes, if I granted it freely, as a royal favor, rather than submit to their demands . . . no precedent would be set of Crown yielding to Parliament, being subservient to it. That was the way, the only way.

"Tell them that I am grateful for their having brought these dreadful abuses to my attention and that I will remedy them immediately."

"Your Majesty?" Cecil was perplexed.

"I will end the most egregious of them now, and suspend the others until their legality can be tested in court. I will draw up a proclamation to that effect and put it in their hands straightway. Then I will receive the Privy Councillors and some members of Parliament to thank them."

"They will be stunned. As am I," he admitted.

"If one must concede, one should do it in all generosity. It is not only the Lord who loves a cheerful giver. Away now, away. I have a proclamation to write."

I needed to reclaim the love of my people, so tried and tarnished by the Essex affair and money troubles. But I could not mortgage the ancient privileges of the Crown to do so. The proclamation would fulfill both needs.

---

Jubilantly Cecil read out to Parliament the royal decree, entitled "A Proclamation for the Reformation of Many Abuses and Misdemeanors Committed by Patentees of Certain Privileges and Licenses, to the General Good of All Her Majesty's Loving Subjects." The monopolies on salt, vinegar, alcoholic drinks, salt fish, train oil, fish livers, pots, brushes, butter, and starch were abolished.

"Every man can have or make cheap salt!" he announced. "For those whose stomachs need it, they can now have all the aqua vitae they like. The same for vinegar to treat your indigestion. Those of you who love your ruffs, rest assured that you can starch them cheaply now. You can start sowing woad dye again, though Her Majesty hopes the stink of it will not make your towns so unpleasant she cannot visit you on Progress. She does forbid it in London or near any palace." As each item was announced, a cheer went up. Finally he cautioned, "The Queen does not abjure her ancient prerogatives." Then he went on to list the monopolies that would be examined in court: saltpeter, Irish yarn, steel, and many others. Furthermore, copies of the proclamation would be printed and distributed to the members immediately.

Commons asked to send their speaker and a dozen members to me to thank me. I sent word back that it was I who wished to thank them, and that they should come in two days. They began to select the deputation to come, but members from the back of the House cried out, "All! All, all, all!"

I was absurdly pleased that they all wanted to come and told William Knollys, now the comptroller of the household, to invite them all, assuring them I had originally limited the deputation only because of the size of the audience room. But we would find room.

So I would speak to them and thank them. I began to write my speech. But somewhere in the making of it, it changed. I had spoken to Parliament many times, but always with the assurance there would be more speeches in the future. There was no longer that surety. Whatever I wished to tell them, whatever they needed to know, I must say it now and in this speech. It had little, or nothing, to do with the monopolies.

I thought of my early days as a princess; the days I lived outside London, removed from the seats of power, but always with vital contact with the people. They cheered when I came to London, sick and wan, in a litter. The only way to show disapproval of a regime was to cheer the successor or alternative, and that they did. By the time I came to the throne I was buoyed on a wave of love that carried me straight to my coronation. Every time I had ventured out beyond London, beyond the quarreling ministers and courtiers, I had felt that love. I drew strength from it as a plant draws strength from sun and soil. What were the Progresses, after all? A personal visit with my people.

What did I want for them? And how could I tell them what I felt?

This would be my last parliament. I knew that. I do not know how I knew it, but I did. Even if I survived until another one, my words would not be so completely my own.

Was I ill? Was I failing? How, then, could I know this so surely?

There is a day in autumn—often a warm one, as warm as summer—when something seems to turn. The wind comes from a slightly different quarter. The light has a different slant. It shines from an angle through the windows, falls on things it has not picked out for months. It has a different glow. It in itself is harmless, innocuous, but it portends a shift and warns us to prepare. Just so I felt this tide in myself. I must address my people when I could say what I wished, in my own words. Even if I lived another thirty years, I would not be so able.

I worked through the night on my speech. I poured all my feelings about my people, my realm, my kingdom, and myself into it.

---

Only ten days after the debate had begun, on the last day of November, the speaker and some 150 members of Parliament came to Whitehall. I sat waiting for them under my cloth of estate in the council chamber, and they filed in. Their speaker, Sir Edward Coke, bowed low three times and then gave a long speech about my majesty and glory, rather embarrassing in its fulsomeness, calling upon my sacred presence, my sacred ears, and my sacred sovereignty. When he was finished, the entire company knelt to hear my answer.

I looked out over them. They were of all ages and came from all parts of England. But that was what Parliament was meant to be, to reflect the people over whom I ruled, and through them every man and woman in the land.

First I thanked them for coming and for their appreciation. Then I said, "Mr. Speaker, I assure you there is no prince that loves his subjects better, or whose love can countervail our love. There is no jewel, be it of ever so rich a price, which I set before this jewel—I mean your loves." I nodded. "For I esteem it more than any treasure or riches, for that we know how to prize. But love and thanks I count invaluable, and though God has raised me high, yet this I count the glory of my crown: that I have reigned with your loves."

Few rulers had been so blessed. I watched the expressions on their faces. "Please do rise, for I will speak a bit longer and do not wish you to be uncomfortable." They got up from their knees. "Mr. Speaker, you give me thanks, but had I not received knowledge from you, I might have fallen into error only for lack of true information. That grants should be grievous to our people and oppressions to be privileged under color of our patents, our kingly dignity shall not suffer it. Yea, when I heard it, I could give no rest to my thoughts until I had reformed it." I then went on to explain I was always keenly aware that I must answer to God as judge if I failed my people.

"To be a king and wear a crown is a thing more glorious to them that see it than it is pleasant to them that bear it. For myself, I was never so much enticed with the glorious name of a king or royal authority as a queen, as delighted that God has made me his instrument to maintain his truth and glory, and to defend this kingdom from peril, dishonor, tyranny, and oppression." And how many ways I had employed to defend it—diplomacy, marriage flirtations, spies and intelligence networks, all before the last resort of arms.

"There will never queen sit in my seat with more zeal to my country, care to my subjects, and that will sooner with willingness venture her life for your good and safety, than myself. For it is not my desire to live nor reign longer than my life and reign shall be for your good. And though you have had and may have many princes more mighty and wise sitting in this seat, yet you never had or shall have any that will love you better."

Oh, it was true. I touched my coronation ring, rubbing it softly. "I have been content to be a taper of pure virgin wax, to waste myself and spend my life that I might give light and comfort to those that live under me."

There was silence in the room. Then I said, "Thus, Mr. Speaker, I commend me to your loyal love, and you to my best care and your further counsels. And I pray you, Mr. Comptroller and my councillors, that before these members depart for their home counties, you bring them all to kiss my hand."

I sat and waited as they filed up, one at a time. I extended my hand for them to kiss. Each took his leave, until the chamber was empty.

# 89

# LETTICE

*March 1602*

*have been a widow for a year today,* I thought with stunned wonder. There was supposed to be a magic in crossing that threshold, the equivalent of applying a soothing bandage to a wound. No longer was it open and raw, but sealed up and healing. That was the belief, in any case. I say it depends on how deep and how wide the wound was.

I had worn black ever since the black day on which Robert stepped onto the scaffold platform. Gradually it had come to seem odd that I would wear any other color.

I had not, of course, been able to visit Christopher's grave. I was not even sure it was marked. He may have been thrown into a trench beside the church. I could not visit Robert's grave either, but I had heard that he had a plaque marking it. But since the Tower was royal property, I could not be admitted to the church inside.

My first husband was buried far away in Wales, my second in Warwick, along with our son. So I could not be one of those widows who haunted graves like a ghost. As a three-time widow, I could say that it is far more hurtful to lose someone to politics than to nature. In a sense, Christopher brought it upon himself, but that was no comfort. It meant he could have avoided it, still be here with me. Neither Walter Devereux nor Robert Dudley had a choice in the matter.

People still sang ballads about Robert, still wrote an occasional slur against Cecil on walls, but it was dying away. Memories are short. The Queen counted on that. Her popularity sagged in the aftermath, but her latest performance in Parliament has restored her to the people's goodwill. She graciously gave in and abolished the hated monopolies, then gave what is being called her "golden speech." It was an elegy, a farewell. She expressed her bond to her people—her version of a marriage vow—and reflected on what it meant to her to be a queen. It was rapturously received.

But people wondered: Does she know she is ill? It had that ring, the tone of an announcement of mortality. She, who had seemed eternal, was reminding her people that she is not.

And they were preparing for the change. Eyes were looking to Scotland, and King James, as Robert's had done. They were looking discreetly, but they were looking. I had heard that even Cecil had put out feelers. He will need to secure his place in the next reign. If James brings his own councillors, then Cecil may find himself dismissed. He must gain the future king's confidence now.

The Queen had been her inconsistent self in regards to the people involved in what was being called "the Essex rebellion." Southampton still languished in the Tower, although he was pronounced guilty alongside Robert. No execution date had been set, no fine announced. Many others were fined and freed. Will got off with a questioning from the Privy Council about the special performance of *Richard II* but seemed to have suffered no consequences. His plays were still shown at court and he was received there. Charles Blount, Lord Mountjoy, for all the incriminating evidence that he had had knowledge of the plot and was even toying with contributing troops to it, got off completely. Doing so well in Ireland meant that he was too valuable to sacrifice, and so the Queen looked the other way.

Then she did the oddest thing she has ever done. No, I cannot say that. But it was the oddest thing she has ever done in regard to our family. When Robert had returned without permission from Ireland, Frances had gathered up letters and papers she thought the government might confiscate to incriminate him. After his death, the people to whom she had entrusted the papers blackmailed her. At first she paid the fee, but they kept demanding more. Somehow the Queen got wind of it and had the blackmailer arrested, tried, and fined. She gave the fine to Frances, as well as the papers, saying, "I would have my winding-sheet unspotted." Elizabeth never loses the power to amaze and surprise us.

Frances, who cried to Elizabeth that she would not draw breath one hour after Robert had been executed, still lived and breathed. She, too, wore black, and busied herself with her children, especially the youngest, who had just begun walking. But I had the feeling that, at thirty-four, she would lay it aside before long and consider a third husband. She was the sort who should be married.

But for myself, no. I was well past that now.

---

I had withdrawn to Wanstead, six miles outside of London. I would grow old here. It was a house free of all the dark associations that Essex House had for me. Here there had been laughter and lovemaking, music, summer's pleasures, and happy liaisons. After the opprobrium died down, I would be welcome enough for charitable work. Since I had become an outcast myself, I saw unfortunates in a new light. Looking down upon them from my heights of wealth and safety, I had shrugged them off. The poor you have with you always, Jesus had said. If they were poor, they must be lazy. Or happy. Odd how to assuage our own consciences we assume they must be happy, and spin tales to ourselves about their dancing and singing and laughing. We even envy them! Drowning in our obligations and worries, we ride past them and imagine their lives free of striving and competition, and sigh with longing.

But I knew now they were not to be envied for the weight of poverty that left them unrecognized. It was the children I most wanted to rescue; it was too late for their parents. I would make them my mission.

I was visited occasionally by my respectable daughters. Dorothy seemed far removed from both court and family, still married to the "Wizard" Earl of Northumberland and spending most of her time at Syon House, on the other side of London, upstream on the Thames. Penelope was the acclaimed woman of the hour, the consort, if not the wife, of the hero of Ireland.

Yes, Charles Blount had done the seemingly impossible, had achieved what Robert had so signally failed to do. His hard-fought campaign in Ireland had brought victory. The great turning point came in December. Charles and his forces had been in the north, chasing The O'Neill, when the Spanish landed at Kinsale with their reinforcing units. Suddenly his mission was not to smash the rebels in Ulster, but to prevent their joining forces with the Spanish in the south. He executed this brilliantly. But as always, fate played a part. O'Neill suffered a lapse in judgment and chose to meet the English in the field, in a traditional battle, handing them the victory. He was ill suited for it and was soundly routed. The Irish fled north once again, and the Spanish set sail, never to return. Now all that remained was to capture O'Neill and extract his surrender. He was a beaten man, and the Irish rebellion was smashed.

Elizabeth would be able to add the subjugation of Ireland to her victory over the Armada in the annals of her reign. A worthy achievement for a woman warrior, no matter how reluctant a one she was.

To be honest, for all his blustering, his engraved armor, and his golden tents, her father achieved nothing militarily. His excursions into France were costly and pointless, yielding nothing permanent. She, on the other hand, has saved her realm from invasion and has slammed the back door of Ireland shut to foreign meddling. And she knew what she wanted. In order to press ahead in Ireland, she was willing to overlook Charles Blount's transgressions to get the important job done. Her father would have focused on the "treason" of Blount. Elizabeth wanted to use him, treason or no. Who, then, was the better monarch? Elizabeth would demur even at hinting at a competition between herself and her father, but that might be because in her heart she knew she had surpassed him.

---

I was shocked to receive a letter from Will, two months after the anniversary of Christopher's death. It was very short, saying merely that he wished to offer his condolences and that, on his way back to Stratford, he would like to pay a call. Would that be acceptable?

I had received few condolence visits, and even fewer guests had come to Wanstead, although in the heady days twenty years past they had begged for invitations. Part of me wished to say no, to keep myself away from anything that smacked of the old life. The other part of me wanted to say yes, still to be connected to the world beyond Wanstead.

I said yes.

---

He arrived on a May day, one of those so fine that we would not want to be anywhere else. Let Rome and Sicily have their wildflowers and warm, sweet evenings; we had May in England.

"Will," I said, taking his hat. "I appreciate your coming."

He stepped in. "I have wanted to ever since . . . You understand."

"Yes. You had to be careful." I looked at him. He had aged little, and he had a contentment about him that I noticed. "Shall we go out in the garden?" Let me add another pleasant memory to it.

I guided him outside, and he exclaimed over the profusion of gillyflowers, hollyhocks, and climbing roses and the neatly trimmed maze. It was odd, but I did not feel awkward around him. It was as if he were from another life, another version of myself. The Lettice who now stood before him owed nothing, had nothing to apologize for. The stroke of the ax on Tower Green had severed my past from my future.

"Will you sit?" I indicated a bench, wreathed all around with climbing vines twining overhead in a protective canopy. He nodded and did so. I sat beside him.

"I was sorrowed by what happened," he said.

"Thank you," I replied. "I still have difficulty believing it. I wake up expecting Robert or Christopher to be there. Then I remember." I smiled. "But there is less and less time between the expectation and the remembrance."

"The gap will always be there," he said.

"Will the realization always be painful?" I asked him.

"As long as you live," he said.

"You give no balm," I said. "Should not a friend do so?"

"A friend must not lie," he said.

"Ah, Will. You were always difficult."

"I was always honest."

"Always?"

"As far as I could be."

I did not desire him any longer, yet I loved him. This confused me. Far from losing him forever, as I had once thought, I knew now he would be a part of me forever.

"Tell me of your life. Mine you know already. I am sorry you were caught up in the rebellion."

"All that was an accident. I wish I had never written that play! But as for my life now, I have been buying property in Stratford. I find my thoughts turning more and more to my old home."

As I had retreated to Wanstead. The past pulled us back with urgent hands.

"My father recently died," he said. "Only a few months after your son."

"His life was not cut short."

"No, he was almost seventy."

"The same age as the Queen."

"Yes. But . . ."

It must go unsaid. "Is your mother still living?"

"Yes. And they had been married forty-four years."

"And you?"

He looked uneasy, embarrassed. "I've been married since I was eighteen," he said. "I am now almost forty."

And I almost sixty. I had forgotten how much younger than I he was. When we were together, he had seemed the elder.

"And how is your wife?" I asked primly.

"The same." He suppressed a smile.

"Shall we not speak of her?"

"That is agreeable to me."

"Why do you return to Stratford, if not to see her?"

"My mother, my children . . . It is odd. When I was a child, I wished nothing more than to escape it. Now I find that if I wish to leave any sort of legacy, it will exist only in Stratford. London swallows me up. I will not survive there. In a generation, I will vanish. The country has longer memories."

"But your plays . . ."

"For the moment only," he said. "They amuse the crowds. But plays are not the stuff that endures. My company owns the scripts. And we dare not publish them, else others would enact them and rob us of our rightful earnings."

I looked hard at him, trying to memorize his features, his fine nose and penetrating eyes. I wondered what women had loved him, and where they were now.

"My younger brother is here now," he suddenly said. "Edmund. He, like me, was afire for the theater. He has played bit parts, but nothing that would make his name. I should write something for him. But I cannot construct a play around such a need. I can only write a character that calls me. Edmund cannot play the ones that are clamoring for me to give them birth. They are too old for him. A Scottish noble who is drawn to murder to fulfill a prophecy, an old king who realizes too late that he cannot give away his office and retain its privileges, a Moor who is undone with jealousy—no, a young man from Stratford cannot play any of these." He broke off suddenly. "But all this is talk. Laetitia, how are you? My heart wants to know." He grasped my hands so I could not pull away.

How could I answer? I was empty; I was a changed creature. "I survive," I said, aware of his hands, their warmth, their hold.

"Can you forgive me?" he said.

"For what? For warning me what to expect from you, and then following through?"

He smiled, a slight smile. "I was a coward."

"It was better for us that you were. You were wiser than I. You could see what must ultimately come of it. And you did not want it."

"I could not endure it. I can write about it, but I cannot live it."

"Better, then, for others. You can leave them something."

"I told you, Laetitia. I leave nothing behind for anyone. My works will not survive me. They are played to crowds at the Globe, then forgotten. I can behold tumultuous emotions, record them—but not fall victim to them. My weakness."

"Never mind, Will. You are here now. Few have come. You have given me a precious gift. Now kiss me. In friendship." I leaned over to him, closed my eyes.

# 90

# ELIZABETH

*July 1602*

I looked up at the threatening sky; black and blue clouds were racing past, and the wind had picked up. I steadied my hat to keep it from blowing off and turned in the saddle.

"Ladies, we are like to have a wet welcome!" I called to my companions.

"How far are we from Harefield?" asked Catherine.

"Five or six miles, at least," said my horse master. "Perhaps it will hold off that long."

A blast of wind tore at my skirts, and I clutched the reins. The horse's mane was flapping. "Let us gallop, then," I ordered, spurring him on. He leaped under me and it was all I could do to keep my seat.

We were on an abbreviated summer Progress. Originally I had intended to go west, leaving London and stopping first at Elvetham House, then on to Bath and Bristol. But the journey was too ambitious and I had to curtail it, substituting an eastern Progress. We had stopped first at Chiswick and now were heading for the house of Thomas Egerton and his new wife, the dowager Countess of Derby. Two years ago he had begged to be released from supervising Essex at York House, because his wife was dying. Now both his prisoner and his wife were gone, and he had taken a new one, a lady with literary tastes—or pretensions. Well, he deserved his happiness. Good for him.

I took less with me on this Progress, and fewer people. People grumbled about the inconveniences, so I had jokingly said, "Let the old stay behind and the young and able come with me!" That had given the ailing ones an excuse to stay home.

There were a number of "young and able" along. I had, as I wished, invited Eurwen back to court, and she rode now in company with some of the younger maids of honor, and there were handsome young men, like Richard de Burgh, the Earl of Clanricarde, one of the "good" Irish. I found myself disliking him, though, and it took me a while to realize it was because he resembled Essex. That was not fair to the man, but the other ladies made much of him, so he was not lacking. There was also the saturnine John Donne, Egerton's secretary and lately a member of Parliament, who skulked in the back and did not seem eager to reach his master's home. He had been jolly enough at Chiswick, but every mile closer to Harefield drew his already long face even longer.

The ride here had immersed us in the glory of a high English summer. Rich midsummer flowers had replaced the delicate hues of spring in the meadows, and fledglings were practicing their flying, swooping skillfully from their nests. Cottage doors stood open, and housewives were spreading linens out on hedgerows to dry. Boys practiced archery in the open fields. Summer was the time of village festivals, and we passed several on our way. It was also the time of weddings, and from a distance I saw a bridal party making its way through the fields to a little stone church. The fields stood high, and this harvest promised to end the run of poor ones.

My realm was faring well. It grew and prospered under the sun.

Now the weather had turned. We dashed to the shelter of Harefield Place, just beating the rain. Our horses were whisked away to the stables, and Sir Thomas and his new wife, Alice, welcomed us into the house. Just as Alice was making her curtsy, the skies opened up and rain pelted the courtyard.

"Even the skies hold back their anger for you," said Sir Thomas.

"Or release it on cue, as they did for the Armada," said Admiral Charles.

"It was an English wind," agreed Raleigh.

---

The rain having blown itself out to sea, the next day was fair. Sir Thomas had planned an outdoor fete, so it was hurriedly arranged, lest the weather prove fickle. The country theme continued, with long tables set up in the adjoining meadow and servers dressed as shepherds and dairymaids pouring local ale and syllabub from crockery pitchers and presenting bowls of possets, curds, and clotted cream for fresh-picked strawberries. An enormous warden-pear pie was carried out, its pastry emitting steam, and hastily carved up. Afterward there would be dancing for the young people under the trees and games for the higher ranking. The central amusement was a huge cut-glass tub brought in by a man costumed as a mariner, who announced, "In order to fish, one needs calm waters. These our gracious Queen has provided for us—security, quiet, and bounty." He placed the tub on the table and withdrew. Twenty or so red ribbons trailed over the side, and the ladies were to take a ribbon and pull their prize "fish" from the depths of the tub. Each prize had a verse that miraculously addressed the concerns of its mistress.

Eurwen, being the youngest, was most excited about the prize, while the novelty of the stunt had worn thin with more experienced women. She extracted a jeweled hair comb and a verse that proclaimed her fortune did not lie with a dark-eyed man.

"How dark do you think his eyes should be to exclude him?" she asked anxiously.

"At least as dark as coal," I assured her. "They should be so black you cannot see the pupils." That left in most of the men she was likely to encounter.

Catherine, Helena, and the rest pulled their prizes out and dutifully examined them. I extracted a pair of delicate rose-colored gloves that fit me perfectly. The verse attached to them merely proclaimed that I was prudent and had many admirers.

"A whole world full of them!" said Sir Thomas, peering over my shoulder.

"Indeed, Your Majesty has become a sort of eighth wonder," said Raleigh. "Forget the pyramids and the hanging gardens."

"Are you saying I am as old as those things?"

"No, but you are as mighty as they. Besides, they have all vanished but the pyramids. Where lives the man who can stroll through the hanging gardens? Can a sailor still be guided by the lighthouse of Alexandria? No. But you will survive longer than they have."

Perhaps in memory. Long ago I had stated that my only desire was "to do some act that would make my fame spread abroad in my lifetime, and, after, occasion memorial forever." It had been one of those offhand comments that, later, I realized was more revealing than I had meant it to be.

"I shall choke on my clotted cream if these flatteries continue," I said.

"I have another gift for Your Majesty." I turned to see John Donne standing behind my chair. "It addresses this subject." He looked around furtively and withdrew a paper from his doublet.

"Thank you, John." Just then I saw Sir Thomas glowering at him, and before I could open the paper, John scurried away.

It was entitled "The Autumnal," and it began, "No spring nor summer beauty hath such grace, / as I have seen in one autumnal face."

I jerked my head up. He had dared to say it, dared to say what everyone pretended was not true. But the phrase "one autumnal face" . . . What a harmonious sound. And was it really so frightening? Did we not celebrate autumn? My eyes darted down the page. "Here, where still evening is; not noon, nor night" . . . "If we love . . . transitory things, which soon decay, age must be loveliest at the latest day. / But name not winter faces, whose skin's slack, lank, as an unthrift's purse . . ." He had not called me a winter face but an autumnal one. He differentiated between them—one desirable, the other pitiable.

Sir Thomas gently tugged at the paper. "Do not read anything he writes," he said. "He has proved an untrustworthy man. I mean to dismiss him after this visit."

"Why, Thomas, what do you mean?" He had seemed diligent and intelligent.

"A climber, a man who does not know his place! He has abused my trust and eloped with the niece of my late wife—a woman far above him in station. If he sought to make his fortune that way, he is sorely disappointed. Our families have cut them both off. And he will lose his position. Let the lovers stew on that!"

"You are not very poetic, Sir Thomas. And here your new wife is a sponsor of literary efforts. I wonder that she does not take the young lovers' part."

"Marriage is not a matter of love but of necessity and common sense," he said. Spoken like a man who had lost two wives—both dearly loved—to death, and now barred the door against further loss. It was not only Pharaoh who hardened his heart. And it was not only a face that made someone autumnal.

"Think before you punish him," I said. "Remember your own youth."

---

That night the rains returned, driving sheets that made it hard to see out the windows. The steady sound of it, beating as if on bronze, drummed into our ears.

"It does not bode well for the rest of the Progress," I said to Catherine and Helena as we prepared for bed. "Perhaps we should give it up. It is hard enough to house a royal Progress, but in foul weather it is too great a strain."

"It's July," said Catherine. "And did it not rain on the fifteenth? St. Swithin's Day?"

"I believe you are right," said Helena. "I knew it then. I knew we were in trouble."

"We should cut our travels short and return home," I said.

Catherine stood closer to me. "My dear, I want to suggest another, private Progress later in the year. Do you remember, we were going to visit Hever?"

"Yes. We talked about it. We had never been there, for all that our mother and grandmother were born there. Thank you for reminding me. We should not delay, but go before winter."

"There is another who should join us, who belongs there." Her round face, usually so placid, looked solemn. "You know who that is."

Yes. Lettice. I nodded.

"She is as close to Hever and the Boleyns as we are."

I closed my eyes. The she-wolf. Wife of my despair, mother of my sorrow.

But my cousin. Autumn. Was it time? Was it time for all that to be over? I had told Sir Thomas, "Think before you punish him. Remember your own youth." Was I bound to obey my own orders? We did not have forever, and Leicester and Essex were as vanished as the hanging gardens. Soon we would follow them. "Very well," I finally said. "You issue the invitation." I could not bring myself to do it, but I could let our mutual cousin speak for me.

---

After several more days of incessant rain, we took our leave of Harefield. Sir Thomas presented me with a multicolored cloak to represent a rainbow. "From St. Swithin," he joked. "For there can be no rainbow without his rain."

# 91

fter I gave Catherine my order—or my blessing—for her to tender the invitation to Lettice, I did not refer to it again. We returned to Greenwich and I busied myself with the usual duties of the realm. Feeling more energetic than I had in ages, I went hunting after a ten-mile ride, causing much comment at court. I announced that I felt better than I had in twelve years. I went to bed feeling I did not need to rest at all.

But when I awoke, oh, what a change. My legs ached and my knees felt as though they were encased in a brace that would not bend. As for my arms, I must have strained my shoulders, for they stung when I reached up. Catherine, who had long since given up vigorous hunting, inquired timidly if I felt as well upon arising as I had upon taking to my bed the night before.

"Never better!" I said stoutly. "In fact, I think I shall take a long walk this morning. I cannot get enough fresh air." Then I forced myself out to walk briskly through the orchard and up the rising hill behind the palace in full view of strolling courtiers, who remarked how vigorous Her Majesty was this morning. Appearing so was my aim.

The park, its big oaks framing both sides of the walk, rose to a goodly height. Resolutely I trudged on, not wanting to stop, but my legs were burning. I was puzzled by the extent to which the ride yesterday had affected me, causing aches and pains all over.

Reaching the summit, I could look down at the river, see the many palace buildings huddled on the shore, and just see London upstream on the other side. Workshops, businesses, and homes all humming, creating the products and commerce that made the city prosperous. And this year, our improved harvest should end the poverty in the countryside; 1602 had been a good year. Why had I feared the new century?

Invigorated, and the stiffness and aches disappearing from my limbs, I returned to the palace.

That evening, sitting quietly in the privy chamber with my ladies, I leaned over to Catherine, whose head was bent over her reading.

"Have you written the letter?" I asked in a low voice, not to be overheard by the others.

She nodded. "Yes, dear Cousin."

"Have you had answer?"

"Yes, while you were out walking. It came from Wanstead, where she has retired."

"Let me see it."

Obediently Catherine rose and went to her little chest, drawing out an envelope, its seal broken. Wordlessly she handed it to me.

Lettice would beg to be excused. Lady Essex—Lady Leicester—Mistress Blount—would plead ill health, or a conversion to perpetual prayer. And I would not have to see her, would not have to act on my impulse to settle all unresolved matters in my life. The urge to do so, brought on by a combination of sentiment and fear of time running out, had dissipated. Did I not feel better than I had in twelve years? That changed everything.

I opened it and read, "Lettice Knollys is grateful to accept Her Majesty's gracious invitation to visit their ancestral castle together. May God have her in his keeping until the day we meet there." Lettice Knollys, her girlhood name by which I had first known her. She was laying the rest aside, like an old gown. Was it a ploy?

But I was weary of trying always to interpret the motives of others, when knowing my own was difficult enough. She had said yes. She would come. We would meet in the courtyard where our ancestors had played together as children. I would try to look out through young eyes, when the world was fresh and unspoiled.

We set out on a bright October day. St. Swithin's rains were long past, but their legacy was a deep greenness lingering long past its time in meadows and grass. Fruits had swelled, drinking up the bounty, and this year's apples were bigger than tennis balls, pears were the size of a burgher's purse, blackberries in the brambles, sweet, glistening globes. Hever Castle was thirty miles south from London toward Kent and equally far from the south coast. It lay in a blessed, protected part of the country.

There were hundreds, no, thousands, of little castles and moated manor houses in the land. There was really nothing remarkable or unusual about Hever Castle. My mother was born here; my father pursued her here in the heat of his ardor. After his failed fourth marriage to Anne of Cleves, he gave it to her, but she never lived here. She preferred being closer to London. At her death it was purchased by a wealthy Catholic family, the Waldegraves.

"She will meet us here?" I asked Catherine, for the fifth time.

"Yes. She said it was easier for her to travel directly from Wanstead, it being on the east side of London."

Like me, she was obviously nervous about the meeting and had, sensibly, shortened her time with us by traveling there on her own.

"When did she plan to arrive?"

"She said the sixteenth."

It was only the fourteenth. We would have time to explore Hever by ourselves first. Just as well.

"Look! There it is!" Catherine sat up straight and pointed to a structure in the distance. The sun hit the moat so that I saw only a sharp, shining rectangle. What it framed was not visible.

I felt my heart rise. My father used to blow his hunting horn from this crest, to let everyone know he was almost there. I felt apprehension as I approached. I did not know what would happen next.

---

We rode slowly down into the dale, crossing the little bridge over the river Eden, and as we did so, the reflection of the moat shifted to reveal the stones of the castle glowing honey colored, shimmering on its tiny man-made island. It beckoned, promising beauty and secrets within.

"I think we have found Astolat," murmured Catherine. "Is the Lily Maid inside?"

It did look as I had always imagined an Arthurian castle would—small, contained, exquisitely lovely, with a high keep where a maiden could look out and see her knight below. "I do not think your grandmother Mary or my mother qualifies as a lily maid," I said with a laugh, and the spell was broken. Inside these walls had lived two very human girls, neither of them pining away for lost loves.

We clattered across the heavy wooden drawbridge, our attendants following. Ahead loomed the great gate with its triple portcullis, raised now but with teeth gleaming.

Sir Charles Waldegrave, the present owner, stood at the entrance to welcome us. He was a tall man, as grave as his name. He bowed low, lower than was necessary. He led our horses through the thick gate into the courtyard.

There was little space in the courtyard; it had shrunk when modern apartments, hugging the old defensive walls, had been built. Half-timbered structures ringed the courtyard, making it look like a narrow London street.

I stood a moment, looking. Could I have been here once before? It felt familiar. But even as I thought it, the memory slid away and was gone.

"It is my honor to welcome you," Charles was saying. "How long has it been since you have visited this family seat?"

"Once when I was very young I saw it from the outside, but that's all," said Catherine. "I was born after it left the family. But it lingered long in our imaginations."

"I may have come here once," I told him, "but how and when I cannot tell you." Had I seen Mary Boleyn here? Had she brought me here to see my grandparents? They had died not long after my mother. Was that why it was vague to me?

"If stones could recount their stories . . ." He smiled. "Let me show you to your quarters. I warn you, for all that Hever housed a queen, it was before she was queen, so it is not very queenly. . . ."

"You need not apologize, Sir Charles," I assured him.

---

He housed us on the second floor, in the west wing, overlooking the orchard and, beyond that, meadows. It was cozy, embracing. We settled ourselves. Our attendants would be housed beyond the moat in outlying buildings. We were alone—or as alone as a queen and her cousin could ever be. The tidy folded blankets and stand with its ewer and pitcher saw to our needs in the simplest manner. A plain candlestick sat on a polished table.

I walked about the room, taking its measure.

Something in my mother's spirit had wanted to soar beyond this homely comfort and security, to seek adventure. It was not her parents who had driven her, but she herself.

And Mary, her sister, progenitor of Catherine and Lettice? She may have danced and bedded with kings, but she had been content with an untitled soldier in the end. She had escaped ignominy but also immortal fame.

The choice of Achilles: Go to Troy, have a brief life but eternal fame; stay home, have a long, safe, uneventful life but be forgotten. My mother and Achilles had chosen the brief but stirring life. When she was born, no one noted it, and no one was sure of the exact date today. When she died, the whole world knew. I would have made the same choice.

"Thank you, Mother," I murmured. "Thank you for your courage."

---

We passed a restful night. There was still another day before Lettice would join us. We explored the house and asked Sir Charles for the records. And all the while the shadows of former owners dogged our footsteps, doubles that followed us about.

"Lettice will arrive tomorrow," said Catherine as we readied for sleep.

"I know," I said.

"Are you ready to greet her?"

As ready as my father had been when he rode to Hever, I supposed. "Yes," I answered her. I blew out the candle and pulled the bed-curtains shut.

# 92

I slept more soundly than I had thought possible behind these old walls. I was untroubled by ghosts or dreams and awoke just before dawn, when any specters would have vanished.

I thought of meeting Lettice after such a long time. Had I ever liked her, my younger cousin? We had once been close. I had known her as a child, her blazing red hair a tie between us, her spirit and daring still more of one. She was more like me than my half-sister Mary, whom at that time I was trying to soothe and reassure. Lettice did not have to do so; her parents left England rather than submit to the reintroduced Catholicism. As heir to the throne, I did not have that luxury. I had to stay here and survive.

When it was safe to return, the Knollyses did so. Lettice was fifteen then. The girl who came to court to serve as my maid of honor was no longer the winsome child who had gone to Protestant Europe; now she was sensual and sly. She spent her time at court trying to captivate men, and soon she was married to Walter Devereux, the future Earl of Essex. Had she been like most others, that would have been the last of her.

But she was not like all the others.

I needed to see her, this creature whom my Robert Dudley had once held so dear, this renegade cousin who nonetheless mirrored me in so many ways. And together we needed to touch the base from which we both sprang, and which would explain much. That was why I had come.

---

While waiting, Catherine and I crossed the drawbridge to stroll in the gardens outside. The water came up to the very edge of the walls, making the castle appear to float. On firm ground beyond the moat, there was an orchard and a formal garden, with flower beds and box borders and a worn sundial in its center.

"What did your father tell you about Hever?" I asked her.

"He was not one for describing houses," she said. "He would just get a smile when he mentioned it."

I wanted details, memories.

"It is a beautiful setting," I said. "It is hard to imagine what lured anyone out of it. But court is a piper, playing melodies only some ears hear." That was the real difference between people—those who heard, who were susceptible to its glittering promises, and those who were deaf to them.

---

"She comes," Sir Charles came to tell us. "From the tower I saw a rider on the road, approaching slowly. I think it is she."

It was midafternoon. Catherine and I stood with our host and waited. Eventually a slight dust cloud signaled someone coming over the rise, and a dun horse appeared, its rider swaying, her hand on her hat. She was dressed all in black. Behind her rode an attendant.

Servants rushed out to welcome her and take her horse. She dismounted, stiffly, and walked toward us. She was no longer young but had not crossed the line into appearing elderly. Her expression was masklike, and the smile she gave as she came closer seemed as false as one drawn on a sheet of paper.

She bowed, tipping the top of her hat upward. Its black feathers trembled. "Your Majesty," she said. She stayed bowed a long time.

"Please rise, Cousin," I said.

She did so and stood looking at me, face to face. Then she truly smiled, and her face became fluid. "Catherine. Your Majesty."

"Welcome," said Sir Charles. "I am pleased that you honor me by gathering here."

"It is you who honor us," I said. "This house has been closed to us ever since we were scattered in many directions. Now we have come home."

We stood awkwardly until Sir Charles said, "I will be pleased to show you every corner and niche. The house has many secrets."

---

While he directed Lettice's attendant to her room with their baggage, I turned to her. I decided not to comment on the black, but we made an odd contrast, for I was all in white, my favorite "color." Both were equally flattering to red hair. Her choice signaled mourning, mine virginity—the only two colors that served as definitive labels for others to read.

"Shall we sit?" Several benches were scattered about the garden; we sought one under the shade of a sycamore tree. "You must be tired," I said to Lettice. "Would you prefer to rest in your room?"

She cocked her head. "No. I am not to that stage yet." She walked, straight-backed, to the bench.

As we settled under the tree, several birds flew off, rising with a rush of wings.

"I would make a comment about three old crows frightening off the sprightlier birds," said Catherine, "but I fear it might seem rude."

"I give you license to say whatever you please," I said. "Lettice, do you agree?"

"Yes," she said, but her voice was icy.

"Very well, then!" said Catherine. "It's sad that, cousins though we may be, Lettice, I cannot remember the last time I saw you."

"Nor I, you." Then silence. Diplomatic silence, for they knew very well when they had last met.

This was even worse than I had imagined. Why had I let Catherine talk me into this? I would plunge in, break the barrier, for better or worse. "I remember," I said. "It was when you accosted me in the passageway at Whitehall and attempted to give me a gift."

As I knew she would, she rose to the bait. "Accosted you? You had avoided me, insulted me, after your invitation to meet with you." Her eyes, beneath the brim of her hat, were narrowed.

"The invitation I was forced to extend, because of your unruly son, who never knew when to cease and desist. You have heard the old country saying 'Lead a horse to water, but you cannot make him drink'? I wanted to teach your son that lesson. Alas, he was a slow learner."

"I did not come here to hear my son insulted." She stood up.

"Sit down, Lettice," I said. How fine to be a queen and for that to be a command. She sank down. "I have no wish to insult anyone. He was headstrong, as we both know. But he was loyal to his mother, thoughtful of her feelings, and I honor that. So many children disobey the fifth commandment. He did not, and we both appreciate what that meant."

"But before the meeting in the passageway, I cannot think when last I saw you," said Catherine, ever the peacemaker.

"I have not been at court since 1578," she said. "Ten years before the Armada."

"Then we must search our childhood," I said, "and that is what we are here for. Lettice, did your mother ever speak of this place?"

Lettice smiled for the first time. Was she relieved to have the obvious stated and over with? "Yes. In her memories, it was an idyllic time. The country. Butterflies. Fields. Horses. Hawking. When her father, William

Carey, died, she was only four. She remembered him swinging her over wildflowers in a great circle, her feet flying out.

"You are the only one who met Mary Boleyn," continued Lettice. She was addressing me. "You are the only one of us alive when she was."

Was she asking me a question? Underlining my age? "Yes, I did. After the—After I lost my mother, I was shuffled around from one house to another. Sometimes I was brought to court to see my father and his newest wife. Mostly I was kept in the country, far from where the sight of me might give offense. I loved Aunt Mary Boleyn. She was warm and encouraging, and I wanted to call her 'mother.' She had a way of looking at me, paying close attention, that spun my little head. No one else paid any attention to me in those days."

"Well, they've made up for it now!" said Lettice.

The bold remark made me laugh; it did not anger me. I was relieved that she had felt free to say it. We were finally making headway.

"I think those first twenty-five years of vicissitude prepared me well for the flattery that followed," I said. "It should be a requirement for rulers: be castigated, ignored, and insulted. It teaches you to weigh the adulation that comes with the office, to know its true worth."

"Was she—was she pretty?" asked Lettice. Of course she would want to know that.

"To me she was. But I was inclined in her favor because of her kindness to me. I remember she had golden hair—unusual in an adult. And that her skin was exquisite—pale but all one hue, no mottling." I thought hard. "Her voice was low, confiding." I paused. "I am so sorry you never knew her. Yet both of you carry her traits. Catherine, your voice is very like hers, and you have her kindness. Lettice, she was catnip to men, and so are you."

Lettice laughed. "I am not in her category," she said. "She indulged herself with two kings, and had two husbands."

"And what two kings!" cried the normally staid Catherine. "The young François, King of France, and the King of England!"

"Yes, and in short order," admitted Lettice. "It earned her a vicious reputation. You know how the French are. No sooner do they bed you than they discard you and mock you."

"And you know this personally?" I teased her. I—teasing Lettice! A miracle—a miracle wrought by Catherine.

"No. I stayed far away from the French. I was satisfied with the English."

"And they were satisfied with you," I said. "A good bargain." I laughed. "In any case, you had three husbands. So you need not apologize for finishing behind her."

"Was it a race?" she asked.

"Always," I said. "We seek to outdistance our forebears."

"Have you done so?" Oh, she was bold.

"Even to ask myself that question is to be unfilial," I said. "But let me say that if my father, who never imagined I would come to the throne, or if I did, that I could manage even to hold it, could visit us now, I think he would be—surprised. And pleased."

"He would be in awe!" said Catherine.

"I do not think my father would be in awe of his own child," I said. "But I do wish I could see him, could show him what I have done in his footsteps."

"He would be in awe," insisted Catherine.

"We will never know," I said. That was the sorrow of it—the final barrier of death. We can imagine, but we will never know.

"Did she leave you anything?" asked Lettice.

"No," said Catherine. "By the time she died, she had little to bequeath to grandchildren. She was the wife of a poor man. True, she inherited the lands and manors in Essex from the Boleyns, but that is not anything to leave a child."

"She left a few personal things to my mother," said Lettice. "Gowns, letters, a necklace—as you well know!"

"Lettice, I am sorry about that," I said. "I was unkind, and I apologize."

"It is well enough," she said. "I am happy still to keep it."

"What if I demanded it now?"

She looked me in the eye. "I would say, 'He who will not when he may, when he wants, he shall have nay.' You are fond of country sayings, are you not?"

"And now you turn them on me," I said. "As well you should. A gift can be offered only once. And as I told you, I have a similar necklace. I brought it," I admitted. It had seemed fitting, since I would be in the place where it originated.

"So did I," she said.

"We must wear them together," I said. I reached out and touched her arm. "I would like that."

Leicester, Essex, my father, all the men dividing us seemed ghosts, ever present but impotent.

Catherine looked from side to side. "We are the three patterns of womanhood," she said. "One of us has had three husbands and been widowed three times. Another is unmarried, and a pure virgin. And I have been wife to the same man for forty years next spring. What other variation can there be?"

"I think that is all," said Lettice. "Both of you are happy, and so you can recommend the path you have followed. But to be widowed three times—no. If being catnip to men leads to this, I would not wish the trait to be passed on. Alas, my daughter Penelope has inherited it in full. It seems undiminished as it passes down the generations."

Catherine stood up. "I need to rest," she said. "We can meet again at dinner."

Her abruptness puzzled me. She did not seem unwell. Perhaps she wanted to leave Lettice and me alone. She made her way along the graveled garden paths toward the house.

Lettice echoed my thoughts. "She wants us to be alone."

"Perhaps. She does not seem ill, but—"

Lettice leaned forward. I looked at her face. Older, but still lovely. Well, that is the way of nature. It ebbs slowly. "You are a beautiful woman, Lettice," I said. "The most beautiful in our family."

"Much good has it ever done me!" she said.

"I would argue it has done you much good," I answered.

"As you like," she said.

"It is better to be beautiful than to be ugly," I said. "There should be a Scripture verse about that, but never mind," I said. "We all know it is true."

"You envy me," she stated.

"I envy your face," I said.

"Well, it is fading now," she said.

"But only after it awarded you prizes," I said.

"Oh, Elizabeth!" she said. "That was so long ago. All of it. I had my face; you had your office. I would rather have been a queen than to have bewitched men, or been the mother of lost sons."

Yes. So would I. I had had the better lot.

---

That evening Sir Charles and his household invited us to a formal supper. In the dining hall we took our places at the table, glowing with candles down its length. Sir Charles had set up a thronelike chair for me at the head.

Across the table and a bit farther down, Lettice was wearing her *B* necklace, as was I. Jeromina, Charles's wife, commented on them, saying that she felt the Boleyns were with us tonight.

"My wife sees ghosts," said Sir Charles. "She is prone to a fiery imagination. Pay her no mind. But I often feel their presence."

"Tomorrow, good Sir Charles, you must show us some of these remainders."

"You are surrounded by them now," he said. He pointed to the walls, festooned with antlers and hunting trophies. They cast long shadows in the candlelight, reaching toward the ceiling like winter branches.

Lost hunts, forgotten triumphs. My father had loved hunting. But it was not game he had hunted here at Hever. He had pursued my mother, sending passionate letters—secret, he presumed. My mother had kept them; someone had stolen them and sold them to the Vatican.

After supper we returned to our rooms, escorted down the dark corridors by lanterns.

# 93

hen I awoke, I was surprised to see Catherine already sitting and sewing in the early-morning light. She paused several times to rub her forehead, as if she were feeling for something under the skin. As soon as she saw me looking, she rose and came to my bedside.

"Did you not sleep well, Catherine?" I asked. "Did the ghosts disturb you?"

She smiled. "No." She rubbed her forehead again. "Just a pain here, behind my eyes."

"Then you are foolish to try sewing," I said. "Such close work is known to give headaches."

"I'll set it aside, then," she said. "I've never liked embroidery, mainly because I am not good at it."

"It has nothing to do with your character," I assured her. "After all, the Scots queen was a superb needlewoman."

In the room next door, we could hear Lettice stirring.

---

After breakfast, leading us like children, with his youngest in tow as well, Sir Charles showed us the older portions of the castle.

"Not as pretty," he said. "But the Boleyn children and grandchildren loved to play in the old rooms, so I was told. The old kitchen, next to the dining hall, had a deep well. The cooks had to order a stout, thick cover for it because Anne, Mary, and George liked to hang over the edge and let down toy buckets, and they were afraid one of them would fall in."

He led us out through the courtyard and toward the great gate with its portcullis. "Now, this was their favorite," he said. "This old keep has three floors, and up top there's two chambers. Come!" He led us up a spiral stone staircase, onto a landing, and then up some narrow steps to the battlements. As we emerged, we could see far across the fields and hills. Indeed, to be here atop the keep was to feel invincible.

Now I could discern the layout of the gardens and orchard below. Thick hedges, wooden palisades, and brick walls enclosed grounds of varying sizes. They spread much farther out than I had realized.

Outside again, Sir Charles told us about the grounds, mentioning that there was a walled and neglected garden on the far side of the orchard. "I do have to tell you, although this makes it sound more exciting than it probably is, that for the longest time we could not find the key to that door. Princess Anne of Cleves had never gone into it, and one of her servants told my father that a stipulation of the King's royal bequest of the castle was that she not visit or meddle with the garden. She was happy enough to obey. Eventually we located the key, in a crevice beneath the windowsill in Anne's room. The stricture forbidding entrance to the garden had long expired, along with the King and with Anne, so we felt free to go into it. There was not much there after forty years. All overgrown. We closed it up and left it. Jeromina had ambitions to replant it, but—" He shrugged.

"Eleven children diverted her attention," said Lettice.

"You might say that," he said.

"Get the key, Sir Charles, if you will. We would like to see it," I said. I felt strongly there was something inside that I should see.

"If you wish," he said, sighing. *Foolish old woman,* he was doubtless thinking. Perhaps so, but a determined one.

We trudged down the paved paths and past the neatly laid-out geometric gardens open to the sun. The four orchards—of pear, apple, plum, and medlar—empty of their fruit now, rustled as we passed, as if they wondered what we sought. Down where they ended, an ivy-grown wall came into view. It was high enough that we could not see over it but low enough that trees inside were visible.

"Oh dear. The ivy has covered the door." Sir Charles plunged his hands in and felt under the leaves. "Ah . . ." He groped along the bricks underneath until he felt wood. "Here it is." He tugged at the tendrils, tearing them off the door where they clung fast. Eventually a faded and warped door revealed itself. It was quite low.

"I think the garden may initially have been built for children, with everything scaled to their size," he said. He fumbled with the key, straining to get it to turn. Finally it did, with a groan and a shower of rust falling from the keyhole. He pushed; the door shuddered but refused to move. He put his shoulder against it and shoved. It creaked open a few inches, an oyster reluctant to open.

"Harder!" I said, putting my hands on the door with him and pushing with all my strength. Slowly it gave ground, its angle of opening growing wider as it cleared a flagstone at its threshold.

Finally it stood open, revealing a tangle of bushes and trees inside, a carpet of fallen leaves, and old pink brick walls, their tops moss-covered, surrounding it all. Shafts of yellow sunlight fell like filmy curtains through the twining tree branches overhead. It was a hushed and sacred place.

"I almost believe I see the Ceryneian hind of Artemis here," whispered Catherine. "Behind that thicket."

"It is a trick of the golden sunlight," said Lettice. "It gilds our imaginations as well as the branches."

"I will leave you," Sir Charles said. "Perhaps you would like privacy here. Oh, let me point out that there is a stone bench over against that wall—hidden now behind creepers. The plot is even more overgrown than when I first saw it."

He left quickly.

"Do you sense that he wanted to get away from this place?" asked Catherine.

"Or from us," said Lettice.

"Or both," I said. "No matter. Now that he has brought us here, it is better to be alone." I walked around, being careful of the uneven ground. A few paving stones peeked out of the fallen leaves, but they were tilted and upended from years of frosts and thaws. Soon I could make out the outlines of old flower beds, bordered by bricks. Strangled by vines, a few old roses drooped, straggly and pale, a scattering of late petals on the ground around them.

"Oh, look!" Catherine was standing at the rim of what had been a pond. It had evaporated, and dried; cracked mud covered the bottom. "Once it must have held water lilies," she said.

"There are still some land lilies," said Lettice. "I see some here, close to the wall."

Gradually the image of the old garden began to reveal itself. In the center, the pond, its surface covered by wide lily pads and flowers. Against the walls, roses and lilies. A stone bench under a pavilion at one end. Peeking through the brambles I could see the listing stump of a sundial pedestal.

"A statue!" said Lettice. "Here, covered by vines and brambles." She tore them away, cutting her hands on the hidden thorns.

"Oh, my dear, we should have worn gloves," said Catherine. "Let me help."

But Lettice said, "No, no, no need." She yanked the last of the vines off, revealing a crumbling stone statue of a young girl gathering flowers but looking over her shoulder in distress. One or two of the flowers were falling, dropped from her hands. She stood on tiptoe.

The girl's face was exquisite but very young. She was somewhere between girl and woman.

"Is there anything else there?" I asked.

"Nothing, but—" She stepped back and looked behind the statue. "There's the base of another one here."

Catherine and I joined her, using branches to beat the weeds and creepers down. Soon a fallen sculpture revealed itself. It was broken in three parts, but the lower part had wheels, and the top fragment depicted a man's head.

"It's Persephone." I suddenly knew. "She was gathering spring flowers, and then Pluto in his chariot grabbed her. This must be Pluto, broken into three parts behind her."

"Serves him right," said Lettice with a laugh.

"Look, you can see the fierce implacability on his face," Catherine said. "He was determined to have her." The lean, square-jawed face, marooned on the ground, stared resolutely at dirt and pebbles in front of him.

"Perhaps the flower beds are planted with Persephone flowers," I said. "Hesiod says she was picking crocuses, hyacinths, violets, roses, narcissus, and lilies. If we cleared the beds and waited until spring, that's probably what would bloom. If any of them survived. But we see that the roses and lilies have."

Catherine caught her throat as if she could not breathe. I saw her face go white, and then she said, "I remember. . . . I understand it now. My father told me, once, that there was a place, a place where each of the sisters had met the King secretly and dallied with him, and that his mother had been there first and then given it over to her sister . . . and that it was a cruel reminder to the parents and so they ordered it destroyed, but it was locked up instead. And how he and his sister sneaked in there once and got a terrible beating. He said, 'It was a garden from Hades, that's what it was.' I didn't understand. He didn't mean me to. It was like he was talking to himself."

"Hades. A garden of Hades, where Pluto swooped down and took them, first Mary Boleyn and then Anne," said Lettice. Her face had gone almost as white as Catherine's. "They could not protest openly, so they spoke through these statues. The King was too besotted, or too oblivious, to notice anything that subtle."

Yes, the King could be frightening. I had experienced that as a child, when he was old and ill and fighting off demons. But I had never thought of his being frightening as a young man; I had seen too many portraits and read too much about the glories of his youth. And, as a queen, perhaps I had forgotten, or willed myself to forget, the terror a ruler's power can induce. I had never considered that to the Boleyn sisters he might have seemed like Pluto, sweeping down on his chariot, carrying them off, trampling them underfoot.

They had converted their children's garden into a place to meet him, walled off, away from everyday life. But whether to receive him or not they had no choice. Their only choice lay in where.

And it was here, then, that the very heart and center of their courtship with him was rooted. "Perhaps he did," I said, feeling the need to defend him, "but was as helpless in his need for them as they were helpless to protest."

"That is a flattering interpretation," said Lettice. She looked sharply at me. "Perhaps you say that because he made your mother Queen."

"Perhaps you should be more forgiving of him because your mother died in her bed," I shot back.

"Cousins!" said Catherine. "The dead are gone and do not feel. We need not be angry on their behalf. It is done. We know the gods—and love—can induce madness. Come, let's find this bench Sir Charles told us about before it gets dark."

The weeds were especially thick in that part of the garden; the wall absorbed sunlight and warmed the area. There seemed to be a trellis or pergola set up against it, enveloped by thick vines, their ends trailing down like a brittle curtain.

"It must be under there," I said, pointing to it.

"All I see is a mound of dead vines," said Lettice. Her hair hung in disarray from her efforts at clearing the statue, and sweat shone on her face.

"I will clear it," I said. "You have done your part."

Gingerly I picked my way over to it, being careful not to catch my hem on brambles. I heard the scurrying of small creatures that made their home in the underbrush. I hoped there were no snakes.

Something waited under the dead vegetation; I felt stone beneath the stems. Carefully I pulled the covering away, revealing a finely carved bench with feet like lion's paws. A curved back, with an inscription, beckoned us.

"Here they sat," I said. I was, unexpectedly, quite overwhelmed at this private withdrawing place, which did not figure in palace inventories or gossip. It was as if they had outwitted history, kept something back from all the chroniclers and ballad makers. This was *theirs*, no one else's.

"Can you read it? What does it say?" asked Catherine.

I brushed my fingers across the lettering, filled in with dirt. "No. It is obscured. We need to clean it out." We took twigs and began scraping the matter out, carving the letters afresh. Gradually it revealed itself.

"The Bower of Love," I read.

I expected Lettice to laugh or deride it. Instead she was silent.

"They believed in it," I said. "Whatever happened later, this moment in their lives was pristine."

Now came Lettice's comment. "For him."

"No, for all of them." Dear Catherine, the peacemaker. "They were young. All the things we see, knowing how it ended, they did not. We have to honor that innocence."

Lettice laughed. "Mary Boleyn is rarely credited with innocence," she said.

"But she *was* innocent," insisted Catherine.

"I will embrace that," Lettice said. "I am weary of having my grandmother branded a whore. Or a fool."

"She was neither," I said. "You have carried that far too long." I made up my mind about something. "Let us sit here and be with them." It was the nearest we would ever come.

We brushed off the seat and sat down together. Overhead the old trellis protected us from the breeze that had sprung up, its dead vines stirring, murmuring.

I rested against the back, feeling the letters against my spine. *The Bower of Love.* I felt for the small gold ring on my little finger, one that I had worn for seven years. I tugged, slid it over my thickening knuckles. Finally I held it between thumb and forefinger. "Lettice, this is for you. Your son gave it to me when we went to Wales." Green Wales. *Dwi yu dy garu di.* I handed it to her.

She took it, strained to see it in the fading light. "You kept wearing it? Even through—?"

"He was close to my heart. That never changed."

She slid it onto her finger. "It is rare to receive a new gift from someone so long after the fact."

"It is from both of us. He would want you to have it. And I want you to know that my care for him never ceased. It was a tragedy. We all must walk our paths. Even a queen cannot depart from them. A queen, sometimes, least of all. At the end of the path, perhaps, is understanding."

"Thank you," she said, no trace of anything hidden in her voice. Then she moved her hands behind her neck and fumbled with a clasp. Slowly she withdrew the *B* necklace, which had been hidden beneath her bodice. "Catherine, I want you to have this," she said. "It is time I give it away. You will treasure it more than my daughters or grandchildren. Here." She handed her the necklace.

Before Catherine could respond or say no, Lettice turned to me. "I had vowed never to let you see this, or even know about it. It was my revenge. But now there is no point. You should have it." She withdrew a folded, puckered envelope from a battered purse she carried and thrust it at me.

I took it, not understanding what it was. It was too dark to read. I turned it over in my hand.

"It is one of the King's private letters to Anne Boleyn," she said. "The Vatican spy did not get all of them. Some were entrusted to Mary Boleyn, although this is the only survivor of the lot. I told you she gave my mother some personal things, and my mother passed them on to me. You have earned this."

"I do not know what you mean," I said.

"My son's wife, loving him and wanting to help, gathered up family papers while he was imprisoned in York House. She feared some might incriminate him, so she entrusted them to a servant, Jane Daniel. Now do you remember?"

"The blackmailer," I recalled. "This Jane had a husband eager for profit, so he withheld the papers and asked for payment."

"Whom Your Majesty graciously punished, and returned the papers unread to Frances, in addition to his fine. Within that casket of papers lay this very letter. Now it is yours."

"Oh." This priceless treasure! An unseen, uncensored exchange between my mother and father, in the hopeful green time of their lives. "I thank you. It is a gift beyond all other gifts."

"Your charity toward Frances merits it."

I was humbled. I had done it not out of policy but only out of pity and justice for Frances. And to have this, now . . . "Perhaps all recompense is not delayed until heaven," I said. "But, Lettice, your charity far exceeds mine. I am stunned."

"I hated you," she said bluntly. "But I know that to be a queen requires cruelty sometimes. I do not understand it, or grasp what alchemy transforms a person into the substance of a ruler, but I accept it. I am thankful we could meet and speak of these things. Otherwise I would have gone bitter to my grave, and that would have made an uneasy rest."

"I hated you, too," I said. "You took my Robert Dudley away!"

"I made him happy," she said, "when you could not."

"Perhaps that is what love is," I said. "To give over to someone else a precious thing. My love was incomplete at the time. So, only now, long after he is gone, can I render him into your hands. I no longer begrudge him to you."

"All that was long ago, and what we have done, we have done," she said. "Our story is as old as what happened here in this garden."

"You speak as if it is over," said Catherine.

"For me it is," Lettice said. "I plan to withdraw to Drayton Bassett."

"The country!" I said. "Oh, Lettice, you had always railed against it!"

"Things change," she said. "If we are privileged to live long enough."

I slumped back against the bench, turning the unread letter over and over between my fingers. "At my coronation, there was an arch at Little Conduit portraying Time. Truly, I have come to believe that Time is the greatest gift of all. Lettice, may you live long at Drayton Bassett. Even longer than old Tom Parr." I wondered if he was still in his house.

"Look," said Catherine, pointing to a gleaming white flower opening at the foot of the bench, a vision of hope and delight. "A night-blooming flower. They must have intended the bower to be visited in the evening."

I leaned forward and touched its stem. "What have you seen?" I murmured. "What do you remember?"

---

In the dim light of my room, late that night, Catherine sleeping, I opened the envelope with trembling fingers. The paper was so stiff it cracked on one side, but I extracted the letter inside and drew it out.

"Mine own darling, what joy it is to me to understand . . . the company of her who is my greatest friend . . . Written with the hand of him that longeth to be yours . . ."

It had all been real, and it had led to me, their daughter. I felt both their hands resting on my head, saying, *Our dear daughter.* Perhaps they had not wanted a daughter, but I had fulfilled their highest hopes. If only they could have lived to see it.

# 94

*December 1602*

e were huddled close in the royal box overlooking the chapel, Catherine and I. The seeping cold of winter, with Whitehall being so near the river, ate into our bones.

It was fitting for Advent, the time of preparation for Christmas. Cold and dark. The blue twilight descended early, wrapping us in what seemed continual night, with just a lightening in the sky halfway through the cycle.

Always at Advent, guest preachers—usually renowned for their oratory—were invited to court. This Sunday it was Anthony Rudd, Bishop of St. David's.

He rose up in the pulpit and began preaching on Psalm 82, verses six and seven: "I have said, Ye are gods; and all of you are children of the most High. But ye shall die like men, and fall like one of the princes.

"Yea, the princes fall. Where is Nebuchadnezzar? Where even Solomon? They all vanish, shrivel like grass in a hot furnace!"

He looked at the congregation. "If even David met his end, how can you hope to escape? Examine your lives. What if the angel of death appeared tonight?"

He looked around, moving his head slowly from right to left. "Some of you will leave here, go home, lie down to sleep tonight—and not awaken."

Beside me, Catherine gave a violent shiver. I pulled her closer to me.

"And a ruler has a double responsibility. For the 'things' a ruler leaves behind are not grain in a barn, or livestock, but the very security of the kingdom. He—or she—has a duty to ensure a smooth passage into another's hands."

This was too much. I stood up, wrenched open the little privacy shutter that shielded me from the people below, leaned out, and bellowed, "You have preached me a good funeral sermon! I may die when I please!"

Heads swiveled to see me.

"That is enough!" I shouted. "Proceed with the service, which is your main duty!"

---

Afterward, in my apartments, Catherine divested herself of her layers of cloaks and furs. "I take it you will not invite him again," she said.

"Indeed. He can depart for Wales and stay there. Impudent cleric." I hid my disquiet under indignation.

The realm was waiting for my death—my transition—my passage. Bishop Rudd had slapped me in the face with it today. They were holding their breaths, wondering when the scepter would slip from my hands, to be grasped by another. I was well aware that Robert Cecil had a clandestine correspondence with James in Scotland and that one of his stipulations to the Scots monarch had been that he not press me on the succession. Be patient, he had advised. All things come to him who waits. He thought himself so clever, but he was transparent to me. Once a packet had arrived for him from Scotland and been handed to him in my presence. Rather than open it, he sniffed it and declared it had a "strange and evil smell" that might indicate it had been in contact with an infected person. Therefore, he insisted on sending it outside to have it fumigated. It was all I could do not to laugh and say, *When it has been purged of the secret message from James, bring it back in to be read in my presence.*

But they were wrong, all of them. I was not like to die soon. There was nothing amiss with me. Nor was I ready. James would have a long wait.

---

In the meantime, Cecil at his new house on the Strand, Catherine and her husband, the admiral, at Arundel House, and my cousin George Carey in his London townhouse all entertained me in honor of the Christmas season. I was pleased to see the heirs of Burghley and Hunsdon so ensconced in their dwellings, but I enjoyed most of all having the admiral show me his mementos from his victories at sea. Catherine presided by his side but seemed pale and weak. My repeated inquiries as to her health were brushed aside.

---

Just before New Year's, an old face appeared. John Dee, down from his post at Manchester, presented himself at court.

"My dear magus," I said, taken aback by the change in him. He looked beaten down, a smaller version of himself. "Your duties at Manchester release you for the holidays?"

He bowed, his long white beard flopping, almost hitting his knees. "They were relieved to see me go," he said. "I am sure of it." He straightened. "It has been a tedious few years. They will let me go next year, I am sure of it."

"We all either die in office, John, or are let go," I told him. I was not sure which was preferable.

He looked around my privy chamber, his dark eyes taking in every object. "Your Majesty trusts me?"

I laughed. "Have I not let you guide me in crucial things? My coronation date, my future with the French prince—God rest his soul." François—I still missed him. Missed what I was with him.

"Indeed you have," he affirmed. "I came because I saw danger for you here. I was consulting the star charts and the glass, and they both told me you must leave Whitehall for Richmond. Death lurks here!"

His surety took me by surprise. He usually softened his warnings. "Indeed?"

"Yes. You must transfer immediately. Do not linger! Whitehall is a death trap for you."

He was fierce about it. In fact, I had never seen him more committed to a prediction.

"But we have New Year's celebrations planned, and plays for Twelfth Night," I argued.

"You must not let festivities be an obstacle," he said. "Just so those eating and feasting are often swept away."

"John, you are sounding like one of those tedious prophets crying in the wilderness. I will not upset my court by leaving in the middle of celebrations I have invited them to. What talk it would cause! They are already murmuring about that sermon. I will not give them any more food for gossip."

He crossed his arms, glared at me. "Your stubbornness imperils your precious royal self."

"It has before, and it will again. But I do not want to cause alarm, and a hasty removal will do just that."

"I have done my part," he said. "I can do no more!"

That night I told Catherine, Helena, and the other ladies of the chamber to ready themselves for a move. "As soon as the Twelfth Night play is done, we will depart for Richmond."

"At night?" Catherine cried in alarm.

"No, but as soon as dawn breaks." It would be cold then, but I felt impelled to do it. Dee's eyes had frightened me.

---

Daybreak on January 6 revealed a drizzly mist enveloping the buildings so thickly that I could not see the great gatehouse across the courtyard. The river was invisible, masked by a fog that lay over it like a cloud. Cold gripped the rooms as we passed through them on our way out to the water steps. As our footsteps sounded, they seemed to drum out, *Flee, flee, for your father died here in just such weather.*

It was true. My father had kept to his sickbed at Whitehall for three weeks in January, and then, just as the month was about to end, he died. Perhaps Dee had felt that time reverberating, wanting to repeat itself.

"Are you sure you want to transfer now?" asked Helena.

"Yes," I replied, walking faster. Let me find a plausible reason. "It is warmer there. The heating system at Richmond is better."

"Perhaps so," said Catherine, struggling to keep up. "But the fifteen miles of river in between are colder than either palace."

"We shall bundle up in the royal barge," I assured her.

Behind them trailed the other ladies of the chamber, as well as Eurwen. I should have sent her back to Wales before the weather turned, but I had promised her a festive Christmas at court. Now it was too late; she would have to come with us to Richmond and wait until spring to return home.

Torches lit our way down the mossy steps to the barge, its oarsmen waiting. As we pushed off, I saw the mist swallow Whitehall, obliterating it.

Soon it began to sleet, the icy particles hurling themselves against the windows. We were going with the tide, but still it would take hours to reach Richmond. Suddenly the heaps of furs and heated bricks seemed a pitiful defense against the elements.

*Oh, John Dee,* I thought, *are you sure you saw what you saw? This is folly.*

Beside me, Catherine began to shiver violently, and everyone huddled together for warmth.

Past Lambeth, then past Barn Elms and Mortlake. I tried to see the little landing at Mortlake, but it was curtained by fog. After Mortlake willows and reeds lined the banks, making lacy patterns. And then the towers of Richmond behind their guarding wall, spires piercing the mist, their vanes glinting. At last.

"Ladies, you have been hardy travelers," I said. "Soon we will be warm."

I could not have guessed I would not be warm again.

---

The dreariest part of the year now commenced—holiday gaieties over, roads iced and dangerous, seas stormy and almost impassable, wood and food carefully husbanded. The court was skeletal. Many courtiers were at home, attending to neglected business. Helena departed for her own family, as they lived nearby.

The Great Hall all but begged for an entertainment; it was a wonderful setting for plays. But there were not enough people at court just now to warrant it. Eurwen was particularly lonely, as many of the younger people at court were missing.

"I fear I have done you a disservice," I said. "It is boring here for anyone but the old. As soon as the weather breaks, you shall leave and return home."

She did not look as pleased with that as I expected. Oh, so that was the way the wind blew. "I see," I said. "And when this young man returns?"

She blushed and found something very interesting to look at out the window.

"The Eve of St. Agnes is almost here," I said. "Perhaps you can get an answer."

"I must have a room to myself, then," she said.

"So you know the rite?"

"I am Welsh, and we know every magic rite there is!"

I laughed. "Very well. On the night of January 20, you shall have your own chamber. What else will you need?"

"A small cake made of flour, eggs, water, and salt. Two white candles that have never been lit. And I shall have to fast all day, so please excuse me from dinner."

She must be very fond of this young man, whoever he was. "Those wishes are easily granted." I smiled, studying her eager eyes. "Do you really believe in it?"

"Oh, yes!" she said. "In my village, a woman who performed the rite saw three men, not one, and the last had a wooden leg. It all came true. She married three times, and the last had a wooden leg. He had been married to someone else when she dreamed the vision."

"Tell me how you perform the ritual in Wales." Blanche Parry might have once done the same.

"You have to go without food all day. Then you make the cake and set it by the hearth. You mark your initials on it, then walk backward to your bed. It is very important not to speak a word all day. Then you go to sleep. While you are sleeping, the apparition of your future husband will come in, mark his initials in the cake, then appear in your dreams. When morning comes, you can see what is on the cake. Then—if the boy is to your liking—you eat a piece of the cake. That breaks the spell. Then you can speak to others again."

"Oh, my, you will be hungry by the time morning comes. And can you reveal who you saw in your dreams?"

"Only if you don't like him. Telling a dream means it won't come true."

"So if you won't tell me who you saw, that means it was the one you like?"

"Yes, Godmother."

"Then I hope you cannot tell me."

With such frivolities I hoped to distract this young and lovely girl from the sense of heaviness and endings that hung over us. *It is the weather,* I kept telling myself. But the truth was, Dee's warning had rung a tone of doom, even though we had fled Whitehall.

Catherine seemed to grow paler by the day, and she confided that she had never warmed up after the boat ride, no matter how high the fire or how many furs she wore. I was stabbed with guilt for dragging her here.

Robert Cecil, who never even hinted about being needed at home, kept loyal company at Richmond, as did Admiral Charles. John Harington and John Carey came to court. But Raleigh was away on his estate at Sherborne, with Lord Cobham as his guest. Egerton was at his London home, and so was Lord Buckhurst.

Thus, the absent courtiers missed the most exciting news in years. Mountjoy had captured The O'Neill at last, and he was at our mercy. Ever since the Spanish had surrendered after the Battle of Kinsale and sailed away, he had been on the run, refusing to give in. Gradually my forces had smothered the resistance in the south and west and chased O'Neill north to Ulster, cornering him in a little area of forest near Lough Erne. His lands were destroyed, and the old coronation chair at Tullaghoge was smashed to pieces. Famine ravaged the land, and stories of people eating weeds and even resorting to cannibalism turned the stomach. At last O'Neill, the erstwhile Earl of Tyrone, surrendered unconditionally to Mountjoy, writing, "Without standing on any terms or conditions I do hereby both simply and absolutely submit myself to Her Majesty's mercy."

I held the letter in my hand and kept rereading it. Cecil stood obediently before me.

"I see this did not require fumigation," I said. "I would have imagined it to stink of death." Before he could stammer out a ludicrous explanation, I added, "But good news, even if it comes from an ill place, needs no perfume." He looked relieved.

My head was spinning. It had been spinning before, from a headache that had plagued me for two days, along with aching bones from the cold. But this spinning was one of exultation. We had done it. We had broken the Irish rebellion. What everyone had said was impossible we had achieved. And in spite of the evil Spanish aid!

"What shall our conditions be? What shall we demand?" he asked.

I knew the answer to that. "He must abjure the title of The O'Neill, High Chieftain of Ireland. He must renounce all loyalty and adherence to Spain. He must order his son to return from that land. He must accept whatever lands I grant him, with no argument. And he must swear his loyalty to me, as my faithful subject. Then and only then will I grant him his life." I paused. "We shall consider liberty and a pardon as separate issues."

"Depending on his behavior?" asked Cecil.

"Of course. He has made many political promises in his career and kept almost none. Let us see if this is any different. Oh, and—inquire about Grace O'Malley. I know we subdued the Connaught region in the autumn, but I would be glad to know of her whereabouts—and her fate." Had she fought for me, had she fought against me, or had she abstained from fighting for anyone?

"I shall carry out your orders with no delay," he said. He fished in his leather dispatch bag, drawing out another letter. "And here is more good news."

I took it, feeling a heavy seal on the seam—the crimson wax seal of the Most Serene Republic of Venice. In the slick parchment letter inside, the doge requested that we open diplomatic relations between our two countries. He wished to send an ambassador as soon as possible.

"Oh, Cecil!" I said. This was most unexpected, and most welcome. "A Catholic state breaks rank with Rome!"

"The first to do so," he said. "It has been a long time coming. Of course, the French have never completely cut us off. But they have been too busy fighting one another for the past generation to worry much about diplomacy abroad. But this is a slap in the pope's face. His allies desert him. They recognize that you are Queen of an untouchable realm."

"Before we know it, Spain will be suing for peace and sending an ambassador." It was long overdue.

"I hope so. We have been working for it. And since Essex has . . . gone . . . the war faction has lost its way. Now imagine, if Spain made peace with us, and France already has, and Venice, you would be entirely vindicated."

"It has been a long fight, my friend," I reminded him. I handed the letter back to him. "Tell the doge yes, before he changes his mind."

# 95

lated by these two coups, I almost skipped down the long gallery toward the royal apartments. I could have asked the guards at the end of each chamber to dance a measure with me.

The O'Neill, bowing his head in defeat. The man who had mocked, defied, and tantalized me for years, draining my treasury. The man who was directly responsible for my selling my father's Great Seal and jewels of my own. Now he was mine. Unless he escaped again. He was a master of that, like a snake, able to slither through any opening.

And the pope. I hoped he was frothing at the mouth in anger. I had outlasted seven popes. Clement VIII was my eighth. With their rapid transits, I could say—if I were sarcastic—that the rock of Peter seemed to be teetering on sand. This pope was no better than the others. He had eagerly pursued the Inquisition, burning the philosopher and astronomer Giordano Bruno at the stake, and appointed his relatives to the Vatican, even making his fourteen-year-old grandnephew a cardinal.

Outside, the palace orchard sparkled with icy branches. It would be a long time until spring. But I could wait. It did not feel so cold now.

---

I traversed the audience chamber, empty and echoing, but when I reached the outer privy chamber, a knot of people were huddled together inside. Admiral Charles detached himself and interrupted my steps. His face was a welter of wrinkles and anguish.

"Catherine—she's taken ill," he said. "Just in the last hour."

She had seemed well enough this morning as she helped me dress, beyond the weakness she had complained about for weeks. "In what way?" I asked.

"Fever—confusion—nausea," he said. "The physician is with her."

"In the bedchamber?"

"There was no time to take her anywhere else. She was tidying up in that chamber when she collapsed."

"You needn't apologize, Charles. After all these years, the bedchamber is as much hers as mine."

I did not ask if I could go in. As Queen, no one could deny me entrance. But as a friend, I must allow her and the physician privacy. The afterglow of the news about Ireland and Venice still cocooned me. On this day, everything would be well.

After some time, the physician emerged, closing the door softly behind him. He tiptoed over to us, bowing to me.

"Tell me!" said Charles.

The physician shook his head. "I have changed the linens and put extra bottles of water on the table. She must drink, to offset all the sweat. She feels as hot as a new-baked loaf of bread. No food. A fever must be starved. And besides, she has no appetite and cannot keep anything down."

"Is she in pain?" I asked.

"She moans and says her joints ache, that her head is throbbing, but that is usual with a fever."

"No spots?" Charles asked.

"No. It is not smallpox, or plague."

"Thanks be to Jesus!" I cried. Either of those could be lethal.

The physician looked at me, almost pityingly. "This is a most virulent fever, even though we cannot name it. She will need strength to withstand it."

Strength. But she had been weak of late. She came to this duel ill prepared.

"Keep the young girls out of the chamber," he said. "Although the young are more resistant to it. She was well last night, you say?"

"Yes," said Charles. "As well as she has been."

"What do you mean?" he asked.

"I would say that she has been . . . dragging ever since autumn. That is the only way I can put it. And then this move, in the cold, and the harsh winter . . ."

Now I berated myself again. I had hurried everyone here out of concern for my own safety, never thinking of theirs. But, I argued with myself, we had made such moves all our lives. Why should this one be different?

"She was well this morning," I said. "When I left her to meet with Cecil, she was humming and gathering her sewing."

"Perhaps she was pretending," said the physician. "Perhaps she kept it from you."

I shook my head. "If it was just beginning, perhaps she was keeping it from herself. After all, if we took to our beds every time we felt a bit off, all the beds in the realm would be full. No, she must have been stricken suddenly."

"And it is increasing in strength."

"What do you mean?" cried Charles.

"I have no way of measuring heat except with my hand, but I am certain her fever increased just in the time I was in there."

"Should she be bled?" said Charles.

"I don't think it helps in such cases. I'll have ice brought in from outside and rub her with that to fight the heat coming from inside her. Lucky for us it is winter."

Lucky for us. If it had not been winter, she would not have been weakened to begin with. "Do whatever you think best. Shall I ask a fellow physician to attend you?"

"I would welcome any assistance," he said. "In cases like this, only a fool scorns help. I am going to consult my texts to see if there are any remedies I am overlooking." He bowed and took his leave.

I turned to Charles. "Let us go in." The other ladies were gathering anxiously but I told them, "Pray wait."

Catherine lay on her bed, her hair matted with sweat. But she was awake and smiled when she saw us. "Forgive me," she whispered. I had to draw close to hear her. From a foot away I could feel the heat radiating from her face.

"Why do sick people always apologize?" I retorted. "You have committed no offense."

"Save not being able to serve you," she said.

"You did this morning," I replied. "You will again, in a few days."

She took a long time drawing in her breath. "Perhaps not so soon."

"Catherine, we have had jubilant news. The Irish war is over."

She merely looked at me, as if she did not understand. Or as if it were no matter. "Oh."

I shot a look at her husband, standing helplessly by the bed. "Charles and I are elated."

"Yes," she murmured, and closed her eyes. "I am glad for you."

"Be glad for England," I corrected her.

"Indeed." Her eyes stayed closed.

Charles took her hand, stroked her arm. "Dearest, open your eyes."

She tried, but the lids seemed to have weights on them, drawing them down. "Forgive me," she whispered. "I need . . . I must . . . sleep."

I reached out and touched her forehead, which felt like a heated poker. I jerked my hand away. "Jesus!" I cried. Could anyone be this hot and live? "Water! Water!"

Together Charles and I raised her head and tried to make her drink, but she could not.

Now fear gripped me. I looked around the chamber, at its shadowed corners, and suddenly felt a darkness waiting there, waiting to creep out and fasten itself on Catherine.

"Let us carry her into the private withdrawing chamber off this room. She will have more privacy there," I said. As if a change of room would banish the specter in the larger room. With the help of the attendants, the bed was lifted and moved into the smaller room. She had spent many an hour in this little room, laughing and arranging my linens and ruffs.

The physician returned with a pail of ice and began rubbing her arms and legs with jagged pieces. One icicle was ideal, being slender, allowing him to rub one leg down its entire length. She moaned and cried, "Cold, cold, cold!" but otherwise did not stir.

Charles, standing beside the bed, burst into tears. I took his hand and led him out into the larger chamber.

"She's gone, she's gone," he cried. "She has passed the boundary line. She has gone over *there*. There's no pulling her back."

"No, Charles." I argued fiercely. "Let the ice do its work. They gave me up for dead when I had smallpox. But I came back."

"You were twenty-nine. She is nearing sixty."

"She is strong."

Charles kept shaking his head. "Not so strong," he said. "She kept much from you."

The physician emerged from the chamber. "She seems to be weakening. I cannot get her to drink, and without that, she will lose all her water in the sweating."

"What *is* it?" I cried. "Is it the sweating sickness?"

"I do not know," he said. "I have never seen a case of that. It has not struck in England for twenty-five years."

Was he that young? God's teeth, was I served only by children?

"But does it not cause just such a sudden collapse, and much sweating?"

"So they say," he said.

"Some recover from the sweat," I told Charles. "I remember."

"Not many," he said. "It left thousands dead in London, Oxford, and Cambridge. Half the students perished."

"Perhaps it is not the sweating sickness. Perhaps it is just tainted food." But I had eaten the same food and I was well.

Catherine moaned from within the room, and we rushed in. The bed was soaked with sweat, the linens looking dark around her. Touching them, I could feel the moisture. "Oh, my dear." I smoothed her brow, slick with sweat.

I had fed Burghley in his final days. I had seen Walsingham's sickbed. But

I had never witnessed as swift and complete a collapse as this one. She seemed changed from just the few minutes we had left her.

The young physician's assistant arrived, but together they stood helpless at the foot of the bed. "Make her comfortable," one said. "We must change the linens again."

I knelt down beside her. If there was little time left, then I must use it to speak. Later I could not. "My dearest companion, my cousin, do not hurry away," I said. I took her hand, like a burning coal. "I have lost so many, but I cannot lose you."

I felt a slight squeeze on my hand. Her eyelids fluttered open. "I feel my feet slipping away. I am being pulled down, into a tunnel. I promise you, I do not wish to leave. Help me. Hold tight. Keep me here!"

I gripped her hands, together. "I have you. I will not let go."

"They are pulling . . . pulling . . . I slide . . ."

"No, no." I tightened my hold on her. "You are right here. In the bed. You are lying flat. No slant, no slide. It is a bad dream." I looked around. "The room is here. You are here. Why, just beyond is the water closet we laughed about. It is still here. All is just as it was. Nothing is changed."

Charles knelt on the other side and put his big hands on her forearms. "I will keep you here. I can hold you. I am stronger than the tunnel."

For a few moments her eyes closed and I could feel the resistance in her limbs, as if she were pushing against the lid of the opening beneath her. She squeezed my hand and whispered, "They call. I must go. But I cannot. I remain here. Get the pillow."

"No," I said. "Not that."

"It will ease my going," she said. "I must go, but it is hard. I pray you, as one last favor, get the pillow."

Charles looked quizzically at me. But I knew what she meant.

If I sent for it, I was acquiescing in her death. But it was her last request. I stood up, my body stiff from the odd position it had been in. I went out into the privy chamber and told one of the guards, "Go to the Bishop of Ely. Request the black lace pillow. He will know what I mean."

The black pillow of Ely: It had been woven by a nun in that village, and when death approached, it was placed under the sufferer's head, then gently pulled away. When the head hit the mattress, the person was released.

---

Within an hour the pillow was delivered. I turned it over gingerly. The pillow of death. But no, it merely eased death. It could not cause it. As some babes come into the world with difficulty, some of the dying have difficulty leaving it. Both are hard passages.

The pillow was a small one, worked all over with lace. It was black as a moonless night. I carried it into the room and held it before Catherine.

Her sunken eyes opened and she smiled, as if recognizing the pillow, although she had never seen it before. "My friend," she murmured. "I have long expected you, and dreaded you. Come here." She seemed to be seeing only the pillow, not anyone else in the room. She stared at it in rapture, as if it were the Holy Grail.

Carefully Charles and I placed it under her wet head. Then, each of us taking our leave of her, kissing her forehead, together we pulled it out from under her. Her head fell back on the bed.

She gave a little sigh, a muffled cry. Then she was silent, and her breathing stopped.

I clutched the pillow, digging my fingers into it. She was gone.

In the privy chamber, the letters from Ireland and Venice sat on my desk, my triumph of the day, of the decade. But matters of state and matters of the heart run on different tracks. It would be days before I would think of them again.

---

I could not order the court into mourning, for Catherine was not royalty nor a personage of state, but its mood was one of mourning nonetheless. For myself, I dressed all in black, but my thoughts were darker still.

Filled with grief, I noticed Charles, who showed the strain of mourning. He was bent with despair and suddenly looked much older than his sixty-seven years. He looked as old as Old Parr. Charles looked at the black pillow with loathing and kept muttering, "It should be destroyed. It should be destroyed." Once he tried to throw it in the fire, but I took it away, reminding him that it belonged to the Bishop of Ely and was revered in that region.

"We destroy papal relics, and this is worse," he said.

"It has helped many people, and Catherine asked for it," I reminded him.

---

John Harington attempted to amuse me, kneeling before me with some of his satirical verses, but I waved him away. "When you feel creeping time at your door, such frivolities will no longer please you. I am past my relish for such matters." My relish for everything had fled, leaving a featureless landscape of the mind as bereft of life as the wintry one surrounding us. I felt a stab of regret at robbing my godchildren of care and company, so I summoned Eurwen and told her, "I give my first and last godchildren to one another. John, take Eurwen under your wing, and look after her. Eurwen, consider him your older brother at court."

"Ah, but this sounds too biblical!" said John. "Surely we are not at the foot of the cross, being told, 'Woman, behold your son!' and 'Son, behold your mother.'"

"I told you, I am in no mood for jesting," I warned him. "Begone!"

---

The remaining ladies of my chamber moved like shades drifting through fields of asphodel in Hades. Helena had returned. She was my last companion from the old days, and she acknowledged it.

"I cannot make up for all the ones who have left us," she told me, "but I will never desert you."

"I will not hold you to it," I said, attempting to smile.

"After almost forty years at your side, I have learned to disregard your low moods," she said.

She did not understand. This was not a low mood but an unflinching look at what lay ahead.

It was time. I heard the summons, not far off, like a rumble of thunder when I dined outdoors.

As she helped me prepare for bed, brushing out my hair—contrary to rumor, I still had hair, quite a bit of it, but gray now, no longer red—Helena was solicitous. She told me what her children were doing and inquired about the coming season at court.

*It does not matter,* I thought, while answering her as best I could.

Lying in bed, I wondered what I had left undone. Nothing that others could not finish. There was Ireland, but only the surrender treaty, with its terms, remained to be signed.

The succession. It was obvious that James would succeed me. I did not regret never having named an heir. There always was an heir, of the body or not, and the kingdom went on. The only problem came when it was disputed. But my adversary the Scots queen had solved that for me admirably, providing only one candidate.

Parliament. It was growing in strength, demanding to be elevated into an arm of government, no longer content to style itself advisory only. That was an ominous development, but I had done my best to retard it. Another challenge for James.

Religion. In spite of predictions, the Catholics had survived. Not everyone had been won to my sensible middle way, to the Church of England. The Puritans found it still too popish, the Catholics, heretical. Well. One cannot satisfy everyone.

Finances. I had begun my reign with a dismal financial situation, had rectified it, only to find myself dragged backward into desperate straits by the wars. Now the kingdom stood as I had first found it—in debt, sliding toward bankruptcy, despite my personal sacrifices to stem it.

But with the Spanish war essentially over, and the Netherlands launched as a successful independent entity, those expenses should vanish. Ireland, too, would no longer drain us. James should have no trouble restoring the treasury to solvency.

Had I pleased people? Certainly the protection from civil war had conveyed a great blessing upon them. Perhaps that was my greatest gift—years and years of quiet at home, so English life could flourish. The French, torn by religious wars, did not enjoy the theater, country fairs, or taverns. Ordinary life—that was what civil war robbed people of.

The defeat of the Armada had given the people the conviction that they were protected by God, that England was a chosen land, for it was the "English wind" that had saved us in the end. Our seamen were skillful, but it was the wind that had destroyed the Spanish fleet. And not once, but over and over again, in the Armadas of 1595, 1596, and 1597, as if to make a point.

---

And the question others would ask long after I was gone: Was I wrong not to marry? Wrong politically, that is? And I could answer that one resoundingly: No, I was not wrong. As the Virgin Queen, I had united my people far more than I could have done with any consort. They knew they had my undivided loyalty.

I touched my coronation ring. This bound me to them. It had from the beginning, and I had never betrayed those vows. I twisted it. It had, lately, been difficult to move, as if it were adhering to my very flesh.

All the doubts—of not having loved enough, not having given enough, not to my country but to one person, one beloved person who might have reigned with me as my consort. Those doubts—it was time to let them go now.

What was done was done.

# 96

## *March 1603*

y pervasive sadness did not depart, and the coming of March, with its promise of spring to follow, made no difference. I forced myself to grant an audience to the Venetian ambassador, Giovanni Carlo Scaramelli, a charming young man, as the best Italians are. One part of me delighted in the belated diplomatic recognition; the other part barely grasped it, as if something far away tugged at my hem.

I heard from Ireland. The O'Neill would acquiesce to my terms. We had won. Along with the dispatch, a chunk of stone from the smashed coronation chair of Tullaghoge was enclosed.

I withdrew it from its pouch and fingered it. It was about the size of my palm, irregular and gray brown. Within it lay the mystery of what made a king in Ireland. Had we the right to destroy it?

"It seems a simple enough thing," I said.

"So was the bread at the Last Supper," said Cecil.

"This is more easily destroyed," I answered. How prescient of Jesus to leave behind no relics, no holy of holies, merely a piece of bread that must be baked, over and over, in its own time.

I pointed to my own coronation ring as an equivalent. I tried to pull it off, but I could not move it.

Cecil tried to help me, but he only succeeded in irritating the finger. "It has grown into the flesh," he said.

"As it has grown into my soul," I said. It was part of me.

"I fear it is cutting off your blood. Look how the finger swells."

"It has done so before," I assured him. "It is my blood rushing out to unite with my people."

"Symbols must not disguise dangerous events," he said. "I must call a physician. We need his opinion."

Over my objections, he called the physician. One look at my red and throbbing finger, and he shook his head. "It must come off, Your Majesty."

"Never!" I snatched my hand away and enveloped it in my other one for protection.

"It will cause your finger to die and rot," he said.

"I am wedded to my people, my land, and my realm," I said. "The ring is my pledge of that."

"It will kill you," he said.

"I accept that. I have always known it. Did I not tell my people at Tilbury, 'I will lay down my life in the dust for you'?"

"A swollen ring finger is not the same as a Spanish invasion. Be reasonable, Your Majesty."

"No!"

"It is only a piece of metal. Do not risk your life."

"Please, my dear Queen. My father's voice joins with mine, as we would not lose you for such a trifling thing," said Cecil.

Before I could hide my hand, the physician had his pliers out, pulled my finger, and cut the metal. Warmth flooded my finger.

"There. You are saved." He handed me the twisted remnants of the ring.

I took it sorrowfully. Its intricate pattern had been severed. Then I picked up the stone fragment from Tullaghoge.

"So we are both shorn of our authority, The O'Neill and I," I said.

"Nonsense," said Cecil. "He lost his by military defeat. No one has deprived you of yours."

But I felt naked, disenfranchised, as though the realm had divorced me, revoked my power.

The place on my finger where the ring had been was deeply indented. I rubbed it; the mark felt engraved, stamped on the flesh. Perhaps it would remain.

The heaviness of soul did not depart from me, and in its wake came heaviness of body. My legs were cold, my bones ached, and I was troubled with sleeplessness. Then my throat was seized with pain, developing an abscess that made speaking torture. I put off a meeting with De Beaumont, the French ambassador. I did not feel up to it. Instead, I wrote a letter to my old fellow ruler and friend Henri IV, admitting that bit by bit, the fabric of my reign was beginning to tear and fade away. Somehow the confession was easiest to make to another monarch.

My physician tried to dose me with potions, but I refused them all, despite the urgings of Helena, Cecil, Harington, and cousin John Carey. "Poison!" I said. "It will hasten my end." I saw them exchanging pitying looks, agreeing silently that the Queen had lost her wits. But I had no wish to prolong whatever road it was I had embarked on.

Charles came to see me. It was difficult to see who was in a worse state.

"They told me Your Majesty was not well," he said, bowing.

"I—" I clutched at my throat. It stung to talk. "They have yoked my neck with an iron chain," I croaked out. "I am tied, I am tied. All is changed for me."

"It is changed for us all, dear friend," he said. "Catherine, your companion and cousin, my wife, is gone. Rather than feeling bound, I feel cast adrift."

"Oh, Charles," I rasped. "We have lost so many. It grows harder, not easier."

"Perhaps there comes a point at which losses no longer matter," he said. "I have not attained that wisdom yet."

"Nor I," I admitted. "Nor I."

---

My conviction grew that I would never leave Richmond. I glanced around me, imprinting it all in my mind. The privy chamber, with its inlaid writing table. The frieze of blue plaques ornamenting the passageway. The ridiculous flush privy in the bathroom. At the same time, these things seemed to be receding into a past that grew ever more ghostly.

John Dee begged audience, and I allowed him in. As soon as I saw him, I rasped, "You sent me to Richmond to preserve me. But look! I fail, I am languishing. You misread the charts." I glared at him. "You sent us here to die! Catherine has fallen already, and I am not far behind. This place has undone us."

He grasped his bony hands, twisting them fiercely. "Perhaps I misread the signs. Forgive me! The devil tricks us. Richmond may prove another Samarra! You must leave tonight!"

"You will have me chase throughout the kingdom?" I smiled. "I am done with hasty removals. And what do you mean by Samarra?"

"It is an old tale I learned in Europe, from an Arab physician. It goes thus: A servant went to the Baghdad market for his master. There he saw a pale woman he knew instantly was Death. He turned away, rushed back to his master, and requested permission to flee to Samarra. His master granted it, and the servant set out on a swift horse. Troubled, the master went to the marketplace himself and confronted the pale woman. 'What did you do to frighten my servant so?' She demurred and said, 'I was startled to see him here in Baghdad, for I had an appointment with him this afternoon in Samarra.' That, my Queen, is the tale."

"So this is my Samarra," I said. "I will remain and greet the dark angel."

Dee looked distressed. I attempted to assure him. "Sooner or later we must stand our ground, or be branded cowards. That is not a label for a queen."

Richmond it was to be, then. Death would stride forward, and I would greet him courteously. Someone had once told me that death is most unthinkable, most heinous, when we are in the blush of health and life. And Archbishop Whitgift had said, "We are not granted dying grace until the moment comes. It is the final gift of Our Lord. We cannot claim it betimes."

Had he granted it to me? Was I ready?

"You must not go to bed," said Dee. "As long as you stay out of bed, you are safe. That is what I came to tell you."

"Safe?" I laughed, although it tore my throat. "There is no safety for one of my years."

---

But the admonition stuck in my mind. *As long as you stay out of bed, you are safe.* I had meant to attend a service in the chapel royal, but I did not have the strength. So they laid cushions for me on the floor. I could hear it all, could hear the sung prayers, through my little balcony window that overlooked the chapel.

Afterward, John Carey and Harington tried to make me rise. But I did not have the strength. I wanted to lie there.

"Dearest friend," urged Helena, "please at least let us put you in bed."

I turned on her. "Bed! No! That is the end!"

"Ma'am! The bed is your friend," she said.

"No, it is my enemy. Bring me tapers here!"

I was still Queen, and they had to obey. They brought candles and set them all around me, a glowing fence of slim beeswax tapers.

"A taper of pure virgin wax," I said, touching one nearest me. "Such I have been. Tell them. Tell them. I have poured myself out for my people, and kept myself only for them. Burned my store of life for them."

"I will, I will," said Helena. Her face was gathered and puckered. Weeping. It wreaks havoc on a woman's face. I wanted to tell her so but somehow could not speak.

The day ebbed. I watched the sun leave the windows I gazed upon. And then, like a whisper, I saw the first of them. My visitors.

Peeking cautiously around the screen set up to shield me, the face of William Cecil. But he was not the old man I had attended on his deathbed but the young man who had sat at my first council meeting the day after I had become Queen. He grinned impishly and said, "Good work, my lady, good work."

Politely he stepped to one side. Another face peered around the screen.

"The Spaniard eats dust at last!" Francis Drake stepped out, his cheeks glowing apple red. "I knew it was a matter of time." He joined Cecil, standing reverently beside him.

Dimly another figure resolved himself in my vision, a dear sight. Robert Dudley. He came to me and took my hand. I swear I felt his touch, felt the warmth of his fingers. Then he receded.

Marjorie Norris came next, her hair dark again, as it was when she earned the nickname "Crow." She was laughing, beckoning to me.

A young, glowing face. Small mustache. "*Ma chérie,*" he whispered.

François.

A sad, accusing figure, dressed in blue velvet. He shook his head, waving his spade-shaped beard. Robert Devereux, Earl of Essex.

Grace O'Malley's figure resolved itself, her red hair tumbling over her bodice. She smiled down at me. "My adversary," she said. "You have triumphed—for now. But it is all one. We shall see. The story of Ireland is never finished."

Then Catherine, the most recently departed. Her image was strongest of all. I could swear she stood in front of me. She held out her hands silently. I could feel their touch, could feel them pulling me up. I rose from the cushions.

"Her Majesty rises!" All around me the living, more invisible than the dead, cried out. "Escort her to her bed!"

The bed, no, not the bed. Suddenly, in my ear, Robert Cecil was speaking. "Your Majesty, to content the people, you must go to bed."

I turned, fixed him with my eye. "Little man, 'must' is not a word to be used to princes." I lay back down.

And so I remain. Here on the floor, on the cushions, not submitting to the shades, not going to bed. Anxious people watch over me. I still see the departed ones, crowding around, jostling against the living ones crowding my chamber.

"Did I not say, did I not promise you, I do not wish to live longer than my life can serve my people!" I cry. But no one can hear. I have become silent and invisible.

My reign has ended. I have kept my promise.

EPILOGUE

# LETTICE

*November 1633*

I am touched. Ten of my grandchildren and five of my great-grandchildren have come all the way to Drayton Bassett in honor of their *grandmère*'s ninetieth birthday. This proves that time bestows the ultimate gift of respectability upon all scoundrels. If one lives long enough, one becomes venerable. It is a recompense for all one has lost.

I have outlived all my children and some of my grandchildren. Time passes both slowly and quickly here in the country, and it is hard to believe that we have had another king after James. The suspense about what James would turn out to be was answered rather quickly: dull. Following the gaudy splendor of Elizabeth would not have been easy for anyone, but this awkward, gauche man made a dreadful contrast. It did not take long for the people to become disenchanted with him and to resurrect the idol of Elizabeth in their minds. The phoenix indeed rose again, and she soars ever higher as the years pass and nostalgia grips the people, even—or especially—those who were not alive when she reigned.

*Tell me, tell me, what was she like?* Even my own grandchildren and great-grandchildren pester me with the question. I suspect they may have come here less for my birthday than to hear about Elizabeth from a true witness.

There were some surprising turns of events after King James arrived. The Earl of Southampton was released from the Tower and appointed to court offices, even—oh, deep irony—the monopoly of the sweet wines that had broken Robert. If only Robert could have waited! It was barely two years between his rebellion and the end of Elizabeth's reign. He could have passed that short time studying, playing with his children, and when James arrived, all would have been restored. Even the mellowness of time cannot dull that sharp edge of regret when I think upon it.

His widow, Frances, who swore to Robert Cecil that if her husband died she would not wish to draw a breath for even an hour afterward, remarried. Her new husband, Sir Richard de Burgh, the Earl of Clanricarde, bore an eerie resemblance to Robert. Like the widow who married seven brothers in succession in the question put to Our Lord by the Sadducees, Frances seemed to marry different versions of the same man: Sidney bequeathed his sword and his wife to Robert; Robert's successor looked like his twin. They had three children. Frances died just last year. It is quite true, I have outlived everyone.

Some of the pardoned conspirators in Robert's rebellion involved themselves in the most shocking assassination plot ever uncovered in England: the Gunpowder Plot. They tried to blow up not only the King but all of Parliament as well. No one was hurt, due to a timely tip, but this time the conspirators were executed. A certain Guy Fawkes has given his name to the entire plot, but there were many more involved.

King James was not popular, and since he died after twenty-two years here, his son King Charles I has proved even less popular. He tries to rule with the imperious will of the Tudors, without a spoonful of their charm, tact, and wit. Trouble is brewing, as Parliament is not the docile creature it was in the past.

My memories. What of them? I can barely remember Walter, my first husband. Robert Dudley, too, is fading. Christopher is the strongest presence, the one I yearn to talk to, to have him explain what happened. Will Shakespeare. I saw him once more, at Southwark Cathedral, where I stood staring at a burial plaque of Edmund Shakespeare, born 1580, died 1608. So he had come to London, acted, and died. That saddened me greatly. While I was reading it, I became aware that someone behind me was quietly reading it as well. I turned to see Will.

"Your Edmund?" I asked. It seemed natural to see him, in this place, to speak again after eight years.

He nodded. "He should not have come to London."

"Had you died young, they would have said that of you," I said. "But how could you not have come, regardless of what would have happened one way or the other?"

He smiled, that slow, thoughtful smile. "I had to come," he agreed. "We both had to." He looked older—much older. "I am thinking of retiring," he said. "But as always when I think about something, I test it out first by writing about it. What would happen if a king were to retire?"

"Many people wish our present one would consider it," I said.

He laughed. "Laetitia, always stay as you are," he said.

Because I liked the sound of it, I did not ask him what he meant by it. In the years since I have often repeated *Laetitia, always stay as you are* to myself when I face disheartening times or people.

I never saw him again. He died eight years later and is buried at Stratford. I do not visit his grave. After all, I cannot visit my son's or my last husband's, so I cannot insult them by visiting Will's instead.

I wander. The past has a way of welling up and gripping me, especially when there is so much of it.

"Great-Grandmother, tell us about Elizabeth," says seven-year-old Henry Seymour. As I suspected he would ask.

"Did she really wear armor and lead her troops?" asks Susannah Rich, shaking her copper curls.

"No, stupid!" says her brother Robert. "Everybody knows she sailed ships and sank the Armada."

I put my arms around them. "It was not quite like that," I begin. "You see, once upon a time there was a red-haired princess . . ."

"Like you?" Susannah giggles. "Like me?"

"A bit like us," I say. "After all, we are her cousins. Now this princess grew up to be a queen, and this queen was quite remarkable. But she didn't sail ships or wear armor."

"Oh!" says Robert, his face falling.

"But she did something better than that. She made her people feel as if they were wearing armor or sinking ships. Only a very special queen can do that. It isn't easy, you know. It takes a kind of magic." I look at them. "Do you understand?"

They look blank. Henry shakes his head.

"You will, my children. You will."

# AFTERWORD

lizabeth Tudor—the Virgin Queen—is the supreme mystery woman. It is safe to say that no one knew, no one knows, and no one will ever know exactly what went on in her mind, and she wanted it that way. That has not stopped everyone from trying, for over four hundred years, to solve that mystery. "What Her Majesty will determine to do only God . . . knoweth," William Cecil, her principal secretary, said. A master of the rolls of the next generation, Sir Dudley Digges, wrote, "For her own mind, what that really was, I must leave, as a thing doubly inscrutable both as she was a woman and a queen." She famously said, "I will make no windows into men's souls," and that may reflect less her religious tolerance—as is usually assumed—than serve as a warning sign to others about herself.

History collaborates with her to hide her true self. We have almost no private letters of hers, no diary, no memoirs. The poems attributed to her are of doubtful authenticity. She is also a mystery because of the blatant contradictions in her behavior. She was a Virgin Queen who encouraged lovemaking (up to a point) and all the outward signs of rapturous love. Her motto was "*Semper eadem*"—"Always the same"—yet she was famous for changing her mind several times over the same decision. She was known to call her sailors back after they had already set sail. Her image is one of leadership and decisiveness, yet she loved to give "answers answerless." She was fastidious, hating the smell of scented leather or bad breath, but she swore and spat. She was stingy but loved jewels. She exercised stern control over her public image, permitting only approved portraits to be released to the public—ones that showed her looking quite different from how she really did—yet she could lose her temper and put on a show of fireworks. "When she smiled, it was pure sunshine, that everyone did choose to bask in, if they could; but anon came a storm from a sudden gathering of clouds, and the thunder fell in wondrous manner on all alike," John Harington wrote.

The only trait that was consistent throughout her life was a superb ability to judge character and to select exactly the right people to serve in the right capacity, thereby getting the most out of the varied talents that surrounded her. She kept the same ministers throughout her reign. Because she listened to these wise advisers, in some ways her reign was a collaboration. But here again is a contradiction, because she, like all the Tudors, had a sense of majesty and would not allow it to be questioned. At the same time, she was in many ways "the people's Queen" and famously declared herself to be married to England. She seemed to have no illusions about her own limitations as a human being and had inherited her father's common touch, but never forsook her majesty—a difficult balancing act.

Although Gloriana, the Faerie Queen, is eternal, each age fashioned her after its own needs. After Elizabeth's death, people quickly tired of the Stuarts and looked back on her reign as a golden age, pointedly celebrating her Accession Day of November 17 on into the eighteenth century. They rousingly celebrated her as a Protestant heroine. In the next century, the anti-Catholic fervor had died down, and they were more interested in Elizabeth the woman, her private life and (suppressed) passions. They saw the tragedy of unfulfilled love, the suffering woman inside the jeweled gowns. By the 1800s, when England had grown into the British Empire, Elizabeth changed into Good Queen Bess, the embodiment of Merrie England (along with her father, Bluff King Hal).

The Victorians saw her as the founder of England's greatness, with its naval prowess, English trading companies, and explorations of exotic locales. She and her "sea dog" adventurers provided wholesome models for the new children's character-shaping literature.

More recently, Elizabeth has been seen as the ultrasuccessful female CEO (or action heroine, take your pick), as well as the ultimate English celebrity in an age that is fascinated by the mystique of celebrity, of being famous for being famous. Just her outline—with full skirt, ropes of pearls, high ruffed collar—is instantly recognizable as an icon everywhere. Indeed, her brand recognition is such as to make a commercial product weep with envy. Thus *Eliza Triumphans* continues to exercise her power over us.

Although I have tried, as always, to be true to historical facts, some things come from my own imagination; usually they also have some factual basis. I want to sort some of them out here for you. First, the Spanish Armadas. History focuses on the first, and most climactic, Armada of 1588. But there were at least three others after that. As in the novel, for one reason or another (usually weather) they did not reach their objective. However, they caused a great deal of worry in England, their target. By the time of Elizabeth's death in 1603, both sides had tired of the fight, and peace was concluded the following year, 1604. So the famous first Armada, the clash that became a national myth, was the beginning of the war, not its end.

Next, Lettice Knollys, Elizabeth's cousin. Elizabeth's animosity toward her started when, during one of Elizabeth and Robert Dudley's spats in 1565—long before the novel opens—Lettice began a flirtation with him. Dudley, never one to pass up a liaison, became her lover. The enraged Elizabeth dismissed Lettice but forgave Dudley. Lettice had much in common with Elizabeth, and this made their rivalry sharper. Both fancied themselves irresistible to men, both were vain and passionate, both were ruthless. But Elizabeth, being the Queen, could quash Lettice whenever she liked. The animosity between the two played out over Lettice's son Robert Devereux, the Earl of Essex.

In her day, Lettice was thought of as a schemer, a social climber, and shared Dudley's reputation as a poisoner. Her numerous children and grandchildren played active roles in the next reign and on into the Civil War, fighting on both sides of the conflict. Her great-grandson, Gervase Clifton, composed this epitaph for her: "She was in her younger years matched with two great English peers; she that did supply the wars with thunder, and the court with stars." She retired to Drayton Bassett, and there the former femme fatale redeemed her days with charitable works, dying at the age of ninety-one in 1634. She has many famous descendants, including Diana, Princess of Wales, in whom her allure survived intact.

Several of the men involved in the Essex rebellion were caught up later in the Gunpowder Plot of 1605. The leader, Guy Fawkes, really did serve in the household of Sir Anthony Browne in the 1590s. However, the episode of Elizabeth meeting and dancing with him was invented by me—although she well could have done so.

There really was an Old Thomas Parr who lived near Shrewsbury. He is buried in Westminster Abbey and his tombstone says that he was born in 1483 and lived through the reigns of ten monarchs, from Edward IV to Charles I. He died in 1635 when he was brought to court to meet Charles I. The change of diet and environment was too much for him at the age of 152. The episode of Elizabeth and Essex going to visit him is fictional, as is their stay with the Devereux relations and Elizabeth's goddaughter Eurwen. However, Elizabeth did have over one hundred godchildren, and I wanted to show her special ability to relate to them. Usually they were presented to her, and I thought I would show her actively choosing one herself.

Shakespeare really did have a younger brother Edmund who came to London to be an actor and died young.

After Elizabeth's death, Francis Bacon earned honors in the Stuart court, becoming Viscount St. Alban and lord chancellor. But he fell from power when he was accused of corruption and bribe taking. He reportedly died from his own curiosity, following a scientific experiment using snow to preserve meat. He took cold, got pneumonia, and died—a death oddly in keeping with his character.

Frances Walsingham had an unexpected life after the death of Robert Devereux, the Earl of Essex. She remarried within two years to Sir Richard de Burgh, the Earl of Clanricarde, an Essex look-alike. Surprisingly, she converted to Catholicism. One can only imagine her staunch Protestant father spinning in his grave over this turn of events.

There is a lot of speculation about Christopher Marlowe and his espionage activities. Was he murdered to silence him? It seems the standard explanation of his being "killed during a tavern brawl" is far from the truth. But at four centuries' remove we may never know the truth. Apparently Christopher Blount was involved, at least peripherally, in some espionage, especially around the time of the Babington Plot of 1586, involving Mary Queen of Scots.

I have allowed myself a little leeway in some of the timing of events. Jesuit father John Gerard's escape from the Tower (which really did occur in the swashbuckling way it is described in the novel) took place in October 1597, a few months later than in the novel. John Donne's poetry was not published in his lifetime. No one knows what Shakespeare spoke at Edmund Spenser's funeral, so I used a passage from the funeral in *Cymbeline.* It is true that the poets threw their pens, and possibly their writings, into the grave. In 1938 the grave was opened in hopes of finding them (and possibly an unknown Shakespeare work), but the attempt ended in failure. There really was a "black pillow of death" at Ely, made by a nun and handed down through the centuries, used to ease the passage between life and death. It was burned in 1902 by the son of the last woman who owned it. In the novel I had it in the keeping of the Bishop of Ely, who had a house in London. Catherine Carey requesting it on her deathbed was my idea.

So many books have been written about Elizabeth I and her reign that I can only list the ones I have personally found most helpful in writing this novel.

Certain biographies of Elizabeth herself I kept going back to. J. E. Neale's *Queen Elizabeth I* (Great Britain: Jonathan Cape, 1934), is the granddaddy of all basic biographies, elegant, concise, and definitive. More modern ones are Alison Weir, *The Life of Elizabeth I* (London: Jonathan Cape, 1998); Alison Plowden, *Elizabeth Regina* (London: Macmillan, 1980); Paul Johnson,

*Elizabeth: A Study of Power and Intellect* (London: Weidenfeld & Nicolson, 1988); and Lacey Baldwin Smith, *Elizabeth Tudor: Portrait of a Queen* (London: Hutchinson, 1976). Editors Leah S. Marcus, Janel Mueller, and Mary Beth Rose, in *Elizabeth I: Collected Works* (Chicago: University of Chicago Press, 2000), let Elizabeth speak in her own words.

Books with a wider range, encompassing the age, include the very helpful Edward P. Cheney, *A History of England: From the Defeat of the Armada to the Death of Elizabeth,* vols. 1 and 2 (London: Longmans, Green, and Company, 1914 and 1926). Although almost a hundred years old, it has details missing in newer accounts that favor broader analysis. Others are Wallace T. MacCaffrey's *Elizabeth I: War and Politics 1588–1603* (Princeton, NJ: Princeton University Press, 1992), and Susan Brigden's *New Worlds, Lost Worlds: The Rule of the Tudors, 1485–1603* (London: Penguin Press, 2000). John Guy, ed., *The Reign of Elizabeth I: Court and Culture in the Last Decade* (Cambridge: Cambridge University Press, 1995), and J. E. Neale, *Elizabeth and Her Parliaments,* vol. 1, *1559–1581,* and vol. 2, *1584–1601* (New York: St. Martin's Press, 1958), add to the picture. There is also Lacey Baldwin Smith, *The Elizabethan World* (Boston: Houghton Mifflin, 1966), which captures the exuberant spirit of the era.

The Folger Guides to the Age of Shakespeare, a series of pamphlets, cover many subjects. Adrian Prockter and Robert Taylor's *The A to Z of Elizabethan London* (London: London Topographical Society, 1979), enabled me to walk the streets of London as if I were there. Other books that take you to London are Liza Picard's *Elizabeth's London* (London: Weidenfeld & Nicolson, 2003), and C. Paul Christianson's lovely *Riverside Gardens of Thomas More's London* (London: Yale University Press, 2005). Roy Strong's *The Cult of Elizabeth: Elizabethan Portraiture and Pageantry* (London: Thames and Hudson, 1977), is a pioneering study in the evolving symbolism in her portraiture.

More specifically, palaces and places are described in the following books. Hampton Court has three: Roy Nash, *Hampton Court: The Palace and the People* (London: Macdonald, 1983); R. J. Minney, *Hampton Court* (New York: Coward, McCann & Geoghegan, 1972); and Walter Jerrold, *Hampton Court* (London: Blackie and Son, no date). This last one is quite old and has delightful watercolors by E. W. Haslehust. Ian Dunlop's *Palaces and Progresses of Elizabeth I* (London: Jonathan Cape, 1962) supplies many details of architecture and setting. June Osborne's *Entertaining Elizabeth I: The Progresses and Great Houses of Her Time* (Great Britain: Bishopsgate Press, 1989), provides additional information.

Books dealing with the personalities who loom so large include Benjamin

Woolley's *The Queen's Conjurer* (New York: Henry Holt, 2002), a biography of John Dee, Elizabeth's astrologer; Robert Lacey's *Robert, Earl of Essex: An Elizabethan Icarus* (London: Weidenfeld & Nicholson, 1971); and Robert Lacey's *Sir Walter Ralegh* (London: History Book Club, 1973). Francis Bacon's *Complete Essays* (New York: Dover Publications, 2008), allows us to experience firsthand his dazzling intelligence and observations about life, as relevant now as when he wrote them. Neville Williams's *All the Queen's Men: Elizabeth I and Her Courtiers* (London: Weidenfeld & Nicholson, 1972), is a good overview and includes portraits of many people, allowing us to picture them more easily. Lacey Baldwin Smith's *Treason in Tudor England: Politics and Paranoia* (London: Jonathan Cape, 1986), throws light into the murky—and foreign to us—depths of the Tudor-era mind. Finally, for details about the personal lives and situations of the men who sat in the House of Commons, there is P. W. Hasler's *The House of Commons 1558–1603*, 3 vols. (London: Her Majesty's Stationery Office, 1981). This series was commissioned by the History of Parliament Trust.

Lettice Knollys is due a biography, and no doubt one will appear soon, as her story is important and absorbing. At the moment, a novel by Victoria Holt, *My Enemy the Queen* (New York: Doubleday, 1978), fills the void.

Books on the women who served Elizabeth include the newly published biography by Ruth Elizabeth Richardson, *Mistress Blanche, Queen Elizabeth's Confidante* (Great Britain: Logaston Press, 2007), along with Dulcie M. Ashdown's *Ladies in Waiting* (London: Arthur Barker, 1976) and Anne Somerset's *Ladies in Waiting: From the Tudors to the Present Day* (London: Weidenfeld & Nicolson, 1984).

Books about Shakespeare abound. I found James Shapiro's *A Year in the Life of William Shakespeare: 1599* (New York: HarperCollins, 2005); Charles Nicholl's *The Lodger* (New York: Viking Penguin, 2008); and Stephen Greenblatt's *Will in the World* (New York: W. W. Norton, 2004), good at reminding me that Shakespeare was a man before he turned into the Bard.

Statesmen deserve their own studies, and Conyers Read's *Mr Secretary Cecil and Queen Elizabeth* (London: Jonathan Cape, 1955) and *Lord Burghley and Queen Elizabeth* (London: Jonathan Cape, 1960) give the great man his due in exhaustive detail.

Studies about the Armada have been undergoing a new popularity. The original analysis of what happened was Garrett Mattingly's brilliant *The Armada* (Boston: Houghton Mifflin, 1959). But newer works, adding to this, are Patrick Williams's *Armada* (Great Britain: History Press, 2000); John Barratt's *Armada 1588: The Spanish Assault on England* (Great Britain: Pen & Sword Military, 2005); and Neil Hanson's *The Confident Hope of a Miracle:*

*The True History of the Spanish Armada* (New York: Knopf, 2003). The latter has an unfavorable view of the English, particularly Elizabeth.

People are fascinated by espionage in the Elizabethan era. I found Stephen Budiansky's *Her Majesty's Spymaster: Elizabeth I, Sir Francis Walsingham, and the Birth of Modern Espionage* (New York: Viking Penguin, 2005); Alan Haynes's *The Elizabethan Secret Services* (Great Britain: Sutton, 1992); and Charles Nicholl's *The Reckoning: The Murder of Christopher Marlowe* (London: Jonathan Cape, 1992) to be very instructive.

Finally, there are books examining the perception of Elizabeth through the ages. These sociological/popular culture books remind us that history is not a static thing but constantly changes—or at least the interpretation of it changes—as the mind-set of a society changes. Michael Dobson and Nicola J. Watson's *England's Elizabeth: An Afterlife in Fame and Fantasy* (Oxford: Oxford University Press, 2002), is particularly recommended for this.